BY SUN AND CANDLELIGHT
SUMMER VISITORS

SUSAN SALLIS

BY SUN AND CANDLELIGHT

SUMMER VISITORS

GUILD PUBLISHING
LONDON · NEW YORK · SYDNEY · TORONTO

This combined edition published 1989 by
Guild Publishing
by arrangement with Transworld Publishing Ltd

Copyright © *Summer Visitors* 1988 by Susan Sallis
Copyright © *By Sun and Candlelight* 1989 by Susan Sallis

CN 3365

Typeset by Colset Private Ltd, Singapore
Printed in West Germany by
Mohndruck, Gütersloh

CONTENTS

SUMMER VISITORS

CHAPTER ONE

1964

Madge had never imagined St Ives could be so cold. Of course it was January, and they'd never been down later than October, but sometimes even in the summer the wind and rain had been such that they'd yelled into it: 'Like November, isn't it?'

But at its worst it had been exhilarating, never depressing. Once, just before war was declared, when she was expecting Rosemary, the skies above Clodgy had split open in a spectacular thunderstorm that had been intoxicating in its Wagnerian magnificence. Madge recalled standing on Old Man's Head, mouth open, trying to drink the rain, and shrieking, 'it's warm! It's lovely, warm, sky-water!' And they had laughed together because water at St Ives, whether it were sea or rain, had a special unifying effect on them.

Now, twenty-five years later, she did not smile at that particular recollection. Her grimace – or so she told herself – was in response to the biting wind that shrivelled – not exhilarated – and scoured the tiny cobbled streets and sandblasted the granite cottages. No wonder St Ives looked so clean if all winter long it was subjected to this brand of sterilisation. Suddenly St Ives itself felt very old. And so did she.

She turned from Rose's window and went to the one-bar electric fire in the immaculate hearth. She could not remember feeling so cold. Even in the war when there had been no coal to speak of, she'd kept warm by working or piling on clothes. Now, dressed in her respectable camel coat, there was no room beneath for more than a twin-set and silk scarf. She looked at the borrowed black hat waiting for her on the corner of the dining table. She wore scarves or knitted caps at home during the winter. That hat was going to offer no protection at all.

Rose came in from the kitchen across the hall and caught her

9

expression of misery before she could wipe it off with a smile. Rose did not feel the cold any more than she felt the heat. Her nature, physical and mental, was not so much hard as completely resilient.

'Have they opened up yet?' she asked. She went to the window which afforded a perfect view of the chapel. She answered her own question. 'No. Well, they'll hang on to the last minute this weather I suppose.' She had no time for funerals and Etta Nolla – even Philip – had been shocked that she did not attend her husband's. But she never missed watching one from her front room window, just to see who was there and what they were wearing.

She glanced over her shoulder at Madge and gave her the same open smile she'd given her forty years ago.

'So. You've come all this way for old Philip Nolla's send-off. Seems daft to me. But you've got some guts, I'll give you that.'

Madge raised her brows, surprised. Guts had not been needed, though resolution had. To come to Cornwall in January on her own entailed making complicated domestic arrangements, and organising her own travel arrangements too. But there had never been any doubt in her mind that she would come.

She spread her hands to the pale glow in the hearth and said, 'I had to come. I've known Philip and Etta all my life.'

There was a funny little pause, then Rose coughed and said, 'Yes. Well . . .' and rubbed at an imagined smear on the pristine window. 'I really meant coming here to stop. To me. Folks who knew me when I was Rose Care, still don't have nothing to do with me now I'm Rose Foster!'

'Oh, Rose.' Madge could still feel embarrassed by Rose's determined frankness. 'Where else would I go?'

'There's plenty of room in the town at this time of year, young Madge. And what will Etta Nolla say when she knows you're here?'

They both knew that Etta's comments would probably be condemning, but Madge said quickly, 'I should think she'd be pleased. Philip always spoke very highly of you.'

'Aye. He would.' Rose rested her hands on the sash and stared through the window. 'He would that. He was a good man. And there's going to be a good turn-out for him, too.'

Madge stood up and turned her back to the fire, hoping that

some of its feeble heat might find its way inside her coat and struggle past skirt and petticoat to where there was a gap between stocking-tops and knickers. She looked at the ramrod back at the window and remembered the young woman Rose had been; supple and carelessly beautiful. The town's scarlet woman.

Madge said carefully, 'I wish you'd come. Philip told me how well you looked after Martin Foster when he was dying. And I could see – that day you introduced us – that you made him very happy.'

Rose turned and smiled and for a moment was the old Rose Care, thumbing her nose at her world.

'I expect Philip told you too that I didn't go to Martin's funeral. My own 'usband.' She laughed. 'They all wanted me to go so they could cold-shoulder me. But when I didn't . . . oh my dear Lord, you should 'a seen the faces that day when they went into the chapel!'

'You watched? From the window?'

'Aye, I watched.' She turned back. 'Like now. I'm an outsider, Madge. Always 'ave been. An' certainly where Martin was concerned . . . dear Lord, I was married to him just over a twelvemonth. He married me to look after him when he was dying. And I did that. And this house is his, thanks to me. I'm a lot of things, Madge, but I'm no hypocrite.'

There was a long silence while both women thought about times they had shared and could not talk about.

Then Rose said, 'Here they come. Nearly time.'

Madge joined her at the window. Two men were unlocking the chapel doors and latching them back with great difficulty. The wind ballooned their sober overcoats and they held their hats beneath their arms.

Madge murmured, 'Poor Etta.'

'She'll enjoy it,' Rose assured her hardily. 'She's Cornish from the year dot and they all enjoy a good funeral.'

Madge was silent. Rose had called herself an outsider. That was certainly what Madge was. A summer visitor, like the swallows. Not used to this scouring wind and freezing cold. Would Etta resent her presence?

Rose darted her a look, then almost as if she'd picked up Madge's thought, she said, 'Philip Nolla will be glad you've come, at any rate. And looking so nice too. That hat . . . and the

11

coat. The sort of thing they wear at Mennion House. County. You've done him proud.'

Madge swallowed sudden tears and both women stared out of the window stolidly, waiting for the embarrassment to pass.

People began to arrive. The Trevorrows in identical black overcoats, she with a veiled hat, he with a bowler. They tried to enter the chapel with dignity and were routed by the wind turning them inside-out.

'Black boots *and* stockings,' Rose commented. Then, as the bowler was only just saved, 'Such a mortal pity men can't use hat-pins.'

She was rewarded by a laugh from Madge. She turned briskly. 'Well. If you're going, I reckon it's time to go.' She surveyed Madge critically. 'Bring the hat forward a bit so that your bun is outside. That's better. Funny, there's a bit of you that hasn't aged at all. I can still see you with that long plait hanging down your back. And now you're knocking on fifty.'

I'm forty-five,' Madge protested humorously because she could have wept at Rose's words.

'Aye. I can give you a few years. Fifty-two next birthday. Ah well.' She went ahead and opened the front door just wide enough for Madge to slip through. 'Don't you take no notice if they're funny with you,' she said into the wind. 'Come straight back 'ere and we'll 'ave a cup of tea or something stronger!'

Madge held her hat and turned to smile up into those bold black eyes that hadn't changed in forty years. Strange, this feeling she had that Rose had always been there in her background. Yet she'd never seen her more than half a dozen times in all those years.

She went down Bunkers Hill bent almost double into the wind. Her own personal grief for Philip was just below the surface of her thoughts and was very deep; she dared not try to imagine how Etta must be feeling. Deep emotion always had made Etta tetchy; if she was short with Madge today, if that strange all-seeing stare was cold, then Madge must understand. Whether anyone minded or not, she'd had to come. She represented so many people whose lives had touched Philip's briefly and had been changed by the contact. She had to forget herself. She had to be . . . thankful.

The chapel was packed, literally to the ceiling. The gallery was tiered so that the congregation in the back row had to wear flat hats to fit beneath the planked roof. Those in front hooked umbrellas over the balustrade and arranged veils and skirts. Madge wished she'd gone upstairs where her camel coat wouldn't have stood out quite so much. Thank God Rosemary had lent her the black hat. She had refused it at first. 'I'll wear my brown felt. It's warmer and just as suitable.' But Mark, who understood the Cornish like a native, had said, 'Don't be daft, Ro. Mum can't go to Philip's funeral in a brown felt hat.' And Rosemary had gone upstairs to fetch the hat she had bought for herself only five years before.

How right Mark had been. And, in spite of Rose's approval, what an idiot she had been not to borrow a black coat from somewhere too. Camel might be respectable but it was a glaring contrast to the all-pervading black. She tried to sit lower in her seat, caught Mrs Trevorrow's eye and was treated to a strange kind of smile. Pitying? Surely the Trevorrows could have no idea what Philip's death meant to her? However, any kind of smile was better than the frozen stare she was getting from everyone else, and she returned it warmly. Immediately, like a light, it was switched off. Madge shrank into herself. So Rose was right; they were going to be 'funny' with her. Philip was a local hero and they were jealous of him, possessive, resentful of 'outsiders' like herself who might try to claim something of his memory. Yet she and all her family had been closer to Philip and Etta Nolla than anyone else. It was an acknowledged fact. They might be just summer visitors, but they'd been the Nollas' only visitors and there had always been a special bond between them. And she, Madge, was representing all of them. She mustn't forget that. And she mustn't forget what else Rose had said: Philip would be pleased to see her, camel coat or no camel coat. He'd glint up at her and say slyly, 'Fancy up-country 'at for fancy up-country woman!'

She straightened her back and smiled as she conjured up a picture of him. If he were sitting by her side now he'd reach to her shoulder and she'd catch his expressions in fleeting glimpses when he chose to lift his head and show her what he was thinking. He did not do that with anyone else; she'd realised that a long time ago. He was a very closed-in man. But he had opened for her. He teased her and let her know that she was special.

Someone stopped by her side and looked at the empty pew next to hers. It was Jim Maddern. It was years since they'd exchanged a word, but she knew him. He had been on the periphery of their group when they were children; a link between them and Rose Care. Now his dark eyes met hers without recognition and he walked on to the front pews reserved for the close mourners, though he had little to do with the Nollas. She felt a flush break through the crust of cold over her face. She had been deliberately cut and by Jim Maddern of all people! This was what Rose had meant. As soon as the service was over she'd get back to the safety of Bunkers Hill and wait till this evening for a quiet word with Etta.

Then the harmonium squeaked to a stop and everyone began to stand up. The wind gusted into the chapel and the minister's voice began. 'I am the resurrection and the life saith the Lord. Those who believe . . .' Madge dropped her chin and held her breath. She no longer thought of Philip alone; the words dealt with the whole of humanity, the quick as well as the dead. As the procession came slowly up the aisle it was as if she could see them all . . . more than a dozen of them, all caught and held in Philip's net.

The coffin went past her. Cheap elm because Etta would have no money to spare. The lifeboat crew bore it on their shoulders. Then came Etta who was older than her husband, so must be nearly eighty. She was walking alone and leaning hard on her stick. Surely there was someone to walk with her, childless though she was?

She drew level with Madge and stopped. The mourners following, neighbours mostly, shuffled to a halt and exchanged glances. Etta lifted her stick and tapped Madge sharply on the arm. Alarmed, Madge looked up and saw that familiar, toothless grin.

'I thought as 'ow you'd come,' she said in a voice audible above the minister's incantations. 'I saved you your place.' And she transferred her stick to her other hand and held out her arm for Madge. As in a dream Madge stepped sideways out of the pew and took the arm. Etta gave a grunt of relief and surrendered her weight to Madge. Together they walked up the aisle and took their places in the front row, and watched in silence as Philip's unwanted physical body was lowered gently on to the coffin rests in front of the minister. There was Etta's wreath in the obligatory shape of an anchor, lying the length of the wood; and above it, as

14

if holding it in place, was a circlet of Christmas roses which Madge had chosen on her arrival yesterday when she had walked down Tregenna Hill from the station.

The last time she'd seen him was five months ago; last summer. She should have known then. Perhaps she had known and not been able to face it.

She'd been sitting with her back to the harbour wall, dreaming. The tide was coming in and Maddern's pony and trap waited patiently on the shore for the first of the boats to bring in its catch. Madge wondered idly about mackerel for tea. Etta would pickle them in vinegar and they could have salad, and a mountain of bread and butter. Then, if the weather held, they could drive to Marazion and watch the sun go down behind St Michael's Mount. It was so hot. So gloriously hot. She closed her eyes against the healing sun and could still see the white sand and the glass-green of the sea; but not exactly where the sea became translucent blue and merged with the sky.

She opened her eyes to check on this, and there was Philip signalling to her from the Fisherman's Lodge. She moved, getting to her feet with some difficulty, gathering up handbag and book and shuffling through the sand barefoot to meet him. He opened the gate for her. Strangers were not allowed in the Lodge but she had gone there with Philip as a small girl and was reluctantly accepted.

They sat outside, backs to the wooden shack with its leaning chimney, the milling crowds shut away behind them. They could still see Maddern's pony and trap waiting patiently by the glinting sea.

'Here they come,' Philip said quietly. And around Smeaton's Pier came the first of the diminished fishing fleet, a big tub-like boat, broad in beam with a wide stern, like a child's toy boat bobbing down a bath of water.

'Good catch by the looks of 'en.'

The boat was wallowing under its load of fish. It berthed alongside Smeaton's Pier with much shouting and leaping about from its crew. A boat put off from the harbour beach and the business of unloading began. Madge was reminded of an oil painting by Sargent in one of the galleries. Painted over a hundred years ago, it bridged time to the present.

Philip said, 'Broodin' over young Mark, are you, woman?'

'No. Thinking of time. Some things never change.' She smiled down on the ancient trilby. 'I don't think of Mark all the time, Philip.'

'But most of it, I reckon.'

She was silent, remembering the heartache for Rosemary not long ago.

His hand came out and rested for an instant on the skirt of her sun dress. It was gnarled as the twisted ropes tethering the boats to the shore. Then he leaned forward, elbows on knees, fingers hanging loosely. 'I think O' young Mark as my own son. You know that, dun't you?'

She swallowed. There were things between them that were never said.

He did not wait for a reply. 'You dun't need to worry about 'im, woman. Like I said . . . my own son.'

He did not look up and she stared down at the crinkled neck above the blue kerchief, realising how much of her anxiety for Mark Philip had carried over the years.

She cleared her throat. 'I wish there was some way I could tell you how grateful . . . you've always been *there* . . .'

'The shoe is on the other foot, woman. Entirely.'

But he did not look up to reassure her and she felt a pang of concern.

She said, 'Are you all right, Philip?'

At last he flicked her one of his quick smiles.

'Course I'm all right, little woman. Etta and me, we've allus been all right.' He looked at the sea again. Jim was bucketing fish into his cart. Mackerel, silver and blue and fluid as mercury. 'Our needs are small, d'you see. Our bodies thrive on sameness. Fish and tea.'

It wasn't what she had meant but she was glad that the conversation was back to everyday things. 'You should have fruit and vegetables, Philip.'

He laughed with genuine amusement. 'Woman . . . woman. We're both nearly eighty years old. Whatever we've ett, whatever we've done . . . must be right, mustn't it?'

She laughed too, ruefully. Neither of them wore glasses, neither of them had ever been to a hospital; they were bent with rheumatism, but they still walked the beaches daily.

16

Their silence was companionable from then on. They watched people gather around Jim's cart to buy the mackerel; he pocketed the money eagerly. His father still paid him pre-war wages for his part in the fishing business. Another boat came around the jut of Smeaton's Pier and the whole business of berthing began again. The heat soaked into them like balm and Madge closed her eyes, reliving the total security of childhood when there had always been someone else to plan tomorrow.

The cemetery, clinging to the cliff above Porthmeor beach, was a nightmare of freezing wind, but it was exactly the place Philip would have chosen; within sight of the sea but far above its clawing fingers. Madge supported Etta at the graveside, unable to slip away, physically held by those black-gloved fingers.

Afterwards they gathered in the house: the Trevorrows; the Gurnards and the Madderns; old Mrs Peters and Miss Lowe who delivered pamphlets and tracts. Mrs Fosdick from next door had pushed chairs in anywhere, and they sat back to back, cheek by jowl, while cups of hot sweet tea were passed over their heads and potted meat sandwiches put on their laps. When Etta saw a free hand or knee she would place a photograph in or on it. 'That's Philip when he was with Jem in the ole lugger.' 'There's Philip there, behind that easel thing. One of they artists was always painting him.' She handed a bundle to Madge. 'Take them. They're mostly your brother and your pa. Used to make my life a mis'ry they did.' But she drew her mouth inside-out as she spoke, in silent, reminiscent mirth.

Mrs Fosdick passed Jem Gurnard a plate of sandwiches and ignored Madge. Etta immediately took the plate from her and sat down on the slippery sofa, sharing the sandwiches solely with Madge and talking to her alone.

'I well remember they cricket matches on Porthkidney sands. Your pa. 'E liked bowling best. Yonkers didn't 'e call it?'

'Yorkers,' Madge said faintly, wishing she was in the kitchen at home, cutting up vegetables for the casserole they always had on a Thursday. For the first time in her life the cottage's smell of fish made her feel queasy.

'Ah. That were it. Yorkers. 'E bowled 'em sort of lovingly, didn't 'e? D'you remember that, my girl? 'E'd put us all over the beach, jus where 'e wanted us, then 'e'd run up ever so careful-like an'—'

Mrs Trevorrow said, 'Well, if everyone is ready, I think Mr Trevorrow had better begin. We have an engagement this evening.'

Madge would have made her excuses then, she had no wish to hear Philip's last Will and Testament. She half rose, but Etta pushed her back down and put photographs and sandwich plate firmly on her lap.

She said, 'Let's hear it then. Though I reckon there's not many 'ere what doesn't know it already.'

Mrs Trevorrow addressed the chandelier which hung so incongruously above the table.

'If you are imputing that my husband discusses the business of his clients—'

'Oh be silent, woman. Philip wrote his wishes on a piece of paper in this room with the help of Mr Fosdick for a scribe, and with two witnesses who could 'ave told anyone. The paper was put in your man's safe. That's not being a client!' She hunched an irritable shoulder. 'Get on with it. Get it over.'

Whether or not Philip had been a client, Mr Trevorrow was determined to do him justice. With much shoving, he ousted Jim Maddern from his place at the plush-covered table, made enough elbow room for himself to scatter a few papers around, picked out the relevant one, adjusted his pince-nez, and proceeded to read.

'I, Philip John Sebastian Nolla, being of sound mind, do hearby bequeath all my wordly goods to Mark Briscoe, on the understanding that my wife, Etta Margaret Nolla, may continue to live in Zion Cottage until her death.' He paused until the various muttered exclamations had died down, then went on without expression. 'I know this will disappoint my partners in the *Forty-niner*, and I ask them to understand. I am going to make it all legal-like with Mr Trevorrow, but I want them to know that this is my real true wish and they would oblige me by not questioning it.' Mr Trevorrow looked up, avoiding Madge's gaze, and commented, 'It was indeed witnessed by two friends, and again by my two clerks. Although it is not couched in legal terms, it is, nonetheless perfectly valid.'

There was a long silence in Etta's parlour. Madge understood now why she had been ostracised during the funeral and since her arrival in the house. She could understand their resentment;

18

Philip was giving away a slice of St Ives, and to an outsider; a summer person.

And then Mrs Fosdick said cuttingly, 'Well. Well, now we know, I suppose. We often wondered whether young Mark's trouble was anything to do with the St Ives hip. Now we know.'

Madge's stomach heaved against the fish smell. It was dying out now, but in the old days many St Ives people had been born with dislocated hips and, untreated, had swayed their way through life accepting their disability without question. Philip had been one of them. But how on earth could anyone, however evilly inclined, associate Mark's 'trouble' with the St Ives hip? She choked and put a hand to her mouth.

Etta said loudly, 'Now listen to me. This is Philip's last wish. I knowed about it and I agreed to it. Philip an' me, we 'ad no fam'ly as you all know. *They* was our family—' she put a hand on Madge's shoulder, 'an' better than most real fam'lies they was too. All we've bin able to give 'em is their 'olidays. An' they've 'elped us over all our 'ard times agin and agin. We couldn't do nothin' in return. Till now. They're summer people and that's the way they will allus be. But young Mark is summat different. 'E en't a summer visitor. We can give 'm summat. An' that's what we want to do. An' if I 'ear anything more about it, I'll start a spate of gossip myself. Oh yes. I know a bit about most of you. We all know a bit about each other I reckon, and we keeps our counsel. But counsels can be unkept. If necessary.'

Madge sat with bent head. But Etta did not actually deny what Mrs Fosdick had implied. And Philip himself had said that Mark was like his own son. Had Philip twisted the truth until he deluded himself that that was true? Did Etta believe it?

Madge concentrated on controlling herself while the mourners filed out. The very air was full of their resentment and anger. Some of them managed a civil farewell to Etta; no-one spoke to Madge. She might not have been there.

When she and Etta were alone at last she still could not look up. She put one hand over her eyes.

'I don't know what to say, Etta. Your home. The *Forty-niner*. *We* can provide for Mark. You must know that. He won't be able to accept this – he *can't* accept it. It will confirm . . . people will think . . . he *can't* accept it!'

'Don't you be too sure, my girl. Philip knew what he was doing.'

'If *only* he hadn't done this, Etta. Don't you see – don't you realise what Mrs Fosdick meant? We can't ever come here again!' Her voice rose to a wail of despair, but Etta, as always when confronted with anguish, chose to ignore it.

'Don't talk rubbish, girl. And help me put these chairs back in the passage. Ernest Fosdick will come and take them tonight. I think Philip would have been pleased with it all, don't you?'

'Yes. I'm sure. But Etta—'

'I'm not talking about it no more, Madge, and that is that. My strength is all gone somewhere, and I want a proper cup of tea and my kitchen fire.'

She led the way into the back quarters where the range glowed comfortingly, shoved the kettle on to the trivet and sank into the chair that had always been Philip's. Madge saw that her face was a network of deeply etched lines and her eyes were red-rimmed with weariness.

'Etta, I understand how you feel . . .' She stood miserably in the doorway. 'But you do realise what people are thinking? They're not just angry because Philip willed his property to an outsider. They think he's done it for a reason. They think . . .'

'That young Mark is Philip's son?' Etta laughed grimly. 'No, they don't. They want to think it, yes. It makes it more int'restin'. But if they think that, they've got to take Philip off that pedestal they put 'im on. An' they wun't do that!'

The kettle began to spit into the coals. She hauled herself up.

'Dun't be 'ard on them, Madge. Folks is only 'uman. There's allus bin a bit o' gossip round Philip an' me. It never worried us, you know that. An' Mark will revel in it – all of it. Philip knew that. That's why 'e did it. It will give Mark a *place* 'ere, like 'e's allus wanted. A place to live and a right to live in it.' She made the tea and sat back down with an audible gasp. 'Now. Are you 'avin' this pot with me, my girl? Or 'ave you got to be packin' up your traps to get back 'ome tomorrow?'

It was crystal clear which reply she wanted, and Madge knew that any further discussion would be dismissed as 'useless talk'.

She said in a small voice, 'I suppose I must go and pack. I'll write to you. I'm only round at Rose Foster's if you . . .'

'Rose Foster? What possessed you to go there?'

'She's respectable now,' Madge said defensively. 'Philip thought a lot of her too.'

20

'Aye. He did. He thought a lot of most people. He valued people. Even the bad ones. Even . . . even himself.' She glanced up. 'That's something you could learn from 'im, Madge.'

'I . . .' Madge wondered how much Etta knew. 'Yes. But Philip was good. Through and through.'

Etta smiled into the fire. 'Aye. Perhaps he was.' She sighed sharply. 'Now get off to Bristol, Madge, and tell 'em what's 'appened. I want young Mark to come 'ere afore I joins Philip. I can do for 'im till then. An' after . . . well, after will take care of itself.'

'Mark is working, Etta. He can't give up a perfectly good job and just come here like that.'

'Why not? This is 'is 'ome now. An' 'is share o' the *Forty-niner* will bring in enough for 'im to live on, if you'll 'elp 'im out now and then.' She sipped gratefully. 'Goodbye, Madge. Close that door as you go out, there's a draught like a knife coming down the passage.'

Madge did as she was bid and walked for what she knew would be the last time down the long passage to the front door. In spite of the funeral, it was as cluttered as ever. Sheets, probably Philip's sheets, hung over the line to air, and the borrowed chairs took up most of the floor space. The tears, which she had held in check all day, started to flow. She walked into the centre of the cobbled court, and tipped her head to stare blindly up at the dormer window which had been a lookout in the days when the cottage was first built, and Philip's bedroom every summer when 'the family' had come to stay.

'Philip,' she whispered. 'What have you done?'

She swallowed her tears, afraid that Mrs Fosdick would see her in the gloom, then she walked slowly to the harbour wall to gaze across the wind-chopped water to where the *Forty-niner* tossed on her anchor. She understood why he had left everything to Mark, she understood only too well. But what would happen now? Was this the end of her summers here? And was that perhaps what Philip wanted too?

CHAPTER TWO

1924

The train journey from Bristol was endless. Eight hours of sulphur-tasting salmon sandwiches and bitter Thermos tea, itchy liberty bodice and pencil-and-paper games with Neville which she never won and never expected to win. Her role as baby of the family and a girl at that, was clearly defined.

She was dazed when they reached the tiny junction of St Erth; she had almost forgotten that there was a world outside the railway carriage. But as she tumbled on to the platform conscious only of the elastic on her hat biting into her chin, the enchantment started to work. There were trees lining the station; they did not have leaves, they sprouted sabres. There were enormous pebbles bordering the burgeoning flower beds – obviously they were magic pebbles because they glinted crystal and blue in the fast-setting sun and the flowers were laying their heads on them as if they were pillows. And the air was different. She'd never considered air as an entity before, not in the whole four years of her life. It was part of the world; she breathed it; there could be lots of it, especially in Park Street in the winter; or there could be not much of it, in which case a feather filched from one of the sofa cushions would float up to the ceiling and bob around like a paper boat on the River Avon. This air was completely different. It did not only smell different, it actually tasted. The awful aftermath of sandwiches caking up her mouth began to dissolve; her hair, stiff and tight under her panama, loosened and lifted; her soot-lined nostrils were soothed, and her ears heard it.

'Oh . . . oh . . . oh,' she sighed. 'It's like Fairy Twinkle Land.'

Neville scoffed loudly, and her father smiled in his lofty indulgent way, but her mother, who read nightly from the big book about Fairy Twinkle and who had sewed a sampler for her daughter which read 'Be good sweet maid and let who will be

22

clever', hugged her and said, 'You've been such a good little girl all day long. Such a good, good little girl.'

They climbed wooden steps, crossed a bridge, and found what Mother called 'the little train' waiting for them. People sat with picnic baskets and dogs and shouted to each other. Not because they were angry, but because that was how Cornish people conversed. Father's colleague at the office who had recommended St Ives had warned them about this. And he had also said they wouldn't understand a word that was said. Marjorie understood everything and found it fascinating. They shouted about the weather and the pilchards and the luggers up north. Marjorie knelt on the seat so that her mouth was close to her mother's ear, and whispered, 'It's a shame the poor buggers won't be here to see the pictures, isn't it Mama? They must be such pretty pictures.'

Mother glanced apprehensively at Father who did not always appreciate Madge's mis-hearings.

'Little girls shouldn't listen to grown-up conversations. But luggers are boats, my darling, fishing boats. And they won't miss seeing pictures. It's the pilchard catch they're talking about. Now, no more listening.'

But Marjorie loved listening, and it was irritating that many of the grown-ups she knew, talked in whispers or spelled out words as if deliberately trying to shut her out. The Cornish people weren't like that. They shared what they said; she didn't have to listen, not really.

Mother turned her towards the window. 'Look, darling. There's St Ives. Isn't it beautiful?' And Madge looked, and listened, and breathed, and fell in love.

They had booked in at Zion Cottage with some trepidation. The Nollas had never taken summer visitors before and the Bridges had only stayed at boarding-houses in Weston-super-Mare and Rhyl. Father's colleague had told them that 'rooms and service' was the best way to do it in Cornwall. You got the full flavour of the place without having to put up with their fish diet. The rooms came at seven and six each per week, and you bought your own food for the landlady to cook. She also cleaned, made beds and put up with buckets, spades and sandshoes in her hall. He had given them the address where he and his family had 'gone native' last summer; but Mrs Warner had decided that foreigners weren't worth the money and had passed Alfred Bridges' letter on to the Nollas. They had had two bad pilchard years and although Philip Nolla took his lugger up to the North Sea each summer, the income was always uncertain. Etta Nolla decided to supplement it with summer letting. But they would have to take her as they found her.

The hall which would accommodate their holiday impedimenta was a passage boarded with ship's timbers and strung with washing lines. The sitting-room, suspended above the fish cellar, creaked like a boat's cabin and wasn't much bigger. Above the circular plush-hung table a delicate chandelier swayed and tinkled when anyone breathed, and curios of a lifetime spent by the Atlantic were packed on shelves, window-ledges and fireplace. Shells, driftwood carvings, ships in bottles, sepia photographs, lace antimacassars, polished crab claws, ships' bells . . . all jostled for place. Mother breathed something about the amount of dusting, but it soon became apparent that Mrs Nolla did not dust. Madge knew that it was the original Aladdin's cave.

Phillip Nolla was still 'taking herring' off the Northumberland coast; with the slackening of the pilchard harvests most of the St Ives luggers went north for the summer months. He might well be home in time to look over the foreign family who were paying so handsomely to share his home. It became obvious very quickly to the Bridges that they were on approval. If they gave satisfaction they would be welcome next year. If not, no amount of rent would secure their rooms again.

Etta lived in the back in conditions so primitive that at first Marie Bridges was shocked, and then full of admiration. The 'back' was built right into the living rock and had no window. Light came from the open door into the passageway, and from the trap in the floor which led via a ladder to the old fish cellar. One wall contained a cooking range, another a long table and storage shelves. Dry goods were kept in an airless little pantry beneath the stairs, perishables down in the fish cellar. Water and toilet arrangements were also down there. In the bedrooms above were elegant chamber pots, china basins and ewers. Etta was won over immediately by Alfred Bridges' first edict. 'Neville, you will take down the slops each morning and bring up fresh water for Mrs Nolla.'

24

She showed her gratitude plainly when she told him, 'There are a litter of Nollas in St Ives. My name is Etta and my man is Philip.'

She was a small, wiry woman, all bone and sinew. Her hair was already turning grey and screwed painfully into a bun on the top of her head. She wore black; high necks and long sleeves; a shawl for outdoors. She was one of nature's stoics. And she preferred men to women; Neville and Alfred got smiles from her, however grim. Marie and Madge were usually treated to a tight-lipped approach which could soften into indulgence or explode into exasperation as the situation demanded. That first evening it was the latter.

Madge, as a reward for being such a good, good little girl, was kept up late and allowed to join in the family walk to Porthmeor. Directed by Etta, they strolled up Virgin Street to Barnoon and walked along the top of the cemetery. The view was breathtaking; the sun just drowning in the sea. They lifted Madge on to the wall to get her first glimpse of the Atlantic.

'America is over *there*—' Alfred told her, jabbing a finger at the horizon.

But as she peered, a fly, drunk with sun and summer evening, zoomed straight into her eye.

'Oh it hurts,' she sobbed. 'Oh it does so hurt!'

'That's because it's come all the way from America!' Neville joked.

'Do be quiet Neville,' Marie begged. 'Oh my darling!' She appealed to her husband. 'What can we *do*, Alfred?'

'Her own tears will wash it out,' he said sensibly. 'Home to bed. That's the answer.'

As they entered the cottage, Etta emerged from her back room at all the commotion. She screwed up one corner of a not-too-clean handkerchief and poked at Madge's eye. The commotion increased.

'She should have gone straight to bed,' Etta declared, giving up. 'No good ever came of keeping a child out of bed after six o'clock!'

Madge wept anew at this lack of sympathy and Marie said, 'Oh Etta, she's been such a good little girl all day long – such a shame—'

Etta was mollified by the use of her name. She said, 'Come and

25

sleep in the little truckle bed I've made up for you, my maid. 'Tis like a canoe.'

Suddenly, just as Alfred had said, the fly was washed out on a wave of salt tears, and the pain went away. Madge gave her wide, painful smile, and held out her arms to this new friend.

'Come with me. Please come with me, Etta. You're a real proper Cornishwoman.'

The words were filched from her father, but Etta did not know that.

'From the mouths of babes . . .' she murmured, herding Madge up the stairs. They knew they would be welcome next year.

Alfred Bridges was a strange mixture of modern and Edwardian. He revered, even worshipped, his wife, but his treatment of Etta Nolla was as one man to another. Etta – and later Philip – became his henchmen, and as such came with them on most of their expeditions. Etta baulked at sitting on the beach; she was averse to sand. But she was soon taught how to hold a bat and how to field a cricket ball. When her advice was sought about good picnic sites, she would smile her grim smile and say, 'It do depend on whether you're taking the bat and stumps. If not, there's a little rocky cove just beyond Zennor there.'

'Caves?' asked Neville, wide-eyed.

'I reckon. They caught smugglers there when I were a girl.'

'Golly!'

'But if you want a proper cricket match, you can't beat Porthkidney. Just b'low the golf links.'

Alfred considered. 'Not really enough of us for a proper match, Etta. We'll go and look at the smugglers' cave.'

Neville whooped his delight and Etta said seriously, 'Reckon we can make up a team when Philip gets 'ome, Mr Bridges. There'll be six of us then. And we could get little Jim Maddern along, an' p'raps Jem Gurnard. Dependin' o' course.'

Everyone knew that meant depending on whether the Bridges were considered acceptable or not. Meanwhile the picnic hamper was lugged along the cliff path and for the last mile Madge was carried on her father's shoulders. She could see Neville's dark brown head bobbing among the fern in front, closely followed by Etta's topknot, while behind, her mother's old-fashioned boater floated genteelly over the top of the foliage like one of the many gliding gulls, and her voice emerged from it in ecstatic exclamations at the view.

Since that first night when Madge had been adjured to admire the view and had succeeded only in collecting a fly in her eye, she had been suspicious of views. But now, quite suddenly, the sheer magnificence of the meeting of land and sea hit her in the eye with far more force than the fly had done. She rode her father's shoulders as if they were the wings of a bird; she saw the cliffs and the ocean as her true environment. She was four years old but already she knew that the beginning of human life had happened here, on the edge of the water. She felt it in the bones of hands and feet, in the bellows inside her chest. She was conscious for the first time of her physical being, its wonderful intricacies, its oneness with everything else. At that moment she thought she could have taken flight from her father, dived into the sea with the seals, dug her fingers into the ferny earth and grown roots. Instead she cradled her father's skull in her plump arms, lowered her cheek to the bald spot on his crown, and wept.

Her parents were concerned.

'Madge, what is it?' Father lifted her down and held her away from him commandingly. 'Tell me why you are crying, child. Come along now.'

'I don't know . . .'

'Alfred dear – let me hold her. My poor baby—'

'Marie, she must explain properly. She is quite old enough to identify a problem causing her such distress. Now, stop crying, Madge, and think. No, I'm not cross with you, dear, I merely wish to discover the trouble so that I may alleviate it.'

'Alfred. She cannot possibly understand—'

But Madge understood that her parents were disagreeing, and she was the cause of it. She swallowed her tears, gulped, then gasped, 'I was so sorry for everything. The world. It's so beautiful, you see.'

For a moment Alfred stared at this child of his who, please God, would never know war, then he clasped her to his shoulder, rested his chin on her ordinary brown hair and closed his eyes. Somehow she had inherited the things he knew; the shadow behind the sunlight.

He said firmly, 'No need to feel sorry, Madge. It will always be

27

here. However much we try to muck it about it will always be here.'

Marie put her arms around them both.

'She is so sensitive,' she murmured, deeply thankful that Alfred understood.

Madge had already lost her moment of epiphany. She dried her face briefly on her father's linen jacket and lifted her head.

'Don't tell Etta,' she begged. 'Please don't tell Etta that I cried again.'

They smiled and assured her they would do no such thing. Marie took her hand and began to lead her through the shoulder-high fern.

'I think you and I will have to work hard to gain Etta's respect,' she said.

It was the first time she had acknowledged that she and Madge were equal females. Father often referred to Neville and himself as 'We men', but to Mother, Madge had always been a very precious, very little, girl.

The picnic was a great success.

There was a great deal of driftwood on the enormous pebbles at the shoreline, and Madge scurried about with Neville, slipping and sliding on the rocks unheedingly, to build a huge pyre. Neville tried to shock her by asking her to look for a dead gull – 'Give it a proper funeral, Sis,' – but she shook her head and said inspirationally, 'It's a signal fire, Nev. Like in your comic. We're shipwrecked, see, and we have to keep a fire going day an' night—'

'I know about signal fires, Madge! It's my comic!' But Neville was just as keen as she was and he prevailed on Etta to feed the fire while he and Madge climbed a finger of rock and waved the picnic tablecloth.

Marie would have ordered them away from such dangers, but Alfred restrained her smilingly.

'They won't try to do more than their capabilities,' he murmured. 'Neville must be permitted to chance his arm. And this is an important step forward for Madge. She's coming out of her chrysalis.'

'Yes. Well. I want them to be good friends in spite of the age difference,' Marie conceded.

28

'When he's twenty-four and she's twenty, there will *be* no age difference,' he said strongly. And she smiled, believing him.

By the time Philip Nolla returned from the north, Madge had established a reputation as a budding tomboy. Neville, sensing competition as well as companionship, tested her to the limit. She could climb cliffs, scramble around rock pools and walk the cliff paths as well as he could himself. Neither of the children were allowed out of their depths in the sea, but Madge was not scared of the giant rollers and would either bob over them like a cork, or sit on the sandy floor of the ocean and let them guggle harmlessly over her head. She did not realise as yet that Neville removed himself hastily when a wave built itself up above his head; so far he had managed to cover his retreat with war whoops, but Madge's courage – which obviously came from stupidity – annoyed him greatly.

One afternoon towards the end of the holiday, they were on Porthmeor beach as usual, the children in the sea, Alfred and Marie in deckchairs outside the canvas bathing tent which they had hired for the fortnight. The picnic hamper, covered with a damp towel to keep the contents cool, served as a footstool for Marie, who if the truth were known, partially shared Etta's dislike of the all-encroaching sand. Etta was not with them; she rarely joined them for their afternoon bathes and that day was awaiting Philip's arrival from his three months at sea.

A wave broke beyond the children. It looked enormous but Madge knew it would flatten out by the time it reached them. Neville never quite believed that and began to retreat. 'Come *on* Madge – it's coming!'

'It's only little, don't run away, Neville.'

He said furiously, 'I'm not running away, stupid! It's a game. Don't you know that? You have to see who can go the fastest. The wave always catches you. You always lose!'

But he stood his ground and sure enough the wave surged around his waist harmlessly. The next one began to pile up inexorably. Madge paddled legs and arms like fins and watched it coming. Neville said nervously, 'It's the seventh. The seventh wave. I've been counting. We ought to race this one, Madge. Come on.'

Against all instincts Madge put her feet down and tried to

stride back to the shore. Neville, much taller than she was, lifted his legs crazily clear of the water and leapt ahead of the wave like an ungainly ostrich.

That was how Philip Nolla first saw them all. The boy leaping clear of the clawing sea; the girl suddenly and horrifically disappearing beneath it; the parents, either indifferent or totally ignorant, sitting placidly high up the beach drinking tea from Bakelite cups.

Like many others who get their living from the sea, Philip could not swim. And his respect for the moods and vagaries of the ocean was akin to fear. But his instinct to save the small girl surmounted all that. He struggled through the dry sand frantically, then tore along the firm wet shoreline and plunged fully clothed into the next wave. His heavy boots filled with water and his trouser legs pressed coldly against knees and thighs. He shuddered convulsively and pushed on. Then, just to his left, a white bathing helmet suddenly bobbed to the surface, and beneath it a small face, curved and dimpled like a sprite's, smiled beatifically at him.

'Isn't it bootiful?' Madge asked. 'All bubbly like lemonade sherbet!'

He hardly heard her words. He grabbed her and lifted her to shoulder height; her knitted costume provided a good grip; he turned and struggled out of the water and there were the parents and Neville, wide-eyed and alert at last.

Philip put Madge down carefully.

'You all right, my girl?' he asked.

'Yes.' Madge thought it was all a game. She surveyed this small, soaking new arrival with delight. 'Are you Philip?'

'I am.' He looked at Alfred with a mixture of pity and censure. 'You did not see the maid go under. Good job I were coming down the path just at that moment.' Then he turned to Neville. 'Never leave your sister like that again, young man. It is your job to look after her.'

Marie spoke. 'But Mr Nolla – there was no need – Madge always goes under the big waves—'

And Alfred said quickly, 'It was damned good of you, Philip – mind if we call you Philip? You deserve a medal!'

Neville, red-faced, said, 'I told her to run. She's silly. I told her. I did. Honestly.'

'Then you must listen to your brother, my girl. Listen and pay heed.'

Madge nodded, wide-eyed, realising now that she had been rescued from drowning. She remembered some words from her Fairy Twinkle book.

'I am eternally grateful to you,' she said.

Everyone laughed except Philip, who smiled gravely. Neville, vindicated and won over completely, said manfully, 'I say. You're a good egg, Philip. A really good egg.'

He shook Philip's hand, so did Alfred, then so did Marie. When it was offered to Madge she took it and did not let go. They all walked back to the bathing tent together.

'Etta sent me to tell you that she is putting tea on the table in half an hour,' Philip told them.

Marie said, 'But we've had our picnic. We can't eat any more.'

Philip said seriously, 'This is my first meal in my house since the beginning of the summer. I would be honoured if you would eat with me.'

They all loved him. He was so different from Etta; Alfred recognised all the qualities of a top-rate sergeant – reliability, initiative, loyalty; Marie thought he was biblical; Neville reiterated at intervals that he was a good egg; and Madge knew he was her rescuer.

They got to know him well during their last three days. He took them around the *Forty-niner* and showed them how to rig her two big sails. They watched as he spread the drift nets and mended them with a fat-packed bobbin, throwing it back and forth, knotting the line, snipping with the knife kept inside his boot. They listened avidly to his tales of old St Ives. He could remember the hurricane of '93 when four steamers had been wrecked in the bay and he had gone over in a bosun's chair on one of the rocket lines to help with the injured. The following year there had been the flood, and just before the war a winter blizzard that had buried the little town and cut it off from all its neighbours.

'What about the war, Philip?' clamoured Neville. 'Tell us about St Ives in the war!'

'Same as everyone. Short of food and too much talk. There was a German woman over to Zennor way – trouble there. But

31

then she went away and we settled down to sit it out. Or was it the other wars you was meaning, young Neville?'

'Other wars?' Neville was round-eyed.

'The Turks landed 'ere y' know. And them Spaniards, and that Mr Warbeck who called himself Richard the Fourth or some-such. And there's always bin the smugglers.'

He entertained Neville; he never tried to entertain Madge. They were quiet companions, perfectly at ease in each other's company, sometimes talking, sometimes happily silent.

They sat together like that beneath Old Man's Head on the last day of their holiday. Neville, fired by Philip's stories, was trying to climb the big square rock that sat high on the headland, so like a human skull. Philip made no attempt to call him down as his parents would have done. Neville expended all his energy on the hopeless attempt, and was content.

Madge was nevertheless anxious.

'Is he all right, Philip? Etta says only grown-ups can climb Old Man's Head.'

' 'E won't get nowhere, my maid. But 'e's enjoyin' the attempt I reckon. An' when 'e's a bit bigger, Philip will show 'im the proper way to go up the Old Man. There's a way at the back.' He looked down at her beneath the brim of his trilby. 'I could show you too, little maid. Anyone can do it.'

She smiled at him. 'Neville first,' she said.

And he touched her shoulder as if congratulating her. 'Aye. Neville first.'

They were silent; behind them Neville dropped to the ground and surveyed the rock face for concealed toeholds. He had seen people atop the Old Man and wanted quite desperately to climb it.

Madge said, 'We've got to go home tomorrow, Philip.'

'I know that, my girl.'

'Will you miss us?'

'Will you miss me?'

'Oh I shall, Philip – I shall.'

'Then that is a question you don't have to ask of me. But that doesn't mean either of us must be sad for very long. A bit of you will stay here in St Ives and next year you'll come back and it will be just the same.' He looked round to check on Neville. 'Next year Philip will take you out in the *Forty-niner*. We'll go and look at the seals.' He raised his voice. 'And next year I'll teach you to climb that there rock, Neville! But not now. Come on, the pair of you. Mackerel for tea!'

He did not wait for any discussion but plodded off towards the wishing well at the top of Porthmeor. Madge watched him for a moment, then took out her handkerchief and ran after him.

'Here you are, Philip. Put it in your sleeve.'

He looked at the scrap of cambric in puzzlement.

'What's this, my maid? 'Tis not big enough for me to use!'

She said very solemnly, 'That is the bit of me that will stay in St Ives with you, Philip. And I'll come back for it when I'm a big girl. I shall be five years old when I see you again.'

He folded the handkerchief carefully and put it into his pocket. Then he took her hand and they walked sedately together. After a few more fruitless moments of token defiance, Neville gave up rock-climbing for a year and galloped along the sandy path to join them.

CHAPTER THREE

1932

The fact that the National Government was in did not console Alfred Bridges for the fact that Ramsay MacDonald was still Prime Minister.

'How can it be a National Government with a Labour chappie at the top?' he harangued his family as he flapped the *Daily Mail* over the breakfast table, making the chandelier tinkle madly and causing his wife to replace the cover over the bacon and eggs before the children had helped themselves.

Neville could not resist picking up the challenge and riposted with: 'Well, what's the alternative, Dad? If Mr Baldwin took it on, it would be no more nationalistic than it is now.' He looked at his mother for support and received an admonitory shake of the head. 'Would it, Tagger?' he asked of his schoolfriend Clem Briscoe who had no father and had come with them on this holiday.

Clem was torn between loyalty to his friend and diplomacy towards the man who was paying for the holiday. He made noises in his throat.

Twelve-year-old Madge, sentient beyond her years and over-flowing still with a compassion that frequently annoyed Neville with its solemn piety, said quickly, 'Does it really matter, Daddy? You said last week that so long as MacDonald has proved beyond doubt that a Labour government cannot possibly work in this country . . .'

Her memory was a little too accurate for Alfred and he flapped the paper again, this time across the marmalade jar.

'We'll see. We'll see how long he can stay at the helm. A year at the most. I'll give him a year at the most.'

Neville lifted the cover from the eggs and shovelled two very slippery ones on to his plate. Over the years Marie had introduced

34

her own cutlery and crockery to supplement Etta's basic supply and – with enormous tact – insisted on laying the meal tables herself. But she could do nothing about Etta's cooking and the eggs were always floating on a bed of liquid dripping.

'I doubt that, Dad.' Neville wasn't going to give way in front of Tagger Briscoe. 'I'd give him four. Wouldn't you, Tagger?'

Clem made more sounds which Neville chose to interpret as total agreement.

'Right. Then he'll have proved he can do it and the country will send in another Labour government, and *this* time—'

Clem glanced at his host and said quickly, 'Steady on, old man. Remember the vote of confidence before . . . remember the plus-four boys and all that.'

'Thank you, Clement,' Alfred said, smiling jovially over the newspaper. 'Thank you for saving us all from Communism. Yours is the voice of reason and I am glad to hear it these days!'

Neville dropped his knife and seized Clem's free hand. Beneath the level of the table-top he began to exert vengeful pressure on Clem's little finger. Clem laughed, so did Alfred and Etta appeared from the back kitchen to enquire whether the teapot should be 'drownded' yet again.

Alfred folded his paper and turned in his chair. He was, in his own words, a pre-war man, and at breakfast he always wore his iron-hard collar and his waistcoat. But he was also a jocular man, and this morning he was in a particularly good mood.

'Etta, the teapot is full and the leaves are by no means drowned. Please sit and have a cup with us.'

Etta favoured them all with her grim smile. This was the eighth holiday the Bridges had spent at Zion Cottage, and they were her only summer visitors. Alfred insisted on increasing the rent each year, and he was always giving her presents. She would have accepted them from no-one else, and she looked on all of them – even Neville's friend – as her own.

'I 'ope you'll excuse me from that, Mr Bridges.' She took the paper away from him and put it on the window seat. 'I like my tea to taste like tea.'

Madge looked at Neville, half-hoping he might make a jokey reference to what he called Etta's 'cup of black treacle'. But he was concentrating on something else. She saw that beneath Clem Briscoe's unfolded napkin, the boys had linked their little fingers and appeared to be trying to tear them out by the roots. Her eyes watered sympathetically. Neville often recounted the trials of strength undergone by new boys at his school, and she knew that this was one of them. There had been a harrowing story about an important old boy who had come to Speech Day and proudly displayed a crooked little finger; legacy of his first day at the school when it had been broken during this frightful initiation.

Etta went on, 'I might as well ask you now, Mrs Bridges. What is it to be today? Hot or cold?'

Marie Bridges knew that this was no reference to possible weather conditions. It was misty outside the small parlour window, but it was a heat mist and would probably disperse by the time breakfast had been cleared. She in turn raised her brows at her husband.

'Well, dear? What are our plans today?'

Alfred was the one who made the plans.

He looked at the two straight-faced boys, his daughter – solemn as usual but with her eyes suddenly enormously blue in her round brown face – his wife smiling and beautiful, Etta at his right shoulder, a ready henchman. He smiled, letting his love for them shine through like the sun through the mist.

'We'll have a cricket match,' he pronounced. 'We'll take a big hamper on to the dunes at Porthkidney and we'll make camp there. And after lunch we'll have a cricket match.'

'Two-a-side?' queried Neville, relaxing his hold on Clem for a moment.

'Etta will come, won't you, Etta? And we'll ask Jim Maddern. Is there anyone else to make up the numbers?'

'Rose Care,' Neville suggested quickly. 'She's home again and was helping Jim with the donkeys yesterday.'

Alfred looked repressively at his son. Rose Care's name was bandied around the Sloop sometimes; she was purported to be short on underwear. Alfred wondered how much Neville might know. He was sixteen after all, and boys talked a lot at boarding school.

Etta picked up the paper again. 'Ah. She's home again because she's bin dismissed from the big house at Hayle.' She brought the folded paper down smartly on the napkin between the two boys. 'Stop that silly finger-wrestling this minute, you two. There's a chap over Helston lost both his little fingers that way. You should

36

know better, eddycated lads like you!' She replaced the paper on the window seat. 'No need to worry about numbers. Philip bin sighted just off Five Points. 'E'll be 'ere in an 'our or two. 'E'll be wicketkeeper just like usual.'

Neville and Madge both cheered, Neville to take his father's attention away from finger-wrestling, and Madge because her St Ives was never complete without Philip Nolla.

In spite of losing the toss that afternoon, Alfred settled back among the picnic paraphernalia, knowing that he was probably the luckiest man on earth. Some of that luck he had made for himself, that was certain. He had gone against family wishes by joining the Engineering department of the Great Western Railway straight from school instead of going to a respectable redbrick university. And now he was the Assistant Divisional Engineer with a good salary and enough first class rail passes each year to enable him to bring his family here, go up to Scotland, or even across to France. He'd made that luck himself. And marrying his beautiful Marie – that had gone against the family grain too – but that had been the best thing he had ever done. She had been a pupil in the girls' school opposite his own, unnoticed in her uniform among two hundred others. But she had come to his Sixth Form Leavers' Dance and floored him – quite literally – by dropping her lemon ice in his path. When she had picked him up, her beautiful dark eyes full of apology, he had known he must marry her and be with her for the rest of his life. But her father was a jeweller from Amsterdam and she was destined to work in his shop. The Bridges did not consider it a suitable match at all.

That was in 1908; he was eighteen, she was sixteen. By 1912, established at the Engineering Office in Bristol, he was seeing her every day, although his father believed they met only on Sundays. And in September 1914 when he went to be measured for his uniform, he arranged a registry office wedding and married her before he went to France. His parents had flung up their hands, but when her father died, they had had her to live with them and had learned to love her before they too died. He thought of how he had bludgeoned his way through those years, and smiled.

But his luck in getting through the war was not self-made. He had not thought he would make it and on his leave before the battle of the Somme he had ceased to be 'careful', wanting a child quite desperately to be his immortality when he was gone. And he had got a child. And he had survived against all odds. There was the gas of course, but he had still survived. And Madge was no armistice conception; they had considered the advisability of another baby and decided for it coolly. Madge was not luck, she was judgement, but she was a privilege too.

That day it seemed to Alfred that the privileges rained thick and fast. It was good to see Philip Nolla. Short and wiry, his beaky face hardly visible beneath the brim of his ancient trilby, Philip had become over the years like a family retainer. Etta cared for their bodily needs as best she could, but there was always an element of grim reluctance about her fondness for them. They were foreigners and always would be. Philip's feeling went deeper and was very near to devotion. He treated Marie like a goddess, and probably thought of Madge as the child he'd never had. Now, as he crouched behind the makeshift wicket, he glanced sideways to check on her.

'Keep your eye on that ball, my maid!' he called. 'It might be a tennis ball, but it'll 'urt ee 'ard if it catches you.'

And Madge smiled blindly into the sun and called back, 'You keep your eyes peeled too!'

Alfred smiled again as he leaned against the hamper and watched young Clem Briscoe taking his run-up to the crease. Etta waited for the ball, bat held casually at knee height, voluminous skirts kilted into her belt revealing black stockings and men's boots. What a character. She and Philip were individuals down to their toenails. Typically Cornish.

Neville and Clem took their cricket very seriously, and Neville, waiting to bat with his father, felt bound to yell 'Well bowled sir!' in spite of the fact that Etta hit an easy six with one hand behind her back. Mrs Bridges fielded the ball from below the tide-line and returned it to a flushed Clem.

Alfred said, 'Seems a nice young chap, Briscoe. Glad you brought him along, Neville.'

But Neville would not permit himself to be conciliatory with his father. He grunted.

Alfred persevered. 'Mother a widow, I believe?' He narrowed his eyes to watch his wife lope back to her out-field position. She was still startlingly beautiful with her jet-black hair and dark eyes. Unexpectedly he saw her in a different perspective: as a widow. His heart thumped with a terror he hadn't experienced since the trenches.

'Don't think so.' Neville almost grinned at the chance to shock his father quite legitimately. 'Husband couldn't take any more. Tagger doesn't say much but she does nag him. And if she did that to her old man, it's not surprising he did a bunk.'

Alfred frowned but decided to make allowances for his son. After all, sixteen was a tricky age.

'Why do you call him Tagger?' he asked mildly instead.

'Don't know. He said something about tagging along on his first day at school and that was that. He calls me Bridal Chamber sometimes.'

'What?'

'Bridges. Bridal. You know.'

Alfred let it go. He could imagine the two boys sniggering about it.

'Yes. Well. Have you thought any more about your future, Neville? If engineering doesn't appeal, I could get you into the office, you know.'

'Pen-pushing.' Neville made a face.

'You'd start *off* as a clerk, of course. But the promotion would be good. Especially if you'd get some qualifications first.'

Neville was almost overwhelmed at the impossibility of explaining anything to the older generation, but he made a gigantic effort.

'I want to *do* something first, Dad!'

'Give me a clue, old man. I'm fogged at the moment.'

'Well. Like *you* did! The war!'

'My God. I put up with that so that no-one else – especially you – would never have to go through anything like it!'

It was a hopeless task. He'd never make his father understand that he was suffocating already; if he went into the Great Western offices at Temple Meads, it would be the end of him. He became argumentative again.

'The war to end wars. Well, we know what happened to that ideal, don't we?'

Alfred looked at his son with resignation. Why was there never a way to pass on experience? He said, 'There's not been another war so far.'

'What about China's appeal to the League? I don't expect they think much of our kind of *peace*.' Neville made it sound like a dirty word. But Alfred refused to lose his temper.

'That's on the other side of the world, Neville. They have a different set of rules. Everything is quite different in the East.'

'And Spain?'

'There's no war in Spain.'

'This new republic isn't going to work! Surely that's *obvious*?'

'Not to me I'm afraid, old man. In any case, Spain and China are none of our business. You're sixteen, Neville. Full of romantic ideas. Which is fine. But until you can make up your mind properly, I want you to get a good matric result and start working towards a university entrance. You can do it.'

Neville flushed darkly. It all came down to the same old pep talk in the end, however reasonable his father might sound. He felt rebellion bubble and simmer in his chest like bile.

'I'm no Einstein – I don't think I *can* do it.'

'Look here, Neville—'

'Okay, okay. I didn't say I wouldn't try. It's just that I'm an outdoor man. Swotting . . . all that stuff . . .' He saw his father's chin begin to jut and tried to turn the subject slightly. 'Taggers now, he's a different kettle of fish. In fact if you want to do him a good turn, Dad, take him into the Engineer's office with you. He's forever drawing plans for this and that, and maths is his favourite thing. I do believe if he had the choice between cricket and maths he'd choose . . .' Etta caught the tennis ball on the edge of her bat and it soared into the air. Neville held his breath. Philip wasn't quite underneath it and he never ran on the sand; Etta was going to get away with it. Then Philip reached out and took the ball from the air as if it had been sitting on a shelf. Etta began to walk back to the 'pavilion'. Neville was forced to say, 'Oh well *caught*, sir!' And the subjects of his matriculation and Clem Briscoe's mathematical mind were dropped.

Alfred leaned back, determined to remain unruffled. So far Neville was a disappointment to him, he had to admit it. But there were so many other privileges, they kept coming. And Neville was still so young. As for Clem Briscoe, yes, he would mention him to the powers that be. It might go towards paying some of his debt to a strangely benevolent fate.

Tiny, bow-legged Jim Maddern was bowling to Clem who had

put himself in as first man to boost morale. It was an easy ball but he stonewalled it anyway. Neville was standing ankle-deep in water, waiting for the mighty swipes he was certain would come his way. He booed loudly. Clem grinned. He wanted to give Mrs Bridges, young Madge and Philip time to recover.

Philip puffed some more air in the deflating cushions and put them against the hamper to make a back rest for Marie Bridges.

'Jest you close your eyes for a few minutes, m' 'ansome,' he said, holding her paper Japanese sunshade while she settled herself in the shifting sand. 'You can go in as last man which will give you 'aff an hour at the very least.'

'So kind . . .'

'Philip is like a courtier, Mummy, isn't he?' Madge's single plait fell over her shoulder as she crawled around gathering up books and knitting and a stray Thermos cup. 'D'you remember that book we were reading called *Queen Bess and her men*?'

'Really, Madge dear. Philip is just a natural gentleman. Courtier indeed!' Marie Bridges fussed with the parasol, embarrassed on Philip's behalf.

But he was delighted.

'I've allus looked on your ma as a sort of a queen – you're right there, my girl. Funny thing, this summer I took a coupla days off the lugger and went along to this 'ere 'Adrian's Wall. 'Ave you 'eard of 'Adrian's Wall, my girl?'

'No. And I wish you wouldn't keep calling me a girl, Philip. I'm as tall as you now, you know.'

He said solemnly, 'Then I shall call you woman from now on. Is that all right?'

Madge dimpled, then ducked her head and laughed.

Marie Bridges said automatically, 'Don't giggle, dear. And you *should* know about Hadrian's Wall. It was built by the Romans when they lived in Britain. It was to keep the Scots out of northern England.'

Philip nodded. 'Goes right across the country, coast to coast. And parts of it is still there.'

Madge flipped her plait back and sat down.

'Tell us about it, Philip. And what has it got to do with Mummy being a queen?'

'Ah . . .' Philip removed his pipe from his top pocket and

41

knocked it experimentally on to the palm of his hand. 'Well, it were just one o' they trains of thought, little . . . woman. See, there's bin a lot of – what d'you call 'em – groups of people—'

'Societies?' supplied Mrs Bridges.

'Umm . . .'

'Civilisations? Clubs?'

'Civilisations. That's it. An' some of them 'ave looked after their women. Which they should do because . . . well, you'll understand about that later, woman. An' others 'aven't. They've treated them like workhorses.'

'Slaves?' Madge looked eager. 'There was a bit in the *Windsor* magazine about white slavery. It was really exciting—'

Her mother said, 'You're too young to be reading the *Windsor*, Madge. I've told you before—'

'Oh, it was ages ago. I haven't since you said not to. Go on, Philip.'

'Well. The civilisations what 'ave looked after their women-folk 'ave prospered. Them Romans. And the Cornish King Arthur. And them Elizabethans in the 'istory books—'

'Only for a time, Philip. The Roman Empire collapsed, remember. And King Arthur isn't true. And—'

' 'E certainly is, woman! If your pa will allow, I'll take you along to Tintagel in the lugger and you can judge for yourself whether King Arthur were true or not!' Philip made this point emphatically, the stem of his pipe held towards her like a small pistol. Madge was remorseful.

'I'm sorry, Philip. I do believe in King Arthur, of course. And it would be marlovely to see Tintagel. I'm sure Daddy will permit it, won't he, Mummy?'

'Madge, don't pester. And kindly use decent King's English.'

Philip said, 'Let me tell you about this 'ere 'Adrian's Wall, woman. Our port up there is Seahouses as I've often told you before. Different from the harbours round 'ere, but just as inter-esting. Just as . . .' he hesitated, then chose an unusual description. 'Just as businesslike.'

Madge understood very well. A port was always a business, a form of co-operative. She buried her bare feet in sand, keeping a weather eye on Clem at the wicket, and listened to Philip's impression of Hadrian's Wall. Years later when she viewed it for herself, she was able to see it through his eyes; not as an archeological treasure, but, like Arthur's Tintagel, a clever piece of tactical engineering.

After the cricket match there was the bonfire.

Alfred was in his element.

'Children, we need kindling. Search up in the dunes, it will be really dry there. Neville, keep an eye on your sister. Etta, can you take young Jim here and find us some decent logs to keep the whole thing going?' He turned to his wife. 'Dearest, I need your expertise with building the fireplace again. Did you bring the grid? We need something long enough to take the frying pan and the kettle . . .'

He deployed them well. Etta needed someone to command, and Jim needed to be commanded. Madge and the two boys wanted to be on the move, running up the dunes and sliding down, looking for basking snakes on the golf course, hiding in the thickets of coarse grass, and wrestling more or less amiably. And Philip, the real power behind making fireplace and fire, was more than willing to give all the credit to smiling Marie as she passed him flat stones and the old footscraper they always used as a hob.

Distant shouts from the shore reminded the wood-gatherers of their task. Neville piled hastily snatched twigs and stalks into Madge's arms.

'Off you go, Sis – keep the old man happy!'

She tightened her face at him to show her disapproval of this remark in front of Clem Briscoe, but launched herself heels first down the next dune towards the fire-makers. When she got back Neville and Clem were trying to suppress furtive laughter and kept their backs to her as they bent to pick up more kindling.

'Daddy says that's not half enough and we are to hurry,' Madge informed them. 'What's the matter? Why are you making those grunting noises?'

'Nothing,' Clem managed in the face of Neville's red-faced inarticulateness. 'Just couldn't help laughing at something.'

Neville exploded and knelt in the sand with lowered head and watering eyes.

'Nothing is right,' he gasped. 'Clem was right first time. We were laughing at nothing. Honestly, Sis. Nothing.'

Madge said primly, 'It was something rude, I know. It's always something rude when you look like that.'

Clem turned bright red. 'I'll just get some of that dry bracken,' he said quickly and giant-strode up the dune and out of earshot.

'Now look what you've done,' Neville snapped resentfully. 'Honestly, Sis. You and Dad between you can put a blight on anything!'

'I wish you wouldn't talk about Daddy so disloyally in front of Clem,' Madge said even more prudishly. 'And I know exactly what you were laughing about. And it's horrid. Unkind and horrid.'

Neville looked wary. 'What was it then, sister dear?'

'It was because Rose Care doesn't wear any knickers! You shouldn't laugh at people's misfortunes, Neville! If she hasn't got enough money to—'

'Who told you *that*?'

'Jim Maddern. That's why she was dismissed from Mennion House. And it's not fair.'

Neville was shocked into silence. He was furious with young Jim Maddern for talking to his sister in that way. She was twelve years old and didn't know a thing. And he was angry with her for not knowing a thing; it made her vulnerable and unprotected and . . . *stupid*!

He said roughly, 'You little idiot. Rose Care was sacked because she's pregnant.' He saw her incomprehension and said succinctly, 'She is going to have a baby.'

Madge didn't turn a hair. 'I know what pregnant means Neville! I know that babies grow inside their mothers' tummies!'

'And who told you *that*? Jim Maddern?' Neville knew he would kill Jim if he had acquainted Madge with the facts of life.

'No, he didn't. I wouldn't listen if he did.' Madge turned her back and began to fill her held skirt with twiglets. 'As a matter of fact, Rose Care told me that.'

Neville said tightly, 'You have talked to Rose Care? You have actually talked to her?' He took a deep and ragged breath. 'What else did she tell you?'

'Nothing. Just that babies grow in their mothers' tummies. I knew she was right because of Timbo.' Timbo their cat, had been hastily spayed when it was discovered she was female.

Neville felt all his dissatisfaction and frustration come to boiling point. His carnal knowledge was one of the few things that gave him any pleasure recently and he and Clem – but mostly he – had been very preoccupied with the plight of Rose Care and

44

how it had come about. Somehow, Madge, as usual, had got in first. Madge had talked to her, in all innocence, doubtless had all the facts at her fingertips and did not even know it.

He probed roughly. 'Didn't she tell you how they get in their . . .' he raised his tone to falsetto . . . 'mothers' tummies?'

'Oh, Neville.' Madge looked round, indulgently amused. 'They *grow* there. I just told you.'

'Hmm. You have to plant a seed to grow things, don't you? Who planted Rose Care's seed, d'you think? And . . . *how*?'

She was still completely assured. 'God, of course.' She tucked the hem of her skirt into her belt to hold the sticks and dusted her hands. Far away now, Clem began to run down his dune towards the fire-makers, his arms full of brushwood. She waved to him, then turned to her brother and held out a friendly hand. 'Come on, Nev. Let's get back to the others.'

He knew he should leave it there, but he couldn't. Initiating Madge gave him a certain satisfaction. He did it as kindly and gently as he knew how, but to watch her disbelief change to horror made him feel slightly less . . . lonely. Her primness had been an adjunct of her innocence, and they had gone for ever. But he felt guilty too as he watched her face turn jaundice-yellow beneath its tan.

'I have to tell you, Sis,' he said earnestly. 'I have to tell you in order to protect you. You understand that, don't you? I mean, Mother should have said something. You'll be starting your monthlies any minute now – or have you started?'

'Mummy said it was all right. Nothing to worry about.'

'Well, it isn't. It's when it stops you have to worry!' He tried to laugh and couldn't. 'Look if anyone – if that Jim Maddern – ever asks you to show your knickers . . . you'll know what they're after and you just run a mile. Okay?'

'I don't believe you. God wouldn't have invented anything so horrible to make his little children. God's gifts they're called. So how could they be made like . . . you say?'

Neville stared at her. With her bulging skirt she herself looked eight months pregnant. It could be her. That bloody Jim Maddern . . . it could be her. Neville hardened his heart.

'Look, Madge. Think. You've seen dogs do it. You've studied birds and bees in your silly nature lessons.'

'But people are people, not animals!' She sobbed suddenly,

45

not able to meet his eyes, so that he had a view of her long brown lashes pearled with teardrops. But he had gone too far to draw back now.

He said very gently, 'Listen, Madge. How do you think the parents had us? You? And me?'

She was deeply shocked all over again. Her sobs checked and she looked at him with appalled eyes.

'Mummy and Daddy?' Her voice was a thread of incredulity. 'Mummy and *Daddy* doing . . . what you said?'

'Yes. Doing what I said. So that first of all I grew. Then you grew.' Neville pulled a dirty handkerchief from his pocket and touched her cheek inexpertly. 'There. That makes it all right, doesn't it?'

She shrank away from him.

'Mummy would never . . . Daddy would never . . . Daddy *loves* Mummy!'

'Of course he does. That's what I'm trying to explain. It's love. It's called *love*!' He whistled with exasperation. 'Listen, idiot. You sleep in the same room with them. Haven't you seen them jumping about on the bed at night?'

She said faintly, 'It's dark . . .'

'Oh I *know*! But you must have heard something. Bedsprings or something.' Her silence confirmed this. He said encouragingly, 'What did you think they were doing?'

'I thought . . .' Her voice was a whisper. 'I thought . . . they were . . . bouncing.'

Suddenly the tension was too much for Neville. He began to laugh almost hysterically.

'Yes. Of course. That's what they were doing. Bouncing!' He bent double, eyes streaming. 'Oh that's a good 'un. Bouncing. Oh I like that. Oh Madge, that's rich!'

She did not laugh or speak. She stared down at the sand.

Neville controlled himself with difficulty. 'Anyway. You know now. And if anyone tries anything – just shout for your big brother. Promise?'

She ducked her head in what might have been a nod of assent.

'Come on then.'

'In a minute. You go on.'

He went, glad it was over. When he was halfway down the dune he thought he could hear her retching and half turned. Then he shrugged. Best to leave her alone. Get over it in her own good time. It was too bad though. Really, Mother should have said something to her before now. It just wasn't fair to leave it all to him.

The sausages tasted wonderful and no-one seemed to notice that Madge ate nothing. After the food had been partially digested, Alfred suggested to the boys that they should have a swim. They had brought no costumes or towels, but the weather was halcyon and Jim Maddern, grinning like a monkey, ran into the sea in his shirt and trousers while the discussion was still going strong. Neville followed suit, ignoring the female protestations, longing to feel clean again. Alfred and Clem retired behind a rock, stripped to their underwear and entered the water more discreetly. Marie Bridges began to shake the sand off the rugs so that they might be used as towels. Madge sat very close to Philip.

'You not going in?' he asked with a measure of relief.

'No. I don't feel like it.' Madge darted him a swift look and said in a low voice, 'Philip, why did you never have children?'

'Hey?' Philip darted a look back. 'May patience guide me, woman – that's not for me to say. That's the Lord's work as you should know.'

'Is it? Is it really, Philip?' She gave him another more searching look, saw the honesty in his face and moved closer to his side. 'Did you not ask Him for children, Philip? Did you not want any?'

Philip squinted at the horizon.

'No. I don't reckon I did, woman. I reckon I left that in the hands of the Lord and din't ask nor want.'

'You're a very godly man, Philip, aren't you?'

He lowered his head so that the brim of his hat hid his face.

Then he said in a steady voice, 'I dun't know about that, my little woman. But I reckon 'E's allus around somewhere. An' I reckon 'E knew I wouldn't be much of a full-time fayther, because of the fishing d'you see. So 'E let me 'ave a share in you. An' 'E made sartain sure that your dear ma and pa would *let* me 'ave a share in you.' He lowered his head still further but she could hear laughter in his voice. 'I 'ope that meets with your approval, woman?'

For the first time in two hours she smiled. She was going to tell him not to tease her, then she pursed her lips to seriousness and said sedately, 'If it meets with His approval, that is all that matters.'

Alfred swam strongly out to the rocks at Carrick Gladden and hauled himself up. He was out of breath and there was a sharp pain across his chest which he thought must be indigestion.

'Serve you right for swimming after a meal, my lad,' he addressed himself, forcing a grin to his face. He puffed the breath right out of his lungs like the army doctor had told him to do after the gas exposure, and the pain blessedly subsided. He watched the three lads cavorting in the shallows and felt deep thankfulness for the day, the hour, the minute . . .

Neville waited for a roller to pass, then he dived and grabbed Clem's feet. They spluttered beneath the surface, grinning hideously into each other's faces, their hair floating above their heads like weed. They surfaced, shouting.

'Rotter!' Clem was enormously relieved, knowing that everything was now most definitely all right again.

'Rotter yourself!' Neville fell on to his back and splashed with his legs. Clem flung himself on to his friend and they both went down again. Another roller tossed them about like flotsam, and Jim Maddern grabbed them by the hair and hauled them up.

'Don't mess about with the sea!' he admonished them. 'You should know better after all this time.'

Neville threw him off furiously. It was all his fault that poor old Madge had had to throw up in the marram grass.

'Clear off!' he yelled. 'And keep away from my sister too – d'you hear?'

Clem looked surprised and Jim staggered into another wave and got a ducking. He came up spluttering.

'No need for that. No need at all. I thought you young gentlemen wanted me to take you to see Rose Care.' He sounded belligerent; the implication was that if they didn't play their cards right, there would be no such meeting.

Neville turned his back.

'I never want to hear her name again!'

'Neither do I,' Clem backed him up staunchly.

Jim said philosophically, 'You'll change your tune,' and swam off.

Neville floated over an unbroken wave. 'We'll show 'em. We'll

48

join the Foreign Legion. We'll see the world.' But even as Clem applauded this enterprise, Neville was thinking of Rose Care and wondering what he would say to her when he saw her.

That night Alfred and Marie went candle-less to bed as usual so as not to disturb Madge. On the other side of the stairwell, Clem and Neville could be heard sniggering and moving about.

Marie whispered, 'I do hope those boys are safe with their candles. I don't know what we'd do if there were a fire.'

Alfred whispered back, 'We'd evacuate very quickly, my darling. But I think we can trust the boys with their candles.'

Marie, sentient to near-telepathy where Alfred was concerned, breathed, 'Meaning we cannot trust them in other ways?'

Alfred might have laughed if it hadn't been for waking Madge, and if there had been light enough he would have smiled reassuringly at his wife. As it was he said softly, 'Dearest, I love you very much.' He reached for her in the darkness and kissed her tenderly, then with greater intensity.

'Darling, wait. I'm not undressed and I cannot find my nightgown.'

'You won't need your nightgown,' he murmured automatically. But he released her and completed his own undressing, putting his pyjamas carefully on the ladder-back chair by the bed ready for afterwards. Most nights one of them had to get up to use the various china chamber pots under the two beds, and after her first exhausted sleep Madge might easily wake. He peered in the direction of the truckle bed. His eyes were becoming accustomed to the darkness and he could see the humped silhouette of his daughter beneath one of Etta's patchwork quilts. He smiled. She was truly a manifestation of his love for Marie; a perfect combination of his nondescript fairness and Marie's vivid dark colouring, of his practical nature and Marie's saintliness.

He whispered, 'Madge overdid it today, I felt. She was so quiet this evening and she couldn't wait to get to bed.'

He saw his wife's teeth flash whitely.

'After one of your cricket matches we are all tired out, Alfred!'

'But not too tired, dearest?'

She whispered submissively, 'Not too tired if you are not, my darling.'

He lifted the unbleached calico and slid in beside her. Her

49

breasts were heavy in his hands and after a very little while her submission gave way to a compliance that he knew from delightful experience would quickly mount to passion. He was a lucky man; there had been many anecdotes in the army of wives who lay rigidly beneath their spouses, eyes tightly shut in horror, putting up with the frightful indignity by 'thinking of England'. Those wives had been unwittingly responsible for much of the popularity enjoyed by the French prostitutes, and Alfred was grateful too that because of Marie he had been spared that.

He waited until her breathing quickened to desperation, then carefully clambered between her legs. The brass bed creaked a protest but the hump that was Madge did not stir. Gently he impregnated his wife and stifled her gasp with his mouth. And then, with no warning at all, the pain was back. It was like the point of a bayonet sliding between his ribs. For a split second he reviewed his supper: simple cheese and lettuce, it could not be that. Then he succumbed to the pain, collapsing over his wife and muffling his groans to a kind of wheeze.

Marie was terrified but competent. She rolled him away, knelt above him lifting his body and ramming pillows behind him until she had propped him up.

She panted, 'Alfred . . . darling. Just nod. Is it your heart? Just nod.'

He shook his head. His grip on her wrist was strong but not frantic.

She was reassured and leaned closer.

'Show me where the pain is. Here? Here?' She moved her hand across his bare chest. He grunted. 'Does that help? If I massage gently?'

'Indigestion,' he managed after a while. 'Stupid of me to eat cheese before bed.'

She left him and went to her handbag.

'I could make you up some bicarb, but these are just as good and less horrid. Suck one gently, darling.'

She put a minty sweet in his mouth and continued her massaging. He closed his eyes as the pain receded.

'Dearest, I'm sorry . . . sorry . . . so very sorry . . .'

'Don't you ever apologise to me, Alfred Bridges,' Marie said fiercely. 'Just get better. That is all I ask of you and all I shall ever ask.'

'My darling girl.' He was ashamed to feel tears behind his eyes; he was weaker than he'd imagined.

At last he could murmur, 'It's gone now, Marie. Absolutely gone.'

She was still. 'Are you sure? Perhaps it was indigestion after all.'

'I told you that's what it was, darling.'

She said soberly, 'It was more than that. We both know it.'

He sighed. 'Maybe the gas, my dear.'

'Oh Alfred.'

He breathed a laugh. 'Hooray for the Hun, eh?'

'Darling—'

'It's a small price to pay, Marie. A small price.'

They were quiet; there was nothing to be done about it, after all.

At last he said, 'Our night clothes . . . Madge.' They both looked over at the truckle bed. 'She's slept through it all. A quiet mind.'

Marie reached for their things and helped Alfred with his pyjama jacket before she slid into her nightdress. Then they lay side by side, holding hands beneath the rough calico sheets.

When their breathing became loud and even, Madge moved at last. She ungummed her eyes with spitty fingers and stared at the grey outline of the window where she had seen her mother's breasts, pendulous and bell-like against the curtains. She had tried to take Neville's advice and not to listen, but she had not been able to miss her father's agony.

Slowly and carefully she turned on to her side and faced the wall. Once, many years ago, Etta had described the truckle bed as a canoe. Tonight it seemed storm-tossed. She closed her eyes tightly and thought of Philip. Her rescuer.

CHAPTER FOUR

1936

Madge had borrowed the beach pyjamas from her friend at
school. Her father did not really approve of them, but had to
admit that sixteen-year-old Madge looked like someone in one of
the magazines Marie loved – not even an English magazine;
Vogue or *Harper's Weekly* from America. But of course Madge
wasn't like that really, and she knew it. She still wore her hair in
a single pigtail and her blue eyes, though no longer full of wonder,
could widen with bewilderment that was almost innocence.

She said, 'Don't worry, Daddy. I'm wearing them to go rock-
climbing with Philip, that's all. You have to admit they're very
practical.'

'Hmm,' was all Alfred could manage, but Marie smiled. 'It is
amazing how such practical clothing can look so chic,' she commented. 'How long before women realise that, I wonder, and
take to wearing workmen's overalls?'

'Oh Mummy,' chided Madge.

Neville had no wish to go rock-climbing. He had been initiated
into the Old Man's Head route two years before, and such childish feats no longer interested him. He had failed his matriculation and gone into the sooty offices just outside Temple Meads
station, where he felt sometimes he could smell his own soul
gently rotting away.

'Have you seen the latest from Spain, Dad?' He flapped the
Mail before his father. 'The army is still in a state of mutiny. It's
civil war, no less.'

Alfred shook his head. 'I thought they wouldn't take to a
republic. And that President Zamora was too weak.'

'Weak? What about when he put down the uprisings in
Madrid? I told you then there would be trouble.'

'Well, they can't bring back the king. What else is there?'

'I don't know.' Neville looked through the parlour window. 'But if the army takes over it will be a dictatorship. They won't like that.'

Alfred shook his head again. He wasn't that interested. He was busy putting his own affairs in order, making certain that Marie would be all right if the pain in his chest finally got him.

Neville said with a kind of yearning, 'The Ruskies ought to help. If they really believe that a country belongs to its workers, then they ought to do something.'

'D'you mean the Bolshies?' Alfred was roused from self-absorption. 'Don't talk about them to me. Murdering devils. There was a chap – white Russian – talked to us at the annual luncheon last year about the trans-Siberian Railway and its maintenance. He could tell you about the Bolshies, my lad!'

'There's rot in all idealisms, Dad. But the Communists are *right*. Dammitall, you're supposed to be a good churchgoer. Surely Christianity is based on the same principles as Communism! Or t'other way round!'

But Alfred had learned that this kind of heated discussion was not good for him and he shook his head yet again and went into 'the back' to consult Etta about the catch of mackerel he had brought in that morning. Philip had brought the *Forty-niner* home early that summer and he took Alfred out regularly on local fishing trips. Marie had asked him to do so. It relaxed Alfred and made him sit still. She hoped very much to avoid a cricket match that year.

Madge trailed self-consciously along Porthmeor beach, her black jersey trousers whispering oddly against her calves. Neville had accused her of fancying herself these days, and perhaps she did. She tilted her chin in the way Hedy Lamarr did when she was provoking Charles Boyer, and lowered her eyelashes until they brushed her cheek.

'Ello there Madge! Coo. Looking proper growed-up this year, en't we?'

It was Jim yelling halfway across the beach as he led the two donkeys towards the customers outside the beach tents. Madge flushed with annoyance and assumed her normal expression as she walked towards him. There were plenty of people in family groups at the top of the beach, but nobody Madge recognised from previous years. She was thankful; she had no wish to be told

53

by anyone else how growed-up she looked now she was sixteen.

'Good morning Jim,' she said formally. 'How are you?

'Okey-doke.' He waited hopefully while she untied the strings of the Bridges' tent, but it was early in the day for parents to be spending money on donkey rides.

' 'Oo wants a go on Brownie? Best donkey this side o' Newquay sands. Can gallop as fast as an 'orse but twice as safe.' Children's voices were raised in frantic pleas, and Jim, encouraged, continued his patter. 'Or 'is mum 'ere. Jennifer. Quiet. Docile as a kitten.'

Two small girls prevailed on their parents to pay for a ride. Jim left, and Madge breathed a sigh of relief and erected two chairs just to show she was expecting company. She rummaged in her beach bag and extracted dark glasses, then settled herself down with her book. After the prescribed literature of the last year at school, it was bliss to open the pages of an Ethel M. Dell.

Ten very short minutes later, Jim was back.

'Neville with you this year?'

Madge lifted her glasses reluctantly.

'Oh. Hello Jim. Yes, he is. I think he might have gone fishing with my father.'

'What about that other one. Came once with Neville. Clem wotsit.'

'He's not with us. I believe he is very well.'

'Both of 'em working now I suppose?'

Madge sighed and closed her book.

'Neville works with Father . . . well, he works for the Great Western Railway. In the office in Bristol. And Clem is a trainee draughtsman at the Aircraft Corporation.'

'Suit 'im. Bet Neville 'ates and loathes bein' in an office, don't 'e?'

Madge was surprised that Jim knew so much about her brother, but she was admitting nothing.

Jim tried again.

'What about you then? You left school too?'

'Not yet.' Madge glanced around. 'Isn't that little boy interested in a ride, Jim?'

'Naw. 'E 'ad one yesty an' they're mean as mice. So what you gunna do then, Madge? Nurse, I bet.'

Madge was surprised again. 'What makes you say that?'

54

'Dunno. You'm always lookin' after folks.'

Madge, who felt useless and knew she must be a great burden to all her loved ones, opened her face in complete astonishment.

'Me? Who – whom – do I look after, Jim?'

'Well, nigh everyone it seems. Ole Philip Nolla for a start—'

'Philip?' Madge's embarrassment and surprise began to merge into irritation. 'Philip? I can assure you, Jim, that the shoe is on the other foot entirely!'

But Jim was not going to give up.

'Well then, your Neville.'

'My Neville as you call him, would have a lot to say about that! Neville is as independent as Philip. I wish I *could* look after them. Neither of them would permit it.'

'I din't mean look *after* zackly.' Jim at last realised he was putting his foot in things. 'I meant . . . oh it don't matter.' He hit Jennifer's coat and sand rained from it. 'I just wunnered . . . See, I knows your Neville thinks the world o' you—'

It would have been laughable if it hadn't been so annoying. Madge interrupted stiffly, 'I'm his sister.'

'Ah. But I reckon 'e'd do a lot for ee, which en't the case with all brothers and sisters as I know very well.'

Madge recognised Jim's typically diplomatic turn, which usually heralded the end of a conversation. She began to polish her sunglasses on a scrap of handkerchief preparatory to resuming her novel.

'So I wunnered . . . that is *she* wunnered . . . whether you'd 'ave a word with 'im about meeting up.'

Madge looked up in utter incomprehension.

'Your sister? She wants to meet my brother?'

'*Naw* . . .' he laughed. 'Not my *sister*. Rose Care. You know Rose Care – you used to chat with 'er at times when she 'elped me with the donkeys. She thought the world o' you, Madge.'

'Well, yes. I liked Rose. I haven't seen her for a long time. I thought she must have left St Ives.'

'She got a cottage out Zennor way. Makes enough out o' it to keep 'er goin' nicely.'

'She lets rooms?'

'In a manner of speaking 'er does. 'Er's a good girl is Rose.' He laughed again. 'In a manner of speaking that is.'

Madge vaguely remembered old gossip. She frowned. 'And she

wants to meet my brother?' She put her glasses on top of her book again. 'In that case why does she not call at the cottage and state her business?'

' 'Er's done that. 'E weren't in at the time. Philip Nolla did say 'e'd pass on a message, but Neville en't been up to see 'er yet. She'd be mortal grateful, Madge, if you'd press 'im into goin' along one day. She don't want to make no trouble. Tell 'im she don't want to make no trouble at all. She wants to see 'im for 'aff an hour of 'is time. Dun't seem much to ask now, do it?'

She looked up at him. He was silhouetted against the sun so she could not read his expression, but he did not sound underhand or sly, which was unusual for Jim Maddern.

She said slowly, 'No. No, it doesn't. I had no idea . . .' She picked up her glasses and put them on. 'All right, Jim, I'll tell Neville that Rose would like to see him. Then it will be up to him, won't it?'

'I reckon so.' Jim shoved Brownie and he meandered over to the small boy who was still pestering his parents for a ride. 'Be sure and tell 'im she don't want to make no trouble. Dun't forgit that, will you Madge?'

Madge pretended she was deep in her book.

Jim said, 'All right then. Come on, youngster. 'Aff price 'cos you're a good customer. 'Ow's that?'

The parents had little choice, Jim was already lifting their offspring into the saddle. As they wandered down to the firm sand, Madge hurriedly moved her two deckchairs back to the flaps of the beach tent where Jim would be unable to bring the donkeys. She was hot and uncomfortable now in the pyjamas and wished she'd stuck to her usual cotton frock until she actually went rock climbing with Philip. She made herself think about clothes and rock climbing and Ethel M. Dell so that she would have no room for puzzling thoughts about Neville and Rose Care.

That afternoon Philip led her carefully over the tumbled rocks to the very edge of the cliff itself. Fifty feet below, the sea snarled and waited.

'Looks dangerous, woman, but t'ain't at all – leastways, not yet. Ketch 'old o' the finger rocks and feel with your foot. Got it? That ledge runs right along to the back of Man's Head and the finger rocks follow it if you look for 'em.'

It was like the running board of a car hidden by sea grass, but wide and firm. The tumbled rocks above it presented handholds here and there. She shuffled along in Philip's wake, glad at last of her trousers. The weather was as warm as this morning but there was a breeze now and then which would have lifted a skirt to waist level.

'Is this a secret way, Philip?' she asked.

'Aye. We tells it to the children when they gets old enough. Saves 'em breakin' a leg or an arm that way.'

'They could break their necks if they fell from here,' Madge commented, taking an unwary glance into the depths.

'That's why they mustn't know about it till they got a bit o' sense!'

Philip paused. He was beneath the looming mass of rock that sat apparently casually on a thin neck of stone. It did not move like many such monoliths, but it looked as unsafe as Pisa or the Chesterfield spire.

Madge eyed it apprehensively.

'Why do people – nearly everyone really – want to climb Old Man's Head, Philip?'

'Not everyone do, my woman. But them as do, does. So they might as well learn 'ow and save some cracked bones, I reckon.' And he began to climb.

Madge had watched him often as he climbed the iron ladders along Smeaton's Pier; she had seen him scale the side of a boat and go aloft to fix a damaged sail. He was not a graceful man, he climbed like a monkey, bow-legged and claw-fingered, but he always made it look easy. He paused now, halfway up, and instructed her as to hand and foot holds. Then he went on to the top, turned and came down again. This time she went first and he waited. It was an easy climb and would have been simple if it weren't for the dizzying drop beneath.

'If you feels giddy, woman, just spread your arms and lean into the rock. Looks plumb vertical, but 't en't. If your foot slips, do the same. You'll slide down and skin yourself, but you'll land right 'ere on the ledge, no bones broken.'

So she reached the top and waited for him, grinning and triumphant.

'I've always wanted to do it. And it *looks* just terrible, Philip! How clever of you to find such an easy way.'

'Not me, woman, not Philip Nolla. All these ole ways was found by the smugglers long time since. That ledge do go on round to one of they ole mine adits. An' comes up in a cellar in Ayr.'

'Oh Philip. I shall come and sit up here and sketch. I don't know whether to be an artist or a nurse, Philip. What do you think?'

'Whatever you wants. Don't matter what you do s'long as you're 'appy.'

They were silent, sitting in the natural eyrie, feeling one with the gulls. Far below them the beach was crowded with tea-time deckchairs. Madge thought of Jim Maddern.

'Philip, did Rose Care come asking for Neville?' she asked.

'Aye, she did. I told 'im.'

'Well, it seems he took no notice. Jim asked me to have a word with him. What d'you suppose Rose wants with Neville?'

Philip's hat brim hid his face as always. He said in a flat voice, 'The usual I s'ppose.'

Madge felt her face becoming warm. She swallowed and said nothing.

Philip sighed. 'Well. Time we weren't 'ere, Madge. I'll go first. But just remember, unless you push yourself back'ards, there's no way you can fall down the cliff. Ready?'

'Yes.' Madge's voice was small. She cleared her throat and said over-loudly, 'Philip, when I was a little girl . . . ages ago . . . you said something about you and Etta not having children.'

He replied without embarrassment, 'I remember it well.'

'Do you? I just wondered . . . it's such a cheek, I know, to ask you this, but I just wondered if there was a reason. For you not having children.'

'You asted me that before, woman. Dun't you remember what I answered?'

'You said it was the Lord's Will.'

'So I did. And so it was.'

She said desperately, 'Yes but . . . I was a little girl then and now I'm grown up. I mean I understand things. And I wanted to know if there was a - a clinical reason.'

'You mean is Etta barren? Or me likewise?' He rolled round on to his hands and knees and felt with his right boot for the first foothold. 'I dun't know about that, woman. I'm not really a medical man, y'see.' He began to descend and when his eyes were on a level with her plimsolls he looked up for a moment into her red face. 'We knew it weren't the Lord's Will for us to 'ave children. So we didn't try.' His hat brim disappeared from view and she turned and backed towards the edge herself. She began to follow him down. Her feet found the toeholds, her fingers the niches. The thought of Neville and Rose Care was frightening. It was comforting to know that some people . . . didn't.

Madge did not have to broach the subject of a meeting after all. Neville, furious with Rose for actually coming to Zion Cottage, backed out of the afternoon on the beach and went to Prynn's in Tregenna Hill to hire a bicycle. He knew he could be as late as he wished; his father had approved of his cycling trips last year and was pleased to hear Neville was proposing to take some similar exercise this holiday.

As Neville strained the ancient cycle up Trevalgan Hill he changed the word exercise to hard labour. Unless it was something really vital, he'd murder Rose for getting him out to Zennor on a day like this. He was hot, sticky and fed up. If Rose thought they could go on with the affair year after year, she'd got another thing coming. At the moment all he wanted to do was get out of the office and go to fight in Spain. He wished to God the Ruskies would organise some kind of foreign intervention. He couldn't simply land at Bilbao or wherever, and ask for a gun. When he got back he'd write off to the London Comintern and see what they were going to do about it all. Or better still he'd get Clem Briscoe to write. Clem could put a letter together better than anyone he knew.

He dismounted and pushed his bicycle up the slopes of Boscubben to Eagle's Nest. There he wedged his buttocks against the crossbar and rested, looking over the enormous expanse of land falling into the sea beyond Wicca's Pool. Last year the excitement of this trek, the feeling of becoming a real man at last, had filled his head completely. He had shown Rose an illegal copy of one of Lawrence's books and told her that they would live in poverty here, just as Lawrence had with his German wife in the Great War.

It had seemed wonderfully romantic at the time. Now he saw it as just another trap. Everything in this country – even St

Ives – conspired to hold him down, to stop him doing anything exciting. Clem had said wistfully last week, 'God, I'd love to be coming down with you and your family, old man. Mother has booked a holiday for us in Yarmouth, of all places.' He'd grinned with some affection. 'She's always hunting for the Peggottys' boat, y'know. Security, warmth, that kind of thing.' Poor old Tagger, having to explain his awful mother.

Neville had said to him glumly, 'Glad you're not coming, actually. We'd probably have a row, then I'd have no friends at all.'

'Rubbish.' Clem had looked uncomfortable. 'Why should we have a row?'

'You'd take over with Rose where I left off. And I'd have to challenge you or something. Oh God, I don't know Tagger. I'm at odds with everyone and everything. We should have done what we planned and joined the Foreign Legion.'

'We were silly kids, weren't we? When I remember some of the things we said and did . . .'

Neville straightened and swung his leg over the bicycle. That was the trouble. Clem had put all that behind him and settled for the humdrum. And Neville hadn't.

He freewheeled down the hill to the village, and the scented air blew away some of his ennui so that he could begin to anticipate the pleasure of seeing Rose again. She must be desperate for him if she'd come knocking at Zion Cottage. Good job Philip had answered the door. Etta would have told her where to get off and his parents would have been bewildered by her enquiry, then horribly suspicious.

He smiled, remembering last year and the year before that. Jim Maddern must have reported to her ages ago that Neville Bridges was 'h'intrigued and h'interested' as he put it. And Rose had lost no time in accosting him and inviting him to see her cottage. Her brazenness was such that it was almost innocent; the master at Mennion House had told her she was beautiful, and she knew he would not lie about things like that. Her confidence as she undressed was enormous. She pointed out violet threads around her abdomen. 'Them's stretch marks from the master's babby. Oh 'e were a lovely babby. 'E went to someone out 'Elston way and the master do pay 'ansome an' 'e's bein' brought up like a li'll gentleman.' She had laughed unaffectedly. 'Think o' that! Rose Care's babby – a gentleman!' Then she had sobered and said, 'I 'aven't 'ad no more babbies. Nor I shan't. It do 'urt 'aving of 'em, and it do 'urt givin' 'em away. I got some stuff to put up inside me what stops anything 'appening.'

Neville had been horrified at first and then she had kissed him and said, 'You can do it for me if you like.' And it hadn't been sordid any longer. Nothing was sordid with Rose. Everything was 'natural'. Morals and ethics were words in the dictionary; if you wanted to do something, then it must be 'natural'.

He walked his bike around the back of Skinner's Cottage and propped it on the dry stone wall which kept the encroaching thistles and fern of the clifftop from the tiny neat garden that Rose tended so expertly. A clothes line ran from the privy roof to this wall, and the laundry on it was still dripping. Rose must be in.

He knocked on the back door. Nothing happened. He knocked again. She could have popped to the Tinners' Arms for bread. Or . . . she could have someone with her. Neville was under no illusions as to how she paid the rent of the cottage. This could be damned embarrassing.

There was a click from above and the scraping of the sash being lifted. He stepped back and looked up at the window. Rose was framed there, her shoulders bare, hair down. She did have someone with her.

'Sorry', he began. 'Was just passing and thought—'

'Neville Bridges! I thought you'd never bloody well come! Wait!' She stood up to pull the window down and he saw she was naked at least from the waist up. He felt hot, then cold. Supposing whoever it was came down with her and chose to be aggressive? Neville was spoiling for a fight, but not in these circumstances.

Bolts were pulled at the back door, and Rose opened it. She wore one of her usual unsuitable dresses, bright red silk, much too short, but at least she was clothed and buttoned. Her normal high colour was hectic, her dark eyes flashing all kinds of messages, her glorious mass of black hair all over the place as always. She gave off a smell; not Roses of Attar, or Evening in Paris. Slightly sour.

'Where the hell have you *been*? I told Jim to tell you and I thought you'd be up the next day! Christ, I began to wonder if you were trying to get out of it or something!' She stood aside. 'Get in for God's sake. You look 'alf gormless.'

61

He'd heard Rose had a temper and could be sharp, but he'd never seen her like this. He stepped meekly past her into the dark scullery. The smell wasn't here; she'd been scrubbing, and everything was damp. The smell came from her. He wondered if she was ill.

'Have you got someone with you?' He resisted her prodding hand, looking at the door of the room with some trepidation. 'I mean, I don't want to make things awkward for you, Rose.'

' 'Course I ain't got no-one with me! 'Ow can I 'ave anyone 'ere *now*?' She shoved him impatiently and he went through the door with a rush and stood blinking in the lighter room.

It was as he remembered. Rose was a good housekeeper, properly trained at Mennion House; the grate was black-leaded, the rag rug shaken and the window diamond bright. On the big round table which took up most of the space, she had plonked her laundry basket; that wasn't like her.

She flounced past him impatiently, and he saw with something of a shock that she was unbuttoning the bodice of her dress; this was carrying naturalness a bit too far, surely? Then she leaned into the basket, scooped out a baby and sat herself in a chair.

'I was feedin' 'im. 'E'll go mad if I don't finish off. You'd better sit down, 'adn't you? Stop gawping as if you'd never seen my titty before too!'

He drew out a chair and sat down very slowly while she poked one of her nipples into the baby's avid mouth. She flinched as the small lips began to suck, then sighed and settled herself more comfortably with elbow on the table.

Neville said, 'What on earth – I thought you said – what happened?'

' 'E's yours, you great lummock! You couldn't 'ave put that stuff in proper! All that messin' about instead of getting on with the job – I told you at the time—' the child came up for air and she waited until he was feeding again. 'I nearly bloody died when nothin' 'appened that next month. If you'd bin 'ere, you'd 'a got the rough edge o' my tongue, I'm tellin' you!'

Neville realised his jaw had dropped and he put his teeth together with an audible click. The scene before him was incredible. He could not take in that he was responsible for it. Quite simply, he had never seen a woman breastfeeding before and the sensuality of it took his breath away. He cleared his throat to speak, then said nothing.

Rose gave him another look.

'Well? You gunna pretend it can't be yours, I s'ppose? That's what Mr Trewyn said before.' She put on a mincing voice. 'Oh it can't be nothin' to do with me, my dear, and as you go with anyone 'ow you goin' to prove it's mine?' She removed the baby from her breast forcibly and held him forward. 'Look at 'im, Neville Bridges. Look at 'im and tell me 'e's not yours!'

The baby opened its mouth and let out a piercing yell of frustration. It was practically bald, and with its eyes screwed tight there was no gauging the colour of them. But Neville could see that this mewling infant was his. There was nothing of Rose in the furious face; but there was a ludicrous look of Alfred, and both Marie and Madge had that dark line of down following the jawbone.

He muttered, 'Oh my God . . . my God . . .'

She was satisfied. 'Ah. I've called on 'Im too. 'E don't do nuthin' about it, Neville. This is something we done, and that's that.' She turned the baby and put him over her shoulder; he burped a mouthful of milk on to her bare neck and his cry reduced to a grizzle. She rubbed his back.

Still he watched, horrified yet fascinated. The discarded breast hung flaccidly, the nipple wet and shining. She saw him looking and said sharply, 'There's none there for you so you can stop that!' And he turned, revolted by his own thoughts, and stared at the rag rug with burning eyes.

She went on doing things; he heard her murmuring to the baby, fiddling with it's clothes, then standing up to put him back in the basket. The chair creaked as she sat down again and he realised she was buttoning her dress. He looked up.

'Oh lor' . . .' she was still sharply impatient. 'Dun't look like that, man – like a beaten dog. What's done is done. What we got to think about, is what we do next!' She laughed suddenly with a flash of her old provocative sensuality. 'Aye, we can do *that* o' course – though I'll see to the jelly this time if you dun't mind! But what we gunna do about the babby? I can't keep 'im. My callers dun't like it, y'see.'

'Oh God. Rose. Why didn't you tell me? Going through all that on your own! Why didn't you let me know?'

Her face softened again.

' 'Ow could I? I cain't write, Neville, surely you knows that? An' if I'd 'a got someone to do it for me – what could you 'a done? Eh? Left your job and come down 'ere to be another mouth for me to feed?' She laughed. 'My lover . . . all that talk about living in a cottage on cabbages . . . that were talk. Nuthin' more.' She touched the back of his hand. 'I got my ways and you got yours, my lovely.'

He muttered, 'I can't bear it.'

'That's laughable, that is!' She showed him that it was, throwing back her head, exposing the magnificent throat and white teeth. 'You din't 'ave to bear nuthin', m' 'ansome. I dun all that.' Her mood changed again and she left her chair and sat on his lap. 'We'll think o' somethin', never fear. 'E's 'ealthy and 'appy enough. Someone 'll 'ave 'im for us. What about your mam?'

He was appalled, and she laughed again, pressing him against the chair back, covering his face with her hair, enveloping him in the smell of sour milk.

'I were just 'avin you on, my lovely. Give us a kiss now.'

'But Rose – how did you – where did you go – who looked after-'

'Jim Maddern.'

He was appalled again. 'But Rose – darling – stop it – Jim Maddern is a kid! He's younger than Madge!'

That made her almost helpless with laughter and she did indeed stop doing what she had been doing and lifted her face to look at him.

'Oh Neville Bridges! You're younger than any of 'em and you dun't even know it!' She controlled her laughter with difficulty, then cupped his face in her capable hands. 'Don't worry, my 'andsome. Jim and me managed very well, no 'arm to either of us. And the babby's lovely. Nuthin' wrong with 'im at all. I do swear I never tried to get rid of 'im. I wanted 'im to be good.' She lowered her mouth on to his very gently. The front of her dress was open again and he felt her warmth and a dampness against his shirt front. He put his arms around her and held on as if he were drowning. When she let him, he cried out, 'Oh Rose . . . Rose . . .' and she crooned, 'There there, my lovely boy, there there.' Just as if *he* were the baby in the laundry basket.

*   *   *

64

This holiday Madge had Neville's old room and Neville slept on the sofa in the parlour window. It gave Alfred and Marie a privacy they needed more and more as his chest pains worsened.

That night he lay gasping for breath, the pills easing the burning in his lungs only slightly. Marie lay quietly by his side, trying to control the thumping of her heart. Since that awful attack four years ago, he had definitely deteriorated. But it was twenty years since he had been gassed; surely he should have got over it by now.

She whispered, 'Is it getting any better, Alfred?'

'Yes,' he breathed, so that she knew it wasn't.

'Let me get you a drink. Cocoa. Something soothing.' She was halfway out of bed as she spoke. He put a restraining hand on her arm.

'No. It's going. Really. Don't leave me, Marie.'

Terror knifed her. 'Oh my darling. Never. Never.'

'Talk to me, Marie. Talk to me about . . . us.'

Her eyes filled but she would not let them spill over. This might be the end. It really might be the end. He had always treated her like a queen, and like a queen she would be.

She murmured, 'We've always loved each other, my darling, haven't we? Since we met that night at the school dance. You were so handsome, like the old king, blue eyes, and always smiling. And you danced beautifully. Beautifully my darling. It was one of the reasons my papa thought so highly of you. He was a good dancer. Many Dutchmen are. Not that he thought of himself as Dutch. Always British.'

Alfred squeezed her hand gratefully. She took three breaths in time with his. They were very shallow.

'It was the war that made us marry so quickly, wasn't it, Alfred? And it was the war that made us decide to have dear Neville. And then Madge was a thanksgiving for – for – survival. She still is. All her life she will be . . .' The tears were there but she forced herself on. 'Every time we look at Madge we remember the years we have had together. Which others did not have.' She stopped and swallowed hard, then went on quickly, 'And coming here . . . how lucky we've been, Alfred. Always. So lucky. So much more than a holiday here with Etta and Philip. A sort of renewal each year. A summer tryst.' She measured her breathing to his again; it was deeper. Her low whisper grew stronger. 'You'll get better here, Alfred. I know it. The air is soft and will soothe your chest. You must give it a chance to work, dearest. No more fishing trips, I beg of you. Let us sit quietly and allow St Ives to do its work.'

His grip on her hand was firm now. She waited, straining her eyes through the darkness to read an expression on the grey-white face.

At last he said very quietly, 'Marie. Darling. You are right. You are always right. We have borrowed so much time together. We are so very, very lucky.' He held her hand hard as if she would protest. 'It is always borrowed, Marie. Always. We had an over-draft!' He tried to laugh and stopped. 'Marie, listen. If it should . . . if the bank will not extend the overdraft . . . it is important not to cavil. Not to become bitter. To keep the sweetness. Can you do that, sweetheart? For the children's sake? For my sake?'

She took a breath and held it for a long moment until the tears subsided once more. He lifted her hand and put it to his face. His skin felt chill and clammy.

'I think . . . this will be my last time in St Ives,' he said simply.

Her body jerked involuntarily but she said nothing. After a while he went on, almost musingly. 'Neville is a man and will protect you. I have no need for anxiety on that score. And I would like to think . . . it would be a triumph for our years together, if the happiness could go on. Especially here. Especially in St Ives.'

She hardly heard his words, she was concentrating so hard on his breathing. It was better. His words emerged in two's and three's instead of singly.

She whispered, 'I think it's going. I think you're getting better, Alfred.'

He gave a shallow sigh. 'Yes. I am better, Marie. Lie down now. We are together at this moment and nothing can change that.'

'And we will be together tomorrow too,' she said stubbornly. 'It is eighteen years since . . . nothing is going to happen now. Not after eighteen years.'

She lay by his side and let the tears slide silently down her face and into her pillow. She had been brought up to believe that a woman was never complete without a husband and though she had faced widowhood during those four terrible years of war, the thought now was unbearable.

In the end it was Philip who 'sorted it out' for Neville.

The next day Alfred did not go out with the *Forty-niner*, and Neville had Philip to himself. He did not enjoy confessing his sins to the old man, but at least he wasn't completely Bible-bound like Etta. And Neville had to tell someone.

'God, Philip. When I think of her all alone in that cottage – just Jim Maddern, would you believe it – couldn't let me know!' Neville dropped his head in his hands and remembered again the utter deliciousness of Rose Care. It gave him the strength to go on. Alter all, that deliciousness was known by many others beside himself.

'She still . . . I mean there are plenty of *friends* . . . they'd have taken the child. But she wasn't sure . . . and anyway she wanted me to see him and have some sort of say in where he should go.' He darted a look up and was comforted to see that Philip's shaded face was not expressing anything but listening silence. He put his hands on his knees and said earnestly, 'What I'd like, Philip, is to come down here and marry Rose and keep the baby. But she won't. Can you *believe* it—' he asked for the second time. 'She won't hear of marrying me or keeping the baby!'

There was a silence and Neville wondered whether Philip was going to react at all to his shattering disclosures.

Then the old man took his pipe from his mouth and said unexpectedly, 'She's a good girl is Rose Care. Stupid in that way. But in other ways, very sensible. You shouldna gone with 'er, Neville, but if you 'ad to go with someone you coulda done worse. There's lots 'ud 'ave made trouble for ee, boy. You know that, dun't you?'

'Yes. That's what I've been saying! I love her, Philip! I want to marry her!'

'Well, she d'know that's impossible even if you dun't. An' a good job too. 'Ow long d'you think it would be afore you were fed up with our way o' life? Then you would leave a lot o' misery be'ind you. Whereas now . . .' Philip put the pipe back between his teeth and drew experimentally. It had gone out. 'Now I think we can do something for the littl'un. Cos that's 'oo we got to thing about. Nemmind you, young Neville. Nemmind Rose

Care – she'll be all right whatever do 'appen. It's that young 'un we got to look out for. 'E's your son so 'sno good puttin' 'im where 'e'll end up in the mines or even on the sea. 'E's got to 'ave a good chance in life. Some'ow. Somewhere.'

It occurred to Neville that Philip was making the problem more complicated.

He said, 'He's Rose's child as well, remember, Philip. Wasn't her father a miner?'

'Aye, and killed afore he could look after Rose properly. She won't want that for her son any more than you.'

'Yes but . . . what's the alternative?'

Philip said quietly. 'Mr Trewyn. That's the alternative. 'E's done it for Rose before and 'e'll do it again. I'll 'ave a word with 'im this very afternoon.'

'Mr Trewyn? Mennion House? Never! I'm not going cap in hand to that . . . lecher! If it weren't for him Rose wouldn't be . . .' Neville's voice faded. Rose was born to be a jezebel. Her first employer had merely discovered as much. He cleared his throat. 'No, Philip. Not the Trewyn man. I can't face him. Sorry.'

Philip made no comment on Neville's lack of courage. He simply repeated. 'I'll 'ave a word with 'im.'

'But—' Neville searched for tact. 'Look. Philip, old man. He won't *listen* to you. Or if you manage to tell him your errand, he'll think – he might even think – you're the father! Either way he'll throw you out. Sorry, but he will.'

Philip sucked on his empty pipe and grinned.

'He might at that. But I shall convince him in the end. Make him see that in the circumstances he ought to help Rose again.' He glanced at Neville. 'His young wife is expecting their first child. He wun't want 'er to be upset like.'

Neville looked at the man of whom his mother had once said, 'He's never done a bad thing in his life.' He swallowed. 'That's a kind of blackmail, surely, Philip?'

'Aye. I reckon it is.' Philip pulled his hat down over his eyes. 'I'm not doing this for you. Understand that, boy. I'm doin' it for your ma and your pa. And for young Madge.'

'Madge. I'd forgotten Madge. Oh God, I'd die if ever Madge found out.'

'Well, she won't. So stop calling on God unnecessary-like.'

Philip removed his pipe once more and knocked it out on the gunnel. 'That's another reason for me goin' alone this afternoon.'

Neville put his face back in his hands. 'I think I'm going mad, Philip.'

'You're certainly not doin' that neither, boy. Once we got this arranged you can put it be'ind you and get on with your plans. Next year you'll 'ardly remember it.'

Neville said with sudden assurance, 'I'll never come back to St Ives, Philip. This is the last time.' He lifted his head. Philip was already clambering over the wide stern into the dinghy and probably hadn't heard him. Neville stared out at the glassy sea and wondered at his own words. Were they true? Surely he would come back next year and the year after, ad infinitum? Yet he had spoken with a kind of prescience not easily dismissed.

He stood up to follow Philip and the thought suddenly struck him forcibly: whatever happened to him, wherever he went, he would leave part of himself in this corner of England. His son would be a Cornishman. It was the one good thing to come out of this mess.

CHAPTER FIVE
1938

Marie Bridges maintained she never wanted to go to St Ives again. She insisted that the memories would be simply unbearable. If Alfred had been spared to her, they might have gone without Neville and found comfort in the familiarity of the place; if Neville had lived she would have gone for his sake. With both of them dead it seemed the last place on earth for a holiday.

But Madge felt differently; and surprisingly, so did young Clem Briscoe. Madge set great store by the physical and mental doctoring of Etta and Philip Nolla. She and her mother had tried a very good private hotel in Bournemouth last year and had both been miserable and rather frightened. They might well feel sad in St Ives, but they would not be miserable nor frightened. Especially if Clem Briscoe was with them.

Clem was quite simply desperate to go. He had been standing next to Neville when he had been killed at the siege of Madrid and he felt a mixture of guilt and bewilderment at the whole 'Spanish interlude' as his mother now called it. The happiest two weeks of his life had been spent at St Ives with Neville Bridges and his sister and parents and he had some obscure idea of recapturing that holiday; if possible recapturing it for ever. Besides his doctor had told him that if he could get away for a while and completely relax, the dreams would cease and he would be able to start work again. He owed it to Mr Bridges to start work again; it had been Neville's father who got him into the drawing office at the aeroplane factory.

He broached the subject himself on one of his many visits to the Bridges' tall house in Clifton.

'Neville would be so disappointed to hear you say you'll never go to St Ives again.'

Since he had returned home, wounded, he had an occasional

70

stammer which came on him when he was anxious. He stared at Mrs Bridges hard, willing his tongue to command speech.

'You know how he kept on about the place. On-and-on-and-on—' he clamped his mouth shut and looked away, flushing.

Marie Bridges pushed her constant grief aside for a moment and concentrated on feeling protective towards this old friend of Neville's. His hair was already thinning and now that he could not meet her eyes his gaze flicked everywhere, at the floor one moment, then, with a nervous flick, at the ceiling. On his last visit to London to see the army doctors at Woolwich, he had collapsed in the Mall. Nerves. They did frightful things to people apparently, a bit like shell shock after the war. Alfred had not had shell shock, that was one good thing. He had just had gas.

She turned to the empty summer fireplace with its arrangement of fir cones.

'We all love St Ives, Clem. You did too, didn't you? We've had such happy, happy times there.'

Clem looked at young Marjorie Bridges, then quickly away. But not before he had registered every last detail of her. She was four years younger than he was, and with her newly bobbed hair held back on one side with a tortoiseshell slide and her fashionable sleeveless dress, she looked all of her eighteen years. But with his inner eye he still saw the twelve-year-old innocent.

He stared at a point between the two women and saw that they were both looking at him with identical expressions of sadness and understanding.

He stammered, 'That's why I'd like . . . that's why I want . . . the chappie in London says a fortnight's rest and change before I go back to work.'

He saw Marjorie turn and look at her mother pleadingly and his heart leapt. She wanted to go to St Ives with him. She wanted to be with him as much as he wanted to be with her. It was going to be all right. At last something was going to be all right. She knew all about unhappiness, but it had not dimmed her own joy and youth. She could give him some of her assurance, some of her . . . essence. He had to have her; he had to.

She said softly, 'It would do you good, Mother. It would do all of us good.'

Mrs Bridges murmured, 'I thought I'd never go back there.'

Marjorie seized her mother's hands and held them tightly.

Sometimes she could hardly bear the sheer weight of the pain borne by Marie; now this feeling was extended towards Neville's friend. She wanted to put her arms around both of them and physically lift them away from their burdens.

She said gently, 'You *thought* you'd never go back, Mother? And what are you thinking now?'

Marie sighed very deeply.

'I daresay it is what your poor father would like us to do.'

Marjorie said rallyingly, 'Neville would like it too, darling. They would both want us to carry on, you know that.' She stood up and came to Clem's side and held his arm. 'And they'd certainly like Clem to come with us. It will set him up for the winter.'

She used a phrase spoken often by her father and was rewarded by a rueful smile from her mother.

'I suppose it will set us all up for the winter,' she said.

They caught the Cornishman from Temple Meads and got a first class compartment to themselves. Marie liked to travel with her back to the engine and Madge settled by her side. Clem sat in the corner seat opposite the two women, at first grateful for their silence, then sweating at his own thoughts. As the train pulled out of Taunton he had reached the usual impasse: Mr Bridges had talked his mother into allowing him to take the Technical College course, and then had got him the job with National Aeroplanes. He had repaid him by letting Neville persuade him to throw it all up and join the Comintern army in Spain. Perhaps he had been the cause of that final and fatal attack, perhaps Mrs Bridges actually held him responsible for the death of her husband.

The train drew in to Exeter and Madge went down the corridor and bought some fruit from a trolley on the platform. He jumped up to follow her and the pain in his leg made him gasp. Mrs Bridges said, 'Do sit down, Clement dear. Madge promised me she wouldn't actually get off the train, so she'll be all right.' He collapsed again, feeling stupid and ineffectual. He wished he could ask her whether she realised that it had been Neville who had wanted to go to Spain; perhaps she thought it was the other way round?

He darted one of his surreptitious glances at her. Her black hair was turning dramatically white in places; two wings of ermine swept away from the centre parting and beneath her

Queen Mary toque. How old would she be – mid forties? Younger than his own mother, that was certain. And so different. No bitterness here, no inversion of mouth, nostrils, eyes, cheeks. Rather, a late flowering. He couldn't bear it if she thought ill of him.

Madge came back in and offered him an enormous Comice pear. A whistle blew and the train started forward, then paused while the locomotive tried to grip the rails a little better. Madge smiled. 'The rule of necessary friction,' she quoted at him. He smiled back; they were her father's words. She was including him in the family. He bit into his pear and did not panic when juice ran down his chin.

They went into the corridor as the train ran along the coast to Teignmouth. Madge's enthusiasm was boundless.

'I remember that heron from the last time we were here! No honestly Mother, it's the same one. Of course they don't all look the same. You might as well say we . . .'

Mrs Bridges said apologetically, 'Take no notice of Madge, Clement. She sometimes forgets she is eighteen and not eight years old!'

He had heard that phrase before too; Madge had used it to Neville once. He smiled and said without a trace of stammer, 'I hope she can always forget her age and be like you are, Mrs Bridges. Herself.'

Nobody knew quite what he meant, but it was an obvious compliment and Madge dimpled delightedly while Mrs Bridges inclined her head and murmured, 'Dear Clement . . .'

His confidence grew. At Plymouth he undertook to fetch tea. At St Erth he found a porter and shepherded the luggage across the line to the branch train while the women used the footbridge. When he joined them Madge was already stationed at an open window.

'Come on Clem, you can get your head above mine. This is the best bit. D'you remember? We shall go right past the place where we had the bonfire.'

The train moved off and almost immediately they were running alongside the Hayle estuary where Madge claimed to see cormorants, kittiwakes and sandpipers within the first five seconds. Her hat had long been discarded and she now pulled out her slide so that her short hair blew up into his face. He closed his eyes

73

against the rushing air and breathed the scent of Cuticura soap. The train slowed a second time.

'Carbis Bay,' Madge announced. Two sedate ladies in spotted voile and carrying parasols, embarked. Madge turned her head. 'Very see-lect here,' she whispered conspiratorially. He opened his eyes and looked at her. She was so close he could see each individual freckle on her nose. He closed his eyes again.

Mrs Bridges said sharply, 'Sit down Madge! Clement's leg must be aching by now!'

Clem sat down abruptly and Madge withdrew her head and looked at him, all concern.

'Clem, I'm so sorry. I didn't think. Is it very bad?'

He couldn't very well tell them why he had closed his eyes. He forced a smile. 'No. I'd forgotten it. Honestly.'

'Are you sure?'

'Absolutely.'

The train jolted carefully against the buffer stops and Mrs Bridges announced, 'We're here. Are you all right to get to the taxi rank, dear boy?'

Madge said, 'Look at the boats. I can see S.S.48 but not the *Forty-niner*.'

'You know very well Philip and the lugger will be in the North Sea grounds now.' Mrs Bridges gathered her handbag, umbrella and picnic basket close to her. The porter appeared at the open door and drew out the cases. 'Has the trunk arrived yet?' she went on anxiously.

Madge said, 'I thought he might have been here to meet us. That's all.'

The porter looked at the label on the cases.

'Bridges,' he recited. ' 'Tis 'ere already. Bin delivered this morning.'

Madge said, 'Don't forget your mack, Clem. And where are the books and maps?'

'In the picnic basket.' Mrs Bridges tried to adjust her hat and knocked her glasses askew with her handbag. Clem picked up the picnic basket, his mack, Madge's mack, his umbrella and a roll of newspapers, and followed the two women on to the platform. There were flowers everywhere. The air seemed to tingle in his nose and chest. Above him the cliff rose perpendicularly, shelved by a road and villas and a sumptuous hotel. It was a different world here; everything would become all right again here; he was certain of it.

They struggled to a taxi and he loaded the cases methodically.

'Oh it is so nice to have you with us, Clement.' Mrs Bridges settled herself comfortably. 'You are so reliable.'

Clem thought he had never received such a wonderful compliment in his life.

They walked a great deal. Etta Nolla and Mrs Bridges would ensconce themselves on the seat by the harbour wall and talk about Neville and Alfred and do some knitting, and the young people were expected to amuse themselves. Madge would have been happy to lie on the beach all day and take a dip in the surf of Porthmeor just before they went in for their high tea. But Clem was restless and eager to explore.

'You've had so many summers to get to know this place,' he told her. 'I've only been here once before, remember. I want to see it through your eyes.'

Madge smiled instant reassurance. She knew he was shy about swimming because of his leg. When he had reluctantly come in with her on their second day, she had seen that he had hardly any calf on his left leg. The skin had been stitched tightly around his shinbone, giving the appearance of a peg-leg. It did not stop him doing most things; he could clamber around the rocks and he was a very good walker. He used a stick with which he slashed at encroaching nettles on the footpaths.

Madge said, 'Actually I've never explored around here either, Clem. Father liked the walks up-country better and Philip always warned us about the old mine-shafts along here. So you're opening up new territories for me.'

He flushed with pleasure. 'Well, you were rather young for walking much when you were here before.'

'I don't know about that. I was expected to keep up with whatever was happening. But Father was such an organiser. And walking didn't satisfy his urge to organise!' She laughed. 'He loved a good picnic. We all had to carry something – I managed the cushions and sunshades.' She paused for a moment to look over the Atlantic. 'And of course there were the cricket matches. You must remember the cricket matches.'

'Yes. Whenever I think of Neville, it is always playing cricket.'

75

She turned to him, her eyes very bright, but happy. 'How lovely! How perfectly lovely! I know just what you mean. And I think of him here too. Always here.'

He nodded, mesmerised again by her eyes. She was so like Neville in a feminine way. She kept Neville alive. Somehow.

Impulsively she took his arm and led him to an outcrop of rock which made a natural seat.

'D'you know, that's the first time you've mentioned Neville. I think if you could talk about him more, you'd begin to feel better.' She glowed at him, her eagerness to help flushing her face. 'How much do you remember of that cricket match, Clem? Tell me – talk to me!'

He said hypnotically, 'I remember bowling Mrs Nolla and Neville congratulating me even though she whacked it to the boundary. I remember Neville saying he didn't want to join the G.W.R. with his father. I remember him suggesting we try to get into the French Foreign Legion.'

'Did he really? Even then . . . sorry. Go on, Clem. Keep going.'

'I remember Neville talking about some girl and you telling him that this girl did not wear knickers and then—'

Madge said quickly, 'No, not that bit. Just the bits about Neville.'

He realised with a start what he had said to this eight-year-old girl . . . no, eighteen. His stammer came back with a rush.

'I – I – I – I—'

She looked away from him but kept his arm between her hands. 'Not if it hurts you, Clem. I shouldn't have asked you.'

'It's not . . .' He wanted so desperately to explain to her that it wasn't enough to talk about dead people. Somehow you had to link them into the present and the future. But he couldn't find words. Maths had been his subject at school; it had been Neville who had been good at English. They were so different in every way. Thrown together for alphabetical reasons – Bridges and Briscoe sat together, ate together, prayed together – Neville had called him Tagger Briscoe because he always tagged along. Now, somehow . . . however impossible . . . he had to make certain that Neville could tag along with him.

'It's not that it hurts. But I – I – I – I want to do more than

76

just talk. I want to *do* something to make them remembered always.'

There was a silence which both thought was one of complete mutual understanding.

Madge said quietly at last, 'Is that why you wanted to come to St Ives?'

'With – with – with – with *you*,' he blurted.

She tried to ignore a stab of unease; she had always felt awkward with the opposite sex. But not with Clem Briscoe; she must not feel awkward with her brother's friend.

She said slowly, 'I don't think we can suggest another cricket match, Clem. There aren't enough of us. And it would hurt Mother unbearably. Perhaps a cooking fire though?'

'It's all right. You don't have to . . . it's too soon. Just to be here together, you and m-m-me. That's enough for now. Isn't it?'

'Oh it is, Clem. It is!' She clasped his arm and through the thicknesses of his shirt and jacket he could feel faintly the thump of her heart. Then she released him and gave him a sisterly pat. 'Come on, let's move off. Mother is trying to teach poor Etta how to cook mutton chops. I really should help. It's an uphill task!'

He was disappointed; he wanted that moment of complete understanding to go on for ever. But as he followed her back along the cliff path to Clodgy and Old Man's Head, he accepted that he mustn't hurry her. The pat had been a promise as well as a caution. They both knew that their salvation lay in each other.

That evening Mrs Nolla told them that she'd had a message from Seahouses in Northumberland. Philip would be home before the end of their holiday and was looking forward to seeing them. Madge's joy was obvious; Clem remembered that Philip Nolla had been her special friend. For some reason Clem felt a foreboding that with Philip's arrival the wonderful easy solution to everything would go wrong. He bit his lip and shifted his leg to an easier position. He must settle things with Madge. He must settle things quickly before this other permanent figure from the past returned.

Marie Bridges and Madge took their candle up to the front room at nine-thirty and got ready for bed back to back. If either of them felt distaste at sharing the big feather bed, they said nothing.

Marie blew out the candle immediately they climbed between the sheets, then said anxiously into the darkness, 'Darling, did you make sure you'd brushed all the sand off your feet?'

'Yes Mother. In fact I washed them under the cellar tap before supper.'

'Good girl. It's just that the bed felt slightly gritty when I put my legs down. It's this unbleached calico. Honestly, Etta and Philip do not move with the times.'

Madge said comfortably, 'That is what is so absolutely mar-lovely about them.'

'Oh that silly word again . . . You're looking forward to seeing Philip?'

'Oh yes. It doesn't seem right without him.'

The words fell deadly into the darkness and the women thought of the other two men who would never be with them again.

Mrs Bridges sighed. 'No. Not right at all.' She heaved her shoulder over so that she was facing Madge. 'You know, darling, Philip made a specific point of being home when we were here. He never had before we began to come in August. Most of the luggers stay away till mid September.'

'Yes, I know.'

'I sometimes think that as he and Etta had no children they thought of you and Neville as their own family.'

This seemed so obvious to Madge she did not reply.

Marie went on musingly. 'Etta must have written to him about Clement. He'll be coming back to meet him again, I expect.'

'Why on earth should you think that, Mother? Philip is coming to see us, surely – not Clem.'

'Well . . . oh I know you're still very young, my darling, but you must know why Clement was so insistent on this holiday. And actually you are older than I was when I met your father first of all.'

Madge went hot then immediately stone-cold.

'I'm sure you're wrong, Mother. Clem wants to be with us down here because of Neville. Nothing to do with me. In that way.' She flushed hotly again.

Marie said soothingly, 'I expect you're right, my dearest. Please don't let it worry you. It's just that . . . it would be so suitable. And your father liked him.'

'I'm never going to get married, Mother. When you . . . when we . . . feel strong again, I wondered whether I would go to a

78

teachers' training college. I know I'm not good enough to be a real artist, but I think I could teach art.'

Marie gave a low laugh. 'We'll think about that later, Madge dear. Meanwhile, don't set your face against marriage. It's a natural state and you are a very natural person.'

In the darkness Madge set her lips hard.

Marie said suddenly, 'What's that?'

They both listened. Above the sound of the waves came a sudden scrabble on the roof.

'Gulls,' whispered Madge.

'Yes.' Marie Bridges settled her pillows beneath her head. 'Turn over and sit in my lap, Madge. We really should go to sleep. Those blessed birds will wake us at the crack of dawn!'

Madge turned over gratefully and closed her eyes. Once Philip came home everything would be all right. Anyway, Clem Briscoe was ill and looked on her as his nurse. That was what she was: his nurse. And if she could persuade him to talk about Neville, she would have done a good job.

Clem was in the room he had shared before with Neville. He lay on his back, staring at the candle shadows which leaned and leered across the planked ceiling as if they were reaching for something. He felt very tired, but sleep meant nightmares and he always fought it for as long as he could. He concentrated on thoughts of Madge Bridges and forced a smile at the candle flame. She wasn't really beautiful but in her way she was so . . . perfect. Her hair was abundant though its mouse-browness meant it was not sensational. Her blue eyes were clear and untroubled, yet at the same time full of sympathy and understanding; they were never provocative and they rarely 'sparkled'. Her nose was small but it had a definite bump in the middle, and her mouth was too big for beauty. She had the sort of attraction that he was certain he alone could see; only he could see that the sum total of all her slightly imperfect parts, was perfect. He could make that full mouth tremble, those eyes fill with tears. He wished her hair was still uncut so that he might remove the pins and let it tumble around her shoulders.

He must tell her the truth about Neville and himself. He nearly had today, then his tongue had stuck to the roof of his mouth and prevented proper speech. But if he could be completely honest

79

with her she would understand about the necessity of bringing Neville into the present and carrying him with them into the future. They could do it together. Between them they knew everything about Neville; good and bad. They could cherish it all, nourish it, make it possible for Neville to live through them so that his terrible, stupid, unheroic death wasn't wasted.

His muscles were knotted rigidly beneath the sheets and agonising cramp sheathed his left shin. He tore his thoughts away from Neville with a physical wrench of his body, closed his eyes on the candle flame and muttered aloud, 'Madge . . . Madge . . .' And as if she had heard him and was coming immediately to his summons, the bedroom door opened.

He felt his eyelids snap open and then real terror gripped him. The figure who stood in the doorway was not Madge. In its long gown and with its veined hands outstretched and its hair a wispy halo, it reminded Clem of a picture in one of his mother's books: Marley's ghost from *A Christmas Carol*. He moved at last, clutching the sheet up to his chin and crooking his legs, ready to leave the bed at a moment's notice.

Then Etta Nolla advanced into the room, went straight to the candle and snuffed it between thumb and forefinger. He shrank further into the bed and waited for the next horror.

'You've laid awake quite long enough, my 'ansome.' Her voice was low and unexpectedly gentle. 'I 'ad to come and put out your candle before – d'you remember?' She put a rough, fish-smelling hand on his forehead, forcing him to close his eyes again. The bed dipped as she sat on the edge of it.

'Now. Just you listen to me and pay attention. You 'aven't got no need to take everything on your shoulders. No-one else thinks it's your fault and you musn't neither. 'Tweren't your fault that the ole Kaiser decided to go into Belgium and start the war, were it? You was only a twinkle in your daddy's eye then, I reckon.' She gave her horrible cackle. 'So it certainly weren't your fault that poor Mr Bridges got that gas poisoning. An' it weren't your fault that young Neville was headstrong neither. If 'e 'ad to find a war to fight in, then I reckon it was best you should go with 'im. Try to 'old 'im back a bit.' The hand cupped his cheek and Clem turned his head slightly so that he could smell the fish. It was a clean, good smell.

She paused and he could tell from her held breath that she was fighting tears. When she spoke again her voice was lower still.

'I'm chapel. You know that, my 'ansome. I believe what they believe. An' a bit extra too.' She tried to laugh again and failed. She leaned closer. 'Oh I know they're in 'eaven. I know that. But where did they think 'eaven was? Right 'ere. In St Ives. Every summer.' She paused, cleared her throat and went on, 'We can't see 'em, I knows that. But they're there. On Porthkidney. 'Long the 'arbour. Porthmeor beach. Everywhere.' This time she managed half a cackle. 'So you keep coming, my 'ansome, an' you'll never lose 'em. Marry young Madge – and do it quick before someone else gets her – and spend your summers down 'ere. You'll be all right. Etta Nolla's telling you. You'll be all right.'

It sounded like a gypsy's promise, and Clem's mother hated gypsies almost as much as she hated her absent husband and the Hun. But when Etta stood up to go, he whispered hoarsely, 'D-d-d-don't go. Don't leave me.'

She cackled properly this time.

'Not many men said that to me, young Clem.' Then she moved her hand from his face and gripped his shoulder. 'Your stick be hard by the bed. I'm right above you. If you need aught, just jab the stick on the ceiling and I'll be down. But you ain't goin' to 'ave no more marbid thoughts.'

She tightened her fingers, then released him and padded out of the room. She must have left her own candle on the attic stairs and he watched her silhouette bend and pick it up before she shut his door.

Suddenly and inexplicably his limbs creaked loose and peace was with him. He thought of the tall thin house built into the rock, with its fish cellar below and its loft above; the simplicity of it engulfed him. It would be like this always; if Madge would marry him.

The next day some old friends from ten years before were discovered during the morning shopping trip. The McGoverns had spent two months in Penzance in 1928. Mr McGovern had inherited a cotton mill from an uncle in Lancashire and though he had moved his family down to Todmorden from Stirlingshire, he had no aptitude for business and left a manager in charge while he indulged his hobby of 'taking pictures'. He found the ideal light for photography in Cornwall and during one of his expeditions in search of the perfect composition, he and his wife had met the Bridges. Mrs McGovern had been so attracted by them all that they had made a point of meeting up with them each day during their two weeks' stay. Now, suddenly, they were walking down Fore Street, Mr McGovern shouldering his tripod, naturally more stooped than before, but otherwise amazingly unchanged.

There was a great commotion. Mrs McGovern fell on Mrs Bridges, and Mr McGovern pumped Clem's hand under the impression he was a grown-up Neville. Madge stood back smiling anxiously; they did not recognise her and she had time to wonder about the explanations that must follow and how they would affect her mother and Clem. Like any good nurse she was doubtful about having too many visitors around the bedside.

However Marie Bridges had no reservations about the meeting. She and Etta talked all the time about the past. It never hurt. It cocooned it and made it all the more precious. The McGoverns suggested a picnic on the beach as soon as they learned the tragic news about Alfred and Neville, just like the good old days. It couldn't be the same of course. Alfred was no longer there to organise things: decide where the chairs should be placed, what time the food would be unpacked, who would swim and when. There were no games. No small tête-à-têtes between the women. Clem was much too embarrassed to swim with such an audience, and Madge would not get into the sea without him. The five of them sat in a large semi-circle facing the incoming tide and conversation soon flagged.

Mr McGovern gestured towards the Island where the enormous stretch of Porthmeor sands deteriorated into the town's rubbish dump.

'Proper mess. It wasn't like that ten years ago.'

Marie peered short-sightedly. 'Etta tells me that the beach has been leased to a local builder. He might tidy it up.'

'He's making a pretty penny out of the tents.' Mr McGovern gestured again, this time towards the canvas swimming tents behind them. 'Half-a-crown a week he wants for one of those. Can you credit it? How much were they when we were here before?'

'A shilling,' said his wife. 'The bathing machines at Porthminster were more expensive, of course. But this beach has never been developed for bathers.' She smiled at Mrs Bridges. 'That's why we liked it so much.'

Everyone smiled. They waited for Mr McGovern's next lead, but he was squinting at Old Man's Head trying to see it as a print.

Mrs Bridges said desperately, 'Why don't you young people look for cockles? The tide is only just coming in. You should be able to find buckets of them.'

Clem jumped out of his deckchair as if shot.

'S-s-splendid idea. How about it, Madge?'

'Yes of course. Will you be all right, Mother?'

Mrs Bridges laughed with relief. 'I've got plenty of company. Most congenial company.'

Everyone laughed with her, and Mrs McGovern murmured, 'Compliments, compliments.' And Madge suddenly took to her heels in the sand, calling, 'Race you to the sea!' Then halfway down the beach remembered Clem's leg and stopped abruptly.

'Is there going to be a match there?' Mrs McGovern murmured archly.

'I rather think so. As I told you, he was a friend of Neville's. They were the same age. He was actually with him when . . . he can't talk about it properly but . . .'

'My dear, don't upset yourself. Let's have a cup of tea, shall we? Angus, why don't you stroll over to the Head and see if there are any likely camera shots the other side?'

Clem took off his shoes and socks and rolled his trouser legs to his knees. The hem of Madge's shantung dress was already dripping, but she did not seem to care. Her bobbed hair hung over her face, and her hat dangled down her back on its elastic. He thought how good it would be to look after her. To tell her she might catch cold or get sunburn.

He opened his mouth and blurted suddenly, 'It was a day like this. It had been raining and we waited for fine weather. And it was a day like this.'

She was suddenly still. She had been bending over a rock, pushing experimentally at the covering of shellfish. She stayed where she was, not looking at him; waiting. He wondered whether to tell her what they had carried. Her hat, lying on her shoulders, was an odd reminder of his own gas mask that day. But how to convey the sheer weight of his 220 rounds of ammo, the Mills bombs, the water bottle and extra rations, the three empty sandbags and his rifle and bayonet? She could not possibly imagine such encumbrances; and he did not want her to.

'It was jolly hot in boots and uniform,' he said heartily. 'The sweat dripped from under our tin hats. And then when we got to the outer defences, it started to rain!' He tried to smile, then she looked up at him and he tried no more. Her eyes were enormous and very serious. 'But then it was hot again. Like this,' he repeated lamely.

She did not speak or take her eyes off his face. When he paused she sank slowly to her knees in the wet sand, and waited. A tiny rivulet of sea washed around her skirt, obviously soaking her to the thighs; she ignored it. He bent laboriously and squatted on a low rock, then, unable to meet that gaze any longer, he stared down at his submerged toes. They still bore the marks of his army boots.

'There was a village. It was called . . . I don't know . . . something like Tarantella. But that's a dance, isn't it? The church had been shelled and one of those statue things was hanging out of it. Some of the other chaps said it was blessing us. They crossed themselves and sort of bowed . . . it seemed to me it was cursing us.'

He remembered the Madonna and Child far above their heads. Neville had wanted to know if anyone could spot her knickers. But he couldn't tell Madge that. Typical of Neville.

He said, 'There were barrage balloons all around the city. They were supposed to stop the dive bombers, but they didn't. The Condors were a crack Fascist squadron. Nothing could stop them. They shot up the balloons first, then came in.' He stopped and closed his eyes.

Madge said, 'You don't have to—'

'I want to.' The words started pouring out of him, running into each other but overcoming the stammer. 'You should have heard your Neville. He started cheering at the top of his voice and he turned to me and said, this is it old man, we're as good as out. And he was right of course . . . oh God he was right. The whistles went but Nev and I, we had to wait because of the wire. We had a roll of it on a stake – he had one end and I had the other. It made us slow and clumsy. Perfect targets.' He opened his eyes wide. 'It was like a fairground. Those ducks that swim along in formation at all the rifle ranges. Making it so easy to pick them off.'

Yet no-one had faltered except himself. Some Russian captain had strode between them all, waving encouragingly, and Neville had glanced sideways and grinned mockingly and Clem knew exactly what he would say when he got the chance. 'The dusky Rusky is somewhat husky' or words to that effect. But Neville would never utter those words or any others. Because there had been a sodden smacking sound then and his end of the wired stake went down. There were bits flying. Earth. Clothing. Flesh. Neville's tin hat spun back down into the trench they'd just left. Amazingly, his smile, like the Cheshire Cat's, hung for a moment in the air. Then someone else picked up the wire and went on walking.

Clem thought he'd dreamed it. He thought when the face looked round at him it would be Neville's. When it wasn't, he knew he had to look for Neville. There must be something left, and he had to find it.

'That is why I was shot in the calf of my leg,' he said in the same gabbling voice. 'Because I'd turned around and was heading back to the trench. The bullet caught me behind the knee and I fell down. No-one seemed to realise I was facing the wrong way. The chap who picked up the wire – perhaps he knew, but he was probably killed anyway. I didn't tell anyone I was running away.'

Madge interrupted him. Her voice was hoarse, but she did not pause to clear her throat.

'You weren't running away, Clem. You were looking for your friend!'

'Our orders were not to stop to help the wounded. And certainly never to go back for the dead.'

'What do you think Neville would have done if it had been him? He'd have gone back to look for you!'

He said morosely, 'It's what I've tried to tell myself ever since. Every day. And every night. Especially nights.' He looked again at his toes. 'If anyone had twigged, I would have been shot for cowardice.'

'Oh Clem – no! You were helping a friend.'

'I knew Neville had gone. I was running away.'

She said stubbornly, 'I don't believe that.'

He was silent, staring at his feet, letting her words soak in and comfort him like the water. She must be right. She was young and saw things properly.

She said in a thin voice, 'You never found. anything? You said his tin hat . . . did you pick it up?'

He thought of the number of tin hats that day and laughed. Then he checked himself and shook his head.

'Someone picked *me* up and dragged me back to the trench. Then there was a dressing station. Morphia there. We were laid on straw in the sun and someone put a newspaper over my eyes . . . No, I didn't find Neville's tin hat.'

He took off his panama suddenly. 'Can you see the cross? They put a cross on your head when you'd been pumped up with morphia. An indelible pencil. It wouldn't come off.'

He thrust his head towards her and she looked at his forehead as he pushed back his hair. There was nothing.

'It's still there!' He heard his voice rising. 'It won't go away. My mother saw it and thought I'd got the plague or something! You must see it, Madge!'

She peered. 'No . . . No, I can't.'

'Here. Put your fingers just here . . .' he grabbed her hand and put it to his head. 'Feel the imprint – go on, feel it!'

Obediently she made a sign of the cross on his forehead, kneeling upright, looking scared. She would have sat back on her heels but he held on to her wrist.

She said quickly, 'Yes, I think I can feel something, Clem. But it will fade. Gradually.'

'No, it won't! Not unless you—' He tightened his grip, feeling her pulse thump beneath his fingers. 'Madge, listen to me. I love you. I love you, Madge.' He kissed the back of her hand frantically as she tried to pull away. 'Madge, you must have guessed . . . why do you think I wanted to come here?'

'Well, I thought . . . Neville's favourite—'

'To be with you. I want to be with you all the time. When I'm with you it doesn't happen.'

'What? Clem, I don't understand.'

'The nightmares. Delusions they call them. I don't get the delusions. Of course the people who call them that, weren't there.' He laughed wildly and when she pulled away again he dropped his forehead to her wrist, feeling tears flooding out. And worse than tears; his nose was running. She stopped pulling and leaned over him protectively.

'Oh Clem.'

'It's all right. Don't worry.'

'It's just so awful that you . . . I mean, I feel so safe with you.

Mother and I – we've been *leaning* on you instead of – we've been burdens!'

He screwed his eyes tight to wring out the tears and said gruffly, 'You could never be burdens, either of you. You make me feel . . . I don't know – like your father. Whole.'

'Oh Clem.'

'That's what I want to do for the rest of my life. Look after you. Protect you.'

'Clem, you're wonderful. You talk about cowardice but you're a hero. That's what you are. A hero.'

He looked up at last and saw her face ablaze with exaltation. He wanted to grovel at her feet, but heroes did not grovel. He stood up, pulling her with him, and water poured from his trousers. They both watched as the rolled flannel at his knee unfurled heavily.

His voice full of consternation, he said, 'My lord, just look at my flannels. What a mess.'

But nothing could dim Madge now.

'Clem, don't bother about that! Look at my dress! And shantung is much worse than flannel when it's wet – it sort of shrivels like liver in a frying pan!'

'Liver?' Under cover of his flopping hair he knew his face was beginning to look slightly more heroic.

'Yes. Haven't you noticed how liver sort of cringes when it goes into hot fat? No, I suppose you haven't. Men don't cook, do they?'

He started to laugh, and after a second so did she. Once started they couldn't stop. Their laughter was near hysteria, but it unified them. Clem had a jumbled vision of frying liver, crumpled shantung, waterlogged trousers; images which obliterated the other unspeakable sights of his mind. He gasped, 'Oh Madge, I do love you. I really do love you.'

She was eighteen, had lost all the men in her life, and was being offered so much. All she could say was 'Oh Clem. But it was enough for him; it was acceptance.

He said, 'What can we *do*? We ought to do something special so that we'll never forget this moment even when we're old and grey!'

She held out her hands. 'Come on. We're wet already. Let's do the job properly!'

Clem had no time for the bright young things cavorting in fountains in London; but this was no drunken splash. This was in the nature of a baptism. He and Madge leapt over the small waves and then strode strongly into the deeper water. Clem felt his flannels cloyingly heavy around his calves and had a momentary misgiving: what would Mrs Bridges say? But Madge still held one of his hands and she looked up at him with that brilliant smile of hers and led him deeper. A roller was creaming towards them.

They cast a look up the beach and saw Mrs McGovern and Marie Bridges on their feet, staring anxiously. Jim Maddern had led a single donkey down the cliff path in another effort to make some pocket money. Silhouetted against Old Man's Head, Angus McGovern framed his hands around possible photographs. Madge started to laugh just as the roller engulfed them.

Mrs Bridges was cross but not angry. She had also read about the bright young things in London and had hidden a smile even while agreeing with Clem's censorious mother that it was a crying disgrace.

'You need not keep pretending it was an accident,' she said, pushing one of the towelling robes over Madge's cumbersome wet dress. 'I saw you go in quite deliberately. No, I don't blame you, Clement, whatever you say. I saw – we both saw – Madge dragging you further and further – it's not funny, Madge, so just stop that silly giggling.' But she did not dare meet Mrs McGovern's eye and that lady was forced to hold the day's newspaper over her mouth at the sight of Clem, miserable and stuttering again, trying to give some cogent explanation.

'I'll run for dry clothes if you'll keep an eye out for donkey riders,' offered Jim Maddern, his eyes as bright as two three-penny joeys.

'We'll go ourselves, thanks all the same, Jim.' Madge treated him to a smile as well. 'We won't be long, Mother darling. And sea water never hurt anyone. Don't you remember Father saying that?'

'I do. And if you think you're going to swan off like that . . . excuse me, my dear. I won't be long.'

Mrs Bridges swept ahead of them up the cliff path, parasol like a banner. There was nothing for it but to follow her back to Zion Cottage like two naughty children. But Clem recognised this as yet another bond. He could not take Madge's hand again because Mrs Bridges, like all mothers, had eyes in the back of her head, but he knew they were still joined. When they reached the cottage and he struggled out of his ruined flannels, he thought suddenly, 'My God, we're engaged. *That* is what has happened this afternoon. Marjorie Bridges and Clem Briscoe are engaged to be married!'

He was so happy he forgot to worry that his spare trousers were rather too short.

Madge was delighted that somehow she had comforted Clem. The word 'comfort' was used a great deal when it came to soldiers, wounded or otherwise. Comfort for the troops consisted of anything from smokes to socks. Words, looks, hand-holding were all used by nurses. But underneath her pleasure, she knew very well that the comfort had gone much deeper than that. When he had told her he loved her, she had almost told him that she loved him too. And she did. At that moment. He had been dear companion, hero, a substitute for her father and her brother, and she had wanted to fling her arms around his neck and hug him desperately. But after her mother's words she saw only too clearly what would then be expected of her. It seemed suddenly as if everyone was standing around waiting for her to marry Clem: her mother, Etta, even Mrs McGovern. And she could never marry, not ever. She shuddered, not allowing herself to remember Neville's words, not allowing herself to recall that night when her father had collapsed on top of her mother. All she knew consciously was that marriage was not for her.

When Philip arrived the next day, she felt happier. It was wonderful to see him again anyway; she had been sixteen when they'd come to St Ives last, now she was an adult. It made no difference. He seemed shorter than before but he'd always had to peer up at her from beneath the brim of his trilby, so that was the same as ever. There was a slight change of roles; he was no longer the family retainer, right-hand man to Alfred Bridges. In many ways he stepped into Alfred's shoes. He was no organiser and he still went about his own business most of the day, but subtly he was the final authority now, just as Alfred had been.

The day after his arrival, Madge got up very early, took her wrap and costume behind Smeaton's Pier where the ebb tide had left a tiny private beach, and swam quietly in the tingling water until Philip appeared above her to spread his nets. Then she got out, dried roughly and slipped her still-crumpled shantung over her head. In the old days Father had encouraged a before-breakfast swim; it would not be remarked upon. She climbed the slippery weed-covered steps to the pier head and greeted Philip as if the meeting were a happy coincidence.

'Hello, woman,' he returned, giving her one of his quick upward smiles before going back to the nets. 'Mad as ever, I see.' He had never come to terms with the family's habit of immersing themselves. 'Do you do it as early as this every morning?'

She was going to lie, then knew she would be easily discovered. 'No. The tide hasn't been right just here and I don't like going to Porthmeor on my own.'

'Sensible.' He held up an enormous hole for her inspection. 'Etta and me'll be busy for a week or two, I reckon.'

'What did that, Philip?'

'Wrasse.'

He began to tell her about the summer in the north-east and about the people of Shields and Seahouses and Berwick. She sat on the wall while the sun gained strength and her hair dried. The first train of the day arrived from St Erth, crawling along the side of the cliff above Carbis Bay, its plume of smoke spreading among the trees and rocks. In the harbour the boats lay on their sides as if resting and the town cats prowled and chased the gulls.

'D'you remember telling me about Hadrian's Wall?' She smiled at him. 'I must have been nine or ten. I went home and read and read about it. The Roman Legions. The sort of country around it. I'm sure that's why I got a place at the Girls' College. When I had my interview they were terribly impressed by my history and geography!'

She laughed and Phillip glinted a grin at her.

'Thought as how you were at a paid-for school, woman. Was it a scholarship you got?'

'No. It was paid for. But they wanted to make certain their standards would be kept up. So there was a sort of exam and the interview at the end.'

'You did well?'

'At school? I matriculated. It doesn't mean much. I need to get some more training. Office stuff. Or . . .' she sat on a bollard so that she could look into his face, '. . . what I'd like to do, Philip, is to train to be a teacher. I'd like to teach art. There's someone called Dalcroze – a German I think – and he says that all art is good for people. Therapeutic is the word he uses. So if I taught art to people who . . . weren't well . . . I don't know . . . I thought I might do some good.'

He grinned. 'Saint Madge', he said but without mockery. He shook his head. 'People do not always want all that sympathy you've got, my little woman. Go steady with it.'

She was stung into replying, 'Clem does. Clem *appreciates* my sympathy – he – he's grateful for it.'

'Ah. So it's Clem we're going to talk about.' He kept looking at her quizzically until she was forced to give him a brief rueful smile.

'It's not funny, Philip.'

'No, it isn't.' He looked at the toe of his boot. 'That young man needs help. But afterwards, when he is whole, he will need something more. Have you got anything more for him, Madge?'

'I don't know what you mean.'

'I mean friendship. Love. The sort of feeling your mother had for your father. Can you give him that?'

She blurted, 'No.'

'Then be careful, woman. Don't let your sympathy run away with you. You understand what I am saying?'

She swallowed. 'Yes.' It was what she felt herself, and she knew he was right.

He sighed sharply. 'Right. That's good. Come along then, back to breakfast.' He picked up his bag and threw it down to the harbour beach, turned and began to clamber down the iron-runged ladder.

She waited until he was at the bottom and then called, 'You think I should train as a teacher then, Philip?'

He picked up his bag and looked up at her.

'I wouldn't presoom to say any such thing, woman!' He looked quite shocked at the thought, then he added, 'Madge, don't you know that whatever you do you can give . . . what you have to give . . . to people.' He shook his head impatiently. 'I ain't got the words, but you are one of life's givers. You don't have to look for your work. It will always be there.' Then he quickly negated what he'd said with an even more vigorous shake of his head. 'Take no notice of me, woman. I'm getting old and I was never much good . . . take no notice of me.'

He tramped away from her and she stared after him, puzzled and a little hurt. Only much latter did she recall that he had talked of her mother's love for her father. Not of his for Etta.

Clem too got up early and almost joined Philip when he saw him going down Smeaton's Pier to begin the interminable task of net-mending. Then Madge's head appeared above the wall, her hair damp and clinging to her scalp like a cap. He should have joined her immediately and talked openly about their adventure two days ago, but he hovered uncertainly for too long. The two of them looked more and more private, more and more intimate. He did not want to share Madge and their wonderful experience with anyone. First he must cement it permanently in both of their minds. Eventually he walked along the wharf in the other direction and threaded the narrow streets of the town until he reached the Malakoff where the telescope turned its eye over the Bay, and the buses took on passengers.

Again he was caught in the trap of his own indecision. It was rather like his sudden and unexpected stammering; he knew what he wanted to do but the action would not somehow materialise. A bus to Land's End was waiting, engine running. Its long bonnet was hooked up at one side and the driver, with a man in greasy overalls, was surveying the hiss of steam which threatened to lift off its radiator cap. But half a dozen passengers were already seated inside. Clem stood four yards off, one eye on the bus, the other gazing unseeingly at the opalescent sea with Godrevy light-house sitting so gracefully in its midst. He wanted to get on the bus. He wanted to do something on his own, something worth-while, something especially his, not even to share with Madge. Yet if he got on the bus he would be gone at least all the morning; a whole morning away from Madge. The weather was perfect, they might go swimming.

The man in the overalls leaned over the engine with a long screwdriver and did something. Steam came from another source for about three seconds, then the whole bus ceased to fume and settled down to a rythmical bumping. There were congratulatory shouts from within. The driver put down the bonnet and fastened it with two leather straps. The mechanic kicked the wheels affectionately. Clem thought, it's now or never. And into his head came Neville's impatient voice: 'For Pete's sake, old man! Don't wait for me any more – you're out in front!' There was a moment of terror when he thought he was having another delusion, immediately followed by enormous relief because even if he was he was in full control of it.

He got on the bus.

It climbed up the Stennack with difficulty, Trevalgan hill with more difficulty. At Boscubben the passengers got out and let it groan on alone to the Eagle's Nest. It cooled down a little while, waiting for them, and free-wheeled down to Zennor like a cumbersome bird. Clem alighted at the Tinner's Arms and looked around him with more misgivings.

There was nothing to Zennor. The pub, the ancient church next door, half a dozen cottages and a Methodist chapel. The pub was closed and there wasn't a soul about. A few hens strutted around his legs as the bus snorted away and on the churchyard steps a cat surveyed him lazily. He went towards it and it stood up, stretched mightily, pushed against his proffered hand then dissolved beneath the gates and disappeared among the overgrown tombstones.

Clem sat on the steps in the cat's place and checked his watch against the sundial on the church tower. He couldn't think whether to add or subtract an hour, but anyway it was ten o'clock and the bus wouldn't be back till gone twelve. He couldn't think why he'd come, it was another wrong decision. He tried to summon up another Neville-delusion. Nothing happened. But if it were Neville here, he'd certainly not be sitting on the churchyard steps waiting for time to pass. However, he knew where to go in Zennor and what to do! For a moment a smile flickered on Clem's face at that very Neville-like thought. Then it died. He wasn't Neville. He did not know where to go, nor what to do.

After another timeless span had been bridged, he got up and opened the gates and walked along the path to the church. The doors stood wide and he walked through them into the cool darkness of the interior and stood still, waiting for his eyes to see again. When they did he gazed around with pleasure, his draughtsman's eye revelling in the ingenuity of design and material, his nose consciously enjoying the smell of ancient wood. Suddenly filled with purpose, he walked up the centre aisle searching for the pew-end which was supposed to be carved with the figure of a mermaid. Not just any mermaid; the one who actually came out of the sea at Zennor and bewitched one of the choir. He found her and traced the rough-hewn outline with his finger. She was not beautiful; she was squat and utterly determined and she reminded him of someone. Etta Nolla. Yes, she had magical properties all right! He smiled again. He must remember that Etta was on his side.

A sound came from the sun-filled doorway and two women came in carrying trugs of flowers. They were talking in low voices and did not see him; he stood up from the mermaid and coughed discreetly. They both squeaked in unison, then began to laugh. He went towards them, smiling apologetically. They were easy and pleasant with him; he felt his confidence growing.

'You must 'a thought it was a village o' the dead!' one of them said jovially. 'All the men out on the fields and the women indoors. If it's the footpath to the headland you want, you can walk back with us in a few minutes.'

'We're doin' the church up for a weddin'.' They displayed their trugs and, in case he hadn't followed them, 'There's a weddin' 'ere this Satty.'

He had a sudden feeling. 'Would that be Miss Care?' he asked. 'Miss Rose Care?'

The pleasantness vanished, wiped from their faces in an instant. One of them said, 'Rose Care married? Who'd 'ave 'er? I ask you – who'd 'ave 'er?' Then the other said expressionlessly, 'You know Rose Care?'

'Not personally. I was looking for her as a matter of fact.'

'Ah.' They exchanged glances. 'Ah. Yes. 'Course. You should 'a got off the bus last stop. Skinner's Cottage. That's where Rose Care keeps 'erself. Or is kept.' They brushed past him to the altar. That was that. It hadn't occurred to him that Rose's reputation would still be bad. Neville had thought such a lot of her that Clem had assumed she must have reformed. He did not like the idea that these two village women assumed he was one of Rose's 'paying guests' either. He turned as if to follow them, then realised he could not. He left the church feeling as unsatisfactory as when he had entered.

It was not difficult to find Skinner's Cottage; there was only one road in and out of Zennor, and he walked back the way the bus had brought him until he came to the gate of a tiny hovel set in a neat garden hedged around with encroaching thistles and weeds of all descriptions. It was so appropriate he did not even bother to read the name on the gate; like Neville before he followed the path to the back of the house; like Neville before him he was nervous – not only that someone might already be with Rose, but that his stammer would put an end to what he had to say to her.

She was gardening. The sight of her bent back above a row of broad beans was reassuring; his mother was a keen gardener and there was something universal, almost sexless about people who dealt with the earth. She was picking the beans and hoeing at the same time and as he paused, about to give his introductory cough, she stabbed at a particularly recalcitrant dandelion and said loudly, "Come on, you little bugger!'

It made him laugh, it was so unusual to hear a woman swear, though he would have been shocked to the core if it had been any of the women he actually knew. Rose Care still had the amazing frankness Neville had spoken of so often. Though Neville had called it 'basic innocence'.

She twitched a little with surprise, but turned to look at him with a twist of her supple waist that had little to do with innocence. She was wearing an old stained cotton skirt and an unsuitable satin blouse 'gone' under the arms. Good enough for gardening and, he suddenly realised, anything but sexless. He started to stammer apologies for startling her, but she ignored him and studied him carefully from head to toe. When he stopped speaking, she said slowly, 'You're Tagger. Neville's friend. I can't remember your other name. He spoke about you.'

Her voice was almost free of accent, which was not how Neville had described her. And that name, Tagger, wrung his heart. He said clearly, 'Yes. I am Neville's friend. My real name is Clem Briscoe. You are Rose. He spoke about you. Often.'

She seemed to sag. 'Oh my dear lord. Oh my dear, dear lord. Philip told me he'd gone. I thought he would have forgot me entirely. Oh my dear, sweet lord.'

'Miss Care – I'm sorry – old wounds – I do understand—'

She said automatically, 'Rose. Call me Rose. No-one . . . oh my lord. Let us go inside. Please.' She dropped her hoe on to the path with a clatter and went through an open door. He had to follow. He was conscious of a dark, damp-smelling scullery, then there was a lighter room. Small; a typical cottage parlour, not unlike the Nollas' but much less cluttered, and sparkling with what his mother called 'elbow grease'. Rose stood by a table, supporting herself with her knuckled hands, head down, mass of dark hair falling about her face. She said, 'He asked me to marry him. Did he tell you that?'

'No.' Clem cleared his throat, not from nerves this time but because it was clogged with tears. 'He told me nothing personal, Miss . . . Rose. Before we went to Spain I knew that you and he . . . he told me that. But then, nothing until the siege.' The satin blouse was ancient, but it was beautifully pressed and he knew that satin was difficult to iron. He could understand why Neville had found this girl so attractive. He said inspirationally, 'I think you were too private, too precious, to be . . . talked about.'

'But you said he spoke of me often.' She turned and faced him defiantly. Bland words were not enough for her.

'I meant, before Spain. When we were . . . younger.'

'Children. That's what you were. Schoolboys.' She was angry. 'So why have you come here today? You want a bit of what Neville talked about? Is that it?'

He was suddenly so hot he thought he might faint.

'I'm no good at words. I'm sorry. Neville . . . he was like a brother . . .' he cleared his throat again. 'It's just that – just before we broke out of the siege – he said if anything happened, would I try to find you and tell you. That's all.' He turned. 'I'd better go. I'm so sorry if I've . . . I'm so sorry . . .'

She said sternly, 'Philip Nolla told me. Neville would know that Philip Nolla would tell me.'

'Not that he was *gone*! Not that.' Clem felt desperate. 'He wanted me to tell you that he loved you. Really loved you. That's all. He wanted you to know, you see. That it wasn't just . . . he wanted you to know that he *loved* you!'

She let him stumble back through the scullery and into the open air. He paused at the corner of the cottage, clung to the granite and took deep breaths. She was by his side, earthy hand beneath his elbow. Her voice was different, no longer her best and carefully tutored accent.

'Come on back inside, m'dear. Or better still, sit 'ere on the

96

stones while I make you a cup o' tea.' She piloted him backwards and pressed him down on to the wall. Her hair brushed his face. It smelled like hay. She smiled right into his face and he saw that her dark eyes were no longer angry and certainly not sad. She looked happy.

He waited there while thistledown from the fields floated about his head. He wondered what would have happened if Neville hadn't been killed. Would he have come back here and made Rose Care a respectable married woman? Already Clem suspected that was impossible.

She came back with strong sweet tea in a decent china cup with a saucer and a silver spoon. There was a crest on the spoon – he felt it with his thumb when he stirred the tea. She waited while he drank it, pulling up a weed within arms' length, already eyeing up the bean-row again.

When he said, 'I'd better go,' she did not try to delay him. She took the cup and smiled knowingly.

'It's Madge Bridges, isn't it?'

He was shocked by her prescience and began stammering again.

'I could 'a tole you that six year ago. She and me used to 'ave a little chat now an' then.' She drooped very slightly. 'She 'asn't 'ad nothin' to do with me since she got to know about Neville an' me. Still . . . I know a lot about most people.' She laughed. 'The ole biddies 'oo talk so much about me 'ud be surprised if they knew 'ow often my visitors come for a chat and a cup o' tea.' She opened the gate and stood behind it. 'You an' Madge, you're right for each other. Me an' Neville weren't, nor never would 'a been.' She sighed sharply and transferred his tea-cup to the other hand to enable her to scratch her shoulder. The satin blouse fell back to reveal no shoulder straps, just bare brown flesh. Clem averted his eyes.

She said, 'You need 'er. That's for certain. An' I reckon she needs you too. But she prob'ly don't know it, so you better do something quick afore she sets off on another course.'

She closed the gate. He moved off down the road, wondering where he heard those words before. Then he remembered. Etta Nolla knew that he and Madge were 'right' too. He propped himself against the stone hedge by the bus stop, feeling heartened. He must start looking on the positive side of things. He was as good as engaged to Madge. Etta Nolla approved. Rose Care approved. He did not think Mrs Bridges disapproved. He had spoken of Neville's death; he had *faced* Neville, stopped him being a delusion, made him into a thought, a memory, which he could himself recall or banish at any time. And he had carried out Neville's wish: he had been to see Rose Care.

In due course the bus came along, snorting and steaming like a dragon. He hadn't looked at his watch; it could be late or early, it didn't matter. The flowers thrusting from the drystone walling left their pollen over his jacket and trousers. He didn't worry about that either. As they began the descent into St Ives, he made another decision. He wouldn't walk back to the cottage through the Warren this time, he'd go down Tregenna Hill where all the shops were, and he'd buy a ring. A proper, diamond engagement ring. And as soon as he could get Madge to himself again, he'd put it on her finger. And all would be well.

But it was difficult for Clem to get Madge to himself any longer. Etta Nolla, presumably secure now that her husband was home again, succumbed to Mrs Bridges' pleas, and joined them for their beach picnic each day. Philip had his business to see to, but he too usually appeared about mid-afternoon and then Madge pestered him to 'show Clem the old mine', 'show Clem the secret cove'. He was not an obtrusive companion, he did or said nothing to come between Madge and Clem, but more often than not, he was just there. It was like the comic song – and Mother came too. Except that the presence of a chaperone would have made the situation more definite; Philip was just one more valued companion.

Clem tried referring to their 'baptism'.

'It was marvellous of you to listen to me the other day, Madge dear.'

'Don't be silly. It wasn't marvellous at all. It was a privilege.'

'D'you know, when we went into the sea together like that, it was as if we were starting a new life.'

'That's St Ives for you.'

'Yes. But together. A new life together.'

'Philip says we're all intertwined. Like the fishing nets. We make a pattern. If the pattern gets torn we have to mend it as quickly as we can.'

98

'He's right. I was in a hundred pieces. You're mending me, Madge. Mending me.'

'No. That would make me too important. Self-important.' She scrambled ahead of him through a mat of rhododendron bushes which met overhead. 'Come on. Here's the monument I was telling you about. There's a terrific view from up here.'

He told himself it was all right, nothing had changed since that day in the sea; but he felt his nerves beginning to stretch again, and at nights he would wake sweating and think for a terrible moment that he was in that field hospital again, believing his leg had been shot off.

On their last day the weather was not so good. A vicious little wind had sprung up overnight and whipped the sand everywhere. The McGoverns came to say goodbye, Mrs Nolla declined to go to the beach, and Philip and the Gurnards were repairing the *Forty-niner*. Clem knew this was his opportunity.

They walked along the farm footpath at the top of Ayr, picking blackberries as they went and tying them in Clem's handkerchief. Then they dropped down over the cliff fields to the first of Five Points. The wind flapped Clem's trousers against his legs and threatened to take his hat altogether. Looking at Madge bracing herself against it, her hat hanging down her back as usual, he had a miserable sense of doom. She was enjoying the change in the weather, he was not. He felt as if he were in a pit, looking up at her playing in the sunshine miles away.

He said abruptly, 'Madge, let's sit over there out of this blasted wind. And watch that blackberry juice. I don't want your mother blaming me for another ruined dress!'

She looked round, surprised, but followed him to the over-hanging rock and crouched there obediently, holding the stained and dripping handkerchief away from her flapping frock.

He said tensely, 'Look Madge, I know you're quite happy with things the way they are. But I'm not. I don't like secrecy. Not for long. It begins to smack of underhandedness.'

Her sheer bewilderment increased the distance between them. Was he sinking deeper into his pit or was she being elevated towards the stars? Whichever it was he was forced to raise his voice to be heard.

'Well?'

She flinched. 'I don't know what you mean, Clem – have I done something?'

We've done something, Madge. As you very well know. And I want it made public. Official.'

Her eyes became enormous and the blueness of them darkened with anxiety. He would have liked to have put his finger on the bump in the middle of her nose but she was too far away.

'Clem, I honestly don't know what you mean.'

'Stop pretending, girl! Or woman, as *he* says! Have you told him? Does he know about our engagement?'

'*Engagement*? Clem, how can we be engaged? You've said nothing. And I'm only eighteen!' She took a step away from him and the wind came round the corner and fluttered her dress frantically. He thought she might take flight at any moment.

He said furiously, 'I – I declared myself, Madge. And you let me think . . , we agreed on it. We got baptised together, didn't we? We started a new life together, didn't we? I want to announce it. I've been patient, waiting for you to say something. But before we leave I want to go up Tregenna Hill and buy a ring. I want it to happen at St Ives. It's our special place now. We'll come here every year until we're quite old and it will be like a celebration each time. Neville and your father and you and me and—'

'Clem, stop it!' She had her hands splayed on the rock behind her as if he were attacking her. 'It wasn't like that. I wanted to hear about Neville, but he's dead! I thought if you told me – got it out of your system, you would be able to realise that – accept it. We could talk about them like Mother and Etta talk about them, lovingly and without pain—'

'Never mind all that!' He shook his head to clear it. 'You're prevaricating again. You keep doing it. Holding me off as if I were a mad animal or something! Let's go back and get a ring and tell everyone . . . come *on*, Madge. Come down. Come here. Don't keep going away.'

'I am here. Right here. I'm not going away.' She took a step back towards him. 'Listen, Clem, you've got it wrong. I'm honoured – yes I am honoured – that you want to marry me. When you told me you loved me the other day I was so honoured I wanted to make everything all right for you. Immediately. And no-one can do that. I takes time and patience—'

'We've got time. We've got our lives. And when we're together

I can be patient. Is that what's worrying you, Madge? My dear, I can be so patient . . . you've no idea. I'll look after you. I'll protect you and be your friend—' He put his arm high in the air, reaching for her, and she stepped back.

'Clem, *please*. I can't get married yet. I haven't *done* anything. I want to train to be an art teacher—'

'You're not saying you don't love me?'

'Clem, I just don't know.'

'You like me?'

'I like you more that anyone I know.'

'That's what it is. That's what love is. Liking someone very very much. You do love me, you see. I knew you did – I could tell. Don't worry, I'll help you to train. I'll—'

'They don't *have* married teachers!' She took a deep breath and said loudly, 'No. I'm sorry, Clem, but no.'

It was like a death knell. Her voice was sonorous and her eyes were black with pupil beneath the short mane of brown hair. If she were wearing a tin hat she would look like a feminised Neville. And she was leaving him, just as Neville had.

He said with great conviction, 'I can't manage this. Not again.' And he turned and began to walk towards the edge of the cliff.

He heard her gasp a scream and knew she was coming after him. It was the same as before. When he'd turned to flee.

'Clem – what are you doing? You can't—' Her fingers tore ineffectually at his sleeve. They left stains like blood. 'Clem – please come back with me now.'

He marched on. She got in front of him and he pushed her aside. She hung on to him physically until he stumbled to a stop, then she wept and said she was sorry she had misled him but . . . He disengaged himself and began to run. As he reached the long finger of rock pointing out into the Atlantic, her voice came to him on the wind, screaming like a gull's.

'All right! All right, Clem. We'll make it official! Come back. I do love you. I can't live if you do this, Clem! I can't live without you!'

He fell in a heap on the hard limpet-encrusted rock and she came to him and took his head in her lap. She was weeping as if she'd never stop.

'Oh Clem, I'm sorry. Sorry. Oh my dear . . . I do love you. Really I do. Honestly. Oh Clem . . . Clem.'

His jacket was covered in blackberry juice, and so was she. First baptism and now blood. She had come down into the pit to be with him. A sacrifice. They held each other, and the sea, green and angry, rushed along the rock as if it would engulf them; then fell back, hissing.

CHAPTER SIX

1944

It was almost September and already the sun was autumn-warm after what Etta called 'the invasion summer'. With the D-day landings, they had all assumed that the war was as good as over. It was a shock to hear of the doodlebugs arriving over London and to realise that the German snake was scotched but not yet killed.

Madge sat on the harbour beach, her back to the warm wall, her writing things on her lap. She was supposed to be writing to Clem; she had been trying to write to him each day since she arrived here. She knew exactly what she had to say; she had to find the words for telling him that she forgave him and that it was all because of this rotten war and he could come home at the end of the month and everything would be just as it had been before. The first two items were perfectly true, of course. If it hadn't been for the war, Clem would not be on 'important war work' in Canada, so he could not have met this Other Woman. Madge looked again at his letter. The Other Woman's name was Julie, apparently. Madge wondered why she could never remember it. She'd come down here with Rosemary especially to think about what Clem had told her, to write to him telling him that she forgave him. The least she could do was remember the name of the woman who had . . . what did he say? The woman who had captured his heart'.

Madge looked up to check on Rosemary whose white sun-bonnet seemed to flutter along the distant shoreline like a cabbage butterfly. Of course she must forgive him and of course he must come home when they sent him back next month – for Rosemary's sake. But she hoped very much that things would not be as they'd been before. She remembered all those nights before Rosemary's conception and her eyes widened behind her pre-war sunglasses. He had said he would be patient . . . he would be her friend. But his patience had been short-lived and his friendship had taken on an aggressive quality when she failed to respond to his engulfing ardour.

She simply hadn't understood. After, all, she had made no protest. She had lain beneath him, rigid with horror, letting him do unspeakable things to her, and when he accused her of 'not responding' she had wondered whether he actually wanted her to scream and fight.

She remembered with deep shame the underlying relief she had felt when they had listened together to Mr Chamberlain's speech on the wireless nearly five years before. 'A state of war now exists . . .' War was terrible. Her mother had told her so often enough and even gone so far as to say that Daddy had been a 'delayed war casualty.' But she could do nothing about it, it had happened and she would have to bear it as Mother had borne it. Clem would go away to fight just as Daddy had. And there would be no more bedtimes.

But Clem had not gone away. His Spanish war wound had seen to that. So bedtimes had gone on until she knew she was pregnant. Then Clem himself had called them off.

'This is our dream come true, Madge. We must do nothing to put it at risk . . .'

She wondered as she sat on the sand that mellow misty morning, whether Clem had been glad of the excuse to give up on her. She knew more now. The Americans had joined in the war and there had been many girls willing to risk disgrace for what they called 'love'. She knew now what Clem meant when he accused her of being unresponsive. She knew there was something wrong with her.

She picked up his letter once more and skimmed through it, feeling again the terrible drag of pity she had always felt for Clem. It was so easy to forgive him; and where else would he go except to her and Rosemary – they were his home now. But to go back to how it had been before . . . Madge bit her lip. She loved Clem. But if she loved him in her way then she couldn't 'love' him in *that* way. The two simply did not add up. She did understand now about the pleasures of the flesh, but they had nothing to do with friendship or pity. They might perhaps be indulged in with a complete stranger whom one would never see again afterwards, otherwise it was simply impossible.

104

She lifted her sunglasses and rubbed one eye. If only Clem hadn't written 'You and Ro are everything. Without you life is simply unbearable'. If he'd said 'I still love Julia but I'm willing to come back to support you' she could have told him to stay. She could have been warm and understanding then. And if he wanted to come back so much, why had he told her about Julia in the first place? She sighed for the umpteenth time and looked up to check on Rosemary's sunbonnet again. It was all worth it for Rosemary. It had to be.

At nearly four years old Rosemary was beginning to 'take shape' as Mrs Bridges put it. She was in fact very shapely; her nose, chin, eyebrows and mouth were all dimpled or tip-tilted or delicately arched; her shoulders were little apricot-coloured pads of fat above rounded arms, her belly was thrust out like the belly of an African child; her buttocks and thighs were strong and thick, and her pudgy little feet made Madge laugh.

She was old enough to want to make her mother laugh. She pouted and lifted her wonderful brows and lowered her lashes. She wriggled her bottom and looked at Madge, waiting for the smile. Then she would come and lay her head in Madge's lap and wait for all the grown-ups present to say, 'What a little darling!'

Neither Etta nor Philip said that, and consequently Rosemary was behaving impeccably in an attempt to win approval. It meant that the holiday was going really well; there were no tantrums and so far she had not declined any of Etta's eccentric meals. Yesterday Madge had had over an hour to herself while Rosemary helped Etta to shake the sand out of the mats. And when the child came down to the beach with her bucket and spade, she would play happily with the local toddlers and never attempt to bite them or snatch their toys away. When she did that sort of thing at home, Mrs Bridges said she needed a father's strong hand. Maybe Rosemary knew that if she played up at Zion Cottage, Philip – or Etta – were quite capable of administering that strong hand.

The sunbonnet was bobbing up the beach now. Madge smiled, glad to be able to forget her letter to Clem yet again. She had written, 'Of course I shall say nothing to my mother nor to yours. Your mother called last week to wish us a happy holiday. I think she might have come with us if she'd realised that my mother was not coming. However this did not crop up in the conversation until it was time for her to leave and then it was rather late to change our arrangements. Father's old colleague, had secured me a seat on the West Country Express . . .' Madge's smile deepened guiltily as she remembered her mother's adjurations. 'Now darling, don't say a word when Mrs Briscoe arrives. Wait until she is leaving and then mention it as if we'd already told her. I think you and Rosemary should have time alone. Without me. And without Clem's mother. We both spoil her. She needs Etta's firm hand!'

Dear Mother. She always said to her friends 'How I'd manage without Madge, I do not know. She is a tower of strength . . . an absolute tower.' And the boot was on the other foot entirely.

Rosemary arrived, lugging a bucket of sea water. She poured it carefully into a prepared hole. It disappeared.

'Oh damn!' she said vexedly.

Madge protested automatically, then explained. 'The sand up here is too dry, Ro, it soaks up the water. When I've finished Daddy's letter I'll come and dig a hole in the wet sand and you'll be able to fill that up and make a lovely lake!'

'Come *now* Mummy. I want you to come *now!* You're always writing to Daddy!'

The truth of the last statement overrode the petulance of Rosemary's voice and Madge began to put everything away in the beach bag while Rosemary goose-stepped on the spot.

'Come on then. Back to the sea. Don't forget your bucket. Left right, left right . . .'

'Sojers, Mummy. Like the sojers.' Rosemary pointed and Madge paused to look over her shoulder.

A platoon of the Marine Commandoes appeared on the wharf behind them, shouldering a life raft. It was a familiar but still exciting sight. Eight men, four to each side of the raft, ran in perfect synchronisation down the slipway and along the sand to the water. Without any audible order being given they then slowed to a loping wade through the water until they were waist deep. The boat was lowered from shoulder height to the surface, and the men hoisted themselves aboard with hardly a ripple disturbing the sea. They knelt and leaned over the side, paddling smoothly with their hands. In less than three minutes from their first appearance, they had disappeared silently into the mist.

'Bye-bye,' sang Rosemary sweetly. 'Bye-bye sojers.'

Madge smiled sentimentally, and the two of them went to the

water's edge where Madge began digging and Rosemary filling. The 'lake' was taking shape nicely when Rosemary looked up and commented, 'A nunny sojer, Mummy,' and Madge glanced over her shoulder and saw another camouflaged giant pounding down the beach. He was making straight for them, but Madge, with complete faith in the trained reactions of all the Mountain Warfare regiment, watched smilingly until almost the last minute. As the booted foot was lifted above the water-filled hole, she gasped a warning. It was too late. The marine, his eyes on the invisible horizon, had seen neither them nor their lake. At the sound of a voice from beneath his raised boot, he managed to gather himself in a kind of writhing knot in mid-air for a split second. Then he crashed into the hole, emptying it of water instantly and soaking the two females on its edge. Rosemary screamed piercingly and began to wail. Madge dashed water from her eyes and picked her up to jiggle her against her shoulder. The marine scrambled to his feet without so much as an exclamation and climbed out of the hole. He marked time experimentally.

'Okay,' he said of himself. Then to Madge, 'You okay?' She nodded above Rosemary's head. 'What about the kid?' She nodded again. 'Sorry.' He stopped marking time and looked out to where the sea merged with the mist. 'Where are the others? Did you see them?'

'Yes. They launched about five minutes ago. You'll never catch them.'

Rosemary lifted a head to protest furiously at her mother's wandering attention. The man ignored her.

'I'll have to try.' He leaned down and ripped at the laces of his boot. 'Look. Can I leave these with you? And this?' He tugged off his flat hat and battledress top. 'Where are you staying?'

'Zion Cottage.'

'Right.'

He ran into the water, staggered, plunged, and was gone.

'There, there, darling. Everything is all right. No need to cry.'

'I'se all wet Mummy!' Rosemary, who got wet regularly of her own volition, decided to object this time. 'That nasty sojer wetted me!'

'Well, I'm wet too. It's our part in commando training I suppose!'

Rosemary stopped crying, intrigued. Madge followed up

quickly, 'Let's take the soldier's things back to the cottage and have a drink. It's time for your rest.'

'No rest Mummy – I don't want a rest!'

Madge put down her daughter and gathered up the enormous boots and clothing. She said with unusual severity, 'You will have a rest, Ro. Remember, there's a war on!'

Rosemary wrestled with the logic of this all the way up the beach and was still frowning when Madge picked up the beach bag.

'Is having a rest doing my bit, Mummy?' she queried then.

'Yes.'

'Orright then. And shall I carry the sojer's hat? That would be doing my bit too, wouldn't it?'

'It would.'

Madge tucked her letter to Clem at the back of the bag and capped her fountain pen. Maybe the encounter with 'the sojer' was going to be another bonus about this holiday. She smiled as she watched Rosemary gallop across the cobbles towards Philip. Whatever was happening, it was terribly difficult not to be happy in this place.

Normally they would have spent the afternoon on Porthmeor beach with a picnic. Etta ate well at midday and liked to rest afterwards. Philip and Jem might take the lugger into the bay to fish sometimes, but they were both over sixty now and officially retired. This afternoon, Madge was strangely unwilling to move out of sight of the cottage.

Etta said, 'Get you off, my maid. I'll give that commando 'is stuff when 'e comes for en.'

'It's rather hot, Etta. I think I'll stay near the house if you don't mind. Then if Ro needs a drink or anything I'm handy!'

'Not got an eye on that there commando, 'ave you, my maid?' Etta said sharply. 'You'm a married woman, remember!'

'Oh Etta. Don't be silly.' Madge looked at the silent Philip. 'Are you going out with Jem today, Philip?'

'No.'

Etta was on to him instantly. 'What d'you mean, no? You tole me you was trawlin' all af'noon and ev'nin' – I dun't know where I be to with you these days, Philip Nolla.'

'I'm staying ashore.' Philip looked at her with his clear blue stare. 'I kin please myself now, wife. An' I'm stayin' ashore this afternoon.'

Etta was silent. Madge felt her neck warm with resentment. It was as if she were an unmarried girl again having to be chaperoned. She recalled how Etta had snuffed Neville's candle in the old days; she had wondered at his annoyance then; now she did not.

She took up her position near the harbour wall again and looked at her letter to Clem. Rosemary sensing her mother's uncooperativeness joined a litlle knot of local children who were playing a complicated game among the beached boats. She toddled after them, crouching obediently when they screamed that Jerry was coming. She was beginning to feel part of the big world.

Philip came slowly down the slipway from the Fisherman's Lodge. His trilby hat was looking too big for him, which Madge saw as a sign of age. This and his diffidence forced an unwilling smile from her.

He said, 'That's better. How did I offend you, woman?'

'Oh . . . sometimes you still treat me as if I'm a child. Come and sit down here.' She made room on the rug. 'Where's Etta?'

'Feet up, snoring away. Minister's calling later. Can't abide him so I'll have to stay out.'

'That's why you were going trawling with Jem.'

He nodded and gave her one of his upward grins,

'True. True.'

'So you did cancel it to keep an eye on me?' She was cross again. 'Honestly Philip, it's too bad. I'm twenty-four, you know. And there's Ro to chaperone me if I should go berserk!'

'Ah . . . it's not that, woman. Did you think I didn't trust you?'

'Then why?'

He was silent, getting out his old clay pipe, then his oilskin tobacco pouch. He looked inside. Tobacco was scarce and after a moment he closed it again and put everything away.

'I can't find words, woman. Once before I din't keep you close and you was pushed into something . . . maybe not right for you. I don't know. I en't aimin' to interfere . . . only . . . only to be at hand if you need someone.'

She was silent for a long time, trying to remember all the tiny events that had led up to her marriage to Clem.

At last she said in a low voice, 'Philip, tell me honestly. Do you think I shouldn't have married Clem?'

109

He did not lift his head again. The rim of his trilby was ridiculously wide, almost like a cowboy hat.

'That's what I don't know. I know you're not 'appy. But you've got your little girl and there's much more to life than bein' 'appy. But . . . I shoulda liked you to be 'appy too, my maid. I shoulda liked that.'

'Dear Philip. I'm happy enough. Really. And if I weren't . . . you must never feel responsible.'

'Responsible, aye.' He seized on the word. 'That's what we are, woman. Responsible for one another. Your pa, and now you and your ma . . . you feels responsible for Etta and me. You – you *keeps* us.'

'Rubbish, Philip!' Madge laughed uncomfortably. 'We remember you at Christmas and—'

'I don't mean keeps. Not like that. Not pays us. I mean you keeps us, like a keeper keeps sheep.' He lifted his head. 'Isn't that right, woman? Don't we keep one another?'

'Oh Philip. Yes.' His flattened vowel sounds gave the word even more meaning. She remembered how he had dived into the sea twenty years before to pull her out. He had indeed become her 'kipper' then.

He patted her hand quickly and looked back to where Rosemary was playing. 'Ah. Well then. Kin I sit 'ere for a bit and talk to you?'

'Of course. And I'm sorry I was touchy about it.' She too patted his hand. 'Tell me one of your stories, Philip. Tell me about the flood of '94.'

'That weren't no story, woman, not in the sense o' fairy tales.' He got out his tobacco pouch for the second time and looked into it. 'Great rocks a — ' urtling down the Stennack. In the front doors, through the walls, out the back. Terrible it was.'

She said, 'I used to pretend I was sitting in the train when the Malakoff walls broke. And I had to get up steam and get the train out of the station before it was washed over on to Porthminster.' She paused. 'What is Rosemary up to now?'

They both squinted into the bright mist. Rosemary was talking to one of the soldiers.

Philip said, 'Is that your commando? The one who gave you his boots?'

'I don't remember.'

Philip turned and gave her a level stare quite unlike his usual glinting looks. Then he faced front again.

' 'E's a-pickin' 'er up. I'd better go and see.'

'No. Stay here, Philip. He's bringing her up. She's teliin him that we're here. It must be the same man.'

'Aye. Must be.' Philip's voice was as dry as the sand.

The soldier, with Rosemary on his shoulders, approached them. All the commandoes were hefty, muscular young men, but this one seemed especially so. His dark red hair was stiff with salt and sprang out from his beret like wire wool, his brown eyes were not large but very round and shiny, like boot buttons. His nose might have been broken at some time, it took a sharp turn to the right halfway down and seemed to pull his top lip up towards it. When he smiled, as he was then, it showed his two front teeth and made him look like a schoolboy.

Rosemary yelled, 'Shoes, Mummy! Sojer wants his shoes!'

Madge said, 'They're at the cottage with the other things. I'll get them.'

The man knelt and bent his head forward and Rosemary stepped off his neck on to the rug. He looked up.

'Don't go yet. I must thank you. For this morning. I was supposed to go in uniform but I'd never have caught the others with my boots on!' His grin made him look about fifteen. 'I'm the sort of cox.'

'Cox?'

'Coxswain. Of the raft. Four a side and one directing ops. The blighters pulled a fast one on me.' He did not move from his position on all fours in front of her. 'My name is Edward Nicholls. Everyone in St Ives calls me Ned.'

Rosemary was goose-stepping again and Philip reached for her hand.

'Pull me up, young lady.Come on. Heave-ho.' He got to his feet. 'This is Mrs Clement Briscoe who is staying with my wife and me. An' 'er daughter, Rosemary. I am Philip Nolla.'

Madge looked up in surprise at Philip's dignified formality. She had expected him to discourage the young marine, in his efforts to 'kip' her. Here he was lifting the whole chance encounter into something more . . . important.

Ned Nicholls straightened his back but stayed on his knees. He was almost as tall as Philip who was on his feet by now.

'I've heard of you, sir. You went to Dunkirk, didn't you? And they talk about you at the Clipper – you went over on a rocket line to one of the steamers in the hurricane when you were just a kid.'

Philip avoided Madge's gaze.

'I'll take Rosemary up for her tea,' he said instead.'You two come on later. Give me time find a cloth for the table.'

'Oh Philip—' Madge began, and Ned Nicholls said at the same time, 'Really, sir, there's no need . . .' Then they both stopped speaking and looked at each other.

Philip started up the slipway. ' 'Alf an 'our,' he stipulated. Then he bent his head to listen to something Rosemary was saying and they crossed the cobbles together.

Ned Nicholls sat back on his heels and said, 'He wants us to get to know each other. Is he a relative of yours?'

'No. But more than a relative.' Madge felt herself flushing at Philip's obviousness. She said, 'He's has always . . . well . . . kept an eye on me when I'm here.'

'You come regularly?'

'Yes. Since I was four.'

The boot-button eyes were full of questions, but he must have decided that they could wait. He unfolded his legs and sat on the edge of the rug.

'I'd never been until I came on this training course. A week in Weymouth each year when I was a kid. That was as much as they could manage.'

'Your parents?'

'Barnado's. I'm a Banana Boy.' He grinned. 'Isn't that why your Mr Philip Nolla is being kind to me?'

'No. I'm sure . . . I don't know.' It made Philip's actions much more acceptable, though it couldn't be true. Even so she relaxed slightly. 'What did you think of St Ives when you arrived?'

'Beautiful. Wonderful. I couldn't believe such a place existed. What about you?'

'The same. Quite literally I thought it was fairyland.' She smiled into the sun. 'When I'm here it's as if it's the only reality. Everything else seems like a dream.'

'Perhaps it is. A dream. Or a nightmare.' He laughed to take the seriousness out of the exchange, then went on, 'I gather from your daughter's remarks to me that you were both thoroughly wetted this morning when I emptied your pool of water.'

Madge laughed too. 'It was so funny. The whole thing was like a Marx Brothers farce. Did you catch the others?'

'Yes. They knew I would. I'm fairly fast in the water.'

The dark eyes were laughing right at her. 'I'm glad no harm came to you. Do you swim, Mrs Briscoe?'

'Yes. Philip doesn't approve. He worries about the sea claiming all of us back. But I love swimming. Mostly I mess about in the surf round at Porthmeor beach.'

He looked at her covertly. Her hair was brown with lighter bands of colour from the sun. There was a lot of it and she had it tied on her neck with a blue ribbon. There was nothing remarkable about her, yet he had a job not to stare rudely. She was the sort of girl who would never get boring. Her face was so mobile, laughing one minute, solemn the next. And the way her neck went down between the clavicles, leaving little shallows each side . . . it was so endearing. He wanted to tell her she must eat more because she was too thin.

He said, 'The sea is treacherous round there. Safer at Porthminster.'

'But tame.' She smiled. 'That's what makes St Ives so special. It seems civilised, but only just under the surface it's dangerous and exciting.'

He laughed aloud. 'That is what the artists see, of course. I know someone. A painter. She would agree with you. She says she has seen one of the standing stones marching over Trencrom hill!'

'Are you an artist, Mr Nicholls?'

'Ned. Please call me Ned.'

'Oh. Well. Ned, then. And you had better call me Madge. Mrs Clement Briscoe is rather a mouthful.' She smiled and he wondered why he had thought her unremarkable.

'Thank you . . . Madge.' It was such a stupid, ordinary name. What sort of parents named their child Madge? 'Well then, no, I don't paint. I mean I don't earn a living by painting. I was hopeless at school. But these people – Mr and Mrs Scaife – they say I could paint if I tried.' He laughed. 'They don't realise I am trying my utmost!' He sifted sand through his fingers and Madge noticed the bluntness of the nails. 'Do you paint, Madge?' he asked.

'I draw. I used to have an easel at the cottage and set it up like a

113

real artist. I played at being one, I suppose. Mother encouraged me but Father thought I made a much better wicketkeeper!'

She began to tell him about the cricket matches. He listened, his eyes going from her hand to her face. He noticed the blue veins along the back of her hand, the small bump in her nose, the way her mouth curved, her rather long chin.

'I wish I'd known all of you. It sounds great fun. We played lots of cricket, but it wasn't like yours. We were in teams and if we didn't win, we'd let our team down.'

'Oh crikey, it was the same for us. Father was livid if anyone on his side dropped a catch or got a duck.'

'Did your husband play cricket with you?'

'Yes. He came down here with my brother once when we were all much younger. He was at school with Neville and then in Spain. Neville was killed out there. And the cricket matches finished.'

There was a small silence. Madge began to gather her things together. Ned got to his knees again.

'It's rather marvellous that you draw. Would you like to meet the Scaifes? They hold classes, you know. Half a dozen of us go along. Keeps us out of mischief.'

'Well . . . I . . . yes. Thank you.' She stood up. 'That is if Etta will stay with Rosemary. Sometimes she won't go to sleep until I go to bed. I suppose the air raids have made her nervous.'

He picked up the rug, shook it and folded it.

'She's so pretty. It's hard to think that she will miss so many things if this war goes on much longer.'

Madge thought of Clem coming home next month. She shouldered her bag. 'I think we'd better go up to the house. Philip obviously wants to do the honours. Do you mind? Can you spare the time?'

'I'm off duty now until three, and I don't mind one bit. It's good to get out of the mess.'

'Three? In the morning?'

'It's the best time for our sort of training.'

'I suppose so.' She glanced at him. I should have thought . . . with the war nearly over . . . the commando training wasn't quite so necessary.'

He shrugged. 'If we can hurry this last bit it will be worthwhile.'

114

She knew better than to ask more, but she wondered if the training could have anything to do with the new doodlebugs. Strange . . . Clem's important war work had something to do with a different kind of bomb, and this young commando was trained to destroy a different kind of bomb. It was all so . . . unnecessary.

He followed her to the cottage, the rug over one arm. It was the usual fisherman's dwelling, built on and into the rock; a fish cellar at one level, a flight of steps to the living area, bedrooms above and the attic like a lookout perched on top. There were no ceilings – the floorboards above occasionally snowed flakes of whitewash on to the plush-covered table. A crystal chandelier incongruously tinkled from one of the heavy timbers, and every nook and cranny was filled with bits and pieces. Rosemary was ensconced in the window seat among cushions, two pieces of driftwood on her short lap. Etta and the Methodist Minister were at the table, an open bible between them. Philip cut bread at the sideboard.

Rosemary greeted her mother vociferously.

'We bin singing, Mummy. A woodin cross, Mummy.'

The minister said sonorously, ' "The Old Wooden Cross", my child.' He looked at Madge. 'A hymn, Mrs Briscoe. We cannot start too early with hymns.' He nodded at Ned. 'One of our brave men. May God be with you, my son.'

Ned nodded too. 'Thank you, sir.'

Etta said, 'Sit down then. Making the place look a muddle. Don't let the child put that in her mouth, Marjorie. It will splinter.' She gathered cups around her and began to pour tea. 'Help yourself to jam, minister.' She pushed his cup towards him and smiled dourly as he shovelled the bible hastily away. 'And you're Private Ned Nicholls, then? Where you from, young man?'

'Wiltshire, Mrs Nolla.' Ned sensed animosity in the lard-like stare. He smiled frankly. 'I haven't got a family, ma'am. I was found in a railway waiting-room twenty-two years ago. Doctor Barnardo took me on.'

The wind had been taken from Etta's sails, but she managed a broadside even though becalmed. 'Mrs Briscoe's 'usband is doin' very important war work in Canada. He's always been a friend of the family. A great friend.'

Ned nodded gently and bent his head to look at Rosemary's driftwood. He was intrigued. They hadn't known he was an orphan, so Philip Nolla's invitation had not been given from pity. He wanted Madge to have a . . . friend? Was that because her marriage to Clement Briscoe wasn't happy? Etta Nolla's aggression might bear that out. And Etta had called Madge Marjorie. That was much more like it; there was something satisfying about three equi-syllable names. He repeated it in his head: Mar . . . jor . . . ie. On the wild country between Zennor and St Ives there was a bank of purple flowers, tall and strong, yet unbroken by the wind, so very supple. He thought they might be marjoram. Perhaps he could take her there.

He glanced up at her and discovered she was looking at him. Her eyes were navy blue with a kind of intense sympathy. He realised she was sorry for him because he had been abandoned as a baby and he grinned at her, trying to reassure her. Without conscious thought his blunt fingers reached out and touched hers.

Philip plonked the jam pot in front of him.

'Better take some jam, Mr Nicholls. Before the littl'un 'as the lot.'

Ned sat up straight with a jerk and was thankful to see that Etta was still attending to the chapel wallah. He met Philip's stare for a brief moment, then mumbled, 'Oh . . . thanks,' and applied himself to spreading jam on his bread.

A week later he took her to see the flowers, and she agreed they were marjoram.

They were into September and the mist on the high cliffs above Zennor had deteriorated into a sea fret and was cold and wet. But the weather proved an ally to Ned. Rosemary's halcyon existence on the beach was suddenly interrupted. Limited to twice daily walks in wellingtons, she became obstreperous. The Mountain Warfare Group came to the rescue and held a party for all the children they could muster. Their mess, high above Bamaluz Point, was transformed from its grim bareness to an Aladdin's cave. The bar looked like a Wild West frontier saloon, the billiard and ping-pong tables covered with hardboard and cloths and laid as one enormous banquet-cum-buffet, the girdered roof was hung with fishing nets, shells and pre-war balloons. Rosemary, escorted by Philip, was entranced. She dismissed her mother instantly. Ned seized his opportunity, and one of the jeeps.

Madge, walking behind Ned through the shoulder-high fern, the sea either side, the mist pearling her hair, knew one of those moments of conscious happiness. The excitement of St Ives, which she had thought gone for ever with the terrible deaths of her father and brother, was tangible again. She smelled it, felt it vibrating through the soles of her feet as they contacted the springy turf, heard it in the scream of the gulls, saw it in the looming shape of the enormous headland pushing into the Atlantic.

When Ned Nicholls paused and quested about in the fern for the flowers in which he seemed so interested, she began to laugh.

'What's up?' he asked, looking at her with brows raised ridiculously above his round eyes.

She couldn't explain. 'I was remembering you landing in our lake,' she improvised lamely. 'You're almost as wet again.'

'So are you,' he came back promptly, grinning like a schoolboy. 'It's rather good, isn't it?'

She recalled Clem's unwillingness to get himself wet, and nodded. It was something to do with becoming part of the earth, a one-ness with the elements that was completely delightful at this moment.

'Here they are.' Ned disappeared among the sodden fern and she followed somewhat cautiously. Philip had warned her frequently about the many old mine shafts on the cliffs. But Ned was only a few feet from the path. And there, almost buried by the burgeoning fern, was a clump of purple flowers growing strongly and independently.

'Well!' She was genuinely surprised. 'Yes, I think they are marjoram plants. Why here? I suppose a bird must have dropped the seed.' She held the heads between her fingers and sniffed experimentally. 'This is wild marjoram. The other is much smaller. Called sweet marjoram.'

Ned took a lethal-looking knife from his belt and crouched by the flowers.

'What are you doing?' Madge asked.

'I'm going to dig a root. That bit of land behind the mess – I'm going to try to get it going there.'

'But why? It's not the kind used as a herb. It's really a weed.'

117

He looked up. 'I wouldn't dream of using it as a herb. And it's certainly not a weed in that sense. It's your flower. Marjoram. Marjorie. Wild marjoram too.'

Suddenly Madge understood. She felt the dangerous heat tiding up her face and felt a sudden pang of anger with Philip. Surely he must have realised what he was risking when he so carefully began this friendship? Ned Nicholls was a young man – a boy practically – with no family; he was in imminent danger of idealising Madge, Rosemary and the Nollas and even feeling a kind of romantic attachment to Madge herself. And in a few days or weeks he was going off to God knew what . . .

She said flatly, 'I'm always called Madge. People never use my full name unless they're annoyed with me.'

He was struggling with the matted roots, determined not to tear them.

'I heard Mrs Nolla call you Marjorie that first day,' he panted. 'It seems so right for you. Natural, liking seclusion. Yet . . . a little wild.' He grinned. 'Wouldn't you agree with that character assessment? That's what they call it in the Marines – character assessment. If there's no wildness there, they won't look at you!'

She was forced to laugh with him, though already she was wondering what to do next. How to get away from this lonely place and back to the safety of Ro.

Ned gave up with the knife and knelt in front of the tottering flowers, easing them out of the ground with his hands. She stared at the top of his head; it was the colour of dark rust; why on earth should it remind her suddenly of Neville's head? Neville had been older than her and this boy was younger. But Neville had been the same age as Ned was now; Neville would always be twenty-two.

She said hoarsely, 'Ned. Is this . . . is your next mission very dangerous?'

The roots came away from the shallow earth with several snapping sounds and Ned fell back into the fern, buried in flowers and scattered soil. He kicked his heels in the air clownishly until she laughed again.

'Come and get me up!' he spluttered, pretending complete helplessness. 'Your contribution to this exercise has been . . .' he struggled to his feet with her help and met her eyes through the enormous bush of flowers. '. . . Oh Madge. I haven't had such fun since I was about ten years old. Thanks. Thanks so much.'

118

She didn't risk looking at him for too long, but as she turned back to the path, still laughing, she was reassured. After all, that's what it had been for him: fun. No more than that. And it had been fun for her too. More than fun; a marvellous experience. She was reminded of a time way back in the past . . . hadn't it been on this same path? Then she had been allowed a glimpse of the rightness of things, their intricate simplicity, her own place in such an amazing scheme. She smiled. Of course, it was the place. It had always been the place. Nothing at all to do with Ned Nicholls.

Yet that night as she listened to an unsleeping Rosemary discoursing on the glories of the party, she recalled that Ned had not answered her question. She had known he wouldn't even as she asked it; but then he had thanked her in the way people thank you when they are leaving a party.

'I thanked that nice captain-man. Mummy. I said "thank you for having me". Was that good?'

'Very good, my darling.'

Madge kissed the top of her daughter's head and told herself she was a fool.

Ned continued to spend all his off-duty time with them. Madge, well chaperoned by Rosemary at all times, subtly changed their relationship to avoid any sudden awareness. She referred to him humorously as 'Uncle Ned' and would scold him in a Auntly fashion – 'dry off after those night exercises' and 'keep your sweet ration for yourself' as if he were in the Boy Scouts and she were indeed an anxious aunt. She did not mention the marjoram plants again, and neither did he. Presumably they had withered and died on the thin soil behind the Commando Post. He called her Madge, never Marjorie.

She did not mention her departure date either, and the day before it he took her to meet the Scaifes.

They had a studio on the neck of the Island, overlooking Porthgwidden cove. It had been a small boat store and the smell of tar had soaked into its wooden walls and still wafted about in the high room. Gerald Scaife was very avant-garde and painted enormous abstracts. They caught him halfway up a pair of paint-spattered steps with a huge paste brush, looking for all the world like someone sticking an advertisement to a hoarding. He did not

119

hear their arrival, owing in part to his concentration, but mostly to the fact that the wind-up gramophone in the corner was going full-blast with an Offenbach piece. Madge, who had 'done' Paris for a month when she was seventeen, was transported to the area around Sacre Coeur. She put her fingers on Ned's sleeve as if she expected to be whirled into a mazurka.

Then a small figure on the other side of the studio turned and saw them and darted for the gramophone, brush still in hand.

'Ned! How delightful. Gerald dear, it's Ned Nicholls come for tea. Get down and put the kettle on.' This small figure advanced and became obviously female in spite of trousers, shirt and a man's cap. 'You must be Madge. Ned said he'd bring you along. And Rosemary – where is Rosemary?'

'I didn't think it was safe to bring her. With all your stuff about.' Ned glanced down, saw Madge's hand on his sleeve and covered it with his own. She shook hands with her spare hand, then laughed as Mrs Scaife remembered the condition of her own fingers and apologised. Ned said, 'Don't worry, Barbara. Madge is used to sand, jam – whatever comes.'

Madge said, 'Rosemary is just at that age.'

'Oh, I wish we could have seen her. Ned says she is so sweet. Gerald and I were going to have a baby last year but then we didn't and we're getting rather old anyway.'

By this time Gerald was on the level and encircled his tiny wife with an enormous arm.

'We're all right as we are,' he said. 'Let's all sit down in the window and look at the rain and drink tea. Shall we?'

The two of them led the way to the large windows beneath the skylight. There were steamer chairs and a card table, and Gerald settled everyone with great care. Ned linked Madge's hand in his between the arms of their chairs. Gerald shifted her a little nearer to Ned. 'It's all right, we don't want to split you up,' he chuckled as if it were the most natural thing in the world for two comparative strangers, one married and much older than the other, to hold hands. Madge did not want to make a fuss about releasing her hand, but a blush started at the neckline of her cotton dress and began to work its way up.

'Tea à la Scaife,' announced Barbara, staggering from behind Gerald's canvas with a loaded metal tray. 'Very strong and very Indian. With rock cakes practically from the beach.' She plonked the tray on the table and picked up one of the cakes in question to tap it in the edge of the teapot. It did indeed have a geological sound to it.

In spite of that initial embarrassment, Madge began to enjoy herself. It was one of the happiest tea parties she could remember. And it was bliss to be away from Ro and talking with adults; the Scaifes were very adult and very interesting. They were trying hard to bridge the gap between the slightly Bohemian arts and crafts set in St Ives and the rest of the population. Like many outsiders they were more aware of the town's traditions and history than its natives, certainly more determined to preserve and respect both.

'We want to start something. A society or something – to stop developers coming in and changing the place,' Barbara explained. 'Once the war is over there will be a building boom. It's always the same. They'll ruin St Ives.'

'That's why we started art classes for the commandoes,' Gerald put in. 'It was our bit of war work of course, but we hoped some of the locals would come too and join us.'

'And did they?' Madge asked.

'Yes. A chap from Zennor, invalided out of the Navy, he cycles over twice weekly. And of course we've got Alfred Wallace to prove that it's never too late to start painting.' They told Madge about Alfred Wallace the fisherman and his curiously childlike paintings on bits of wood and card.

'Philip has told me about him,' she said, dipping her rock cake in the tea as Ned was doing. 'Philip said that one day when they were mending nets on Smeaton's Pier, Mr Wallace stopped work and just stared and stared at the net for ages. Then at last he said – I don't know – something about everything being there, the whole world, intertwined like a net.'

Barbara Scaife smiled. 'I suppose one always feels that where one lives is the centre of the universe, but I'm sure that a place like this, bringing people from all corners of the globe together, gives them a common denominator if you like. They have time in their busy lives to look and appreciate.'

Gerald said, 'It's a microcosm as all communities are. This microcosm reflects man's purpose and fulfilment in a special way perhaps.'

Ned nodded. I'll go for that. Even in wartime I've never been happier in my whole life.'

Gerald said, 'Yes, well old chap, you've had a fairly grim time of it up to now, haven't you? Barnardo offers bread and butter, but not much jam I imagine.'

Ned shrugged. 'It wasn't that bad actually. Just a feeling of marking time until real life began. I thought real life was the war. But no. It didn't make sense until I came here.' He leaned forward and let go Madge's hand. She brought it surreptitiously on to her lap and put it under her plate. He said raptly, 'I remember when we arrived the lorry spilled us out at the top of the Stennack, and we had to come down in full kit. I was dreading it. It had been a long haul and one of the chaps had been sick in the lorry – God it was awful. But as we started down I looked over the tops of all those funny old roofs and saw Godrevy sitting in the middle of the sky, and I breathed the air . . . it must have been a Monday because all the washing was out on the Island, bleaching in the sun. And it was January!' He laughed. 'By the time we got to the mess we were sweating like pigs. We chucked our stuff into the corner and went straight into the sea. It was like being born again.'

Everyone laughed. Madge thought that she was glad his happiness did not depend on her. She'd been right. It was the place.

'A baptism,' she murmured, remembering Clem.

'That's it exactly!' He turned to her joyously. 'A baptism!'

Later Gerald took them the length of his enormous painting.

'It's to do with the relationship between land and sea,' he explained to a mystified Madge and Ned. 'The way the Island pierces the ocean. Then Old Man's Head. Then the Five Points . . . all those lovely headlands pushing back the rollers. Next time you walk along the coast, look at them. The way the sea tries – it throws itself on each of the rocks. Then slips back.'

Madge said soberly, 'Philip says it will win in the end.'

'Perhaps he's right. But not in our lifetime.' Gerald took his brush and drew another line. The effect was of a comb with one tooth much longer than the others. He said, 'There. That concedes his point.' He put down the brush and turned to Madge. 'Remember – when you see this picture in the Tate one day – remember that line is agreeing with Philip Nolla. The sea has won.'

Madge shook her head and Ned said, 'No, it hasn't surely? If the lines are the land then surely that bit of land going farther than any of the others means that the land has won?'

Barbara appeared, drying her hands on a piece of rag. 'I think it means that we've surrendered. Like we do when we bathe. We surrender to the sea.' She opened the door and looked out. 'Still raining. And you've no umbrellas. You're definitely surrendering to the general wetness!' She danced outside, holding her face upwards and opening her mouth to the downpour. Gerald reached out and grabbed her back.

'You've got to look after yourself,' he grumbled, holding her tightly to him. Her cap caught on his arm and was pulled off. Unexpectedly her head was revealed covered in grey stubble. It was a shocking sight and Madge looked quickly away, understanding the reason for the endearingly ridiculous man's cap. When she looked back, it was in place again and Barbara grinning her gamine grin.

'Fare thee well, children,' she said. 'Come next week and have some more rock cakes.'

Madge did not look at Ned. 'I'm afraid I am going home tomorrow,' she said.

Ned did not tighten his hold on her arm. 'And my posting is the next day,' he said levelly.

'Never mind!' Gerald held out his free hand and pumped theirs in turn. 'We'll meet again. I know it. I feel it in my bones.' He smiled at Madge. 'Like Alfred Wallace's net, you know, Madge. We're going to be entwined.'

Barbara kissed her paint-stained fingers at them as they moved into the rain and Madge gave a final wave before they were enclosed in the high wall of Teetotal Street. She saw them silhouetted in the strange grey light of the studio door: a big, bear-like man, holding his tiny wife as if he would never let her go.

He said, 'Why didn't you tell me today was your last day?'

'I thought it might spoil it. I hate last days.' They turned into Back Road West and were met by gale-force winds. 'You didn't tell me about your posting date either.'

'I'm not supposed to.' The words – sounded cold and he grabbed her upper arm and held it to his side.It wasn't that, of course. I hate last days too. Let's abolish them.'

She laughed with relief, thinking they were back to their bantering footing. 'All right, Uncle Ned. How do we do that?'

'Well, we make next week happen now.'

'Sounds interesting.' Her laugh became indulgent. She was terribly conscious of his hands above her elbow, pulling her to him. His strength was there, manifest. She could not resist it. She said breathlessly, 'And what are we going to do next week, d'you think, Uncle Ned?'

'The weather will be okay again. So we'll have a swim at Porthmeor. The wild beach.'

'Lovely.' Rain trickled inside her mack and she moved her neck to block it, then gave up. She remembered something Barbara had said about surrendering. Surrender. It need not mean defeat. She saw suddenly that it could mean more than victory itself. She was breathing very quickly now, though they were not walking fast. 'Yes. Lovely. We'll ask Philip to come with us so that he can mind Ro. And we'll swim right out past the old wreck and look at St Ives as if we're seals.'

He stopped and turned to face her. Rain streamed down his face like tears.

'Madge. Marjoram. My marjoram. We haven't got next week. We haven't got much time left. Only now. And Ro will be in bed. Philip will look after her. He understands.'

She was aghast. This was the moment she had tried to avoid, knowing, beneath her superficiality, that it was unavoidable.

Nevertheless she panted, 'What are you saying, Ned?'

'Come swimming with me, Madge. Please. Now.'

'I can't! Rosemary. And the weather! It'll be like a seething pot at Porthmeor in this wind! And Philip hates me going into the sea.'

'Just tell him. Get your things. And come.' He shifted his grip and pulled her up so that their eyes were level. 'A last swim, Madge.'

But she knew it would be more than that. Total immersion in water had always had a special significance for her ever since Philip had 'rescued' her.

She said on an upward note, 'We're *friends*, Ned.'

'Oh, we are.' He grinned unexpectedly. 'I've never had a proper girlfriend before. I didn't know what it was like.'

She did not know whether to be reassured or not, but when he put her down and turned back the way they had come, she walked slowly down the court, certain she had no choice in the matter.

*   *   *

124

Philip and Etta were in the kitchen and Etta had put Ro to bed and announced with grim triumph that there had been no fuss, nor bother, and the child was already fast asleep.

When she said she was going for a swim, they both looked up at her, startled and disbelieving.

'Oh no, you're not,' said Etta. And Philip said, 'In this weather?'

'I have to. Ned is being posted somewhere tomorrow. I think it must be dangerous.' She sobbed suddenly. 'I have to, Philip. I have to.'

Etta said furiously, 'Yes. This is all your doing, Philip Nolla, and don't you ferget it!' She rounded on Madge. 'You'll be drownded and worse!'

But Philip said, 'Do you really have to? You're married to Clem Briscoe.'

How could she tell Philip that her marriage was for Rosemary's sake only? How could she explain to Philip that Ned was her best friend? And he was also the stranger in the night that she would never see again.

She sobbed, 'It will be all right. I will make it all right.' And she turned and grabbed her costume and towel from the passage lines and shovelled them into the beach bag of American cloth. Then she was out in the rain again and running for the deserted expanse of Porthmeor beach.

They changed in adjacent canvas tents which creaked and groaned around them in the wind. He made no attempt to come into her tent and when she emerged he was waiting outside for her, staring at the incoming tide as if calculating their chances of survival. The surf was creaming in perfectly but mountainously. Not a living soul was in sight. If they got into difficulties no-one would know. Madge wondered if that was to be the end of it: she and Ned lost in the sea for eternity. Her calf and thigh muscles shook momentarily and then were still. Surrender. To the sea. To events. To fate itself.

Ned turned and smiled. 'Ready?'

'Ready.'

He took her hand and they lowered their heads and walked into the wind and rain. There was one moment of caution; as the sea rushed up to her knees, she gasped and pulled back and would have run ahead of the next breaking wave as Neville did in the old days. But Ned leaned down and picked her up bodily and ran forward before it could lay them flat. They were both lifted high to its crest as it gathered itself into a crescendo of water, then it was past them and they were both wirnming for the next one.

For ten glorious minutes they were one with the ocean. Occasionally a wave would threaten to break right upon them and Ned would shout a warning and they would both sit on the sea bed. It was the usual immediate and strange translation; sound became something felt and not heard through the ears. They were rocked where they sat and above them was a turbulent madness. Then they would bob to the surface like corks, hold hands, laugh crazily, all tension and fear gone. She felt part of this different element, as if she could live like this for always. All too soon Ned was pulling her into the white water again, making her body-surf for the shore. A roller took them to the edge of the dry sand and left them slowly, almost with regret.

Madge rolled on to her back and sat up in the shallows.

'It's over,' she gasped, but not sadly. She was warm now, invigorated, her blood coursing fast through her veins.

'No. That was the beginning,' Ned gasped back at her. And she knew what he meant and at that precise moment was not afraid or even reluctant. But that couldn't last. By the time they had dragged themselves back to the tents, she was beginning to shiver again.

She stammered, 'Ned. I have to explain. There is something wrong with me. I'm sorry. I should have told you sooner. Oh Ned, I'm so sorry.'

He came inside her tent and fastened the fly-sheet with great care. After the wind it was warm and in spite of the flapping canvas there was a sort of cosiness in the small space.

He misunderstood. 'It's all right, Madge. Don't worry.' He put his arms around her and held her tightly. 'I'm just thankful you came swimming. I know some girls won't when they're that way.'

She almost laughed. 'Oh Ned. It's not that.' She pushed her face into his shoulder, then put her arms around him and held him to her. She explained.

'Madge. Darling. I can't hear. Did you say . . . what *did* you say, my dearest?' She said it again and he shouted, 'Frigid? You?

126

Oh Marjorie-marjoram.' He laughed very tenderly. 'You're not frigid, my love. My only love.' He began to kiss her.

She could respond to kisses; friends kissed. Her hands slid from his waist to his neck. There were cords there going from his scalp into his back. She was reminded again of his strength, yet knew that he would never exert it on her. She moved her fingers into his wiry, rust-coloured hair.

He lifted his head and she could see the white of his smile. 'Oh Madge. I wouldn't care if you were made of ice. I do love you so.' And then, incredibly, she heard her own voice say very steadily, 'I love you too, Ned. You are my friend, and a stranger. And I love you.'

This time she cupped his face and kissed him herself, then dropped her hands long enough to slide off the shoulder straps of her costume. They came together naturally; it was all so easy, so uncomplicated. Madge recalled the twanging bedsprings of long ago and smiled blindly over Ned's shoulder. She had been right in the first place, before Neville had enlightened her. It might be serious, but it was fun too. And it was the ultimate giving; the ultimate surrender; the ultimate triumph.

She kissed his neck and lay within his arms, calming her own breathing while his calmed too. She wanted to rejoice with him that she was not frigid, but she waited for him to speak first.

At last he said in a low voice, 'You have given me my whole life in this past hour, Marjorie. Do you know that?'

She held him more tightly. 'No. That cannot be. You will live and know love often. Often.'

'Perhaps. But if I don't, it won't matter.' He stroked her hair back from her face. She had let it grow again because Clem had asked her. It was out of its knot and everywhere. He whispered into it, 'You have made me immortal.'

'Oh Ned. You must not talk like this. Please.' Tears ran down her face and he felt them with his own and kissed them with a kind of reverence.

'Listen, my darling. We both know that you would never leave Rosemary. And that is what it would mean if you came to me, wouldn't it? Your husband would be the injured one . . . he would be given the child . . .' She was sobbing now and he soothed her with shushing sounds as if she were a child herself. After a while he went on. 'That is what I meant, my Marjorie.

We have done all the living we can do. Like Barbara Scaife.'

'Barbara Scaife? I don't understand.'

'Couldn't you tell from the way Gerald looked at her? She had a brain tumour, Madge. It will probably recur.'

She cried out at that, understanding now the shaved head, the crazy cavorting in the rain.

He whispered, 'Don't be sad, Marjorie. They've had more than most people have in their three score years and ten. Just as we have.'

'Ned, I'm frightened. I feel now as if I cannot live without you. And tomorrow . . .'

He kissed her silent.

'There are no tomorrows. I am just with you from now on. Whether it's one day or ten thousand. And because of us, everything will be better. Believe that.'

'I'll try.'

Suddenly he laughed again. 'You don't have to try. You know it! You thought you were frigid—' his laugh became a shout. 'And now you know you are not! You thought you were frightened, and you are one of the bravest people in the world!' He got to his knees, drawing her with him. His hands moved over her like a sculptor's making a new creation. He whispered, 'Be proud, Madge. Be proud because of me.'

And she knew as she kissed him that in spite of her own innate humility, she would always be proud because of Ned. And at last she would understand. She would understand her father. And . . . Clem.

CHAPTER SEVEN

1945

Clem had never been so happy. His special war work entitled him to one of the new Mayflower cars and he drove the whole family to St Ives as if he were leading a triumphal procession.

It was September again and he'd been home almost a year. He couldn't believe it; time had telescoped for him. The long years of his depression, his constant striving for the sunshine, had seemed endless. The last year, so full of joy and incident, had gone before he'd been able to savour it. Now, here they were, back at Zion Cottage with a whole month in front of them. He could gather up all the scattered pictures in his mind and assemble them; gloat over them. Even Julia; he could even think about Julia again and feel no guilt.

His mother said grudgingly, 'Well it's certainly quaint, I'll give you that.'

Rosemary, tired and peevish after six hours on the road, whined, 'Where's Philip? I want to see Philip!'

'Do be quiet, darling.' Madge sounded edgy too. 'Here, hold Mark for me while I take his things up to the house.'

Clem would have liked to hold Mark himself, but it gave him even more pleasure to see Ro with her baby brother. Ro was so like her Uncle Neville, discontented, always chasing rainbows; but her love for Mark could make her forget all imagined tribulations. She smiled now, cooing down at the tiny round face, smoothing back the pale, gingery quiff.

Mrs Bridges said, 'I do hope you like it. The quaintness includes candles, I'm afraid. And no bathroom.'

'I expect I'll survive. As a girl we had an outside toilet. In fact we considered it unhygienic to have such things inside the house!' Mrs Briscoe actually laughed. 'It'll be like putting the clock back forty years!'

Clem felt another surge of pleasure. He had thought it impossible to make his mother happy again. He took the heavy case from the boot and staggered up the courtyard to the house. Etta was already on the steps to welcome them. Clem heard her say straightly to Madge, 'You all right, my maid?' then before Madge could reply, she put her arms around her – Mark's basket and all – and held her for a moment. It was an unprecedented action from Etta. Clem put the case down on the steps and stared.

'Don't I get a hug too, Etta?' he asked with mock plaintiveness. 'I'm the one who's home from the war, doncha know!'

Etta opened her eyes and looked over Madge's shoulder for a long moment. She seemed to come to some conclusion and went from Madge to Clem.

'Oh I'm that glad – that glad I am!' She was almost in tears. 'Philip said it would be all right! The old fool – 'e's never wrong, is 'e? Oh my boy, my boy—'

Clem said, 'It's all right, Etta. I wasn't in any fighting. Safer than you, I expect.'

'Ah. There's fightin' and there's fightin',' she came back cryptically. 'An' where's the rest o' you then? Where's your ma and Madge's ma? An' where's this new babby oo's so good no-one knows 'e's around? And that young flibbertigibbet of a Rosemary!'

Madge said, 'She was asking where Philip was just now, Etta. Is he inside?'

'Naw. 'E's a-gone down to 'elp Jem tar the *Forty-niner*. Couldn't face ee, I daresay.'

Clem wondered what on earth Etta meant. He dumped the case and looked at Madge with raised brows. She was still deathly pale. Worse than usual, if anything. She'd had a rough time with Mark, but everything would be all right now.

'I'll get everyone inside, darling,' he said reassuringly. 'Go on upstairs and lie down until the rush is over.'

He expected her to turn down that suggestion on the spot. She would want to find Philip, or take Ro down for a paddle, or make sure her mother was all right. But she said, Yes all right, Clem. I'll do that.'

He was disappointed, but then told himself he couldn't expect St Ives to work its miracle immediately. Madge had changed anyway; she had grown up and matured in those two years he was

130

in Ottawa. The way she had forgiven him; there had been none of the old sentimental pity; she had wept, certainly, but with understanding. She had kissed him repeatedly and when he'd made love to her – so diffidently – her kisses had become fiercely possessive and she had cried out, 'Darling I do love you – is it too late?'

He remembered again his joy in trying to reassure her. He was still trying to reassure her. It was part of his happiness – to protect her, to enfold her in his love, to make her realise that now, with Mark's birth, they had everything – everything on earth it was possible to have.

He helped the older women out of the car and passed them their handbags and scarves and magazines. Then he reached inside again for Rosemary and Mark.

'I can carry him, Daddy – I can *do* it!' Rosemary insisted, emerging rear first, her small body arched protectively over the baby. Already, at three months, Mark was too big for her to hold properly and his head hung awkwardly over her elbow. Clem hovered anxiously.

'Go 'way Daddy! I want him to see the sea an' you're in the way!'

'Well he can't see a thing if you hold him like that, honey.' Clem supported the heavy, gingery head on his palm. 'There. Now tell him all about it.'

Rosemary rattled off in a strange cooing voice, 'That's Smeaton's over *there*. Ahd that's Westcott's. And there's the train just coming into the station. And back there again is the commando's big house where we had the party.'

Clem had heard about the commando's party ad nauseam and he said hastily, 'See the boats, Mark? And the little waves splashing up on the sand?'

'Oooh! There's the *Forty-niner*! An' I think it's Philip! Daddy, hold Mark for me—' she thrust the baby at him and went flying along the wharf. Clem watched her indulgently. She'd been two and a baby when he'd gone to Canada; now she was almost five and a proper little girl. He'd pictured her as another small Madge while he was away, but she wasn't a bit like Madge. She was wayward and often very selfish; but she was lovable too. Very lovable. He held Mark above him and looked at the round placid face. 'You're going to have to understand your sister, young man,' he said, grinning, one male to another. 'Women are the very deuce and she's going to be particularly difficult.' He lowered him and kissed the tiny nose. 'But if you remember that she loves you, then you'll manage.'

The dark eyes, changing from blue to brown crinkled in real smile and Clem felt his heart lift with the brand of proud happiness which was still so new for him.

He turned and went quickly towards the house.

'Hey Mother – Hey Marie! Guess what? He just laughed at me! No, it wasn't wind. It was a real laugh!'

The two grandmothers exchanged glances. Baby Mark had bound them together in a way none of them would have believed possible. He looked around the tiny parlour now, as if he'd seen it before and was checking on its furnishings. Etta, coming in with a big pot of tea, paused to look at him with an approval she had never given Rosemary.

' 'E's at 'ome already,' she said, well pleased. 'Look at 'im staring around! Oh 'e's just like 'is father.'

Clem was delighted. 'No-one's seen that before, Etta! You always were a dab hand with the compliments!'

Everyone laughed except Etta. But they were used to her dourness.

It was dusk when Madge walked down Teetotal Street and into Porthgwidden Place. There were no lights in the studio. The gaunt old tarred-wood building rose stark against the evening sky, its windows reflecting the nearby street lamp emptily. Madge felt every muscle in her body tensed against incipient shaking; she kept swallowing though her mouth was without saliva. She had rested until tea-time, then fed Mark while her mother put Rosemary to bed and sang her to sleep. At the familiar strains of 'Golden Slumbers' Madge's eyes had filled with tears, and Clem, coming upstairs to check on all the family, was concerned all over again.

'Darling, I won't go out. Philip is no drinker and we were going along to the Clipper simply to get to know each other again.'

'Of course you must go. You'll enjoy it, Clem. And Philip wants to re-introduce you to everyone . . . please go.'

'If I do, will you promise not to do a thing? Let the grandmothers cope with the children?'

'Of course. Now go. There's nothing wrong with me. A touch of the nostalgia!'

Her mother's head appeared around the door.

'Neuralgia? I knew something was wrong. Get into bed, my girl, and I'll bring you some warm milk.'

Madge exchanged a smile with Clem but she accepted the milk and lay on top of the bed for half an hour while the house settled around her and Clem and Philip finally went for their glass of stout. Then she got up very quietly, leaned over Mark's carrycot for a long time and eventually fetched a cardigan and left the house. She mustn't be long. She hardly knew why she was here, but she knew she mustn't be long. No-one had seen her leave and no-one must know where she was. She put a hand to her throat and knocked on the door of the studio.

It was all of a piece with her foolish behaviour over the past year – it was quite obvious no-one was in the studio. Just as it had been obvious that Mark couldn't be Clem's baby; she had known herself she was a month ahead of her doctor's diagnosis and that the baby was not premature. Yet she had refused to face facts until she had looked at Mark's round, honest face, and fingered the dusting of rust-coloured hair.

Hopelessly she waited, then knocked again without urgency, like any polite visitor making an unscheduled call. Then she turned the handle and pushed, and the door swung inwards on to impenetrable blackness.

She called shakily, 'Hello! Is anyone there? Mrs Scaife? It's me. Marjorie Briscoe.'

There was complete silence for a long half-minute. In that time her eyes could make out the dark shapes of several small gigs up-ended for tarring. The studio was back to being a boat store. She began to close the door.

'Madge Bridges that was?'

The voice was female and as politely formal as her own, yet her bunched muscles tightened further then collapsed into uncontrollable spasms. She could hear her teeth chattering and she made a small involuntary whimpering sound.

'Oh my dear God. I made you jump, did't I? 'Tis on'y me. Rose Care. You d'remember me, don't you? We used to 'ave many a word on the beach when I helped Jim Maddern with them there donkeys.' The laugh was rich and untroubled. 'Then I went

133

to live in Zennor, and I don't think I've seen you since . . .' the voice paused fractionally ' . . . since then.'

A shape detached itself from the gigs, and came to the door. Madge was conscious of a great deal of very black hair and very white teeth. She was perilously close to tears.

'I was looking for—' she drew a long breath that got hitched on a sob. 'Barbara Scaife. She and her husband used to . . . they were artists . . .'

'Oh my 'ansome. I'm sorry. That Mrs Scaife, she died. Oh my dear Lord, you en't goin' to faint are you? Come on in now and sit on one of these boats. Come on now. Put your 'ead down. That's it. I'll get you some water. 'Tis all there is, but . . .' the voice went away for a while, then a cup was held to Madge's mouth. She drank. The water had the indefinable St Ives taste, straight from the mine where Madame Curie had procured her radium samples. Madge sat up straight.

'I'm sorry. Just a little weakness. The shock, I expect.'

Rose squatted in front of her. The place seemed full of silvery light now; Madge could see that Rose's garish red dress was covered in dust and her bare feet were dirty.

'I really do apologise.' Her voice was steady now. 'Barging in like this. You must be living here.' It wasn't a question, Rose would only be dressed like this in her own home.

But the older girl gave her careless laugh again.

'Here? In this boat store? Not likely. I've still got my cottage up Zennor way. Nice it is.' She paused, then said with a mixture of defiance and frankness, 'Jim and me meet 'ere sometimes. 'E won't come up to the cottage – dun't like most o' my callers.' She hugged her knees. 'I'm fond o' Jim. 'E's been a good friend to me.'

Madge felt colour flood her face. She made inarticulate noises.

Rose said, 'That's 'ow I am. You've always known it, so dun't pretend you 'aven't.' She turned so that she was looking out of the window. Below them the small waves lapped up the sand on Porthgwidden beach. The arms of the cove seemed to embrace and welcome the moving water. Madge was reminded of Gerald Scaife's enormous abstract canvas. Rose said very quietly, 'It din't stop me lovin' your brother in my own way. An' 'e loved me too. 'E was the only one who asked me to marry 'im. Did you know that?'

134

Madge cleared her throat. Rose waited. Madge said hoarsely, 'No.'

'He would have told you one day.' Suddenly the rough voice was soft and the consonants clear. 'You were still a schoolgirl, but he would have told you when you were grown-up. He thought you were pretty well perfect.'

Madge drew another shuddering breath and the tears began to run down her face.

Rose went on in her different voice, 'I sometimes think . . . if I'd said yes, he wouldn't have gone to Spain and got himself killed. He was such a boy. A stupid, headstrong, wilful boy. But he would have been a lovely man.'

Madge forced herself to speak through her closed throat.

'If he'd not gone to Spain there was the war.'

'Yes. Yes, there was that.' She glanced up at Madge. 'And you got married to Neville's friend, didn't you?' Her teeth flashed whitely again, nostalgia over. 'See? There's not much Rose Care dun't 'ear about!' She laughed. 'Cheer up, little Madge Bridges! That Mrs Scaife did what she wanted to do in life – that's the main thing, in't it?'

'How do you mean?' Madge could hardly speak for the tears. The way Rose ignored them, let her weep freely, was a wonderful relief. She thought she might cry aloud any moment: 'Daddy's dead! Neville's dead! Now Barbara Scaife is dead! And I love two men and my baby belongs to the wrong one!'

Rose said matter-of-factly, 'Well. She 'ad a babby. She left 'er man with a bit of 'erself as you might say. To be goin' on with. An' she were lucky I reckon. She knew that babby would be loved and looked after always. That's the trouble for a woman left on 'er own. Tidn't easy earnin' a livin' and bringing up a strappin' boy.' She hesitated then added, 'Nor a girl, neither.'

Madge took in half of this and stammered, 'She died having a baby, d'you mean? But I saw her just a year ago! I'm sure she wasn't . . . Ned said she had a brain tumour!'

Rose's eyes flashed blackly at her for an instant, then she said, 'The baby was born two months ago. The brain tumour grew again, you see. An' I s'ppose she wanted . . . well, like I said, she got what she wanted.' She paused again, then went on slowly as if Madge might be deaf, 'She knew she 'ad got the tumour. She knew she 'ad to leave 'im anyway. An' she wanted to leave 'im something of 'erself like.' She stared directly into Madge's face. 'I don't think that is anything to grieve over, Madge Bridges. If it 'appened to me – if it *'ad* 'appened to me – I reckon I'd be thankful.' She waited while the tears dried stiffly on Madge's face, then she asked very quietly, 'Wouldn't you?'

Madge whispered, 'I don't know.'

Rose said, 'People thinks I haven't got deep feelings, and mebbe they're right. How should I know? I only know the feelings I got, not the ones I ain't got!' Her laugh rolled out again. Then she said seriously, 'What I do know is, you can go on making other folks 'appy, even when you ain't *that* 'appy yourself. An' that sort of . . . makes the wrong all right. In a way. Surely?'

Her voice on that last word was a plea for reassurance and Madge responded instantly.

'Yes. Oh yes, Rose. I'm sure you're right. Up to a point.'

'An' another thing.' Rose was crouching forward now, very earnest, 'You dun't tell no-one. You keep it to yourself. So that no-one else 'as to carry any burdens. See? It's like a lightning conductor. Takes it straight into yourself like.'

'Barbara Scaife was so open—'

'You dun't know that. She might 'a bin lonely and frightened and in a lot of pain, and kept it to 'erself.' Rose unhooked her arms and stood up lithely. But we weren't talking about Mrs Scaife then. We were talking . . .' She brushed her skirt vigorously and began to feel around the floor. 'We were talking *generally*.' She found what she was looking for and began to fit ridiculous high-heeled shoes on to her bare feet. 'I reckon you should be getting back to your family, Madge Bridges. Before they start wondering where you are an' feeling worried about you.' She put a firm hand on Madge's shoulder and through the wool of her cardigan and the cotton of her frock, Madge could feel the warmth of that palm. 'I should thank God for a husband who loves you. An' who you love too. Put everything else to one side. That is what is important.'

Madge smiled ruefully. 'Live for today,' she murmured.

'What's wrong with that?' Rose teetered to the door and opened it, and the cool air of the evening swept through the boat store. ' 'Tis all we got when all's said an' done!' Her laugh rang out. 'It's not been a bad day for me. An' it's brought you back to

S'nives, so it can't be a bad one for you! I reckon you've prob'ly made that young Clem Briscoe a 'appy man. An' . . .' her laugh became a gurgle of innuendo. 'An' I know I've made Jim Maddern very 'appy indeed! So sit you there a minute and think about that. Then go back to your fam'ly.' She half closed the door then pushed her face back through the opening. 'If you need anyone, you know where I am. Skinners' Cottage. After all—' a final laugh echoed around the upturned boats. 'Things bin a bit diff'rent and we might 'a bin sisters!' And she was gone.

Clem had been almost too gentle with Madge since the birth of Mark and her unaccountable depression, but that night she clung to him as if she could not bear to let him go and he made love to her with a deep and tender passion that transcended even their reunion last autumn. Then he was frightened.

'Darling. Did I hurt you? Oh Madge, I do love you.'

'And I love you, Clem. Oh I do. I really do. And I am glad and thankful you persuaded me to come to St Ives again.'

'Are you sure? You needed a holiday and if we'd gone anywhere else we weren't certain we'd be all right with such a tiny baby.'

'I'm fine, Clem. Please don't worry about me.'

He was silent for a long time, staring at the outline of the window and listening to Mark's steady breathing from the basket. From the room next door a strange humming sound started up.

'What the dickens – ?'

Madge said with a smile in her voice, 'It's Mother. Ro must have roused when they went to bed and Mother is singing to her. "Golden Slumbers".'

'Sounds like a vacuum cleaner.'

Madge actually laughed and Clem was so delighted that he laughed too at his own feeble joke. They clung to each other giggling foolishly until Etta – or Philip – thumped irritably on the floorboards above them. Then for a moment they were silent before pulling the sheet over their head in an effort to suppress incipient hysteria.

Clem did begin to wonder whether he might explode with his own happiness. As he held his wife through each muffled paroxysm of mirth, there was a part of him that was quietly, deeply thankful. At last he had done the right thing and the fates had smiled on him. He had confessed his brief affair with Julia so that Madge could get out of their marriage if she wished, and incredibly, that confession, which could so easily have been another barrier between them, had somehow melted Madge's inhibitions at last. And that all-pervading, confounded pity of hers had gone, too.

He held her close now, his mouth full of her hair, and remembered his arrival at Temple Meads station. His own loneliness had seemed to hold him in a vacuum; post-war Bristol had been unutterably bleak and hopeless. And then, through the grim-faced crowds, he had seen Madge and she had seen him and there had been no hesitation. She had started to run towards him, arms outstretched. He hadn't moved from his pile of luggage; even then he had thought she would weep over him, tears of forgiveness. But her face had been shining. She had thrown herself on him, laughing, kissing him with little excited pecks. Then she had said, 'Darling. It's all right. I understand – at last I understand. Can we start again?'

And they had done that; they had made a new world together. Slightly dimmed since Mark's premature birth, but still there, waiting for them while Madge regained her strength. And she would do that down here. A whole month down here. It was wonderful.

She stilled her laughter long enough to whisper, 'D'you think Ro will be all right in there?'

'With two grandmothers? One a singing vacuum cleaner?'

He wanted to make her laugh again, but she did not. Instead her free hand came up and cupped his face and her thumb moved down the channel from eye to nose and so to the corner of his mouth.

She murmered, 'You are such a good man, Clem. I loved you all the time and did not know it until . . . the war, I suppose.'

He did not reply. She knew he wasn't that good a man, but that she loved him in spite of it was wonderful.

She left her thumb on his lips and kissed him.

'Oh Clem, I wish . . . I wish . . .'

'What do you wish, my darling?'

'I wish I hadn't wasted so much time. Time is all we've got, darling. We must never waste it again.'

Her hand slipped to the back of his head and her kisses became urgent, almost desperate.

138

For an instant he held back. A sudden terror seized him that she was warning him her time was limited. He thought of the two lonely women across the landing and felt a new compassion for them both.

'Madge – Madge, you'd never leave me?' he panted, even as he returned her kisses.

'No, Clem. We must stay together. Whatever happens. We must.'

Then they were lost in the maelstrom of their own passion again. And afterwards they slept.

The days fell into an unplanned pattern as they always did. The mornings were short; there was shopping to be done, Mark to be bathed, fed and 'settled'. They tended to stay on the harbour beach within easy reach of the house while Etta cooked a lunch for them. Afterwards the two grand-mothers packed a picnic and joined the younger generations on Porthmeor beach for a long afternoon in the sun. They were lucky with the weather; one day it was grey and overcast and they left their deckchairs and strolled along the cliff to Old Man's Head. Another day a sudden squall blew up and they piled into the beach tent with much laughter and ate their sandwiches while they watched gigantic waves pound the beach unmercifully.

Mark accepted whatever happened to him with equanimity and absolute trust in his family. Clem was amazed – and delighted – that he was so different from Rosemary. She had been a difficult and discontented baby, and even now caused more trouble than her brother. With two grand-mothers at her beck and call, she could still have spells of stubborn boredom so that no diversion on earth could please her. After one such day, Clem was forced to come the heavy father and send her to bed as soon as they got back to the cottage. Mrs Briscoe and Etta nodded their approval; Marie and Madge did not meet Rosemary's outraged face and fussed around Mark's cradle; Clem hated himself. As soon as Madge took the baby upstairs and the two older women settled down with their knitting in Etta's small back quarters, Clem went up to make his peace with his daughter.

The truckle bed, which Madge had occupied for so long, had been shifted into the back room and the bedroom door opened right against it. Rosemary, against her will, had sunk almost immediately into a deep sleep, exhausted after a day of exercising her contrary will against the lesser ones of her family. She woke with a jerk as the door knocked against her bed and immediately began to cry bitterly. Clem, under the impression that she had wept continuously since being sent upstairs, crouched by the bed and took her in his arms.

'Darling. Daddy's sorry. There . . . it's not as bad as all that, surely?'

Rosemary clung to him thankfully.

'Oh Daddy, I'se all right. I'se really all right. Is Mummy all right?'

'Of course Mummy is all right, baby. She's just across the landing putting Mark to bed.'

'She's not drownded?'

Clem smoothed the ash blonde hair away from the small hot face. 'Mummy hasn't even had a paddle today, Ro. Have you been having a nasty dream?'

The sobs slowed to sporadic hiccoughs.

'Was it a dream? I thought Mummy and Uncle Ned were drownded in that great big sea. Etta said they shouldn't ought to go swimming when it was so rough, but Philip said they ought to be young once. An' I dreamt they were both drownded, Daddy!' She started to cry again and Clem soothed her automatically, frowning slightly above her head.

'Listen, Ro,' he said at last, settling her on to her pillow again. 'I want you to have a nice dream now. I want you to pretend this little bed is a boat, and you're bobbing over the harbour with Daddy and Mummy and Mark—'

'And Philip?'

'And Philip. You know Philip wouldn't let you do anything dangerous. So your last dream was very silly, wasn't it?'

'Yes Daddy.' Rosemary's voice was sleepy again. 'I only dreamt I heard him let Mummy and Uncle Ned go swimming. 'Cos I was only a little girl last year, see.'

'I know. I know . . .' Clem made his voice into a drone. 'And now you're a big girl, so you won't have any more nasty dreams.' Next door Madge was crooning some Bing Crosby tune at Mark, and Clem took it up quietly. Rosemary's hold on his finger began to loosen. Downstairs Jem Gurnard tramped through the front door and he and Philip held a rumbled conversation in the passage. Clem wondered whether to mention Rosemary's dream to Madge . . . or Philip. No. It was too ridiculous for words. As if Philip would permit Madge to do anything even slightly dangerous. Though of course, years ago he had shown her the way to climb Old Man's Head, and she had continued to do so until she was expecting Rosemary.

Still singing quietly, Madge crossed the landing and put her head around the open door. It was just light and he could see her conspiratorial smile. For a moment he did not move. Then he rose and crept outside with her. They stood at the top of the stairs; she struck an attitude and sang, '. . . Someone, waits for . . . me.' He hesitated another moment then, when her outflung arms collapsed to her side, he forced a smile, put a hand to his heart and warbled softly, 'Where the blue, of the night . . .' She put her face against his shoulder, laughing silently, and he held her there, while above her head his smile slowly died.

For some reason he did not understand, Clem stuck close to Rosemary the next day. She was delighted. She had accepted that her parents stayed with Mark and her grand-mothers took it in turns to play with her. But there were very many limitations to grandmothers. She enjoyed her father's exclusive company and was a biddable and charming companion. Together they clambered over the more inaccessible rocks with bucket and shrimping net. He did not scream when she managed to shovel a tiny crab from beneath a stone, and when a wave splashed her shorts there was no suggestion of an immediate return to the beach tent for a change of clothes. He just laughed.

When Madge signalled to them from the beach that tea was ready, he picked Rosemary up and said,' Shall we have a quick dip before our picnic, Ro? I'll show you how Mummy and I had our first swim here, shall I?'

'What do you mean, Daddy?' She leaned back to reveal a huge wet patch on his shirt. 'I'm making you all soggy, Daddy – look!'

He laughed again. 'That makes it even easier. Come on, let's do the job properly.' And he began to advance into the sea.

Rosemary screamed pleasurably.

'We haven't got our costumes on! Daddy – your trousers are *soaking*! Grandma Briscoe will be so *cross*!'

141

For answer he advanced into a wave and jumped up and down until his leg ached. Then he waded out and put Rosemary on to the firm sand.

'Off you go then. Run and tell Grandma Briscoe what we've done so that she can be cross.'

Rosemary was thrilled that her careful, conservative father could behave so outrageously. She laughed and capered about, one pudgy hand over her mouth, the other swinging her bucket madly. Only when she discovered that her crab had disappeared did she sober slightly.

'All that time, and we've lost the one thing we catched,' she mourned.

'But what an adventure we've had!' Clem reminded her.

'Yes. Oh just look at your trousers, Daddy. Why don't you roll them up?'

He wouldn't do that and expose his wasted calf.

'Run! Go on – before you start to feel cold!'

He chased her half-heartedly up the beach. He was already feeling idiotic. Madge would understand of course, though she would wonder why. But his mother would nag and nag about the kind of example he was setting, et cetera. He slowed and let Ro go on ahead. Why on earth had he repeated that 'baptism' business? Was he trying to remind Madge of something? Or remind himself? He mustn't be possessive. There had been Julia . . . Madge had been so marvellous about Julia. Only when she had been so marvellous had he realised that Julia had meant nothing. Nothing at all. Madge – and now the children – were at the very core of his being.

A ball landed at his feet and he kicked it automatically, his heavy wet flannels spoiling his aim so that the gaily coloured ball rolled just a few yards away.

'Well done, old man!'

The voice was slurred and as its owner broke into a shambling trot, Clem could see a wine bottle dangling from one hand. The man gave a mighty kick, even more unsuccessful than Clem's. It landed him flat on his back, wine bottle held safely high and away from the sand.

'Christ almighty!'

The expletive was humorous and was greeted by a great deal of feminine laughter. Other players converged and looked

142

down at the supine man, who made no attempt to get up.

'Come on, Gerald!'

One of the women leaned above him and removed the bottle from his hand. He yelled a protest but did not move.

'Gerald, get up and behave yourself.' The woman sounded severe. 'You can't play football when you're sober, let alone when you've been drinking this filthy plonk all afternoon.'

'Slander!' bawled the man at the top of his voice. 'You witnessed what my tyrant-sister just said! I've been on this bloody beach for exactly one hour! Is that all afternoon? Is it? I demand an answer! And you're all sworn to tell the truth, the whole truth and nothing—'

'Gerald. I am going to take the baby back to the car and feed it.' The woman was not seeing the joke at all now, though the others still laughed. 'If you are not there when I have finished, I shall drive back to Penzance and you can walk it for all I care!'

Clem did not hear his answer but the tone was conciliatory. He obviously took his sister's threat seriously. Clem smiled, remembering Madge and Neville. And then stopped smiling because the memory snowballed into something painful. For an instant he wished he'd stayed in Canada, sent for Madge, made a new life away from all the old entanglements. Then he saw his mother and Marie Bridges fussing over Rosemary and knew that there was really no escape.

'Daddy's wetter 'n me!'

Rosemary was thoroughly enjoying being on the carpet with her father. She was wrapped in a towel and he was despatched into the beach tent to manage as best he could. Madge, knowing how he felt about wearing his costume and exposing his leg, poked her head through the tent flap.

'Darling. I'm going back to the cottage for some fresh milk. Etta has scalded this lot and you know Ro won't drink it. I'll bring your linen trousers, shall I? Or would you rather the other flannels?'

'Oh . . . linen please.' He grinned at her gratefully. 'It seemed the thing to do at the time.'

'Of course.' She smiled back. 'There are times when you have to go into the sea. It's unfortunate if you're fully clothed, but really there's not much choice!'

They both laughed. Clem felt ridiculously reassured and no

longer foolish. Madge disappeared and his mother's nagging voice fell silent as she and Marie moved away with Ro to dig a sandcastle. And into the sudden silence came another voice; that of the erstwhile footballer. It seemed he too was being nagged.

'Di. If you don't shut up I'll let you go back to Penzance without me and stay without me! Got it? Christ, if the bloody baby wasn't part of Barbara, you could have it for good and all and bring it up how the hell you liked!'

The voice passed close to the tent; shuffling steps began to climb the sandy path to the top of the beach. Di began, reluctantly, to apologise. 'I'm sorry I get on your nerves, Gerald, but I think even you must realise I do it for your own good. All this drinking – would Barbara approve? Of course she wouldn't!'

Gerald's voice changed to utter weariness.

'She'd understand. That's what Barbara would do. She'd understand.' And on the last word it changed again and lifted. 'By all that's holy! Is that – hey! You! Turn around!'

Clem was curious enough to push up the roof awning and make a peephole. Through it he saw 'Gerald' and 'Di' sitting on the grass of the cliff, struggling to put shoes over salty feet. They were surrounded by the usual beach paraphernalia plus a basket – presumably containing the baby. Gerald was waving to someone at the top of the path. Someone who obviously obeyed his summons and turned round.

'Good God, it *is* you! Marjorie, wasn't it? Young Ned Nicholls' girl, at any rate!' Gerald struggled to his feet half shod and hobbled out of sight. Clem dropped the canvas and stared blindly at Rosemary's spare sunbonnet dangling from a cup hook by its strings. In spite of the tent, in spite of the distant roar of the surf, in spite of them meeting halfway up the cliff, he had no difficulty in recognising Madge's voice.

'Mr Scaife? I thought you'd gone! I went round to your studio the first evening we were here—' Clem closed his eyes tightly. She had gone to lie down that first evening. She couldn't have walked down the stairs and along the passage without him knowing. Except . . . after Ro went to bed he'd taken Philip down to the Clipper for a glass of stout. He tightened his eye muscles until he could see stars.

The man was speaking again and he couldn't catch everything he said.

'. . . had a baby – did you know?'

144

Madge's voice, familiar in its cadences, was clearer. 'I heard . . .'

Gerald's voice was suddenly high and forced.

'She went into premature labour and died.'

'I'm so sorry. So terribly sorry.' Clem could imagine that terrible pity of Madge's; her eyes filling, her hands reaching out.

'I'm glad you know. After Ned was killed I always felt . . . Barbara wanted to see you.'

There was a pause then Madge's voice, slightly breathless, said, 'Ned? Killed?'

'Christ, didn't you know? He was off to Arnhem that following week. His name was in *The Times*.'

'I didn't see . . .'

'Are you all right? You're not going to faint, are you? Hey – Di—'

'No, I'm fine.' Madge's voice did indeed sound much stronger. 'Look, I have to go.' Now she sounded formal. 'It was . . . good . . . to see you, Mr Scaife. I'm terribly sorry about your wife. But you have the baby. That is what is important – she was right there, you know.'

The voices receded. He must be walking up the path with her. 'Di' was not long starting up again. 'Gerald! How long have I got to sit here waiting for you? Gerald!' And then he must have returned because there was a muttering, mumbling period, and they scuffed off. He heard 'Di's' voice say, 'You sound better, my dear.' And the man answered with a kind of surprise, 'Yes, by God. I feel better. I feel . . . my perspective coming back. I might paint tomorrow.'

'Good.'

They were gone. Clem found he was crouching on his haunches, both hands clutching his wasted calf as if it were paining him. He lowered his forehead to his knee and tried physically to blot out the thoughts cascading through his brain. After some time he stood up slowly. His muscles were shaking after the enormous tension, but he had in fact succeeded in pushing the whole peculiar incident out of his head. He began to roll his wet clothes into a bundle, changed his mind and hung them over the hooks next to Rosemary's sunbonnet. Outside he heard the three females return from their labours and his own mother commented, 'He's still in there – it always took him an age to change his clothes.'

He pushed his head through the flap.

'Just waiting for Madge to bring me some trousers,' he explained. 'Start on the picnic – she won't be long now.'

They all looked at him and smiled. Rosemary still with collusion; Marie Bridges with affection; his mother with a kind of exasperation.

'Honestly, Clem. You're not tanning at all, are you? You look as white as a ghost still!' She stooped and peered into the cot, where Mark, so placid, so unlike Rosemary, gave her one of his now-famous gurgles. 'Even the baby is a better colour than you are.'

Unbidden, Madge's words came into his head. 'You have the baby. That is what is important.'

Madge said nothing about her meeting with the man Gerald Scaife. Clem found himself watching her like a hawk. He remembered the sister had mentioned Penzance, and he waited for Madge to suggest a shopping trip there. She did not. At times he found this even more suspect than her clandestine walk around to the Scaife studio that first night. After all, she liked shopping in Penzance; they always had a day there; why was she avoiding the place this year? The answer was that her sole connection with the Scaife man was through . . . he had to force himself to think of the overheard name . . . this Ned Nicholls.

In quite a separate way, Clem also watched Mark. There was no doubt about it, Mark was a model baby. He slept all through the night, and during his waking hours he would wave fists and legs occasionally with a kind of joyous abandon that was utterly endearing. When he cried, it wasn't as Ro had cried, in anger or frustration; it was a wail of despair because no familiar face was in sight, no bottle of milk was available, no comforting hands were reaching for him. Once these needs were supplied, the tears dried instantly and the magical smile reappeared. Marie Bridges said he was like Madge. Maybe he had her nature, but he didn't look like her. His hair had a coppery tinge and his eyes were small and round and his ears were big and flappy. He didn't look like Clem either.

The twin mysteries of Madge and Mark seemed insoluble. Mark did not even know there was a mystery, and Madge suddenly and inexplicably 'went down' with a kind of flu which kept her in bed for a whole day and then forced her to rest frequently

146

until almost the end of the holiday. Not that Clem could have cross-questioned her anyway; more than half of him did not want to know precise details. But he might well have asked casually, 'Who is this Ned Nicholls that Rosemary keeps talking about?' and seen what kind of reaction she would register.

And with that thought came an idea. He would ask Rosemary some questions. Obviously Rosemary would not know exactly what had happened last year – which was good because of course he must remember he didn't want to know – but she might be able to slake partially the terrible thirst he had for a picture – a knowledge – of this man.

Utterly confused, he began a careful pattern of questions the day after Madge's illness began. He decided to limit himself to one question per day so that Ro did not become suspicious. He even listed them in the back of his diary.

1. Was Uncle Ned a soldier?
2. Did he take you swimming every day?
3. Did Mummy mind you having a grown-up friend?
4. Depending on the answer to 3, did you stay with Etta and Philip when Mummy and Uncle Ned went out?

He wasn't certain about 4. It might have to be changed or omitted altogether. He did not want to put ideas into Rosemary's head for later years.

Responses to 1, 2 and 3 revealed a lot. Rosemary was still enjoying her fathers' company and wanted to keep his interest, but allowing for this, it was obvious that Ned Nicholls, soldier and great swimmer, had not been Rosemary's friend. She had liked him and admired his physical prowess, but had been conscious even at four years old that he was her mother's special property.

'But he arranged the party, Daddy,' she said as they paddled around the harbour to Porthminster at low tide. 'Oh it was a lovely party, with real b'loons and presents. Philip took me and I held his arm like a grown-up lady and made him play musical chairs an'—'

'Didn't Mummy come with you?' interrupted Clem, bending down to roll up his trousers. He had no wish to get a second pair wet.

'No. She went for a walk along the cliff. They found some flowers what had got the same name as hers.'

147

'Oh.' He did not need to ask who 'they' were. 'I've never heard of Madge flowers, have you?' He laughed loudly and Rosemary joined in. 'Race you to the raft!' he suggested, not wanting to talk about Ned Nicholls any more.

'Okey-dicky-dokey,' spluttered Rosemary, knowing that he would let her win.

He watched her climb up to the beached diving raft and caper about on it before he broke into a loping run. They'd been after marjoram. It told him everything he hadn't wanted to know and it linked the mysteries of Madge and Mark for evermore.

They went for a sedate walk along the Carbis Bay footpath. It was the first time Madge had been far from the cottage since her rather odd illness, and she leaned heavily on the hired pram and let her mother take over when the footpath became narrow or overgrown. Clem and his mother walked behind with Rosemary, who had suddenly decided she wanted to collect wild flowers. She darted about like a gadfly, ignoring Grandma Briscoe's requests to look for blackberries, running on to put a bunch of cow pars-ley on the pram, then hanging right back so that they all had to wait for her.

Clem wasn't sorry. He did not want to be with Madge or Mark. Somehow he was behaving normally, but he had no idea how he was managing it. At night he lay by Madge's side not daring to move until she was asleep, then he tossed and turned for hours while his brain chugged monotonously around getting nowhere, like the old Hornby steam engine he still had from his boyhood. Eventually he would fall into an uneasy sleep, conscious all the time of a headache. Each morning he woke late after Madge had crept downstairs, taking Mark with her. He welcomed his new pairing with his daughter because it avoided the former arrange-ment of him and Madge sitting in deckchairs with Mark between them. Now his mother was an added barrier. When Rosemary galloped ahead again and demanded to push the pram, he talked quite animatedly to Mrs Briscoe in an effort to keep her with him. She, sharp as ever, was quick to notice his unusual enthusiasm for her company.

'You never talk about your proper job like this, Clem,' she commented, lifting her gaze from the ground for a moment; she believed in looking to see where her feet were going. 'Anyone

148

would think you preferred war work – my God, anyone would think you were sorry it's all over!'

The remark was so absolutely typical of his mother, he ignored the criticism. 'My job at the factory is interesting, of course. But this atom bomb is going to open up new fields entirely. There will have to be some kind of international control. It'll be centred in America, of course. As a matter of fact I've been approached—'

Mrs Briscoe looked up again and stumbled on a pebble. 'Teach me to look where I'm going,' she grumbled. 'And are you trying to tell your mother you're going off to America – deserting her just like your father did?'

He said impatiently, 'Oh for goodness' sake, Mother!'

'I mean it, Clem!' She paused and her voice suddenly lost its sharpness. 'You don't know what it means to me – coming here with all of you, being part of a family again. If you all go and live on the other side of the world, I'll never see Rosemary and Mark again!'

'Don't be silly, Mother. I wouldn't try to transplant the children like that. It would be a temporary thing anyway. There will have to be some kind of commission. It'll be like a committee. We shall meet – discuss certain aspects – then permanent staff will carry out recommendations—'

Mrs Briscoe stopped short in order to survey him properly and with amazement.

'You would leave Madge and the children behind? You would go off and leave them here?'

He wanted to throttle her. 'Mother. I've already explained that it would be for short periods only!'

'You men have always got excuses for what you want to do, Clem.' Her face seemed to shrivel with obstinacy. 'If you accept this – offer – whatever you like to call it, you will be deserting Madge. Just as your father deserted me!'

He looked at her helplessly, seeing all the years of bitterness in her as she stood there. He wondered if Madge could go the same way, then knew she couldn't. It wasn't in her nature. And immediately followed a thought worthy of his own mother: she consoled herself when I was away before, presumably she'd do it again.

He said aloud, 'Come on, Mother. You know damned well I'm not going to be deserting anyone. Take my arm over this rough bit and let's talk about something else. Did I ever tell you that

Ginger Rogers came to entertain the troops when I was in Toronto?'

'Yes. Several times,' she said, but she took his proffered arm grudgingly and got under way. And he changed the topic of conversation yet again and told her about the work at the Aircraft Corporation, which always pleased her. But the back of his mind still dealt with the conversation he'd had with his contact in the Admiralty, a man called Bill Penney, who foresaw enormous peacetime possibilities for atomic energy. If he *was* offered some kind of place on a commission, it might well mean protracted absences from home; protracted absences from the intolerable situation he had discovered.

As if she could read his thoughts, Madge finally surrendered the pram handle to Rosemary and came back to him and his mother.

'Are you all right?' She spoke to both of them but she looked at Clem. 'Is it too rough for you, Mother?'

'Not a bit.' Mrs Briscoe let go of Clem's arm and straightened her shoulders. 'My goodness, I used to walk almost into Keynsham when I was a girl – along the river bank!' She put a hand in the small of her back. 'It's not far now, is it?'

'No. We shall be at Carbis Bay station in a few minutes now. I was just saying to Ro that we could catch the train back if you were tired.'

'I'm not tired. But of course she is only five and I daresay . . .' Mrs Briscoe listed reasons for returning by train while Madge continued to look at Clem. He smiled vaguely over the top of her head and quite suddenly could bear it no longer. He left the two of them in the middle of the footpath and went on to join Rosemary. That wasn't much better. Mark was propped on a pillow so that he could see over the edge of the pram, and his contented round face looked foreign now. Clem remembered his own bursting pride in the child and wanted to groan aloud. There was another week of the holiday to go. How could he stand it? As soon as they got back he would ring the Admiralty and let it be known he was willing and eager to go to San Francisco . . .

Marie Bridges said, 'Clem, you're a million miles away. I just asked you if you'd got a handkerchief I could put these blackberries in.'

'Sorry . . . yes. Sorry.'

He fished out a clean handkerchief and they bound up the

150

blackberries Marie had collected. She went on chattering.

'D'you remember that awful windy day you proposed to Madge and she accepted?' She laughed. 'You came back to the cottage covered in blackberry juice, and so happy you were incandescent!'

'Yes. I remember.'

'And before that you'd gone into the sea, the two of you, and got soaking wet. And you've done the same this holiday with Ro! Talk about history repeating itself!'

'Yes. Yes I suppose, in a way . . .' Madge hadn't really wanted to marry him. He had known that and not faced it till now.

Marie smiled at him fondly. 'Dear Clem. You were made for each other, you and Madge. Etta could see it – I think she knew it the very first time you came with us on holiday. That year you came with Neville.'

'Did she?'

'And it would have pleased Neville, of course.' Marie was waxing thoroughly sentimental now. Her smile was faraway. 'You were such a good influence on Neville, Clem. Don't think we didn't realise it and appreciate it. He was a madcap and you kept an eye on him . . . I was always so grateful you went to Spain with him. So grateful.'

It was as if she was spinning a cocoon around him and holding him down. It hadn't been like that anyway. He had followed where Neville led, always. Tagged along. Tagger Briscoe he had been.

He heard Madge scream his name and looked back at her in amazement, convinced she really had read his thoughts this time. She and his mother were clutching each other; she was pointing. 'Clem! Look!'

He turned his head. Rosemary had wheeled the pram on to the footbridge which spanned the railway line. It was very high up. At its other end a flight of steps led down to Carbis Bay bridge and from its parapet there was a magnificent view of the perfect cove, the Hayle estuary, and the dunes of Hayle itself. Rosemary was lugging Mark out of the pram. It was quite obvious what her intention was. She was going to sit him on the parapet to admire the view.

Clem did nothing. He could not remember afterwards whether he was paralysed with terror, or whether, quite cold-bloodedly, he decided to leave it all to fate. Whatever the reason, he stood still while Rosemary lifted the heavy baby and got its flaccid legs the other side of the parapet high above the burnished railway lines. Madge screamed again, and still he did nothing. Then Rosemary held the child into her shoulder with one hand and pointed with the other. She must have heard her mother and with Briscoe obstinacy she ignored her. They all heard her as she said in her baby-voice, 'See the pretty boats, darling? See the pretty red sails?'

Clem was conscious that Madge was running; he could feel the thud of her sandals on the footpath like a heartbeat. Twenty yards in front of him Mark responded as always to Rosemary's cooing voice; he stiffened his plump legs and threw out his arms. Madge stopped and choked out another cry: 'Clem – Clem, please!' And at last he moved.

It was too late. Mark's sudden spasm had jerked him free of Rosemary's restraining arm. He pushed himself forward slightly to look at her pointing finger, and he had gone. Rosemary started to scream, she grabbed, her small fingers grasped Mark's matinée jacket and clung on, the matinée jacket slid off the plump shoulders and dangled in her hand. She went on screaming and screaming so that nobody heard the sickening thump of the body hitting the rails beneath.

Now Clem could not stop moving. He crossed the bridge without pausing by Rosemary, without looking over the parapet. He took the steps half a dozen at a time and leapt over railing and barbed wire on to the ballast. Mark lay, a small globule of humanity, on one of the sleepers, neatly between the two metal lines. Amazingly he was upright, his head undamaged, resting on his chest. Clem thought fleetingly that he looked like a small buddha.

He crouched and peered. There was a great deal of noise; he had no idea whether it was inside his own body or sounds of distress from the bridge above. Mark was breathing. It was shallow, a kind of panting snort, but air was going in and out of his lungs. There was no blood as yet. The snorting was horribly loud; Clem put his hands on the tiny body and a voice said, 'Don' ee touch 'im, m'boy. Someone be gettin' th' ambulance. Leave 'im be till they gets 'ere.'

Clem looked up. Standing in the station was the small train

which served the branch line. The man speaking to him was the guard, navy blue uniform, gold braided cap, whistle, carnation . . . and the snorting came from the square-boilered locomotive.

'Oh God – oh no – it's not Mark—' Clem flung himself full length and put his ear to the soft body. He could hear nothing. He looked up and could no longer see the railwayman through his tears. 'I thought he was breathing and it was the bloody engine all the time!'

The man got down on his knees. From his waistcoat pocket he produced a silver half-hunter and turned it shiny-side to Mark's mouth.

' 'E's breathin' all right my 'ansome, never fear. 'E landed feet first like a kitten. We was just drawin' in an' I saw 'im fall. 'Tis 'is back we got to be careful of. I'm an ambulance man myself an' I know that's the danger.' He straightened. 'I'll go an' tell your wife an' by the time I gets back, the men will be 'ere and they'll take 'im straight to Camborne General. Best 'ospital in Cornwall. They'll take care o' the babby there, never fear.'

He went and Clem put his head as close to Mark's as possible. The pudgy cheeks were pushed up into an unconscious smile and the round eyes closed; there was a passing resemblance to Neville . . . or rather a universality about his babyhood.

Clem whispered, 'I'm sorry. Oh God I'm so sorry. It doesn't matter . . . after all, it just doesn't matter. I love her. And you belong to her. Oh dear God . . . dear God . . . what have I done? What have I done?'

Someone lifted Madge over the barbed wire and she crouched by him. She looked terrible. He thought of what she had had to bear this last year. She had been down in that pit and he had been wandering about in the sunlight on top, never realising she was down there.

He said, 'Madge, can you forgive me?'

She stopped looking at Mark and turned her gaze on him. She must have seen that he was down there in the darkness with her, and she lifted a hand and touched his cheek with a kind of gratitude. From the top road there came the familiar clanging of an ambulance bell. Marie's voice came down to them from the bridge: 'Go with him, my dears! We'll look after Rosemary.' And the blessed bustle of the experts took over.

*   *   *

They never saw the ambulance men take the crumpled body up the station approach to the ambulance. They were ushered ahead, and in any case Mark was swathed in a sheet before he was lifted. But at two o'clock the next morning, when the surgeon, grey-faced and weary, saw them, they were allowed to look into the incubator where Mark lay on his stomach, stark naked. He had no recognisable legs. They had been quite literally concertinaed into his trunk and the surgeon had removed them. Whether the child could survive the twin shocks of fall and operation was doubtful. They could stay in the hospital with him but he would not know they were there, and no-one would think badly of them if they preferred to return to their other child.

They stayed. They sat by the incubator and watched. And Mark did not die.

CHAPTER EIGHT

1948

That year they went down in July. Grandma Briscoe was not well, but they took Grandma Bridges with them to help with Mark. He was still small enough to be carried upstairs, but he was fascinated when Philip outlined plans to make a bed for him in the window seat.

'For next year that'll be,' Philip said, holding the truncated body tenderly on his knee. 'When you're a big boy.'

Mark looked into the sea-blue eyes close to his own and gave his contented smile.

'Like a bunk in a boat, Philip?' he asked.

'Just like a bunk in a boat!' Philip agreed. 'And it'll be your boat too. Your very own boat. You can come and sleep in your bunk whenever you want to. Not just in the summer. Any time.'

Mark said in his clear, precise voice, 'That will make me very happy.' And, as usual, everyone in the room smiled at him.

At three years old Mark was surprisingly mature. Sometimes, when the pain in his stumps was bad, he would cry, otherwise nothing seemed to upset his sunny disposition. He found his circumscribed life full of interest; already he could read and write, but mostly he communicated through his drawing. His father brought him home unlimited supplies of paper from the drawing office at the factory, and he used charcoal, pencils, even ancient stubs of wax crayons to record what he saw around him. The world through Mark's eyes was invariably optimistic. This had been made plain to the whole family about three weeks previously when Rosemary had come home from school with a face as long as a fiddle. She had borrowed her best friend's fountain pen, crossed the gold nib, and now the best friend wouldn't speak to her.

Mark had drawn her with fiendish accuracy: the stubborn set

of the mouth, the flaxen, day-long plaits fraying at the ends, the angry eyes. And then when his mother said, 'Oh dear, yes. I'm afraid that's how you are looking, Ro,' and Ro herself was protesting furiously that it wasn't in the least like her, he had gently stroked one of her eyelids down so that she was winking. Immediately the whole thing became a joke. Rosemary was duping the world; making everyone think she was cross and hard-done-by when really she was laughing at her own performance. He looked surprised when she hugged him, and pleased when she laughed and relaxed in front of his chair, combing out her hair with her fingers. He wasn't old enough to work things out logically, but his instinct often led him unerringly to the right action. More than anything he wanted his sister and his parents to be happy. Already he knew that sometimes when they looked at him, they weren't.

Marie Bridges clambered the last few steps to Saint Nicholas' chapel and leaned on its retaining wall, recovering her breath with some difficulty. Etta Nolla, older than her friend, but as spry as she had ever been, grinned smugly.

'Might look like an old crone, but I've got more puff in me than you, my 'ansome.' She commented as she shoved stray hairs beneath her trilby hat. 'Now just raise your eyes and look at the view for a spell and you'll feel like a young woman again.'

Marie did as she was bid. The long line of Porthmeor beach soared away beneath her, the black promontory of Old Man's Head a silhouette against the grey morning sky. She drew a deep breath and thought of Alfred. Was he out there somewhere, hovering between land and sea perhaps? She believed implicitly in an afterlife and was certain she would see him again, but where *exactly* was he? Supposing he wasn't? She shivered. Mark's terrible accident had put her off St Ives, and for two years now Granny Briscoe had accompanied the young people. This year, when she had been ill, Marie had come with them reluctantly. There was something about that huge sweep that made her think that Alfred might not . . . was not.

'Well?' prompted Etta.

'It's very beautiful,' Marie temporised prosaically.

'Dun't it take the years off your back?' Etta straightened her own back as if to prove the point.

156

Marie said apologetically, 'Not really. But it's different for you. You and Philip. You . . . you're indestructible. And this is your place – it belongs to you. We're just summer visitors.' She attempted to laugh. 'Like the swallows.'

'We've 'ad to fight to stay 'ere – oh not Philip mebbe. 'E's allus bin a bit of an 'ero,as Philip. But I were a stranger from Menheniot, an' I din't give 'im no children. There's bin times they'd 'a stoned me out.'

Marie was aghast. 'Surely not? This is the twentieth century, Etta!'

Etta tugged at her hat brim and cackled. 'Not then it weren't. When I kem to Snives first, there were plenty o' folks 'oo still believed in witches.'

'Oh no! Etta – no.'

'An' why not?' Etta stared up from beneath the trilby with a kind of defiance. 'I looked after young Clem Briscoe din't I? I fixed it so that 'im and your Madge would get 'itched.' She turned and gazed across to the headland. 'Couldn't do nothing about the other. Philip wouldn't let me.'

'The other?' Marie made the query wildly; she wished Madge were here so that they could laugh about it afterwards. Hearing it tête-à-tête with Etta gave it a certain horrific credibility.

Etta dived another glance around, then looked down at the tumbling rocks and said quietly, 'Mark. I couldn't do nothing about Mark.'

Marie put her hand on the ancient black shawl. 'He lived, my dear. Maybe your prayers tipped the balance there.'

'Oh aye. 'E 'ad to live.' Etta covered Marie's hand with her horny one. ' 'E 'ad to live so 'e could bring you all down 'ere.' She grinned again. 'You bin swallows long enough, my 'ansome. Mark en't no swallow. Mark is a native Cornishman. 'E'll bring you all down 'ere one O' these days. You'll see.'

Marie smiled back. What else could she do? One of the many aspects of Mark's tragedy was that he was never going to be independent. He would never be able to decide his own destiny. Dear Etta, full of folklore and barren of children. No wonder she took such an interest in all of them, especially Mark. She looked back at the enormous view and it was as if loneliness, cold and tangible, entered her very soul.

Etta said briskly, 'Best be gettin' back now. They'll want their dinner early if they're going up to Knill's to see the dancin'.' She began to clamber down the steep slope of the Island, then looked back up at Marie. 'Don't you get tryin' to find 'im out there, my 'ansome. 'E's right with you, lookin' at all that from 'ere. 'E'd 'ardly be out there lookin' at *us*, would 'e?'

But as Marie followed the black-shawled figure through the tumble of rocks, she wondered whether she wanted Alfred to be as close as that. He would grieve so for Mark, and for Clem and Madge who were just as much victims as the child. And as for Rosemary, naughty one minute, angelic the next . . . she had never spoken of the frightful accident since she had said to her two grandmothers, 'I know Mark will get better because I've prayed to Jesus.'

Marie caught up with Etta and they strolled through the town together.

'I hope it's not going to rain,' Marie said as they came down to the harbour. 'Hayle looks awfully near today.'

'They'll 'ave the dancin', rain or no rain, never fear.'

'I do hope so. Ro is looking forward to it so much.'

The rain started when they were in the middle of their mutton stew. Rosemary pretended to choke on one of the small bones. Etta, coming in with another dish of potatoes, thumped her on the back with unnecessary force.

'Best end o' neck is that,' she announced. '*And* I took all the bones out after I'd boiled 'en. Just like your ma asked me to!'

'There was a bone!' Rosemary whimpered, looking at the rain lashing the window.

'Where is it then? Show it to me – go on!'

'I've swallowed it.'

Clem said quickly, 'That's all right then. No harm done. This is delicious, Etta.'

'Duff afterwards. You'll want somethin' to stick to your chest this weather. Take your brollies and wear some good thick boots. It gets muddy up at Knill's.'

'I don't want to wear boots! Mummy, you said I could wear my rosebud dress – how can I wear boots with my rosebud dress?'

'I don't know about the dress either this weather, Ro.' Madge retrieved a piece of carrot from Mark's shirt front and returned his smile. Rosemary, infuriated by her mother's lack of real interest, said loudly, 'I'm not going then! If I can't wear my dress I'm not going!'

Philip had come in behind Etta to clear the empty dishes and he said peaceably, 'You can wear your dress, my maid. I'll get a donkey and jingle down to take you up there – 'ow's that?'

Happiness was restored instantly. Rosemary demanded to be told the old story of John Knill yet again and Philip obliged.

'I know about the ten maidens and two widows dancing around his monument,' Rosemary chipped in. 'But what do they ackcherly *sing*?'

'The Old Hundredth. And some kind of rhyme.'

'What are the *words*, Philip?'

'Strange they are. Dun't know 'em for sure.'

Etta chipped in. 'If you 've finished messin' with that good food, you'd best go and change into this 'ere dress, my girl.' She watched her scrabble down from the table. 'Anythin' for a bit o' peace and quiet,' she commented. Marie glanced at Madge and tried to look reassuring. She really must explain some time about Etta's 'magical powers'. They might be something anyone could learn!

It was Jim Maddern who arrived with the donkey cart. Jim had gone through the war as a submariner, but it had not changed him. Even when he shook hands it was with palm upward as if hoping for a tip.

They piled into the jingle, Rosemary between her parents, Mark on Madge's knee. Marie had asked to be left out of this trip and was thankful as she watched them move off along the harbour, Jim leading the donkey. The four of them positively bulged out of the tiny cart and with umbrellas held above them they looked like a bursting flower pot of petunias. But there was a snugness inside the little cart and a sense of adventure which they could all share. Mark sang 'Jingle bells, jingle bells . . .' and Rosemary shivered in her thin frock and her father put his arm around her and held her into his hairy jacket.

Disaster threatened when they had to pile out at Skidden hill and walk ahead of the donkey until they reached the Catholic church. They sat on the bench where John Payne had been hung four hundred years before and waited damply for Jim's arrival – the donkey took mincing, three-inch steps – and then everything was redeemed by a most enormous rainbow which materialised out of the mist over the Malakoff. They climbed back into the jingle and folded their umbrellas. Jim yelled, 'Told ya, din't I?' Rosemary said, 'He didn't tell us at all!' And her father whispered, 'Don't spoil it for him. He wants another tip for being a weather forecaster!' And Rosemary giggled helplessly.

It was the first of the Knill's Dancings since the war, and in spite of the weather hundreds of people turned up and stood among the rhododendrons at the base of the tall spire. Rosemary could easily have been mistaken for one of the maidens had it not been for the pink rose sprigs on her white dress. As it was she stood in the front, smiling and curtseying when they did, very aware of being the object of much admiration. When the 100th psalm was sung she made a great to-do of inclining her head every time the Lord was mentioned, just as Grandma Bridges had taught her. And she joined in the Gloria with great aplomb. Clem whispered, 'I don't know where she gets it from. Neither you nor I, that's for sure.' It was by pointing out Rosemary's uniqueness that Clem somehow avoided even noticing Mark's.

Then it was over, and the mayor was distributing the monies and conducting his little band back through the rhododendron grove. The rest followed more slowly, and Clem and Madge lingered to climb on to the plinth of the monument and show Mark the tiny huddle of houses that was St Ives. Rosemary, uninterested in views, held her skirts wide and circled the monument, reciting a parody of the little rhyme she had just heard.

'Give a bun to your daughter today . . . hum, hum, hum . . . Give a bun to your daughter today . . . hum, hum—'

'Give a *what*?'

She looked up, startled. A big boy – but still in short trousers – stood behind her. His question was asked of another boy, smaller, in shorter shorts. Both boys were grinning widely, but the big boy's grin was full of confidence, the other's more diffident.

The big boy looked back at her.

'Yes. You,' he said. 'Give a *what* to your daughter?'

'A bun. They were just singing – give a bun to your daughter—'

Her words were lost beneath the big boy's guffaws and the smaller boy's whinnies.

160

'I thought you said *bum*! It sounded like *bum*!'

Rosemary primmed her mouth. 'I don't say rude things. You're horrid.'

The big boy controlled his mirth with difficulty.

'A bun, is it? To your daughter? Is that it?'

'Yes,' Rosemary came back with dignity. 'It's what they've been singing this afternoon.'

The big boy doubled up again and Rosemary seized her umbrella from the steps of the monument and whacked him hard across *his* bum. He yelped and rounded on her furiously, wresting the umbrella from her and hurling it into the rhododendrons.

'You . . . you little termagant! If you weren't a girl I'd give you a good hiding!'

'Steady on, Rory,' said the smaller boy, 'her mother and father are up there.'

It was that fact which was giving Rosemary her sang-froid. She smiled at the furious face above her and said, 'I gave *you* a good hiding – and you deserved it. You're a very rude boy. And if I can't find my brolly, I shall tell the police about you.'

The smaller boy said quickly, 'I'll go and find it.'

'Let her find it herself, Jan,' ordered the bigger boy who had the fascinating name Rory. But 'Jan' was already leaping into the undergrowth like an eager puppy.

Rosemary, enjoying her unexpected victory, smiled pityingly at Rory.

'All because you were poking fun at the dancing maidens. You really are a silly boy as well as a rude one.'

Rory looked as if he might explode on the spot. After a boiling, inarticulate few seconds, he swallowed and said with tight calm, 'You little idiot. For your information, the words are "Shun the barter of the day, Hasten upward, come away". You can't be expected to understand what that means, I suppose, at your age. But you could at least listen and get the proper *words*! Or are you deaf as well as daft?'

It was Rosemary's turn to boil. Jan, arriving with the retrieved umbrella, took the situation in at a glance and spoke in his clipped precise voice. 'Here it is. And no damage done. And I think you look pretty in that dress. Were you one of the dancing maidens?'

'No,' was all Rosemary could manage.

'How could she be? She didn't know the proper words.' Rory

161

forced another scornful laugh. 'Give a bun to your daughter indeed! I've never heard anything so stupid in my whole life!'

'Well, the real words aren't much better, Rory,' Jan said pacifically, smiling from one to the other.

'Well not to you, of course. You're a foreigner. You can't be expected to understand. That man, John Knill—' he gestured towards the monument, 'was a customs officer or something. I suppose he's telling us to give up trading and arguing and money and things, and think about heaven. And she thought he was telling us to give buns to our daughters!'

Rosemary raised her umbrella again. And her father's voice came sonorously from above.

'Ro! What on earth d'you think you're doing?'

Rosemary shouted with devastating honesty, 'I'm going to hit this boy!'

Her mother's voice from much nearer said, 'Hang on, darling. I'm coming.' And there she was, not trying to take the umbrella away, stooping down to Rosemary's level and looking at the boy with mild surprise. 'You can't hit people, darling—'

Rory burst out. 'She already has! She walloped me and I took the umbrella away and threw it into the bushes and Jan found it and gave it back and she thinks she's going to do it again!'

'He's rude, Mummy. He said bum. And he called me an idiot—'

Jan, red-faced and worried, intervened, 'We were teasing. That was all. We must say sorry with great sincerity—'

Rory yelled, 'Stop being so – so – *Polish*!'

And Madge picked up smoothly, 'Ah, you are Polish? I thought I recognised a slight accent, though your English is perfect. Please let us dispense with apologies on both sides, shall we? Misunderstandings often happen and should be ignored, I think.' She stood up and held out a hand to Jan. 'My name is Madge Briscoe. This is my daughter Rosemary. And here is my husband with our son Mark.' She indicated Clem coming down the steps, then shook Jan's hand and turned to Rory. 'And you are?'

Rory allowed his hand to be taken but said nothing. Jan said, 'This is . . . I mean, allow me to present . . . Rory Trewyn. My father and Rory's father were together in Lancaster bombers, and now I live with Rory because my father is dead. My name is Jan Frederic Grodno. I am delighted to make your . . .'

162

his voice petered out and Rory supplied gruffly. 'Acquaintance.'

Madge and Clem exchanged a glance. Mark said happily, 'Hello.' Clem said, 'How about an icecream? To – er – heal the breach.' And Mark said, 'Yes please.'

Everyone laughed except Rosemary and Rory, but Rosemary couldn't resist a smile up at her brother and Rory saw it and fell in beside Jan as they began to walk back down the hill. But by the time they reached the lane Rosemary had skipped and flounced too much for his taste.

He said stiffly, 'Well . . . we'd better get back, Jan. The parents will be expecting us.'

Madge glanced at her daughter and smiled right at Rory's dark face. 'I think Rosemary would like to apologise first, Rory. Wouldn't you darling?'

Rosemary's face was a picture. She wanted the boys to stay very much. She did not want to apologise. Eventually she addressed the rhododendrons. 'I'm sorry I hit you with my umbrella.'

Jan said enthusiastically, 'I say. That's so very English. Yes, Rory? I think your parents will not mind if we are a little late.'

Rory said nothing but he shrugged a kind of resignation and fell into step with Jan as he escorted Rosemary down the lane. Behind them, Mark looked deeply into the faces of Clem and Madge in turn and smiled. Madge suddenly hugged her son and husband, then they all three laughed.

Marie Bridges walked with her granddaughter along the harbour shoreline.

'Just how do you mean, darling? Surely it's rather difficult for a small boy to look like a pirate?'

'He wasn't *small*, Grandma! He was very tall. And he was very strong. And he was really, really dark. Black hair, black eyes – they flashed!' Rosemary stooped and picked up an empty crab shell. 'He is one of the Trewyns from Mennion House and Philip used to say that back – back – back years ago, they were famous smugglers.'

'I don't know whether a smuggler ought to be famous exactly, Ro. Surely nobody should know about them? They're very secret people.' Marie could smell the crab shell. She took it from Rosemary's sandy fingers, cast it away and scrubbed with a handkerchief. 'And you *did* say, they were small boys. You said they were in short trousers.

'Well they *were*! But they weren't *small*. They go to a school in Truno and after the summer hols they go into longs.'

Marie felt her brows go up into her hairline. Rosemary must have listened hard to glean all this information; and Rosemary was no listener.

She finished – or gave up – the task of cleaning Rosemarys hands and they resumed their walk. 'Tell me something about the Polish boy, darling. He sounds far more interesting.'

'Jan? He's very fair. His hair is like wet straw – he's a real Brylcreem Boy.'

'His father was an airman, I believe. He is doubtless copying him. So sad that he is alone in the world. The Trewyns must be good people to give him a home and a family.'

'Yes. Philip says they're philanderers.'

'Phil – ? I expect he said philanthropists, darling.'

'I don't know, Grandma. Rory's father and Jan's father were in the same aeroplane and when it was shot down Jan's father was killed.'

'What about his mother?'

'She died in Poland, I think. Anyway he's English now and not all that interesting really. He keeps saying yes sir and being polite. Rory is really *rude*!' She giggled.

Marie had heard the tale of the bun already and had a definite feeling Rory Trewyn might prove to be a bad influence. She said, 'So you enjoyed the Knill's celebration?'

'Oooh yes. Rather.' Another new expression. 'When I'm old enough I'm going to be one of the maidens.'

'I think you have to be born in . . .' Marie's voice died away as a motor boat came creaming around Smeaton's Pier and began to zigzag perilously between the moored craft. 'Goodness, look at that idiot – showing off I suppose.'

Rosemary looked up and screamed ecstatically.

'It's Rory! Look Grandma – it's the S.S. *Lancaster*! The Trewyns' boat! He said he was 'llowed . . . oooh he's going to . . .'

The boat was heading right for them. Marie clutched Rosemary to her and closed her eyes. The next moment they were sprayed with water, the engine cut, the shallow keel planed over the last

164

six inches of water, and the boat came to rest within arm's length of the two females.

Marie opened her eyes and released the wriggling Rosemary. Two grinning boys were sitting in the boat, one dark, one fair. The dark one tried to get his grin under control as Rosemary cavorted excitedly. The fair one called, 'It's all right, we know Rosemary. We met yesterday.'

Marie had lost her voice which perhaps was as well because irate boat owners and fishermen were converging from all directions and their voices were loud and clear. Phrases ranging from 'damn young idiots' to 'bluggy fools' surrounded Marie. She hated it. She wanted to grab Rosemary and rush away, but that was very much easier to think than to do; Rosemary was loving every searing minute.

She experienced again the feeling of Alfred's complete absence. Last night, as Ro slept beside her, she had put one arm out of the bed and extended her fingers until they ached. She had thought quite consciously that if Alfred was anywhere, he would take that supplicating hand; just brush it with his, breathe on it . . . something. Nothing had happened, nothing whatever. If he were anywhere at all, he would help her now, surely? He would not allow her to be embroiled in a situation so completely distasteful?

A voice behind her spoke. It said, 'The wee girl is enjoying herself, my dear. Come away now and wait for the fuss to die down.'

If it hadn't been for the accent she would have been quite certain Alfred was responding to her need. Even so she wondered if the voice belonged to someone he had sent.

She turned and there was Mr McGovern; Angus McGovern, a voice – a face – from her past. Surely sent by Alfred.

She smiled more warmly than she would normally have done and held out a hand still clutching the crab-smelling handkerchief.

'Mr McGovern! After all this time!'

She let him lead her up the beach to an upturned rowing boat. He took off his linen cap and swiped at the planks before seating her with old-fashioned ceremony. Below them the furore was already dying down. Dear Philip had arrived on the scene and was dealing with it.

'Ten years – I'm sure of it. If not more. Your man had not long . . . how are you keeping, Mrs Bridges?'

'Well. Really very well. And you and Mrs McGovern?' Marie was inexplicably glad she was wearing her pre-war voile with penny-sized spots.

'Brenda died. It was the Blitz. We were in London – my wish. I wanted to photograph some of the work being done by the rescue units. Went out with my camera in the thick of it – completely unscarred. She stayed in our boarding-house.'

'I am so *sorry*!' Marie's distress was genuine and compounded too by guilt of her own vanity. She wished she could be wearing sackcloth. 'I can't believe . . . oh dear, how simply awful. Poor Mrs McGovern! And you too. I really am—'

'You lost husband and son in one year. And your husband's illness – I was spared that. Brenda could have known nothing at all. The house was simply gone.'

'Well. Yes. But . . . it's so sad. All of it.' She looked at him with swimming eyes. He must be in his middle sixties now; his cream linen cap covered thin white hair, his face was beaky and somehow tired and his hands a mass of liver marks. But he retained his Scottish hawk-like look which gave him a passing resemblance to Raymond Massey.

He took her hand again. 'We all have to go eventually, Mrs Bridges. We must make the most of the time left to us. That was why I came back to St Ives. I'm looking for contentment, Mrs Bridges. Actively looking for it.'

She wondered exactly what he meant and felt rather too warm. She disengaged her hand gently in order to wipe her eyes with the disgusting handkerchief. If only she hadn't been wearing her voile: it was too young for her, too frivolous.

'I think I can go and collect my granddaughter now, Mr McGovern. Madge's child, you know. Rosemary.'

'Please, my dear. Call me Angus.'

'It's been so pleasant meeting you again after all this time.'

'Fate. Kismet. Weather permitting I am hoping to take some of the cliff walks. Perhaps you would give me the great pleasure of your company?'

'I really can't say, Mr McGovern. I like to help with the children, you see, and—' Marie was already standing and edging away from him.

'There are other children?' He stood up too and moved with her. 'And please – Angus, remember.'

'Er. Yes. Angus. And you must call me Marie, of course.' She looked towards the shore. The *Lancaster* was chugging its way very sedately between the boats; Philip and Rosemary were walking up the slipway towards the cottage. She stopped again. 'Actually, Angus, there was an accident – here – three years ago. Mark, the baby, was terribly – was *terribly* injured.' Even now it was almost unbearable to talk of it. How had they all been there and let it happen? She swallowed. His legs are amputated just above the knee. Until he stops growing there will be a lot of . . . pain. He is good – contented and sweet – and very advanced for his age. But obviously Madge and Clem need help.'

She stayed where she was, staring after Rosemary and Philip, conscious of him by her side but deliberately not even glancing at him. He said nothing for a long time, then he gave a long-drawn out sigh.

'A-a-gh. I wondered if there was something . . . more.' He moved so that he was in front of her. 'Look, my dear. It's not just random coincidence that we've met again. Let's take the child out. I've never had much to do with youngsters. Perhaps he could teach me a thing or two.'

Until he spoke she had no idea that he was on any kind of trial. But when he said the right thing, she knew he was vindicated; his presence here was vindicated. Perhaps this was Alfred's way of keeping in touch with her – I can't come myself but . . .

She smiled mistily at the silhouetted face above her.

'Oh Angus. That would be . . . so nice.'

Jan was waiting in the crab rocks at the far end of Porthminster beach as arranged, but there was no sign of Rory. Rosemary was furious. It had been Rory who stipulated Porthminster – 'We'll have to come on the train and I'm not walking right over to Porthmeor just to see you.' It had been difficult for Rosemary to get away from the usual family picnic outside the beach tent, especially when Grandma Bridges and that Scotsman had taken Mark off in the pram. Mummy had kept offering to come crabbing with her as if she didn't want to be left alone with Daddy and eventually she'd had to say she wanted the lavatory which was at the top of the cliff by the well. She ran like the wind but she knew she'd be at least half an hour and either Mummy of Daddy or both of them, would come looking for her. She'd have to say she'd gone to the other end of the beach to talk to Jim Maddern and help him feed the donkeys. After all the fuss about the *Lancaster* last week she hadn't mentioned her assignation. Rosemary liked intrigue.

She panted along Westcott's Quay beneath the church wall and plunged into the Warren with an agonising stitch in her side. A train was pulling out of the station; it must be the one they'd come on. She pumped her legs harder past the putting green and on to the footpath. That was when she saw Jan and realised he was alone.

'Damanblast,' she gasped under her breath. 'Dammit to all hell.' She tried to think of something even worse to say and could not. Her wide blue eyes filled with childish tears and she bent over to touch her toes and get rid of the stitch with a groan of sheer disappointment.

Jan was delighted to see her, however.

'Oh Rosemary. We wondered so much about you. Are you all right? Was there a severe telling-off for you?'

'Course not. Wasn't my fault. Where's Rory?'

Jan gave a Polish shrug. 'There was trouble for us. Mostly for him because he drove.'

'You let him take the blame?'

Jan flushed slightly. 'He is always . . . the ringleader. They know that. Now that there is no school he is grounded.' Jan smiled. 'That is what Mr Trewyn calls it. It means he cannot—'

'I know what it means.' And she also knew that if Rory had really wanted he would have defied all orders and become ungrounded. She did not wonder why or how she knew that; it was simply a fact. And it was like a challenge to her, a gauntlet thrown by the piratical Rory. She had another week in St Ives. In that time she had to get him to travel to St Ives to see her. And if she could somehow make him do that, it would be so much more than the way she'd described it last week: 'a secret meeting'. It would mean he would become hers. For always.

She smiled blissfully up at Jan.

'So long as you could come, that's all that matters,' she took his hand confidingly. 'Mummy says you are a true Polish gentleman.'

168

His face turned puce. He gripped her hand and said ardently, 'Your mother is so beautiful.'

'Beautiful?' Rosemary could not control her incredulity. 'Mummy?'

'I hardly remember my own mother, but Mrs Briscoe – it is her long hair looped up so . . . just so . . .' he gestured with his free hand. 'I thought we might see her last week, but then your grandfather—'

'That was Philip, not my grandfather.'

'And she is not with you today?'

'Course not. Don't you remember? I said we could have a secret meeting.'

'Yes. But you are so young, Rosemary, I did not think your parents would permit you to go about alone.'

'I'm eight years old,' Rosemary said levelly. She remembered what she had been working out in her head ever since the dancing around Knill's monument. 'When you've finished your National Service thing, I shall be nearly seventeen. You can get married at seventeen you know.'

'Can you?' he asked doubtfully.

'Yes. And I shall get married as soon as I can so that I can have my own house and eat what I like and go where I like.' She gave him another smile. 'P'raps I'll marry you, Jan. And Mummy would be your mother too then.' She hugged his arm. 'We're like a brother and sister now aren't we? Look at our hair. It's zackly the same colour!' She swung one of her plaits over her shoulder and reached up with it into his hair. Then she drew it down his face slowly. 'I'll have to go now, Jan. They don't know I've come right over here.' She looked at him very solemnly. 'Shall we seal out promise with a kiss?'

Jan's high colour receded and he looked bleached white. 'Rosemary . . . you are just a little . . . you are so sweet. If only we were brother and sister. Oh Rosemary.'

'We will be one day. There. I promise.' She planted a kiss on his mouth. Then threw her arms around his neck. 'This is our secret, remember. Don't tell Rory!'

She kissed him again, turned immediately and ran off. The stitch came back before she reached the station but it did not seem to hurt so much this time and she did not stop. When she got to the harbour she slowed to a walk; she was so hot she thought she might explode. But she still smiled.

At eight years old, she was enough of a psychologist to know that Rory would eventually come to her to investigate Jan's attachment. What she had not foreseen was that Jan would not be able to keep away. He saw no need for secrecy, either. The next afternoon he arrived at the beach tent before any of them. He had a picnic and his swimming stuff and was obviously prepared to stay for the afternoon. His manners were exquisite; he could talk to Mark or Angus McGovern with equal ease; with Clem he was perhaps a little too formal. It was obvious to everyone that he worshipped Madge.

Rosemary was piqued. She had not hesitated to use her mother as bait when she 'proposed' to Jan, but that he had risen quite so ardently was affronting. When he appeared the next day – this time at the door of Zion Cottage to help them round with their things – she decided that their groupings should be changed. She loaded him up with beach bags and towels, picked up the bag containing Mark's spare jumpers and drawing things, and announced that they would go ahead and open up. 'We'll get out the deckchairs and hang the wet costumes up, Mummy,' she said, almost shoving Jan down the steps. Madge, who had found Jan's adoration slightly embarrassing, nodded happily. Clem had gone off with Philip in the *Forty-niner* and taken Angus McGovern with him. It promised to be a restful afternoon with her undemanding mother and son.

So Jan spent the afternoon digging sandcastles, searching for crabs in the rock pools beneath the Island, and, in a confused way, coming to believe that he had actually asked Rosemary to marry him. His reward was a swim with Madge at the end of the day. She had a battered three-ply surfboard, and they shared it, three waves each.

'No, really, Mrs Briscoe. You didn't have a good ride on that one. Have another go.'

'Jan, we agreed three waves each whether they were any good or not! Take it, go on! I'm going to swim out to the rocks.'

'It's not safe – please don't.'

'It's not safe to dive from them because of the current underneath. But I'm not going to do any diving.'

But Jan could not let her take any risks and swam behind her just out of her vision, clutching the surfboard and pushing it ahead of him with some difficulty. It was obvious even to him that if there was any rescuing to be done, she would have to do it. When she pulled herself on to the rocks and saw him, he was thankful for her out-stretched hand.

'Jan!' She was panting as she pulled him up beside her but all he knew was that she was next to him, water flowing from her hair and shoulders. You are a quixotic idiot!'

He drew in a deep breath and wished he could bury his face in her costume; the top half.

'Quixotic? This I do not know,' he gasped.

'Courteous to the point of foolishness.' She scooped her hair back, pressing out the water. 'Like my husband.'

'Your husband is foolish?' Jan was ready to fight him.

'He is quixotic.' She looked at him without smiling. So many English people smiled when they looked at him; as if they saw his Polishness and found it amusing. 'Like you. Very . . . honourable.'

'That is bad?'

'No. That is good. But if it stops him doing what he should do . . . is good at doing . . .' she sighed sharply. 'It doesn't matter.'

'Please. Please, Mrs Briscoe. I would like to understand.'

She looked at him again very seriously. 'Yes. I am being rude. Either I must explain or not say anything at all.' Now she smiled, but not at him, at herself. 'It is silly, Jan. My husband is a clever man. He has been asked to go to America and sit on the committee which is investigating peaceful uses for the atomic bomb. He wishes to go. But he will not leave his family.'

Jan said ardently, 'Neither would I!' then, seeing her smile beginning to become indulgent, he added, 'But it is Mark, yes? He is anxious for Mark.'

She nodded. 'Yes. It is Mark. Always Mark.'

'He is worried for you, because of Mark,' Jan said wisely, 'It could not be that he does not trust you.'

Her eyes went past his and studied the outcrop of the Island with it washing bleaching in the sun. No. No. I'm sure you are right,' she said quietly.

*   *   *

171

Rosemary sat with Mark and her grandmother and watched the swimmers with thin lips. She needed to do something really electrifying to shock Jan, and then Rory. Perhaps Jan actually *had* kept their 'secret' and Rory knew nothing about the marriage pact, so she had to think of something so shocking, Jan would be forced to tell Rory, and he would be forced to come to St Ives and see her. She began to gnaw at her bottom lip.

The next morning, she went round to Porthmeor by herself. It was easily arranged: Grandma and Mr McGovern thought she was with her parents and Mark, and they thought she was with Philip and Etta. Rosemary – unusually – wanted to be by herself. There were two emotions she could not bear: one was guilt, the other was shame. The guilt she felt about Mark sometimes came between them so that she could not meet his happy face nor let her gee wander to the blanket that covered his stumps. She would get up and walk away from him on the flimsiest excuse. Today she felt shame, and it was just as unbearable to be with any member of her family. She walked across the neck of the Island and knew she was a wicked girl and would never go to heaven. She glanced up at that thought, as if checking on it, and saw without surprise that the cloud layer was getting thicker. Philip had said earlier, 'Don't worry, this sky will clear by'safternoon,' and she said categorically, 'No it won't, Philip, it will get worse.' She nearly added 'And it's all my fault' but stopped herself in time. Philip would not ask questions but the way he would look at her from beneath the brim of his horrible old hat, would make the shame even worse.

She surveyed the beach from the tumble of rocks at the town end, and for the first time in her life saw it as a place of desolation. The sea was flat calm and the colour of Grandma Briscoe's kitchen spoons, the beach tents had their canvas rolled halfway up the frames anticipating a very high tide later, and looked like a row of tired herons. Not a soul in sight, not even Jim Maddern and his donkeys. Well . . . just one. Someone slicing the wet sand methodically with the long hooked knife that pulled up sand eels for bait.

Rosemary had excellent eyesight but she made funnels with her hands and applied them to her eyes like binoculars in an effort to focus the one figure away from the enormous expanse of sea and sand.

It was Rory Trewyn.

She lowered her hands and stayed where she was. Triumph

172

writhed inside her but could not emerge as a shout of recognition or a crazy run across the beach. Her ploy – her shameful ploy – had brought him to her just as she had hoped, but now he was here the shame was no longer so private. Before, Jan had known and she had known, and that was all. Now Rory knew. She began to climb down the rock-fall slowly and carefully; she jumped the last three feet, landed badly in a patch of very wet sand which splashed her socks and shorts, and began to walk towards him. After a few yards she stopped, took off sandals and rolled her socks into them, and left them where they were. The sea was iron cold that morning and she shivered as she entered it. But it stiffened her spine and gave her some sort of courage. And it meant she could approach Rory from the seaward side. What possible difference that made she could not say, but it did make a difference.

He was wearing thigh-high waders and an oiled-wool sweater and with the wicked, slashing knife, looked more like a young pirate than ever. He could hear her splashing in the shallows ahead of him, but he did not look up. She refused to speak first. She bent down and started to flick the water in the air. There was no sun and it did not sparkle as usual. She flicked it higher and further. It rose and fell like molten lead. She scooped a double handful and hurled it. Rory looked up, his black hair dripping.

'You little . . . *bitch*!'

The word shocked and startled her, it hung in the air between them; fishwife talk.

She stammered, 'I – I didn't mean to! I was just . . . you were in the way-'

'Not that!' He advanced towards her, the knife held like a dagger. 'Christ, not that!' He took a deep breath and almost shouted – '*Jan!*'

She felt colour flood her face. So he did know. She had hoped – hoped so much – that he had come to see her simply because he wanted to come. But she had succeeded in shocking Jan out of his vow of secrecy. He knew.

She tried to brazen it out. 'Jan? Where is he? Are you going fishing? I don't know how you can bear to cut the sand for bait like that. You slice the eels in half most of the time, poor things.'

He stared at her for another furious moment then suddenly leaned over and slashed vigorously at the flooded sand until the bright silver of an eel came up on his knife.

'Like this, d'you mean?' The creature wriggled in his fingers. He used the knife and severed it completely. The two halves continued to wriggle. Rosemary screamed and put her hands over her face. Rory splashed towards her, caught hold of one wrist and pulled it down. 'Like this?' he repeated, shoving his palm in front of her. 'Like you're doing with Jan?'

She stopped struggling abruptly. The smell of fish was sickening. She knew it came from his jersey but it was as if it all emanated from the tiny creature on his hand, now, mercifully, still.

'What do you mean?' she asked in a small voice.

He was so angry he shook her by the wrist. She fell to her knees and he lugged her up, threw away the fish and seized her in both hands.

'Making him think you'll marry him and hand over your whole family on a bloody plate!' She had never heard so many dreadful words uttered aloud before and she quailed before him. 'Your mother will be his mother! Your father will be his father! Your grandmothers will be his grand-mothers! Your brother will be his brother!'

It had the rhythm of a liturgy, each phrase accompanied by a single spine-clicking shake to give it emphasis. She felt tears somewhere and concentrated on not letting them rise to the surface. She would not cry in front on him. She would not.

'And now . . . this!' He spat the word almost in her face.

She panted the truth. 'I did it to shock you. I did it to make you come to see me. Really.'

'Christ – d'you think I don't know that? That day – Knill's monument – I knew what you were thinking! I knew we could be friends even if you are just a kid! I pinched the *Lancaster*, didn't I? Just to come to see you and show off!'

His honesty matched and surpassed hers. The tears were at the top of her nose.

She gasped, 'And you promised you'd come with Jan to Porthminster beach. And you didn't!'

'Dammit, Jan told you I was grounded. Anywhere outside the perimeter fence was out of bounds!'

'You could have sneaked out—'

He shook her again, this time with a violence that was colder than his previous temper.

'I'm adopted – d'you know what that means, little girl?' He

174

almost sneered the words.It means I'm no better off than Jan. I've got no real mother. I've got no real father. I've got no real grandmothers. I've got no—'

'Shut up!' She screamed. 'Shut up! I'm sorry – I'll see Jan and explain and say I'm sorry and—'

'No you won't. Because that'll make you into some kind of bloody plaster saint as far as Jan is concerned. I know. Because I'm like Jan. I want someone to look up to, to – to – *belong* to—' the words were savage, blurted out against his will. He shook her again as if it was all her fault. 'No. I know exactly what will convince Jan. I know what will put him off you for life, little girl.'

He released one of her hands, turned and pulled her up the beach after him. His knife lay where he had discarded it, already covered in a layer of sand and water. He picked it up and threw it into the pail of sand eels and continued along the shoreline. It was a struggle because Rosemary pulled back at every other step. Occasionally his iron grip would tighten and he would jerk her to his side so that she wondered her arm did not come out of its socket. But at least the pain stopped her tears.

They came to the small cove only uncovered at low tide. Above them towered the dark rocks, culminating in Old Man's Head. Rory shoved her ahead of him now and again she stumbled to her knees.

'Take off your shorts,' he ordered curtly.

'Take off my –?' She turned and looked at him, her eyes very wide and blue and uncomprehending.

He explained in a voice that reminded her of Dr Barnes back home.

'You showed Jan your knickers. You're going to show me what is underneath your knickers. Then I'm going to tell Jan what you did. And he'll know that you are no better than Rose Care.'

She'd heard that name. She had no idea what it signified, but she knew she did not wish to be associated with it.

She said on a frightened sob, 'I'll do no such thing! I think you're a horrid rude boy, Rory Trewyn! I never want to see you again!'

'Don't worry, you won't. And you won't see Jan either.'

He stood above her. In his waders he looked like a giant.

175

'Now do as I say. Or d'you want me to do it for you?'

She tried to run before she was properly on her feet and he leaned down, put one hand on her heel and brought her smacking into the sand again. A pebble bulleted into her cheek. She squeezed her eyes shut.

The elastic on her shorts was not tight and he pulled them off her legs without difficulty. Her knickers were a different matter. She clutched at them desperately and kicked at him with her sandy feet. But he was twice her size and she was lying prone, quite unable to use her fists or teeth. When it was too late she rolled on to her back. Immediately the bunched-up knickers slid to her knees and she lay there, exposed.

He was shocked. She saw his black eyes widen with a kind of appalled disbelief at what he was seeing. And she knew only too well what he was seeing. One of the big ten-year-olds at school had told her that she would bleed from there when she was older and she had borrowed her mother's gold-edged hand mirror that very night and examined herself most carefully. The girl must have been right. It was like an open wound. She wondered if some ladies healed over eventually. She had put the mirror back on her mother's dressing table and gone to play dominoes with Mark who had a nice neat healed-over place through which he passed his water.

She could not bear Rory Trewyn, of all the people in the whole world, to see that open wound. She scissored her legs to her chest and grabbed at her knickers. And he stared even harder.

From high above them came a shout.

'Rosemary! Rosemary – what on *earth* are you doing?'

Her shorts were flung over a rock somewhere, but she pulled up her knickers, got to her feet and turned to face the voice in one fluid movement.

It was Grandma Bridges with Mr McGovern. They must have gone for one of their walks again; they were always going off for cliff walks.

'Nothing, Grandma!' she called.

'You . . . you're . . . undressed!' Grandma Bridges shouted back in horrified tones.

'I was just . . . just splashing in the water.' Rosemary stood squarely in front of Rory. She scoured her brain frantically and added, 'I was being a mermaid.' She recalled how keen Mr

176

McGovern was on Cornish legends. 'I was the Mermaid of Zennor!'

Grandma Bridges was silently nonplussed. Mr McGovern saved the day by emitting a hearty laugh and calling down jovially, 'See you at the beach tent, Rosemary. First there buys the icecreams!'

The icecream shop was shut anyway but Rosemary laughed too, waved and turned casually for her shorts. Rory was standing like a statue, head bent.

'Go away,' she said in a low voice.

'I . . . sorry. 'He looked like a beaten dog.

'Go *away* I said!'

'I can't I must come with you and – and—'

She turned on him. 'If you don't go away I'll tell them what you did! I'll get you into trouble! I hate you! Just go away from me! *Now*'

She watched him go, the tears pouring down her face at last. He did not straighten; he looked cowed, whipped. She imagined how sickened he must feel, seeing what he had seen. Shame was like a weight across her chest and shoulders.

She waited until he had picked up his pail of sand eels and begun to lope towards the Island, then she dragged on her wet shorts, buttoned them and began to make her way across the rocks towards the tents. Grandma Bridges and Mr McGovern were already there and he was bemoaning humorously that he was unable to buy icecreams 'all round'. She knew he was really pleased about it because he hated what he called throwing his money around.

Grandma Bridges said sharply, 'Where are your sandals and socks, Rosemary?'

'I left them in the sand up there,' she gestured vaguely towards the Island. For two pins she would have told them the truth and hoped that her punishment would clean the slate somehow.

'We'll walk home that way then.' Grandma Bridges was stiff and unhappy. She would have been devastated if she knew what had really happened. Rosemary squeezed her soggy nails into her equally soggy palms.

'Getting in the water like that—' Grandma Bridges ignored Mr McGovern's attempts to normalise things. 'Your shorts are soaking too. You deserve to catch a nasty cold.'

A tear fell down Rosemary's nose and plopped onto her blouse. 'I think I've got one, Grandma. I don't feel very well,' she whimpered.'

It worked like a charm, but it did not make her feel any better. Grandma encircled her with one arm and clucked her sympathy and helped her on with her socks. Rosemary felt worse and worse.

'It's all the fault of that Trewyn boy,' Grandma snapped eventually. 'He's old enough to know better!'

'Oh it wasn't Rory, Grandma,' Rosemary said innocently, her eyes as wide as she could force them. 'It was Jan. And he's Polish. He doesn't understand, you see . . .'

Both Grandma and Mr McGovern seemed strangely reassured by this. They nodded and said something about Continentals and the romanticism of an orphaned boy so far from home.

'Don't worry about it any more, darling,' Grandma said in quite a different voice. 'And don't say anything to your parents either. We'll say you caught the sniffles coming for a walk with us. All right?'

Rosemary nodded vigorously. And just at that moment a watery sun broke through the cloud.

CHAPTER NINE

1951

It was Festival of Britain year and Mark, who loved the sound of words, drove everyone mad by singing 'Fest-i-val of Bri – tain' at intervals from dawn to dusk. It was also the year his father was made the Chief Designer at the Aircraft Corporation, but try as he would Mark could not make a satisfying cadence of those words. However, when Jan Grodno called to 'pay his respects' as he always did, he said, 'If the United Nations Atomic Energy Commission ask for your advice, sir, it seems to me you are much more than a designer. I'd call you a boffin extraordinaire!'

That pleased Mark much more. He set the words to waltz time and sat on the harbour beach with his drawing things, waiting for the arrival of Jem Gurnard junior and trying out the new jingle.

'He's a boffin, he's a boffin, he really is a boffin, a boffin extraordinaire! He's a boffin, a boffin, he really is—'

His sister jumped from the harbour wall and landed with a dull thud by his side.

'What are you singing now?' she asked, squatting on her haunches to look over his shoulder at his drawing. Clem had made him a table which would fit over his wheelchair or stand on the floor in front of him, and adapt for almost any purpose. At the moment it was an easel.

'Didn't you hear what Jan called Dad? Jan says Dad is very clever and very important.'

'We already knew that,' Rosemary said tersely.

'Yes but I'm glad Jan knew it too.' Mark glanced at his sister. She was wearing her flaxen hair in one of the new pony tails; Clem called it her skinned-rabbit look. 'Jan's nearly seventeen now, Ro. Grown-up.'

'Huh.'

'You can get married when you're seventeen, so you must be grown-up to get married.'

'Did he tell you that?'

'He might have done. I knew already.'

'Huh,' she said again.

Mark added two strokes of his HB pencil to the drawing, then licked his fingers and smudged them into greyness.

'Why don't you like Jan any more, Ro?'

'I do. It's just that . . . he's always *around*.'

'He comes to see you. I think – when *you're* seventeen, he'll want to get married to you.'

'Rubbish. He comes to see Mother, you know that. He hasn't got a family and he likes to pretend he's related to us, or something. But he isn't. And sometimes he seems so foreign. And he looks at you as if he knows all your thoughts. And I just wish he wouldn't keep coming over.'

'Grandma Bridges doesn't like him either.'

'I know.'

'D'you think Grandma Bridges will get married to Uncle Angus? I heard him say to her yesterday that it was their anniversary. What did he mean by that?'

Rosemary said glumly, 'It's three years since they met. Down here. When Rory drove the Trewyns' speedboat over and got into trouble.' She sighed. 'Yes. I suppose they will get married.'

'You don't like Uncle Angus, do you?'

'Not much.'

Mark licked his finger again and smudged. 'Nor me,' he said. Rosemary was amazed.

'That's the first time I've ever heard you say you don't like anyone. You even like that woman doctor who keeps hurting you!'

'Old Fizzy?' Mark grinned. 'That's what Denver Richards calls her.' He looked earnestly at his sister. 'Fizzy. Short for physiotherapist, see?'

She rolled her eyes. 'Yeh-yeh-yeh. And Denver Richards' father comes from Denver Colorado wherever that is—'

He began to sing excruciatingly, 'He comes from Denver Colorado so they call him Joe—'

She began to get up. 'I'm going.'

'Oh don't go, Sis. Please. Jem will be ages yet. I promise I won't sing any more! Sit there. I'll draw you if you like. With your new hair.'

She subsided, giggling in spite of herself. He discarded the drawing of Mount Zion and fitted more paper on to his easel.

She picked up the drawing.

'How do you make it look as if you could go right into that little street there?' she asked.

'Shading. You can shade really well with these very soft lead pencils Dad gets me.' His eyes flicked from her face to the paper and back again. His voice went up a semitone as it always did when he was anxious. 'Will it make any difference when Uncle Angus marries Gran, Sis?'

She shrugged. 'I s'ppose so. She'll go away and live with him in Todmorden.' She saw his face and said quickly, 'Or he'll come and live with her in Bristol maybe.'

He said nothing and after a while she added, 'But they might not get married. They seem quite happy to visit each other and have their holidays down here.' She leaned forward and caught a glimpse of someone waving from Westcott's Quay. 'Oh damn,' she said crossly. 'It's Jan again. I thought he said he was going to revise for exams or something today.'

'Be nice to him, Ro.' Mark put his pencil down and passed her the portrait. It showed her with eyes and mouth pulled slightly upwards, looking like a waif. She studied it, frowning. Mark went on, 'He doesn't mind when you're horrid to him, but it's just . . . horrid.'

She looked up and met his bright brown gaze. She said slowly, 'Do I really look like this?'

'Yes. Your hair is pulled right up, you see, and it takes the edges of your face with it.'

'I didn't mean that. You've made me look sort of . . . lost.'

'Have I?' He too stared at the cartoon. 'Well, that's how you look, Sis.' He smiled suddenly. 'Why don't you write a letter to Rory and give it to Jan to deliver or something? Ask him to come to tea.'

She sprang back as if he'd attacked her.

'No!' I'd never do such a thing!' She looked at him sharply. 'What made you say that? You can't even remember Rory Trewyn! You were only three years old when . . . what made you *think* of something like that?'

181

'I don't know. You've told me about the speedboat often enough. And you say you never want to see him again in your whole life. That's what you say when you quarrel with Sheila Patten at school. And the very next day—'

A voice hailed them from above. It was young Jem Gurnard, the same age as Mark and his holiday companion for the past two summers.

'That Polish bloke's a-comin' along the quay, Rosemary Briscoe. 'E tole you about wrecking the Trewyn boat yet?' He read their silence correctly. 'Naw. I reckoned 'e wouldn't.' He chortled. 'S'prised Philup Nolla en't said nuthin' though. My dad do know all about it. Fine ole do it were. Las' winter when it all 'appened and the insurance en't paid up yet. Reckon 'tisn't their li'bility cos the boys shouldna bin driving of it.' He jumped down and squatted by Mark. ' 'Ow you doin' then? I go to the big school now an' we dun't break up till bank 'oliday—'

Rosemary said, 'Who was actually driving? Was it the *Lancaster*? Was anyone hurt? How did they *do* it?'

But Jem had already lost interest. He wanted to tell Mark about being in the cricket team and going out crabbing with his father in the *Forty-niner*.

Rosemary ran to meet Jan with an eagerness she had never shown before. She had long ago discovered that Rory had never mentioned the terrible incident in Porthmeor Cove beneath Old Man's Head but she still felt ashamed of herself for showing her knickers to Jan; indeed the whole awful business was something she could hardly bear to remember. Rory had been right, she had been completely selfish to suggest to Jan that by marrying her he could become a member of her family. She had tried to show him her true feelings by cold-shouldering him ever since, but it had little effect. In fact Grandma Bridges was the only one who did not thihk of him as part of their annual holiday. And she would usually relax by the end of the fortnight and say to Mr McGovern, 'Well, I suppose he is foreign, and they are different.'

So all Rosemary's ploys had been unnecessary; even at eleven years old she could see the irony of that. Jan had a place among the Bridges without any kind of favours from her, and the only effect those 'favours' had had, was to cause an unbridgeable chasm between herself and Rory. After what had happened she never wanted to see him again – that was obvious. Even so, she knew there was a connection between them; she did not know what it was, but she knew it would never be broken.

She almost pounced on Jan as he hung over the harbour rail talking to Philip below.

'Why didn't you tell me? Were you hurt? Was Rory hurt? What *happened*?'

Jan pretended to cower, putting his hands over his head protectively. Philip called up, 'I'll go and get the lugger ready then. 'Bout two o'clock? The tide'll be right then.' He trundled down to the shoreline and the *Forty-niner*'s dinghy. He was walking badly, rolling from hip to hip.

Jan lowered his hands, laughing.

'We're going to have a cricket match, did you know? Philip is going to take us all over to the Towans and we're going to have a cook-fire. Your father is going to resurrect an old custom apparently.'

'Cricket match? Don't be silly. Mark can't play cricket. Daddy would never suggest such a thing.' Rosemary shook her head impatiently. 'Never mind that. Why didn't you tell me about you and Rory and the *Lancaster* and the insurance? Were you hurt? Was Rory hurt?'

Jan's fair skin blushed the unbecoming red it always did when he was embarrassed.

'Did Philip tell you?'

'No. Jem Gurnard. Just. What *happened*?'

'I . . . nothing really. But the consequences were bad. I cannot tell you, Rosemary. Please do not ask.'

She was so angry she almost struck him. She clenched her hands into fists and her arms into rigid poles by her side.

'I've got to know. Everyone else must know. I can ask Philip.'

'He won't tell you.'

'Then I'll ask Etta. She will tell me.'

'She does not know.'

'If Jem Gurnard knows—'

'Oh, they all know that Rory and I took the motor boat without permission . . . we'd done it three or four times. We got into trouble of course but Rory said it was worth it. It *was* worth it. Rory can handle it better than Mr Trewyn and it's the most splendid feeling—'

'Then how did he manage to wreck it?' she asked succinctly.

'I . . . don't know. Exactly. I mean, I can't explain.' He began to walk towards the slipway. 'Shall we join Mark? Your mother will be down soon I expect.'

She caught him up and walked by his side without a word until they were outside the Sloop. He gabbled on about the weather being ideal for cricket and the Towans the ideal spot for it and the sea ideal for sailing across to the Towans. And eventually she put a hand on his arm and pulled him up.

'Who was driving the *Lancaster* that day?' she asked.

He looked across at the cottage but no-one was emerging from the front door.

'Rory,' he replied at last.

'That is what Jem Gurnard knows. And Etta knows. But not what Philip knows?'

Jan looked at her at last with a kind of despair.

'I had to tell Philip the truth. I had to tell someone. Besides, he was like you. He knew Rory wouldn't have wrecked the *Lancaster*.' He took her hand. 'I'm sorry, Ro. I should have insisted on taking the blame. But Rory wouldn't let me and you know what he's like when he gets a – a – how do you say? A bee in his hat.'

Rosemary knew only too well.

'But why? It doesn't make sense.'

'I do not do very well at school. The Trewyns were displeased with me. Rory – for him it is different. Everything is easy. He thinks they will not be so angry.'

'But they were.'

'Yes. Also he grieves for the boat. There is no scrap of it left, you see. Nothing. Not even a plank.'

Rosemary was horrified.

'Did it explode?'

'Ah no. The vortex at the mouth of the river, it was very bad. A storm came up and the boat was caught in it and turned round and round. We jumped clear. We had cork jackets and we managed to swim to the sandbank. The boat . . .' Jan made a very Continental gesture indicating that the boat had gone straight down.

Rosemary shivered. 'You could have both been drowned.'

'The Trewyns said this to Rory when they stopped being angry.

184

But it is no good. Some wrecked boats are beached many weeks later over at Lelant, and he keeps going there to search, but nothing turns up.' Jan's colour was normal but he looked worse than before. His pale skin did not tan and against Rosemary's honey colour he looked sickly. 'You see, Ro . . . it is my fault. And I am not happy for some time. That is why it is so good to see all of you again. I have tried to persuade Rory to come over with me, but he will not.'

Rosemary's shoulders slumped. 'No. No, of course not.' She turned towards the cottage. 'Come on then. You'll want to say hello to Mother.'

He followed a pace behind.

'I thought you would be . . . I don't know . . . angry. I thought you would despise me. I am a coward.'

It had not occurred to her that if Rory was a hero – or sort of hero – then Jan must be a sort of coward. She looked round at him. He was the same as ever, taller and his ears much bigger than they'd been last year; but just as pale and anxious and diffident. She had always known he would do anything for Rory. She had not known that Rory would do so much for Jan.

She pushed her sandy hand into the crook of his arm.

'Of course you're not a coward. You're an idiot. Just like Rory. Two idiots.' She grinned. 'Listen. If we're really going over to Hayle Towans for a picnic this afternoon, why don't we look for signs of the *Lancaster* that side?'

'I don't know. It's something to do with the current in the estuary. Wreckage is thrown up on the Lelant side. Always.'

'But if nothing's turned up there, surely it's worth looking somewhere else?' She ran up the steps ahead of him. 'If you could take something back for Rory tonight, wouldn't that cheer him up?' She turned and looked down on him. He had three pimples on his chin.

'Oh yes. Most certainly,' he agreed fervently.

'Then we'll look.' She went on staring at him. His eyes were very blue. For the first time she considered seriously whether she could marry him. She smiled with genuine affection. 'Mark has just drawn my portrait. It makes me look more of a skinned rabbit than usual. But would you like it?'

'Oh . . . yes!'

'Okey-doke. I'll get it in a minute.'

'I like your hair up, Ro. You look like a ballerina.'

'Do I?' She was delighted. She leaned down and pecked his cheek, taking care not to let her face touch the pimples. 'You are nice, Jan. You really are nice. All the boys at home are horrid. They shout or they laugh at you – they're really awful. You are a gentleman. Daddy always says that.'

'Does he?' Jan was bright red again. It gave ground cover for the spots. 'I value your father's good opinion most highly.'

It was a pity he talked like a pompous politician. But she knew he couldn't help it. After all, as Grandma Bridges said, he was foreign.

Madge was of the same opinion as Rosemary about the cricket match.

'It will make Mark feel so out of it, Clem,' she said when he came out of the butcher's with half a dozen pounds of sausages. 'And really darling, how many are you catering for?'

Well, there'll be your mother and her Angus. Mark and Jem Gurnard. Ro and Jan. Philip and Etta – and you and me, Madge. That's . . .' he counted under his breath. 'Ten altogether. And if there are an average of eight sausages in each pound that's forty-eight sausages, which means—'

'Clem—' Madge was laughing ' – you're not doing mathematical calculations for picnics now, are you?'

'It was how your father organised his cricket matches. I well remember that day at Porthkidney Sands – he delegated jobs like an army captain—'

'He *was* an army captain, darling. And he didn't have to bribe the butcher to let him have six pounds of sausages either! How did you do it?'

'Charm.' He smiled blandly at her and took her arm. 'As for Mark. He'll enjoy himself whatever we do. You know that.' He pressed the inside of her arm. 'I thought if we went over to Hayle in the *Forty-niner* it wouldn't be too much like history repeating itself. For your mother, I mean.'

She didn't look round at him.

'No. We never went there. Philip was often away in the *Forty-niner*. We used to go on the train because of Father's privilege tickets.'

'Yes. I remember.' He guided her down Court Cocking. 'Let's go into the milk bar and have a coffee.'

'Such extravagance!'

'We're well off now. We'll be able to afford the very best for Mark.'

'And Ro,' Madge said quickly.

'Swiss finishing school if she fancies it!'

Clem held one of the high stools steady while she perched on it. Further along the harbour Jan was leaning over the rail, talking to someone on the sand below.

Madge said, 'That's what Ro will be doing. Never mind finishing schools. She's only eleven and she's got that boy exactly and precisely under her thumb.'

'Jan?' Clem handed her a frothy, almost white coffee. 'He's in love with you, Madge, not with Ro.' He ignored her protests. 'Besides, that wouldn't do for Ro. She doesn't really care for people who allow themselves to be put under thumbs.'

'I don't know about that.' They both watched almost guiltily as Rosemary arrived and cast herself on Jan. When the two of them had walked past, Madge sipped her coffee and said in a low voice, 'She needs someone . . . special. It would be Mark – she adores Mark – except of course . . . it can't be Mark.'

Clem also sipped. 'She's over all that guilt business now, Madge. If that's what you're thinking of. I told her at the time it was my fault. And we've talked since, too. She realises that a five-year-old child cannot be held responsible for that kind of accident.'

'But—' Madge flicked him a sideways glance. 'It wasn't your fault, Clem. How can she accept that? She must realise you're just trying to comfort her.'

'I don't think so. I was in charge of both children. I simply didn't move fast enough.' He swigged the last of his coffee. 'Don't let's talk about it again, Madge, it does no good. Mark – Mark copes with it somehow. And at least I'm in a position to make sure he will never lack for anything material—'

She caught his arm. 'Clem, wait. It wasn't *your* fault. I've always thought you took it upon yourself for Ro's sake. Of course it wasn't your fault. As for Mark – perhaps he wouldn't have been the boy he is if it hadn't happened. How can we know? And once he's stopped growing and can have artificial legs, he'll

187

be able to do so much more – become independent of us—'

'Is that what you want?'

She hesitated fractionally. Then nodded fiercely. 'Of course. Of course I want Mark to be independent.'

Clem got off his stool and pecked her forehead. He had accepted a long time ago that without the unknown Ned Nicholls his wife might never have been able to express physical love. He had also accepted that without Mark she might well have left him. Mark anchored Madge to him.

He said gently, 'I know. It's just that he does bind us so closely as a family. The other night I listened to his prayers. He listed all of us, then said, "Have I forgotten anyone, God? If I have, can you put them in. And don't tell them I've forgotten in case they feel hurt!" '

She laughed, though he could tell she was moved nearly to tears. He looked at Jan Grodno and worked out his age: sixteen. He had been sixteen when he first noticed Madge as a separate feminine person, not just Neville's sister. And now Jan Grodno loved her. And Ned Nicholls had loved her. He wondered what he could do to make certain that even if Mark ever did become 'independent' she would not leave him.

He said heartily, 'It will be like turning the clock back this afternoon, Madge. It will be like that other time. When I was sixteen and you were twelve and everything was so simple and so sweet.'

They walked slowly back to the cottage and he wondered how he could have considered living without her. And it never occurred to him that he was just as trapped in this marriage as Madge was.

The engine had been fitted into the *Forty-niner* in 1939, just in time for Old Jem and Philip to take her over to Dunkirk the following year. Clem had overhauled it two years ago, but it still burnt too much oil, and they were glad to anchor it off the Towans and take it in turns to row ashore in the dinghy. The sands appeared completely empty and they felt they were staking a claim in an unexplored continent. There were summer bungalows, asbestos, corrugated iron, wood all built into the dunes, but the beach was so vast and undulating they knew they would probably see no-one else all day. They toiled up a dune and Clem looked down on a gigantic bowl of sand.

'This will do nicely,' he announced. 'It's a natural sun-trap.'
He cleared his throat self-consciously and deepened his voice.
'I claim this sand-saucer in the names of Nolla, McGovern,
Bridges, Grodno and Briscoe! May God bless all who make fires
in her!'

Rosemary whooped with joy and Philip looked up from
beneath his hat brim with one of his quizzical smiles. Etta said,
'My good Lord. You d'sound so zaccly like old Mr Bridges it fair
turns me 'eart.'

For a moment Marie looked startled, then she smiled and
moved down into the saucer and away from Angus McGovern.
He and Clem held Mark's sling-chair between them; they followed more sedately. Everyone else, even Philip and Etta, went
crazy, and either ran about their new territory or announced
plans in loud voices.

'We kin build the fireplace here – the smoke'll be took away
from us then—' so said Etta, arms akimbo across a black dress
which might well have been the same one she wore to the
Porthkidney cricket match nearly twenty years before.

Jem bawled, 'Plenty o' wood over yonder—' and Rosemary
shouted, 'Where? Is it a wreck? Could it be – ? Oh that's old
stuff. Driftwood.' Burns better, dunnit?' 'Yes, I know but—'

Jan called, 'Will this do for the cricket pitch, sir? Wickets here.
Crease here—'

Rosemary spoke to him in slightly lower tones. 'Don't bother
with all that. I thought we were going to look for some sign of the
Lancaster?'

Jem yelled, 'Bring Mark over 'ere, Mr Briscoe - quick -
quick - look, there's a kind o' slide in the sand! 'E'll be able to
shoot right down there into the bloody sea!'

Etta shrieked, 'Language! I'll 'ave your 'ide for that, young
Jem Gurnard! If your father coulda 'eard that—'

Philip said, 'I'll sit up top. We should need a lookout.' And
trudged off on his own.

But Jem was right. A funnel of smooth sand led into deep
water and Mark was a natural swimmer and stronger than
most. They watched him tumble down it, laughing hysterically
and closely followed by Jem and Rosemary. Madge smiled.
'You were right,' she said softly to Clem. 'He'll always enjoy
himself.'

The adults left the younger generation to it, and began to collect wood for the fire.

The cricket match lasted most of the afternoon and, like others before it, left plenty of opportunity for conviviality among the waiting batsmen. Mark sat in his chair, folding table across the arms, and did a series of lightning sketches. They were more graphic than anything produced by Madge's old box camera. Jim's expression was caught absolutely as he knocked off his own bails; Philip's fifth run revealed that his legs were as bowed as a cowboy's; the best catch of the match was the one 'held' by Etta's spread skirt; Clem, arm upraised, shouting 'Owzat?' was indeed beginning to look like old Mr Bridges, though young Mark knew his grandfather from only faded sepia photographs. And Madge, jumping for a ball, hair coming down her bare freckled back, looked no more than seventeen.

'May I have that one please Mark?' Jan asked hoarsely, looking over the boy's shoulder.

'If you want to.' Mark was too young to value his own work, he drew by instinct, his hand often discovering things his eye did not see. 'And Ro said you wanted a sketch of her too. I've got it here somewhere.'

Jan put the drawing of Madge carefully inside his shirt. 'Thank you, old man. Don't worry about the other if you can't find it.'

'No, here it is.' He frowned at it. Rosemary did look sort of lost; it must be the skinned-rabbit hair after all. He said, 'Jan. D'you think you might marry Ro one day?'

Jan laughed and shifted about in the sand. 'Perhaps. I should be honoured, of course. If she would have me.'

Mark's frown deepened. 'I don't know whether she would or not. But it might be a good thing.' He handed the drawing over. 'Anyway. She says you love Mother, not her.'

Jan laughed again, rather more loudly.

'I love all of you, Mark. As if you were my own family.' He shoved the second drawing into the other side of his shirt. 'I have to go now. I am in next.'

Rosemary stood by Philip's supine figure on the lip of the saucer. Philip had hoped to have forty winks before their side went in to

190

field and he opened one eye and surveyed her menacing length without pleasure.

'Well, miss?'

Rosemary was aggrieved. 'You only call me miss when I've done something naughty. And I've been an angel all day. Even Etta said that.'

'Etta called you an angel?'

'She didn't say I wasn't when Mummy called me it.'

He sighed and closed the eye. There came panting, thudding sounds from just by his ear. He opened it again and saw that Rosemary was doing handstands. It was very hot; not only that but if she misjudged the effort she put into each push, she might collapse on his body.

Philip groaned. 'Dun't keep doing that, my 'ansome. All the blood do rush to your face and you look fit to burst.'

Rosemary sat on her heels, breathing deeply.

'All right. Can I talk to you then? Ask you something?' He groaned again and she hurried on, 'Listen. Philip. Please listen. Jan's told me about the *Lancaster* and everything and I've been thinking and thinking. I mean the whirly pool at the mouth of the estuary isn't there today, is it? We came right across there and it was as calm as glass.'

'Certain times it isn't. When there's storms brewin' up or when ole Neptune pulls the plug out.'

'Pulls the plug out?'

'Nex' time you 'as a bath in that posh washroom you got at 'ome, jest look and watch when you pulls out the plug. You'll get a whirly pool all of you own then.'

'Oh *Philip*. I'm not a little girl! There's no plug and there's no Neptune.' She stood up and did a furious handstand. Philip watched her legs, wondering which way they would fall. When she righted herself, so did he.

'There's allus a vortex there when the weather is bad,' he said. 'An' if you want to know how it happened, I cain't tell you. The boat was pulled down and the boys jumped clear. That's all I know an' all I'm saying.'

She was aggrieved again.

'I don't know why you're cross with me. I wasn't going to ask you about that. I was going to ask you something quite different. Something you might know because you've been a

191

seaman all your life and you know the sea. That was all.'

He eyed her suspiciously. 'Well?'

'Well. It was just . . . where has the wreckage of the *Lancaster* gone? It hasn't come up along the Lelant side because Rory keeps looking for it. And we know there's no Neptune and no plug, so it can't have disappeared down that!' She looked at him sardonically. 'So where is it?'

He had to grin. With her hair scraped back from her face, she had a look of Etta as a young girl. Lonely. In need of an ally. And aggressively sarcastic to hide that need.

He said, 'Well now my maid, that's a question no-one can answer, not me, not no-one. Prob'ly 'tis all churned up down under the sea and won't never be seen again.'

She gave him one of her special smiles.

'Just supposing it had been washed-up this side of the river. Just *supposing*. Where d'you think it might land up?' She put a hand up to shield her eyes and gazed over the featureless dunes. 'It could be anywhere. But someone who knows about the currents and things – like you, Philip – might know where it would be . . . *if* it was.'

He said dryly, 'This sand keeps a lot of secrets, my maid. You could search for a year and not find a thing. Or you could put your hand under the surface and come up with anything. A precious di'mond. Old coins . . . all sorts are found on these 'ere beaches.'

'Yes, but that's all luck.' Rosemary took his arm and pulled him along the lip of sand until they could see the mouth of the Hayle river. 'That's where the whirly-pool was, Philip. Now can't you tell where a wreck might have landed? Allowing for . . . the wind . . . and the currents.'

'The sand moves too, you know. But I reckon if 'twere this side, and if there were anything to throw out, it might be worth looking t' other side o' that flat rock down there.'

'Come on then, Philip.'

'I reckon 'tis almost my turn to face the bowling.'

'No, not yet. Jan's next and he'll be ages.'

When the cricket match was over, they lit the fire and laid half the sausages on the old footscraper. It would not be dark for another two hours, yet the afternoon was well and truly over and they gathered round the pale flames with a sense of coming together for the night. Rosemary had lugged Philip off for yet another 'walk', but the others kept close in spite of the smoke – or perhaps because of it. Angus McGovern announced it kept off the gnats and as Etta said, it was better to be kippered than eaten alive.

Madge felt wonderfully at peace. The terrible guilt she had felt for so long was often eased by the day to day business of her happy life. And today had been very special. Clem had turned back the clock for her, made her young and innocent again. She remembered another cricket match and, for the first time, let herself recall its sequel: that awful attack her father had suffered which had put a stop to his sexual advances on her mother that night. She stared into the fire unsmilingly and knew that if it hadn't been for Ned, that experience might have made her frigid for always. Was it sufficient justification for everything that had happened since? She would probably have never understood Clem, and his brief affair with the Canadian girl might well have poisoned their difficult relationship in the end. But . . . Mark would not have been born; and therefore Mark would not have been injured.

She looked at him now. He was eating sausages with his fingers, grinning at Jem who was drunk with sunshine and cricket and food. The two of them had swum before tea and would swim again later. In the water they were equal; if anything Mark was faster. But out of the water . . . Madge looked across at Clem who was laying out the next batch of sausages. How much did he know? Did he feel trapped by Mark's complete dependence? She shivered suddenly.

Her mother said, 'Cold, darling? There's a spare cardigan in the bag.'

'No. Not really. Just one of those moments.'

Marie smiled. 'A goose walked over a grave, perhaps. Most of our memories are happy ones, Madge. We're very lucky.' She glanced at Mark. 'He might not have been the person he is if . . . it . . . hadn't happened.'

If anyone else had said it, Madge might have felt angry. But she smiled at her mother and nodded slightly.

Clem called, 'Anyone for more sausages?'

And Rosemary came running down the dune, a piece of planking clutched to her chest.

'Look what we've found! Jan – look!' She held out the plank. It looked like any piece of flotsam, except that the letters A.S.T.E in scoured black paint appeared on its length.

Everyone stared incomprehension.

Rosemary said impatiently, 'It's the nameboard from the *Lancaster*! Jan – surely you can see—'

Jan took the board and moved into the direct sunlight with it. He looked at the others.

'She is right! That's what it is – see how the S curls back under the A? Rory's father painted that himself!'

Madge said quickly, 'Never mind, Jan. Let's give it a Viking's farewell – throw it on the fire!'

But Jan was delighted. 'We have wondered so much – the *Lancaster* was like a friend. Rosemary, how can I thank you!'

'It was Philip really.'

Philip himself came lumbering down the sandhill. He pulled his hat on more firmly.

'She kep' on an' on. I gave 'er some idea where it might be an' she dug like a terrier!'

The mood of the party soared again. Rosemary and Philip were fed sausages as if they were returning heroes. The women made more tea. Jem and Mark began to pester for another swim.

'You must wait another half an hour at least!' all the adults said in unison.

'Stink-bombs!' Mark said loudly.

Jem screamed with laughter. Mark pulled his mouth down with one hand and pushed his nose up with the other and made retching noises. Jem collapsed on the sand.

'Really Mark. Behave yourself,' Madge admonished automatically. But Clem was laughing too and Jan and Rosemary were capering about like lunatics and her mother was looking at her with raised brows as if to say 'What did I tell you?'

The following day it was as if they had a hangover. None of them could face Etta's midday meal and she removed the untouched plates in thunderous silence. Philip was taking some visitors around the bay in the lugger and after an interval while they waited for the pudding which did not arrive. Etta's voice bawled up from the cellar – 'Just off to Bright Hour!'

'Thank goodness for that,' Rosemary said.

'Now dear,' said her grandmother.

'I meant as it's such a horrible day it will do Etta good to go to Bright Hour!'

Not even Mark smiled at that.

Madge said, 'I'll make some tea and you take a pill, Mark. Then you can lie down for an hour.' She saw rebellion on his face. 'Dad and I are going upstairs for a rest and Grandma and Ro said they were going for a walk.' She looked meaningly at her mother who nodded immediately.

Rosemary said, 'I'll bring you back some of that funny sea-weed you wanted, Mark.'

Clem groaned. Mark had a large collection of dried seaweed, but the drying process was smelly to say the least.

Mark grinned, accepting the inevitable with good grace as usual. Besides, the window seat was not like going to bed prop-erly. He had a framed view of the harbour and when Jem arrived back on the *Forty-niner*, he would be able to raise the sash and talk to him face to face. Philip had been as good as his word and the window seat had the cosiness of a ship's bunk with the free-dom of the out-of-doors. He took his pill, setlled back and lis-tened to his parents creaking about above him. The next instant, he was asleep.

Angus McGovern was sitting on his usual seat above Porthmeor. He too looked the worse for wear, especially as he was in yester-day's clothes – shirt and trousers and no jacket. He looked at Rosemary without enthusiasm.

'Shall we go back into the town, find a teashop and have some tea?' he suggested hopefully.

'We could do that. Or we could have a brisk walk to Five Points and back along the lane – that would warm us up.' Marie smiled at him. 'I think it would also help to blow away the cob-webs,' she added.

Rosemary said, 'May I play on the beach until you get back, Grandma? I want to look for some seaweed for Mark, remember. And I could help Jim Maddern with the donkeys. I'd much rather do that.'

'That's a good idea,' Angus said, remembering Rosemary's lagging steps on other walks. 'Then I'll buy you an icecream in the beach shop before you go home. How's that?'

Marie agreed with some reluctance. She had never quite got

over the shock of seeing her granddaughter cavorting with that boy three years ago. Rosemary had said it was Jan Grodno, and Marie had forgiven him because, being Polish, he knew no better; but Jan was fair and she was almost sure that the boy on the beach had been dark. It was all most mysterious.

'If it starts to rain, go straight home, darling,' she cautioned. And she said to Angus, 'She's only twelve, after all.'

'Quite.' Angus was of the school that thought children should be seen and heard as seldom as possible.

They walked single file along the cliff top. Angus went ahead, swinging his arms fiercely in an effort to get warm. When he turned round Marie was a hundred yards behind and breathing audibly. He would have waited but she gestured to him to go on, and he did so, accelerating his pace so that he could wait for her in the lee of Old Man's Head.

Marie watched him with an over-objective eye. Every year since they had re-met he had proposed to her, and every year she had asked for more time. It was so stupid; at the beginning of each holiday she was delighted to see him and quite certain she would accept him this year. By the end of the fortnight she had these silly doubts. What did it matter that he was looking so idiotic at this precise moment? So was she probably, panting along like an old woman. He was older than her but he had more energy than she'd ever had. Wasn't that what she needed? And when she was with him she never felt that awful alone-ness that had swept over her so forcibly that day on the Island long ago. She might feel slightly irritated occasionally, but she never felt alone.

She caught him up under the enormous hanging rock and leaned against it, getting her breath back. He swung his arms, smacking his shoulder blades rhythmically, then ran on the spot.

'I'd like to show you some of the mountain walks back home,' he said at last, blessedly ceasing his flailing. 'Cornwall is very beautiful, but Scotland leaves it standing.'

'I can imagine,' she murmured. 'Very hilly though?'

'Hilly?' He laughed boisterously. 'Mountainous, not hilly.' He looked at her seriously. 'If you liked it, Marie, I'd give up the Todmorden home and we could live there. We could live any-where, in fact. Another country—'

'I wouldn't want to be too far from Madge and Clem, Angus.'

'Bristol?' She knew he didn't like what he called the 'middle-lands'. Then he smiled and reached for her hand. 'Anywhere with you would be paradise.'

She was suddenly and inordinately touched. He had talked of companionship and shared interests, but never in a romantic vein. Perhaps he hadn't noticed her laboured breathing and pepper-and-salt hair. One thing, she didn't wear curlers. But what about her teeth? She had a vision of them magnified a thousand times in their tumbler of water.

He said, suddenly ardent, 'Marry me, my dear. Say you will. Now. We're not getting any younger. Let's have our last years together.'

'Oh Angus . . .' She was only just sixty, but he was probably ten years older than that. How would she feel if he died this winter and she'd kept him hanging on for so long?

He put his arms around her and made the ultimate declaration. 'I love you, Marie. I love you. Don't make me wait any longer.'

He smelled so wonderfully masculine. No man had held her like this since Alfred's death. Clem might give her a quick hug, but it was wonderful to be able to lay her head on a man's shirt and feel his warmth through it.

She murmured, 'It would be lovely to be married on Sundays.'

'You mean get married on a Sunday?'

'No. I meant . . . Sundays are such lonely days.'

He held her more tightly. 'They are. Oh they are, Marie. Every-one involved with their families.' He kissed the top of her head. 'Does that mean yes? Does that mean you will?'

She closed her eyes. After all, why not. There would be adjust-ments on both sides, but if he was willing to make them, so could she. She moved her head up and down.

'Oh Marie. I'm the happiest man on earth!'

He also sounded surprised. After a moment he loosened his hold enough to kiss her mouth. It was a chaste kiss, for which Marie was thankful. She knew from novel-reading that kissing these days was quite different from how it had been with Alfred. She wasn't quite sure how her teeth would fare with anything even slightly 'probing'.

Rosemary was so bored she thought she might actually start to cry. Her best friend Sheila had a favourite phrase, 'I could weep with sheer boredom,' and until now Rosemary had thought it just an affected remark. But even the smell of the donkeys' coats was depressing and as she set off under the lowering sky to search for the seaweed which reminded Mark of his therapist's alligator handbag, she could hardly drag one foot after the other. She deliberately recalled the complete euphoria of yesterday, but it had gone, and the discovery of the *Lancaster*'s nameboard now seemed pointless.

She left her sandals and socks above the tidemark and crossed the firm damp sand to where it became sloppy. The water was no colder than it had been yesterday, but it seemed to eat into her feet; the blister on her little toe shrieked for a moment then settled into an ache. She stood still, her knees knocking, and gazed out to sea. 'I hate you,' she whimpered and squeezed a single tear on to her cheek. 'I hate you,' she said again, then noticed a fishing boat off Bamaluz Point. 'Not *you*,' she said hastily in case it sank before her very eyes. 'I just hate . . .' But she did not quite know what it was she did hate and when she failed to eject another tear she turned petulantly to walk back to the seaweed rocks; and there, coming down the beach towards her, was Rory Trewyn.

Three years was a big hunk out of her life, and in that hunk Rory had changed. She knew that Jan was five feet nine inches tall and that Rory might be even taller, but Jan was so slight and pale that he never looked big. Rory looked big. His shoulders were wide and powerful and his head was leonine. His features were large too; eyes, nose, mouth and ears all declared themselves vividly. His hair was as black and copious as ever. She knew before he left the cliff path that this was Rory. And she knew too – he made it so obvious – that he had come to find her. Her boredom went as if it had never been; her feet tingled and she felt her face come alive. She forgot the terrible shame of their last meeting. Quite untypically, she went up the beach to meet him. They halted with a yard of no-man's-sand between them.

He said, 'Jan told me how you pestered Philip to find something that was left of the *Lancaster*. I want to thank you.'

His voice was so deep it was hoarse. She felt a flutter of panic. He was grown-up. He'd left her behind in the realms of childhood and gone on to something deep and mysterious. Yet he was the same age as Jan; and as rude as ever.

'I didn't pester. I asked his advice and . . .' She couldn't be bothered to go on justifying herself. Even though she tried to hold it back she felt a grin lifting her eyes to her hairline. She said directly, 'I'm glad you're pleased.'

'Who said I was pleased?' He tried to sound truculent but he was grinning too.

'No-one. I just knew you would be.' Then she remembered that this time she must be absolutely truthful. 'Jan said you were grieving for the boat. I would have too. Not to have anything of her at all must have been awful.'

There was a pause while he seemed to weigh up her new openness. Then he shrugged.

'It was. That's why I wanted to thank you.' He didn't move but it seemed the end of the exchange and she felt another twinge of panic in case he turned and left. Then he said flatly, 'You've changed.'

'Yes.' The smile disappeared and she swallowed painfully. 'I was only eight . . . then.'

'Yes. I know. I've thought of that often. Rosemary . . . Ro . . . I'm sorry. I shouldn't have . . . I can't think why . . . I was so damned angry—'

'You were trying to protect Jan,' she said swiftly in case he actually mentioned *seeing* her.

But he snorted a sort of laugh. 'I wish I could think that. It was only part of it.' His black eyes went past her and stared at the indeterminate horizon. 'I'd just found out about my adoption. I was angry. I took it out on you. And you were eight years old.' He made another snorting sound. 'I'm sorry. It's all I can say. I could have mucked up your whole damned life and that's all I can say. I'm sorry.'

She was grinning again. 'You didn't muck up my whole damned life.'

'I shouldn't swear in front of you either. You're still only twelve.'

'I'm quite old for my years. I know lots of worse words than damn.'

There was another pause. She wondered whether to prove her maturity by voicing some of the words she knew. The awful thing was she couldn't remember them just for the moment.

He said tentatively, 'What were you doing? I saw Etta outside the chapel and she thought you'd gone for a walk with your grandmother. I couldn't believe it when I saw you down here all by yourself.'

'Oh . . . Grandma and Mr McGovern were going all round Five

Points and it's so boring. I came down to look for some seaweed for Mark. He collects it.'

'Jan has told me about him. He sounds a great kid.'

'He is. You should see some of his drawings.'

'Jan had a couple. One of you. With your hair up. It made you look much older.'

'Oh. Really?' She felt herself blushing. 'Daddy calls it my skinned-rabbit look.'

'Yes. That too.'

She didn't mind his bluntness. He had been like that before; it was his form of honesty.

She said, 'D'you want to help me look for Mark's seaweed? It's flat and about a foot wide and it looks like crocodile skin.' She turned and moved again towards the rocks, talking over her shoulder. It gave him the opportunity to leave immediately without embarrassment. Or to join her.

He joined her.

'I know the stuff. It'll stink while it's drying.'

'Oh it does. All of it. Last year on the way home Daddy said the car was so full of fumes it was a wonder it didn't take off like a hot-air balloon!'

He laughed. It was another of his harsh sounds and somehow made her feel very protective towards him; as if he were the young one and she was the elder.

He had lost none of his expertise among the rocks. He kicked off ancient, lace-less plimsolls, and walked easily across the sharpest ridges and spongiest weed-beds without losing his footing once. Rosemary used her hands as well as feet, her hair hanging in rats' tails on either side of her face and making conversation very difficult.

His physical strength was no surprise; she recalled only too vividly how helpless she had been in his grip that awful day three years ago. When she tugged hopelessly at the trunk-like roots of a sea kale, he leapt over to remove it with one enormous heave.

She said, 'I thought you might have a knife.'

'I never carry one now.'

'What about . . . don't you cut for sand eels any more?'

'No. Couldn't stand seeing them . . . you know.'

'Oh.' That was a surprise. She herself had long learned to accept this culling of bait.

200

He shrugged and said frankly, 'You don't know how I felt afterwards. To tell you the truth, I didn't think I'd ever be able to face you again.'

She looked at him directly. And understood.

'That's how I feel about Mark sometimes. I can't bear it. And I have to.'

He frowned. 'It's not your fault the poor kid is crippled.'

'But it is. Surely you know? Everyone in St Ives must know. I feel they look at me – point me out—' She swallowed and turned to stare out to sea. The fishing boat was still there. At least that hadn't sunk.

'All I know is there was an accident. He fell from the railway bridge on to the line. At Carbis Bay.'

She breathed deeply. 'Yes. That's what happened.' She wouldn't say any more. She couldn't. Not even to her father had she spoken the actual words. 'But you see I lifted him out of his pram and propped him on the rail to look at the view. And then . . .' her voice shook. 'I dropped him.'

There was a moment of sheer astonishment at herself for speaking out at last, then a kind of enormous relief. Her body began to shake with her voice. She stammered, 'I didn't mean to. Daddy says it was his responsibility . . . but I *did* it! Whatever anyone says, I did it! And Mark – he's so good. I mean *good*! A good person. Not good like Etta. A bit like Philip. He's more like Philip than any one of us. He doesn't seem to *mind*! I mean even when the pain is bad he never grumbles – not really – not like me. And his physio woman – she's horrible, but I think he really loves her!'

She was weeping. Rory said uncomfortably, 'Look here, steady on old girl.'

She dashed the tears away, pushed her hair behind her ears and mumbled, 'Sorry.'

'I didn't mean that, you idiot. I meant, it's not much good going overboard with the sackcloth and ashes, is it? It would be different if you'd been mad jealous of the kid and tried to do him in. But it *was* an accident – just like everyone says. And Jan says you're good friends – better than we are. Maybe you wouldn't have been such friends if Mark was . . . well, you know . . .' His voice petered out. He was red from the effort of thinking everything out, couching it in terms he thought a twelve-year-old might grasp.

She took a deep breath, hiccoughing on a sob like a baby. She

said, 'So . . . if I . . . if I give my whole life – a bit like a nun – to
Mark – if I sort of implicate myself—'

'D'you mean dedicate?'

'Yes. Dedicate myself to my brother. Then it might be all
right?'

He said doubtfully, 'I suppose it might.'

'That would be the right thing to do, wouldn't it Rory?'

'Ummm, well, yes. I suppose it would.'

She took another shuddering breath and looked again at the
fishing boat. It was making towards Cape Cornwall and looked
as safe as anything could on that wide sea.

She smiled suddenly and turned to Rory confidingly.

'I've never told anyone that before,' she said. 'Sheila Patten
who is my best friend, is a Roman Catholic and she goes to
Confession and says she feels it's like putting down a bag of
potatoes.' She laughed. 'It is.'

Rory, not displeased with being cast in the role of father con-
fessor, held up the sea-kale like a banner.

'Onward Christian soldiers . . . looking for a croc!'

Rosemary couldn't stop laughing now she'd started. 'Oh I
must tell Mark that one – he'll love it!' she said as she scrambled
after Rory towards yet another bed of seaweed.

Marie Bridges undressed in the dark as usual and slid into bed
beside her granddaughter. One of the few snags about staying
with the Nollas was that she did not have her own room, yet had
to retire early so that Mark could be settled for the night down-
tairs. She supposed rather glumly that all that would change next
year when she was married to Angus. He stayed at one of the big
hotels at the top of the cliff and never retired before midnight.
That would suit her all right, but then she wondered what would
happen at night; would he expect anything of her? Her mouth
turned down with distaste. She might like the smell of his shirt
and the warmth of his arms around her, but that was as far as she
could possibly go. Well . . . she had told him that they would talk
about it properly before they made any announcements, and that
must be one of the things she must bring up.

She sighed deeply and put one arm behind her head in an effort
to ease the tension in her neck. Alfred had frequently massaged
her neck; would Angus do the same? Did she want him to? And

what about undressing in front of him? But of course that was as nothing compared with the enormous problem of her teeth. Surely she couldn't change her mind about marrying him for such a frivolous reason? But then, to her it was no frivolity; to her it was a matter of enormous seriousness. Every time she thought of her teeth the word 'enormous' cropped up. Strange, inside her mouth they fitted comfortably and she never thought about them. Outside, in the glass which she could just see on the bed-table, they looked . . . enormous. It must be the water acting as a magnifier. Although when she simply held them in order to scrub them, they still looked . . . enormous.

Her head was about to drop off. She removed the arm and flung it over the edge of the bed. Rosemary felt like a furnace, yet it hadn't been all that warm today so the child couldn't possibly have sunstroke. Of course yesterday she'd been out in it all day looking for that silly piece of wood. As if Marie's concern had communicated itself, the child rolled towards her and snuggled into her side.

'Gramma . . .' she slurred.I'm so h . . . appy.'

'Oh darling.' Marie accepted the small warm body as best she could and tears filled her eyes. She knew – quite sharply – how Rosemary felt; the ecstasy that had nothing to do with content, the breathless anticipation for the morrow, and when that came for the next minute – the next second. That was how it had been with Alfred. And that was how it could never be with Angus.

She was telling herself that she must be sensible and accept the companionship and security that Angus undoubtedly had to offer, when the palm of her outflung hand tickled. She brought it over to the other one which was imprisoned under Rosemary's head and managed to scratch it. Then she cast it wide again in an effort to release the mounting heat, and immediately it tickled.

She lay very still in the bed, suddenly rigid with concentration. This was how she had imagined it; she would reach out her hand and Alfred would find a way to touch it. Her palm was being caressed, perhaps . . . perhaps kissed! She clenched it suddenly to try to hold it in. But it had gone. The tears spilled over and down her face, warm and salty, and her body relaxed creakingly, telling her it was old. Even if Alfred were here, alive and vital, they were both past the years of ecstasy. She was a silly old woman, a silly toothless old woman, still expecting too much from life.

She turned her head on the pillow and her eyes, accustomed to the darkness now, saw that her teeth were grinning at her in their glass. She blinked the tears away and grinned back. After all, everything had its funny side. She remembered her wedding night when the gas in the boarding-house bedroom had unaccountably flared up, revealing her in her stays and Alfred in his combinations. She nearly chuckled aloud at the recollection, and as she closed her lips tightly over her gums, the ends of her fingers tingled sharply. She did not tense herself again. She left her fingers where they were, drooping almost to the floor, and felt the weight of her head now quite comfortable on the pillow.

After a while her fingers tingled no more, and she put her hand on the outside of the covers.

Rosemary murmured out of the blue, 'I do love you. So much.'

And Marie whispered, 'I know, darling. Oh I do know that.'

Then she slept.

CHAPTER TEN

1957

That year they arrived in St Ives as many pilgrims arrive in Lourdes. Mark's first pair of aluminium and wire legs had proved useless; worse than useless because his stumps had been damaged by his perseverance and had to be dressed daily. He had a lightweight folding chair with an electric motor, designed by his father, but he had to be carried up the steps into the parlour of the cottage, and he was well aware that at twelve years old *he* was no light weight.

And there was the death of Grandma Briscoe last winter, which felt like a corporate wound shared by all four of them. It had been so different when Grandma Bridges died. She had actually told them she was excited at the prospect, and half convinced them too. And, strangely, her death had been kind; no pain, simply an inability to eat anything. Even her thinness had been ethereal and at the end, when she had hallucinated, she had been smiling all the time. In the four years since, they had come down to St Ives half expecting to find her there.

Grandma Briscoe had become senile and vicious. One night she had appeared outside the house, hair streaming down her back, shouting that her son was a coward and a deserter just like his father. She called Madge a whore and Mark a bastard cripple, then collapsed and was taken to hospital where she kept muttering about 'the sins of the fathers'.

It was unbearably distressing. They did not know how to cope with it and felt guilty and inadequate. That same winter they took in a refugee couple from Hungary, but the language barrier and the anxiety about Mrs Briscoe made that a short-term business. Madge, who was in the house with the Dravas all the time, became ill herself and though Mrs Drava tried to look after her, she must have realised herself that it was hopeless. They applied for emigration papers to Australia and left Britain in June.

And then Mark's left stump had become infected, and he had run a fever . . .

Etta said, 'Let 'im stay with us till the winter really sets in. Jem Gurnard and 'is lad will 'elp fetch 'im in an' out.'

For a moment Mark's face lit up, then he shook his head. 'No, Etta. I'm almost better now. And I want to go back to school in September and let Fizzy work on me a bit more.' He grinned. 'One day I'm going to walk along the harbour with you and Philip. Walk.'

Meanwhile the weather was not good that year and he was glad of his new chair. It was a bumpy ride over the cobbles and he was bounced around like a dummy each day as he manoeuvred up Fore Street and around by the war memorial, but it kept him warm and gave him new pictures to draw. He was still a cheerful soul, but he knew he needed something good to happen this holiday. It couldn't be anything for himself because all he needed personally was St Ives and Ro and his parents and the Nollas. Perhaps he needed something to happen for Ro? He thought about it as he worked on a packed sketch of boats in the harbour.

Ro was going to training college in October to learn how to be a teacher. Of all things. Jan said he'd like her to have a proper profession all of her own, though it seemed he didn't want her actually to work. Jan was a strange chap really. All these years he'd maintained the illusion that he and Ro would get married one day and he talked about their future life together as if it were all settled. As if by talking about it often enough he could make it happen. Yet surely he could see – surely everyone could see – that Rory was the one for Ro?

Mark frowned at his sketch. He had obeyed water-colour rules and started with the foreground. But he saw now that he should have broken that rule and started way back where the jumble of beached boats became a forest of masts. Sometimes the foreground just didn't make any sense without the background.

Jan said solemnly, 'I am very sorry to hear you have been ill, Mrs Briscoe. Rosemary said nothing about it in her letters. I would have sent flowers.'

'Oh . . . really Jan . . . no need . . . weakness . . .'

Clem said firmly, 'Mrs Briscoe is anaemic, Jan. She needs plenty of rest and good food.'

'Then I could have sent some – some fresh fish perhaps,' Jan suggested doggedly. 'Or some grapes. We grow our own grapes at Mennion House.'

'Actually Mrs Trewyn did send me some wine which she had made from the grapes,' Madge said almost apologetically.

'You wrote to the Trewyns? They said nothing.'

'It *was* nothing! Please Jan, don't mention it again. I want to forget it this holiday.'

Clem said, 'Why don't you go and find Rosemary, old man?' He saw hesitation in the pale face and added, 'You could take her mack if you would. She's gone out without it of course, and it's going to tip down at any moment.'

They watched from the window as Jan departed reluctantly along the wharf, holding the mackintosh carefully over one arm.

Madge said, 'Darling, that was cunningly underhand of you. Is that how you get your way when you go to those awful conference things in America?'

'I don't get my way there, I'm afraid, my love.' He turned down his mouth, then adroitly swung her on to the window seat which was already made up as Mark's bed. 'There. Now lie still like a good girl while I make some tea. Be like Mark. Watch the world go by and relax.'

'What if Etta comes back and finds you in her kitchen?'

'I can wrap Etta around my little finger,' he assured her airily. He grinned wickedly. 'I never told you she came into my bedroom many years ago, sat on the edge of the bed, talked to me for a good half an hour, did I?'

'What did she *say*?'

'A-ah. I think she blessed me. Told me I'd be safe. Something. She was always on my side.'

He disappeared into the kitchen and Madge lay and listened to the sound of kettle and cups, letting her mind drift into an idle neutral. This was where Mark slept; or lay awake in pain. This at any rate was where he drew on the deep well of acceptance that he had inherited – from Ned? She had known so little of Ned except that schoolboy happiness. But there had been something else; she had sensed it. And he had wanted to be an artist. She'd hardly thought of Ned for years until that ghastly night when Mrs Briscoe called her a whore and Mark a . . . Madge turned her head, unable to think the word. Poor Ned, forgotten, somewhere in Holland. Yet living on in Mark. And poor Mark. Poor, poor Mark, with only half a life to lead. And Mother. Darling Mother, sending Angus McGovern away so calmly with the words, 'I'm still married, you see. Actually married. I've never been unmarried.' Poor Mother.

Clem came into the room carrying a tray which he put on the round table beneath the chandelier. He glanced at Madge as he poured tea.

'Do you do everything in life because you're sorry for someone, darling?' he said lightly, as he passed her a cup. 'No – I shouldn't have said that.' He tried to make her smile, bringing his face close to hers and putting on a woebegone expression. 'After all, if you hadn't been sorry for me we'd have never got to the altar!'

She still did not speak and the cup was unsafe in its saucer. He held her wrists lightly; her pulse fluttered beneath his thumb.

He said quietly, 'When I came back home, after the war, you were no longer sorry for me. That's what I remember. That is what makes me so thankful.'

'Thankful?'

'Yes, darling. Thankful. Just as I am thankful that Mark lived. Thankful that your mother's cancer was so . . . gentle. Thankful that my own mother did not live to remember her cruelty. Thankful that we still have each other.' He grinned. 'You never imagined Clem Briscoe could talk like that character in Ro's old book, did you?'

'Pollyanna.' She began to smile at last. 'No, I never imagined that.'

He looked at her for a long moment. Then he stood up and went back to the tray to pour his own tea.

Ro and Rory walked the length of Porthmeor beach from Island to Old Man's Head without saying more than half a dozen words each.

At eighteen, Rosemary had not quite fulfilled the beauty that had promised at eleven. Her hair was pale rather than blonde, her eyes too light a blue to be noticed, her lips invisible without makeup. Her mother's individual features were imperfect, yet their total became beautiful. Rosemary was the opposite; each individual feature was exquisite; together they added up to a kind of perfect plainness. Perhaps that fact explained her stubborn determination.

Rory Trewyn, at twenty-two, was so good-looking he literally made her heart ache. It ached now as she looked up at him; the pain across her chest made her breathing shallow. But her voice when she spoke was hard and firm.

'I've never heard anything quite so stupid in my whole life! Sacrifice yourself if you must. But not me. Certainly not me!'

He turned from her wearily.

'Look. We went into all this last year when you informed me you were seventeen and intended to marry me. I am not sacrificing anyone, Rosemary—'

Suddenly her iron calm disappeared. The pain across her ribcage intensified to bursting-point, and she caught hold of his arm and pulled him round.

'Don't look away from me, Rory Trewyn! Are you afraid to meet my eyes? It's not just what you said last year by any means! You've written to me since – have you forgotten? I've got it in writing, Rory! You want me to marry Jan. You've told me often enough that you love me – and heaven knows I love you – yet you can't marry me because it's always been understood—'

'That's it exactly, Ro!' His anger rose to meet hers. 'I can't marry you. Leave it at that. Please!'

Her nails dug into his arm.

'No. I won't leave it at that. I want to know why you can't marry me! Don't you love me any more? Why can't you be honest? Have you met someone else?'

'For Christ's sake, Ro! You're eighteen! You'll meet other men when you go to college – like I met other girls when I did my National Service! It doesn't mean much, but it's all part of – of—'

'Go on, say it. Growing up. You think I'm still a kid! I'm not! I haven't been a kid where you're concerned for years! And I know you love me – I *know*!'

She released his arm and threw herself on him. Her mouth found his more by accident than design, and she clung to him desperately. He tried to remain icily still, to repel her with sheer indifference, but after a while his hands went around her waist and he held her to him for an instant before thrusting her away.

'Dammit, Rosy. That's not fair!'

209

'Anything is fair to me.' She looked at him with her soul in her pale eyes. 'Rory. Please marry me. It's all I've wanted, all I've lived for. It's not just this—' she touched his lips with butterfly fingers' – it's more. We should be together, Rory. Always.'

He said miserably. 'I can't, Ro. Jan and me – we're more than brothers. And he has believed all these years that you would marry him.'

'Oh God. We're back to that. The sacrifice. Just like I said. You want me to sacrifice myself—'

'No. I just don't want to be the one to muck up Jan's life. You must do what you have to do, Ro. But I cannot be part of it. Don't you see?'

'No,' she replied flatly. 'No. No. No. I don't.'

'Darling. It's so straightforward. If I marry you – tomorrow. Or ten years' time. Jan will always know that it was me who came between him and his family – yes, he calls you his family!'

'And you called me darling. You do love me.'

'I don't know. I don't even know. There's something between us, but is it love? I don't know – and whatever you say now, you certainly don't.'

'I know I don't love Jan.'

'You get on well. He says you kiss him.'

'I let him kiss me sometimes. I want to find out what it's like. So that I can do it properly.'

She was speaking for effect, watching him for signs of jealousy. That kiss years ago on the steps of the cottage had been the first of many such greetings; Jan had made sure of that. But on the other hand she had never put a stop to it.

She was not prepared for his anger.

'You haven't changed, Ro, have you? Not really. You're still using Jan. Still leading him up the garden path.' He shrugged coldly. 'I can't stop you any more. I can't even shame you any more, can I?' He turned and began to walk back along the shoreline. 'He loves you. Perhaps you could learn to love him? Why don't you try?' His voice was tossed over his shoulder at her on a squall of wind and rain. She ran after him, hating herself yet unable to give him up.

'Rory, I didn't mean . . . I'm *fond* of Jan! You know that!'

He kept walking fast so that she had to skip along like a child to keep up with him.

'In that case it should be easy to grow fonder. Until one day he becomes the knight in shining armour you obviously need—'

'Oh shut *up*!'

She stopped but he went on walking. Down the steps from the Island appeared a figure clutching a mackintosh.

She said fiercely, 'Here he is now. I'm going to tell him. Right here and now. Tell him I don't love him, I love you.'

He slowed, waved to the distant Jan, turned and walked back to her.

'Do what you like, Ro. Say what you like. It's entirely up to you. I'm going away at the end of the month. I've got a job crewing on a charter boat. I meet up with it at Rhodes. That's a Greek island—'

'I know where Rhodes is. And you're running away.'

He shrugged. 'Call it what you like. I prefer to think I'm leaving a clear field.' He looked at her levelly. 'By all means send Jan packing, Ro. But is that what you really want? Honestly? Jan's doing very nicely in the family auctioneering business. You could end up living down here. Maybe with Mark. Think about it carefully. Before you burn your boats.'

She stared at him. 'You haven't got a very high opinion of me, have you, Rory?'

'If I didn't have a high opinion of you, I'd never want you to get hitched to Jan, would I?' He smiled almost affectionately. 'Ro . . . you can be devious to the point of dishonesty. But I have a very high opinion of you.'

She wanted to wake up and find it was a bad dream. His last words convinced her as all the previous arguments had not. Yet they were so close; like peas in a pod. Certainly, more often than not, Jan was with them, but she had assumed always that Rory knew just how the triangle was balanced.

Jan arrived at a gallop and came straight to her. He wrapped the mackintosh around her shoulders before pecking her cheek and putting a friendly arm around her shoulders.

'You two! I suppose you haven't noticed the rain?'

Rory ginnned across at him. 'This isn't rain, it's a sea fret.'

Both of them laughed at what was obviously an old joke, and Rosemary felt the balance of the triangle shift. She was way out on the apex and the two of them were either end of the solid base. She tried to look up to check on Jan's expression and caught what

211

seemed like a wink. For the first time it occurred to her that the two of them might be manipulating her instead of the other way round. Her father had teased her for so long about having both boys 'on a string', she had come to believe it. Supposing they were playing some macabre game with her?

She said, 'Isn't this exciting about Rory going off to Greece? I always told you he looked like a pirate, didn't I, Jan?'

She knew that would annoy Rory; it made the whole expedition sound melodramatic and pretentious.

Sure enough he said, 'It's a job, Ro. Just a job. I tried to join the family firm like Jan, and mucked that up. I didn't go to university after the Navy and that disappointed the parents. I've got to get out – I've got to get away from Cornwall before she smothers me!'

He was deadly serious. She said in a small voice, 'But you love Cornwall. You *are* Cornwall.'

'No. I'm not. I'm me. I'm going to prove it!'

Jan squeezed her shoulders. 'He has to go. He has to cut the strings, then come home and tie them up again himself! Is that not so?'

'That is so,' Rory mimicked solemnly.

Jan laughed but Ro persevered. 'You went away before. When you did your National Service in the Navy.'

Rory sighed theatrically. 'Tell her, Jan. I'm off. I'm going to catch the train to Lelant and walk from there. See you tonight, old man. Cheerio Ro-Ro.'

She did not reply but it didn't matter because he was off across the beach like a cheetah and wouldn't have heard her anyway. She felt terrible; almost as bad as she had before when he'd pulled off her knickers. This time she had stripped away her own pride; she had begged and pleaded and argued; and he had still gone away.

Jan said, 'National Service was the opposite to being free, Ro. If Rory thinks Cornwall is a prison, then National Service was a dungeon.'

'But you don't feel in prison, surely?'

'Ah. It is different for me. My father is dead, but I knew him. I know who I am and what I am. I choose to stay here.'

Ro watched Rory disappear over the Island, then turned to look at the sea. Everything was so grey. It was hard to find the horizon. She could almost hate it herself.

Jan said rallyingly, 'You will be coming over to Mennion House to supper one night as usual. You will see Rory then. He is not leaving for another week.'

'A week? I thought . . .' She swallowed fiercely. 'Surely if he tried to find his real parents, it would help?'

'Ah. We have talked about this. Often.' Jan gently pressed her towards the cliff path. 'Come on, we shall get our shoes wet, the tide is coming in.' He drew a breath. 'It is perhaps embarrassing to speak of this. You are still so young. But you will understand the delicacy—' he hurried on at her explosion of impatience '—Rory considers it likely that his father – Matthew Trewyn, you understand – was disloyal to his mother – Mary Trewyn. And therefore he is not able to enquire about the matter for fear of hurting his mother.'

Ro stopped to dig her arms into her mackintosh. The rain was coming in with the tide in swathes of heavy mist. She glanced at Jan's face. It was puce.

'You mean Matt Trewyn had an affair with someone else? So he is Rory's real father, but Mrs Trewyn is not his real mother?'

'It is conjecture of course. But it seems possible.'

Ro said thoughtfully, 'I heard Etta telling Mummy once that Mrs Trewyn had miscarriage after miscarriage. That was why they adopted Rory.'

'Gossip,' commented Jan distastefully. 'She is not a popular woman – we are aware of this. But gossip is unpleasant.'

'Yes. I suppose so.' She smiled ruefully. 'You have high standards, Jan. If you knew me properly I don't think you would want to marry me.'

'Aah. That is not so. I accept you as you are.'

For a moment she was tempted; terribly tempted to do what Rory expected of her and slide into an easy marriage with Jan Grodna. It would be second best certainly, but plenty of marriages were, and it would mean she could live down here always and surely see Rory sometimes.

She felt her smile die.

'Thank you, Jan. But you must know . . . I love Rory. It's Rory I want to marry. I'm sorry, Jan. I must be honest with you.'

The colour drained from his face.

'I think I knew already.' The Adam's apple moved in his throat. 'It makes no difference. I still love you. More than ever because you have said this so frankly.'

'But you must see, surely, that I cannot marry you?'

'I do not see that. No. I think, one day, you will accept me.'

'Oh Jan . . .' she literally clasped her hands and wrung them desperately. 'I'm so miserable.'

He went to her and held her tightly. It was what she needed. She pressed the side of her head against his shoulder and felt the thump of his heart.

He said in a low voice, 'I too am not happy. But together we will be happy. Have patience, little Ro. It will be all right.' He tried to lighten his voice. 'We do not need to run away to sea like poor Rory. We know who we are and we shall be happy here.'

He held her for a few moments more, then said bracingly, 'Come. We must go back and see the others. Your mother will be worried.'

She walked ahead of him up the path. He was always anxious to get back to her mother. If she did not marry him she would be depriving him of that too. She began to feel trapped, just as Rory must feel trapped.

She said, 'Have you and Rory had a miserable time of it with the Trewyns? You never talk about it much.'

'Miserable? Oh no. They have been good to us. Very good. Just. And kind.' He caught up with her and they walked past the well beneath the cemetery. 'And we have had each other since the war. I came to live with Rory in 1941 – we were both six. We do not remember much before that. We are closer than brothers.'

Ro hunched into her mackintosh. Whatever she did it seemed she would make Jan and Rory unhappy. Either by coming between them, or by depriving Jan of his 'family'. She wondered, fleetingly, whether she had the strength to sever herself from both boys and look for something else. But she did not let the thought linger.

Supper at Mennion House was stiffly formal as usual. For the last three years the Briscoes had been invited there in acknowledgement of the hospitality they extended to Rory and Jan. Matthew Trewyn had been a bomber pilot during the war so he and Clem got on fairly well by talking exclusively of aircraft. But Mary Trewyn barely hid her boredom, and the boys were never natural in front of her. It was Mark who had saved the evenings before with his insouciant chatter of films and books and fishing. After

214

the meal he had done lightning sketches of them all, unconsciously caricaturing them and making them laugh in spite of themselves. This evening he was strangely lethargic. Madge wondered whether he was incubating a cold. It was more likely that his stumps were hurting him. She bit her lip and tried not to think of the future.

Rory, on the other hand, was unusually bright, helping himself to his father's whisky with a liberal hand and cajoling his mother to play the piano once the meal was over.

'Don't be ridiculous, Rory,' she said dismissively. 'This is 1957. Shall we have the news on the television? Have you got a television, Mrs Briscoe?'

'Er – yes. Just a small one.'

'Really? It makes world events so vivid, don't you think? I was particularly interested in all that business on the Gold Coast. My family have a great deal of property out there.'

'Ghana, Mother.' Rory knelt down to plug in the television set. It was an enormous thing, with doors across the screen to make it look like a cocktail cabinet. 'And surely, now that it is Ghana, foreigners can't own great chunks of it?'

'We're not foreigners, Rory! And it will always be the Gold Coast to me.'

The screen began to come to life and showed a picture of Mr Anthony Eden tending a garden somewhere.

Matthew Trewyn looked at the whisky bottle with a frown, then back to the television without pleasure.

'Macmillan's all right, I suppose. But Eden shouldn't have let that Nasser force him to retire like he did. The whole Suez thing was a disgrace. We should have told the United Nations to clear off and let us sort out our own problems. We bought the Canal fair and square—'

'Ha!' Rory did not try to soften the scorn in the single guffaw.

'Kindly keep your left-wing views to yourself for this evening, Rory,' Matthew Trewyn requested. 'Jan, d'you want some of this? Apparently Rory's fair-shares-for-all policy doesn't extend to his family and friends.'

Madge said quickly, 'I understood Mr Eden had retired because of ill health?'

'And what caused the ill health, dear lady?'

'Well, I—'

'Mr Briscoe, I was hoping you would talk about your visit to Nevada.' Jan accepted a small glass of whisky and sat next to Madge on the sofa.

Clem smiled. 'You will have seen more than I did, actually. The television crews zoom in where angels fear to tread, quite literally.'

'State secret, eh?' Matthew Trewyn suggested.

'It's no secret that we are working on rocket launchers now.' Clem shrugged. 'Plans and designs are another thing, of course. We – I mean America – won't be putting anything up until next year at the earliest. It matters terribly to them that the Russians have beaten them in that particular race.'

'Not to you?'

'There's a long way to go. A lot of time.'

Rory said, 'Anyway, surely the most important race is the human one?'

'Very clever, old man.'

Mrs Trewyn said, 'If you're going to talk all through it, shall we have the volume slightly higher?'

Everyone fell silent.

Jan said, 'May I show Mrs Briscoe the vines, Uncle Matthew? She was saying you sent her a bottle of the wine when she was ill.'

'Certainly. Allow me to—' Matthew offered an arm and Jan's face fell.

Rory intervened. 'Actually Dad, I wanted to show off the new boat to Mr Briscoe. Any chance of me taking him up the river and back?'

'What – after last time? No fear! Come on Briscoe, I'll take you out myself. This weather is enough to give anyone claustrophobia. Anyone else for a spin?'

Rosemary stood up unobtrusively and moved alongside Rory. But Matthew Trewyn had other ideas.

'Not you, old man. Stay and keep young Mark company. Rosemary, did you ever hear about *Lancaster I*? I expect the whole of St Ives was buzzing about it. That great oaf back there took it into the middle of the vortex – you know, the whirlpool at the mouth of the estuary.'

'I do vaguely remember . . . it was six or seven years ago, surely?'

'Seems like yesterday to me.'

216

Rosemary fumed. Matthew had hold of her arm and her father was practically treading on her heels. She wanted to snap that it was Jan who had had the wheel that day, not Rory at all. But why should she care?

Madge said, 'What a lovely old-fashioned word. The vinery. And it's so pleasant too.'

Jan said, 'May I call you Madge?' He tried to laugh. 'After all, if I am to marry Ro one day, I suppose I ought to drop the Mrs Briscoe as soon as possible?'

Madge took a step towards the house and was confronted by a huge stone basin.

She said, 'I wish . . . you are both very young, Jan. And Rosemary could meet someone at college . . . I don't want you to be hurt.'

She turned from the basin and walked out of the vinery into the wild, rock-strewn garden high above the Hayle estuary. Below she could see Rosemary running down one of the sand burrows towards the Trewyns' jetty. She was reminded of a cricket match on the Towans years ago, when Mark had found a similar burrow and used it as a water chute.

Jan said from her shoulder, 'D'you remember that day we made a fire on the dunes? The day Rosemary found the old nameboard from the *Lancaster*?'

She smiled round at him. 'I was just thinking of that same day. How strange.'

'No. I have noticed often this thought-link between us. It is the reason I am so certain that one day Rosemary and I will marry. I have been part of the Briscoes for a long time.' He laughed, but she had no doubt of his seriousness.

She said quietly, 'That is hardly fair to the Trewyns, Jan. They took you in and treated you as their own. You see us each summer, that is all.'

'Ah . . . Madge . . . there, I have spoken it!' He laughed again and she wondered whether the whisky had gone to his head. 'Madge. My father left all that he had to me in Matthew Trewyn's trust. That is all. I stay now because of Rory. They are good people, we – we – rub along well enough – that is how Rory says it. We rub along very well. But you are my family. I wait for the summer. And then I am happy.'

217

Madge could have wept at his transparency. Nobody took him seriously. Certainly Ro did not. And Clem teased her about her Polish admirer; he actually teased her.

Instead she said in the most matter-of-fact voice she could muster, 'Then you are independent financially. I am glad.'

'Ah yes. Of course. And though my work is with the auctioneering company, actually I work with the partner. Jeremy Stockton. Yes, I am thoroughly independent, Madge. I can promise that.'

He had misunderstood her, but it did not matter. His mind, his heart, was so set on its course that whatever anyone said would make no difference. She stiffened her spine consciously and refused to feel sorry for him.

She walked along a footpath between samphire-cushioned rocks, to the side of the house.

'Now I can understand why the Trewyns built their house here.' She stopped, confronted with the enormous view of dunes and sea. 'It – it's magnificent.'

'Yes.' He was right behind her, cutting her off again from Clem and safety. 'Yes, but actually it was built here to be close to the rope factory down on the estuary. Also to bring up the brandy from the contraband boats.' He laughed again. 'The Trewyns do not want views. One needs special eyes to see views. Briscoe eyes.' He urged her on. 'See? Down there somewhere is where we played cricket that day. The weather was perfect. Do you remember?'

'Of course I remember.'

There was another narrow path to her right. It must lead back to the vinery and the house.

'I knew you would. I knew that day was special for you too.' Another laugh, then he suddenly started to unbutton his shirt. Madge was horrified and he saw that and quietened down to the seriousness of before. 'I carry this everywhere with me. Inside my shirt. Always.'

He withdrew some paper. It looked like old parchment, yellow and veined. Then she saw it had been varnished and the varnish had cracked.

'I photographed it and have it in my room. But this – the original – goes with me to my grave.' With enormous care he began to open it and smooth it down. 'I had one of Rosemary also, but that was lost. This one is safe.'

218

Madge stared at it with incomprehension. It seemed to be the figure of a woman leaping into the air.

'One of Mark's sketches?' She leaned closer.

'Yes.'

'It – is it – me?'

'Of course.'

She looked up at him, shocked out of her careful facade. And as he met her eyes the shock transmitted itself to him. He stared at her, horrified, realising at last that he was in love with her.

He said hoarsely, 'Madge – oh Madge – I thought – I didn't *know*—'

She straightened abruptly. She could not afford to be honest.

'I'd throw that old sketch away if I were you,' she said. 'It must be horribly scratchy inside your vest all the time. And not hygienic.' She was amazed to hear her voice emerge steadily and with a hard edge to it.

He said, 'Madge. My God. What shall I do?'

She folded the paper in new lines and it crackled ominously. 'I'll take it. I'll burn it. You'll . . . forget.'

She turned and took the path to her right. She thought she heard him sob, but she did not look back.

The weather improved slightly, and with it the pain in Mark's stumps. He would not permit anyone to lift him more than necessary, but the small stone slipway at the end of the wharf could take his chair right down on the sand and he made sure that he was there most afternoons at the end of the school day. Jem never kept him waiting. He lay prone now alongside the chair, incurious about Mark's painting. Other painters worked on the harbour beach and down Smeaton's Pier. They were taken for granted even when they sat in a wheelchair.

Jem said, 'The *Forty-niner* will come in with the tide and unload straightaway. No reason why we cain't take it out. Just for an hour. Christ, I kin manage that engine. Any kid could. You can take the wheel.'

'Don't be daft, Jem.' Mark was experimenting with a touch of bright cobalt in the green of the sea. He wasn't sure. He tried another, then another. It was too much, he'd have to whiten it out. That was the best of oils. He said, 'Your father would go crazy. As for Philip . . . it would be stealing, Jem.' This was how

219

Rory and Jan must have argued when Rory planned their escapade in the *Lancaster*. Mark half smiled. If he had legs he'd do it, stealing or no stealing. It must be terrific to take control; make things happen.

Jem, already giggling at the thought of his father going crazy, spluttered, 'Rowlocks!' Then rolled over in the sand, convulsed. He knelt up, spluttering and spitting.

Mark said laconically, 'Serves you right.'

'All I said was rowlocks. The things you put the oars in! That's all.'

Mark imitated the slippery Cornish accent.

'Oh ah.'

'I'd kill you if you could fight. D'you know that?'

'You'd try.'

'Everyone in the town's scared o' me.' Jem wiped the sand off his face with the back of his hand, grinning boastfully. Then he looked at his friend who came to St Ives once, or twice a year, yet seemed so much part of it. ' 'Cept you,' he added. 'An' you're only not scared cos you know I *cain't* fight someone'oo cain't even stand up!'

Mark took his eyes off his painting for a moment and grinned at Jem Gurnard who was his best friend.

'Rowlocks!' he said.

Jem fell backwards laughing, squirming like a sand eel, unable to keep still for longer than a few minutes. It made his friendship with an immobile companion even stranger.

When he recovered he went on with the conversation which was also unusual. Jem wasn't much for conversation.

'No, but 'ow could I? I'd 'ave to kneel down to get at you. Then you'd prob'ly run me down with your bloody wheelchair.'

'Good idea.' Mark went back to his painting, still thinking of fighting Jem. Thinking longingly of fighting Jem. He shrugged. 'You wouldn't fight me anyway. We've got nothing to fight about.'

'We 'ave now. I want to go out in the *Forty-niner*. Just you an' me. It'd be the greatest adventure. Like pirates.'

Mark moved the easel to one side, suddenly losing interest in how much cobalt there was in the greys, greens, whites and blacks of his static sea. That was the trouble with Jem. Every now and then he was just plain stupid. Perhaps he only really understood fighting.

He said with exaggerated patience, 'How could we? How could I?'

Jem looked at him wide-eyed. 'You come out in the *Forty-niner* often enough. What you on about?'

'Your father carries me. Or my father carries me.'

'I'm talking about when the tide is full. You can swim better 'n me. You can get yourself over the gunn'l. You got arms like a bloody gorilla!'

'Oh shut up, Jem!'

But after a moment of glaring futilely at each other, both boys started to laugh. They did not know why. Maybe it was Jem's description of Mark's arms. Maybe it was the thought of boarding the boat illegally and actually taking it to sea. Whatever it was, they couldn't stop. Jem rolled and squirmed and Mark put his head in his hands and made noises like a foghorn.

Madge, shaking an eiderdown from the bedroom window at the cottage, paused and watched. It was an unlikely friendship between Mark and Jem Gurnard. The town's tough boy. But it worked. She smiled as she listened to their cracked, animal sounds. Mark seemed better. And that awful business with Jan Grodna had come to a head and burst. He had gone with Rory to the Aegean; he would heal. Everything would be all right again.

Rosemary was not so sure. She wished now she hadn't been quite so honest with Jan. She had lost both of them; at least Jan would have kept a link with Rory. She felt a strange physical emptiness just between chest and abdomen as if she needed a nourishing hot drink or one of Etta's sandwiches. She tried both and neither helped. She was glad she was going to college. She'd show both of them that she didn't care. Meanwhile, as the weather got better, she spent all her time on the beach or in the sea. Mark was a comfort, his acceptance of the situation held none of the anxiety she sensed in her parents. He did not understand, of course, but he was a comfort nonetheless.

They were swimming together one afternoon. She had wheeled him along to the end of Smeaton's at high tide and tipped him out into the full harbour as if he were a sack of coal. It was his usual method of entry, though he could in fact manage an undignified crawl into the shallow water. The harbour suited him best: he could not manage the surf on Porthmeor beach, he needed deep water, still water.

There was usually an audience and today was no exception. It was an amazing sight, more spectacular than watching the local boys dive for pennies. At first, strangers were horrified to see the truncated body plummeting into the sea. And then they stood in admiration as Mark's powerful arms sliced him through the water without apparent effort. He and Rosemary used the deep clear water like dolphins, turning and twisting side by side then weaving around each other and breaking the surface gaspingly to laugh and take more air.

Rosemary said, 'I'm going to swim under the *Forty-niner* I'll bring you a barnacle!'

She upended herself, her legs kicked the air and she was gone. Mark followed.

The next time, he led the way and she clung to his waist. His arms shouldered the water; he turned and saw Rosemary's face slightly flattened by pressure, her hair out of its pony tail streaming behind her like his stumps. He would paint her like that. It was glorious . . . he felt drunk on sea water.

They came up on the other side of the old lugger and hung on to its mooring rope, getting their breath.

A female voice said, 'I heard what you were saying the other day. When are you going to do it?'

Mark and Rosemary looked round in surprise. One hand on the rudder of the boat, the other sluicing water from her face, was a girl; though apart from the voice there was very little to support that claim. Her hair was shorter than Mark's and rather bristly. Her voice had a twang that was deeper than the Cornish. From hair and accent they deduced she was American.

'Well?' She sounded impatient. 'I've got to get back. When are you going to do it?'

Rosemary said, 'Do what, for goodness' sake?'

The girl flicked dark blue eyes past Rosemary without much interest. She was talking to Mark.

'When are you going to pinch this boat? It is this one, isn't it? I've kept watch on it all week and you've not been near it. But I heard you say—'

Mark chipped in quickly, 'No-one is pinching any boat. You heard Jem Gurnard talking rot. That's all. He does it often.'

The girl looked disappointed. 'Oh. I thought . . . I might have guessed. This place is so *dull*.'

Rosemary swam a little way off and floated on her back.

Mark said, 'It's not dull at all. And I wish you'd keep quiet in front of my sister.'

'Oh, is she your sister?'

'Who did you think she was, my wife?'

The girl giggled. 'Well now, maybe she could be at that.' She stopped giggling and stared at Mark. 'I've watched you. You're paraplegic, aren't you?'

Mark opened his round eyes very wide. It was a medical term which most people had not heard.

He said, 'No. My legs were amputated above the knee.'

She blew her nose inelegantly into her hand.

'Same difference I reckon.'

'I don't. I'll be walking one day. Paraplegics can't.'

'Say. I like your spirit. How will you walk for Godssakes?'

He ignored the question. 'Are you a Yank?'

'Not by birth. I go over there a lot.'

'That might explain it. Though my father says most Americans have perfect manners.'

He turned casually on to his side and disappeared beneath the surface without a ripple. He surfaced next to Rosemary and they swam off together without a word.

The girl shouted coarsely, 'What's your name?' And when he didn't reply, 'It's all right, I'll find out from Jem whatever-you-said. Gurnard.'

When Jem arrived that afternoon after school, Mark swore him to secrecy, but he knew it wouldn't do any good. The girl had appeared to be the same age as they were, but she had the tough assurance of a forty-year-old woman.

When Jem said thoughtfully, 'D'you think she could be trusted to take the wheel?' Mark felt only deep resignation.

'What does it matter if you're never going to speak to her?' he asked.

'Oh. Ah. Yes. Anyway girls are no good on boats.'

Mark said unguardedly, 'She would be. She's tougher than most boys.' He looked grimly at Jem. 'If you try anything with the *Forty-niner*, I'll half-murder you, d'you hear me?'

'How d'you think you'd do that, big-bonce?'

'Don't bother to find out. That's Philip's boat. It's all he's got.'

'It's my father's boat as well.'

'And it's all *he's* got too. Don't you dam-well forget it.'

Jem said no more. It was so unusual to hear Mark Briscoe say even a small swear-word like damn, that he was shocked into silence.

But obviously not for long.

The day before they went back home, with Mark's stumps well and truly healed, Madge looking pink in spite of the absence of sun, and Rosemary already planning strategies for her time at training college, the awful Yank girl with the crewcut jumped off the harbour wall and landed with a thud next to Mark's easel.

'Hi Mark.' Her grin of triumph nearly split her face in half. She got up, rubbed at her knees and sobered enough to say in robot tones, 'Mark Briscoe. Born 1945. Home town Bristol, England. Ambition, to live here and paint pictures every day.' She grinned again, flumped down by his side and surveyed his current work. 'Not bad,' she decreed. 'Where is it?'

'Hayle Towans,' he told her reluctantly. 'From Mennion House.' He should have told her to clear off straightaway, but he was proud of this painting. It had a Turner look about it. A huge sky, a vast land and sea mass and two tiny, distant figures.

'Who are the people?'

'I don't know. Anyone you want them to be.'

'I like that.' She turned her toothpaste grin on him again. 'Make the viewer work. That's what my father says.'

She wanted him to ask if her father was an artist and he wasn't going to. He began to clean his brushes and put everything away.

She said at last in slightly less confident tones, 'I'm Zannah. That's short for Susannah. I could have been Susie or Anna, but no-one can remember those sort of names. You can't forget Zannah. Can you?'

He rolled the brushes in rag.

'Did Jem tell you my name?'

'Yes.' She glanced at his face. I had to buy him six icecreams.'

'*Six*?'

'Choc ices. When he felt sick he had to tell me so that I'd go away.'

Mark would have liked to laugh. After all, right at the beginning of the month, he'd wanted something to happen.

'Did you talk about the *Forty-niner*?'

224

'His plan? Yeh. Not much of a plan. Just sneak on board, hoist the skull and crossbones and chug around the bay.'

'You've got a better plan, I suppose?'

She said crisply, 'Do it at night. Leave a thank-you note and a couple of dollars for the gas used. Keep everyone guessing.'

'Look. It's dangerous. I'm not bothered about you or Jem. It's the lugger. Philip Nolla is part-owner of it. Has been for about a hundred years.'

'We'll be okay. But if not, the insurance will buy something better. It's an old tub.'

Mark was furious. 'It's his *life*! You don't know anything about the Nollas! Etta is almost a witch – a good witch – and Philip went to Dunkirk in the *Forty-niner* and before that when he was about our age he went out on a rocket line to help with a shipwreck . . . you don't understand!'

She was impressed. 'You're real mad, aren't you? Your hair looks redder than it did before. Listen, Jam Pilchard or whatever his name is, won't do it without you. So what's the ruckus about?'

She had the knack of killing his anger and making him want to laugh. Jam Pilchard. He must remember that one.

But he still said, 'Maybe not now. But if you work on him enough—'

'Listen, I can't *afford* any more choc ices! I'm broke now till Dad turns up again!'

He said grudgingly, 'You don't need choc ices.'

She was silent, wondering whether he'd given her a compliment or not. He followed up his advantage.

'I might have a go at it next summer.'

'Oh.' Sudden desolation was in her voice. 'I won't be here next summer. I have only every other summer with Dad.'

Amazingly, he felt his spirits descend a little too. But then he rallied.

'All right. Not next summer then. We'll make a pact. We won't let Jem do anything about it unless we're both here. How's that?'

'Great.' She looked at him with her purple eyes. 'I've seen you before. When I was just a kid. I wanted to look at your painting. And ask you what it was like to have to sit still each day. I didn't have the nerve.'

'Oh.' There was nothing else to say to that, except that he was amazed to hear she ever lacked nerve.

225

She waited for a long time, staring at him, then she shrugged. 'Okay. So it's a pact.' She stood up. She was already taller than Ro and her arms had visible muscles. She wore boys' shorts and her legs were scarred. She wasn't a bit pretty but he still wanted to draw her.

'Well. So long then. See you in two years. I'll be fourteen then.'

'Same here.'

She began to walk up the slipway and then stopped and looked down on his painting.

'Y'know, that's real good. It's a bit like a Turner. I like it.'

And she went.

CHAPTER ELEVEN

1959

By the time the Briscoes arrived at the beginning of July, the work planned and organised by Clem and Madge the year before was complete. The Nollas showed off the tiny bathroom with some trepidation. It took a big piece off the end of the passage and they couldn't imagine why anyone except Mark would need a water-closet, a basin and one of the new-fangled shower things, right next to the kitchen.

'We 'ad all this – the old bath were better 'n this drippin' thing – down in the fish cellar. You 'ad no need to spend all your 'ard-earned money on such nonsense!'

Clem knew Etta wasn't ungrateful. He nodded his satisfaction. 'Very nice. They've made a good job of it.' He put a hand on the shawled shoulder. 'Save the sand going all over the house. You know how that's always got on your nerves.'

'Be an excuse for that Rosemary not to swill her feet down at the tap! That's what you really mean!' But she grinned up at him toothlessly. He seemed to get better-looking each year in spite of his hair thinning. She knew he was an important man too and though that mattered little to her, she was still proud that he chose to bring his family to her home year after year.

His hand tighten on her shoulder.

'Of course. That was the whole reason for having it done.' He grinned right back at her. 'Was it much of a nuisance? The work-men and so forth?'

'Went out and left 'em to it!'

'Said a prayer for them at Bright Hour, I hope?'

'Said a prayer for you more like! Throwing your money about like a iunatic.'

He was suddenly serious. 'Look here Etta, there's enough of

that these days. If you ever need anything – *anything* you're to let me know. Understand?'

She was well into her seventies, and was surprised and delighted that she could still quiver beneath the touch of a man. Her grin widened, and in the darkness of the passage her gums gleamed.

That evening they walked around the town, rediscovering it yet again with their usual deep satisfaction. They went through the Warren, skirted Porthminster beach and took the footpath as far as the 'crooked bridge' across the railway line. Then they turned back and went in the other direction; over the Island where the laundry was no longer put out to bleach because the summer visitors so often stole it, along the road which overlooked the wilds of Porthmeor beach, and finally up the footpath to Old Man's Head.

Mark's chair bumped ahead of all of them most of the way, as if he were trying to show off his – or its – prowess. Madge knew that was not the reason. Mark's innate sensitivity was still there; she wondered whether he was deliberately and consciously pushing Clem and herself together. Certainly he must know that it would be Rosemary who tore after his chair and Clem and she who brought up the rear. She glanced sideways at Clem and he met her eyes with his usual quick smile.

'Penny for 'em!' he demanded rallyingly, as her father would have done.

'Oh . . . I was thinking of Mark,' she nodded to where he was bouncing up the stony track towards St Nicholas' chapel on the summit of the Island.

Clem looked away again. 'Yes,' he said. Then added, 'Of course.'

She said quickly, 'What were you thinking?'

He gave her another quick smile, this time a wry one.

'I was looking at the gulls. Wondering whether their use of the wind wouldn't be a better bet than our use of rocket fuel.' He shook his head. 'Trouble is, we tend to run out of wind after a few miles up.'

She had thought, when he started making his annual trips to the States, that it meant a new phase of their marriage. They were so close in many ways; a perfect partnership. Yet always there was Mark. She thought of Mark, and – perhaps as an escape from thinking about Mark – he thought about space travel.

He caught her hand and drew it through his arm.

'Sorry, darling. What were you thinking about Mark?'

'Oh, nothing much.' She wished she knew more about Clem's work. He couldn't talk about it, so much of it was 'top secret', but she wished she could make an intelligent comment now and then. 'Just his future. What it will be.'

'There will always be a place for him in the drawing office. You know that. His talent could be very commercial.'

'Yes,' she said doubtfully. 'It's not quite what he wants,' she knew what Mark wanted. It was to live away from them. And how could he do that? She thought with a terrible pang: if he stays with us, working for Clem, dependent on Clem at work and me at home, he will eventually dislike us both. And Clem too . . . Clem will always be burdened by a child that is not his . . .

'I know, Madge. But the training and the discipline will be good for him. And if he wants to work on his own stuff, we can make a studio for him . . . perhaps in the garden . . . How would that be?'

It was as if he were discussing a birthday treat for her. She swallowed.

'Yes. Marvellous. You're so good, Clem.'

'Rubbish.' But before he could add something like 'It's our son we're talking about' they rounded a rock and were face to face with a couple sitting on a bench enjoying the view. Madge's automatic smile of greeting widened almost immediately into recognition. It was Rose Care. And the man sitting by her could not possibly be one of her clients, either. It was old Martin Foster, the basket weaver who lived alone in Bunkers Hill since his wife died last year. How he managed no-one knew. He was blind and crippled with arthritis and as Etta said, 'We takes 'im meals, but there's more to life than eatin' and someone must be a-goin' in to 'elp 'im dress and undress and keep the 'ouse clean.'

Madge said, 'Rose. It's ages since . . .' She held out her hand. 'How are you?' She realised she hadn't seen Rose Care since that evening in the boathouse, the year of Mark's accident.

There was a moment of hesitation. Rose's dark eyes flicked from Madge to Clem and back again. She was still unsuitably dressed; her black two-piece and high heels would have been unremarked in Bristol's city streets; here they were merely an older version of her red dress. But she had lost her wanton look. Her hair was confined in a snood and she looked well-corseted.

She took Madge's hand. 'Well. This is a surprise.' Then, perhaps for Martin Foster's benefit, she said, 'Madge Bridges, isn't it? I remember you when you were just a little girl. We used to chat sometimes when I was minding Jim Maddern's donkeys.'

'Er . . . yes.' Madge swallowed again. 'It's Madge Briscoe now. This is my husband Clem.'

Rose said, 'Pleased to meet you I'm sure.' But Clem held out his hand, shook hers firmly and said. 'We've met before, Miss Care. You've forgotten. It was a long time ago, before Madge and I were married.'

'Really?' Rose tossed the information away from her with a flick of her gloved hand, and turned to her companion still seated on the bench. 'Do you know Mr Foster?'

The old man turned his dark glasses from one to the other and nodded solemnly. 'Any friend of Rose's . . . she's a good girl. A wonderful girl. I don't know what I'd have done without her this past year.'

Madge smiled again. Philip often said quietly in the face of Etta's condemnation, 'Rose Care 'as got 'er good side, and dun't you fergit it.' It was now obvious who was looking after Martin Foster.

Rose misinterpreted the smile.

'Nuthin' like that, Madge,' she said defensively. 'I'm just doin' a spot o' charring as you might say. Till Mr Foster can get 'imself fixed up with an 'ousekeeper.'

But Martin Foster had something to say about that. He stood up with difficulty and supported himself on Rose's shoulder. 'Charring indeed! Oh, she might do that as well. But she's more than that. She's made 'erself my eyes. And my ears too!' he chuckled. 'She's brought all the news o' the town inside my little place in Bunkers' Hill, so's I'm part o' the place agin!' He turned his glasses on Rose who was actually blushing. 'You might as well be the first to know. She's agreed to become my wife. An' I'm honoured. An' I'm proud.'

It was indeed touching. Madge felt tears in her throat and had to swallow yet again. There was a flurry of congratulatory chat. Clem pumped the old man's hand and told him how lucky he was.

Madge found her voice and said it was marvellous, and wondered suddenly how Jim Maddern would feel about it.

'It's good that you will be back in St Ives too, Rose,' she said. 'May I call on you in Bunkers Hill?'

Rose, unusually silent through all this, shrugged with assumed carelessness.

'Up to you. I warn you, if you do, you'll be the only one!'

'Now, Rose,' cautioned old Martin.

'You don't know them like I do m'dear,' she said, patting his arm fondly. 'Like I said to you before, they'll all say I'm after your money.'

'My pension dies with me,' he came back promptly. 'An' whether you marries me or no, I'm still goin' to leave you the 'ouse! So you might as well make me an happy man in the time we got left!'

Rose gave Madge a resigned look. 'You see 'ow it is? 'E's wore me down!' And she threw back her head and gave one of her full-throated laughs.

It was the end of the exchange. In any case Rosemary was hallooing from the chapel steps and they had to move on. Half-way up the steep incline, they stopped and watched as Rose led Martin Foster carefully trough the jumble of rocks.

Clem said with a kind of thankfulness – 'So. Rose Care is going to be all right. Respectability at last. Who would have bought it?'

Madge said carefully, 'I didn't realise you knew Rose. Was that when you and Neville were boys?'

'No.' His eyes went from Rose to the soaring gulls, and she knew he wasn't thinking of space travel this time. 'It was after Neville's death. The summer we got engaged. Neville asked me to find her . . . if anything happened to him. Find her and tell her that he had really loved her.'

Madge remembered Rose saying with pride that Neville had been the only man who had asked her to marry him. And now there was Martin Foster.

She took Clem's arm and followed his gaze.

'D'you know,' she said, 'I should think one day we shall run out of rocket fuel. Then we shall have to come back to using the wind.'

He looked at her blankly for a moment, then gave a shout of

sudden laughter. 'Madge, you're right! Trust you to see it so clearly! We've no choice really – absolutely no choice!'

They went on their way and began to discuss windmills.

The following Monday they made their obligatory visit to Mennion House. 'Let's get it over quickly,' Mark suggested. 'Then we can enjoy ourselves.' Rosemary said nothing but she never missed these visits, boring though they were. Rory and Jan sent postcards but never any real news.

It was easier to deal with the Trewyns in the absence of the two boys. Without them Matthew and Mary Trewyn led pleasant, rather aimless lives, going their separate ways each day and coming together as infrequently as possible. Matthew was beginning to run to fat and he had less hair than Clem. Rosemary watched him covertly and thought he probably was Rory's father and hoped Rory wouldn't go the same way.

He caught her eye and smiled gallantly.

'More sherry, Ro? You could do with some colour in your cheeks! How is the teaching going?'

'I don't begin actually until September.' She avoided her mother's eye and accepted more sherry. 'I'm applying for posts in South Gloucestershire. Something with a house.'

'Where you can do your own entertaining, eh?'

'Well . . .' She had made friends of both sexes at college but nobody special. She had found Jan's desertion harder to bear than Rory's. Rory had always been as unpredictable as quicksilver; Jan just the opposite. Sipping her sherry now and simpering at Matthew Trewyn, she thought suddenly that if Jan returned and asked her to marry him, she would accept immediately.

She glanced at Mark and he responded as he always did. 'Any news of Rory and Jan, Mr Trewyn? Last we heard they were taking tourists around the Everglades in one of those boats with a propeller above the stern.'

'They've been everywhere, those lads. Done all the things most men talk about doing.' He went to the windows and looked out over the estuary. 'Don't suppose we shall see them here again. Too small for them. Too dull.'

'That's where you're wrong, my darling,' Mary Trewyn spoke up unexpectedly, a touch of acid in the endearment. 'They're coming home this summer, as a matter of fact. There was a letter at the beginning of the week which I left on your desk for you to read. Obviously you have been too busy.'

'Underneath all the bills I suppose? You put it underneath all the bills!'

'No. The bills have arrived since.'

Rosemary said in a high voice, 'Both of them?' Mrs Trewyn stared at her blankly. Rosemary amplified, 'Are they both coming home? Together?'

Mrs Trewyn relaxed slightly. 'Ah. Yes. Yes, apparently they are flying back with a friend of theirs who has chartered a plane. They will be together. They've always been inseparable.'

Rosemary looked again, at Mark.

'Great,' he said enthusiastically. 'Shall we see them? I mean when are they arriving?'

'Oh yes, you'll see them. They're coming to see you actually. I can't quite remember what Rory said in the letter. Matthew, why don't you fetch it?'

He did so with the best grace he could muster and read it half aloud, half inaudibly, until Rosemary wanted to snatch it from him.

'Funny sort of place hm . . . hm . . . hm . . . like the creek at Lelant ten times over and twenty times hotter bla . . . bla . . . Thought we'd time our visit to coincide with Briscoes' holiday so that we can catch up on all the news.' He looked up triumphantly. 'There. So we can expect them some time during the next three and a half weeks.' He skimmed the rest of the letter and folded it back into its envelope. 'Doesn't say why. Nor for how long. They've got another charted job in the autumn. Mediterranean.' He exploded suddenly. 'Why the hell don't they come home and settle down!'

'You just said what a great time they're having seeing the world, darling,' Mary Trewyn reminded him.

'I didn't say that exactly, my dear. I said—'

'I really think it's time we were going.' Madge stood up. 'Etta is expecting us back for lunch. Perhaps you'd care to come over with the boys when they're here? We could dine at the Tregenna perhaps?'

Rosemary got behind Mark's chair and for once he did not slap her hands away. She wheeled him out to the car and fussed about getting him inside as if he'd never done it before. Her mind seethed with questions, the main one being: why were they coming home together? Did that make it entirely casual, or just the opposite? Was it a holiday, or were they going to tell her something? Like goodbye.

Mark said gently. 'I'm all right now, Sis.'

She stopped tucking his rug around his waist and gave him a rueful smile.

'It will be so nice to see the boys again,' she confessed while her parents made their farewells.

'Both of them?' he asked.

'Yes. Oh yes. I've missed Jan more than I would have believed possible.'

He smiled back at her. 'Then you're going to have a good holiday, Ro.' He glanced back at the Trewyns standing well apart on the driveway. 'I hope,' he added.

They arrived a week later, presenting themselves at the door of Zion Cottage with a diffidence they'd never shown before. Then they had belonged to the place and it belonged to them; now they had the same status as the summer visitors. And they looked alike too; Rory had fined down slightly and Jan had filled out. Incredibly there was a smattering of grey in Rory's hair which lightened it; Jan's paleness had weathered, his spots had gone, his formal manner had relaxed. But he would not look at Madge directly, not even when he shook her hand.

There was no room in the parlour so they trickled down on to the harbour beach, Rosemary still behind the wheel-chair. She had deliberately set herself to acquiring a tan over the past few days, and her eyes and hair were startling in comparison. It was the time of pale lip gloss too – fashion was conspiring in her favour. She looked stunning and did not even know it. In fact, faced with the two strangers who were Jan and Rory, she was terrified. She looked back and realised that at eighteen when she had ranted and raved and begged Rory to marry her, she had been just a child. She still felt a child; small and insignificant. She was educated just enough to know how little she knew, which was a good and humbling thing to recognise. Now, suddenly, it was demoralising as well as humbling. While she had been learning and theorising, these two men had been living and forging links between them which she knew nothing about, and might well never understand. It was as if they had fought a war together, side by side.

She trembled inside as she watched them. The quality in Rory which had always wanted to protect Jan, was more pronounced. When her father said, 'Well, what do you think of the States?' Rory started to answer, then stopped himself. 'Go on. Tell Mr Briscoe what we thought of the States, Jan,' he said, grinning encouragement. And Jan, who had always been able to carry a conversation with his oddly foreign formality, mumbled some reply incoherently, then said, 'I haven't stopped feeling homesick yet.'

Rosemary knelt by Mark's chair so that their shoulders were touching. She knew that Jan had gone with Rory after he had talked to her, and her heart bled for him. To be constantly homesick for two years was ghastly. And it was her fault. She wished she could call back those two years and tell him she would marry him.

Rory turned to her directly. 'And what about you, Ro? Have you had a good time at college?'

Her heart began pounding away double-time.

Mark guffawed. 'She's found out what the word work means, Rory! I can vouch for that!'

'You lived at home?' He seemed surprised. Had he imagined her living the life of Riley in hall or something?

'Yes.' She cleared her throat. 'Fishponds is so near home it's not worth living in.'

'And you're qualified now? Or is it a three-year thing?'

'No. Two-year.' She shrugged. 'I don't know about qualified. I've got my certificate.'

Mark said, 'With a distinction in her principal subject too!'

'Well done!' Rory looked sincerely pleased. 'Many congratulations, Ro. I didn't think you had it in you!'

She knew his opinion of her only too well and her face warmed ashamedly. But Mark's biceps tightened with annoyance at the implied slight.

'She did one of her practices at my place,' he said in the same boastful voice. 'You should have seen her with the little ones. Drama. They made a Chinese dragon from parachute silk – dyed it and all themselves – then draped it over the wheelchairs – wow!'

Ro said, 'Come off it, Mark!' She made a face and tried to laugh. 'It wasn't that much of a success! Remember little Chrissie Williams?'

Mark laughed too and Rory said, intrigued, 'Tell me. What happened?'

Mark explained. 'He got carried away – thought it was a real dragon. He's only six.'

Rory grinned. 'I should have thought that reaction was a measure of your success, Ro.'

'Not *my* success. Theirs. They were terrific.'

'Will you try to get a job there?'

'Fat chance. I've not got any experience yet. I did a practice there solely on the strength of being related to Mark.'

'Useful having someone on the inside,' agreed Mark. He looked from Rory to his sister. 'There's Jem. Mind if I push off and see how he is, Sis?' He didn't wait for a reply. His motor hummed and he reversed up the slipway and along the wharf to where Jem capered and swung his satchel over his head. Ro and Rory faced each other.

'Well,' Rory said. 'It's certainly nice to see all of you again.'

'Yes. I'm glad you . . .' Ro brushed at the skirt of her sun dress. 'And your father says you're off to the Mediterranean next?'

'Just me. At the end of this month.'

'Jan's staying?'

'Yes. One way or another. He's staying.'

'One way or another?'

Rory looked at her consideringly for a moment, then took a quick breath. 'Whether he gets a job back in the firm or not, he's still staying here. He hasn't enjoyed it.'

'I gathered . . . I'm sorry.'

'Yes.' He seemed to make up his mind about something and said quickly in a low voice, 'Ro, be kind to Jan. He's in a helluva state.'

'Of course.' She too made a decision. 'Rory, I'm sorry. I didn't mean to send him away before. I didn't mean to hurt him. I promise I won't do that again.'

He shook his head. 'It wasn't that.' He looked at her. His eyes were black and unfathomable. 'Oh God. Ro. I can't tell you.' He shook his head again as if to clear it. She knew quite suddenly that

236

there was still that indefinable something between them; and he knew it. Her heart jumped and started to pound again.

He said, 'It's the same situation, Ro. It's up to you. I can't make anyone else's decisions for them. Forgive me, my dear. It's up to you.'

It didn't make much sense then. She stored the disjointed words away for later examination and looked over at her father who had spoken her name.

'We were wondering about a picnic over at Porthmeor, Ro. How about it?'

She nodded with feigned enthusiasm. And noticed that Jan appeared to be studying her mother's ankles while Philip sat by her side as if guarding her.

Mark did not go with them. The sand was too soft for his chair at Porthmeor and the weather not warm enough for a long afternoon of sunbathing. He made a point of being by himself for part of each day, not only to achieve coveted independence, but to give his parents a break from the incessant burden of responsibility. Besides, he wanted to talk to Jem.

They sat in their usual place almost within the arm of Smeaton's Pier, on the old disused slipway. Behind them one of the many Porter boys was tarring the bottom of a rowing boat and the smell was heady and exciting. Mark watched Philip and Jem senior row themselves out to the *Forty-niner* in the dinghy, Philip standing in the stern with the single oar swaying rhythmically from side to side, while Jem leaned over to grab the mooring lines and pull them alongside. The way the rope emerged from the sea, dripping and weed-laden, was something Mark consciously tucked away for future paintings. There was a sound that went with it; a slapping, watery sound. But then, you couldn't paint sound.

Jem said sulkily, 'I don't see why you couldn't. I've watched you elbow your way down to the bloody sea often enough when you want to.'

For a moment Mark was confused, thinking of his picture. Then he tuned in to Jem's constant beef these days: the 'capture' of the *Forty-niner*.

'There's no point in it,' he said more curtly than usual. He remembered the plan the girl had; there was much more point to that, much more thrill. 'If it's a beating from your father you want, why don't you just go up and punch him on the nose?'

'Don't be crazy. I said it would be *worth* a beating! I don't *want* a bloody beating! It would be *worth* it!'

'What? Worth piling the *Forty-niner* on the rocks? Worth watching her go down? After all the work Philip and your old man have put into her?'

'She wouldn't go down – nor on the rocks. You an' me can manage 'er. We've done it often enough.'

'When Philip's around, yes.' He wished they weren't so near that tar. The smell made him want to jump out of his chair and run down to the sea and take the first boat he came to. Then he wondered how he knew what it would be like to run.

Jem said, 'You scared or summat?'

That was another thing; he'd like to do it just to show he could. Show himself. He couldn't master the tin legs, but you didn't need tin legs to swim out to a boat and haul yourself over the side.

He said shortly, 'Shut up Jem. Just shut up, will you?'

'Please yourself,' Jem came back sulkily.

They sat together in a lowering silence, staring at the *Forty-niner*, as she got under way, with a longing that verged on sheer lust. Mark wished he'd gone with the others now – this whole argument with Jem had gone past a joke and threatened their friendship. The silence was like a dead weight between them. It was pushing them apart and they couldn't seem to dispel it with the usual laughter or stupid remark. The old lugger swung out of sight around Smeaton's Pier and Jem turned on his elbow away from the wheelchair and sifted sand through his fingers. Mark wondered how he could get away. Jem knew everyone was round at Porthmeor so it was no good saying he had to get back to them at the cottage. If only he had some money on him he could offer Jem an icecream, or a Cydrax at the Shell Cafe. Then, like an answer to a prayer, a voice broke into the simmering silence.

'Hi!' They looked behind them. Standing on the harbour wall was a girl in white shorts and yellow sun top. Her caramel-coloured hair was done in the fashionable urchin cut, and her glorious tan was set off to perfection by a number of silver chains: one round each ankle and wrist and half a dozen around her neck. She wore a lot of lipstick and eyeshadow and her finger and toe nails were painted crimson lake. They stared up at her goggle-eyed.

'Hi,' she said again. 'Have you forgotten me? I'm Zannah.'

'Christ,' commented Jem solemnly. And again, 'Christ.'

She jumped off the wall as agilely as she had done two years before. Her chains jangled as she landed between the boys. Mark winced, never able to understand why people used their legs so profligately. He said 'Hello,' and felt very young.

Jem said, 'I thought you were the same age as me?'

'I am. Fourteen. Well, almost fourteen.' She spoke to Jem but she turned and smiled widely at Mark. 'Thanks for waiting,' she said.

'Thirteen?' Jem was incredulous. 'Bloody hell. You look about thirty.'

'Thanks,' she said again, beaming on him too. 'Girls are always older than boys. Our psychology tutor told us that.'

Mark swallowed. Ro had had a psychology tutor; they were definitely for grown-ups.

He said to Jem, 'She's half American, don't forget.'

'Oh. Ah.' Jem looked across the girl's fantastic legs and met Mark's eyes. He signalled a truce. 'Does that mean they wear out quicker?' He tried to control his appreciation of his own wit and failed; he sounded like bath water running down a drain.

The girl said calmly, 'I'd rather wear out quickly and feel I'm doing something with my life than live to be a hundred and eight because I'm mostly vegetable!'

Mark wondered if she was referring to his static existence and felt his neck grow hot beneath the collar of his shirt. Jem, insensitive though he rnight be, drew her fire.

'You calling me a vegetable? You got a cheek turning up here like a field of dandelions and calling me a vegetable!'

'I thought I heard you discussing the same problem you were discussing two whole years ago,' the girl said coolly, ignoring Jem's allusion to her yellow sun top. 'So I have to assume you still haven't made a plan.'

It was the way she spoke as much as the long words. It made both boys feel gauche and ridiculous. Neither of them could think of a thing to say in return; she had assumed quite correctly. However, Mark thought that she certainly wouldn't want to participate in any schoolboy adventure now; she was far beyond juvenile piracy.

She waited, looking first at one, then the other, with the

shadow of a smile on her long mouth. When nothing happened she sat forward in a businesslike way.

'Right,' she said. 'Okay. So we forget the joy-ride. And I think we'd better forget the thing I had in mind – we'd surely wreck the boat if we tried it at night.' But she sounded regretful. 'I think.' she paused until they both leaned forward in an attitude of attention. 'I think we wait for a storm. Or rather, just before a storm,' she added as Mark drew in his breath sharply; 'It'll be dead calm then for one thing. And for another it'll be almost dark. You'll take the wheel—' she put her crimson-lake fingers on the arm of the chair – 'and we'll start up the engine and cast off. It'll be up to you to take us around the harbour buoy and back in again. During which time you can run up your skull and crossbones if that's what turns you on. I shall write a note and leave some money like I said.' She looked serious. 'The trick is, to get away without being seen. We can chuck you over the side before we drop anchor and you can swim around Smeaton's Pier and into the steps by the rocks. No one will be around there if there's a storm brewing. We can hide the chair in the rocks and join you later.'

'Where do we go?' Jem asked.

'We split up. It's always best to split up when you're on the run. I'll go over to Porthminster. You can creep up the drain under the church. I've been through it just today. There's a man-hole in the market place.'

Both boys were still dumb. She grinned her triumph.

'You see the beauty of it, don't you? You two will disappear immediately. Anyway no-one will suspect Mark – and you'll be behind enemy lines, Jem. If anyone's seen it will be me. And by the time they run round to Porthminster, I shall be a girl again and no-one will recognise me.'

Mark said, 'You're going to disguise yourself as a boy.' His confidence returned. 'I saw that film too. Wasn't it Joan Fontaine?'

She flushed angrily. 'Never mind that.' She turned to Jem, sensing where her allegiance would come from. 'What do you think?'

He stared and swallowed. 'Well . . .' He was reluctant to admit that she had taken over so completely. 'What do you think, Mark?'

240

'Same as I've always thought. Why d'you want to pinch the *Forty-niner* in the first place?'

'Because it's sort of *your* boat, so it's not really stealing,' the girl explained with exaggerated patience. 'If we're caught, no-one's going to prosecute us are they?'

Jem said, 'There'll be one helluva row. I think I'd rather go to gaol.'

'Shit,' commented the girl. And both boys gawped at her. 'Listen,' she went on reasonably. 'Do you want to live. Or do you want to exist,' They weren't questions but she waited for answers. When none came, she said, 'Talk it over. See you soon.' And she got up as gracefllly as a deer and strolled off on her long slim legs with all the assurance of a woman of the world.

Jem said, 'Look at that. Did you hear what she said?'

'I've been here all the time, or hadn't you noticed?' Mark felt irritable still, but exhilarated as well.

'She said shit. She actually said—'

'I heard.'

'And that plan! She's got it worked out to the last detail! I don't fancy that drain.'

'Why not? It's big enough. And the cover is hinged.'

'All right for you. Get your backside up the steps and into the chair and who's going to suspect you?'

'No-one. Cos I'm not going to do it.'

'You'll do it. If she says so, you'll do it.'

Mark did not reply. He found he was imagining a dark, storm-filled sky and himself swimming for the steps just below Bamaluz Point. The escape would be the good part, the exciting part. The escape was what made the whole thing worthwhile.

Jem said, 'Reckon I'll go and have a look at that drain tonight. D'you think there's any rats up there?'

'Dunno.' When he was back in his chair he'd take time to look for the girl. She should have reached the sands by then. He must remember to put his father's binoculars in the pocket of the chair . . . He held on to his thoughts and looked down at Jem. 'We can't do it, Jem. Like she said, it's sort of our boat. We can't do that – risk the boat for a lark.'

'It's no risk. You're at the bloody wheel. You won't *take* any risks! Once round the buoys and that'll be it!'

'I'm not sure . . . I've always had Philip standing next to me.

241

Besides if you don't moor her properly and there's a storm coming up—'

'You heard what she said! D'you want to *live*?'

'Yes. And I want to be able to look Philip in the eye too.'

Jem stood up.

'Listen mate. I'm going to do it. She an' me – we can manage it together if you won't come. In fac'—' he paused as if already regretting what he was about to say. 'In fac' we'll prob'ly manage it a damned sight better without you!' He looked away quickly from Mark's face. 'It'd be better if you came o' course – so's you know I ain't lying when I tell you all about it. But . . . you'd better agree to it tomorrow when she turns up. You'd just better.'

He turned and made off before Mark could reply; not that Mark could think of a thing to say. Jem had said it all: they would be better off without him.

For a long moment he wallowed in self-pity. Then he thought of how the girl had smiled at him and said, 'Thanks for waiting.' That was their secret; the pact they'd made two years before when they'd been kids, that was theirs. Mark grinned. He didn't know why he grinned, but he couldn't stop himself.

Rosemary was happier than she'd been in her life before. She was in the place she loved best in the world, and with the people she loved most. As she swam in the surf that afternoon, she looked from Madge to Clem, from Rory to Jan, and loved them all equally. Her long hair darkened in the water and streamed out behind her like seaweed. Back on the beach outside the tent, Etta laid out the picnic, the last representative of her grandmothers' generation. And then the *Forty-niner* chugged around the Island and pulled in as close to the swell as it could, so that they could all swim out to it and be pulled up on to its old-fashioned poop to sunbathe and dive in safety under Philip's cautious eye.

It was a glorious time. In spite of Rory's veiled hints, Jan made no special attempt to be alone with her; she had to make no choices, no decisions. But by the end of the day she had in fact made a big decision. She would no longer try to force events and she would let Rory go without any regrets. And if Jan still wanted to marry her, then so be it. He knew how she felt and if he was willing to accept the fact that she loved Rory first and him second, then it must be all right.

That night in the bed she had so often shared with one of her grandmothers, she thought about it more deeply and discovered something strange. Even if Rory begged her to marry him now, she could not. The realisation was so forceful that she sat bolt upright in bed to consider it. It was true. Rory was strong and self-sufficient; he could go away and make another life for himself somehow. But Jan . . . Jan was different. She understood now why Rory had been unable to claim her two years ago; Jan was intensely vulnerable. She lay back down slowly. It would make Rory happy if she married Jan; and it would make Jan happy too; and . . . yes, it would make her happy! She smiled at the dark ceiling and wondered why on earth she had been so against it all the time.

Having come to such a selfless conclusion, it was deflating when Jan continued to enjoy her company only when Rory and the others were around. He made no attempt to seek her out exclusively, and when Rory deliberately dropped out of a three-some, he said quickly, 'Let's look for Mark shall we, Ro? I haven't had a chance to really *talk* to Mark. He's so different now. Serious. Adult.'

'He's only just fourteen.' Rosemary was reluctant to lose her small brother and had not yet got used to the idea of him as a young man. So long as he was a child his terrible disability could be dealt with by a kind of indulgence; he could still be hugged and pampered with treats; his artistic talent was enough for him; his electric chair was almost a toy. As he grew older he would feel he had to try again with those rotten tin legs; and unless you were some kind of genius how could you earn a living with charcoal and paint?

They walked along to his usual place by Smeaton's Pier, but he wasn't there. Rosemary began to realise that Jan needed to find him so that he would not have to talk to her. The knowledge made her feel peculiar: rejected all over again.

She said, 'He might have gone to Lanham's for some new brushes. He said something about it at breakfast.'

They went on down Fore Street. People spoke to them, asked Jan how he was. A wizened seaman who knew them because of Philip, said they made 'A pretty enough couple', and Jan laughed. 'That is good for you, Rosemary, but not for me, I think.' Rosemary flushed and hurried on. Humiliation followed rejection. She thought of all the girls the two boys must have met on their two-year old adventure. She muttered aloud, 'Oh God,' and Jan said, 'What did you say, Ro?'

'Nothing.'

They found Mark in the market place just by the war memorial. He seemed to be studying the ground.

'What on earth are you doing?' Rosemary's voice was sharper than she had intended. Drooping over the arm of his chair like that, he looked utterly dejected, not like the contented boy he had always been. She tried not to imagine what adulthood must look like from his level.

He was startled out of a deep reverie.

'I . . . nothing, Ro. Absolutely nothing.' He switched on his chair and glided away from a large manhole cover. 'Where are you two going? May I join you?'

'Let's find a cafe without a step and have some coffee,' Jan said practically. They went on up the High Street like a royal procession and were welcomed into the Snuggerie in Gabriel Street with easy familiarity. There weren't that many eating places in St Ives which could admit a wheel-chair. Mark felt in the breast pocket of his jacket, extracted three separate shillings and lined them up on the polished oak table.

'I'm paying,' he said expansively. 'Baps and cream all round.'

Jan grinned, relaxed now. 'You have come into money?'

'I bet Jem something. And I won.' Mark shoved forward one shilling. 'My stake.' He touched another coin, 'My winnings. And—' he picked up the last coin – 'my meagre earnings.'

'Earnings?'

'You haven't heard? A man came up to me on the harbour when I was painting. Offered me this bob for doing a sketch of his kid.'

'That is good, Mark.' Jan smiled congratulations. 'But you must let me pay for this treat. Rory and I are rich after Florida, you know.'

Mark ignored this. 'The joke of it was,' he went on, 'The bloke would never have asked me to do it if I'd been standing up at an easel. Or if I'd been ten years older. So let's make the most of it while we've got it.'

Jan looked at Rosemary and she in turn looked at Mark. Bitterness was foreign to him, but there was no mistaking his tone.

She said softly, 'If you really thought he was giving money to a cripple, why did you take it?'

'Why not?'

She realised that since they had met him in the market place his whole attitude had been slightly aggressive.

She said, 'You've had a row with Jem.'

Jan, unused to their mental shorthand, was completely bewildered. He caught the eye of the waitress and ordered coffee and baps while an incipient quarrel brewed at his elbow.

'None of your business, Sis.'

'Yes it is. You're my brother.'

'What's that got to do with it?'

'And I'm five years older than you.'

'Also I'm a cripple. That's what you really mean, isn't it?' The word 'cripple' had stuck in his throat; he knew she had used it to snap him out of any self-pity, but it lay between them like something obscene.

Jan made room on the table. 'Here we are. Baps, cream, jam . . .' the bill fluttered across the polished surface and Mark snatched it up. 'And coffee.' Jan looked helplessly at the two of them. Mark was red-faced with anger; it was a rare sight. Jan wondered what could have happened. Something obviously had.

Rosemary said pacifically, 'You know I didn't mean that. What I mean is – I'm concerned about you—'

He didn't hear. 'I don't interfere in your life, do I? So why the hell do you imagine you can interfere in mine? Just because you can walk and run doesn't mean you're much good at *people*, Sis! Does it? You've only got to look at Jan to see how much good you are at *people*!'

The whole silly argument was nonsense, but Rosemary still did not relish public examples of her ineptness with relationships.

She said, 'Shut up Mark. Just shut up, will you?'

'You see? You don't like it! You're dithering away between Jan and Rory – can't see the wood for the trees – and all the time you've got no choice! Jan's been in love with Mother since he was my age – he doesn't want to marry you! And Rory—'

Rosemary stood up with a small gasping scream.

'Mark! I said shut up! How dare you – how *dare* you—'

Jan too got to his feet.

245

'Rosemary, that is not true. There was an attraction – school-boy attraction – but in the last two years—'

'I'm going. No, I don't want you to come with me, Jan. And I certainly don't want you, Mark! Stay here and eat the baps! And I hope they choke you!'

She left hurriedly. Her chair collapsed on its side as she pushed past; by the time Jan had righted it and shaken his head at the waitress then smiled apologies at the other customers, she had disappeared. He sat down again.

'Mark. You should not have spoken those words. They are words to be thought, never spoken.' He looked seriously at the round young face opposite him. Mark was as white now as he had been red before; even his wiry auburn hair looked flattened.

He said in a small voice, 'I'm sorry, Jan.'

Jan did not reply. After a while he poured coffee, and by the time he had stirred sugar into his, the normal hum of conversation offered a spurious privacy.

He said heavily, 'I have wanted to die. Often in the last two years . . . I have tried to die. Rory would not permit it.'

Mark looked sick. 'I didn't know. Didn't realise . . .'

'Rory thinks it will be all right if I come back and marry Ro. I will be . . . settled. Ro and your mother will be able to give me new life. You must know that I have always loved your mother – even as a small boy. She gives life – never takes it away. And Ro is charming and happy. We have been close – we had *rapport* since we were small children.'

Mark ventured a question. 'Do you love Ro?'

'Ah Love. It is more than love. It is a need. Perhaps one day you will understand, Mark.'

'And Ro? How does Ro feel about you, Jan?'

To Mark the whole thing was so obvious: Ro loved Rory and Rory was trying to force her on to Jan.

'That I will discover,' Jan said in his ponderous way. 'Rory has a plan. It is like a child's game. Harmless and innocent. But it will help Ro to make up her mind.' He smiled bleakly. 'It will help me also. I am to be the champion knight, claiming the hand of the fair maiden!'

Mark leaned across the table until his head almost touched Jan's.

'For Pete's sake. What has Rory cooked up now?'

'Oh, it is nothing. Nonsense. Ro will climb to Old Man's Head and the one who reaches her first . . . Rory has told me the proper way to climb so therefore I shall be first there. You see, Mark, Rory is very fond of your sister. He wishes her to marry someone who will care for her properly. We shall marry and we shall be happy.'

Mark drew back his head and surveyed Jan incredulously.

'I think Rory is a shitbag!' he said, as much to shock Jan out of his fatalistic attitude as anything. It was a word beloved by Zannah and it certainly had impact. Jan looked up, startled. Mark said, 'He doesn't want to marry Rosemary himself, but he doesn't want anyone else to have her except you. Christ. It's as if he's trying to put her in cold storage!'

Jan stared in horror. 'It is not like that at all, Mark. You do not understand. Rory wants only what is best for everyone. When I said he would not permit me to die, I should have told you that once he saved my life. The Everglades are the natural home of the alligator. We had taken a party off the beaten track and—'

Mark said, 'I don't want to hear about how marvellous Rory is. He knows it – you've told him often enough, I expect.' Mark visibly simmered. 'The thing is, Ro isn't going to get much out of his great plan, is she? And neither is poor old Mum.' He leaned forward again. 'I reckon the best thing you two can do is clear off to your alligator-infested swamp again! Play at being pirates or whatever Rory thinks he is! Leave us to get on with real life!'

Mark switched on his motor and backed out of the Snuggerie with much bumping and manoeuvring. Jan made no move to help him. Alter Mark had gone and the cafe had once more settled down, he picked up the bill and the three separate shillings and signalled to the waitress.

'Oh dear. Was something the matter with the baps, sir?' she asked.

'No. We were not hungry after all,' Jan replied.

The waitress gathered the things on to a tray and said sympathetically, 'Don't worry sir, it's the weather. There's a real big storm brewing up. Gets everyone on edge, doesn't it?'

'That must be it.' Jan felt a certain relief at her mundane explanation for the unprecedented furore of the morning. 'Yes, of course. That must be it.' He stood up, anxious now to get back to Mennion House and find Rory. The sooner they left the better.

Mark was right, it was the only thing to do; if they stayed they were going to mess up a lot of lives.

Ro did not put in an appearance for Etta's midday offering of boiled mutton and dumplings.

Etta said, 'What can I do with her dinner? I cain't a-bear waste!'

'Warm it up for her tea?' Mark felt guilty now; the emotional mess he had uncovered boded ill for Rosemary.

'No-one on God's earth kin warm up dumplin's!' Etta snapped. 'They'd end up bullets, they would.'

Clem said, 'She'll be glad of them even so, Etta. There's going to be a storm and a half this afternoon and if she's gone for a walk she'll come in soaking wet, you see.'

Thunderclouds were piling up on the edge of the sea, sure enough, and the light was poor. Mark glanced nervously through the window.

'Aye.' Etta was mollified as always by Clem. 'I'll leave 'n in the saucepan then and you can warm it all up when you've a mind to. It's Bright Hour's afternoon and after that I'm taking tea with the minister and 'is wife.'

Clem waggled his eyebrows and he and Madge laughed while Etta pulled her mouth in. Mark concentrated on spooning up all his swimming gravy.

Philip put his head round the door.

'Jem and me's going to get the *Forty-niner* in the lee of Wheal Dream,' he announced. 'She's too far out with this storm a-comin' up and there's not enough water in the harbour to float her in there.'

'Wheal Dream?' Mark lifted his head. 'You won't be able to see her from there.' Wheal Dream was behind Smeaton's Pier, within easy reach of the steps in the rocks.

'They'll see 'er from the seaman's mission 'all,' Philip grinned reassuringly. 'Any'ow, the way we shall anchor 'er she wun't pull herself away, never fear.' He peered through the window. 'Flat calm now too. Will be for a coupla hours.'

Mark looked at his plate and wondered whether Jem and Zannah were capable of anchoring her solidly again when they got back. He had a momentary vision of the *Forty-niner* smashing herself up on the rocks around the Island. Not that Jem would do it. If he didn't have the nerve to enter the drain this morning, he wouldn't risk being caught by his father.

When they were alone Madge said worriedly, 'I wonder just where Ro has gone? She never misses popping in at midday even if she can't manage to eat anything. Did she put her watch on this morning?'

Mark tried to visualise Rosemary's wrist but all he could see was a mass of silver chains.

'I don't think she did,' he said. 'But don't worry, Ma. We had coffee and baps in the Snuggerie not long ago. Probably just the thought of dumplings was too much for her.'

'Did she have baps?' Madge looked surprised and pleased. 'I wish you'd get her to do that every morning, darling. She's much too thin.'

'Not as thin as you are!' Clem protested. 'You haven't changed since the day you agreed to marry me!'

'Oh I have.'

Madge gave her gentle smile and Mark tried to look at her objectively. Whatever his father said, she did not look young. She looked sort of ageless; like the paintings they'd been to see in the National Gallery by Rembrandt. She had a way of looking at something no-one else could see.

He said abruptly, 'Would you mind if Ro got married to Jan?'

They turned to him, surprised, perhaps even shocked. He had a momentary twinge of sheer embarrassment in case Jan's crush on his mother was what his father call 'an issue'. Then his father laughed and said, 'Well, we've always thought Jan and your mother might make a match of it one day!'

And his mother said more seriously, 'Oh, don't laugh at the boy, Clem! But Rosemary and he . . . they're not right for each other. Not really. It's a sort of pretend-thing with both of them.'

'I agree.' Clem stopped laughing. 'Have they said anything to you, old man?'

'No. At least I don't think so. I rather got the idea – in the Snuggerie – that something was in the wind. I wondered how you'd take it.'

'Ro's too young,' Clem declared. 'I know she's older than you were, Madge, but that was too young anyway. And Ro . . . Ro wants too much from life.'

249

Madge said nothing; she looked down at her hands and twisted her wedding ring round her finger.

Mark persisted. 'But wouldn't you mind? I mean, if it happened, would you mind?'

Clem said slowly, 'I don't think so. They've known each other for years. I used to think that Ro's attraction for Jan was that she'd come with a ready-made family!' He smiled. 'But since the American trip with Rory, he seems very much more . . . detached. What do you think, Madge?'

She did not look up. 'Yes. He is detached. Certainly.'

But she did not say more, and Mark knew that she minded very much whether Jan and Ro were married or not.

They wanted an afternoon nap and he got them to lift him down to the courtyard before they went upstairs. He insisted that he would go into the fish cellar when the rain started, and at last they gave in. The sky was lurid purple and yellow ochre; he could smell danger. They seemed oblivious to it.

He made straight for the old ruined pier at the side of Wheal Dream. His chair whined louder as he took it down the long ramp. The *Forty-niner* was already close beneath the coastguard's lookout, anchored fore and aft and moored to a buoy as well; there was no sign of Philip or Jem senior, but the dinghy was well up on the shingle so they had gone long since. The water was still calm, but there was a glassiness to its surface, and now and then it lifted on an uneven swell as if shifting position uncomfortably. There was a breathless, waiting quality to the ominous, early darkness; even the air seemed to be thickening.

He stopped the chair and the silence was complete; not even the gulls called that afternoon, no-one was about. It could be all right; Jem had been scared by the prospect of the drain; Zannah had been recalled to Penzance and her careless father. Mark was ready to laugh with sheer relief, when they stood up from the tumble of rocks by the steps and waved at him. His heart sank. Zannah had greased her hair flat and scraped off every trace of makeup. The silver chains were gone and she wore long khaki shorts and a dirty vest. She looked like any of the local boys; she looked like Jem's younger brother.

*　　*　　*

When she left the Snuggerie, Rosemary's instinct was to hide. She ran down to the High Street, then along Fore Street and left into the Digey. She had no idea where she was going, but the town was packed with holidaymakers and she needed emptiness. The only place she would get that was along the stretches of Porthmeor.

The tide was out as far as it could go and the sun was almost covered by massed thunderclouds. Where there were gaps it beamed through like a searchlight, hitting the sea angrily and adding to the menace of the coming storm. Rosemary surveyed the beach almost frantically. People were packing up their towels and deckchairs and moving off; she could go into one of the beach tents and cry to her heart's content. It wasn't quite what she had in mind; she remembered the scene in the Snuggerie and wanted to die. It would serve Mark and Jan and Rory right if she died here and now. She could run out to the tideline and keep running . . . except that she was such an excellent swimmer. But presumably that was the bliss of drowning, you swam until you were exhausted then sort of floated into death like going to sleep.

She tore down the sands at full pelt, her sandals squelching in the pools, her pony tail bouncing hard on her neck. Halfway down she was forced to stop and touch her toes in an effort to get rid of a chronic stitch in her side. Then on she went again and full tilt into the water. It was difficult swimming in her clothes but that was good because it would tire her out all the sooner. In fact she was tired already. There was no surf and she rolled on to her back to float over the swell and get her breath, only to find her water-logged clothes pulling her under. She fought her way to the surface and sucked in an enormous gulp of air; there was a horrid pain in her chest. She struck out for the shore and felt only deep thankfulness when her sandals touched bottom. Drowning was obviously a much more difficult business than she'd realised, and she waded out of the water and lay on the sand face down until the pain went. And then she walked slowly up the beach to their tent, undid the strings, went inside and started to cry.

She was still there, gazing bleakly out at the lurid sky and seascape, when Rory arrived an hour later. She had not seen or heard him coming and she gave a little scream when his face appeared around the edge of the fly sheet.

'It's okay – okay—'

'Is Jan with you?'

251

'No.'

'Oh God . . .' She put her face in her hands and wept again.

He took in the state of her, from tangled damp hair to soggy sand-filled shoes, and got himself inside the tent to put an arm around her shoulders. Immediately, with a wail of despair she turned into him and the next moment he had her properly in his arms, her wet, salty, clothes soaking his shirt, her hair in his mouth and nostrils.

'I can't bear it – I can't *bear* it!'

'It's all right, Ro. All right.'

'You don't understand! You don't know what happened!'

'Jan told me. I came straightaway on the next train. I thought you'd go to the cove. You know, where I . . . you know. Then I heard a sound from the tent.'

'I never thought of the cove! Even then you treated me like dirt! That's what I feel like – dirt! I tried to drown myself—'

'Ro!'

'I did! But I couldn't! I feel like dirt – I had to clean myself, but even now . . . I felt like dirt *that* day too! You've always treated me like—'

He kissed her to shut her up at first, and then he couldn't stop because he'd always wanted her and tried to stop wanting her and now he was practically honour-bound to prove to her that he wanted her. And then he stopped thinking and Rosemary stopped wailing. There was a desperation about their love-making: Rosemary was quite certain she would regain a sense of her own worth: Rory knew that Jan was waiting at the top of the cliff path. The shorts and knickers came off as easily as they had done more than ten years ago. Both of them were panting and clutching at each other frantically; the whole thing was over in less than two minutes. For Rosemary it was a promise, a contract, an engagement. She held him to her, murmuring endearments.

He said, 'You've done that before, haven't you?'

She did not stop murmuring immediately; it took a second for his question to register. And then she remembered the finals dance at college: the girls she admired for their assurance and confidence, looking at her in amazement – 'You mean you're a virgin? You actually haven't? My dear, what on earth is a teaching certificate worth if you haven't learned about *that*!'

She opened her eyes and looked at Rory. He hadn't been trans-

252

ported as she had; she had thought they'd gone somewhere together but apparently not.

She whispered, 'How can you ask that at a time like this?'

'Tell me the truth.'

'I haven't done *that* before. No.'

'But something pretty close to it.'

She felt so tired she almost didn't reply, then he got to his knees and pulled her up.

She said, 'Oh Rory. There was someone's brother at the college dance . . . it was nothing. And if you can ask me that, then you've obviously done it before and know. Don't let's spoil it for each other.'

'No. I'm sorry.'

He smiled and began to help her to dress. He was tender and gentle and she almost cried. Something was wrong somewhere and she didn't know what it was.

They went outside to a darkening day that should have been exciting. The beach looked abandoned; half-finished sandcastles ringed the tent, a paper flag on top of a mound was beginning to flap.

'Let's run down to the sea!' Rosemary remembered one time when she and her father had immersed themselves fully clothed; it had had a wonderful, renewing effect.

'We'd better get back, Ro. It's going to empty down in an hour.'

'That gives us time . . . Rory, we need to do something to celebrate! Come on!'

She would have run but he held her back.

'Ro, I'm sorry. I shouldn't. Even if you have done it before, that's no excuse. I'm sorry.'

'It was nothing. What they called heavy petting at college. You were the first.' She looked up at him and saw dismay in his black eyes. 'Rory, it's all *right*. Honestly.'

'No, it's not. You see, Ro . . . oh God . . . Jan is waiting for us at the top of the cliff. We're going to walk along to Old Man's Head. He's going to—'

There was a loud halloo from behind them and there was Jan coming down the path, smiling and waving theatrically.

Zannah said steadily, 'We're going without you if we have to, Mark. It's up to you.'

253

'I shall go straight back to the cottage and tell Philip.'

'No you won't,' she replied confidently.

'You can't do it,' he repeated for the ninth time.

'Of course we can. Ideal conditions. They've even put the lugger in a more convenient place.'

'You'll never tie her up securely again when you get back. You can see it's going to be a helluva storm.'

Jem said, 'Oh let's get on for Chrissake. By the time we get back it's going to be as black as pitch, and I don't fancy that bloody drain in the dark.'

'If you couldn't go along it in broad daylight this morning with me sitting on top of the manhole cover the other end, how d'you think you'll do it now?' Mark snapped.

'I did do it this morning, clever dick. When I lifted up the bloody cover you weren't bloody there!' He snorted. 'It'll be easier now if anything. There's no-one about for a start so I'll be able to get out without any trouble. And don't forget you owe me a bob!' he added.

Zannah suddenly leaned over Mark's chair.

'You were keen on the idea this morning' she said. 'What happened?'

He couldn't explain about the awfulness of Jan and Rosemary and how it made their escapade seem stupid and dangerous and downright selfish. He remembered years ago how Rory had treasured a piece of a boat he'd wrecked; would it come to that? The dear old *Forty-niner* reduced to driftwood?

Zannah gave up waiting for a reply and straightened with a sigh. She looked marvellous dressed as a boy; more feminine if anything.

'Come on Jem. Let's get cracking!' She ran down the rocks without pausing to look back again. Her legs were strong and brown, her bare feet so assured and confident. Jem followed just as agilely, but Mark had seen him bound around for years. His envy, his damp eyes, were for Zannah, not Jem.

They dived off the end of the little headland and sported around in the dark sea for a few minutes like porpoises. Mark switched on and went as far as he could along the broken pier. Jem surfaced and made rude signs at him – then swam after Zannah. The plan was for them to fool any watchers by swimming towards the harbour, then diving and making for Wheal

254

Dream under water as far as they could. They got as far as one of the red buoys and clung to it, looking back towards the land, then Zannah nodded her seal-like head at Jem and released the buoy. He grabbed at her and pulled him to her. Mark watched with open mouth. He was kissing her. She was laughing and letting him. It had happened before. God . . . that was why she'd got him so completely under her thumb. Oh God . . .

They dived and were gone. He threw off the rug that covered his stumps, tore at his shirt buttons. He hated Jem with an intensity that gave him enormous energy. He left his vest tucked into his pants; it would give him protection if he scraped the rocks. He took his chair back fifty yards, then went into forward gear and steered for the end of the the pier. They came up for air, saw him, waved and went under again. And then the chair, with him in it, was sailing through the air.

There were no rocks and he'd done this sort of thing often before with Ro pushing him. His chair would be gone for ever but he didn't care about that. He needed to be intact himself; that was all. Once in the water he was Jem's equal. And he and Jem had been spoiling for a fight for years.

He caught them as Zannah was clambering on to the old tyres that served as fenders along the lugger's sides. Jem was gulping in the air, waiting his turn to scramble aboard, when something grabbed his ankle and dragged him down. He shouted and there was a quick flurry of water before he disappeared. Zannah crouched where she was, staring in horror. She had not long to wait before discovering what had taken her confederate. Both boys broke water fighting fiercely, Jem flailing punches anywhere, Mark's head under Jem's chin, driving his fists into Jem's chest with the dull rhythm of a machine. Jem used his knee to thrust away and his hand caught Mark's ear. The two of them went under.

Zannah screamed, then raised herself sufficiently to look over the lugger at the land. Nobody seemed to have noticed anything. She got one leg over the side and tumbled after it, crouching low and listening for a hail of enquiry. Nothing. Unexpectedly the boat lifted on a big swell and she felt the first of the rain. She raised her head and saw the swell pile into a wave which crashed on to the shingle. The boat rolled the other way against its mooring line and she had to hang on to the side to avoid being tipped out. The boys came up within arm's reach. Jem had his hands in Mark's hair but it seemed to make little difference to Mark's butting power. His forehead went into Jem's chest with the monotony of a pile-driver. For a split second she looked into Jem's up-tipped face and shouted, 'Give up!' then the old lugger yawed back again and she went crashing against the engine casing as the boys submerged.

Twice more it happened. Each time they surfaced, Jem shrieked, 'Pax! For Chrissake – pax!' But Mark had gone beyond words. All the frustration of today – of a lifetime – went into that fight. He thought he might drown them both, but he wanted to know, when they got to the pearly gates, that Jem had drowned before he had.

By the third roll, Zannah was desperate. She had shrieked herself hoarse and nothing had happened. It was obvious that all their careful ploys to ensure secrecy were a waste of time; everyone had gone indoors to await the storm and the coastguard was probably drinking tea and thinking his busy time wouldn't be for another hour. She saw that Mark did not care any more and that Jem was at his last gasp. So on the third roll she was ready with the boat hook. It was possible she would fetch blood on one of the boys, but the hospital could deal with that and there wasn't much they could do for drowning.

But luck was with Jem at last. He saw the hook and let go Mark's hair to grab it. He couldn't have held on for long, but the sea was an unexpected ally: the boat rolled back on the swell which pushed the boys up its side. For a moment they were suspended, Mark's head thumping a little less vigorously into Jem's chest, Zannah crouched by the engine casing pulling frantically and Jem getting air into his starved lungs in time with Mark's head movements. The boat hovered and began to roll them back into the sea. Zannah leapt forward and seized Jem's arm, leaned over and got his leg. He rolled into the boat holding Mark to him like a lover.

They walked to Old Man's Head because that was the way Jan went, and Rory followed him so Rosemary came after, unable to walk away from Rory now. She knew the boys had cooked up some plan between them and that it must be pretty awful and pretty serious because of Rory's panic down on the beach. But whether he felt guilty or not, he couldn't blot out those two minutes of heaven in the beach tent. It was still awful about Jan, but it had to be all right now, it just had to be.

Jan was talking practically all the time, pausing on the path by the putting green to throw back at them some gem about the purple sky. Once he started to say something about Mark painting a storm sky, then stopped abruptly. When they got out on the cliff top proper, they walked abreast and Rory joined in the unnatural conversation and tried to include Rosemary.

'D'you remember we used to clamber all round these rocks, the three of us? We've had some great times. The terrific trio.'

Rosemary smiled and held out her hand, but he did not take it.

'It will always be like that,' Jan said emphatically. 'Whatever happens, wherever we go, we shall meet here again and be happy.'

'Rather! What do you say, Ro?'

She looked sideways at the two of them and noticed to her surprise that Jan was taller than Rory now.

She said, 'You're trying to tell me that you're both going away again. Is this whole act meant to be a farewell scene?'

Rory said urgently, 'I'm going, Jan's staying. You know that, Ro.'

'Yes. But I thought after—'

'After what Mark said in the Snuggerie this morning? You surely didn't take that seriously? For goodness' sake, Ro – we both adore your parents, that goes without saying. You've met my adopted ma and pa so you can imagine how we feel about . . .' He wouldn't look at her, wouldn't let her speak in case she said something about their love-making in the tent just now. The familiar pain began in her chest again. And the familiar anger too.

She said tightly, 'Let's forget it, shall we?' and hoped he would read the double meaning in her words. He'd probably forgotten it already. She never would. It was true that she had been 'dithering about', as Mark so elegantly put it, before, but not any more. She knew again what she had known two years before. She loved Rory and he loved her.

He said, 'Right. That's fine. Okay, Jan?'

'Okay. Fine. I apologise Ro, if there has been any embarrassment—'

'No need for apologies, old man! You heard what she said. We forget it. Back to where we were before. Okay?'

'Okay.' But it seemed he had run out of words and would have turned back for home except that Rory kept walking.

They came to the Head, balanced precariously on a bed of rocks, looking apparently into the eye of the coming storm.

'This is one we never did. Philip showed you how to climb it, didn't he Ro?'

She looked at him and forced him to look back at her. His eyes were narrowed as if in pain.

She said directly, 'When are you going on the next job?'

'Tomorrow.' He took a short breath. 'That's . . . if I go.' Her heart leapt, but he turned away and grabbed Jan's arm. 'I've got an idea. Seriously. Ro – climb up on to the Head. Go on – do it now!' He looked back at her and said urgently, Please!'

She didn't want to. She knew she should turn and walk back home with dignity and show them that she needed neither of them. But there was that urgent 'please' . . . and before that there had been the tent.

She said, 'It's ridiculous. Anyone can climb it. I'll show you and you can do it if you're so keen.'

'No. We're not going to watch you. Just do it.'

Jan said nothing. He was staring at the ground. Rory's eyes were black holes looking at her.

She kicked at a stone with her sandy damp sandal. 'Oh . . . all right. This is all nonsense. I'll climb it, then I'm going home. I'm hungry.'

They kept their backs to her as if it were a game of hide-and-seek and she went further along the cliff and clambered over the strewn rocks until she found the ledge with her feet. She remembered her mother telling her of the first time she'd done the climb, the excitement of it, the challenge which, once met, was not there any more. Philip was wise; he knew that until it was done it was a danger, once it was done it was safe. She smiled as her hands found the finger rocks; Philip had sworn her to secrecy and she had kept that particular promise. It was surprising that Rory and Jan, being 'local', did not know the smugglers' way, but she was glad she'd never told them. They'd look till the storm came and never find it.

It took five or six minutes to crawl along the top and look over, and she was surprised to see Rory and Jan in exactly the same positions as when she had left; Jan had not lifted his head an inch. She hallooed and they turned in unison like puppets and stared up at her.

'Okay? Satisfied?' She was still on her knees and even so the height made her dizzy. 'I'm coming down now.'

'Wait!'

Rory held up a hand and came closer to the base of the rock. After a quick glance up at her, Jan looked back to the ground. Rory stood directly beneath her and tilted his head right back to look at her.

'Ro. Please wait there. Please. You won't like this – we knew you wouldn't like it, but we couldn't think of another way. Try to understand. We both love you – you must know that. We both want to marry you, Ro. It's always been like we said – the three of us. And it can't be any more, can it?' She made to speak and he held up his hand again. 'Ro, listen. We didn't know what to do – not so long ago we could have fought a duel, couldn't we?' He tried to laugh. 'But there had to be some way to decide.'

Rosemary interrupted fiercely. 'Isn't that up to me? And haven't I made it quite clear anyway? What about just now – in the tent—'

Jan's head did not move but Rory said quickly, 'Of course it's up to you, Ro. We know that. But we also know that you can't make a decision because you love both of us. If you choose me, what happens to Jan?' His eyes held hers commandingly. He did not follow through with a query about his fate if she chose Jan. She swallowed, half convinced in spite of herself. At least some of the humiliation was assuaged; they both loved her.

She said, 'Well?'

She saw his Adam's apple move convulsively.

'We know there's a way up there, but we don't know where it is. The first one to join you . . .' his words petered out. He didn't have the nerve to say, 'The first one to join you, gets you,' but that was what he meant. She did not know whether to laugh or cry. It was so typical of Rory's sense of the dramatic. It was funny and it was sad and it was insulting. But if it was his way of 'claiming' her, then none of that mattered. He was more ingenious and much more athletic than Jan was. He had been born among these rocks; he would find the way. Poor Jan. But even

259

poorer Rory. He could not find a way to tell Jan the truth, that he and Rosemary already belonged to each other. He had to do it like this; make a game of it.

He held her gaze for one more agonising moment, then took her silence for consent.

'Come on then, old man! Who's going to win the princess?'

He spoke rallyingly and indulgently as if to a child. Jan seemed to be trapped in a world of his own and apparently did not hear him. Rory went to him and took his arm and said something in a low voice that Rosemary could not hear. And at last he looked up and after a while reluctantly nodded. Rory gave him a little shove. Rosemary leaned over the edge to see better; Rory's shove was in the direction of the cliff. Away from the rock. The way she had come herself.

It need not mean anything significant; it could simply mean that they had decided to reconnoitre for an easy way up. But when Rory ripped off his pullover, waved it over his head and charged straight for the smooth and unclimbable inland face, she was almost certain. He had seen other people atop the Head, he must know they never tackled it this way.

While he scrabbled among the tumble of supporting rocks beneath, she looked at the top of his head and remembered the feel of his hair beneath her hands not an hour ago. She remembered how they had clung together, devoured each other, as if they were about to be parted for ever. She remembered Rory's guilt immediately afterwards and the way he had tried to make the whole thing cheap by asking her if she'd done it before.

He had reached the Head itself now and he stood there, pressed against its smoothness, searching with his fingers for a hand hold. She sat back on her heels and looked no more. If Jan had found the smugglers' way, she could be certain.

She took her time crawling across the bald crown of the Head. She was feeling sick and remembered she'd had nothing to eat since breakfast. And she did not want to see what she knew she would see. She looked over the seaward edge. Jan was at the bottom of the ledge, his hands already gripping the finger rocks automatically. He must have done the climb a dozen times before; they had both done it dozens of times before. She was – as usual – a dupe.

How long she crouched there she did not know; it seemed an

age. Jan did not appear. There were small scrabbling sounds everywhere but the wind had increased now and there could have been a dozen people climbing up to join her, she would not know. Eventually she uncurled herself and looked over at Jan again. He was halfway up, leaning against the rock as Philip had shown her, spread-eagled there safely enough, but unmoving. Another two footholds and he would be with her; yet still he didn't move. She stretched her legs until she was prone above him and reached over with her arms. She was about to call him and tell him to hang on to her, when there was a shout directly behind her. It made her jump but she knew instantly who it was and what had happened. Somehow, Rory had scaled that sheer face; somehow he had forgotten the grand stupid plan he had worked out with Jan. He loved her and he had climbed Old Man's Head to prove it.

His shout went into the wind and, by some trick of acoustics, was flung back again. Jan looked up at last. She stared into his eyes and saw nothing; no expression; complete and desolate emptiness. And then his foot slipped. He would still have been all right; all he had to do was to keep himself pressed to the rock and he would have slithered back down to the ledge with no more than a pair of skinned hands to show for it. But he pushed himself upright as if to see properly what was happening above him and his body kept going. She felt Rory's hand on her back as he joined her. They both looked in horror as Jan lay back into the wind and plummeted down into the sea. Rory was after him before he had hit the water. With a screamed 'Get someone – get Philip—' he was scrambling down, taking terrible risks himself but never putting a foot wrong. And Rosemary was scuffling along the ledge, over the finger rocks, running . . . running like someone in a nightmare who never gets anywhere.

It took Mark and Jem almost half an hour to recover and begin to grin sheepishly. There was no question of them going on with the escapade. They had no more energy and their appetite for adventure was sated anyway. Besides, the swell was escalating powerfully; the danger was obvious even to Jen and Zannah.

'You were great,' she said simply, looking at Mark. 'You'd have killed him, wouldn't you?'

'No.'

'He couldn't. He tried and he couldn't.'

'He could,' she said soberly. 'But he'd have gone himself too. I rescued you both. You owe your lives to me. And don't you forget it!'

They grinned again, united under their oppressor.

She said, 'Are we going to take our medicine together, or what?' She looked dispassionately at Mark. 'One of your leg bits is bleeding so you'll have to have proper treatment.

He shrugged. 'I'd have to own up anyway. I ditched my chair.'

'You what?' They were agog with admiration.

'No need for you two to say a word. Zannah, you can disappear. Jem, you can pretend to find me and go and tell Dad or Philip or someone. I'll say I lost control of the chair and went off the end.' He sniggered. 'Which is true anyway.'

'Is that cowardice?' she asked.

'It's called living to fight another day,' Mark told her.

She sparkled immediately. 'What can we do next? Something really terrible!'

The boys groaned aloud and Mark said, 'Look, chuck me in and let's get back. If we wait much longer we won't be able to swim against this sea.'

It was raining in squalls by the time he'd got himself up the steps on his bottom. They found his sodden blanket and shirt and bundled him up in the lee of a rock; they were all shivering convulsively.

Zannah said, 'Git – go on Jem – git. I'm staying with him till you get back. Go on!'

Mark was thankful; without his chair he felt completely helpless. Zannah sat close to him and put her arms around him so that their two shivers became one.

He said close to her ear, 'You let him kiss you.'

She managed a stuttering laugh. 'Is that what bugged you?' She turned her face into his and kissed his eyes, nose and mouth. 'There. Does that make it even?'

He said nothing but he let go of his blanket and got his arms around her too.

It was only five minutes until Jem returned with Clem and Jem senior, but each one of those minutes was expanded into an hour of sheer happiness.

And then Jem was babbling something about Jan and a terrible tragedy. And Mark was being lifted between the two men, and his

262

father was saying, 'We'll tell you later, old chap. Lean back now. We'll soon have you warm and looked after.'

And he knew that Jan was dead, and he, Mark, had walked out on him only this morning when he had still been able to use his chair. He tried to tell his father about his chair but no-one was listening. Zannah was trailing behind, mistaken by everyone for a boy. And now, when it was too late, he knew how Jan had felt about love.

CHAPTER TWELVE

1963

Etta put her head through the car window and looked around its interior very carefully before she greeted them.

'So you 'aven't brought 'er again this year?'

They all began to speak at once, telling her in almost identical words and tones that one day Rosemary would come back to St Ives, but not just yet.

Clem laughed. 'Did you get that, Etta? She's fine and sends her love.'

'Ah.' Etta removed her head and straightened her back with difficulty. 'Come on then. Let's get you indoors. I got the kettle on and Philip's waiting for you.'

'He's here?' Madge got out and pecked Etta's cheek, which was all the salutation the old lady would permit. 'He's in the house, d'you mean?'

'Ah,' Etta said again, then answered the unspoken question. ' 'E's not quite so spry on 'is feet no more, so e'll wait till you gets the stuff out of the car.'

Madge hovered by Mark's side while he hoisted himself on to his tin legs; she did not make the mistake of trying to help him. He reached behind him for his stick and thrust himself forward with a kind of fierce aggression. Etta said approvingly, 'Well now . . . you en't got fed up with us yet then, young man?'

He grinned. It was four years since Rosemary had come with them and each year Etta asked the same questions and made the same imputations.

'Not pygmalion likely, Etta,' he said. 'And neither has Ro.' He too pecked the withered cheek. 'Any news of Rory?' he asked directly.

'Naw. An' you won't 'ave to put up with 'avin' tea over at Mennion 'ouse, neither,' she said dourly, walking just ahead of him. 'There's bin-an almighty bust-up there and she's gone orf to Lunnon.'

'Surprise, surprise, commented Mark, and Madge said, 'Oh dear.' Then with one accord they all stopped and looked across the harbour towards Hayle. The sea glittered in the late afternoon sunshine and the beach was littered with the new breed of visitors called hippies. The tide was halfway in and the boats swung gently at their moorings. Godrevy looked as if you could swim out to it in five minutes.

'It's too clear,' Etta pronounced. 'It's going to rain before long.'

And Clem said quietly, 'It hasn't changed. It never changes.'

But Philip and Etta had changed. The shock of Jan's death and Mark's near miss had taken its toll; Philip could no longer climb the iron ladder to Smeaton's Pier, and Etta was at last glad to use the bathroom at the end of the passage. She could cook fish and potatoes and make tea, buf she let Madge take over the kitchen for anything else. And if she thought she was quite alone she would talk aloud; not to herself, but to people who were not there any more. One day Madge heard her addressing Jan.

'You shouldn't 'uv done it. You were allus a headstrong lad – I know that – but you shouldn't 'uv left that girl all on 'er own like that. An' now 'e's gone off the Lord knows where.'

Madge felt her eyes fill. Then Etta said inexplicably, 'Your son. Your flesh an' blood. An' you left 'im.' And Madge turned away, knowing that not even Etta's illusions were logical. She closed her eyes momentarily, praying that Etta would not become like Clem's mother and live in a nightmare world of filth and evil. And then Etta came out of the parlour and saw Madge gathering up the swimming things from the passage clothes line.

'What's it to be today then, hot or cold?' she asked, as she had asked Marie Bridges so often.

'Er . . . I'm not sure . . . we'll have a picnic, Etta.' Madge wondered whether Etta was speaking to her or one of her private people.

'Right then.' The old woman gathered up her apron front and rubbed her hands on it. She gave Madge a lizard-glance and said firmly, 'You might 'ear something you dun't want to,anging about in the passage like that, my girl!' And went into the kitchen.

Madge smiled, reassured. Etta knew full well what she was doing after all.

She missed Rosemary more than she would have believed possible. For years it had been Rosemary who injected energy into their holidays down here, instigating outings, swimming parties, fishing trips. And now, Rosemary would be sitting with her on the harbour beach, making the empty hour into something positive: 'Come on Mummy, stretch out, we've got sixty minutes to get *brown*!' Madge smiled again, closing her eyes and tipping her head back to feel the full impact of the sun. She did not mind her own company and was always glad when Mark and Clem went off together, but there was no doubt about it, Rosemary had been the bit of grit inside the oyster shell.

The heat was glowing red against her closed eyelids, warming all the passages behind her face. She wished it were quieter; her ears did not enjoy the constant chatter of the crowds who thronged the beaches now and she remembered the time when the harbour had belonged exclusively to the local children. But Mark loved all the newcomers. He had already started to sketch them; a hundred or more faces on a piece of card two by one-and-a-half, flowers, head bands, long hair, beads . . . Clem said it was a social document and Mark said it was 'freedom'.

Madge's sentimental smile died; Mark used that word 'freedom' often now, yet never in connection with his own progress on his tin legs. He used it longingly, as if he had had it and lost it. And Clem couldn't understand. Clem thought that by taking him into the drawing and design office, he had given Mark a measure of independence. His own salary and his own work.

Madge took a deep breath and opened her eyes. Clem had taken Mark along to the Clipper for a pre-lunch drink and she knew he would be talking shop right now. She could imagine Mark, perched on one of the tall stools which were exactly the right height for him, looking into his beer instead of the scene around him, nodding and saying, 'Gosh, yes Dad, I can see what you mean,' and trying desperately to match his father's enthusiasm. He thought such a lot of Clem; as well as respecting and loving him, he admired him. He'd never do anything to hurt his father.

Madge pressed her lips together and swallowed another sigh.

266

Neither Ro nor Mark were completely happy at the moment, but as Philip had said once, there was more to life than just being happy. Live a day at a time . . . pile them up until they made some kind of structure that was strong and worthwhile . . . let dreams have a separate place of their own perhaps. Again she smiled, this time self-mockingly. Sometimes she wondered what her mother was making of it all, now that she knew everything.

The tide was coming in and Maddern's pony and trap waited patiently on the shore for the first of the boats to bring in its catch. Madge made herself think about tea and whether mackerel would be acceptable to the others. It would mean that Etta could cope with it, which she would enjoy in her grim fashion. She would pickle them in vinegar and they could have salad and a mountain of bread and butter. Then, if the weather held, they could drive to Marazion and watch the sun go down behind the Mount. Etta and Philip would enjoy that too.

She noticed Philip signalling to her from the Fisherman's Lodge. She got to her feet with some difficulty, gathering up handbag and book and shuffling through the sand barefoot to meet him. He opened the gate for her and they sat outside, backs to the wooden shack with its leaning chimney, the milling crowds shut away behind them.

'Here they come,' Philip said quietly. And around Smeaton's Pier came the first of the diminished fishing fleet, a big tub-like boat, broad in beam, with a wide stern, like a child's toy bobbing down a bath of water.

'Good catch by the looks of 'en.'

A boat put off from the harbour beach and the business of unloading began. There was an oil painting by Sargent in one of the galleries that was an exact representation of what was happening now; painted a hundred years ago, bridging past and present.

Philip said, 'Broodin' over young Mark, are you, woman?'

'No. Thinking of time. And how some things never change.' She smiled down on the ancient trilby. I don't think of Mark all the time, Philip.'

'But most of it, I reckon.'

She was silent, remembering the terrible heartache for Rosemary not long ago.

Philip did not look at her. 'I think o' young Mark as my own son. You know that, dun't you?'

267

She said nothing. Philip must know . . . he must. Was he trying to take on some of her guilt?

He sighed audibly. 'No need to worry, woman. No need . . .'

His voice petered out. Madge felt a pang of concern. He was only a year or so younger than Etta. They were both . . . old. They sat there together and watched Jim Maddern pole his dinghy back to the waiting cart. And Madge clung fiercely to her feeling of timelessness where surely guilt had no meaning at all.

Mark had not seen Zannah since that ghastly evening four years ago, and neither had Jem. The public story of their escapade, that day of the storm, had become apocryphal; their own real version no less so. Jem saw it still as an heroic venture and a wizard wheeze. Mark saw it in lurid colours of tragedy. Even his love for Zannah could not redeem it; there were doubtless reasons for Jan's terrible end; one of them might well have been to reveal to Mark his own impotence.

He looked at his latest sketch, narrowing his eyes so that each individual figure became blurred into the whole. Even so he knew that Zannah's face with its long aggressive chin and short hair was there, as were Jan's and Rory's and Rosemary's. Very carefully he turned the picture on to its face and focused again on the real thing.

Because of the terrible winter, this summer seemed the best for aeons and people were everywhere, no room any more for the artists. There was the usual crowd of families, mostly local, lining the harbour wall, but right down to the tideline the hippies had taken over. Etta was disgusted by them; they slept in the tents or under the arches or under the stars even; they never washed; they threw their rubbish everywhere, and – if reasons and excuses were offered for all of these offences – they were simply a disgrace. Mark was fascinated by them. Their philosophy of freedom – doing their own thing – appealed to him because he saw it as unattainable for himself. He longed to lie full length on the hot sand, eating fruit and buns and letting tomorrow take care of itself. But if he managed to get himself sitting at floor level, he'd never get up again. And their drowsy contentment relied a great deal on smoking 'pot' besides the hot weather. Mark knew from personal experience that drugs had their drawbacks; and of course, the sun was not going to go on shining like this.

So he looked, and envied, and tried not to remember that at the end of this short two weeks he had to return to the drawing office and the discipline of the slide rules.

Meanwhile he waited for Zannah.

She hadn't appeared for two years previously and he had told himself every day since that if she did not turn up this year, he would give her up for good. And they were already five days into the holiday.

The trouble was, Jem and his father had taken the *Forty-niner* up north, so Mark had no-one with whom to share and restructure again and again those four-year old memories. And no-one to act as scout for him when his legs couldn't keep up with what was happening. It was Jem who discovered that Rory had left home in the widest possible sense; no forwarding address, no correspondence, nothing. It was Jem who would have found out all about the latest scandal from Mennion House; why Mrs Trewyn had gone to London and for how long. And when Zannah did not keep her biennial tryst, Jem would have gone looking for her. Although how he would have started when neither of them knew her full name or where her father lived, was a mystery.

Mark tightened his mouth against his own irritation and turned his sketch right side up again. He fished in his jacket pocket and broke off a lump of charcoal from the stick there. In front of him, no more that twenty yards away, a man and girl were entwined and asleep. She wore a leather headband into which were tucked bunches of daisies and buttercups, already wilting in the scorching sun. The hair which flowed from beneath the band was the same colour as his own, rust-red. It was unbelievably tangled and matted so that it looked like an unravelled piece of knitting, and it fell across her face and his, veiling their clinging mouths and surely half-stifling them. Beneath the shawl of hair, his hand appeared to be cupping her breast. It was an erotic pose, made innocent by their unconscious state.

Mark began to draw.

The three of them swam from the end of the pier at high tide. Neither Clem nor Madge were as strong as Mark in the water, and after ten minutes they clung to one of the mooring ropes and watched their son use his whole body like a dolphin as he knifed through the water with a kind of ecstatic energy.

Clem said, 'D'you remember two or three years ago you were talking of Mark's independence? You were right. See how he gets away from us as soon as he possibly can.'

There was an unfamiliar note in his voice; Madge wondered if it was sadness.

She said, 'He always did. When he had his electric chair, he would get down on the beach with his painting things . . .'

'Yes. But he wasn't a loner then. Now he is. Of course he had Ro then. And other years Jem Gurnard was at home in the summer.'

The thought of Mark being a loner was awful. Madge blinked sea water from her eyes and said, 'Is it the work at the office? Can he cope with it all right, Clem?'

'He's marvellous. Especially at the mock-ups. I was going into technical details with a VIP layman the other week, and Mark did a lightning sketch which showed it all without any words. But—' he hauled himself high on the rope to check on Mark. 'He's not keen on the maths side.'

Madge swallowed. 'He'll get used to it.' She wished she could thank Clem for what he had done. 'He likes working with you. You get on so well. So well.'

She met his eyes in a moment of sudden awareness, then quickly looked away. And, with shocking suddenness, something grabbed at her legs. It was Mark of course. He pulled her under and when they surfaced, laughing, the moment had passed.

He said into her spluttering face, 'I was diving again by the old pier. Looking for the chair.'

Clem said, 'Again? The sea had that a long time ago.' Then he added, 'We thought you were leaving home.'

Mark laughed but Madge knew it was the wrong thing to say to him. And she wondered: did Clem sometimes wish he could be free of the terrible responsibility of Mark?

The drawing had gone. He had left it on the harbour in the box which slid beneath his old easel like a drawer. He went through the other things, though he knew he had left it on top. The old water-colours were there and some sketches of Ro as she bent over the desk of one of her pupils, but there was no sign of the hippie drawing. Yet no-one knew about the drawer, and nothing else had been touched. He had some decent brushes and a bag full of tubes of oil paint which were intact. He couldn't understand it. He folded everything up and struggled back to the cottage and the fish cellar where he left what Etta proudly called his 'mess'. He knew he hadn't left the drawing there, but he searched through old paintings anyway, without success. Then went upstairs and questioned his parents and the Nollas. Then stood at the window and looked out, as if he expected to see the drawing floating on the very high tide.

'It's like being grilled by the Secrets people,' Clem commented humorously, raising his brows at Mark's hunched and predatory pose. 'It'll turn up, old chap. You should have left your stuff there. Probably someone looking at it and will bring it back—'

'Bring it back!' scoffed Etta. 'It's they 'ippies what's took it! An' they never bring nothin' back!'

'It was in the drawer,' Mark said stubbornly. 'And no-one knows about the drawer except you and me. And Jem.' He gnawed his lip. And one other. She had to be out there somewhere. He rested his hands on the window and stared through the glass for the crop-haired figure hung with silver chains.

Philip said, 'Why dun't you go an' sit in your usual place and get on with some more work, m'boy? Take your pasty with you and make the most of the sunshine.'

'I'd nearly finished the whole damned picture!'

'Then start again.'

'Oh . . . I can't!'

'Course you can. Everyone can.'

So he went out again, took the steps one at a time, collected his easel from the fish cellar and, using it like a second walking stick, made his way along the harbour. And waited.

When she materialised beside him, it was the same shock as before. He had looked for an eighteen-year-old sophisticate, sleek and sharp to the point of being abrasive. He had expected that the silver chains would be no more, but had been certain that their glinting sparkle would still be in evidence somehow. And the short, beige-coloured hair, the long belligerent chin, would always mark her out.

The girl who suddenly arrived, holding the drawing carefully and reverently between her hands, was certainly familiar. Her rusty, tangled hair, blowing across the lower half of her face like a yashmak, identified her immediately as the female half of the erotic twosome who had been the latest addition to his multi-figured sketch. Her leather, flower-bedecked head band of this afternoon had gone, but the metal rim she now wore like a tiara was looped with a fresh daisy chain, and on top of her shawl of hair was draped a liana of small, reddish flowers. Beneath all that she appeared to be wearing a grey-white muslin dress; no shoes or socks and, apparently, no underwear.

She stood before him, the picture in front of her like an offering, saying nothing, simply looking at him. And then he knew. She could do nothing about her eyes, they were still purple. This creature, a definitive flower person if ever there was one, was Zannah.

He took the picture numbly and went on staring, waiting for that vibrant personality to show through. She lifted one hand and moved the hair away from her mouth; her chin was still prominent, but the mouth was different, not so firm, the lips fuller and tremulous. He continued to wait; her voice would be the same, hard and American and very real.

She said softly, 'You were hurt. You didn't come to me. You didn't wake me. But you still drew me although you were hurt.' The accent was the same but the register was much lower and there were no cadences: she spoke in a monotone. He wanted to shake her physically as if he could empty her of all this rubbish and find the old Zannah behind it.

He tried to smile. 'I didn't realise it was you. Sorry. It was just . . . archetypal.'

'You mean I'm a symbol of the whole peace movement? That's nice.'

He hadn't meant that exactly, but he let it go, and went on smiling politely.

She tucked her hair beneath her chin and leaned back against the wall. She was taller than he was. His tin legs had been cut down as far as aestheticaily possible to make movement easier.

She said in her gentle, middle-C voice, 'I looked everywhere for you, but I was looking for another chair.'

'I never had another one. I wanted to get something positive out of . . . all that.'

'You're a wonderful person, d'you know that?'

'Oh God . . . et tu, Brute.'

'No, I mean it.'

272

'That makes it worse. Look . . . thanks for returning the drawing, though you shouldn't have pinched it in the first place. And
goodbye.'

'You *are* hurt. And angry. I guess I should be flattered, but to
inflict pain on another human being is—'

'Oh for Christ's sake Zannah – shut *up*!'

It was the first time he had spoken her name and as he did so he
knew she was right; he was hurt. He thought of the unknown
man, legs twined around her, hand cupping her breast, and he
wanted to yell aloud his pain.

She said with a touch of urgency in the sibilant murmur, 'We
believe in free love, Mark. Morals – ethics – they're just rules to
make the old society work. We don't have to have them. We can
make our society work with love. Just love. So it has to be free.
Surely you – you of all people in the world – can understand
that? Mark—' She picked up the edge of the drawing and pointed
to the sleeping couple; he noticed with horror that her fingernail
was filthy. 'Listen Mark – I don't even know the name of this
man. We ate together yesterday around a fire at Sennen. We
walked here together. There were a lot of us. Bound by love.
Human beings on the edge of eternity in a beautiful world created
just for us. We slept together on the sand. For an instant in time
we were bound. That is all.'

He said dryly, 'But apparently that is everything too. The
whole bloody credo. Free love? It's free sex, that's all. It's
cannabis so that you don't have to exercise self-discipline. It's
weakness. In the end it's cowardice.'

She flinched. 'You've changed. You are totally reactionary. I
used to admire your free spirit—'

'In a fettered body? And I used to admire the fact that you
never thought or spoke clichés!'

She said with a suddenly hard edge to her voice, 'I've always
been looking for freedom. Ever since I was born. That was the
whole point of the business with the *Forty-niner* – to do something against everyone and get away with it.' She flipped the
drawing back to him contemptuously. 'You had it. Freedom.
Inside your head you were free and when you chucked yourself
into the sea and swam out to stop Jem that night, you proved you
were free *outside* your head too! I thought you could do anything – anything you wanted to! And you've changed. You're

bitter and condemning of things you don't understand – won't understand! You've closed your mind in some way . . . you're just . . . different.'

He put his head back against the wall. He wished she would leave. He did not want to turn and struggle back up the slipway with his stick, but he wanted her away. He closed his eyes and hoped she would take that as dismissal. She did not. He knew she had moved closer because he could smell her. She smelled of Indian hair oil, the awful scent the hippies used, joss sticks, and – faintly – something else. Something which took him back to that evening four years ago when she had held him close until Jem fetched help.

She started whispering, practically into his ear. He could have sidestepped away from her without difficulty with the wall as support, but he did not.'

'I dived and dived off the end of the old pier, Mark. And I scoured all the beaches hoping something would be washed up. And when it was, I took the wheel and got Daddy to cut out the spokes and I wore it everywhere – long before I went to San Francisco – when I was only fifteen. It's one of the small front wheels – the ones that steered the chair, you know? I've got the other one too. I shall never lose them, Mark. I shall never forget that time when we were kids. Everything seemed so . . . possible.'

He pressed himself hard against the rough granite of the wall. The underlying smell from her tawdry, anointed body was pure Zannah.

She whispered, 'Why do you think I dyed my hair red? To be like you of course. Why do you think I joined the Frisco people? To find your – your completeness – your one-ness with the world. You can scoff now, but you had it, Mark. You had contentment – acceptance – Christ, I don't know what it was. But you had it.'

There was a very long silence. She withdrew slightly, but she did not leave, and he no longer wanted her to.

He said at last, wearily, 'I was happy because I was a kid and I was spoiled and everybody made a fuss of me. No mystery. That's all it was.'

'No it wasn't. It was more than that. There was a tale going round St Ives – Jem told me about it. You should have been killed when you fell off that railway bridge. And you weren't.

It was a miracle. You're a special person. You belong to fate.'

'Shut up. Claptrap. Superstition. Etta was going to be ducked for a witch when she was a girl and Philip rescued her and married her. Some people still thing she's a witch – she thinks so herself sometimes. Superstition.' He opened his eyes and turned his head. 'I think that's what I react against, Zannah. Your people – the flower people or whatever they call themselves – let them preach peace and wander around penniless pleasing themselves. Marvellous. But when they start going into the realms of fantasy and illusion—'

'It was the *local* people who said you were a miracle. Nothing to do with—'

'It's the same sort of scare-mongering but yours is brought on by cannabis.'

It's not as harmful as cigarette tobacco!'

'I'm an expert on drugs.'

She stared at him for some seconds, then drew in her breath. 'I haven't argued like this since . . . for ages. We don't argue. It's one of the wonderful things about being one of them. There is never discord.'

He grinned suddenly.

'We always argued. You, Me. Jem.'

'Yes. We did, didn't we?'

A voice from the beach yelled, 'Hey! Everyone! Food! Come and get it if you want it!'

Zannah said,I must go.'

'Where will you sleep tonight?'

'Anywhere. I've got a sleeping bag.'

'Will you sleep with him?' Mark jabbed a finger at his drawing.

'No.' She smiled. 'I'm so glad about the legs, Mark. You and Jem – you must have such fun now that you can walk.'

'Jem's a seaman. I haven't seen much of him for the past couple of years.'

'Well, your sister then.'

'Ro?' He was going to tell her, then changed his mind. 'Yes. It's good to walk with Ro.'

He watched her join the others. Smoke curled up from their midst as they lit a cooking fire. He wondered why he had condemned them so wholeheartedly to Zannah when until today he had envied them their carefree attitude. She turned and waved to

275

him, holding her aluminium crown with her free hand. After a second's hesitation, he waved back.

He did not want to be seen along the harbour the next day. He lurked in the fish cellar until he saw his parents leave for Porthmeor beach with the picnic hamper, then he went back up to the parlour intending to sit in the window and watch the hippies. He knew the parents would be hurt if they thought he was avoiding them, but he had swum with them twice and had a drink with his father at the Clipper, and sometimes their anxiety for him was hard to bear. He reached for his father's binoculars so that he could see if Zannah was amongst the heaving crowd on the beach, and swore quietly when he discovered Clem had taken them with him.

'Langwidge!'

It was Philip, head round the door, smiling slightly. He came into the room settling his hat firmly on his ears.

'Sorry, m'boy. Looking for Etta.'

'She went with Mother and Dad. Porthmeor.' Mark saw the surprise in Philip's blue stare and said defensively, 'I wanted to be by myself for a bit.'

'Fancy a row? The Gurnards left the dinghy. We could go over Porthminster and trail a mack'rel line if you felt like it.'

Mark considered. Unless she came up the court, there was no chance of him spotting Zannah in the crowds and it was hot in the tiny parlour. He nodded and levered himself to his feet.

He was expert at getting into the dinghy, sitting himself on the gunnel and manhandling his legs over one by one, and he was a good oarsman too. He rowed slowly across the bay while Philip fitted spinners on to a pair of lines and let them go off the stern. Then he rested the oars and they drifted lazily towards Porthminster with the tide.

It was another glorious day. Philip was no conversationalist unless it was with his mother, but the silence was never awkward. Mark half closed his eyes and did not think about Zannah; then he did not think about the hippies and his sudden and inexplicable turn against them; then he didn't think about the office and the effort of subduing imagination to inches and angles. It was exhausting. He opened his eyes to find Philip looking at him from beneath the brim of his trilby with unprecedented intensity. He sat up self-consciously and grinned.

'All right, Philip? Anything on the lines?'

'Naw.' The old man turned and pulled experimentally. 'Naw,' he confirmed. He stared at the spinner glinting beneath the water. 'Your mother says you're not so 'appy these days, boy?'

Mark shrugged, then realised he couldn't be seen.

'You know how it is. I suppose when you're a kid you think everything will be rosy when you grow up. And then . . . you grow up.' He laughed. Philip did not join in. The water lifted the boat gently and gave Mark a momentary view of the old pier and the cove at Wheal Dream.

Philip said pensively, 'Sometimes the Lord is cruel, or so it do seem. But gen'lly 'E do leave us some way we kin manage . . . gen'lly 'E does that.'

Mark said, 'You mean my legs? Yes, I am managing very well with them now, Philip.' He wished people weren't afraid of mentioning his tin legs. In a way he'd prefer them to know that he was using artificial legs rather than think that he was naturally five foot five and walked like a drunk.

'Aye, you are that. But I wasn't thinking o' your legs zacktly.' Philip turned and glinted a quick grin, then went back to watching the spinners. 'I were thinking of Etta. Wund'rin' 'ow Etta 'as bin able to manage.'

Mark concentrated on the wizened profile in the stern.

'Etta? I should think Etta has managed very well, Philip.'

Another look. 'You've 'eard the tales then? They thought she were a witch and I kem along on a white charger and saved 'er?' He cackled a laugh. 'I dearly wish it 'ad bin like that, my boy.'

'It's how she sees it, Philip.' Mark leaned forward. For some reason he wanted to touch Philip reassuringly. 'I think it was what she told my grandmother. Ages ago.'

'I don't doubt it.' Philip must have seen Mark's outstretched hand, but he ignored it. 'The truth doesn't sound quite so good you see, boy. Oh, I stopped 'em from stonin' 'er. Aye, that's what they was doin' – an' it were this century too. Nineteen nought four it were. Nigh on sixty year ago.'

Mark frowned, wondering how old Philip actually was and what he was getting at. Was this some kind of allegory? He put his hand on the gunnel and shifted position slightly and the dinghy rocked.

277

'Then I ast 'er to marry me.' Philip pulled on his hat brim so that there was no chance of him catching Mark's eye inadvertently. He said quickly, 'I worked it out with 'er that it weren't too bad a bargain. She wouldn't want to bring children into the world if they was going to be tainted with any kind o' wizardry. An' she wanted to get out o' that part o' the country. Be respeckable. Go to chapel like other people and 'ave a man to proteck 'er. To keep 'er. Keep 'er safe from talk an' that.'

Suddenly one of the mackerel lines began to jerk. Philip ignored it as he had ignored Mark's hand. Mark found he was holding his breath. He had heard stories of Philip's past before; the old man respected and admired by everyone who knew him. But this story was . . . different.

'Aye. She would 'ave quite a catch in Philip Nolla. Quite a catch. 'Cept for one thing. There couldn't be no children – not never. And no-one knew that save Philip Nolla 'imself. An' if 'e brought 'ome a wife then no-one would ever know it. So that were the bargain. She'd protect 'im. An' in return 'e'd protect 'er.'

Mark thought of Etta, grim and loving, yet never loved as much as Philip. He thought of Etta, letting herself be seen as a barren woman, taken on by a good man. And then he thought of Zannah.

He said hoarsely, 'Why are you telling me this?'

Philip began to pull in the mackerel.

'Because we bin 'appy. We've shared everything, troubles and joys and we bin 'appy. Whatever people says, Mark, it's not everything.'

Mark wanted to hurt him; he wanted to hurt someone, anyone. He said deliberately, 'Obviously for you it's nothing.'

Philip ducked his head lower, gripped the mackerel in one hand, removed the hook, tapped the head against the side of the boat; the fish lay where he threw it, quite dead.

Mark asked angrily, 'What about Etta?'

Philip said something inaudible, cleared his throat and repeated, 'I dun't know, boy. I cain't answer for Etta.'

'Do you *care*?'

The head came up at last and the blue eyes were unexpectedly hard. 'I care. Every day . . . every time I look at 'er . . . I care. You got to look further 'n that, boy. You got to think

278

what else would 'ave 'appened if we 'adn't linked up our lives.'

'She could have gone away somewhere else. She didn't have to marry you. You were the one who needed respectability – in a place like this where you'd lived all your life—'

Philip interrupted fiercely. 'She said she loved me! Don't you understand, boy, what I'm tryin' to tell you? She wanted to be with me. Whatever . . .' He shook his head as if to clear it. 'Mark . . . that girl . . . if she says later on that she wants to be with you, you must believe her. If you send her away because you're crippled, she might never be 'appy again! An' neither will you!'

Mark felt his face stretch wide. Philip held his gaze relentlessly for a long time, then he turned and began to wind in the other line.

'Let's go back, boy. There's nuthin' more to be said or done out 'ere. You're too young for what I sed to you this day. But there might not be another time. Keep it in your 'eart for now.'

Mark said stubbornly, 'I don't know what you mean. There's no *girl*. How could there be a *girl*? I'm practically handcuffed to one of you all the time!'

Philip said, 'You gunna row back? Or d'you want me—'

'Are you trying to say we're in the same boat?' Mark realised what he'd said and sobbed a laugh. There were indeed tears at the back of his nose. 'You had legs, Philip! You could have gone away – somewhere else – yourself! You didn't have to stay here where you'd got this reputation for being so bloody marvellous! You could have started somewhere else where no-one expected you to be virile!' He paused, half expecting Philip to say 'Langwidge' at him. But nothing happened. The small man, the man he'd been brought up to admire and even revere, sat in the stern of the boat in an attitude of abject surrender. It was as if, with his bowed head and shoulders, he expected Mark to rain blows on him. Yet Mark – even though he consciously tried – could not summon contempt for him. He looked at him and told himself he was sorry for him. But that was not true either. Strangely, there was still admiration and respect beneath the undeniable anger.

He said curtly, 'I'll row then.' And fitted the oars carefully into the rowlocks. Philip's 'confession' had had one result: Mark knew that he must not see Zannah again.

*   *   *

279

But he could not stay indoors all the time and when he set one of his tin legs outside the door, he was immediately obvious to anyone who might be watching. He left the house early the next morning to buy the Sunday papers and catch the branch train to Lelant where he would feel safe from the hippies. He left a note for Clem and Madge telling them he would be out all day. He knew they'd accept it all right, but Etta would bemoan the fact that he'd taken no sandwiches; and Philip would think it was all his fault. Mark couldn't be bothered with all that; he felt suddenly as if he'd spent his whole life worrying about other people's feelings and now he simply didn't care. The weather wasn't so good, but he didn't care about that either. He'd find a warm spot among the dunes at Lelant and read the *Sunday Pictorial*, then he'd go to a restaurant and have a slap-up lunch. He wasn't used to eating out alone, it would be something achieved.

It was seven thirty when he passed the parish church and the early communicants were just filing out. He remembered going to services there with his grandmothers; Grandma Bridges had sat smilingly and commented at the end, 'It's like being in an upturned boat with the sea swishing away just outside.' And Grandma Briscoe had said they were all shipwrecked sailors with doom just over the horizon. He had been there since but never to a service, and he wondered if he might return home that evening in time for Evensong. It would spin out his absence for another hour at least.

The last worshipper emerged; a hiker already shouldering into a large back-pack. He paused for a word with the vicar who obligingly gave him a hand with one of his straps: it was probably that gesture which made Mark realise it wasn't a man hiker, it was a girl. The next moment she turned away, smiling, and he could see beneath her cap a wodge of red hair.

He sidestepped into the doorway of Prynne's. Always before, she had seen him first and been able to make her appearance when she chose. Now he had that advantage and was thankful for it. He could choose to stay where he was until she went away. If it meant missing the early train, too bad. There were other trains.

She took her time, still chatting to the vicar though she was moving away. He got the impression they were friends. As the man gathered his cassock against a draught from the harbour, he called, 'Good luck then – and be careful for goodness' sake!'

Which was an informal farewell from minister to flock member, surely? Mark realised how little he knew of Zannah. Not even her full name.

She began to lumber down towards the Warren, bent almost double beneath her load. Mark waited until she had disappeared before striking up the High Street and into Tregenna Place. Was she going to make camp along the cliff somewhere? It was more civilised this side of St Ives, and people would surely move her on. But at least she was out of her hippie gear, so she would receive civil treatment.

He paused at the top of the station approach to get his breath and there she was again, her head bobbing up from the Warren Steps in slow motion after the steep climb. He watched her hang on to the rail and stare out across Porthminster. He knew she was making her farewell; she was catching the train like he was, she was going right away.

The pang he felt then was physical. He didn't want to see her, yet the thought of her absence was awful. Last year he had known she wouldn't be here and that had been bearable, but the year before when she should have made one of her unexpected appearances, he had waited for her and had been miserable.

He watched her as she resettled the weight on her shoulders and marched across to the booking office without looking to left or right. He knew how she felt. The sinking misery of departure infected him too. There was no point any more in his day out; he nearly turned and went back to Zion Cottage. It would be the sane sensible thing to do; but even as he thought the thought he was swinging into motion again, passing the booking office and making straight for the waiting train. He could buy a ticket from the guard, and he wanted to keep the element of surprise on his side for once.

She climbed into the long open carriage and began to get out of her pack. He pulled himself up and came up behind her. He braced himself against a seat and took the weight of the rucksack in his hands. She gasped a 'Thanks' and struggled to some avail. When she turned to take the load from him she still did not immediately realise it was him. Then the metal frame slid to the floor between them.

'Mark!' The eyes were almost navy blue this early in the morning and unexpectedly – shockingly – they filled with tears.

281

'Oh Mark!' She tried to laugh and added inanely, 'It's you!'

'Yes. It's me.'

He smiled up at her, then reached behind for his stick and sat down. She stayed where she was, staring down at him, her eyes drowning. He smiled slightly and patted the seat next to him and she sat down.

'I thought . . . I kinda thought . . . we'd said goodbye,' she stammered.

'Did you? Did we?' He had wanted to say goodbye two days ago, but he had not realised she felt the same way. She had been so bloody persistent when they were kids.

'I tried to find you. To explain some more. But no-one answered at the cottage and Mr Nolla had gone out in a boat. So I kept watch on the others, thinking you'd join them when they ate their picnic. But you didn't.'

'You kept watch?'

'Yes. From the cliffs.'

'All day?'

'Sure. Almost. And when you didn't show up I knew it was goodbye. And I couldn't stand that. So I figured I'd go back today. And here you are.' She too smiled. 'How did you know? Did you follow me?'

'No. I saw you come out of church. Then I followed you.'

'Oh Mark.' She swallowed and smeared at her eyes with the palm of one hand. She was wearing corduroy trousers with a lot of pockets but she did not seem to possess a handkerchief. Mark passed her his and she used it vigorously. Then she crushed it between her hands and looked at him earnestly. 'You see, it's not like it seems. I know you must think I'm some kind of whore, sleeping around on the beaches with anyone who comes along. But when it happened it wasn't like that because I was looking through *their* eyes. Now I'm looking through *your* eyes and I've stopped. Honest to God. I'm going back to London and I'm going to work my fingernails off and—'

He said stiffly, 'You mustn't change your way of life because of me, Zannah. I've absolutely no right to—'

'Oh don't be such a pious *idiot*!' The eyes became purple and blazed at him. 'You sound just like you did when you were preaching to Jem and me back in '59! It wasn't a way of life – it was an experiment! Okay. I tried it and it wasn't for me!' She had a corner of his handkerchief round her little finger like a tourniquet. 'I made a mistake. Isn't a person allowed to make a mistake in your book?'

He did not immediately reply and then the guard arrived and he had to explain there had been no time to buy a ticket. By this time they both realised that the train was moving and they were nearly at Carbis Bay.

She said urgently, 'You bought a ticket to Lelant. That's only another three minutes.'

And he said at the same time, 'I only meant that I can't interfere with your . . .' He stopped and looked at her and then said, 'Zannah, d'you have to go on the early train? Get off at Lelant with me. Just for an hour. Please.'

It was as if she unloaded another rucksack. She leaned back in her seat and a smile spread from one side of her face to the other.

'I can go back to London at any time,' she said after a long pause, during which he thought he might have held his breath. Then the smile became a giggle and she leaned forward and put her hand on his knee, felt the metal of his leg and moved up to his thigh. 'And thanks for interfering, Mark Briscoe. I honestly began to think you never would!'

And they both laughed.

There was a cafe open on a Sunday right among the dunes. It was a wooden shack, almost derelict, and the wooden sign announcing 'Teas' swung in the wind with a rusty squeak. The proprietor warmed two pasties in an old Calor gas oven and cut bread and butter. He told them he had served in 'the first lot' and lived here since 1920 on his pension and what he got in the summer from serving teas. Mark said, 'I'm not a victim of the last war actually. I was dropped when I was a baby.'

'Then you're a victim anyway,' the man said gloomily.

'Oh no he's not.' Zannah bit hugely into the bread. 'He's a miracle. He should be dead and he's not. He went off the railway bridge at Carbis Bay.'

'I've heard of you,' said the man less gloomily. 'She's right. I reckon you are a miracle.' He poked Zannah's shoulder with a yellow finger. 'Good job for you, eh miss?'

Mark wanted to cringe with embarrassment, but it did not worry Zannah at all. She smiled sunnily.

'A jolly good job,' she agreed.

As soon as the man had delivered the pasties on thick earthenware plates and plonked a bottle of tomato sauce between them, Mark said in a low voice, 'Let's get out of here.'

Zannah shot him a look then said, 'No problem,' and gathered the pasties into the tear-stained and crumpled handkerchief. 'We'll be back for tea,' she called.Going to eat out in the sunshine.' There was not a glimpse of sun and the unoiled sign seemed to squawk a protest, but the man nodded with unwanted and unwelcome understanding and Mark stumbled thankfully into the dunes and threw himself down among the sharp grasses with a kind of groan. Zannah gave him another look, noted the red face and spread the handkerchief busily.

'Just as well to get out of there,' she said, passing him a pasty and immediately starting on hers. 'I've got loads to tell you. Private stuff y'know. And walls have ears.'

'Zannah, d'you mind if we don't talk any more? You see, there's no real future for me. Not your kind of future. And—'

'Not that kind of private stuff!' She deliberately blew some crumbs at him. 'You've been listening to too many dirty old men in crummy caffs, Briscoe! That's what is good about the Peace People. They're never dirty.' She pretended to sniff under her arm and made a face. 'Not in *that* way!'

She forced him to laugh. He'd never met anyone like her. Most of the women he knew would think she was vulgar. It was as if she knew what Philip had said to him and was trying to knock it all down in the only way she could.

He relaxed and took a bite of pasty. 'Go on then,' he invited.

'W-a-a-l . . .' She chewed exaggeratedly and he wondered whether, beneath the bravado, she was nervous, 'You might not like it. I mean, it might seem like me being nosey.'

'That would make a change.' He looked at her humorously. 'I don't know a thing about you, Zannah. Not even your other name. And you know practically everything about me. Wouldn't that indicate that you are a little inquisitive?'

She flipped some sand at him.

'Okay, okay. 'I'm *curious* about things I like. I'm very curious about painting and sculpture. I find out everything I can about them.' She swallowed. 'And I have tried to find out everything about you.'

284

The compliment was obvious. He wished he could lower his temperature somehow.

She spread her hands. 'Listen. I'll tell you about me first. Shall I? It'll stop you feeling all embarrassed about yourself and put me in the hot seat for a spell.' She sighed. 'I've wanted to tell you anyway. Right from the beginning when we were kids. But you were never interested.'

She paused as if for permission to continue. He realised he had a mouth full of unchewed meat. He said through it, 'I'm interested. I'm really interested. Why d'you think I got on that train?'

She was reassured and gave him a flash of a smile.

'Yeah. You gave yourself away there, didn't you? Oh lordy, I don't know where to begin. Ask me a question.'

He tried to think of something sensible and all he could say was, 'Where were you two years ago?'

It seemed like the key question. She stopped fidgeting and went very quiet. Then she looked down at the sand between her legs.

She said softly, 'I was in Penzance. My father . . . died. We were all there. For the funeral. Then I went back to the States with Aunt Di.'

Something hit the sand by her left ankle. It could have been the remains of her pasty or it could have been a tear.

He said, 'Zannah. I'm sorry. I shouldn't have . . . Please don't say any more.'

She looked up. It had been a tear. But now she was angry. 'Why not? Is that what your family do – bottle everything up so that they can keep the stiff upper lip, the closed family ranks? I *want* to talk about Daddy! I want to talk about him to *you*!'

He wished he could get to his knees and hold her, but it was an impossibility. He said, 'It's okay. I'm here. Talk.'

The tears suddenly spouted from her eyes and on to her pasty. 'Oh Mark. You didn't know him. That is what is so *awful* – you didn't *know* him!' She sniffed furiously. 'You would have liked him so *much*! And he would have liked – he would have *adored* you! The way you know things without having them explained . . . the way you draw your thoughts . . . oh God. He was great, Mark. He was . . . what's the word? Irreverent. He was so damned *irreverent*! He drove Aunt Di almost out of her mind! And he was such fun! He made everything such fun!

285

He wanted to tell her that she had inherited all those qualities, but all he could say was, 'I'm sorry.'

She said in her old fierce way, 'I'm not! I'm glad! He was always talking about Mummy. And painting her. Trying to make her real. He wanted me to know her. But all I knew was that he was unhappy without her. All the time. And now . . .' she broke down completely, crouching over the pasty and sobbing out the words. 'And now they're together.'

'Oh Zannah.'

The best he could do was remove the pasty from her hand and shake out the handkerchief for her. She cried helplessly for a long time, then she took it and scrubbed at her face.

Then she looked at him. All the trace of the peace brigade had gone. Her face was streaked and dirty, just as it had been that night four years ago when she had held him to her tightly to control his shivering body.

She drew a trembling breath.

'You see, Mummy was dying anyway. She had something ghastly growing on her brain and they operated and then it grew again. So she thought she'd have me to be company for Daddy.'

This simplistic explanation had obviously been rote-learned as a child. Zannah gave a watery smile.

'It didn't work out quite like that. He had his work and he had to go all over the world. I went to school in the States so I lived most of the time with Aunt Di. He would join us when he could. And every two years without fail, we'd open up the Penzance studio and spend all summer here. You know about that. They were marvellous times. I can't believe they're over. He never . . . shut me out of anything. When other artists came – or when he met them – I was always there. I expect they hated me and thought I was precocious and horrible. But he didn't. He believed in me . . . he sort of . . . respected me. D'you know what I mean?'

'Of course.'

'Yes. You would. Aunt Di thinks I joined the Peace People as a sort of reaction thing. Grief. Bereavement. But she's wrong. I'd have done it anyway. And he'd have understood. And now it's over he wouldn't crow or anything. He'd say it was another experience under my belt. I want to be like him. Experience things. Get *back* to him.'

286

He said, 'You don't have to go anywhere to find people once they're dead. They are with you all the time then. They *become* you.' He stared at her. 'You say you wish I had known him. Maybe I do. Maybe I'm looking at him now.'

The tears flowed again.

'Oh Mark. How do you know that?'

'I don't. But it's common sense, isn't it?'

She said eagerly, 'And there's his work. You probably know that, too.'

'What was his name?' Mark held his breath, prepared to lie. But when she said, 'Gerald Scaife,' he let it go in a gasp of surprise. 'Gerald *Scaife*? Yes, of course I know him. We've got a rather bad copy of something of his at home. An abstract. My God. You are his daughter.'

She looked slightly more cheerful. 'Ah. A little respect at last!' She stretched out her legs. 'Oh, I'm so glad you know his stuff. There's a retrospective exhibition of it at the Tate starting next week. That's why I have to be in London.'

'The Tate *Gallery*?'

'Sure.'

'Gosh. He must be really good.'

'One of the best,' she said unboastfully. 'That's how I know you're good. I've got an eye trained by one of the best.

'Oh Zannah.' He did not know what to say. 'Thanks. Really. Thanks.'

'I'm at art school too. I mean, I'm not just a gut critic.'

'Tell me about *your* work.' He realised he had known all the time that she was an artist.

'I'm going to sculpt.' She glanced at him with defiance. 'I like techniques. And materials. You know. I like to find out what bronze can do. And how wood looks inside. And the way you can polish stone.' She wriggled her backside into the sand. 'I'm not wonderful actually. I have to work. And work. And then work some more.' She laughed. 'I don't mind.'

'I should think not. You're damned lucky.' He gave her the pasty and she took it and tried to eat.

'Yes. I am lucky. But so are you. I know you must sometimes think you're not. But that's not true. You see, you are able to experience things without actually doing them. You've got some wavelength . . . I don't know what it is . . . that puts you in touch

287

with other people and how they feel and react. It's all there in your paintings. I have to go places, do things, make a damn fool of myself. And you're there already. Do you understand what I'm saying?'

'No.'

'Maybe that's as well. If you did it might go.' She bit a lump of gristle and made a face. 'Shall we ask for our money back?' She removed it and began to take the pasty to bits like a monkey looking for fleas.

'Actually, it was your picture that made me start feeling curious again.'

'Curious?' He tried to grin for her. 'You mean nosey?'

'Well, yes. I think I mean nosey.' She grinned back. Then she began to flick the insides of her pasty to a gull. In an instant hordes of them were screaming and squabbling. It gave him a moment to think about her background and how she had explained it. So much was now clear about this girl: her surface brashness and her inner uncertainties. A child of one parent; an artist; a broken-hearted artist; finally, an orphan. There was something so damned brave about her. He thought that whatever happened to her she would manage to beat some kind of a drum and fly some kind of a flag.

The gulls finished the pasty and wailed disconsolately for a few moments while she laughed at them. Then they were gone and the dunes were grey and quiet again.

He said, 'Go on. Being nosey is a kind of therapy for you. Like my physio. Tell me.'

She shifted sand from one palm to another.

'It was that picture of yours. The one I stole so that I could look and look at it. It revealed your subconscious to me.'

'Listen, Zannah. I didn't know it was you. I told you that already.'

'No. And probably you didn't know that most of the people there had faces I recognised. Your sister for one.'

'Oh come off it. You don't know my sister that well.'

'Yes I do. And your mother. I've seen her lots of times talking to old Mr Nolla.'

'Rubbish.'

'And the boy who died in that fall from Old Man's Head. And his friend, Rory Trewyn.'

'Zannah. You're into all this stupid psychology thing. And you'd been smoking dope. I could smell it on you.'

'They were *there*. In your picture. I've seen photographs of Rory and Jan.'

'Newspaper photographs. They're never any good.'

'Daddy and I – we've called at Mennion House in the past. Daddy knew Mr Trewyn quite well. The boys were always at school, but Mrs Trewyn gave me a photograph album to look at. They haven't changed much since they were at school. And they were in your picture.'

He surrendered without grace. 'All right. So what?'

'Well. It showed what was on your mind. Then I heard about the split at Mennion House. And I wondered if it was anything to do with that accident four years ago.'

'Possibly,' he said gloomily. He hated talking about Jan and Rory. It was like walking around a maze with no exit. He tried to change the subect. 'I can't get over you going to Mennion House. We always went, each holiday. It was awful.'

'Yes. It was a sort of armed truce between them. It's better really that it all blew up in the end. And nothing to do with Rory or that Polish boy. Did you hear about it?'

'No,' he said cautiously.

'Jeremy Stockton – the partner at the auctioneering firm – turned out to be Matthew Trewyn's son!' Her eyes were wide; in spite of the Peace People and her penchant for shocking people, he realised that Zannah Scaife still had some pre-war morals.

'How on earth did you discover that?'

'Everyone – all Daddy's old friends – is talking about it. Actually they think that Matthew did the decent thing really. He fostered the boy out till he was fourteen, then took him into the business and eventually made him a partner. If only it hadn't come out it would have been all right I suppose. But Mrs Trewyn couldn't stand everyone knowing. At the golf club and things.'

'Yes. I can imagine. Poor woman. And poor Mr Trewyn too. How did it come out? Or couldn't you quite discover that?' He couldn't take it too seriously. It was like one of Ro's magazine stories.

'That was easy. This guy Stockton, he wanted to find out about his real parents. Do you know Mrs Foster who lives in Bunkers

Hill? She's a widow now, but her husband used to make baskets. He was blind.'

'Martin Foster. He married Rose Care and Etta went on and on about it. Rose had a reputation . . . oh no, not Rose *Care*?' It became more and more like a story and drew him in almost against his will.

Zannah nodded. 'He found that out from the parish records. And he kept asking her about his father. And at last she told him and someone heard—'

'Mrs Trevorrow! I bet you anything it was Mrs Trevorrow!'

'I don't know. But Mrs Trewyn heard about it the next day. And she packed up straightaway and left.'

They stared at each other, amazed that adults could weave such tangled lives.

'But that's not what I wanted to tell you.' Zannah sat forward now, confident in her interest. 'I thought if Matthew and this Mrs Foster were in *love* . . . you know, like your parents and mine then they probably had *more* children. Rory. He's dark and Mrs Foster is dark. So I went to see her.'

'You . . . *what*?'

She sat back again. 'You're mad? Maybe it was kind of nosey, huh?'

'Nosey? It was impertinent! Oh God – it was insulting! What did she say? What did she do? You absolute idiot, Zannah!'

'Well, she took it better than you're taking it. She sort of smiled all the time. Like she knew something I didn't. And she called me mettlesome! That's one of Daddy's words – he had old-fashioned kind of words. He used to say all my adventures were ''scrapes''! Anyway, Mrs Foster thinks I'm mettlesome.' Her smile was different, begging a response.

He shook his head resignedly. 'All right. But she didn't tell you anything.'

'No. I think if she was tortured she'd never grass on anyone.' She dug her hands deep into the sad. 'But she went to make me a cup of coffee. It was like cough medicine, but I drank it nicely and thanked her. Because while she was outside I flipped through her photograph album and found an old snap of Rory and your sister. Rosemary looked about ten, and Rory no more than fourteen.'

He said, 'That doesn't prove a thing, Zannah. Anyway, it's

none of our business who Rory's real parents are. What difference does it make?'

'Surely you can see?' She arched her brows impatiently. 'Once he's over this Jan thing, he'll come back. He's a Cornishman. His roots are right here. And your sister will come down on holiday and it will be all right!'

'Zannah . . .' He lowered his head, faced with the impossibility of conveying to her the strange emotional ties between Rory, Jan and Rosemary. He began to scrape sand into walls between his tin legs. 'Zannah. I know the verdict of the inquest was accidental death. But . . . it wasn't quite like that. Ro and Rory both know . . . *I* know . . . Jan deliberately pushed himself off that rock.'

He heard her swift, indrawn breath, but did not look up. His left leg was almost covered in sand. He began on the other one. And he started to tell her.

At the end she said angrily, 'It certainly wasn't your fault! You – you – bird brain! Just because you spoke your mind in that damned cafe place . . . my God, when I think of that day! And we expected you to join in that stupid *game*!' She took a deep and shuddering breath, then went on, 'And you know it wasn't your sister's fault! Or Rory's!' She leaned forward and put her hand on the pile of sand which now completely buried his tin legs. 'Oh Mark, don't you see – it makes it better! He chose to die! Not like my mother who had no choice in the matter! He'd had a good, normal life with the Trewyns. And he chose to end it. It was probably something to do with his *genes* dammitall! If he told you he'd tried it before, then how on earth your sister can imagine it was anything to do with her . . .' She stopped speaking quite suddenly but went on looking at him with total concentration. Then she said on an indrawn breath, 'Oh Mark. I do love you.'

Thoughts of Jan disappeared on the instant. He too was caught in that look. Gulls wheeled and cried and the waves broke beyond the dunes, but they were trapped and held in a timeless moment.

He whispered desperately, 'You mustn't. You mustn't.'

And she whispered back, 'You can't stop me.'

He knew that, and a terrible thrill wrung his heart.

He said, 'You're still a kid.'

'So are you. But you love me too.'

His voice rose, 'I . . . *can't*!'

There was a long silence. Her hand had worked through the

sand, and his thigh told him it was pressing on his tin leg. He felt tears behind his eyes.

She said, 'Would you like to come and see Daddy's work in the Tate?'

He couldn't reply. The tears gathered in his eyes.

She said, 'Fine. Two weeks tomorrow. I'll meet you at Paddington and we'll have a taxi.'

He found his voice and said hoarsely, 'I shall be at work.'

'Take a day off. You need to see my father's stuff.'

She started to get up and when she was on her knees she touched his leg again. Much higher up. And she smiled right into his face with blazing triumph.

'Oh Mark. Oh darling. I think you can. I think you can.'

CHAPTER THIRTEEN

1964

Etta and Mark sat over the drawings until a large orange moon hung over the harbour, making the whole area look like a film set. The chandelier tinkled gently as Etta stood up to fetch the teapot from the sideboard again. It took her a long time; she used her arms on the table to lever herself straight. Philip's death had taken its toll.

'Had enough, Etta?' Mark asked, taking his cup from her. The two of them had long dispensed with niceties; they left the saucers stacked on the dresser and ate their fish with their fingers. 'It's late. We can go on tomorrow.'

'Naw. I like to 'ear your plans, boy. Though why you wants to move down into that ole fish cellar I don't know.'

He said for the umpteenth time, 'Less effort for the tin legs. Anyway it's been my special place for a long time now. I might as well do it out properly.' He looked into her face. 'You're sure you don't mind, Etta? Legally I've got no right to be here at all, you know.'

'What 'ave we got to do with all that legal nonsense, eh? If it's cos o' that, you'll stay right 'ere in the parlour where you've allus bin!' She returned his look through the steam from his cup and her face softened. 'I know you didn't come down 'ere to claim your legacy, my boy – I know that. You came to be with Etta Nolla. That I do know. An' that's what matters.'

'Other people might think differently,' he said gloomily. 'Jem hasn't been near me since I got here.' He looked back at his sketches. 'That's another reason for making a flat downstairs, Etta. No-one can think I've come to oust you out of the house, and no-one will tell you you've reverted to being a nursemaid!' They had both been told that Mrs Trevorrow's heart went out to Etta Nolla who was expected to nurse a cripple.

Etta cackled. Mark had arrived at the beginning of March, just as soon as he had worked out his notice and packed his bags. He had found Etta sitting in the kitchen, staring at the empty range, her lungs audibly creaking. He had ordered coal, made up a bed for her on the ancient horsehair sofa, and fed her beef tea for a week before she pushed it away and demanded ordinary tea, hot and very strong. She had not so much wanted to die, as been unable to find anything to live for. Suddenly, on the verge of pneumonia, she had Mark.

She said now, 'I dun't know as I'll be able to manage on my own.'

'Which is just as well, as you've got a permanent lodger.' Mark looked again at the massive windows he had drawn into his plans and wondered whether a single girder would be able to take the load of the house above them. He had to have the front wall made of glass, there was nowhere else for light. Clem would know. He'd write to him tomorrow.

Etta said, 'It might be too much for you, my boy. I en't getting no younger nor no spryer.'

Mark put his hand over hers; he could feel every tiny bone in it.

'Etta. I've never been much help to anyone. The boot's been on the other foot. The sort of thing I'm doing here – no-one else could stand it. Tea. Fish. Spuds. Bread. It suits you and it suits me. And it makes me feel . . . good.'

'I know. But it still might git too much.' She sucked in her lips. 'Ah well. We'll wait and see. Eh?'

Mark nodded. He was certain it would never be too much for him. He had thought St Ives would be unbearable without Philip, without Zannah, without his parents. It was nothing of the sort. He felt amazingly fit; there had been no warning ache from his stumps, yet the weather had been damp and cold until today. His mother had been tight with anxiety about the whole thing; she had finally wailed, 'Darling, you'll never *cope*!' And he was coping.

The next day he went to see Pearce the builder with his sketches between the pages of the *Comishman*. Nathaniel Pearce had been responsible for the grim rows of council houses above Ayr, but he had been merely taking orders and they were solid enough. He was an old man now, but his married son had taken on the business and shared the bungalow in Orange Lane. Mark was fagged out by the time he'd climbed Porthmeor Hill. He paused on one of the rough unmade roads that terraced the cliff, and looked out across the bay. The sun shone again but the wind was cutting; the horizon was bumpy with white horses and the few fishing boats were keeping close to the shore.

Mark stood still, letting the icy wind cool him down, and revelling in the leaping joy which had possessed him ever since his mother had arrived back home from Philip's funeral. He was going to *live* here. For always. It was what he'd always wanted; not a schoolboy's dream because he had not dared let himself dream of such bliss. It was a need in his very bones. As if he'd grown here at some time and been uprooted against his will. He smiled, permitting himself a whimsical fantasy of his small baby feet rammed into the railway ballast at Carbis Bay station. Maybe that was when he had been 'planted' here. If only he could sell that rubbish to Ro, she might be persuaded into realising she'd done him a favour that day!

He went on up the hill and found Pearce's spanking new bungalow without difficulty. Nat himself opened the door to his knock and stood there narrow-eyed unfriendly.

'Saw you coming up the lane. What do *you* want?'

Mark was rocked back on his heels. He had noted Jem's absence without too much surprise; Jem and his father had a large slice of the *Forty-niner* and had expected to get Philip's. Or at any rate to get it through Etta in a few years. And Jem would come round, he was incapable of harbouring resentment longer than a few weeks. But that other people, who had always been so friendly and who were completely unaffected by Philip's strange bequest, should cold-shoulder him, was a definite shock.

He said, 'I've got some conversion plans here.' He waved the folded newspaper, suddenly conscious that to Nat Pearce an eighteen-year-old was still a child. He began to stammer slightly; a trait he must have inherited from his father. 'I thought of converting Etta's cellar into a flat. W-w-well, a sort of bed-sit actually—'

'She's got the run o' Philip Nolla's 'ouse in 'er lifetime, young man! An' I ain't noticed she's dead yet!'

Mark nearly told him that was no fault of Etta's neighbours; then he decided on diplomacy.

295

'Look, Mr Pearce, I'm there as a friend. A visitor—'

' 'Ten't the season yet. She 'as you in the season an' not before. You're presooming, young man. Philip Nolla treated you like a son, but you en't no son of anyone in St Ives, an' it's no good thinkin' you are!'

Mark felt as if he had been struck physically. No-one had spoken to him so unkindly in his life. And so unjustly.

He said, 'Perhaps I could have a word with your son?'

'No, you cain't. If 'e were 'ere 'e wouldn't want any work from you. But 'e ain't 'ere. So good day to you.'

Mark leaned heavily on his stick, waiting for the door to close in his face. Nat Pearce had another thought and stuck his head through the gap.

'Let me give you a bit of advice, lad. Go back 'ome till feelings cool down some. You came down too soon—'

Mark said, 'Etta would be dead now if I hadn't come down. I didn't come to claim anything! I wanted to be with her—' He wanted to tell this man how Etta had loved her husband; enough to sublimate all her own maternal instincts to protect him. He looked at him helplessly. 'She was completely alone and ill.'

Nat Pearce said stubbornly. 'Someone would've gone in and found 'er and got 'er off to Camborne General.'

'She would have hated that!'

' 'Tis not your con*carn* lad!' But Nat's lined face was softer. 'Look. You go back now. You won't get any builder in the town or out of it, to start knocking Philip Nolla's house about. An' even if you could, the planning folks at Penzance 'ud turn it all down! So just go 'ome like a good boy and wait till the summer. You're a summer visitor, that's what you are.'

He did close the door this time, and after a few, fuming seconds, Mark turned himself and began to trudge back. He knew a sense of defeat waited for him at the edge of his mind and refused to let it come further. He took the top road to the cemetery gates and went in to find Philip's grave. It was too soon for a headstone to have been affixed, but he had no difficulty in finding it because the heaped oblong of earth was smothered in flowers. The blooms in Etta's anchor had long withered but the dark laurel and the berries and the florist's ribbons made it presentable. The Christmas roses which his mother had told him she'd bought, had died and been discarded. Beneath the anchor was an array of flowers. Early daffodils and anemones from the Scillies in jam jars; bunches of snowdrops in fishpaste pots; tiny, flagging crocuses transplanted straight into the soil. Mark stood above them, staring down, actually counting them. Etta had not been here since the funeral, and this was the first time he had visited the grave.

He said aloud, 'Well, you kept your reputation Just like you wanted. And . . . somehow . . . I don't know why . . . you've taken mine.' He stopped counting. There were over one hundred blooms fluttering on Philip's grave, brought by people who loved and admired him. He remembered his mother saying, 'Don't go down, Mark. Please. You don't unerstand how it is. They won't welcome you.'

Again he spoke aloud. 'I don't care. I've a right here. You gave me that right, Philip. I'm not going back. I'm going to fight for that right.'

A thought wormed itself between the determination and defeat. It was, quite simply: Etta will make it all right.

He began to stump back between the tombstones. Of course Etta would bring some of her cynical common sense to the problem. He would tell her about Nat Pearce and she'd cackle a laugh and tell him to take no notice. Next time she got along to Bright Hour, she'd make it quite clear that young Mark saved her life . . . he could practically hear her saying it. But the thought had been more definite than that. Of course, Philip had relied on Etta to make things all right. And by sticking to her role of barren wife, she had done that. Had Philip sent the thought into his head? Did thoughts live on . . . have a life of their own . . . dart into somebody else's consciousness?

Mark came out of the bottom gate and closed it thankfully. What he needed was a swim in the icy Atlantic. Then mackerel and tea with Etta. Then his precious phone call to Zannah.

Before that he spent the afternoon trudging the streets of St Ives, trying to find a builder to look at his plans.

'It's incredible,' he protested to Zannah over a crackling connection to her hostel. 'It's as if they knew I was coming and ganged up on me!'

'You need an older man,' she said. 'Everyone is against us because we're young. I told Aunt Di about us, and she was all for it when she thought you were some kind of war hero. But when I said you'd lost your legs in an accident and you were eighteen, it was a different ball game. Oh.' She started to giggle. 'D'you get that, Briscoe? A different ball game!'

'For Pete's sake, Zannah. What am I going to do? Come up with some answers like you always do!'

'Oh Mark. Darling Mark. What does it matter? Look, when this trustee business finishes, I'll have enough cash for both of us. We can go to Frisco and just . . . live! Darling, we love one another. Let everyone else – everything else – go hang!'

'It's because I love you that it's got to be this way, Zannah. Before, there was just no chance for us realistically. But when Philip gave me an actual *place* here – it's more than the house and the boat, Zannah, can't you see that – then it all became possible. Oh I know I'm still living on the allowance from home, but I'm going to be a working artist, my darling! Soon I'll sell my stuff, and with the income from the boat I'll be really independent! Then I'm going to ask you to marry me. It'll be up to you then. You might change your mind, or—'

'Shut up, bird brain. I know that's how it's going to be. You're as good as Daddy, if not better. It's in your blood and bones, nothing to do with your brain, which is just as well as you're not hot in that department! And I'm going to be a sculptor and we'll be so happy everyone will come and look at us!'

He leaned his forehead against the glass of the telephone box and closed his eyes.

'Will you come down for Easter, Zannah? I want to swim with you. In the cove at Wheal Dream.'

She said, 'Are you unhappy down there, my honey?'

'No. I'm angry right now. But it's good here, Zannah. It's right for me.'

Her sigh rattled his eardrum. 'Put the phone outside and let me hear the waves. A-a-a-ah. Oh Mark.'

'I know.'

'I just wish Daddy were here. I mean I wanted you to know him. That's why it was so marvellous you seeing the Tate thing. But I want him to know you too He would help you, darling. Practical help. He'd find a builder and he'd get the plans passed. And he'd understand He wouldn't say we were too young. He'd love you like I love you.'

298

He could hear her weeping so he said, 'I do hope not, baby.'
And after a second she began to giggle again. He said, 'Darling, I
could ask my own father. He's wonderful. And he'd do it like a
shot. But I want to do this on my own. I mean, I don't mind using
people with influence, but I want to find them and talk to them
and persuade them. And I don't know anyone!'

There was a pause; he could almost hear her thinking.

She said, 'It's so illogical. I mean if they're putting flowers on
Philip's grave, why can't they respect his wishes? He wanted you
to live there. In his house. I don't get it.'

'It's nothing to do with logic.' He tried to ease her frustration.
'Look. I'll go and see Jem. I can win him round. Don't worry.'

'But he's young too. No-one will take any notice of Jem. What
about Dudley?'

'Dudley?'

'The Reverend Dudley. The vicar. He thought the world of
Daddy.'

'Darling. Philip was chapel. Nearly everyone is.'

'I've got it. Really. Matthew Trewyn. He knows everyone in
that end of Cornwall. He'll fix it for you.'

He hated to squash her. After Jan's death and Rory's desertion, how could he ask anything of the Trewyns?

He said doubtfully, 'They say he just sits around in Mennion
House, sozzled most of the time. I don't know whether—'

'He needs something to do! You'll be his salvation, darling!
Get him going – stimulate him – motivate him—'

'Like you did me? Was that what the Act of Piracy was all
about?'

'Could be.'

'You're cunning. And underhand. And completely devious.'

'And you love me.'

'And I love you.'

He came out of the kiosk and propped himself against the glass
for a few moments, savouring the wind and the sound of the
waves. Last night there had been that huge red, frost-moon; now
there were silver-edged clouds moving fast across the night sky.
He wondered what tomorrow would bring. The weather was
all-important down here; a constantly changing character. He
watched Godrevy lighthouse winking in the darkness and knew to
the right of it was Mennion House sitting in the marram grass and

wild thyme of Hayle dunes, ugly and very lonely. And inside, solitary and disgraced, was Matthew Trewyn.

How on earth could Matthew Trewyn help anyone now? He was the one needing help. And Mark was the last person to give that help.

But as he pushed himself off the glass and on to his stick, Mark made up his mind. He would go and see Matthew Trewyn.

Etta thought he should take a taxi.

'A *taxi*?'

Mark was incredulous. Etta would rather walk all day than pay any man for transport.

'You'm looking tired, boy.'

'Am I?' He took the trouble to stand up and study his reflection in the glass above the sideboard. His face certainly looked thinner but it had been too round before. 'Nonsense, Etta. You should see me after I've done a day at the drawing board.'

'You're not 'ankering for your folks then?'

'No.' He felt guilty about that. He loved them more than ever, but sometimes their constant presence was a burden. He said soberly, 'I've never been free before, Etta. probably – after a few months – I shall take it for granted. Not now.'

'Free? With me 'anging like a millstone round your neck?'

He laughed. 'Lifebuoy more like. You're keeping me afloat.'

She sucked her lips in against a smile, then she pointed a gnarled finger. 'That's it. By sea. You kin go over in the dinghy, if go you must.'

He sat down again. The dinghy would be by far the easier way for him to go over to Hayle. There was a landing stage at the foot of the dunes, then steps right up to the house with a hand rail all the way.

'They wouldn't let me have it,' he said slowly. He would like to row the *Forty-niner*'s dinghy. He went swimming most days but the water was icy and the effort of unstrapping and restrapping his legs was gigantic. To row was another way of using the water; just as energetic but more appropriate to the weather.

'Don't ask 'em, then.' Etta stuck out her jaw belligerently. He'd heard those words, or similar, and seen that expression on Zannah's face. Etta poked again with her finger. 'You got a share in the boat. You got a right to the dinghy.'

300

So the next calm and windless day, he went down the harbour beach, sat on the gunnel of the dinghy, lifted his legs inside, unhitched the mooring rope and fitted the oars into the rowlocks. No-one saw him leave and no-one evinced the slightest curiosity as he rowed out of the harbour and across Porthminster and Carbis Bay. It was a marvellous feeling. He'd rowed the dinghy often before, but always with someone else aboard. He took long, slow strokes, resting on every twentieth for a few moments to gaze around him and relish the shouldering swell beneath the boat. The silence then was wonderful; not silence at all, just absence of every human sound. Then came the intense physical effort again when he was conscious of loud breathing and even a grunting groan occasionally. Then more silence.

As he tied up at the Mennion House landing stage, another of his clear, concise thoughts arrowed into him. It was that Ro would find the answers to all her questions and fears down here. He did not shrug that one away as he had done the previous one; it was completely logical and inevitable. He saw that she had been running as in a nightmare through cloying mud, away from the very place which could offer solace. He began to search for words to use in a letter to her. Tranquillity. Simple solutions. Clarity of water moving on the face of the . . . He was at the top of the steps and the conservatory door was open.

He walked through it and into a dark passage cluttered with coats, tennis racquets, golf clubs, old plimsolls. He had never been this way before, his chair would not have got through. He opened a door at the end and was in the kitchen. A loaf and wedge of cheese were on the deal table which took up the centre of the room; the bread was shrinking with staleness and the cheese smelled sharply of its own rind. Under the window the deep white sink was jammed full of crockery and the tap ran gently over the lot; the window itself was slashed with gull-droppings and most of the cupboard doors swung open. Oddly, the floor showed signs of some attention; the coconut matting was rolled neatly and stood on its end in a corner, a broom leaned beside it and beneath the table was a full dustpan. Mark edged carefully around it and opened another door.

He was on familiar ground now. The hall stretched ahead, shabby and untidy but still beautiful in its wide proportions. The stairs curved out of it elegantly; hanging on the banisters was a pile of clothing topped by a dressing gown and a clutter of shoes lay on the bottom two steps. He paused, frowning. Then he cleared his throat self consciously and called diffidently, 'I say! Is anyone around?'

There was just a second of waiting silence, then the sitting-room door opened with a jerk, and a woman emerged and closed it behind her. Mark's frown deepened. He recognised the woman: it was Rose Foster, the woman Zannah supposed was Rory's mother. And he could see suddenly that it was very likely. Her hair and eyes were more than dark, they were black; she had the wild, almost piratical air that Rory carried with him Mark was rigid with concentration. She was here, in Mennion House, and Mrs Trewyn was not.

She came towards him and said in a low but aggressive voice, 'What do you want?' And there was a faint emphasis on the 'you'.

'I – I've come to see Mr Trewyn,' He wished to God he could cut out the stammer, it made him sound a schoolboy still.

She said, 'Why?'

He wondered if he should tell her to mind her own business, but it went against his nature and besides it might *be* her business. All the stuff Zannah had worked out had sounded pretty thin at the time, but it was very probable that Matthew Trewyn's business was also Rose Foster's.

'Er . . . actually . . . I needed some advice. On builders and planning permission and things.'

'I heard.'

She surveyed him a moment longer then brushed past him. 'Come on into the kitchen. I'm clearing up, and we can talk as I work.' She jerked her head at the sitting-room door.

'Mr Trewyn is asleep at the moment.'

Mr Trewyn? It didn't sound as if she'd moved in as his . . . whatever. He followed her back into the kitchen and when she pushed a chair at him, he lowered himself into it.

She gathered up the dustpan and tipped it into a paper sack. Then she did the same with the bread and cheese. Then she went to the sink.

'I put these to soak while I saw to him. I heard yest'y that his daily help hasn't been for over a month, so I guessed he'd be in a pickle. Never could look after himself. When I was here nearly

302

forty years ago, he had to be looked after hand, foot and finger, and men don't improve. They just gets worse.' She glanced at Mark. 'Pull that chair closer and you can dry the crocks and put them on the table.' She rummaged in a drawer and came up with a tea towel, then spread clean newspaper over the table. 'I'll scrub that later. It's not deep dirt. I'll give 'er that. She weren't much of a wife to 'im, but she kept everything nice, and trained 'er staff to do the same.'

So Mrs Foster had worked here years ago. Perhaps that was when . . . but no, she'd said forty years ago and Rory wouldn't be thirty yet. He looked at her back as she tackled the washing-up, and tried to imagine her as young and passionate. It wasn't easy. She'd come down from Zennor way about five or six years ago, married old Mr Foster when he was on his last legs, and inherited his house in Bunkers Hill. Etta said she had 'gobbled up' the old man. But his mother liked her. In fact she had stayed at Mrs Foster's house for Philip's funeral.

'Come on,' she said, already up to her elbows in suds. 'Get on with it. You've got arms like a gorilla – let's see you use them!'

She grinned at him suddenly to take the sting out of the words, and he found himself grinning back. She did have a certain attraction: an enormous energy and drive. Matt Trewyn would be all right if she was going to take him over.

She waited until he'd polished half a dozen glasses, then she said, 'Mr Trewyn is asleep because he is drunk. I don't think he'll be able to help you. But he'd like to see you – he thinks everyone has deserted him, not just his wife.'

He cleared his throat to get rid of any stammer and said brilliantly, 'Oh.'

She stacked half a dozen plates neatly against a tea-cup; her hands were so capable and her bare arms were still round and firm.

'I wouldn't, want you to think my visit here is on a regular basis.' She grinned at him. 'I haven't seen Mr Trewyn face to face since I left his . . . service—' she laughed at the unexpected innuendo, then sobered. 'But I know what it's like to be an outcast.' She lifted her shoulders to her ears. 'Funny you an' me choosing the same day to come calling.'

'Um . . . yes. A coincidence.'

She rinsed the sink, seized another towel and began on the

303

piled crocks on the draining board. They diminished rapidly.

She said, 'I'll make some tea and you can take it in to him and wake him up. I'll finish here.' She filled a kettle at the tap and moved strongly to the gas stove. 'It's only surface dirt. I'll go into Hayle and get a'old of Mrs Vissick and put the fear o' God into 'er. She'll be up tomorrow and at least the 'ouse will be back to normal. As for 'im—' she adjusted the gas flame and sighed.

'Aren't you . . . I mean, don't you . . . what I mean is won't you stay to look after him?' Mark brought out at last, blushing to the roots of his hair.

'Me?' She laughed again; she did a lot of laughing. 'Gawdlemighty boy, 'e'd soon drink himself to death if I stayed 'ere.' She looked at him. 'You're as green as your mum, aren't you, young man?' She put cups and saucers on a tray. 'Listen, Mark Briscoe. If you cain't get no 'elp from poor Mr Trewyn – and I doubt if you will – come 'an see me. A week from today. Eight o'clock of the evening.' She chuckled. 'That's if Etta Nolla will allow it!' She made the tea and placed the pot on the tray. Then she made a wry face. 'Pity poor old Etta couldn't let the rumours stand, my boy. Then you wouldn't be 'aving all this difficulty!'

'Rumours?' He was still admiring her firm, decisive movements from stove to tray and back again. 'What rumours?'

'Surely you 'eard? When Philip left you 'is all, there was folks who thought it was because you was his own kith and kin. But Etta scotched all that by clinging to your ma like a leech all through the funeral, and now taking you in.' She leaned over the table and touched his cheek, quite hard. 'Don't look like that, boy!' Twas only gossip and it's over now. Everyone know your ma . . . and Philip . . . straight as dies, the pair of 'em. Now if it 'ad bin me—' She laughed uproariously. 'What would you have thought of me as a ma? Eh?'

He was still reeling over her last words. No wonder his mother had arrived back from the funeral white-faced and shaking. No wonder she said she could never come to St Ives again. And Philip! If they knew about Philip!

She said, 'Not much, eh? You wouldn't want Rose Care for a ma!'

He swallowed hard and looked at her. There was a kind of brazen innocence about her that was infinitely touching. He said without a trace of a stammer, 'I should be very honoured, Mrs Foster.'

Her colour darkened and her laughter died. She picked up the tray and marched to the door.

'Come on then. All this talk is getting us nowhere.'

She waited in the hall for him to get himself up and moving. Then she went into the sitting-room and put the tray on a low table. Mark, following behind, was back in the past; the big leather chairs with their built-in ashtrays on the arms were the same as he remembered, the piano in the bay window still wore its Indian shawl. Rose had evidently spent time in here; the whole place smelled of lavender furniture polish, and there was a clear, bright fire in the grate. Matthew Trewyn sprawled in one of the chairs beside it, his arms touching the floor either side, his head lolling loosely, mouth open, snores emerging irregularly. Mark hung back, wishing he'd never come.

Rose went over to the sleeping man and shook him vigorously.

'Come on now, Maister!' Her voice became at once hectoring and servile. 'Wake yourself up! You've got a visitor!'

Matthew came to slowly and grumpily.

'You still here, Rose? What would I do without you?'

He reached for her with one flailing arm and she side-stepped neatly.

'Ah Rose . . . Rose. I should never have sent you packing all those years ago. I knew it would come out in the end – and it did. Oh God . . . it did.'

Rose said loudly, 'You've got a visitor, Mr Trewyn!'

Matthew tried to focus his eyes. 'Visitor, did you say? Who . . . Christ, it's the little Briscoe boy, isn't it?' He made an effort to stand up and failed. 'Haven't seen you since . . .' he couldn't bring himself to speak of the inquest and funeral. He relapsed into the chair. 'I heard you'd got some cork legs but I'd never have thought . . . never . . . well done, lad! Bloody well done!'

This was the Matthew Trewyn Mark remembered, bluff and instantly friendly. He looked up and nodded his thanks.

'Actually they're aluminium, not cork. Very light – as light as cork and a lot stronger.'

'Make you top heavy, do they?'

Mark could cope with what he called the techniclinical approach. He grinned.

'I have been known to turn turtle! They make them shorter to counteract that. Apparently my natural height should be six two. Not two six.'

Matthew laughed loudly. Rose did not.

'You're a fine figure of a man,' she said with a hint of reproach.

'Let's have some tea, Rose! Eh lad? Eh . . . er . . .'

'It's Mark,' Rose said clearly. 'And the tea is here.' She marched to the door. 'I've got work to do,' she announced, and left.

Mark noticed she had put the tray near a high chair which would do nicely for him. He made some remark about being mother and sat himself by the teapot. Matthew eased himself upright by degrees, talking all the time.

'What *about* your lovely mother – how is she these days? And your father going from strength to strength? It's the quiet ones who get there, my boy – Mark – every time. The quiet ones. And you . . . that Mrs Vissick told me a tale about you. I won't repeat it.' He guffawed. 'So . . . old Philip Nolla left you his all, did he? No wonder the tongues are wagging.' He leaned forward at last and took a cup from Mark's outstretched hand. 'It's like old times this, Mark. Bit more civilised than I'm used to nowadays, I'm afraid. Good job you came the day Rose took pity on me. Things had got rather run-down here. Mrs Vissick – the daily help you know – she was taken on by my wife . . . you've heard about my wife?'

'Yes. I'm very sorry, sir. I hope it will—' Mark sipped his tea and practically scalded the roof of his mouth '—eventually blow over.'

'Don't know. It's not actually finding out about my lurid past you see, lad. She always knew about that. It's the disgrace. Golf club. That sort of thing.'

'Er . . . yes. Quite.'

'It's worse for a woman, you see. You . . . me . . . we'll soldier on. People accept us again, seven days wonder, all that sort of rubbish. Women . . . they let these things fester inside them.'

Mark sipped again and decided to take the bull by the horns.

'Actually, it was about that kind of thing. Indirectly. I mean . . . I came to see you because . . . I want to make a sort of flat out of Etta's fish cellar. The services are down there – a lavatory,

306

sink, gas – lots of people are converting their fish cellars and it's not difficult. But until I can get the corroboration of a builder I can't get any plans together to submit to the Council.' Once he'd started it wasn't too bad. He pulled out some of his sketches and began to talk enthusiastically about his ideas. Matthew became interested and stood up at last to take a sketch over to the window.

'Ideal,' he muttered. He looked up. 'You could be independent down there,' he commented. 'No trouble to the old girl – Mrs Nolla – yet within earshot of each other if anything went wrong.'

Mark nodded vigorously, surprised that this insensitive man could see immediately the advantages of the plan.

'And it might help to scotch all this talk of me ousting Etta,' he added. 'I don't want to do that of course, but she needs someone.' He smiled for the first time and with a certain pride. 'She needs me,' he admitted.

'Yes.' Matthew grinned back. 'Yes. She's damned lucky.' He flapped the sketch. 'I don't know what I can do to help. Lost a lot of my contacts . . . Got a copy of this?'

'Yes. You can keep that if you re interested.'

'I am. I'll see what I can do. Perhaps someone from further afield . . . Truro.' He sucked in his breath consideringly. 'They won't like that. The local men. Could make it very difficult. But I can certainly get you planning permission. No trouble at all.'

'It's very good of you. I mean in the circumstances—'

'Do me good to think about something else. Nothing's gone right since . . . Why the hell Rory had to banish himself like he did, I'll never know. Never understand. That's why Mary was so bitter. Christ, we were cut up about Jan, but we didn't run off to God knows where, did we!' He recalled himself. 'Sorry, old man. I forget your family was involved. Did your sister get over it all right?'

'I . . . yes, I suppose so. In a way. She's just different. I'm going to try to persuade her to come down again. She's never been back since.'

'Why? If she doesn't want to come, won't it just open old wounds? I suppose that is why Rory stays away.'

'I rather think she should face things, sir. *Look* them in the face.' The moment of vision on the surface of the water had gone. He fumbled for the certainty he had had then. 'It's still so beautiful down here, so . . . eternal.'

'Yes.' Matthew Trewyn came back to the table and poured

himself another cup of tea. 'Perhaps that's what Rory should do. If I knew where he was, I'd write and tell him so.' He looked at the sketch again, unseeingly. 'You know, Mark, when Philip Nolla asked me to take in another of Rose's children all those years ago, I thought it might be his. Mary lost her child, and it seemed the best thing to do. Any stock of Philip Nolla's would be hard-working and clean-living, and if Rose passed on her energy and laughter . . . well.' He shrugged. 'No doubt about Rose being Rory's mother. But Philip? Philip would never run away from anything like Rory has done.'

Mark said involuntarily, 'Then you're not Rory's father?' He put his cup down with a clatter. 'I'm sorry. I shouldn't . . . none of my business.'

'Not at all, old man. My business belongs to the world and his wife now. I'd rather you heard it from me. No. I'm not Rory's father. I did my best. So did Mary. But I think he must have known.'

Mark revised some of his impressions. Perhaps Matthew Trewyn only seemed insensitive.

He stood up and leaned on his stick.

'I'd better go. I've rowed myself across, and the tide will be dropping soon.'

'Good to see you. Good of you to . . . Come again. Any time. I don't go into the office often now, you know. I'm usually somewhere around.' He grinned. 'Jerry keeps things going for the old firm. At least I've done something right.' He seemed to have forgotten his promise to take Mark's plans to the Council. He went to the mantelpiece and pulled a bottle from behind a large carriage clock; it was empty. 'I say old man, tell Rose to bring in some more whisky, would you?'

Mark went back the way he had come, but there was no sign of Rose anywhere. A note on the table said, 'Casserole in oven with rice pudding. Expect Mrs Vissick in the morning.' He smiled, thinking how he would tell Zannah about this visit with all its surprises. And then he stopped smiling. There was too much unhappiness linked to each of the surprises.

He went back to the sitting-room to tell Matthew that Rose had left.

'That's all right. I'll get my own whisky.' The older man straightened away from the mantelpiece. 'Glad you came, Mark.

I'll do my best for you.' He sketched a comic salute. 'Everyone used to come to me if they wanted anything done. Who sent you?'

'Er . . . Miss Scaife, actually. You knew her father.'

'Miss Scaife? Susannah Scaife? My God. She must be nearly your age now. And Gerald . . . Gerald was a fine chap. Never the same after his wife died, but a fine artist. Susie Scaife, eh. Imagine that child remembering me.'

Mark felt as if they were talking about someone other than Zannah. He remembered her saying a long time ago, 'My name is Susannah. I could have been Susie or Anna, but no-one remembers names like that. You'll never forget Zannah.'

All the way home he thought of Zannah Scaife, who had been determined from the moment she met Mark Briscoe, that he would never forget her.

The next day when he came out of Philips' Dairy, Jem fell into step by his side. He was delighted, about to hand over the heavy bag of groceries, then changed his mind. Jem's face was stony.

'If you need the dinghy again, perhaps you would mention it to me or the old man first. You might 'ave part share in the *Forty-niner* but Philip Nolla 'isself wouldn't a' took it without our say-so.'

Mark was suddenly so angry he could taste his own bile. Without a word or a thought, he put his stick neatly between Jem's feet. Jem stumbled to his knees. Mark waited till the furious face was raised to his. Then he said very quietly, 'I should have drowned you when I had the chance. Keep your bloody dinghy. I'll sell my share of the *Forty-niner* to one of the summer visitors and buy my own dinghy!' And he swung himself away with his seaman's roll, leaving Jem staring in sudden consternation.

During Bright Hour Etta sat as close as she could to Mrs Trevorrow, and afterwards asked for her arm to the bottom of the hill. It was an unprecedented request; Mrs Trevorrow did not know whether to be flattered or alarmed.

'Weather's still unkind, Mrs Trevorrow,' Etta said in a voice that still trembled with weakness. 'If it dun't come soon, I reckon I wun't see another spring.'

'It's the wind,' agreed her companion. 'But the sun must come nicely through your passage door and—'

'That boy of my Philip's will need good friends after I'm took. Like the son I never could 'ave, 'e is. So good about the 'ouse too, and a real Cornishman for all that.'

'Philip's boy?' asked Mrs Trevorrow faintly, almost holding her breath in anticipation.

'Did I say. . . ah well, you guessed all along, didn't you. An' I kin trust you to keep a secret. After all, the wife of a solister—'

'How can you bear it? Poor Mrs Nolla. All these years. And butter wouldn't melt in her mouth. I don't blame your Philip. He was a good man. It was her. It's always the woman.'

'Do you mean Mrs Briscoe? Oh no, you got the wrong one there. It was Mr and Mrs Briscoe what took the child on and gave it a 'ome. Saved Philip and me from disgrace y'see. But he's allus bin like a son to us. Oh no, the mother were as Cornish as Philip. The boy is a proper Cornishman. That's why I rely on you to befriend 'im after I've passed on. 'Tis your secret, Mrs Trevorrow. But you will know. And you will see that justice is done. I am quite certain of that.'

'But dear Mrs Nolla, how could you stand it? My heart goes out—'

They came to the harbour and Etta took a deep breath.

' 'Twere partly my fault after all. I couldn't bear my 'usband no kith and kin. 'E were a natural man, Mrs Trevorrow. A natural man. I dun't want to say more. You unnerstand.'

'Oh my dear, I do. Oh I do. And we all thought you were. . . well, unsympathetic perhaps. And all the time . . .'

'And you will keep my secret?' Etta smiled gently at the gulls quarrelling over some fish heads on the wharf.

'. . . Rest assured . . . and the boy will be one of us . . . one of us, my dear . . .'

Etta disengaged her arm. 'I can manage now, thank you Mrs Trevorrow. Excuse me from asking you into the cottage for tea—'

'In any case I am in a hurry. I have to call in to see Mrs Peters. And Miss Lowe. Are you sure you can manage?' But she was already walking back up Fore Street. And as Etta went up the cobbled court, she said aloud, 'I 'ope you're satisfied now, Philip Nolla!' And she began to laugh.

It was a week since Mark's visit to Mennion House and he had heard nothing from Matthew Trewyn. These things took time, but he wished he knew whether anything was happening. He hardly liked to call again so soon. Even Zannah counselled patience. He hadn't told her of Rose Foster's invitation yet; he did not know why.

That day the strangest thing had happened. He had taken his swim very early to avoid anyone witnessing the business of removing his legs and wriggling into the sea like a sand eel. The church clock was striking eight as he started across the bay to Porthminster and the intense cold of the water was making his stumps ache so that he got no further than the first buoy. As he duck-dived for the return, he saw another swimmer running down the harbour beach, clad in singlet and shorts. Mark paddled with his hands until the swimmer reached him. It was Jem.

'Gawdlemighty!' The small bullet head broke water, spouting like a whale. 'It's bloody cold! D'you do it every morning?'

Mark felt his heart lift in his body. This was the Jem he knew. But he kept his voice sour. 'You probably know the answer to that. I suppose you've spied on me before?'

'Not me.'

'But others have.' Mark began to move towards the shore. 'What are you doing here anyway?'

Jem swam alongside, still gasping convulsively.

'Well . . . I thought . . . mebbe . . . I ought to give you the chance you wanted. To drown me.'

He met Mark's round brown eyes, and suddenly grinned. 'Not that you'd catch me o' course.' And he was gone, arms flailing, legs kicking frantically. Mark could have caught him easily with his dolphin stroke, but he did not. He watched Jem pant his way up the sands, grab a towel and run up Jinty Passage.

Now, as he swung himself from side to side along Fore Street on the way to see Rose Foster, he wondered for the umpteenth time if it had been Jem's way of apologising for his words about the dinghy. In which case Mark would have to find some way of acknowledging that he shouldn't have tripped Jem up with his stick. Damned childish anyway. And he could do with Jem's friendship; he *needed* Jem's friendship.

There was a flight of ten steps to Rose's front door and steps were difficult. He hooked his stick over one arm and used both hands on the rail to pull himself up. It was dark; he wondered if that was why Rose had stipulated eight o'clock. No-one to see him struggling.

She didn't make the mistake of opening the door before he reached it, either. She gave him time to regain his breath and composure and knock twice. Then she put on the hall light, opened the door and immediately preceded him so that if he stumbled he'd do it in private.

'Close the door after you, will you?' She pushed at another door further down the passage. 'Go on in. I'll just put the kettle on.' And she exited left.

Mark realised immediately that someone else was in the room as he edged into it, but after the outside darkness the brilliance of Rose's lighting dazzled him and he could not see who it was. He assumed for a second that it was Mr Trewyn again and that Rose had got him over here to sort out the business of Mark's cellar conversion. Then he knew it was too tall, too wide for Matt Trewyn. He blinked and leaned on the back of an armchair. It was Rory.

For a long moment, neither of them spoke. For Mark the initial shock of recognition was repeated several times as he noted the changes in Rory. And Rory had never seen Mark out of a wheelchair.

Rory spoke first.

'Come and sit down, old man. It must be hard going. And Rose's steps are tough enough anyway. Here. Have this high chair. I take it a high chair is easier than an armchair?'

'Thanks. Yes.' Mark sat down carefully.

Rory laughed. 'Sorry. It's your voice. It hadn't broken when I saw you last. I can't get over . . . sorry. I'm being more than rude. Insulting.'

'No. It's almost five years. And you've changed too.'

Rory made a face. 'Old, you mean. I'm thirty now, Mark. And a lot has happened.'

'But you've come back.'

'Not to stay. I gave Rose a forwarding address. She wrote and said my father was in a state and demanded my presence. So here I am.'

Mark's mind churned. So Rory knew Rose Foster was his mother. And still thought Matthew Trewyn was his real father.

He said lamely, 'It's good to see you, Rory.'

Rory did not respond to this. He sat down close to the small electric fire and shivered, which was, perhaps, response enough.

312

Mark noted that his neck and the back of his hands were weathered to a burnt sienna brown so he must have come from somewhere warm. And his hair was sprinkled liberally with grey. He did indeed look very much older.

Rose came in carrying a tray. She put it down on the table and began to pour tea. It occurred to Mark that this was where his mother must have sat for her meals two short months ago.

She said briskly, 'Bit of a shock, Mark? I didn't tell you Rory was on his way home in case it put you off.'

Mark took a cup of tea gratefully. 'It wouldn't have done that, Mrs Foster. I'm very pleased to see Rory again.'

'I wasn't sure. You Briscoes are a funny lot.' She put a cup near Rory and sat down herself. 'This is the one to help you, Mark. He's been building houses for the past four years. Working with construction firms all over the States. What he doesn't know about building isn't worth knowing. Right, Rory?'

Rory looked up. 'Probably.' He picked up his cup and stared into the steam. 'Crewing on charter boats gave me too much time to think, Mark. I started off as a brickie. But I can do a bit of everything. Carpentering, plastering, even electrical work.' He looked through the vapour at Mark. 'Rose has told me your difficulty. I'll stay long enough to do the flat. No longer.'

Mark hardly knew what to say. He stammered delighted thanks and mentioned the planning permission.

'I'm going over to see the old man tomorrow. We'll get something going between us.' He turned his hooded gaze on to Rose. 'Satisfied?' he asked.

'For the moment.' She sipped. 'I want you to stay here for good though. That's what I've got in mind.'

'You're incredible. D'you know that? You had two children by Matt Trewyn. Do you nag the other one like you nag me?'

He was only half joking and Mark glanced apprehensively at Rose, expecting her to flinch away from the implications behind the question.

She said very straightly, 'I had one child by Matt Trewyn, and he is Matt Trewyn's responsibility. Your father is dead, Rory. You are my responsibility. And you'll never solve anything by running. You ran away from Rosemary. Now you're running away from that Jan Grodno. It's so . . . *silly!*'

He was silent, staring at Rose for a long moment, shocked

by the news that Matthew Trewyn was not his father. Then he shrugged as if it didn't matter. 'Rosemary obviously feels like I do. She's never been back either.'

Mark said suddenly, 'I think she should. She feels it was her fault. But of course it wasn't. And she needs to come back to believe that.'

Rose said swiftly, 'You see?'

Rory looked from one to the other, then sighed deeply. 'I'll tell you why Jan jumped off that rock, shall I? Then you can tell Ro and perhaps one of us will get some peace. It was because of me. I climbed the rock that day . . . somehow I got to the top of Old Man's Head the wrong way. And Jan knew what that meant.'

'It was a stupid *game*!' Rose said angrily. 'Good God, Rory, if he was such a fool – he must have known that if the girl really loved him she wouldn't have cared if fifty others got to her first!'

'He didn't love Ro.' Rory stared at the single glowing bar of the fire. 'He didn't even love Madge Briscoe, though he longed to have her as a mother.' He sighed deeply. 'He loved me.'

Rose and Mark were shocked into silence for a long minute; then Rose said, 'Oh my God.'

'Exactly. He told me how he felt, begged me to let him stay. I thought the only answer was to push him into a marriage with Ro – as if that could cure him. Give him the family he wanted. I was willing to push Ro into it too, just to get free. It was ghastly. Awful. I loved him too, but not like that. And after a while I began to hate him. And I was the only one he trusted. Oh God. You're right, Rose. It was awful.'

She said strongly, 'You shouldn't be telling us. You should be telling Rosemary Briscoe. My good Lord. 'Tis always the way. The men do fight it out between themselves and the woman is supposed to take what's left. You must tell that girl what you've told us, Rory. And soon, too.'

'I thought of it, Rose. But she couldn't stand it being raked up all over again. You don't know what it's like between us. The link – the ties. She's cut them now. Let them stay cut.'

Rose made an impatient gesture that nearly sent her tea flying. 'You cain't cut blood ties, my boy!' She folded her arms furiously. 'You didn't show much surprise just now when I told you Matt Trewyn weren't your father!' Her voice had slipped into Cornish again. 'You must 'a guessed that there was different blood in you! Well, does it come as a surprise to 'ear that you 'ave got Rosemary Briscoe's blood – Mark's blood – a-coursin' through your veins?' She stood up and went to the sideboard. She picked up a photograph album, flipped it open at a well-worn place and handed it to Rory. 'There's your dad, my boy. Neville Bridges. 'E wanted to marry me. An' I turned 'im down because it wouldna done. An' 'e went off to that Spanish war and got 'isself killed!' She sat back down again. 'An' if I 'adn't done that, 'e might 'ave bin 'ere today!' She shook her head. 'Never mind that. Water under the bridge. But you *are* part of the Briscoe family – something Jan would have been pleased about. You cain't deny it by staying away! All this business about love – what's love in the end? A few hours o' 'eaven, then payment. Marriage and blood-ties – them's what counts. I dunno whether you and Rosemary Briscoe are more than summer lovers. Mebbe you are, mebbe you idn't. But you're linked all right. Whether you like it or not – you're cousins. And the sooner you accept that, the better!'

Rory sat holding the album, looking at Rose then at the faded photograph. Her colour was high, defiance was in every line of her body.

He said, 'I can't really tell . . . it's a sepia snap. But he – he – looks a bit like Madge Briscoe.'

'Philip Nolla gave it to me.' She seemed to relax a little. 'Neville din't know which way to turn. I couldn't look after you, my boy – I din't 'ave no feelings that way – and it 'ad to be a secret. It would 'ave killed old Mr Bridges, and Mrs . . . oh, it would 'a broke 'er 'eart. Things was so diff'rent then. 'Tis 'ard to imagine.' She sighed. 'So Neville told Philip Nolla, and 'e went to see Mr Trewyn. An' when madam lost 'er baby, they talked it over and said they would take you on themselves. It was best. Philip allus said it was best. They gave you the sort of schoolin' . . .' She looked away. 'It was best.'

There was a long silence. Then Mark said quietly, 'I think you're marvellous, Mrs Foster.' It sounded so silly and kiddish. He cleared his throat. 'I'm glad Uncle Neville . . . I mean, Mother and Dad talk about him often to us. I'm glad he knew you. And had Rory.' Rory was still staring at the photograph. Mark tried to sound hearty. 'Hope it's not too much of a shock, old man, to learn we're . . .' His voice died. It was all so tremendous, there were no words.

315

CHAPTER FOURTEEN

1965

Etta died quite suddenly and undramatically eighteen months later. She waited until all the gossip was old hat and the Briscoes resumed their pattern of visits, before she called Mark up to her sitting-room to discuss her 'final arrangements'.

'I want you all here,' she announced. 'Nothin' under cover, like at Philip's. You're my fam'ly an' I want everyone to know it. An' that means Rosemary too. An' that young Scaife girl o' yours. An' Rory Trewyn.'

'If Rory comes, Ro won't,' Mark said, trying hard to pretend they were talking about someone other than Etta.

She said grimly, 'That's the only loose end. I've tied the others, an' I depend on you to tie that one.'

'You know very well I've tried, Etta. Be fair.'

Etta nodded sadly. 'She were always a stubborn girl were Rosemary.' She cheered up. But she'll 'ave to come down to look after you, my boy. You cain't stay 'ere all on your own an' that's that.'

Mark was silent; he had continued to keep house for the two of them and last winter had nursed Etta through another bout of pleurisy.

She said sharply, 'You do see that you cain't stay 'ere alone, don't you?'

He scraped back his chair. 'I hate talking like this, Etta. We're neither of us alone. We've got each other and we manage very well.' He held on to the sideboard and clumped a single step to the window. It was a beautiful summer's evening and the wharf was packed with strolling people. St Ives had been well and truly discovered.

He said, 'How can you talk of dying on a day like this?'

She replied in the same sharp tone. 'Because on the day I die I'll be in no state to discuss anything!'

He tried to laugh but she would have none of it.

'I want it all done proper-like,' she insisted. 'I want the Old Wooden Cross – that was the first 'ymn your sister learned and she sat in that there window seat when she learned it. An' I want your mother dressed up in that linen thing she wore up to the Knill's monument last time. An' o' course your faither will look a real gent like 'e allus does. An Rosemary will 'ave to walk alongside young Rory Trewyn, an' look 'im in the eye. An' afterwards, when they've all gone back 'ome and she is 'ere seein' to your meals and suchlike . . . then they will 'ave another chance.'

'Neither of them want another chance, Etta. I've told Ro what happened that night at Rose Foster's, even . . . I've told her everything. And it makes no difference. And though she came down last year to see the flat and everything, Rory made no attempt . . . it's obvious he feels the same as she does.'

He had not told Etta that Jan had been 'in love' with Rory. Indeed he knew little about homosexuality himself and could not imagine the awfulness of Rory's experience. But Etta still had her sixth sense and shook her head, dismissing all arguments.

'Rubbish. She will have to make the first move and if she cain't do it, then you must do it for her.' She puffed her lips out in a sigh. 'That Scaife girl would know what I mean without all this argy-ing. She knew you was for 'er long before you did. An' Rosemary knew that Rory Trewyn b'longed to her right from the start.' Suddenly she looked bone-tired. 'I cain't talk about it no more, Mark. But don't let any more time go by . . . 'Tisn't fair to Neville nor to Jan. They might be dead, but they're still important. I cain't do no more, boy.'

Mark came to her clumsily and put his hand on her shoulder. She turned into him with a sigh.

'Eh, boy. You've got an 'ansome pair of arms. Arms is important . . . to 'old folks up.'

She permitted him to hold her for just a moment, then she raised her head.

'We got it all straight then. We got it all straight . . .' She levered herself to her feet. 'I'm going to bed. 'Tis early, but I'm tired.' She went to the door and paused there, hanging on to the jamb. 'I was angry with Philip, my boy. But if 'e 'adn't let your mam 'ave 'er 'ead, you wouldn't be 'ere now. You make folks 'appy, my boy. That's what you do. You make folks 'appy.' And

318

she left him sitting under the chandelier with tears on his face.

He stayed where he was all night in case she called him. In the small hours he went as quietly as he could into the kitchen where she slept on the sofa now that the stairs were too difficult for her. She was breathing gently, her withered cheek pillowed on her hand, her hair wispily about her face. He went back to the parlour and lay down on the window seat where he had slept when he was a summer visitor. He did not unstrap his legs, but she did not call. At six thirty when the road sweeper came round the court, he went in again to boil a kettle for tea. He knew instantly that she was dead; her body was in exactly the same position, but it was no longer inhabited. He sat by it, weeping like a child because she was the last of that old century's generation: a different breed, hard and honed, yet fey and magical too And now that it was too late, he wanted to ask her questions. What had she meant about Philip letting his mother 'have her head'? And how had Etta borne Philip's celibacy all those years? And what had she done to change the climate of opinion in St Ives so dramatically last year? And why had she adopted them and loved them all so fiercely?

The last question was the only one that had mattered now, and he knew the answer to that already though he could not put it into words, and could only weep anew with gratitude for the strange, illogical bonds which linked them all like one of Philip's fishing nets.

He knew he should go for the doctor, but first he went about making tea as he always did these days; very strong and very sweet, just as she liked it. He poured two cups and drank them both. By then it was nearly eight o'clock and the town was waking up. He poured water into a bowl and shaved sketchily. And he found he was humming some song. It was incredible. He felt his awful grief subsiding physically. He stopped shaking; a new strength surged through his shoulders and arms. He smiled down at Etta's body and finished the song. It was something his mother had sung to him when he was small and could not sleep: a Bing Crosby number. He knew only a few words: '. . . meets the gold of the day . . . someone waits for me . . .' And he remembered the single word Etta had demanded for the headstone in the cemetery. 'Reunited.'

*   *   *

319

They all came just as Etta had wished. Zannah and Rosemary stayed with Rose Foster in Bunkers Hill, and Clem and Madge went to Mennion House. Small, black-edged cards were displayed in shop windows all over the town announcing the time of the service, and the florists were busy with wreaths and sprays of the old-fashioned flowers Etta had asked for: clarkia and marigold, zinnia and wild tulip; bedded in cushions of samphire and sea-pinks.

The chapel where she had sat for Bright Hour was as full as it had been for Philip; Clem, Rory, Matthew Trewyn and Mark were her pall-bearers. It was difficult for Mark, he was so much shorter than the others, but Mr Trevorrow, who was an expert in funerals, solved the problem with a special padded shoulder-rest his grandfather had used.

Mrs Trevorrow said, 'We use it for a footstool now, but that is what it was. A pall-rest. Specially made for Mr Trevorrow's grandfather, who happened to be of shorter stature than many others. It can lengthen or shorten with this screw, and the velvet means it won't slip off the shoulder, or mark the suit.'

Madge, remembering that awful winter's day when the Trevorrows had snubbed her so thoroughly, looked anxiously at her son. But he was used to his acceptance now and nodded gratefully.

'Just right . . .' He put it on his shoulder and waited while Mrs Trevorrow buckled the strap. 'It's very comfortable. I'm sure Etta would be tickled pink.'

She wasn't affronted. 'You've been a good boy . . . a good boy,' she said sentimentally. Then suddenly turned to Madge and Clem. 'And you have done more than most families . . . much more. We're glad. Glad you've come.'

Rosemary watched the four men place the coffin carefully on to the rests and take their place in the front pews. She had been to St Ives twice since Mark moved down here, but this third time she felt different. Mark had said urgently, 'You mustn't expect miracles, Sis. Just keep coming each year like you used to, and wait for it to happen.' And she had done that and felt as if she were visiting a ghost town whose ghosts were strangely elusive. The brash, tanned faces of the summer visitors came between her and the people she expected to see. Philip and Marie, poor old Mr McGovern and Grandma Briscoe, and . . . Jan.

She sat like an invalid day after day, looking at the sea, listening to the summer noises all around her and remembering the thin, albino-pale girl who had tried so hard to force events into her own pattern; and failed. Where did accidents stop being accidents and become the logical sequence of cause and effect? What if the accident of her own birth had never happened . . . would Jan be alive now and would Mark have flesh-and-blood legs? But that was a road her mind had travelled often and she knew only too well it was a dead end walked by everyone with 'paranoid tendencies'. The accident of her birth had happened, just as had the accident of Mark's fall and the accident of Jan's death. She tried instead to think of her Uncle Neville and his summer love affair with Rose Foster. And that brought her back to Rory. And why he had made no attempt to see her during either of her visits.

Now, this third time, this third visit, when she should be unhappy because of Etta's death, she felt . . . different. For one thing the sight of Rory in his black suit came as a shock. He was changed almost beyond recognition, his shoulders bowed, his hair grey, his black eyes sunk into a weatherbeaten face. She knew he had converted Etta's fish cellar into a flat for Mark without any help. He had used a pickaxe to hew out the rock and had mixed concrete and mortar by hand. He had used the forge at St Erth and made wrought-iron gates to hang in the wall, giving the flat privacy without taking away the view. He had turned plumber and installed a sink and a shower. The lighting was subtle, directed on the granite walls with their pictures.

She knew too that he had taken his father in hand and rescued the auctioneering business from bankruptcy; that he had installed a new engine in the *Forty-niner*; that he and Mark went fishing most weekends.

When Mark told her these things, it had sounded typical of Rory. Energetic, ebullient even. He had laid his ghosts to rest by the simple expedient of filling every hour of every day with activity. With achievement. She had imagined him laying his head on the pillow each night, wearily but with satisfaction. He had the family Jan had wanted; he could find it in his heart to be magnanimous – generous – to his adoptive father. He had returned to his homeland and found some sort of contentment.

She realised, as she looked at him kneeling in prayer, that she had painted the wrong picture from Mark's words. If Mark had painted Rory, she would have understood. He had always been driven; as a boy he had been driven outwards, to seek the intangible in the big world outside this small town by the sea. Then he had been driven to escape his own guilt and horror at Jan's death. Now he was still driven. In the context of his true parentage – the wild black haired Rose of Zennor, and the equally wild middle-class boy who had wanted adventure – he was driving himself back into his very roots. Working – digging himself into the land almost physically – still seeking the intangible.

He sat just in front of her and next to Mark, getting off his knees with a small involuntary grunt. His body and head were the same size as Mark's so that now they were on a level, and they turned and glanced at each other as the minister's voice announced the first hymn. It was hard to see that they were cousins; Rosemary was often surprised that Mark took after neither of the parents, but in that glance there was a deep kinship. As she turned to the page in the hymn book, she thought: that is one thing Rory has done, he has established his relationship with Mark: I must tell him that. Then she remembered; there was no relationship between herself and Rory so she could not tell him anything.

Madge too watched the quick exchange between Mark and Rory, and tried to remember Neville on that last visit to St Ives when he must have seen Rory for the first and last time. Poor Neville; immature in the worst possible way, with none of youth's strengths and all its weaknesses. How good Rose Care would have been for him. If he'd stayed with her how she would have bullied and protected him, loved him and laughed at him. Yet from what Mark had told them it had been Rose who had sent Neville away. Perhaps she had known him better than any of them.

They stood up to sing the first hymn, 'Abide with me', and there was a rustle as someone crept down the side aisle and moved into the empty seat by Rory. It was Rose. Madge smiled. Rose, who was so cynical about Cornish funerals and had not gone to Philip's, though she knew that he had valued her more than most. She wore a black blouse and skirt that made her look like a barmaid; luckily she was hatless and her abundant hair, darker

322

than Rory's, was wound around her head like a crown. As Madge looked and smiled, Rory reached out, took his mother's hand and tucked it into his arm, then held his hymn book for her to see. Madge's eyes flicked to her own book as if they were intruding on a personal moment. She tried to sing and could not. Beside her Clem's deep voice reverberated strongly. 'Help of the helpless . . .' She bent her head lower still. Etta and Clem had been as close as she and Philip. Etta had known about Mark; she was almost certain that Clem knew too. Now Etta was gone and Mark was as independent as most people. There was still Ro, of course. But if Ro eventually left home, what was there to keep Clem there any longer?

Susannah Scaife saw the arrival of Mrs Foster and Rory's welcoming gesture, and frowned over the tiny print in her hymnal with a sudden impatience. She was so full of love and curiosity and eagerness that she sometimes wondered why she did not physically burst. Just the thought wiped away the frown and made her smile. She had visions of Mark turning round and mopping at her melting body apologetically: 'I always knew she'd burst one day.'

Mark had told Zannah only half of Rory's tale, and she simply could not understand what was keeping him from the girl he so obviously loved. Nothing on earth would keep her and Mark apart: not Aunt Di, not Mark's tin legs, not his fear that he was impotent, not even Etta Nolla with her lipless mouth and constant menacing presence every time Zannah had turned up for a weekend. Zannah glanced at the coffin and gave a little nodding salute. Last Easter when Zannah had spent three weeks at the cottage, the old girl had personally escorted her to her room each evening at nine thirty sharp. Mark had accepted the situation with an amused shrug, and Etta had ignored Zannah's furious protests and literally herded her up the stairs and put out her light too, with the terse comment, 'Philip couldn't afford this new fangled 'lectricity, and neither can young Mark, so don't put it on again, my girl.'

Zannah had told Mark exactly what she thought about interfering, parsimonious, frigid old biddies; but she hadn't told Etta. And, surprisingly, Mark had said, 'Etta isn't frigid, my love. Etta is as full of love as you are!' She had known in her bones that he

323

was right and she had kissed him sulkily and replied, 'Well . . . yes . . . but if it hadn't been for last year in London, I might well think you *are* impotent!' He hadn't even been put down by that, but his next kiss had been very satisfying and after it he had sighed deeply and said, 'If it weren't for you, Zannah Scaife, I would be.' And, as usual, that had made her cry.

So now she wanted them all to be happy and it was simply maddening that they weren't. She supposed that Clem and Madge Briscoe were okay; though of course they weren't like her parents must have been. But then . . . her parents must have been very special. She lowered her head quickly as she always did when she thought of her father and babbled quickly inside her head: 'Just let them be happy now . . . just let them . . .' Then she blinked hard and looked at her book again. 'Through cloud and sunshine . . .' She breathed deeply and began to sing. That's what it was all about, surely? There had to be cloud as well as sunshine, and though she hadn't known Jan Grodno, she was sure he would want Rory and Rosemary to be together. She stiffened her spine. She'd have to work on it.

Like her mother, Rosemary could not find the voice to sing; she mouthed the words but when she saw Rory take Rose Foster's hand even that automatic lip service trembled to a stop. No wonder Jan had loved Rory more than anyone; no wonder he had leaned back into eternity that day when Rory had shown him that his love had been given to a woman. Perhaps he had known – when Rory's face had appeared at Rosemary's shoulder – that they had consummated that love only an hour before. It must have been so obvious, especially to someone as sentient as Jan was then.

The hymn came to an end and they sat down for the address. Rosemary, unused to chapel funerals, was as surprised as her mother had been last year, at the suddenly popular image of Etta as a sister in God. She heard of her unflagging work for Christ and realised that it added up to Etta's regular attendance at Bright Hour. And the diligent service in God's holy name . . . did that mean waiting each day for Philip to come home with his catch, helping him to mend his nets, shaking rugs and sweeping the court?

The final hymn was announced. She recognised, with a spasm

of her heart, that it was Etta's favourite, 'The Old Wooden Cross'. Mark turned and looked at her over his shoulder and gave her a funny lop-sided smile. He whispered, 'She wanted it for you. It was the first hymn you learned.'

They stood up. It all came back to her; the window seat and the piece of driftwood so light and crumbly between her fingers. The minister like a black crow sitting at the table with his bible before him. A pot of jam going the rounds. Her mother, flushed and pretty. Etta . . . Philip . . . and a man with rusty-red hair in a camouflaged uniform.

Yes. Probably all Etta's 'diligent service' had been in God's name. Even to trying to stop her mother going swimming with Uncle Ned. Rosemary swallowed another treacherous lump and managed to smile back at Mark who also had red hair. And quite suddenly it was all right; quite suddenly Cod and Uncle Ned, and even Uncle Neville, seemed to take the burden of her 'accidents' and make them theirs.

She straightened her shoulders until she was almost the same height as Zannah Scaife, and she began to sing. As her voice climbed the crescendo of notes, clearly and steadily, Rory heard and turned to look at her.

It was a week later and Madge and Clem were returning to Bristol the next day. They had gone for a walk along the Zennor footpath at Mark's request. He wanted to talk to Rosemary.

They sat on the harbour and watched the gulls screaming over some discarded chips. The visitors, anxious to feed them at first, were half frightened by their frantic squawking and tearing of the paper, and backed away in confusion. People laughed and tried to scare the gulls off with flapping newspapers; the old-timers scowled and said you should never feed gulls and what damage they were doing to the marvellous old roofing tiles of the town.

Rosemary said, 'It's changing. It's not the place we used to know.'

Mark looked at her, his face set in stubborn lines.

'It is. Underneath . . . there's a kernel . . . Ro, please listen. You've got to stay. I can't manage on my own – you've just got to!'

'Of course you can manage on your own – don't give me that! You've managed for yourself *and* Etta since you came down to

325

live. You've done absolute marvels and we're all proud of you, so stop looking like an unmilked cow!'

He was forced to laugh, but he noted, not for the first time, that Ro was different. Not so buttoned up.

He played his trump card. 'Etta wanted you to stay and live upstairs. The night she died she sat me down in the parlour and told me exactly what she wanted done. And she wanted you to—'

'You're making that up, Mark!'

'I wouldn't make up anything about Etta. She'd come back and put a hex on me or something!'

'Yes. She might at that.' Rosemary laughed, then sobered. 'How can I give up everything just like that? I've got a job. And there's Mum and Dad. And anyway . . . St Ives. You know how I feel, Mark. I should hate it. I'm only a summer person.'

He held up one hand with spread fingers and ticked off each of her objections.

'You can get a job down here – there's a special school at Helston. They'd jump at you. And Mum and Dad might be glad to be on their own after all these years. It's obvious that was one of the things Philip had in mind when he left me the cottage. As for you being a summer person – what was I? We belong here, Ro. I don't know why, but we're more than summer people. Maybe Grampa and Grandma Bridges put down roots and we grew from them! Everyone knows it. Oh they were a bit funny at first, but it didn't last long. We're wanted down here, Ro. Dammit – we're needed!'

There was a long pause. Some children crawled from beneath an upturned boat and ran yelling down to the sea. Rosemary could remember doing that.

She said, 'You haven't mentioned Rory.'

'Neither have you.'

'I don't love him any more.'

'Oh. I see.'

'Does he . . . I mean, you see quite a lot of him . . . does he mention me?'

'No.'

'Well. That's all right then. I suppose.'

'Then you'll come?'

'No. I didn't mean that. Oh *Mark*—' she picked up a handful of sand and squeezed it hard. 'Can't you see? If he'd go away

326

again it would be all right – *might* be all right. But if he stays . . . we're cousins. How can I avoid him?'

'You can't. But if he doesn't mean anything special to you now, couldn't you get to know him all over again? As a cousin? He – he's a good person.'

'No. I don't think I could.'

'Then I'll ask him to go away. He'd understand. And he'd go.'

'*No!*' She threw away the sand as if it had stung her palm.

Mark said quietly. 'Quite. For you, St Ives means Rory. If he isn't here then you're waiting for him to come back. If you knew he was never coming back—'

'Mark. Shut up. Please.'

'Okay. I only know because of Zannah. I think I know everything I know because of Zannah.' He laughed. 'But if she went, then I'd still have this place. Where she had been. Where her parents had been.' He took a quick breath. 'Did you know that Mum knew Barbara Scaife? She met her once apparently.'

'No.' She touched Mark's arm. 'Zannah is quite a character, brud. A bit . . . weird at times. And you're both so young.'

'Yes. It's good, isn't it? We don't know about time. It's as well to start as soon as possible.' He looked at her directly. She noticed how very brown and round his eyes were. She felt her own filling with tears.

'Oh Mark,' she said helplessly.

'Yes. We're lucky, aren't we?'

He looked past her and saw Zannah coming across the beach. She wore her aluminium 'crown', this time woven with the reddish flowers she had worn around her neck two years before. She looked very zany and he could have wished, for Ro's sake, that she had conformed for once.

'Hi!'

She was carrying a large flat pebble, white and shot with crystal. She held it towards Ro.

'This is what I meant about the stones. You need to see what is inside them. That is why Hepworth makes those holes in her sculptures – so that you get the inside as well as the outside. It's terribly important.'

Rosemary took the pebble and stared at it as if the answer to everything might be there.

Zannah went on enthusiastically – 'We just don't know how

327

far the crystal goes. Or where it came from. I mean it was part of the stone and it changed. But it's still part of the stone. It's obviously different, yet it's essential I mean the stone would be nothing without it.'

Ro said, 'Er . . . quite. You mean, dull and uninteresting?'

'No. Just empty. They couldn't exist without each other.' She took the stone back, realising Rosemary did not comprehend. Then she said in the same voice, 'Rory Trewyn is down on the beach. He said he'd probably clear off quite soon.'

'Clear off?'

'Yes. He seems to think he's a bit . . . superfluous. You know, being a bastard cousin.'

'Zannah!'

She ignored Rosemary's reprimand and went on musingly, 'He's looking for something in the rocks. Where I found my pebble. Some special kind of seaweed. Very wide and flat with frilly edges. He says he's looked for it before and never found it.'

Rosemary glanced at Mark and said, 'Oh.'

And Mark said, 'It's for my collection, I expect. He doesn't know what I mean actually. You remember, Sis. The stuff Fizzy used for her handbag.' He grinned at Zannah. 'Fizzy was my physiotherapist and she had this crocodile handbag . . .' He reached over and put a hand on Rosemary's shoulder. 'Why don't you go and help him?'

Rosemary looked from her brother and back to Zannah. Her face was wide open and she felt an engulfing sense of déjà vu.

She said, 'D'you think I should?'

'Yes. He must feel a bit of an outsider after all. And he shouldn't. You could tell him that for a start. Dammitall, Ro, you could try being *friends*!'

She said, 'Yes.' Though she knew that would be difficult.

Zannah said, 'Look. He doesn't like himself. And you're not keen on Rosemary Briscoe. Couldn't you help each other in that way?'

Rosemary could take advice from her brother but not from this strange creature with a wheel-rim on her head. She lifted one shoulder irritably and moved off. She went in the general direction of Porthmeor; she could change her mind at any time on the way.

*   *   *

328

Madge and Clem rested on a rock above the first of the Five Points. Clem had started off wearing a jersey over his shirt. He was now carrying it carelessly by the knotted sleeves. It was very hot.

Madge said, 'If you screw up your eyes, you can practically see each atom of the air. They kind of dance.'

He narrowed his eyes obediently and sure enough the sunshine swirled before them.

He said, 'Interesting that you knew Zannah's parents. You met them during the war, I suppose?'

'Yes. Just once.'

He felt her stillness through their joined shoulders.

'Were they as crazy as she is?' he asked.

She did not laugh. 'She's not crazy. They weren't, either.'

'I was joking. She's the best thing that could happen to Mark. I just hope . . . I mean she's hell-bent on exploring every experience she can. What if something – someone – else crops up that she thinks is more interesting than Mark?'

'She'll explore it in her work.' She sighed. 'Artists are so *lucky*. They can experience everything that way. Like actors.' She straightened. 'In a play,' she added.

'Yes. I understand that.' She moved away and he pushed himself off the rock and joined her. 'So you think Mark and Zannah will be all right?'

'I don't know.' Her head was down, studying the springy turf at her feet. 'I pray about it,' she said in a low voice.

'Yes,' he said again, tacitly acknowledging that he did the same. 'Meanwhile . . . we don't have to feel that frightful pity for Mark any more, do we?' She stumbled and he put a hand under her elbow and held her up. 'Sometimes – at night when you were asleep – you used to call his name. You haven t done that since . . . for some time.'

She leaned on him. 'That's . . . good, isn't it?' He could hear the sense of loss in her voice. She said, 'And you? You said *we* don't have to feel pity. I didn't know – you've never said—'

'But you *must* have known. That is how I understood you. The way you were so often sorry for people – I didn't like that at first. Then – because of Mark – I understood.'

'Oh.' She gave a small laugh that sounded like a sob. 'He didn't like it either, did he? Philip saw that. Philip gave him his freedom, I suppose.'

'It's what we all wanted for Mark. His independence. And now we're missing him.' He squeezed her arm. 'Darling, it's only natural.'

'Yes. Of course.' They came to the narrow gully leading to Old Man's Head and Madge went in front. She looked up at the massive monolith. 'And we've still got Ro,' she said.

He did not reply. They did not pause by the rock; in fact Madge quickened her pace until she was almost jogging. Clem shouldered his jersey and lengthened his stride. When they were above the line of beach tents they both slowed automatically. Far below them on the wet sand in the rocks, Rory and Rosemary were moving carefully as if looking for something.

Madge breathed, 'My God. That's . . . isn't it?'

'Yes.' Clem started to fumble with his binocular case, then stopped. 'She's been different this time. Stronger. And happier. She and Mark have gone into one of their old slanging matches. Like they used to.'

Madge said, 'I feel so sorry for Rory—' she stopped herself, glanced at Clem and started to laugh. 'Well, I do! Everything was against him from the start. I sometimes think that if Neville had had more time – to get all that discontent out of his system – he might have turned out like Rory. Putting everything into every little thing he does . . . you know.'

'There's a lot of Neville in him.' Clem looked as the two tiny figures on the beach moved towards the water. 'He's so damned polite, calling me sir all the time.' He turned and smiled wryly at Madge. 'I've asked him to call me Tagger.'

'Oh Clem. You always wanted to keep Neville alive somehow. But you didn't dream that it would be like this.'

'No.'

They went on past the putting green and into the town. The summer crowds moved slowly and aimlessly around beaches and shops and icecream parlours, like the moving atoms of air on the cliff top. Still and silent amidst the throng, Zannah and Mark sat on the sand waiting for Jem to arrive with the day's mackerel. Zannah was dressed in her hippie gear, her long hair hanging either side of her face like curtains. Mark hailed them enthusiastically and they paused for a moment on their way to the car park.

'Mum! Dad! I think . . . would you mind awfully if Ro stayed? I think she might. I've put it to her that I can't cope alone.'

'You've got me,' Zannah put in.

'That's why I need Ro. As chaperone.' He hugged her. 'Anyway you're back to art school in September.'

'Ro has school then too,' Madge said quickly.

'She'd give that up.' He shielded his eyes from the sun and looked up at his mother. 'Don't look like that, Mum. She's got to face this place some time. It's where it all happened for her.'

'I don't think—'

Clem interrupted. 'I do. It's been a long time. Quite long enough. I'm for it. If you can persuade her, old man.' He looked at Zannah. 'Don't feel you're not appreciated, young lady. But you're going to have to put up with my son for a long time. Have a break while you can.'

Unexpectedly Zannah turned pink. It was the first time the family had publicly acknowledged that she and Mark were a bona fide couple. She smiled mistily.

Clem said, 'Those flowers in your hair . . . wild marjoram, aren't they?'

'I don't know. I just picked them.' She pulled a blossom from her crown and handed it to him. 'They're growing all over the place behind the seamen's mission.' She indicated Bamaluz Point. 'They're just weeds.'

Clem took the purplish flower carefully.

'We'll have to get back to Mennion House. Packing and so forth.' He piloted Madge towards the steps. 'See you this evening for dinner at the Clipper.' He almost carried her up the steps to the wharf. 'We could have rowed across in the dinghy if we hadn't brought the car,' he went on conversationally. 'It would have been much pleasanter than driving through this traffic.'

She said nothing until they reached the car park. Then she said quietly, 'You've always known, haven t you?'

He unlocked the passenger door and she slid into the hot, leather-smelling interior. He walked round the car and got in beside her, winding down the window after closing his door.

'The first time we brought Mark down. I knew then.' His voice was low. 'That was why . . . when I didn't respond immediately to your warning cry about him . . . along the Carbis Bay footpath . . . that was why I felt responsible. It could have been a subconscious wish to annihilate . . . what had happened.'

They sat side by side, not touching, staring through the

smeared windscreen at the rank of parked cars opposite.

She said at last, 'But the marjoram. How did you know about the marjoram?'

'Ro. She told me that on the afternoon of that damned children's party, Uncle Ned—' he drew in his breath as he spoke her childish words ' – took you to look for marjoram plants. That was when I knew. For certain.' His eye caught the glint of the wing mirror and he saw that she was reflected in it. Tears were rolling down her face. He looked away.

She said, 'He died. At Arnhem.'

'I know that too.' He told her about overhearing the conversation between herself and Gerald Scaife. 'So I met Zannah's father for a moment. Just a moment.' He tried to make his tone lighter.

She said, 'Oh God . . . oh God . . .'

He said nothing, trying to imagine how it had been for her all these years. She had seemed happy, yet underneath, all the time, had been this terrible grief.

She cleared her throat and said strongly, 'And now Mark has gone. And it looks as if Ro is going too. So . . . it's all right, Clem. You're free.'

He did not understand. 'Free?'

'You had to stay. I realise that. But there's no need any longer. You've done your duty – more than—'

'Did you think I stayed from a sense of *duty*?' He was outraged.

'Oh I know . . . we've been close. Good friends. And after . . . after . . . Ned . . . there was more. But you couldn't have liked me very much, surely. There must have been times when you hated me. I understand that.'

He said levelly, 'I have loved you since you were twelve years old, Madge. There was a moment of madness in Canada which I was selfish enough to . . . it was the war. When Mark fell on to that railway line, I knew I loved him. And that meant I loved you.' He put his hands on the steering wheel and gripped hard. 'Has it been pretence with you all these years? Is that what you're telling me?'

'No. Oh God. No. I was so mixed-up. When Father and Mother . . . Father almost died one night making love to her. I thought I would be safe married to you. Then I realised there was something wrong with me. And then . . . Clem, is it really all

332

right? It is, isn't it? I mean neither of us could have put on an act all these years? Clem—' She turned on the seat and took his hands forcibly from the wheel. 'Darling, I love you. And you love me. It's so – simple!'

He too twisted sideways and managed to take her in his arms. They held each other gently with a kind of tender compassion. And then they kissed and held again.

He said into her ear, 'Do you want to go up to Bamaluz and pick some marjoram? I don't mind. Really.'

She pecked his check with infinite gratitude.

'No. That's over now, Clem. The marjoram is for Zannah and Mark. Not for me.'

A red-faced man tapped on the glass. 'You going, mate? Only I bin waiting for your parking space for ten minutes now!'

Madge sat up quickly and started to laugh. And Clem switched on the ignition. They moved forward slowly and the engine stalled. They could not stop laughing.

Rosemary said, 'We looked for this stuff before. D'you remember?'

Rory did not look up. He had rolled his old flannels to his knees and waded through the pools as easily as he'd ever done. But his legs and feet marked him as an older man more than any other feature; his calf muscles were knotted and his toes as gnarled as Philip Nolla's hands had been. Rosemary felt protective and it was a feeling she hadn't experienced for Rory before.

'He said, 'Of course I remember. I remember . . . everything.'

'You came to help me that day. It was your way of patching up our differences.'

He grunted a laugh. 'Differences. That sounds very civilised, Ro. I don't think you and I have differences. We have quarrels. Furious quarrels.'

'But we always made them up.'

He straightened slowly, put his hand in the small of his back, and stared at the horizon.

'Is that what you've come to do today? Make up a quarrel? But we didn't have a quarrel, Ro, did we? We were wrenched apart. There was no quarrel.'

'Our quarrels were always about Jan. This . . . this separation . . . was about Jan too.'

He turned and studied her. She knew she must look a mess. There hadn't been time to get a tan and she was very pale.

He said, 'Did Mark tell you why Jan killed himself?'

She flinched, closed her eyes, then said, 'Yes.'

'Were you disgusted?'

She whispered, 'How could I be disgusted? I love you too.'

He groaned and she opened her eyes to see him bent as if in pain. She made to clamber towards him and he held up a restraining hand.

'I didn't mean . . . I meant were you disgusted by my behaviour? My treatment . . . of you?'

She stood very still, thinking of all that pain and resentment. And she remembered the moment in the chapel when some of Etta's wisdom had lightened her mind.

'Rory. We were all . . . wounded. Damaged,. But it has to end somewhere. Let it end. Now. Please.'

There was another silence and she knew that if he continued with the self-recriminations she would have to go away from him. But after a while he began to move again, squelching over a bed of green weed to a tangle of brown kelp. She did not go with him; she waited.

He bent and pushed at the heavy seaweed; it was a miniature jungle, weighed down with sea water. He felt in the pocket of his trousers and brought out a penknife. He hacked for some time, then he stood up and exhibited a flat piece of weed, the size of Mrs Trevorrow's fox fur, frilled at the edges.

'Is this it?'

'Yes. You've found it at last.'

'Like you found that piece of nameboard from the old *Lancaster*.' He smiled at her. 'Something for my cousin.'

'I'm your cousin too, Rory.'

'Yes. And so much more.'

'Zannah Scaife said that you were intending to leave Cornwall again.'

'I thought it would make it easier for you to stay with Mark if I'm not around.'

She said steadily, 'No. Not any more. In fact it would make it much harder for me if you left.'

He smiled again. 'I don't think I could leave anyway. You said just now that you love me. You spoke in the present tense. I won't

334

try to tell you how sorry I am for . . . things. I'll just say – I love you too, cousin Rosemary. Could we get married, d'you think?'

At last she smiled back at him, then held out her hand. He came to her and took it. Then he waved the enormous piece of seaweed in the air like a banner. And they began to walk towards the sea.

BY SUN AND CANDLELIGHT

I love thee to the level of every day's
Most quiet need, by sun and candlelight.
I love thee freely, as men strive for Right;
I love these purely, as they turn from Praise.
I love thee with the passion put to use
In my old griefs, and with my childhood's faith

Elizabeth Barrett Browning

One

They discovered the empty farm labourer's cottage in the winter of 1940, when, desperate with boredom, they waded single-file and thigh-deep along the muddy brook which meandered across the heath towards Kings Norton.

It stood stark and derelict against the frosty winter sky, its chimney leaning, its downstairs windows choked with briars, gate and door hanging off their hinges. It had everything the girls needed: a roof to keep out the freezing fog, privacy while they dried their legs and tucked-up underclothes; above all, mystery.

Carol at just eleven years old was the youngest of the quartet, but she was also the tallest and could see over the high right bank with ease. Her long face, framed by straggly English-brown hair, looked down at the others who were shivering behind her.

'It's got cabbages growing in the back garden,' she said, awed by the unexpectedness of their find. 'And I think that hut thing is a lavatory.'

'I don't care about that.' Myrtle was the shortest of the four, so her skirt and knickers were soaked. 'Just let's get inside!'

Monica and Liv said nothing, but their grimness spoke volumes. They hadn't wanted to come in the first place. They had suggested alleviating the boredom of the Christmas holidays by window-shopping in Birmingham before the night raids began. Liv was blonde and pretty and beginning to think about boys. Monica was very dark and had been born knowing about them.

Carol dug her bare feet firmly into the mud of the bank, closing her mind against thoughts of leeches and frogs. She grabbed a tree root and hauled herself out. She turned and gave a hand to Myrtle, ignoring the other two. If they couldn't see that wading up a mini-Zambesi into unknown territory was more exciting than ogling boys in the Bull Ring, they didn't deserve any of her undoubted expertise. They scrambled out, panting, getting mud all over their raincoats. The four of them stood shivering and looking at the house.

'Is it all right to go inside?' Liv asked doubtfully. Her parents were chapel and what they and their friends would think of this whole escapade was unimaginable. They would understand window-shopping; they would smile indulgently when Liv received letters from schoolboys. But brook-wading and house-breaking were out of their ken.

Myrtle sniggered her triumph. 'Oh, you've got a voice then!' She wrung out the hem of her coat. 'For Christ's sake! Look at this! Mother will kill me. She sold my clothing coupons for petrol to go and see Daddy last month. Oh God.'

'Don't keep swearing!' Liv said half-heartedly. 'I suppose it's all right to go in? If anyone should be inside we can say we rescued a dog from the water and need to dry out.'

'Lies, Livver Baker! You won't go to 'eaven! Carol put on a Welsh accent, then regretted it when Liv buttoned up her face tightly again. Carol was a much-loved only child. She cared too much about people and it had been she who had persuaded Liv and Monica to come today.

Monica shoved her bare wet feet into her brogues and led the way past the line of willows at a brisk limp. 'Frankly, I'm past caring whether anyone is there or what we bloody well say!' she snapped over her shoulder. 'When I think I spent all last night with my hair in ruddy pipe-cleaners – just like Rita Hayworth I looked first thing this morning! Now look at me!' Her gypsy-black hair hung to her shoulders in rats' tails. The others had worn their school berets, but she hadn't wanted to crush her myriad curls.

They crowded into the tiny square hall behind her, Carol still hopping as she tried to cram on her shoes. It was obvious the place was deserted. The floor was liberally peppered with hen or rabbit droppings, and the smell was not good. But it was dry and comparatively warm after the unpleasantness of the past hour. They began to relax, wrinkling their noses and using phrases they'd heard on the wireless. 'Pooh what a pong!' 'Don't it pen and ink!' 'Kin I do you now, sir?'

The downstairs rooms had been wrecked, either by people or marauding animals.

'This scraping here – that's been done by the horns of a steer,' Carol announced. She read a lot and had just discovered Zane Grey.

'You wouldn't know a steer if you were introduced at a party,' scoffed Liv who read just enough to keep her English grades above average.

'Course she would. It's the wheel inside a car!' Monica said in her funny, off-hand way. Monica also read a great deal because she was so often lonely and frightened and did not want to show it. Ever.

Upstairs it was much better. At the top of the angled stairs was a wide passage with windows front and back. They were still giggling at Monica's wit, and they rushed up and down suddenly euphoric.

'It's ours! It's ours!' Carol sang.

Myrtle peered out of the windows. 'Perfect for keeping a look-out for intruders!'

'It's so light and airy. I could bring my violin here and practise.' Liv ignored the theatrical groans. 'Seriously girls, this could be our private place. A base. A sort of – sort of—'

'Secret society,' Carol breathed.

'Didn't we tell you it was better than parading up and down the Bull Ring?' Myrtle asked.

'Is there any furniture left? I need to sit down and put on my stockings and do something with my hair.' Monica opened doors and peered around. 'Here. This one. There's a box thing, and an old bed.'

They trooped inside the bedroom. The bed's bare coiled springs twanged when they sat on it. Carol, the agile one, stood on it and jumped experimentally, and they lugged her down and pushed her on to the box. They concentrated on getting clothed and damp-dry again. Liv found some hair grips in her pocket and offered to put Monica's hair up.

'If we're going to be a society, we ought to have rules and a programme and things.'

'I could bring my violin. Seriously. We could have a musical afternoon.'

'A soirée.'

'No. An après-midi. 'Cos of the black-out.'

'Be serious.'

'We could have debates. Proper debates.'

'About what, for Christ's sake?'

'The war. Whether we ought to open a second front.'

341

'Not the war again. If I have to hear Stewart Hibberd once more . . . well, actually you sound rather like him at times, Carol. It's true. I can't help it – it's true!'

'We could have games. The truth game.'

'Not pygmalion likely. If you think I'm going to tell you about Denzil McIntyre you've got another think coming!'

'Not about boys. All you think about is boys! Boring, boring, boring.'

'They make the world go round.'

'It's love that makes the world go round. Love!'

'Well?'

'Well?'

'It was you who said "kin I do you now sir"!'

'Well?'

'For God's sake don't keep saying well! You know very well what that means!'

'Actually, it means may I clean out your room now sir. She is a charlady. A cleaner.'

'And it also means can I do you now sir. Why do you think everyone laughs their sides off?'

Monica looked directly at Carol, her beautiful dark eyes challenging. She loved Carol and wanted desperately for Carol to love her. Therefore she had to force her to . . . to face . . . certain things. Because if she didn't, there would come a day when Carol would not like Monica at all. Monica looked away from Carol and thought of her home life and its only warm spot. Giles. Her brother. Giles.

Liv put in the final hair grip and stood back to survey her work.

Myrtle said, 'I say you two, don't quarrel.'

Carol gave her quick, propitiating smile, and shook her head. 'We're not. Not really. Mon, you look marvellous. Different and grown-up.'

Liv presented her with a tiny mirror painted on the reverse side with Walt Disney's Snow-White. Monica inspected herself carefully, then with a quick hand she whipped out the hair grips and let the rats' tails descend to her gaberdine.

'I'm not different. I'm the same as ever.' She grinned. 'I don't know if that was a debate, or part of the truth game.'

Liv was furious. 'I'll never do your hair again, you ungrateful twerp!'

342

Carol said quickly, wanting everyone to be all right again, 'Right. That's settled then. An afternoon of music next week. Okay Liv? Maybe I'll bring my recorder and you two could be percussionists.'

The groans were extra-theatrical and full of relief that bonhomie was restored.

'Then the week after, the topic for discussion will be boys and whether they make the world go round.' She didn't look at Monica. 'And we might find that the truth game comes into that.'

'Sounds interesting,' Myrtle acknowledged. Myrtle too loved Carol, but she wanted quite desperately to be like Liv and Mon. Unfortunately she was short and overweight with strange, fuzzy brown hair that never looked right.

'I shall do that song we sing in the choir,' Liv enthused. It was the sort of thing chapel people did: musical afternoons, discussion groups. Even Liv found that thirteen-year-old boys had limited appeal.

Monica said, 'Why not "In the Mood"? Why can't you learn something decent, Liv? Don't you just love that bit when the music stops and everyone keeps on dancing because they know—'

'Good grief, look at this!'

Carol's raincoat had caught on the edge of the box as she stood up. It was not a box at all; it was a raised piece of the stairwell which gave headroom on the first flight. The lid lifted to reveal a perfect view of the entrance hall and kitchen.

'My God. If anyone came in we could watch them from here!' Monica said.

'And if they came up the stairs, we could all drop through and make our escape!' added Myrtle.

Liv pocketed her Snow-White mirror and the hair grips.

'It really is the perfect headquarters!' she announced. And as she was chapel, it put the seal on the place.

The house fulfilled all their hopes for it. In a world filled with news of war, it was a refuge: somewhere they could be silly and selfish and talk freely. In the summer it was less isolated; the girls were worried in case marauding schoolboys or a walker might discover it, and they repaired the gate and printed 'Beware of the Dog' on its crossbar. In some ways it was better when the winter set in again and they could huddle together on Saturday afternoons and chart the progress of the Allies in Africa, discuss Liv's and Monica's conquests and play the truth game about other things besides what made the world go round. It emerged that Liv wanted a nice house with carpets everywhere and a machine that did the washing-up. Myrtle wanted a better deal than her mother had and a really good career for her baby brother, Boris. Monica too was very close to one of her brothers and talked often of what 'Gillie said' and how Gillie 'fooled the call-up board by faking a limp' and what a constant laugh he was. Carol wanted her invalid father to get strong again and for the three of them to lead a 'really interesting' life.

'You're a typical only-one, Cass,' Monica scoffed. But she scoffed affectionately. 'We've all said at some time or other that we want to get married and live happily ever after. D'you want to stay with mummy and daddy for ever?'

Carol looked surprised. 'I'm not sure. But . . . if we're still telling the truth . . . I don't want to get married. And the three of us – Mother and Dad and me – we get on very well together.'

Myrtle said fervently, 'We don't. When Pa is home on leave they're always rowing. Boris cries about it sometimes. It's awful.'

Liv said, 'Mam and Da are okay I suppose. But I don't want to stay with them longer than I have to. I want to marry someone with lots of money—'

'We all know that, Liv.' Monica was genuinely scornful this time. 'At least Myrtle and I want to fall in love. That's the last thing on your list!'

'Fall in love!' Liv was equally scathing. 'You don't want to fall in love, Monica Cook! You just want to fall into bed! Ever since you started your monthlies you've been different. My sister says you've got sultry eyes!'

Unexpectedly Monica flushed to the roots of her hair.

Carol, not quite thirteen and lagging behind in so many ways, said, 'That's a terrible thing to say, Liv. For someone who is supposed to be a Christian that's – that's – *sinful*!'

Myrtle laughed. 'All that chapel lot are sex mad. I've looked through some of Daddy's notes and I could tell you a thing or two.'

They waited for her to go on, but she was silent, suddenly realising the seriousness of her spying. Eventually she said

344

lamely, 'Anyway, sex is overrated, I'm telling you. The rows at home are always about sex. I don't want any of that. I want to fall in love. Properly in love. I want someone to love me more than anything else in the world. Yes, that's what I want.'

Liv said defensively, 'Well, yes. I want that, of course. I suppose everyone wants that.'

Carol said nothing, not knowing.

Monica said, 'Yes. But not just anyone. Only one person. The person that you love.'

They all nodded slowly and judiciously.

One May night in 1944, crazy with the ennui which was gripping the whole country, Carol and Myrtle took paint from the school caretaker's shed and met outside Northfield's post office at eleven-thirty to daub the wall with the familiar words OPEN SECOND FRONT NOW. Owing to British Double Summer Time, it was still light enough for them to be spotted by a policeman, and they were chased down the alley, across the Bristol Road and up to the old stocks before losing him. Almost weeping with terror they decided they had been recognised, and they went into hiding in the Haunted House – as it was now called.

Monica and Liv found them there on Sunday afternoon, hungry and still terrified.

Monica was immediately reassuring.

'Everyone's daubing that particular slogan everywhere – Good God, you won't be clapped into gaol for that! And your mother thinks you're staying with me, Myrtle, so that's all right. It's your people, Cass. They're going Harpic.'

'Oh . . . I can't bear it!' Carol's father was exempt from the Forces because of a weak heart. 'The longer I stay away the worse it will be. What shall I tell them?'

'Anything. The truth. But do it quickly, because they're going to the police today. Might have already gone.'

'What did you say to them?'

'Liv didn't say a word,' Monica replied with her usual scorn. 'Couldn't tell lies of course. I told them you and Myrt were on one of your expeditions, and I'd come and fetch you. I knew you'd be here.' She rolled her eyes. 'They phoned this morning when they discovered you weren't in bed. You must be mad.'

'We had to make something happen,' Myrtle explained. 'And

if that policeman hadn't seen us, we'd have been back in bed by midnight.'

Liv broke her disapproving silence. 'Why didn't you go back to bed anyway?'

'He'd seen us. We could be identified.'

'Melodramatics.'

Carol sobbed suddenly. 'I'm so homesick!'

'Serves you right.'

Everyone was embarrassed; now they were fifteen they didn't cry any more; they didn't admit to homesickness any more. Especially when they were within two miles of home.

Myrtle said, 'It's worse for me. My father is fighting for our country.'

'Behind a desk. In Wiltshire,' Liv reminded her.

'That's better than pretending that the post office is a reserved occupation like your father!'

Carol couldn't take her eyes off the floor. She knew if anyone said anything derogatory about her own father, she'd break down completely.

Then Monica, staring out of the window so as not to see Carol's shame, said tightly, 'Someone's coming.'

Instantly, they were reunited. They crowded to the window. A man was crossing the field, picking his way carefully around the molehills. So he wasn't a farmer – a farmer would have gone through them like a tractor. This man was dressed in khaki trousers, belted thickly with leather, a greyish-brownish shirt, open at the neck, and a tweed jacket. He carried a tie in his hand. He was bare-headed, his hair cropped roughly.

'My God. I bet you he's a deserter,' breathed Monica.

'I bet you he's a Jerry,' Liv said.

Myrtle peered beneath Carol's arm. 'He's one of those men. You know. The nasty ones.'

Carol swallowed the last of her tears. Her eyes suddenly felt gritty-dry.

She moved sideways and opened the lid to the stairs.

Monica said, 'Don't be daft. There's four of us and only one of him.'

The man had stopped, and was surveying the house. They moved away from the window hastily, except Myrtle; she was too short to be seen.

346

She said, 'I say. Girls. D'you know who I think it is? I think it's Mussolini!'

Scoffing disbelief was muted, though with the window tightly closed he couldn't possibly hear unless they shouted.

'Well, he's disappeared, hasn't he? Since last July when he got out! And where's the best place to hide? In the enemy's bosom, that's where! He's probably got a gun and will shoot us all!'

Monica said grimly, 'Never again let me hear you grumble about nothing happening!'

Carol said, 'Listen. If he comes in, we'll wait till he's underneath the lid, then I'll drop on him and pin him down and you join me as soon as you can. Myrt, you run for the police.'

Myrtle said, 'He's coming through the gate.' After that nobody said anything until much later.

They lowered the lid until they could just see through the crack. As footsteps scuffed to the front door, the tension was almost unbearable. When the door was pushed open against the rock they'd put there, they held their breath.

The man bludgeoned his way in, muttering curses that were English enough. There was a circular bald patch on his head, and below that his nose was a wart-encrusted promontory. He looked around the door, saw the rock and shoved it towards the stairs. There was a splintering, soggy sound, the floorboards caved in and the rock disappeared. The man seemed nonplussed. He stood above the hole, staring down in disbelief. Above him the girls breathed very carefully.

The hole appeared to fascinate the man for some time, and it also seemed to discourage him from attempting to cross it and mount the stairs. After a while he began exploring the downstairs rooms. The girls looked at each other tensely, then returned to their spy-gap.

When the man reappeared, he was talking to himself. It could have been German. It could have been anything. He came again to the hole and peered down it. Then he draped his tie over his shoulder and began to undo his trouser buttons. Again the girls stopped breathing, and Carol closed her eyes. The gushing sound as the man passed water was so indecent she almost shifted her position, but the tiniest movement would have given them away. There was a long pause. Monica's hand came out and gripped her

347

upper arm. Carol opened her eyes. The man was doing something unspeakable. She closed them again. There were a few grunts, pig-like, then a long drawn-out groan, dog-like, then a period of shuffling and muttering, which finally diminished.

'He's gone,' Myrtle whispered. 'Someone look out of the window.'

Liv stood up stealthily.

'Yes, he's gone. Just pushing out of the gate now. We must close that again. And we'd better do a notice on the door and wedge it shut somehow.'

'We'll get some net curtains,' Monica said definitely. 'There are some in our shed. Dad uses them to cover the raspberries. I'll bring them next time.'

Myrtle said, 'Did you see what he was doing? I mean – I thought he was spending another penny, then—'

Monica said stonily, 'He was wanking.'

'He was what?'

'Wanking. Working himself up. Ejaculating.' She said the last word in a high falsetto, a bad imitation of the mistress at school who took human biology and invariably squeaked on the embarrassing bits.

'How do you know?' Liv was indignant. She was the acknowledged expert on all things sexual. Six grammar-school boys had asked if she would let them. She put a cross inside her rough note book for each of them. Like the fighter pilots when they shot down an enemy aircraft.

Monica said laconically, 'I've got two brothers, remember?'

Liv said, 'Well, I've got a sister who is practically engaged.'

Carol took her hands from her face. 'For God's sake!' Tears smudged filth down to her chin. 'It was horrible! How can you talk about it so calmly? It was like – like – dogs!'

Monica put a hand on her shoulder as she went to the door.

'Dry up, old bean. Forget it. It happened – it happens all the time. They can't help it.'

Myrtle said, 'It's because you're so hungry, Cass. Don't worry. We're both weak with hunger. If you two knew we'd be here, why didn't you bring us some food?'

'Because we had other things on our minds,' Liv snapped. 'Like, how to get you two idiots out of trouble.' She kept her eyes off Carol. 'Now. The sooner we get you home, the better. Where

348

have you put the paint tin? There's likely to be more fuss at school about that being taken than—'

'We've buried it in the garden,' Myrtle said, equally snappy. 'We're not daft, you know.'

'No?' Liv ran her hand through her natural curls with a sang-froid so inexplicably aggravating that Myrtle darted at her. Carol, the peacemaker, made no move, and Monica separated them.

'You're so boring!' They were not surprised when she swung at them both. Monica was not known for patience or self-restraint. 'Myrt, you should know better. Carol's always been an idiot, but you should know better. Daubing school paint over the post office walls – it's stupid and childish and – plain boring!'

Liv said righteously, 'And you're over a year older than Carol, too, Myrt.'

Monica swung again, and Liv cowered, a hand over her ear.

At last Carol stood up.

'Yes. Let's go. Come on. We're okay. Nothing terrible has happened. We've hurt no-one – except my parents. Let's forget today – forget it completely. We'll never mention it again.'

And they left.

It was high summer and the Normandy landings were going well. People were already talking about the end of the war.

Myrtle, the eldest of the four, was already sixteen, the others not far behind. The list of adventures grew: bella donna picking for the hospitals when Myrt had pretended to suck her poisonous fingers and had fallen down, twitching violently. The teacher in charge had looked at her solemnly for a long moment while Myrtle's acting ability played itself out, then said, 'All right now, dear? Then let us get on. This is our war effort, isn't it?'

There had been dances at which Carol and Myrtle had been landed with men old enough to be their fathers, and Liv and Monica had 'scored' over and over again.

There had been summer harvest camps, dig-for-victory campaigns, sweaters for Russia, concerts for the Spitfire fund. In between there were exams. Mocks for the dreaded School Leaving Certificate; tests for German and French, Geog and Maths; practicals in Chemistry, Physics and Biology; books – tomes – to read for English and History. They would lug satchels

349

full of work to the Haunted House and sit in the upstairs room supposedly studying.

'My God!' Carol, who wanted very much to get a State Scholarship to university, tended to be genuinely interested in some of her subjects. 'Did you know that if one atom is split, the energy it releases will automatically split every other atom in the world, and this planet will be annihilated?'

'So spake Miss Edgeworth,' Monica intoned.

Carol shook her hair off her face. 'She's a clever woman, Mon. She got a brilliant first from Cambridge in her day.'

'And she's an old maid, too.'

Carol frowned. 'Does that matter? If you mean she's a virgin, does that matter?'

'I didn't mean that. And you know it. You can be married three times over and still be an old maid.'

Carol was silent for a long time. Liv was lying back, eyes closed, muttering French verbs to herself. Myrtle was grappling hopelessly with a theorum. Liv would probably do all right in the exams; her pride would not let her come below average. Then she would get married very well and as quickly as possible. Myrtle was all right too; there was money in her family and they would get her some kind of professional training. That left Monica and Carol. Carol wanted her parents to be proud of her. Monica was a dark horse.

'All right . . .' Carol finally accepted Monica's statement and crossed her legs the other way. The floor in the bedroom now boasted faded old rugs, but it was still unresilient. 'All right. But what about the other way round? I mean, can a virgin – a spinster – not be an old maid?'

'Of course not! Or do I mean of course?' Monica's calculating brown eyes stared at the tall thin girl opposite her; took in her mouse-brown hair, the irregular features, the over-sensitive mouth. Her own face, perfect in its way, broke into a smile that was all affection. She leaned forward and touched one of the bare brown knees; she was an undemonstrative girl, but occasionally she touched Carol as if to reassure her. 'For instance, you'll never be an old maid, kiddo. If Liv doesn't get married, she'll be one. But not you.'

Liv stopped her murmured chanting to say, 'Thanks very much. I won't say what I think of you.'

Carol swallowed visibly. 'I . . . I would like to be a mother. That's the thing. I'd like to live an ordinary, a normal life.'

And Monica, who knew so much, said, 'Give it time, kiddo. Give it time.'

And Myrtle who knew nothing, but was determined to know it all sooner than anyone else, said, 'All this talk. You two—' she shot venomous glances at Liv and Monica. 'You think you're so wonderful. A couple of film-stars. But . . .' she straightened her back proudly, '. . . you will notice I am the only one here with a proper bust!'

Nobody had liked to mention it. For the past year, Myrtle's breasts had blown up like balloons.

Liv said half-heartedly, 'Well, you're older than us.'

And Monica asked, 'What do you do with them, Myrt? D'you wear a brassiere, or what?'

Myrtle was slightly crestfallen. 'No coupons. But Ma says I can have one of hers this summer. You know, when we get out of uniform.' The summer school uniform was stout poplin; when the girls went into their holiday frocks, mostly two years old and let down twice already, the lack of petticoats suddenly became very apparent. Nobody wasted precious clothing coupons on petticoats.

Liv was immediately envious.

'Mam says if you've got good muscles you don't need any extra support.'

It was all too obvious that Myrtle did not have good muscles.

Monica felt the need to touch her plump knees too. She resisted it.

'What you ought to do, Myrt – just when you go to a dance or something – is hoist them up with some sticking plaster. I read somewhere that's what Betty Grable does when she's dancing. Then you haven't got to worry about brassiere straps and you don't bounce about, and you've got a vai-ry interesting cleavage!'

Everyone giggled. And Liv relented.

'Can we see them, Myrt?' she asked tentatively.

Carol's leg muscles visibly tightened. 'Take no notice of her, Myrt! Typical. Just because she hasn't got a bust—'

'You don't have to. Sorry I asked!' Liv was unexpectedly red-faced.

351

'I don't care. Good lord. I'm not embarrassed about anything. Anyway Ma says I should be proud of myself. Little women always get their own way. Ma says that.'

They were all silent, thinking of Myrtle's ma who was under five feet and terribly in thrall to her doctor husband. Myrtle knew as well as anyone that her father 'messed around' with all the Waafs on his station, and she added swiftly, 'I'm really sorry for you and Liv, Carol.'

Liv said, 'I'm not as tall as Carol. I could have died laughing when that little Irishman came up and asked you to dance, Carol. Why on earth didn't you say no?'

'Because she wouldn't hurt a fly, let alone a human being,' Monica replied. 'Come on, Myrt. If you're going to do a strip, let's get it over with.' She ignored Carol's horrified glance. 'We all know you're one up on us – sorry, two up on us, so you might as well prove it.'

Myrtle unbuttoned her blue poplin shirtwaister. The result was electrifying. Her breasts tumbled almost on to her lap and lay there submissively as if waiting for something.

Liv said, awestruck, 'My God. They're enormous.'

Carol looked at the floor.

Monica said briskly, 'Right. Proof positive. Myrtle is one year older than us and four years ahead. Good old Myrt. Now I've got something to tell you. Pin back your ears, girls. I'm not a virgin any more. As of last night, I am no longer a maiden.'

All eyes moved to her. Myrtle shovelled her breasts back into her dress automatically. Carol looked as if she'd been struck across the face. Liv was agog.

'You don't mean . . . a man . . . you let a man do it?'

'Yep.'

'I don't believe you.'

Monica shrugged. 'Okay. I'm certainly not going to have a medical examination.'

'Who? For Christ's sake, who?'

'Swearing, Liv. You won't go to heaven.'

'Tell us.'

'No. Sorry, but that's my business. I'll tell you it happened. And that is all.'

Liv was suddenly indignant. 'You should be struck down.

352

You're wicked. How can you sit there and say you've done it? You're sinful. You're a scarlet woman.'

Monica smiled.

Myrtle fidgeted. 'What was it like? I mean, did it hurt?'

'I'm not saying any more. Wish I hadn't told you that.'

She got up and went to the door. 'I'm off. Anyone coming?'

Liv stood up with alacrity.

'Yes. Why we go on coming to this place, I'll never know. Good God, we're not kids any more.'

'That makes twice you've sworn, Liv.'

Myrtle scrambled to her feet. Her face was red.

'Coming, Carol?'

Carol was still staring at the floorboards and Myrtle repeated her question. Then she looked up and spoke with an obvious effort.

'Not yet. I've not finished this paper. Not yet.'

'Oh . . .'

Myrtle followed the other two downstairs and leapt Mussolini's hole with difficulty. Monica looked round.

'Where's Carol?'

'Not coming yet.'

Monica was suddenly angry. 'Get back to her. Don't leave her there. Go on!'

'I'm not going to be bossed around by you, Mon Cook! Go yourself!'

'She doesn't want me.'

'She doesn't want me either.'

'But she can bear you. Idiot. She can stand the sight of you. Now go.'

Myrtle went, and Monica turned to the front door again. She glanced up. The stair-lid was wide open. Carol must have heard what she said.

She called loudly, 'I don't care. I don't care! Wait for me, Liv!'

And she left.

On V.E. day, Carol came to the house alone. She knew that in the evening she would go into Northfield with the others, and they would have a 'good time'. They would be wonderful to her because her father had died three weeks ago, and they guessed the depth of her misery. Her mother might come too for an hour, and her fixed smile would tremble in the dancing flames of the bonfire, then she would say, 'You stay on, darling. Have a good time. I think I'll get back home and lie down. Bit of a headache.' And Carol would feel the loneliness intensify like a knife point under her ribs, and the magic that had been the future would loom terrifyingly.

She sat in the bedroom window, gazing at the familiar view, and let the hot tears drip from the end of her long nose and equally long chin. She said aloud in a monotone, 'This is self-pity. It's not grief for Daddy, because I believe in God and heaven and all that, so why should I grieve for him?'

The tears dripped faster. She saw the brook with its parallel droops of willow as if it were all under water. The rough fields where anonymous cows sometimes grazed, and the long line of elms which must hide the distant road, were blurred into a yellow-green mass. It was like an oil painting when you were too close to it, all bits and blobs. She was reminded of the constantly moving atom. Were there enough atoms out there to reincarnate her father again? Why couldn't she and Mother have supplied some from their over-subscribed bodies to repair his disintegrating one? Why was death 'the end'? Why couldn't you do anything about it? There weren't many things in life you couldn't change if you really wanted to. What was so different about death?

She said aloud, 'I believe in you, God. But I hate you. All right, I know you gave us free will. I know all that. But you can intervene to change the course of events if you really want to. And you didn't. You damned well didn't. I asked you – Mummy asked you. I know she did. But you didn't do a thing.'

After a long time the tears dried up and she saw Monica crossing the field very clearly. She did not go to meet her. For one thing she was exhausted with her grief. For another . . . she did not know the other reason. Monica and Carol could tune into one another easily. That was not always good.

Monica came closer and started to untie the gate. She could not know that Carol was inside. Carol had not only tied the gate, she had closed the front door. Monica did not glance up at the window. She wound the rope carefully around the gateposts again and came up the path. She looked marvellous, doubtless dressed for the evening's revelries. Her black hair was in about a million small curls, and she wore a saucer hat over one eye. She had

354

updated last year's floral art silk with a contrasting peplum, and her gloves were long and pre-war. She had been the first girl at school to flaunt American nylon stockings, and she must have had masses of them, because she ignored the front door and swung herself through the kitchen window without a thought for their unladdered elegance.

She said quietly to the raised stair-lid, 'I'm coming up, Carol.' Then there were steps along the landing, and she appeared.

Carol moved her head. She said, 'How did you know I was here?'

'Where else would you be? This is our place.'

Carol said tiredly, 'Oh yes. The Haunted House.' She forced a smile. 'It was ours when we found it, wasn't it? We were kids then. Twelve. Wouldn't it be lovely to be twelve again?'

Monica closed the stair-lid and sat on it carefully.

'Yes,' she said unexpectedly. 'Yes, it would.'

Carol looked at her properly, trying to balance that sudden heart-felt agreement with the defiantly smart appearance. Monica met the look for a moment, then stood up and began dusting off her dress.

'We should have brought some chairs or something. Furnished the place.'

'We brought the rugs, and there's the bed.'

'I'm not sitting on either in this dress.'

'You know we decided we'd leave it looking deserted. In case anyone came nosing around.'

'Yes. Well . . .' Monica paced to the other window and stood with her back to Carol. 'I doubt I'll ever come here again, so it doesn't matter.'

Carol tried to laugh. 'Of course we'll come here again. Oh, I know you're all leaving school so you've got to pretend to be grown-up, but that won't matter. We'll come here again.'

'You might. I won't. I'm leaving. Leaving home. I came to find you to say goodbye.'

'But we'll meet tonight. At the victory celebrations.'

'No. I'll be in London by then. I might go to Trafalgar Square or something.'

None of the girls had ever been to London; for so long it had been completely beyond the pale, a war zone. Carol was silent with incredulity.

Monica hunched her shoulders irritably. 'Oh well . . . perhaps in twenty years' time or something. When we're old. But not till then. I don't want to see any of you till I'm really old.'

'Mon. You can't mean it. What has happened?'

There was a silence and Carol waited for a rebuff. It didn't come. Eventually the hunched shoulders relaxed. Monica said without any expression, 'I found out . . . last year actually . . . I'm adopted.'

'Oh.' Carol wondered what her reaction should be. She said, 'Well, that's not bad, is it? I mean, your parents actually chose you. you're more special than the rest of us.'

Monica said nothing, giving Carol time to review her words.

Carol had once told her own parents that the Cooks were like a couple of shunting engines, pulling and pushing their two sons here and there, and vainly trying to get stubborn and wilful Monica on to the rails in order to start chivvying her likewise. Monica's abrupt disclosure explained a lot. She wasn't like them; not a bit. They were all rough and tough and uncaring. Monica could be tough, but in her that quality was more a veneer than anything else.

Carol cleared her throat. 'They must have wanted you quite desperately. I mean, they already had Gus and Giles.'

Monica said softly, 'Giles. Yes, they had Giles. And Gus of course.' She hunched her shoulders again. 'They didn't want me. They wanted the money my real mother was offering. It was a cash deal you see. I don't blame them. Dad had been out of work since the last war with his chest. They had to do . . . something.'

'Oh.' Carol searched her mind frantically. 'I can understand how you feel . . . odd. But you must be fond of them. And they must be fond of you. You can't run away.'

'You watch me.'

Carol said, 'Are you going to look for your mother? Your real mother?'

'She died a long time ago. When I was ten. And she never told Mum and Dad – the Cooks – she never told them who my father was. Maybe she didn't know. Maybe she was a prostitute.'

'Oh, Mon.'

'Well, you never know.' She turned and attempted to smile. 'I don't know her, so I can't grieve for her. Do you realise how lucky you are to be able to grieve for your dad? Grieve

356

properly? So that everyone knows and respects your feelings?'

'No. No, I suppose I don't. I just . . . did it.'

'Oh Carol. I'm sorry. Going on like this. I just wanted to say goodbye. That's all.'

'Listen. Don't go. You can come and live with us. It would do Mummy good. She likes you. Really. I know she'll say yes. Honestly. You don't have to run away.'

Monica's eyes slid past Carol's head and into a future that did not hold anyone she knew.

'I do actually. I'm having a baby. I'm going to pick up the first rich-looking Yank I see in London, and make him marry me and take me back to America.' She shoved out one hip and put a hand on it. 'I look all of twenty-two or three, don't I? Don't I, Carol?'

'Oh . . . Oh my God . . .' Carol scrambled to her feet and moved forward with outstretched arms. 'Oh Mon . . . oh God . . . who . . . what?'

'Keep away!' Monica's voice was sharp. 'You'll mess up my hair or make me cry or something. Just keep away.'

Carol fell back.

Monica said, 'I shouldn't have told you. Damn fool me. That's what I am. A damn fool! You were always soft! God, it's not the end of the world! Other girls have . . . other girls have . . . other girls have . . .'

Carol interrupted helplessly, 'Can't you marry him? I know Miss Edgeworth says they don't respect you afterwards. But surely—'

'No, I can't marry him.'

'Your father would make him. He'd make him, Mon! It's his duty – oh he must be horrible to do this to you and then leave you to take it all by yourself!'

'He's not very nice. But then neither am I. And if Dad knew about it he'd kick me out. I'd rather go under my own steam, thank you very much.'

'Oh Mon. Don't be daft. As if your dad would kick you out!'

Monica sighed sharply and looked at her friend. They were the same age, but although Carol was six inches taller, she was unmistakably years younger in experience.

'All right. You may as well know. Then you'll want to see the last of me too.' She smiled slightly. 'I've always been honest. You've got to admit that, Cass. Not wise, not a bit clever. But honest.' She stopped smiling. 'It was Giles. Gillie. The one I've always loved best.'

'Your . . . brother?'

'Quite. And Dad's favourite, too.'

'But how could you, Mon? Was it when you found out . . . about the adoption? You had always loved him, and when you knew you weren't related, then you discovered your love was—'

'For God's sake, Cass! Shut up!' Monica gave a small sob and turned to the window again. 'It wasn't *Girls' Crystal* or Ethel M. Dell. Nothing like that. He was the one who told me I was adopted. That I'd been sold. That I'd got no-one to call my own. Then he said that I could very easily have someone of my own. My very own.' She banged her head suddenly on the window sash and her hat was pushed high on her curls. 'Yes, you're right. It was like that. I've always loved him. We used to mess about when we were little kids – oh I can't tell you, you've got no brothers. Disgusting, it was. And then I got older and knew it was disgusting and stopped it and . . . that's what happened. I was seduced because I wanted a brother again! And I couldn't have been seduced if I'd known he was my brother! Oh it's too difficult, too complicated. And I'm so tired. I'm so tired, Cass.'

She let Carol approach her and hold her awkwardly in her long arms.

She sobbed, 'Admit you're sick to your soul. I remember how it was for you when that Mussolini man came. And when I told you last year that I wasn't a virgin. I know what it does to you! I didn't want to tell you—'

Carol said, 'You told me because we're friends.'

'I don't want the others to know. Liv. Myrt. Don't tell them. Please, Cass.'

'Of course I won't tell them. One person is enough.'

'But you're not the right person. You can't bear it.'

'I wouldn't have been able to. Before. But now . . . it's different now. It's something to do with atoms and putting life back together.'

'What are you talking about?' The sobs increased.

'I'm talking about my father. I can't do anything about that. Can't you understand, Mon? Something can always be done with life. But death . . . nothing. Nothing.'

Monica allowed herself a small gasping laugh. 'Nothing much

to be done about this life either, Cass. I've tried gin. And hot baths. And running a mile. It's still there.'

'Oh Mon. You shouldn't.'

'No. Well. I had to try. Poor little devil.' She pushed herself upright and unwound Carol's arms. 'Anyway. I'd better be off. There's a train at four-fifteen, and if I don't get a bus into town in the next half an hour, I'll miss it.'

'Mon. You can't. You know you can't.'

'Listen, innocent. I know I can. I know what to do.' She shook her head at Carol's rush of colour. 'It need not mean much, Cass. The actions. It's up here it counts.' She touched her forehead. 'All I have to do is get off the train and join in with everyone else – it'll be nearly eight o'clock. I pick the nicest-looking American I can see, and we start dancing. Who knows, he might make a marvellous husband, as well as a father for Gillie's baby!' Her defiance crumpled again and she fumbled for her handkerchief. Her net gloves were already grubby. 'Oh Cass. I'll never forget this place and our happy times.'

'You won't need to remember them – you can come back – I've got a wonderful idea. All right, you want to get away. I understand that. But you want to come back too. Afterwards. You don't really know my parents. They . . . well, they're good people. And my mother will go on being good. For Daddy as well as for herself. I can't explain it. I know you think I'm pi and stuffy—'

'I don't. I think Liv is pi and stuffy. Not you.'

'Come home with me, now. Please. Mummy will understand. And we've got enough money, you see. Daddy's insurance . . .' her voice petered out. She cleared her throat and said loudly, 'Mummy keeps saying – what shall we do. She wants to go on holiday or something. So we can all go. It'll be all right. Mummy will sort it out. I know she will. She needs to be doing something – to be thinking of something.'

Monica did not immediately repudiate the fantastic idea. She dabbed at her face with her hanky and kept swallowing and looking at Carol as if she'd never seen her before. When she did shake her head, it was without her usual vigorous conviction. Carol took her hand and led her back to the stair-lid and sat her down. And she began to talk in her low, persuasive voice.

Two

Mary Woodford listened to Carol's words and glanced now and then at Monica's white face, and did not speak for a long time. She noted Monica's fixed, defiant smile, and felt something begin to trickle into the vacuum that John's death had left. It was pity, and Mary knew that pity was not a very constructive emotion.

Carol finished, 'Mummy, we can do something, can't we? We can help Mon? She doesn't have to go to London and find a rich American?'

It was the pity that released Mary's vocal cords and made her say quickly, 'Of course she doesn't have to marry a rich American! She doesn't have to marry anyone unless she really wants to! And of course we can help her.'

But she didn't know how.

Northfield was a suburb of Birmingham now, but it had been a village until recently, and it had all the disadvantages of a small community. Monica Cook's life wouldn't be worth living if she stayed here.

Mary said carefully, 'Monica. Dear. How do you feel about Giles? Do you love him?'

'No!' The reply came too quickly and emphatically.

'Have you told him? I mean . . .' Mary herself was too inhibited to be direct ' . . . does he know?'

'No.' The girl hesitated, then said with a rush, 'I can't tell him, Mrs Woodford. I know he would – he would—' she swallowed and came out with a word from a penny dreadful. 'He would repudiate me! I mean . . . what else could he do? He works at Longbridge – he doesn't know anything else – we'd have to stay here. And even if I could – he couldn't!' She shook her head. 'I can't tell him.'

Mary accepted this and nodded. 'All right. Let's go slowly. Step by step. First I ring up your mother and tell her that Carol and I need some company and can she spare you for a week or so.'

'We're not on the phone.' But Monica began to lose some of the tightness around her mouth.

'Then I'll send a note.' Mary smiled, already gaining confidence, already sensing John's approval. 'Then . . . Carol and I were planning a holiday this summer. North Wales perhaps. It would be nice for Carol to have your company.'

'Oh, Mrs Woodford.' Monica's eyes filled suddenly and Mary felt something besides pity. Anger. Anger towards the feckless, stupid boy who had caused all this. Giles Cook of all people. He had developed a limp to get out of the army. He saw no further than next week.

She smiled. 'I'll write the note now and you two can take it down to Turves Green and collect Monica's clothes. While you're gone, I'll get some tea. I managed to buy some kippers in the village this morning. How would you feel about a winter tea in June, Monica?'

'Oh Mrs Woodford.' Monica fished a handkerchief from her sleeve and blew her nose. Mascara ran from her eyes and her lipstick had smudged. She looked what she was, beautiful and ravaged.

Mary stood up and went to John's writing desk, determined to be as matter-of-fact as possible.

'Perhaps later – if you feel like it, girls – we could go to the Green and watch the bonfire. I understand they've made an effigy of Hitler, and they're going to have fireworks too.'

Monica said again, 'Oh Mrs Woodford!' And Carol, bright-eyed and smiling tremulously, said, 'Perhaps we can enjoy it – V.E. day – after all.'

They went to Rhyl for a fortnight in August. Carol and her mother had had a holiday there at the beginning of the war when the place was full of evacuees. Now, in spite of the victory summer, it was almost empty. There was still a war in the Far East, and the soldiers weren't going to be home for a while. There was a terrible food shortage, and the sticky tape crisscrossing all the windows hadn't been taken down yet. They spent the days on the beach, and in the evenings shared the landlady's wireless to listen to Alvar Liddell and Stewart Hibberd reading the news. It was in that plush-insulated parlour that they heard of the atom bomb falling on Hiroshima. Carol and Monica exchanged glances. Carol wondered what Miss Edgeworth would say about splitting the atom now. Monica thought dryly that it was one more male theory gone down the drain. Mary Woodford was horrified and thankful at the same time. Now the war would be well and truly over. She could take the next step in her tentative plan for Monica.

She wrote to an old friend of hers who ran a small boarding house near Paddington, and who – amazingly – had not been bombed out. Miss Drake had been a reputable ladies' dressmaker in Selly Oak and had made Grannie Woodford's clothes for years. She had made Mary's wedding dress, come to Carol's christening, and expected to be part of the family for the rest of her life. And then George Gosling met her at one of 'her' weddings and their own had been announced soon afterwards.

John had thoroughly enjoyed all of it. 'It was absolutely inevitable,' he had spluttered. 'Immediately they heard each other's names, they had to bow to fate.'

When Miss Drake had confided to Mary that it had indeed been love at first sight, and that she called George by his nickname – 'Gander' – and he called her his 'Dilly', John's joy had only just been controlled.

The marriage had worked splendidly. The two families kept in touch at Christmas and Mary had actually stayed at the Albion once, when she'd gone to London to visit an old schoolfriend. It was a nice little place, comfortable and well run. But the Goslings were in their fifties when they married and must be nearly seventy by now.

Mary told Dilly the whole story of Monica and Giles, and asked whether a place could be found for her at the Albion.

'I would not wish you to think I am making a convenience of you, my dear. I will of course meet all Monica's expenses. But I am hoping very much that you might be able to offer her a permanent position after the baby has been born. She is a very presentable girl and adaptable too. If you could teach her the business, I think one day she might make an excellent hotel manageress. We have not discussed this at all, so if it is an unwelcome

362

suggestion, do not think you will be disappointing Monica. As for the baby, we have not discussed its future either. I am assuming Monica will have it adopted.'

Mary posted the letter with a feeling of enormous optimism. Since that afternoon, six weeks ago, when she had been forced out of her reclusive misery, she had been conscious of sudden surges of energy, and she wondered now whether it could be anything to do with the energy released by the bomb. It was ridiculous; she knew nothing of physics. But if all life was energy, and love was energy, then John's love was still most definitely with her. She wrestled with her thoughts as Carol had wrestled in the Haunted House, and returned to the seaside boarding house flushed and exhilarated.

Dilly's reply arrived two days later. She hung on to it until the evening when the girls got out the Monopoly board as usual. It was one thing to make plans and have them agreed; when they were for other people it was another thing altogether.

She shook the dice and moved to gaol. The girls spluttered with laughter. They were so young: Carol completely innocent, Monica probably knowing more than Mary herself. But the bond between them was obvious. Perhaps Monica's baby would strengthen that bond, make it unbreakable, make it survive death itself.

Carol said to Monica, 'Trust you to buy a hotel already – we've only just started the game!' She turned to her mother. 'You see, she'll win again. As sure as eggs are eggs we shall both end up on her square!'

Both girls looked up, surprised by Mary's sudden gurgle of laughter.

'It's just that . . . oh, I must tell you. Perhaps you won't like it, Monica dear, but . . . well it's so apt. You buying a hotel, I mean. You see . . .' She started by telling them about the Goslings: their unlikely but happy marriage, their lack of close family, their staunch commitment to the large boarding house surrounded by bomb sites. She stressed their age and their need for support. Finally she told the girls that she had written to Mrs Gosling.

'I told her the truth, Monica dear. All of it. She is offering you a home and training – and it will be good training. How do you feel about it?'

Monica turned white, then immediately fiery red. She said

363

painfully, 'I suppose, if I'm to be . . . taken in by someone . . . they will have to know.'

Mary said gently, 'Dilly Gosling came from Selly Oak, Monica. She has been lonely in her time. She was a friend of my husband's family and she will look on you as a daughter. But, unlike most mothers—' she tried to coax a smile on to the strained faces opposite her ''—she will be entirely without criticism.'

'I didn't mean – I'm very grateful, Mrs Woodford. I just haven't wanted to . . . look into the future. It's been marvellous with you and Carol. But of course I knew it couldn't go on.'

'Monica. It can go on. If that is what you want.'

'No. That wouldn't be fair on anyone. And my mother . . . and Gillie . . . No. I'd like to go to this London place. Thank you for arranging it all – thank you so . . .' She swallowed. 'Will you and Carol come with me – just to introduce me?'

Carol said stoutly, 'We shall stay with you all the time, Mon!'

And Mary Woodford said, 'Well, we will certainly settle you in. And be with you when it is time for the birth.'

It worked out almost as Mary said. They went to stay at the Albion guest house at the beginning of September, and fortunately, not only did the Goslings take to Monica immediately, but Monica – still inclined to bouts of stubborn pride – took to them. Mrs Gosling had kept her Birmingham accent, which was endearing for a start. And Mr Gosling was from a bygone age, large, lumbering, courteous, and fairly demanding. Mrs Gosling explained to the three women, 'He can rise to the occasion splendidly. Simply splendidly. But he's no good in an emergency.' Where the dividing line between an occasion and an emergency was drawn, was anyone's guess.

Monica knew instantly how to deal with him. She had had a lot of experience in the Turves Green council house. You made sure he had his newspaper, neatly folded, whenever he wanted it. You kept his shoes clean and gave him a constant supply of clean shirts. And you deferred to him. All the time.

'Nice little gel,' he said to Mary. 'Taken advantage of, that's obvious. Can't think what her father was about.'

'You realise that he doesn't know?' Mary said seriously. 'He is not a fit man and Monica wants to spare him. Naturally.'

'Question of pride too. I like pride in a woman.' Gander

364

Gosling smiled approvingly. 'You've got it, Mrs Woodford. Always had it, according to my Dilly, and always will have it.' He passed his cup for more tea. Mrs Gosling was showing the two girls around the guest house. Gander held forth uninterrupted.

'I admit we can do with some help here. Now the war is well and truly over, I might apply for a licence and become a private hotel. Sounds better on the cards, wouldn't you say? And young Monica will be worth her weight in gold. Sitting-down jobs, dear lady, never fear. Cleaning silver. Marking linen. You know the sort of thing. Plenty of company here too. Keep her mind off things. I shall introduce her as my niece. Safety first, Mrs Woodford. Safety first.'

'I am so grateful, Mr Gosling. Obviously I will book Monica into a nursing home and be with her when her time comes. Then you must let me know – honestly – what you think about the future.'

Mr Gosling leaned forward. 'Mrs Woodford. If things work out here as we both hope, there will be a position for your young friend after her child has been adopted. Hotel work . . . good opportunity for a girl. Live like one of the family.' He waxed sentimental. 'The family we never had. Never had. Dear Dilly already in her fifties when . . .'

Mary nodded sympathetically. 'Quite.'

She reserved her opinion. Once the baby was born, any decisions must be Monica's.

It was put about that Monica was training in hotel management. When Mary had first made the suggestion, Mrs Cook had been inclined to look on it as interference. Giles, staring speculatively at the older woman, said, 'We ought to thank Mrs Woodford, ma. Using her influence on our Mon's behalf. She didn't get no school certificate, remember. You'd've 'ad to get her trained at a secretarial school or soomthink.'

Mrs Cook said sharply, 'She could 'a' gone into a shop, my lad. And liked it or lumped it. Our Mon was always too big for 'er boots.'

Mary Woodford murmured, 'My husband was very fond of Monica. He would have liked to feel he was helping her in a career, Mrs Cook.'

'Oh well. If you put it like that. I'm too soft, that's my trouble. Can't help it. That's the way I am.'

It was left to Giles to mutter, 'Good of you, Mrs Woodford. Real good.' But Mary noticed he did not ask if he could see Monica; he did not even want to know her London address. And she was not surprised that during the whole exchange, Mr Cook slept on in his armchair next to the fire. Monica had lampooned him so often: the breadwinner, uninterested in the family.

'It seemed too good an opportunity to miss. An old friend of mine made the suggestion in a letter and while we were on holiday in Rhyl, I mentioned it to Monica.'

'She could 'a' come and talked it over, like. Still, she allus was an ungrateful little 'ussy.'

Mary said inconsequentially, 'Girls will be girls,' then looked quickly away from Giles Cook's sharp gaze.

He said soothingly, 'She'll come back one of these days, our Ma. Flash her money around. Buy you a present I wouldn't be surprised.'

'We'll see,' Mrs Cook said grudgingly.

Liv and Myrt were more curious. They met Carol in the Haunted House just before Myrtle went off to train as an osteopath. The bedroom was icy cold although it was only the beginning of October.

'If it's just you and me left here, Cass, I shan't bother to come any more,' Liv said fretfully. 'I mean, what's the point? I've started at the post office and I don't want to talk about school. I reckon this is the end.'

Carol thought of Mon and the baby; the Haunted House meetings seemed trivial in comparison. She nodded.

'Perhaps we could arrange to come here when we're forty. You know, have a reunion. Just the four of us.'

'Can't see Mon leaving London to meet us in a muddy field.' Myrtle was in a gloomy mood. 'If only this training thing was in London, I could at least keep in touch with her. You two are lucky to be staying at home.'

'You're scared,' Liv said incredulously. She would have adored to be leaving Northfield for pastures new.

'I am. I bloody well am.'

'You and your swearing. I suppose you think it's clever. Anyway you'll soon get used to being away. Though I must admit I never liked Wales.'

'Rhyl was lovely,' Carol said dreamily. 'All empty and wild.'

Myrtle humped a shoulder. 'You've changed. I thought you

366

were like me. Wanted things to happen! And you had Mon for company. I was surprised you asked her to go with you. I thought you and me were partners. You didn't ask me.'

'Oh Myrt, I'm sorry. But you always have a holiday. Mon has only ever been away with the school or the Guides or something. And you know how ghastly the Cooks are – she wanted a break before starting work.'

'Don't be daft, I'm not huffy about it. Just wondered.' She frowned. 'Liv and I were talking about it. Did something happen to Mon? Was she kicked out or something? I mean, it was all a bit sudden.'

Carol looked at her friends, wide-eyed. 'Not really. We left school in June and she didn't start her hotel training until last month.' She was amazed at how easy it was to lie on behalf of others; she didn't even feel a blush coming on.

'Yes, I suppose so. It was Liv really. She reckoned she could smell a rat.'

Liv was furious. 'That's right. Put it on to me. All I said was, the least she could have done was say goodbye!'

'Then you said you could smell a rat,' Myrtle insisted inexorably.

'Some rat! She was a rat! Leaving a sinking ship! It's no good you two looking at me like that, either. I feel it's a sinking ship. We're all leaving—'

'I'm still here,' murmured Carol.

'But as soon as you've done your Higher School Cert, you'll be off too. Leaving me by myself. Nothing ever happens here. It's not as if it's Birmingham proper. There's nowhere to go. Nothing to do.'

'You'll get married, Liv. You know you will.'

'How am I going to meet anyone? I know all the boys round here.'

'What do you mean – you *know* them?' Myrtle sucked in her cheeks against a grin. 'Like the Bible? You know them? You've been through them already? All of them? God Almighty, you must have had a boy a night—'

'Oh, shut up, shortie. Just cos you can't get anyone—'

'I'll tell you something.' Myrtle set her features hard. 'I'll tell you both something. I'll be married before any of you. Before Mon even. That's a promise.'

367

Liv made derisive sounds through her nose. Carol said mildly, 'I wish you wouldn't think marriage is the be-all and end-all of existence, Myrt. Mon is training for a career. So are you. You don't need to get married.'

They both stared at her in disbelief. Then, accepting that it was impossible to explain to Carol about the true nature of marriage, Liv said sharply, 'Well. I bet you that Mon will get married. And she'll marry someone rich. An American probably.'

Carol, remembering Monica's intention last June, started to laugh. That was something Monica would never do; in fact it was doubtful whether Monica would marry at all.

Mary Woodford went to London to be with Monica at the beginning of November. She wanted to be certain the girl was going for regular medical check-ups and that the light duties promised by the Goslings had not increased or become more strenuous.

It was the first time she and Carol had been apart since John Woodford had died, and they were both concerned for the other. Mary suggested that Liv should come to stay for the month, but Carol, afraid that Liv might find out about Monica, was determined to be by herself.

'I can join you on the 28th, Mummy,' she said. 'The History work will be done and I can bring the English stuff with me.'

'All right, my love. I'll book a double room, then you can decide whether to share with me or with Monica.' Mary gave an inverted smile. 'Sure you'll be all right? If anything goes wrong you can call on Mrs Trent next door. And phone me every day.'

They laughed. Carol was sixteen. Mary had been only a year older when she married John Woodford.

Even so, on the train going to London she had a moment of sheer incredulity at what was happening. A year ago John had still been alive, and because of his failing health their lives had been completely introverted. Carol, the house, and the garden . . . there had been nothing beyond that. Not even the war had encroached on their tiny world. John had been interested in Carol's School Certificate, an interest she had shared, but otherwise everything stopped at the front gate. The very few occasions she went shopping she had experienced this feeling of being out of place in the world. Or out of time. Rhyl, with its deserted beaches and barbed wire, had suited her. There she had been able to think and plan and wonder how she could bear the burden for the two girls . . . she knew that the burden was on Carol's shoulders as well as Monica's.

It was on the train, that no-man's-land between Birmingham and Euston, that she made the decision. It had been in the back of her mind for some time, unacknowledged, even suppressed at times, but always there. Now, as she stared at the undulating telegraph wires, and the wonderful pastoral views of ancient Warwickshire, a kind of peace flooded her being. It was so obvious. The next page in her life. If Monica would agree to it, she would adopt the baby.

She waited for Carol's arrival before broaching the subject. Meanwhile she had another holiday, quite different from the one in Rhyl, but just as therapeutic in its way. In the mornings she and Monica walked in Hyde Park. It was full of American soldiers, still jubilant, though impatient to get home. The nannies had returned too, with their high prams and recalcitrant toddlers. And there were old ladies with dogs. After lunch Monica rested and Mary walked around the city on her own. The bomb damage was shocking. Yet it had not devastated normal life. Mary felt she was learning a lesson in survival. She seemed to re-enter the larger world again. She faced reality; acknowledged that she had health and strength to spare, that she wasn't yet forty, that the only work she knew was looking after a family. By the time Carol arrived at the end of November, the decision she had made on the train was part of her life. If Monica turned it down out of hand, or Carol shook her head gently, she would be . . . bereft.

She put it to the girls one evening while they were making paper chains for the hall. Monica was at last wearing one of the smocks she had made for herself out of an old school skirt. She had embroidered red daisies around the neck and it looked amazingly pretty. Cass – dear Cass – was uncompromisingly an overgrown schoolgirl still. Mary experienced one of her moments of passionate longing that John could be here with them all, right now. And, as usual, the uncontrollable surge of feeling was miraculously quietened; as if he were saying with surprise, 'But Mary, darling, you must know I'm with you all the time.'

So her voice was very calm and steady when she spoke.

369

'Monica. Carol. I've been thinking very hard about the future. The future of the baby, as well as our own.'

Monica looked up from a tumble of crepe paper. 'I don't want to worry you for evermore, Mrs Woodford. I shall stay on here – Mr Gosling says there will be a job for me. And I intend to get in touch with the adoption agency immediately after Christmas.' Her dark eyes were very determined. 'Please don't try to dissuade me. It isn't history repeating itself or anything like that. These agencies are very careful to find good homes—'

Mary interrupted firmly. 'I wouldn't talk you into or out of anything, Monica. But I did think of something you might feel would be good. For the baby, and for you. I haven't discussed it with Cass. She might disagree. You might both think I'm mad. Or unfit.' She laughed, suddenly nervous.

Carol folded yet another Chinese lantern. 'We wouldn't think anything of the sort, Mummy. Come on, tell us.'

'Well . . .' Mary put down her scissors. 'It's . . . Monica, would you let me adopt your baby? In other words, Carol and me, but it would have to be me legally. You see, we'd love her because she is yours – as well as for herself. And then – well – if you were ever in a position to look after her again, we wouldn't hold you to any piece of paper.' She swallowed. 'You know what I mean. We'd almost hold her in trust. It would be an honour. I – I don't know how Cass feels about this, but I would look on it as that. An honour and a privilege. And so—' she cleared her throat '—so worthwhile!'

Monica said nothing. She stared at Mrs Woodford as if she had never seen her before. Then she took a sharp short breath and turned her gaze to Carol. Carol too was silent for a long time, but her excitement could be felt as if shock waves were flowing out of her eyes and open mouth. She also stared at her mother, but when she felt Monica's eyes on her she switched in to her and whispered, 'Well?'

Still Monica held herself back and simply said, 'What do you think?'

Carol breathed, 'It would be marvellous – wonderful – Mummy and I . . . oh Mon . . . would you let us?'

And then Monica's dark and determined face crumpled and almost dissolved in tears. For the first time the terrible strain of the last seven months broke its banks; she lost her superficial

370

chic, her gypsy attraction. She creased into ugliness and complete surrender.

Mary and Carol held her as best they could, kneeling either side of her chair, crushing paper chains and Chinese lantern between them, dabbing frantically as Monica's tears washed the dye from the cheap crepe on to her smock.

She spluttered, 'It won't matter . . . it's red . . . like the daisies . . . oh Cass, it would be the best thing that could happen . . . I need never worry. I wouldn't interfere. Not ever. But I'd know the baby was there. Where I lived. Where we lived, Cass. Oh Mrs Woodford . . .' She tried to sit up. 'But . . . what would – will – you say to everyone at home?'

Mary felt her own tears stinging her eyes. Monica had put up such a good front that she had not realised the full extent of the fears the child felt. Monica was as sensitive as Cass, and so careful not to show it.

She said huskily, 'Anything. I'll say the baby is a war refugee – lots of children from the camps are being adopted – I shall say this one's mother died in a Red Cross camp.' She cleared her throat. 'I wish I'd talked to you both before. Do I take it the idea meets with unanimous approval?'

Her attempt to raise a smile succeeded in a watery way. Carol sniffed luxuriously and said, 'I feel so selfish! All I could think of was how exciting it would be. I wasn't looking through your eyes at all.'

Monica scrubbed her eyes with the communal handkerchief.

'But it is exciting. It's the most exciting thing that has happened since I knew about the baby.' She looked from one to the other. 'Oh, I feel it's Christmas now. I feel . . . I feel I can have the baby now. I feel . . . marvellous.' And she started to cry again.

Mary had booked a bed at the nursing home recommended by the local G.P. There was some doubt about the date of the birth: Monica could not remember the date of her last period, and Dr Martin was against internal examinations in someone so young. Monica's smock was still hanging straight when she stood up, and though the older women avoided discussing the pregnancy in front of her, Mrs Gosling did say tentatively that while she naturally had not much experience in these matters, she could not see that the baby would arrive before the New Year. 'You see. January 1946. That's when we shall be celebrating the next birthday.'

Mary nodded, but voiced a reservation. 'You never know with first babies. You just never know.'

A week before Christmas, they went to see the nursing home. It was in a quiet tree-lined road in St John's Wood – 'five minutes in a taxi' – as Mary pointed out. Discretion was in every pointed architrave, in each of the yellow-blotched plane trees surrounding it, in the fine gravel of the car park, and certainly in the thick pile of the carpets in hall and lounge at the front of the house. Here, in enormous, boxy armchairs, the young mothers who were convalescing lounged in satin dressing-gowns and talked about feeding routines and knitting patterns. Mary had deliberately worn a full swagger coat, and it was assumed tacitly by all the loungers that she was the expectant mother. They smiled up at the two schoolgirls. 'How nice. A little brother or sister for you to look after.' Carol looked at Monica and was relieved to see a gleam in the dark eyes. 'Yes,' they said in unison, then had to control incipient giggles. Mary was thankful they had not left their childhood behind them entirely.

There was no delivery room as such in this nursing home. Normal babies were delivered in their mother's bedrooms, just as they would be at home. There was an emergency room which they were not shown. The bedrooms were pink, blue and lemon. Choice was limited to availability.

'Lemon, I think,' Monica murmured to Carol. 'Sharp and acid. Like me.'

Carol whispered back, 'Idiot. I'd rather blue. Goes with my eyes.'

Mary said aloud, 'How very pretty the pink is.'

The receptionist, who was showing them around, said, 'The pink is available at the moment. As is the lemon. But who knows what the day will bring?'

The girls were convulsed. For some time after they were apt to say dramatically, 'Who knows what the day will bring?'

That particular day brought Monica's first labour pains. There was mulligatawny soup that night and she thought at first it had given her wind.

372

'I think I'll wait till my pudding, Mrs Woodford,' she responded to the proffered plate of spam and tinned peas.

'Not very appetising, I agree.' Mary forked a slice of spam on to her plate. 'Actually Monica, when you start working here properly, I think you could well put your mind to the menus. I know we're stuck with spam once a week, but it could be chopped into batter and served as a savoury pancake.' She got no reply and looked round at the silent and preoccupied girl. 'My dear, what is it?' Her alarm infected Carol who leaned over the table.

'Mon. It's the baby. Isn't it?'

'No. It can't be. Not till after Christmas. Wind, I think.'

Carol and her mother exchanged glances. Mary manoeuvred her watch uppermost and noted the time.

'Better now.' Monica took a deep breath and reached for her glass of water. 'It was wind. I'll have a piece of bread and scrape, and go on up to bed early.'

They all smiled at each other reassuringly. But when, five minutes later, Monica leaned over her plate again, eyes closed, Mary stood up.

'I'm going to ring Dr Martin,' she announced, holding up a hand against protests. 'Much better to call him out now than in the middle of the night.'

Monica did not demur.

The doctor arrived an hour later and examined Monica in her room with Mary present. Carol and Mrs Gosling lingered on the landing apprehensively. There was only partial relief when the door opened and the doctor asked them to call a taxi.

'We'll move her into her bed at Denham Lodge,' he said. 'It won't be until tomorrow at the earliest, but you will all feel happier, no doubt, if she is in professional hands.'

'And everything is all right?' Carol was clutching Mrs Gosling much too hard and loosened her hold with an effort. 'We wondered if . . . we were afraid that . . .'

'Perfectly normal.' Dr Martin had been intrigued all along by the trio of women. It seemed that even the boarding-house owner was roped into the drama now. He grinned suddenly. The child might be illegitimate, but it was certain it would never lack a family. 'It might be a week or two premature. No more. Get that taxi and you and your mother can go with her.'

'Of course – of course. We won't leave her . . .' Carol finally released Mrs Gosling who collapsed against the newel post, and ran down to the phone.

They did not leave her. Mary still had nightmare recollections of the casual treatment she had received during her own labour, and was determined Monica should not be left alone. She would have spared Carol, but the girl refused to go, and indeed Monica herself clung to her with the fierce strength of all imminent mothers. All that night and the next day Monica went from one contraction to the next, garnering her strength in between, breathing deeply as Dr Martin had instructed, hanging on to Carol and gasping, 'Stay with me, Cass . . . stay with me . . .' And Carol shifted her position slightly to ease her aching joints and said, 'I'm here, Mon. After this one, we'll drink some tea. And Mummy will rub your back. Oh God. Oh God, please help her.'

Mary took over when she could, holding the gripping hands in hers and murmuring ridiculous reassurances. 'Not long now, dear girl. Hang on . . . not much longer.'

As the short afternoon darkened, Monica lost track of her purpose and shouted wildly, 'Why am I here? Why don't they operate? If you knew what it was like – me and the pain – me and the pain—' Mercifully it was then that Dr Martin appeared with the gas and air machine, and Mary and Carol were banished to the lounge.

Mary tried to make the whole experience clinical.

'It won't be bad at all now, darling. This second stage is when Monica can actually push the baby out.'

'We shouldn't have gone. Why won't they let us stay?'

'Carol, they are all going to be working hard. All of them. Not just Monica. They need the room. Monica understands that.'

'I read a piece in that magazine the American woman left. It said that women in labour should always have their husbands with them. And as Mon hasn't got a husband, we should be there.' Carol's face was pasty white and her blue eyes had gone a strange, pebble-grey colour.

Mary said, 'It's been too much for you, darling. I wish I hadn't allowed you to come.'

'I wouldn't have stayed at the Albion, Mummy. I couldn't. I wish I was back in Mon's room right now.' She shook her head as if to clear it. 'We've been friends since we were seven years old.

374

The four of us – Liv and Myrtle and Mon and me – we've always stuck together.'

Mary felt something like a twinge of envy. She said gently, 'I know, darling. But sometimes, however close we are to others, we have to do something on our own.'

Carol looked up. 'Like Daddy? We have to die on our own?'

Mary forced herself to return the look. 'Yes. Birth and death. They're solitary experiences.'

Carol nodded slowly and was silent for a long time. They drank more tea and ate some sandwiches and still there was no message from upstairs.

Carol said, 'I must go to the lavatory. How much longer, d'you think?'

'Another hour. Perhaps. Everything must be all right, Cass. They haven't gone to that emergency room, we'd have heard.'

'I know.'

Carol went into the hall and turned right for the downstairs cloakroom. An animal cry, muted by closed doors and curtains, came from above. She stopped in her tracks and listened. Another. She pivoted on her heel and took the stairs three at a time. Her entry into Monica's room was unceremonious but very quiet. Monica was on her side, her left leg supported by Dr Martin's shoulder. The midwife held the gas and air mask with one hand, the other was offering the doctor a pair of forceps.

Carol met Monica's drugged and agonised gaze above the mask. She moved swiftly to the side of the bed and knelt down. Instinctively she slid a hand beneath the damp hair and cradled Monica's head. She put her mouth close to the free ear.

'Listen, Mon. The baby is almost here. Almost. Not quite. Dr Martin is going to use forceps. And we don't want that if we can help it. Let's try . . . like in that book we looked at . . . come on, I'll do it with you. A deep breath. Hold it. Now . . .'

Dr Martin glanced above his mask at the two girls. They were children. Yet with a child's instinct they knew what was happening and what to do. He waved away the forceps and rolled Monica on to her back. Brusquely he took one foot and indicated to the midwife to take the other. They crooked both of Monica's legs and held them into their shoulders. Then they gripped a hand each.

'Push!' Dr Martin commanded loudly. 'Come on, girls. Both of you. Push hard!'

It was difficult to tell where the gasps and the grunts came from. Carol pressed the mask hard into her friend's face and then removed it and held her straining shoulders. It was as if she were groaning for Monica. She took a swift gasp of air when she needed it, and Monica did likewise. She let that out in a fierce explosion of sound, and so did Monica. Three times they both bore down together as one, then Monica gave a cry that was independent of Carol, and immediately the coiled-spring tension, the discipline, was gone.

Dr Martin said crisply, 'The head has been born, Monica. Another very gentle push, please. You haven't quite finished.'

Almost dreamily, Monica gave a token grunt. Dr Martin put his two index fingers into tiny armpits and twisted very gently. A baby girl corkscrewed into his hands. Her resemblance to a monkey was striking. Her blue-black eyes were hooded beneath mounds of loose skin, her hair was a black unmanageable thatch, her nose, cheeks, ears – even her mouth – were pushed into her head. Perfect fingers and toes clawed at the new element in which she found herself. The midwife took her and cleared her mouth with an expert finger. While the doctor dealt with the cord, she took her first breath through the parted lips, and let out a howl.

Monica said, 'Is it over?'

The midwife said, 'You've got a beautiful baby girl, my dear.'

Carol said, 'Oh Mon . . . oh Mon . . . she is so *real* – I mean – look at her pink *heels*!'

Dr Martin said, 'We might need a little push for the placenta. But no more contractions. Everything is fine.'

Monica murmured, 'I don't want to see her. I don't want to get fond of her.'

But Carol laughed. 'Oh Mon. Don't be silly. You know what we agreed. Oh Mon, I feel drunk, do you? *Listen* to her!'

The midwife was busy with olive oil and a binder. She wrapped the baby tightly and held her out. It was Carol who took her. Carol who could not stop laughing. Carol who leaned over the ugly face and said, 'Baby . . . baby . . . you're all right with us . . . no need to cry . . . we're all going to look after you.'

Monica whispered, 'I didn't know it was going to be like that. I could never have another one. Never.'

The midwife said cheerfully, 'They all say that, my dear. It'll be forgotten in a few months. Believe me.'

But Carol, distracted for a moment from the bundle in her arms, shook her head.

'No-one could possibly forget this.' She smiled wryly at Monica. 'I didn't go through it, Mon, but I'll never have a baby. Never.'

Mary, entering at that moment in search of her daughter, heard those words. She felt a pang of terrible regret. Then shook herself and hurried forward.

'Is it all right? Let me see. Doctor, I'm sorry, she slipped away . . . oh, what a beautiful baby!'

Dr Martin stripped off his gloves and went to the wash basin. He told himself it was all in a day's work; another youngster in trouble, another baby for the adoption society. But he couldn't help grinning.

Monica was not well for nearly a week afterwards. Dr Martin used some of the very latest drug on her and told Mrs Woodford there was nothing to worry about. 'A few years ago this sort of thing was extremely dangerous. Not any more.'

Mary was worried. 'What exactly is it, Doctor? She hasn't got septicemia, surely?'

'There is some infection in the Fallopian tubes, Mrs Woodford. As I said, with penicillin there is nothing to fear.'

And he was right. Before the week was out Monica was going to the bathroom under her own steam and looking almost the same as she'd done a year ago.

But she could not feed the baby. She'd had no intention of doing so anyway, so was quite glad of her infection which meant there were no arguments. At first she refused to choose a name for the tiny girl, but after pressure from Carol she said carelessly, 'Oh, all right then. Elizabeth. After the princess. You know how we always tried to be like her, Cass.' She looked out of the window. 'I'm not coming to the christening, though. Nothing like that.'

Mary was anxious, but Carol knew that the only way to deal with Monica's pain was to keep it open. Like a wound, the fresh air would help it.

'You might change your mind,' she said. 'We won't have her christened for ages. Will we, Mummy?'

'I won't change my mind. I don't want to see her. You will be

377

her family. And you're more my family than the Cooks. So, you see, that's all right. Honestly.'

'You'll have to come home sometimes,' Mary protested.

'I don't think so. I'm going to work really hard for the Goslings. They've been kind to me, and I can repay them. I might buy a house one day and turn it into a hotel of my own. I never thought I was domesticated, but I'm quite excited about it all. A new life. I'm going to start a new life.'

'Well, we shall come to see you,' Carol said.

'Please don't. Not for ages anyway. Let me get going properly.' Monica held Carol's arm. 'You know I'll be all right. I'm much tougher than you. I've had to look after myself for a long time now. Please don't come down here to see me.'

They had been a threesome for so long, it seemed wrong to split up. But now that Elizabeth was born, Monica could hardly wait to get rid of them. She hurried through the legalities, signing away her child without even reading the document. Elizabeth proved to be a noisy baby and Mary and Carol took it in turns to nurse her through the night. When they found a special brand of milk that satisfied her, they felt they had solved their first problem. Already they were both involved with Elizabeth; Monica's future was as well planned as it could be. They agreed they had better return home.

Monica did not see them off at Euston. But after Carol had carefully handed Elizabeth into the taxi and on to Mary's lap, Monica planted an entirely unexpected kiss on her cheek.

'Listen, Cass You'll never breathe a word . . . I mean, I know you won't, but Liv and Myrt might try to guess, and the kid is so like me – dark and swarthy. You'll fob them off somehow. Won't you?'

Carol grabbed a handful of Monica's jumper, and squeezed it.

'No-one knows except us. And no-one will ever know.'

Monica pulled away the gloved fingers and shook them, as if they'd made a bargain. Then she turned and fled back up the steps of the boarding house.

Three

The church was packed. The Dennings were well-known in North-field and since Dr Denning had come home covered in glory from his last-ditch heroism in the Far East, his list of National Health patients was the longest in the area. He was wearing full uniform for the wedding, though it was doubtful whether he was entitled to do so.

Liv and Carol waited in the church porch, holding Bessie between them. Myrtle had insisted on traditional bridesmaids' dresses, and Liv, who had wanted to wear a New Look dress with a saucer hat, had sulked for ages, then chosen something which would outshine Myrtle and look ridiculous on Carol. Now she realised that whatever she had worn, Bessie Woodford would steal the occasion. At nearly six years old she was as pretty as a picture with long black hair to her shoulders, luminous dark eyes set in perfect olive skin, and a nose, mouth and chin that seemed brushed gently upward in perpetual laughter. Today, Liv noted, her ears were suddenly revealed by the flower circlet on her head which pushed her hair back. They too were perfect. Twin pink shells giving a mother-of-pearl effect as the sun shone through them.

The sun was everywhere. Blazing into the porch, sending beams through the side windows, striking patterns over the congregation who sat beneath the stained glass.

'Myrtle's always been so damned *lucky*,' Liv murmured to Carol. 'Fancy landing that gorgeous surgeon! I mean. . . *Myrtle!*'

'He's an osteopath, Liv. Not a surgeon. And Myrt is an osteo-path too. And she deserves to be happy.'

'Oh . . . you! Myrt's going off to Bournemouth. You're going to Paris. We've heard nothing of Mon since she finished her hotel training. You're all leaving me in this dump!'

Carol looked sympathetic. 'Poor Liv. Anyway I'm not going

379

away for long.' She smiled down at Bessie. 'Can't leave you and Grannie for long, can I, baby?'

Bessie beamed and rubbed her cheek against Carol's fingers. Everyone knew that the two of them were inseparable. Everyone knew that Bessie called Mrs Woodford 'Grannie' though she was the child's adoptive mother. And Liv and Myrtle had seen nothing of Carol after that October farewell in the Haunted House. They could not help but dally with the outrageous idea that Bessie might belong to Carol. So much for Cass and her perculiar inhibitions. They both wanted to know how it had happened and dared not ask.

But Liv, suddenly provoked, couldn't resist a little dig.

'I'm surprised you could go to university and leave Bessie when she was so young. It's not so bad now she's started school.'

Carol looked up, surprised. 'She had Mother. They're the best of friends.'

'Oh yes, I forgot. Grannie,' Liv said.

'Where is Grannie?' Bessie interrupted. 'Is she sitting with Mrs Denning? Will she be all right?'

'We can peep and look at her if you like.' Carol drew the child forward to the inner door and there was Mrs Woodford sitting by the Bakers in the middle of the church, twisting her head like an owl to get a glimpse of the bridesmaids. Bessie waved and she waved back delightedly. Carol thought she looked younger as the years went by. Mrs Woodford was not as tall as Carol but she was just as unbeautiful, and when her husband had died six years ago she had shrivelled into an elderly woman overnight. Bessie had changed all that.

'I wanted her to sit in the front with Mrs Denning,' the child whispered now. 'Then we would have been by her and she could have smiled.'

Carol wanted to hung her. She was still five years old and her prime concern was 'Grannie'.

Liv said at her shoulder, 'My God. Look at him. He's so handsome.'

Carol switched her gaze to the front right-hand pew where Malcolm Chester Lennox waited for his bride. She knew that her father would have turned down his mouth at the obvious good looks, the ridged waves, the toothbrush moustache. But maybe that was unfair. This man's personal presentation was important

380

in his job. Outside regular medicine, outside the new and revered National Health scheme, he had to use all his assets.

She turned away. 'He certainly is.'

'Well, Myrt might have nobbled him, but the best man is definitely mine!' Liv continued to stare down the church and as if her gaze was magnetic the best man turned and looked towards them, and smiled. He was not as obviously handsome as the groom. He was fair and nondescript until he smiled. Then there was something rather special about him.

'I like him best,' Bessie declared. 'Is that why he is called the best man?'

Liv started to explain as the bridal car drew up. There were people waiting at the lychgate and a little cheer went up as Dr Denning alighted and handed out the froth of white net beneath which was Myrtle. She joined her bridesmaids and stood still while Liv dealt with the train, bouquet and veil.

'Now you know what to do.' She was in her element. 'The veil goes up and back, over the combs. It will give you more height. And take it slowly. Those platform shoes are lethal. And give me the bouquet when the vicar says—'

Dr Denning said smoothly, 'I think we remember last night's rehearsal. Don't we, honey?'

Myrtle managed a single nod. Then the organ struck up and everything started. 'Here comes the bride . . . all fat and wide . . .' But Myrtle knew now that she wasn't fat. She was plump and desirable. When she had gone to Malcolm's treatment room with three other students to 'observe', she had known he wanted her straightaway. But she had held out for marriage. For two years she had held out, smiling gently when he boasted of his other conquests. And in the end he had been forced to ask her to marry him.

She moved her laden head with difficulty to look at her two friends. She remembered being jealous of Carol; it had been amazing, quiet Cass having an illicit affair, and an even more illicit baby. Carol had the best of all worlds: her mother taking care of the sin itself, Carol off to university and then landing this job with a firm of publishers who were sending her over to Paris. But now . . . now Myrtle was glad she had waited. And she was glad she was getting married before Liv. Carol and she might have been the ugly ducklings of the quartet, but they'd made it before Monica and Liv. Carol. Dear Carol, looking anxious, putting out a hand which Myrtle could not take because one arm was in her father's and her other cradled the massive bouquet. But she smiled a special smile, and said, 'I wish Mon was here.' And Carol nodded. And Liv said, 'Bessie darling, you in front.' And Dr Denning said, 'Let's get the show on the road,' and they were off.

Myrtle knew the devil was in Malcolm when he merely brushed her cheek with his lips after the ceremony, then murmured in her ear, 'I see what you mean about your sexy friend. Games-captain type on top, and molten lava underneath.' But she wasn't going to let it spoil her day. Instead, she glanced at Bessie standing there like an angel, and murmured back, 'And molten lava burns. As you see.'

But maybe it sounded like a warning, because he wasn't smiling when he gave her his arm, and when they all stood about in the vestry for the signing he kept glancing at Carol and Bessie with that still, aware look that she'd seen on his face before when he'd got a woman patient he fancied.

It was all right again in the car. There was a glass partition between passengers and driver which gave an illusion of privacy, and taking his hand she slid it under the net and along the smooth satin of her dress.

'Can you feel my heart beating?'

'No.' He cupped her breast hard and pushed it up until it was almost beneath her chin. Then at last all his repressed passion came to the fore and he kissed her madly until the car drew up outside the hotel. The driver got out with slow tact, keeping his eyes averted from the mirror. Myrtle gasped, 'Malcolm – darling – we're there!' 'Not quite.' He lowered his head to the satin. 'Oh baby . . . bunny rabbit . . . do you know what these do to me?'

She smiled. It was the realisation two years ago that he thought her breasts were beautiful that had made her start to stand up straight again. Until then she had never quite forgotten her shame in the Haunted House.

'That was when I fell in love with you,' she admitted, kissing his waves which, amazingly, remained undisturbed.

The car door was opened by her completely tactless mother,

and with Malcolm's body on top of her she almost fell into the gutter. It did not help when Mrs Denning, flustered out of her wits, tried to make light of the matter by blaming her daughter.

'Come on now, Myrt! Enough of that! You're not allowed to start on the main course until this evening!'

It was all so utterly tasteless. How could Malcolm know that poor Mother had had to learn this kind of defence because Daddy was a philanderer?

Myrtle scrambled out of the car without a bit of dignity, and had to wait while her new husband straightened his tie and emerged unruffled and smiling urbanely. And – almost without pause – looking around him until he spotted the arrival of the bridesmaids.

Myrtle watched her parents going up the steps to the hotel, and knew that she and Malcolm were younger replicas of them. Mrs Denning, tiny and plump, was clinging to her husband's arm as if he might shake her off at any moment. And he was smiling and smiling. But not for his wife.

Myrtle thought wildly, 'Mother's had to put up with it all these years – but I won't – I won't – I won't!' And she too smiled up at Malcolm and said, 'Look at me, my darling. Just look at me. No-one else.'

Mrs Woodford said, 'I don't really like Bessie being shown around like an expensive doll, darling. It won't do her any good.'

Carol, who had done the rounds as quickly as possible, was sitting by her mother drinking a cup of tea.

'This is lovely. How did you get it?' she asked, looking for Bessie over the rim of the cup.

'I know one of the waitresses. She was in the Girl Guides with me. Many years ago.'

The waitresses were mostly in their late forties; some were even older. These days young girls were used to working alongside men in factories and earning good money.

'Trust you. Everyone thinks you're so quiet and reserved. It turns out you know more people than . . .' Carol put down her cup. 'Oh, there she is. Look at her, Mother. She's so *pretty*!'

'Like a little doll?' Mrs Woodford asked quizzically.

'Well, I suppose so. But, just this once . . . she is so enjoying herself.'

Mrs Woodford smiled. 'Not much we can do about it anyway. Wasn't she marvellous? The way she held the train and stood so quietly. Reverently, almost. I could have burst with pride.'

Carol said softly, 'She's made all the difference to our lives, hasn't she?'

'Oh yes.' Mrs Woodford never dissimulated. She nodded. 'She was a gift from heaven. Literally, I felt.' Her smile broadened to a grin and she looked very young again. 'But I couldn't have coped with her on my own, Cass. How we scrambled through that first year I'll never know. You were wonderful.'

'I loved it. I didn't want to go to Bristol. Thought she'd forget me. Thought you'd be frazzled out! But she . . . sort of . . . grew up, all at once, didn't she?'

'Anyway, you were home so often.' Mary Woodford's smile became wry. 'I'd have hated it – you going away to university – if it hadn't been for Bessie.'

'I don't think I'd have gone. Strange. Everyone thinks we made a prison for ourselves, taking her on. It worked the other way really.'

'Yes. I wonder if Mon . . . how Mon feels about it now.'

'She's ours, Mother.'

'Oh I know, darling. But . . . oh look at her now. Just look. Miss Pears of 1952.'

Bessie was shaking hands gravely with a boy of ten or eleven. He was Myrtle's young brother, and though they lived quite near each other Bessie did not meet him often and was rather in awe of him.

He wore long trousers and a Norfolk jacket, and his hair was so slicked down with brilliantine that his head looked flat on the top. He was not quite old enough to be tongue-tied, and Bessie was too young to cause him any inhibitions.

He said frankly, 'You are very pretty. I didn't want to come actually. But I've got to admit, it was all very pretty.'

Bessie said politely, 'You look nice, too.'

'It took Ma ages to get me up like this. She borrowed the jacket from someone. But the trousers are mine.' He spoke with quiet pride.

'Oh.' Bessie did not understand the importance of long trousers, but she knew she loved the feel of her dress whispering about her ankles.

384

She said, 'You'll miss Aunt Myrt, won't you?'

'Not really. She's never at home.'

'I miss Cass when she goes away. She's going to Paris in September.'

'I know. Myrt's as jealous as anything.'

'They're friends!'

'That makes it worse. What between you and Paris, Myrt grinds her teeth in her sleep!'

Bessie laughed, realising it was a joke, or one of the strange grown-up compliments.

She said, 'Paris is over the sea.'

'Yeah. It's in France.'

'Cass will be a long way away.'

'Yeah.' He couldn't think of more to say on that subject, so he changed it. 'Why do you call her Cass?'

Bessie was surprised. 'It's short for Carol. Aunt Myrt calls her that too.'

'Yeah, but you call Mrs Woodford Grannie. So Cass must be your auntie. But you call her Cass.'

'She's my sister, silly.'

'Oh.' It didn't make sense, but it wasn't that interesting. He heard his father's voice and looked around apprehensively. 'Oh lord. They've cleared the tables. You know what that means, don't you?'

'What?'

'Dancing, I hate dancing.'

'Don't worry. I'll dance with you if you like.'

'Oh. Will you? Thanks a lot. Bessie.'

She remembered a line from her story book. 'It will be a great pleasure. Boris.'

Myrtle said, 'Well girls, what do you think?'

'He's a dish,' Liv said generously. 'Handsome, successful. A dish.'

'It's good that you're in the same profession, too,' Carol added. 'You'll understand each other's problems, be able to talk about your work—'

'He's no talker,' Myrtle giggled. 'He's all action. You should have seen him in the taxi here! He almost had my dress off!'

Carol flushed slightly. Liv said, 'He must be mad for you,

Myrt. Well, you're the first of the four. Who would have thought it?'

Myrtle was conscious that the compliment had a sting in its tail. She tried to pass it on. 'Carol was the first, don't forget!'

Carol was completely uncomprehending. She said, 'To go away from home, d'you mean? Well, it was Mon actually. If you remember, she started her course while I was still at school.'

Liv giggled senselessly, and Myrt said, 'Oh come on, old thing. You can come clean with us, surely?'

Carol still stared wide-eyed, and Liv stopped giggling and said, 'We should go back to the Haunted House and play the truth game. My God, Mon said you'd never be an old maid even if you never got married. And she was right. You're a dark horse, Cass!'

Carol felt a tide of colour start from the base of her neck. She looked to where Bessie was dancing sedately with Boris Denning. 'You don't mean . . . you surely don't mean *Bessie*?' she asked incredulously.

Myrtle might well have passed it off then, because after all she and Carol had always been paired off when Liv and Mon went boy-hunting, but Malcolm and his best man arrived, both – incredibly – making a bee-line for Carol. She managed to get her shoulder between the two of them and laughed up at her husband.

'All right, darling – we were just having a final gossip before life sweeps us away for ever! Such a pity Mon couldn't be here to complete the quartet. We were inseparable at school, weren't we, girls?' She did not wait for an answer. 'Come on then. Let's dance.'

The best man stared deeply into Carol's bewildered face. 'You've forgotten my name. It's Reggie. And you're Carol. Myrtle's very special friend. Shall we dance?'

Carol looked at Liv. Her grey chapel eyes were veiled. But Carol knew her so well.

'Won't you dance with Liv? I really should talk to some of these people.'

And she moved back and away towards her mother, knowing she had done nothing to endear herself to Liv. The glorious curly hair fitted neatly beneath the best man's chin; they were perfect together. But Carol had given him to Liv and that was simply not good enough.

386

Feeling sick and shaky she suddenly decided to avoid her mother, and made for the ladies' room.

Malcolm said, 'Oh really, Myrtle! What's all the fuss about? I wanted to dance with your friend, that's all.'

'You've been looking at her all day. You're married to me. Just now. Remember?' Myrtle knew she sounded shrewish, and could not stop herself.

'You're not going to let me forget it, obviously. Shall I pop along to an ironmongers and get some chains or something?'

'Childish.'

'You're the one who is being childish. And stop shoving yourself against me like that. It's too hot for that sort of thing.'

Myrtle felt tears burn her eyes. 'I thought you liked my breasts?'

'I do.' He looked down at her. 'Oh darling, I do. Are we having our first row?'

'I think so.'

'Kiss me.'

He bent his handsome head and kissed her ardently. One or two people clapped. Myrtle felt her spirits lift. He might be a wanderer, but he'd always come back to her. She was certain of it. She must make certain of it.

Liv tried to quell her sudden dislike of Carol. It was so ridiculous and petty. She searched her mind for one of her provocative remarks the opposite sex usually found so enchanting.

'Reggie? Is there another name to go with Reggie?'

It sounded ridiculous. As if she were talking to her grandmother's canary. She tried tipping her head right back so that he could see her wonderful teeth.

'Reggie Bradbury.'

He really was good-looking. Not so obvious as Myrt's Malcolm, but longer-wearing. She'd noticed him straight-away. It was so unfair he'd been attracted to Cass. After all, she didn't want him.

'Reggie Bradbury.' She rolled the syllables out as if they had some extra significance. Reggie Bradbury. Olivia Bradbury.

Well, Olive Bradbury really. She invariably tried her name with the surnames of new men friends. She very much liked Olivia Bradbury.

'That's right,' he replied, as if she were stupid, or deaf, or something.

'It sounds like a film star.'

'Malcolm tells me it sounds like a cabinet-maker. Actually, I'm an auctioneer. With my father's firm.'

Well, it was better than a furniture-maker. Though with Myrt marrying as-good-as-a-doctor and Cass about to take up a post in Paris, it could have been better.

'I'm just a little clerk. With the post office.'

'Civil servant. Good job.'

'Well, it is, actually. But it sounds so dull.'

'Not at all.'

'I'm a real small-town girl. Myrtle and Malcolm are going off to Bournemouth. Cass is away to Paris. All I want to do is stay here and get married.'

'And what's wrong with that? It sounds very . . . womanly.'

He was looking at her properly now. And yes, he was the sort of man she had known he was when she saw him first. She lowered her lashes.

'I shouldn't have said it, though. Sorry.'

'I don't see why you shouldn't tell me how you feel. I take it as a great compliment.'

'I feel as if I could tell you anything.' She laughed breathlessly. 'I've never felt like that before.' And dammit, it was true. That was why she'd disliked Carol. Because this man meant something to her. Maybe he was the one.

He cleared his throat. 'Anyway, I wouldn't call Birmingham a small town.' He tried to make the conversation less personal. 'It's the second biggest place in the country, you know.'

'But Northfield is still a village, really.'

'Yes. I knew what you meant. Sorry. I was just . . .' He tried to laugh and sounded as breathless as she had. 'You're so simple. I didn't mean that either.' He was rushing into things more quickly than she could have hoped. She lifted her lashes, let him see right into her transparent grey eyes for a moment, then lowered them again. 'You're so *sweet*!' he amended.

'*And* silly. Like you said.'

388

'I didn't say silly. I said simple. And that is something quite different. It's real. And basic. And good.'

'Oh, Reggie.'

Carol sat in a small side room, trying to compose herself. She wanted desperately to run away; go outside, find a taxi and go home to the old, ivy-covered garden behind the trellis screen. The three years at university had been hard for her; she was not brilliant and had had neither time nor inclination for the social life. She recalled endless hours in her room at Bristol, trying to force her mind to grapple with ancient historians who all saw events from different angles. She remembered the efforts of kind fellow students to integrate her into the social life of the university. She hadn't wanted that. She had wanted to keep the inner core of her mind free for Bessie. She loved Bessie with a protective force that surprised herself. She loved her . . . as a mother.

The discovery, forced on her by Liv an hour ago, shocked her. Both she and her mother looked on the adoption as a trust. They were holding Bessie in trust, as it were. Until when or for what, they did not know or ask. The head of their small family had been taken away from them, and Bessie had come. It was ordained that way. On the advice of the local vicar they had told the child she was 'chosen' long before it could mean anything to her. But she knew she was special. That was what mattered.

Carol closed her eyes. She and her mother had been in a room like this when Bessie had been born. It had even smelled of roses like this one did, because the private nursing home made a point of overlaying their disinfectant smells with serried vases of flowers. And Carol had seen Bessie before Monica herself. It was no wonder she had felt like Bessie's mother. She had spent so much time with Mon during the pregnancy. She had shared *everything*.

Not quite everything. It was after all Monica who had conceived and borne Bessie. Carol forced the thought of Monica and Giles into her mind, though she had spent long hours all that time ago trying not to do so. Now she thought quite deliberately . . . Monica and her adopted brother begat Elizabeth Woodford. That was how it had been. Begat. Adopted. Two completely different processes. Carol kept her eyes tightly closed. She knew that there must be something wrong with her. She was conscious at times that her whole being was filled with love; not just for her mother and Bessie and Mon. For the whole of humanity. And then . . . then she would come up against a brick wall. It was as if her love bounced back at her, unwanted and ridiculous. Only her mother and Bessie continued to shine with a kind of reflection of her own feelings. And now, even Bessie's presence was tarnished.

She stood up abruptly and moved to the window as if to escape her own thoughts. The sash had been lifted and the smells distilled by the heat of summer drifted through into the small room. Hot grass and hot leaves and hot cars and hot bodies came at her like sensual gunfire. She said aloud, 'I hate August. It's too brazen,' and then drew back, embarrassed, as Liv and the best man walked across the gravel, possibly within earshot. But Liv was talking herself, so could not have heard.

'Let's find some shade. Somewhere natural. Oh, look at that weeping willow. Like a little house!'

And the best man said, 'It's made for you. It grew there just for you.'

'Rustic, d'you mean?'

'Pastoral. Pastoral and real. And so innocent.'

They crossed the lawn and Carol found herself smiling at last. So Liv had accepted the 'gift'. She had conquered for herself. What a relief. It meant Carol could talk to her properly and convince her that Myrt's ridiculous assumption about Bessie was . . . ridiculous. Not that Myrt really believed it, of course. Myrt said things just to be outrageous, and she was completely loyal. But Liv was different; Liv might say something to others. Carol felt herself growing hot again.

A sudden breeze across the room told her the door was open. She looked up and saw that Myrt's new husband had come into the room and was standing holding the door and swaying gently. For an instant Carol considered climbing through the window, then realised she was being childish and turned into the room, smiling.

Malcolm said, 'It's you. I've been looking for you all day. Were you waiting for me? Here? For me?'

He was obviously drunk. Carol said, 'Where is Myrtle?'

'Talking to Mumsy. While that ghastly Mrs Baker gets off with Dadsy. So we're safe.'

Carol smoothed her long skirt. 'It must be time for you to change. I must go. I promised I'd help Myrtle. Everything is laid out upstairs. Her suit. And her hat.'

'Are you frightened of me? You're as pink as a rose. You remind me of a rose. Not opened. All closed up with thorns at the ready. But when you open up . . . wow!'

'Of course I'm not frightened. You've just married my best friend. How could I be frightened—'

'You're trembling. Just like a rose when the rain starts!'

'Oh Malcolm. Really.' She wanted to tell him he sounded like a soppy film hero, but couldn't quite do it.

He took her prudish protest at face value.

'Yes. Really. You're different. You're special. You're interesting, dammitall! I'm interested in you.' He took two lurching steps towards her and she backed against the wall. It was a mistake. He went on lurching, and ended up leaning on the wall too, an arm either side of her . He smelled of whisky and brilliantine. She closed her eyes.

'Oh Carol . . . Cass they call you, don't they? How old were you? Sixteen? Was it a bloody Yank? Did he hurt you? Oh Cass . . . Cassie . . .'

She opened her eyes and saw his face looming night-marishly. Then she made her biggest mistake of all. She opened her mouth wide to yell for help. And he was literally inside it.

She thought she would choke. Her hands clawed at his shoulders, but he was a big man and he simply stopped leaning on the wall, and leaned on her. His tongue was a solid six ounces of liver pushing into her throat. It was the most ghastly physical experience of her life. She left his shoulders and tried to scratch his neck above the stiff shirt collar. They swayed from side to side. They were both making animal noises.

And then, unexpectedly, he left her. He was wrenched from her. There was a horrid sucking noise as of a bath plug being pulled out, he went staggering backwards, and Myrtle's furious face was visible beneath his flailing arm.

Carol sobbed and tried to say thank you. But apparently Myrtle held her responsible.

'You – you – *bitch*!' she screamed, her voice ripping through the window and alerting Liv and Reggie beneath their pastoral arbour. 'You absolute bitch! My wedding day – on my wedding day – can't you keep your hands off – good God almighty is no man safe from you – should have known back in the Haunted House – pretending to be – never want to see you again! Never! D'you hear me? I never want to—'

Malcolm, suddenly sober, managed to free himself.

'I should think every bloody person in the bloody hotel can hear you! What the hell is the matter with you? Groom's prerogative to kiss the chief bridesmaid!'

'The best man – the best man's prerogative! Not yours – and certainly not Carol Woodford! My God, I've told you about her, and you should know—'

Carol found her voice at last with a giant sob.

'Myrt! Please stop – please don't go on! Malcolm is drunk – he didn't know what he was doing!'

It was her final mistake. She lost the remnant of chivalry Malcolm was throwing in her direction. He made no more protests. He allowed Myrtle to denounce Carol in front of crowding guests. He stood with bowed head while she tore apart the friendship of schooldays, stripping herself as well as her friend. Perhaps if Monica had been there it would never have happened. Or if Mrs Woodford had arrived on the scene sooner, she could have stopped it. But Myrtle ceased ranting at last because she ran out of steam, and in that moment of silence which followed the tirade, the farcical quality which had somehow hovered over the whole wedding day was gone.

Certainly Myrtle had lost her dignity and plump prettiness, and stood there almost indecently naked without them. And Malcolm, his scratched neck beginning to seep blood, was revealed as most definitely drunk. But Carol, silent under her friend's whipped-up scorn, was not ludicrous or overdone in any way. She was no tragedy queen, nor a victim. Embarrassment seemed to have shrunk her so that the dress, chosen by Liv, appeared ill-fitting. But for the first time in her life Carol was beautiful. Her hair had been shaken out of its set by Malcolm's rough handling and haloed her face, making it look smaller than it really was. All her make-up had gone long since, but her fiery skin and sore mouth highlighted the intense blue of her dilated eyes. She stared at Myrtle as if trying to photograph her for posterity. Her throat moved occasionally but she did not speak a word.

Into this appalled silence, Mrs Woodford arrived with an uncomprehending smile. She looked at her daughter, then at Myrtle and her new husband, then she crossed the floor and took Carol's arm.

'Bessie's tired, darling. I think we should go home now.' She looked at Myrtle and her smile had gone. 'Thank you for everything,' she said with great deliberation. Then she led Carol past the gogglers and gawpers to where the music still played and Bessie and Boris were polka-ing, perspiring, and enjoying themselves like young puppies. Surprisingly, it was Liv's father, Mr Baker, who found their coats and offered his car to take them home.

'How very kind,' Mrs Woodford was smiling again, tucking Bessie into one arm and Carol into the other. 'I'm afraid these occasions are a little much for the very young and the old.'

Bessie laughed comfortably. 'You're not old, Grannie. And I'm not very young.' She peered around Mrs Woodford at Carol. 'Cassie, guess what? Boris Denning says I'm the beautifullest creature he's ever seen and he wants to take my photograph.' She giggled with delight and snuggled back into the leather upholstery of Mr Baker's new Armstrong-Siddeley. 'This is the first wedding I've been to. I specks it will be Aunt Liv who gets married next.'

Carol made no reply, and Mr Baker guffawed from the driver's seat. 'D'you want me to book you in as bridesmaid for our Liv then?' he asked in his slight Welsh accent. Then with misplaced gallantry he added, 'It will probably be your Aunt Cass who gets married next!'

Mrs Woodford felt her daughter's shoulder tighten beneath her hand, but Bessie said comfortably, 'Oh no, not yet. Cass is going to marry me when I grow up.'

Back in the hotel, Mrs Denning, incensed by Myrtle's inexplicable command to 'get lost', approached her husband and Mrs Baker.

'You chapel people are all the same!' she snapped, wedging her plump backside between them with great ostentation. 'Give you half a chance and you're up to your tricks!'

She did not explain the nature of the tricks, but Mrs Baker, flustered and furious, stood up and left without more ado. Dr Denning said in a bored voice, 'Oh really, Sylvia. More histrionics? Sounds as if your daughter has taken over in that department.'

'Shut up, Ivan. The whole thing is ruined.'

'And it's my fault.'

'For once. no. It's Carol Woodford's fault. She's been flirting with poor Myrtle's—'

She was interrupted by Dr Dennings' laughter. Once started, he seemed unable to stop. He leaned his handsome head back exposing the manly throat, and laughed and laughed.

Outside, Reggie Bradbury lifted his head hurriedly and listened in astonishment and mounting horror to Myrtle's explicit denunciation of her friend.

'I say,' he murmured. 'Is she really . . . I mean, it's a bit steep, isn't it? Wedding day and all.'

'Well. Perhaps Carol went too far.' Liv did not want to be interrupted at this stage in the proceedings, but she was not entirely displeased at what was happening. It might precipitate events. She suspected that Reggie Bradbury would not be averse to following in his friend's footsteps quite soon, and she knew that she had already made a big impression. A few years ago he would have been another cross in her school rough note book. She waited until Myrtle's voice died away, leaning on Reggie as if her legs could not support her, gazing through the shifting curtain of willow in case anyone decided to come into the garden.

He said uncomfortably, 'Look. Perhaps we'd better go inside now. It sounds as if there is a situation to be retrieved.' He tried to laugh. 'And as best man, I suppose I should be the one—'

'All right, Reggie.' Liv sighed deeply. 'Dear Reggie. So thoughtful.' She leaned more heavily. 'I knew immediately that you were the protective dependable type. What I didn't know was that you would be able to deprive little me of the use of my legs!' She laughed and let her knees sag. He had to hold her up and then she sort of fell back at the waist and her chest pushed against him, almost out of the sweetheart neckline of her bridesmaid's dress. He breathed quickly and suddenly kissed her again, less circumspectly.

And then the unthinkable happened. A breeze lifted the curtain of willow, and there was her mother crossing the lawn purposefully. She saw them. She stopped. Then she advanced very quickly.

'Olive! What are you up to? How dare you! My God, your father has gone off with - with that woman, and now you—!' She grabbed Liv's arm. 'As for you, young man, all I can say is, if you go around practically ravishing every young girl you've just met, you're asking for trouble!'

Reggie stammered, 'Mrs . . . er . . . Baker . . . I do assure you I've never done anything like this before in my life!'

Liv put her hands to her face and began to cry.

Mrs Baker said, 'Then I hope your intentions are absolutely—'

Liv removed her hands and moaned, 'Ma . . . *please!*'

But Reggie said, 'Absolutely. Completely. Absolutely.'

Mrs Baker said, 'Then in that case, I suppose . . .'

The curtain of leaves fell into place like a trap. For a while Liv's weeping was audible. The it grew less and finally only Mrs Baker's voice could be heard.

Four

Bob came to Britain from the States in 1951. He had spent some time in London during the war, and remembered the Albion where some of his fellow officers had stayed. So he booked in there.

Old man Gallagher had died during the war, and Bob had returned home to find his mother trying to carry on the business – which she had started anyway. Bob had taken over immediately and in seven years had made Ideal Patterns the market leaders throughout the States. Now he wanted to go international.

His father had been brought up in the Bronx by his Irish family, and would have been content to live and die there. But he had taken a brawny and unbeautiful Scottish girl to a dance because his mother had known her mother when they were girls, and had been seduced by her in her tiny back kitchen when he took her home. When she announced that she was pregnant, he immediately volunteered to go to Europe and fight in the Kaiser's war. It made no difference. Her father was red-haired and enormous, and the Gallaghers were much too easy-going to put up a fight anyway, in spite of their Irish blood. Liam Gallagher married Kirsty Donaldson in 1917 just before he embarked for Europe, and Robert was born six months later.

They would have stayed poor all their lives just as the Gallaghers had always done, except that Kirsty had a talent and an energy inherited from her Scottish ancestors. The talent was in making clothes. She could cut out a dress with a few basic measurements, and the dress would fit perfectly, hang delightfully, and take less material than you would think possible. Kirsty supplemented the family income nicely until Hildie came along and soon after, Leone. Then it was all a bit too much for her and she began to make paper patterns for other people to sew. They sold like hot cakes. The family moved to Queens and then Connecticut. The children went to good schools. Bob married and divorced and had lots of love affairs. Hildie and Leone married well. Hildie and her husband, George, bought a farm in Connecticut and started to raise a family. Leone married an industrialist from Detroit and moved away. Bob went to war and had lots more affairs.

When he returned home he took his mother to see old Dr Murdoch in the Bronx – the only doctor she trusted. He confirmed what they all knew: she had cancer of the liver. When she died, Bob already held the reins of the family firm. Suddenly, all he had achieved so far in life seemed pointless. He threw himself into making Ideal Patterns one of the success stories of the decade. He had inherited some of his mother's thriftiness as well as his father's wandering eye, and he decided to stay at the Albion because he realised it was value for money.

The first person he saw when he signed the register was Monica. She was then twenty-two; her gypsy good looks had settled into a kind of aristocratic sophistication. She reminded Bob of pictures he had seen of Winston Churchill's mother. It pleased him to think that he might transplant an English girl into American society, just as Randolph Churchill had transplanted American Jenny into his English background. Besides all that, he had to have her.

Dilly and Gander were still at the Albion, otherwise he might have won Monica during that visit. But they took their chaperonage very seriously, and although she virtually ran the hotel, she paid lip service to them in everything. And Monica seemed a cold fish. In spite of her Latin good looks and sultry eyes, he sensed the ice maiden in her. This made her more exciting than ever. A paradox; an enigma; an anomaly.

He lined up some appointments. Harrods and Liberty were out this time around, but there were other shops which could build up a reputation for him, and next year or maybe the year after, the others would come running. He concentrated on shops in Kensington High Street; small, select outlets glad to be associated with a large American company. And in the evenings, after dinner, he talked to Monica about his aspirations. And she listened. He thought it was because she was interested in his money, and he did not mind. After all, it was one of his interests too. She told the proprietress of the hotel about Ideal Patterns, and she was unexpectedly helpful. It turned out that she had been a dressmaker before the war and was able to put him on to some useful contacts.

By asking discreet and individual questions of Mr and Mrs Gosling, he could piece together some of Monica's background. She was an adopted child who had never got on with her family. That suited him well – he had no wish to support strings of hangers-on. Some good mutual friend had put her in touch with her employers when she was leaving school, and they had decided to train her to take on the hotel when they retired. So although she was interested in his money, she was by no means desperate for it. Old Mr Gosling had a way of dropping hints, with one eye closed, that led Bob to believe Monica was probably the illegitimate offspring of a duke. Or maybe that was wishful thinking. She had style. And if Ideal Patterns were going world-wide, he would need a classy wife. And a good mother for his children. He wanted a family. He wanted . . . an establishment. Monica was ideal, in every way.

Monica resisted him without too much effort. Practically all the men who came to the Albion on their own made a pass at her, and she was adept at rebuffing them without giving offence. Even if they came back often, she rarely had any further trouble with them. What she did have was respect, and this was terribly important to her. She knew she was good at her job; she had suggested to Gander that some of the profits could be ploughed back swiftly into refurbishing the hotel after the long and arid war years, and the rooms at the Albion bore witness to her newly restrained taste. She never curled her hair or wore obvious make-up now. The colours of walls and carpets chosen by her were just as delicate as her own appearance. Gander got his licence; at her suggestion he extended the lounge into the long walled back garden so that guests could sit in the sun on the windiest of days. Monica saw him through it all; she insisted that he and Dilly should spend a week in Brighton when the builders were in. The decorators were practically locked in whichever room they were doing so that Gander would not be bothered by them. She cushioned the Goslings and the guests alike.

In 1952 Bob came back to the Albion. This time he had dinner with one of the directors of Harrods. He invited him back to the Albion and consulted Monica about the menu. After the meal, he introduced her to his guest.

'Miss Cook. She runs this place. It's kinda special – don't you agree?'

The V.I.P. did agree, and took a card on the way out. Dilly and Gander were impressed; Monica smiled coolly at Bob. But she too was impressed by his strategy, and before he went back to the States she accompanied him to the theatre to see *Oklahoma*.

The following year he came to England with most of the rest of the world to see the Coronation. At great expense he booked two places at a window on the route and asked Monica to come with him. He was put out when she declined.

'Surely you'll take time off to see the procession?'

He had thought she would have to show some gratitude if he'd bought her a seat, they were unobtainable on that special June the second. For the first time he began to wonder if she would ever succumb.

She said, 'Of course. But I want to be with everyone else. I'm going to find a pitch tomorrow afternoon and stay overnight.' She smiled at him. 'You're lots more ladies to take to the Coronation, Mr Gallagher.'

'You're darned right.'

But his annoyance could not hold out against those black eyes of hers, and he said ruefully, 'But there's only one I want to be with for this special occasion. And please call me Bob.'

'That would mean you'd call me Monica,' she said. Her smile widened. 'Why don't you come and pitch a camp with me? It will be much more fun than standing in a window. Bob.'

His good-looking, open, Irish-American face split into a wide grin.

'Are you asking, Monica?'

She laughed assent.

'Then I'm coming,' he finished.

And he managed to sell his window seats for twice what he had given for them. With some of the profit he bought her a pure silk scarf. She protested, of course – you could always tell a British lady by the fact that she refused presents from a man. He told her it was an old American custom – giving presents when it wasn't a birthday. 'We call it an un-birthday present,' he said solemnly.

And she laughed. He was certain, then, that it would be all right.

Later he was to shock his sisters with the confession that he and his wife had slept together before they were married. He never made that kind of remark in front of Monica, however; her sense of humour was definitely lacking in that department. He might have had reservations about her mothering the large family he wanted to begin as soon as possible, except that as soon as the newly-crowned queen had gone by in her coach, Monica forgot herself enough to throw her arms around his neck and kiss him. And that kiss spoke volumes. She herself drew back from it, startled. Bob would not let her go. He held her by the waist, forcing her to be totally aware of him. And she was aware.

It made her defences all the stronger. Bob eventually gave in after three furious days of intense courtship, and asked her to marry him. Her reply was off-putting, to say the least. 'I can't, Bob. I just can't.'

'Why not? You can't deny we get on—'

'Oh yes. I like you. Enormously. But you see . . . you're American.'

'You don't want to live in the States? Honey, you'll love it. And I'm making enough for us to live half the year there, and half here. Suits me.'

'It's not that. It's something else. You wouldn't understand.' She made a feeble attempt to explain. 'After the war, so many girls got out of the country by marrying Americans. G.I. brides. You know.'

'I don't get it. The war has been over for eight years, for God's sake.'

'I nearly did that. Married a G.I. So that I could get out of England. Then I got this job with the Goslings. And things were better.'

'You were that desperate?' He put an arm around her shoulders and felt her stiffen. 'Poor kid. It must have been rough for you. But surely you're not going to make me suffer because you played around with a crazy idea for a couple of months?'

'Yes. No. I mean, I vowed I'd always look after myself. Not expect a man to do it for me.' She gave an embarrassed laugh. 'You're too well off, Bob. If you didn't have a bean—'

'Can't you see that's why I want you? A lot of girls would be after my money. Listen, kiddo. You want to be independent and so do I. Can't we be independent together?'

'Bob. You're incorrigible. Can't you take no for an answer?'

'If I did, I wouldn't be a millionaire now.'

She took a little breath. 'A millionaire?'

'Sure. I could stay at the Ritz or the Savoy. I chose to stay at the Albion.'

She was silent. Suddenly he wondered what the hell he was doing getting down on his knees to this little slip of a girl who had no background, no money . . . who the hell did she think she was?'

He snapped, 'Okay, honey. I'll not worry you any more.'

He went out and found himself a girl and came back the next day just to say goodbye. She was white-faced and as jealous as all hell. He could feel it in the palm of her hand when she shook his.

He said, 'No kiss, honey?'

'You can buy plenty of kisses, Mr Gallagher. You don't need mine.'

He forced a laugh. 'True, Miss Cook. Very true.'

He stayed away for four months, determined not to go crawling back. Then he did. It was no big soul-searing decision. He simply went into the office one morning and told his secretary to book him a flight. He spent three nights at the Ritz sleeping off the trip and making all the arrangements for a special marriage licence. On the fourth night he went to the Albion to seek her out. She was supervising a Bonfire Bean Feast. Guy Fawkes was unknown in America, but he was glad he'd found her in the midst of another celebration. Her guard was less fierce at such times. When she saw him in the light of the bonfire flames, her face came to life for an instant. He went straight to her, took her hand, and led her into the deep shadow by the garden wall. She struggled against him, but she would not make a scene with so many people within earshot, and he kissed her until she began to respond. Then he held her away from him.

'I've got a ring and a licence,' he said in a low voice. 'If you won't marry me, say so now, and I promise you'll never see me again.'

She was genuinely distressed. 'Bob. Please. I can't make up my mind like that. Really.'

'Do you love me?'

'I think so. I've missed you.'

'Then that's the answer.'

401

'It's not so simple. You've consoled yourself, admit it.'

'All right. I'll admit it. But if I marry you, there won't be any others.'

'How can I know that?'

'By keeping me happy.'

He drew her to him and kissed her again. He hadn't been wrong. There was fire beneath the ice.

She pushed at him. 'You're trying to rush me.'

'Yes. It's now or never. I mean it, Monica. I've never begged.'

'All right.' She looked at him. In the shadow her eyes were black coals. 'You don't have to beg now, Bob. I'm not sure about getting married, but you don't have to beg.'

His face opened with surprise. 'I don't get it. Most women *want* to get married.' He kissed her violently, almost angrily. 'I want to marry you, Monica. I want a wife. Kids. I want to found a – a dynasty!'

'Oh Bob. I know.' He suddenly realised the black coals were shining. She was crying. 'Listen. I have to see my family. I'm not sure. But I have to see them—'

'Why for Christ's sake? What hold have they got over you? I'll come with you. We'll blow them apart—'

'I must go on my own.'

'Tomorrow. Will you go tomorrow?'

'Yes. Oh Bob. Yes. Will you wait for me?'

'Tomorrow night. I'll wait until tomorrow night.'

She was dismayed again. 'They live in Birmingham! It'll take me three hours to get there. And then I've got to talk to them . . .'

'Tomorrow night.'

He kissed her again. And after the party she took him to her room. He was disappointed to find she wasn't a virgin, but, after all, neither was he. He had never known anyone like her. He had thought by taking her by storm he was the victor in their odd little game. But as he lay in her bed, he knew the tables were turned on him. He would wait for a week – even a year – if she insisted.

Monica was under no illusions about Bob Gallagher. She found him very attractive and a good companion and a marvellous lover; but she knew that his energetic and optimistic attitude to everything stemmed from an innate superficiality. It was good to be with him when everything was going well; she wondered how he would be in an emergency. When he had told her that there would be no other women so long as she 'kept him happy', she had sensed an underlying threat. She knew she could never tell him about Elizabeth and Carol; the Cooks and Gilly. He wouldn't be able to take that kind of emotional tangle; he'd run a mile. And he was attractive enough to make her hold her peace.

It was not his money. Strangely, Monica was not ambitious in a worldly sense. She wanted money, not for power, but for security against other people's power. She wanted quite desperately to be loved and cherished, and to belong to a family. And she wanted a suitable father for her children.

Bob could supply all her needs. He wanted to supply them. It seemed such a simple decision. But there was always Gilly.

She caught the Birmingham train at Euston by the skin of her teeth. She had left Bob sleeping; if she was back by dinner time as he had stipulated, she would make it up to him. If not . . . then it wouldn't matter because it would mean that Gilly still wanted her. And wanted Elizabeth too. He couldn't have known about Elizabeth, no-one could have known. Perhaps she had been unfair in not telling him. Maybe he had thought she didn't love him any more when she left home so abruptly and went to live with Cass and Mrs Woodford. Maybe that was why he'd never got in touch with her, never even asked Mrs Woodford for her London address. Maybe he'd retreated into silence because he felt hurt. When she told him . . . when she told him what had happened . . . surely everything would be all right again and she would thank Bob Gallagher for forcing her into this journey.

She took off the silk scarf Bob had given her for her unbirthday present last summer and slid it into the sleeve of her new donkey-brown coat, folded the lot neatly and put it on the luggage rack. She had packed a small overnight bag, just in case. After all, she would surely visit Mrs Woodford whatever happened. And then she'd probably stay overnight. Or something.

She sat down and watched the telegraph wires swaying past the compartment window. She dared not think too much about the future. So she switched her mind to Mrs Woodford and Cass. And Elizabeth.

She had said, right at the beginning, that Elizabeth belonged to the Woodfords; she would not take the role of mysterious and ubiquitous 'aunt'. Nor would history repeat itself yet again – Elizabeth would always know she was adopted, and she would know she had been chosen for love and not for money.

Monica caught herself in mid-sigh, and straightened her spine in the defiant way she had never lost. She remembered that no one of her rare visits to Northfield Mrs Woodford had said hesitantly, 'Monica dear, would you mind – be hurt – if Cass and I called Elizabeth Bessie? She looks like a Bessie. She's round and dark and giggly.'

Carol had put in quickly, 'Not Bessie Bunterish! She's just so cuddly!'

Monica had said, 'Look. Both of you. She is yours. Legally and morally. If you recall, I did not even want to suggest a name.' She looked straight at Cass. Dear Cass, flushed and anxious even then. 'I like Bessie. But if I hated it, it's nothing to do with me.'

They hadn't replied to that. Perhaps they had known that she would never be able to cut through the cord that bound her to her baby. She caught herself sighing again; it was no good, she didn't like the name Bessie.

The ticket inspector slid open the door of the compartment and she fumbled in her bag for her ticket. 'Change at New Street,' he intoned. 'Stopper to Bromsgrove.' She took back her punched ticket, feeling a rush of adrenalin to her heart. She was going home. That was the immediate future; she was going home.

The train was passing the university and she stood up to check her hair in the mirror. She dressed it in a 'doughnut' on top of her head these days and sat her hats slightly forward. In the New Look black dresses she wore at the hotel she looked like a ballerina; in her new donkey-brown hat and coat she gave an impression of subdued sophistication that pleased her a great deal. She had left Northfield a frightened schoolgirl, prone to too much make-up and too many curls. She was returning a mature woman with unmistakably good taste. She drew on her gloves, shouldered her bag, and picked up her case. Dammit, she wanted to be married and have a family, and she'd got two strings to her bow . . . most girls would envy her.

The train drew in at New Street. It was colder than in London, and it had been raining. Everything smelled of sulphur; it was a familiar smell that stoked the excitement inside her. She hadn't felt like this for years. She loved London, loved the fact that she had carved a niche for herself, but this place was where life had started.

404

She got on the Bromsgrove stopper and sat on one of the sideways seats that would give her a view of the canal and then the school. When she emerged on to the high platform and walked down the steps to Turves Green, it was as if she had never been away. The remains of the local bonfire charred the grass and the council estate spread around it like a small village. Every tree was familiar, the small row of shops where Gilly had had his hair cut each month was still there, and the brook which eventually meandered on to the heath and past the Haunted House. Children ran up and down the street collecting the dead fireworks from the night before; they were well wrapped up – quite literally – old scarves bound their necks and chests and were pinned at the back, and what looked like dirty crepe bandages were wound from wrists to fingers. Monica remembered reading somewhere that the Birmingham city council were involved in a big scheme to rehouse some of the slum dwellers from the blitzed city centre. Certainly, even with clothes rationing, the small children of her time had looked less deprived than these.

Number thirty-one was more run-down than she remembered, too. The gate had been propped open because a hinge was off and a bulbous Standard Vanguard was jacked up on the drive, one wheel missing. The front lawn was scuffed bare and muddy, and the holly hedge which she had loved was shrivelled and without a single berry. She hesitated, glancing at her watch, wondering who would be where. If her mother still had her job at the cafe along the Bristol Road, she would be there doing her morning stint. Perhaps her father and both boys would be at the Longbridge plant. That would be unusual; they tended to opt for differing shifts so that they could have the house to themselves when they were home. It was Saturday but they invariably worked at weekends to boost their wages with overtime.

There was only one way to find out. She eased her new coat past the Vanguard and knocked on the front door. The paint was chipped and the transom cracked. It had been like that when she left in 1945.

Nothing happened. She knocked again and heard, faintly, a bellow. Then someone's footsteps came down the stairs. The door opened and there was Giles.

He did not recognise her. She should have unbuttoned her coat or taken off her hat. Even then, with her black hair pinned up and her discreet make-up, she was so different from the flash young miss who had tried to look like Rita Hayworth. She forced a smile.

'Hello, Gilly.'

Her voice had changed too, but she deliberately injected a Brummy accent and the old uncompromising hardness. Anyway, only she called him Gilly. To everyone else he was simply Gill.

'Good God Almighty!' He took a step back as if she'd hit him. 'If it isn't . . . is it our Mon? God, it's our Mon! Where in the hell have you sprung from?'

Pleasure lightened his heavy features and he looked young again. But his eyes were smaller than she remembered. Everything was smaller than she remembered.

Her smile became slightly more natural; unexpectedly she felt sorry for him.

'London. The address I sent Mum.

'For Christ's sake. Come on in. You've got a bag. Give it here!'

He leaned forward and took it from her, and for an instant their shoulders touched. She imagined that through her dress and coat she could feel the heat of him. He had always been warm. In the war when there had been few blankets, and Mrs Cook had thought hot-water bottles to be decadent and on the side of Hitler, Gilly had been so warm in bed. She had crept in with him when she was ten years old and shaking with fear as the enemy bombers went over. And then a year later, when her periods began, she had been given the boxroom to herself and Gilly came to her.

He hefted the bag into the front room which was kept tidy for visitors. 'You've not come for long then, our Mon?'

'Was that why you took the bag? So you could tell how heavy it was?' She tried to make it jokey, but they were bitter words.

'Just wondered. I've got your room now, see.' He glanced at her and she wondered whether he was about to throw his arms around her in welcome. He didn't. He cleared his throat and said heartily, 'So. You've come to see us at last, little Sis. How are you then? How's it going?'

'Fine. And you?' She moved around the table and looked out of the window. This was terrible. Worse than she could have imagined.

'Fine. Doing double shifts when I can. With overtime I can bring home twenty quid a week.'

He spoke without boastfulness and she wondered if he was

telling her that he could support her now. That they could take Elizabeth back and make a home together.

Then he laughed. 'Mind you, I can spend it too! I was always a good spender, weren't I, our Mon? That's mine out there. Getting new wheels for it, then I shall be off every Saturday night – you won't see me for dust.'

She smiled blindly at the window. It really was amusing, the way she had fooled herself.

'Sounds fun,' she said. 'You haven't changed, Gilly. You were always fun.'

He said eagerly. 'That were it, weren't it, Sis? We had great laughs together. God, I missed that when you left. D'you remember Dad got me in at the munitions place so I wouldn't be called up, and we began practising my limp!'

He guffawed heartily, but she wondered now what had been so funny. Bob had fought in the war. She was suddenly proud of that fact.

She said quickly, trying to excuse Gilly, 'You were only fourteen then.'

'Yes, but like you said, the sooner I got used to having a limp the better. What between that and the munitions factory, they hardly looked at me when it came to the medical!'

'No.' She remembered her relief. She had still thought he was her brother then. She couldn't have lived without him. The guilt they shared each night had been a further bond. When he told her she was adopted, some of that guilt had gone; and perhaps some of the bond too.

He started to limp around the tiny sitting room, thrusting out one side of his body in imitation of Alfie Crump, the old snobbie who had a dislocated hip and rolled around Northfield like a wallowing boat; a local character.

'See? It's like riding a bike. You never forget. And the war's been over eight years!'

She turned to watch him and tried to laugh and he said quickly, 'God, you're still beautiful, our Mon. I thought at first you'd changed for the worse, but I was wrong.'

She knew she ought to treat that remark lightly. Maybe whip off her hat and show him her Hayworth hair-do had gone. Or dip a curtsey and say thank you, kind sir. But she did neither. She was turned to stone, looking at him. She forgot he was smaller and still immature and probably a coward. She remembered the warmth and security of his arms, his laughter in her ear, the feel of his mat of curls beneath her hand.

He said roughly, 'Christ. Our Mon.'

And still she said nothing.

It was only natural that he took her silence for acquiescence, because that was what it was. It was more than acquiescence, it was an invitation. His arms went round her and his face crushed hers, knocking off the hat, sending the coronet of hair tumbling to her shoulders. And although the walls behind which she had entrenched herself ever since her pregnancy were shoved aside so shockingly, she let the whole thing go on. She let him take possession of her as he had always done. As if she belonged to him by right. She waited for his left hand to hold the back of her head steady. And it did. She waited for the right hand to attempt to cup her breast through the thickness of winter clothing. And it did. She waited for the full mouth to part on hers and the tongue to demand an entrance. And both those things happened. He was so familiar, so much part of her past, there was nothing strange about it. She was dissolving into him as she had always done. This was why she had come to Birmingham.

And then, from the next room, came the bellow she had heard when she first rang the bell. Gilly withdrew his head and grinned at her without embarrassment. They were the same height so he must have shrunk.

'Gus,' he said. 'You'd better come and show yourself, otherwise he'll say something he shouldn't to Mum.'

She stared at him dazedly, unable to pull away from that moment as he had done. He pecked at her parted lips.

'Come on, Mon. Pull yourself together.'

And he laughed. And in that laugh there was a note of triumph.

He opened the door to the back room and announced her uproariously.

'Our Mon! Proper growed-up now, but just as gorgeous as ever!'

She hardly knew Gus. He was much older than Gilly and had always been 'out at work' when she was home. Also, unlike his clever young brother, he had not escaped the war. When she went to the Albion he had been in Malaya.

She wouldn't have recognised him from the old snaps she had

seen. He was fat and squat like a buddha, and his hairline had receded to a monkish fringe. She did some calculations as she held out a formal hand to him. He must be well over thirty. He looked much older.

'I'd have answered the door myself, girl. Thought it was one of Gill's mates to help with the car. Well. You have grown and no mistake. Just a little thing you was. Now you're almost as tall as that friend of yours.'

'Carol Woodford,' Gilly supplied. 'She's away in France so you won't see her.' He glanced at Monica as if checking her reaction to that piece of information. Did he guess about Elizabeth after all?'

'Oh, I've lost touch with everyone,' she replied airily, 'I was never any good at writing letters, and I've been busy.' She took a breath. 'Actually, I'm thinking of going abroad. This is . . . might be . . . a farewell visit.'

Gus said, 'Abroad, eh? Good for you, girl. Doing well for yourself I reckon. Where you goin' exactly?'

'America. Actually.'

Gilly mimicked, 'Oh, jolly dee. Ackcherly.'

Monica flushed, but Gus took the teasing at face value and nodded lugubriously. 'Aye. Plain to see you're not one of us, girl. Tall and skinny for a start. And a few brains too.'

'Speak for yourself, our Gus!' Gilly wasn't teasing now. 'I'm doing all right, thanks very much. Take a look out of the window at the Vanguard. And I'm taller than you. And this is all muscle!' He pounded at his chest, Tarzan-style.

Monica felt a helplessness near to despair. He was awful; and she still loved him.

She said desperately, 'I suppose I'd better go and have a word with Mum. Is she still at the caff'

'Aye. Come on. We'll all go.'

Gus went into the hall and opened the cupboard under the stairs. Clothes fell out on to the floor. He selected two overcoats and gave one to Gilly. They trooped into the street. Monica was painfully aware of her own clothes. She should have remembered her erstwhile family much better and worn high heels, a short jacket, costume jewellery.

They crowded into the tiny steamy cafe on the Bristol Road where Mrs Cook worked. If Monica had wanted to create a sensation she would have been well satisfied by her mother's range of emotions at the sight of her long-lost adopted daughter. Beginning with shock and amazement, she went quickly from tearful delight to recriminations.

'Why haven't you bin to see us before? Ingratitude is one fault I cannot forgive, Monica. I'm sorry, but that's the way I'm made. Charlie and me, we brought you up like our own – you wouldn't have known otherwise if that great lummock hadn't told you—' She flipped a dirty tea-towel across Gilly's curls, and he pretended to cower. 'And how do you repay us? Immediately you start earning, you're off! What benefit is that to us? I ask you! Sixteen years I slave to bring you up nicely. Grammar school – yes, I know she got a scholarship, Gill, but there was the uniform and all the outings and trying to keep up with her snobby friends!' She collapsed in a chair and fumbled in her overall pocket for cigarettes. 'When I see that Mrs Woodford in town with that adopted kid of hers. I want to tell her a thing or two. No, I'm sorry, Gill, I've got to have my way. That's the why I am. I don't harbour grudges. I up and out with them.' She lit up and drew ecstatically on her cigarette. Then she leaned back, opened her eyes and smiled at the three of them. 'There. I've got it off my chest. We'll say no more about it, Mon. You're home again, and that's all that matters.'

There was a little silence as the boys waited for Monica to confess that she was off to America. She said nothing.

Mrs Cook's smile widened. 'Listen. Sausage and chips on me. Okay? There's half my wages gone for the week, but I can't help it. And bread and butter. And a pot of tea.' She stubbed out her cigarette and stood up, laughing. 'My God, Cookie, stop it, you generous, crazy fool. Well . . .' She made for the kitchen. ' 'Tisn't every day your long-lost daughter rolls up.'

'She's cracked,' Gilly said proudly. 'Bet you'd forgotten how cracked she was, hadn't you, our Mon?'

'No wonder she's cracked, living with our dad,' Gus said. He shook his head at Monica. 'You won't get much out of him when you see him tonight, Mon. It's as much as he can do to open his mouth and shove in his food these days. Don't know how she puts up with it.'

Gilly said, 'He was always like that. You were in the army so you didn't know him like me and our Mon. When Mum was

410

fire-watching and Dad just sat in front of the fire, looking, it was like being in a loony bin. Good job we had each other, eh Sis?'

He grinned conspiratorially, and after a second's hesitation she found herself grinning back. Then the sausages and chips arrived, and Mrs Cook sat down again to watch them eat. It was so familiar: like sliding into a very old and threadbare pair of slippers. Gilly's arm around her; her mother talking non-stop as if frightened to let a silence gather around them; greasy food and greasy smells; Gilly smiling; and the addition of Gus who seemed now strangely avuncular.

She could slip into the pattern of it all so easily. Her voice, carefully controlled for school, could slide up a register and become nasal and Brummy. She could dip her bread into the sauce, blow on the tea, suck her fingers after picking up a chip. They would accept her again and find a place for her, and she and Gilly would take up where they had left off. No fuss, no big now. No wedding.

'Yowse looking solemn, our Mon,' commented Mrs Cook. 'Penny for 'em.'

'Just remembering old times.' Monica forced a smile, then picked up a chip, ate it, and sucked her fingers.

'Ah. It's real nice having you back, love. I'll put up a bed in Gus' room, and Gilly can go back in there. You can 'ave your own room again.'

Monica did not look at Gilly. The clock was slowly and inexorably being turned back.

Afterwards, Gus went to watch Aston Villa play at home, and Mrs Cook disappeared into the kitchen.

Gilly said, 'We'd better get back. Too cold to wander around, and if we run into the Bakers or the Dennings, that will be it.'

Monica certainly did not want to see Liv or Myrtle, but she had half-planned to call on Mrs Woodford. She knew it wasn't the time now. On the other hand she did not want to go back to the mean little house in Turves Green.

'Gilly. Did I ever take you to see the Haunted House?'

'Haunted what? Come off it, our Mon. You're a big girl now.'

'No, really. I'll show you if you like.'

He was easy about it, certain that very soon now they would make love. So they wandered up through the old village, past the

411

stocks and the ancient church, and kept going into West Heath road. Gilly did not take her hand, but when they came to the stile that led to the brook he swung her down and kept an arm around her waist.

'We waded along here. Liv Baker and Myrtle Denning and me.' She did not want to mention Carol by name. 'It was this time of year actually. Cold as charity. We were glad to find this old house.'

'I remember Liv Baker. You and she hung around together a lot. Saturday afternoons window-shopping. Or were you shopping for something else?'

He made her sound like a street-walker. But wasn't that basically why she and Liv had tarted themselves up and paraded the shopping area. She'd had Gilly then, but she had still seemed to need the odd 'conquest' to prove herself. Was that all Bob represented – the odd conquest?

It seemed to take a long time to reach the bend in the brook where the old labourer's cottage squatted among the willows and the wild uncultivated garden. It looked completely derelict now; the front door was gone and several slates were missing, while others hung drunkenly at odd angles. Gilly went first, curious but wary of rotten floor-boards. They explored downstairs, holding their noses but still tasting the smell. Door frames and floor-boards had been ripped away, presumably for firing. The sink was missing in the kitchen and there was no glass in any of the windows.

Monica retreated into the hall. The gaping space into the foundations was still a deterrent to anyone going upstairs. She giant-strode it as she'd always done, and looked up at the stair-lid. It was either raised or missing. She could see the familiar ceiling of the bedroom and that was intact. She took the stairs two at a time, crossed the landing, and went through the open door.

'It's the same!' She ran across to the stair-lid and looked down at Gilly. 'It's just the same, Gilly. Just like it was on V.E. day when I came to tell Carol . . .' she broke off. Gilly was staring up at her and the truth was suddenly clear between them. He had turned away from it for nine years; pretended it hadn't happened. Now he knew. She waited, holding her breath, praying that he would take her in his arms, or tell her that they would go right away with Elizabeth and make a new life.

And then he laughed, that knowing laugh of his that she had always thought was confident and happy. And he said, 'So. It was a kid, was it? That's why you did a bunk. You told Carol Woodford and her old lady looked after you. I did wonder.' He laughed again, this time with a ring of pride or triumph. 'Well done, our kid. Well done. I might have guessed you would come out of it okay.'

He started up the stairs and she gripped the edge of the lid and wondered if she might be sick. It was the Mussolini man all over again. She knew how Carol had felt that day.

He entered the room and she heard him collapse on to the bed. She turned to look at him. He was grinning broadly and expectantly.

He said, 'Come on, our Mon. We've messed about enough. Come 'ere.'

She did not move; she began, quite consciously, to marshal her strength.

'It's all right, our Mon,' he said, sensing a withdrawal in her. 'You're older now. You know what to do. There won't be any more babies to get rid of.'

It was the last straw. She remembered now that there had been times in the past when she had hated him. Love and hate. Inseparable. She forced a laugh.

'Oh Gilly. You haven't changed either, have you? Just a few more slates missing perhaps!' She let the laugh begin to gurgle away. 'Yes, I'm older. And just a bit wiser. And I know what to do.'

She took off her hat and scooped her hair to the top of her head again. She stuck pins in her mouth and began to secure the hair, one pin at a time, talking through them, making it all sound very simple.

'If it *had* been my baby, d'you think I'd have let it come back to this dump?' She shook her head. 'Oh Gilly, I wasn't the little innocent you thought I was. I knew what to do in those days too, and I did it. There was no baby, big brother. Just boredom. Complete and utter boredom.' She stabbed the last pin into place as if she were driving it into him. Then she swung her hat casually from one hand. Protect Elizabeth. She had to protect Elizabeth.

'Why do you think I went to stay with Carol? To look after her, of course. Give her an alibi now and then. And to get away from number thirty-one!'

She sighed dramatically. 'Gilly, I'd better confess. I'm getting married. To a rich American. That's why I'm off to the States. I wanted to say goodbye. And maybe have another fling!' She

413

brushed past him. 'But the old magic . . . it's gone, hasn't it? Even coming to this place hasn't resurrected it.' She started down the stairs. 'You're right, big brud, I am older. Older, and very much wiser. Come on. Let's get back to the house. I've got time for a cup of tea before my train goes.'

He did not protest much. Oddly enough even that hurt. He caught her up when she reached the gate and walked half a pace behind her until they reached the road.

Then he said, 'A rich American, eh? I might have guessed it.'

She waited for the whiplash of scorn or petty jealousy. It did not come. They walked back to Turves Green in silence.

The Goslings, Gander and Dilly, came to the wedding, but Monica did not invite her parents nor Mrs Woodford and Carol. Bob assumed there had been some big bust-up when she told her family of her marriage plans, and she did not enlighten him.

He said 'Listen honey, if you need a family, we'll cut our wrists and become blood brothers, like the Indians. How would that do? Huh?'

And she laughed and rubbed his nose with hers.

She said, 'I'd like my own family, please Bob. How do you feel about children?'

She knew how he felt, but was surprised at his fervour.

'We can give them such a life, hon. We'll have an apartment in town and a place in the country – maybe near Hildie and George – you'll like Hildie and George. Our kids can ride and fish with the boys. Hildie and George have two boys. Oscar and Leo. Did I ever tell you about the time . . .'

She touched the back of his hand. He was at his most endearing when he talked about his sister. It made Monica feel guilty about what she was doing. Yet it opened the way to repay him for his overwhelming love.

'It sounds great, darling. But I'd like some girls as well. How about three girls and two boys?'

'I want more boys than girls, baby. I was the only boy in our family and it was hell. I want four boys and one girl.'

She let herself be led into one of the silly arguments he enjoyed.

'I had two brothers, remember. I insist on three girls at least.'

'Brazen hussy!' He kissed her and then kept kissing her.

Yes, she could repay him. She was good at sex and she would be

414

a wonderful mother too. She would forget all about Elizabeth. She would start again.

But on their wedding day there was a moment, as they stood before the registrar, when she knew she was wrong. It was only a moment, and when she recalled it later she had to smile to herself, because she of all people knew that you could make things work properly just by sticking at them.

Five

It was spring in Paris, and it was raining. Cass wondered whether you could call March spring. It was only four weeks until her mother and Bessie would be coming over for Easter, and that was most definitely spring in her calendar.

She smiled as she glanced out at the grey sky. Things were going so well now, she could barely remember her terrible distress of three years ago. Luck had been with her on that first assignment to Paris: she had handled it well, and when the firm had suggested opening a permanent office here, it had been assumed from the outset that the job was hers. She'd never have taken it if it hadn't been for Myrtle's cruel words. She had run away, no doubt about that. Not the best reason for taking a job. But it had worked out. It had worked out splendidly.

She glanced over to where Gaby sat, typing fiercely. Gaby was another stroke of luck. She had been the first applicant for the job, and though she was everything Carol was not – pert and pretty and an incurable clock-watcher – she suited Carol ideally. They came together at nine each morning and went their separate ways at five-thirty. Carol had no wish for any more close friendships.

Gaby's other advantage was that she was married to a journalist working for *La Planéte* as a foreign correspondent. He specialised in French colonial affairs and had twice put Carol in touch with likely authors. It was a happy coincidence that augured well for the job.

The manuscript he was delivering that afternoon had been written by someone on Carol's own special list, however. She had met Clive Hubert at a dinner given by the British Council; he was on his way to the Shott Plateau of Algeria to teach the Arabs how to extend their animal husbandry into arable farming. Carol had

416

suggested the book and Clive had very diffidently agreed to 'give it a go'. And he had done just that. Jean-Claude Durant, Gaby's reporter husband, was bringing it back some time today after a stint in Algiers.

He arrived at four o'clock when Carol was drinking her English tea. As usual, Gaby completely ignored his entrance into the office; they were an odd couple. He went to her desk and dropped a kiss on top of her gamine haircut, then turned immediately to Carol, smiling warmly.

'I have it here.' He put his briefcase in front of her and extended his hand. As usual she held it as briefly as possible and did not quite meet his intelligent black eyes.

'It is not absolutely complete. He will bring the final chapter when he comes out next month.'

Carol thanked him formally. If he had not been quite so good-looking perhaps she could have been more natural. Though with Gaby sitting in the window, hitting the typewriter keys with unnecessary force, perhaps not. Gaby had not seen her husband for a month; he had been on a potentially dangerous assignment reporting on Algeria's struggle for independence, yet she did not even look round at him.

He grinned suddenly at Carol as if guessing her thoughts, and crept up behind his wife.

She said laconically, 'I know you are there.' She returned the typewriter carriage with a crash 'I am busy. I will see you in just one hour from now. Please go home, light the oven, pour drinks, wait.'

Gaby spoke in English because of Carol, but her accent was so French it was almost comic. Jean-Claude had no accent. Apparently he spoke Arabic without an accent too. Also German and Italian.

He replied to his wife in very colloquial French which Carol did not try to understand. Then he turned back to her desk.

'You will enjoy the book. And be surprised too.' He looked at her speculatively. 'Though I am never entirely certain how much you understand of the Algerian situation.'

'Only what I read in the papers.' Carol slid the bulky parcel out of the case with care. When she handled a manuscript she was always conscious she was handling part of someone else's mind, besides a year's work. In this case, rather more than a year. She

417

smiled quickly. 'And you newspaper people tell us only what you want us to know.'

He shrugged. 'Or what we are commanded to tell you. It is not always the same.'

'You spoke of Clive getting out of Algeria. Is there – might there be – some difficulty in leaving?'

'Possibly. The country is a powder keg. Someone like Clive Hubert could light the fuse.'

Carol opened a drawer in her desk, pushed aside pencils and erasers and a S.C.N.F. timetable and laid the manuscript carefully down. She stared at it. Jean-Claude was already by the door.

She said, 'He – Clive – went there to teach agricultural husbandry. I should have thought the Algerians would be grateful.' She knew Jean-Claude's political opinions from his newspaper articles. He was still a colonialist; Algeria was another part of France to him. She meant nothing inflammatory; quite the opposite. But she knew by the way Gaby's typewriter roller suddenly squeaked a protest that she had probably put her foot in it.

Jean-Claude shrugged. 'Of course. Clive will be all right. But feeling runs high out there. And after Indo-China, Africa . . . perhaps we are too sensitive about Algeria. If the conference can happen in Geneva then perhaps our national pride will be . . .' Uncharacteristically he searched for an apt word and came up with 'appeased'. He went through the door, then stuck his head back into the room. 'It is just that . . . when Clive gets back here, dissuade him from returning to Algeria. If you can. For his own good.'

Carol looked at the closed door. Gaby continued to type.

Carol said, 'Gaby, I'm sorry.'

'What for?' The girl did not stop her staccato stabbing. She underlined something and corrected herself. 'I should say, for what?'

'Well . . . if I put my foot in it about Algeria.' She smiled. 'Made a faux pas.'

Gaby whipped out the envelope, whirled her typist's chair and brought the letter to Carol's desk for signature all in one fluid movement. She was older than Carol but had the childish looks of Brigitte Bardot.

'Boulder Desh,' she said emphatically. Carol correctly deciphered that as 'balderdash' and smiled again. Gaby went on, 'Jean-Claude is too much in the past.' She struck an attitude. 'The Free French Army, headquarters, Algiers.' She made a very French sound of dismissal. 'He should have been here through the war, in occupied Paris. It was not so bad. I am a realist. The word honour means nothing. To survive – that is what is important.' She whirled her chair again and threw a crumpled waterproof cover over the typewriter. 'But Jean-Claude is not so – so – fanatic – as you think. His writing in the newspapers has to be very . . .' she thumped her chest '. . . patriotic. But he is a realist like me in many ways.' She went to the mirror and made a moue at her reflection. 'He might think he married me to save me from certain death!' She rolled her eyes. 'Ah yes, some people imagined I was a collaborator. Just because I was alive and well-fed! So Jean-Claude – who is the brave liberator, you remember – gave me his name and his protection!' She laughed. 'But he was certainly a realist.' Her reflected face became defiant. 'I was nineteen and he wanted me.'

She saw Carol's intense embarrassment and lifted her shoulders in a Gallic shrug of helplessness. 'He wants Algérie for the French, but he knows it cannot be so. Eventually, everyone must be free to choose their own . . . damnation!'

She shrugged again and concentrated exclusively on her makeup, giving Carol time to collect herself, or rather to push the unwelcome images which Gaby had created right to the back of her mind.

At last Gaby was satisfied with her enchanting appearance. 'Now I go and leave you in piss to read this manuscript from Monsieur Hubert.' She shouldered her bag. 'Do not picture the passionate reunion, please, Carol. Jean-Claude will not go to the flat. He will not light the gas. He will go to the Left Bank and sit in Montmartre with other journalists and they will talk for a long time.' She turned with a smile of pleasure. 'Which will give me time to cook his favourite coq-au-vin and soak in a bath, yes?'

'Yes. Of course, Gaby. You go. And thank you.'

Cass watched the whirlwind departure of her secretary and then caught sight of her reflection as she sank back in her chair. She was as plain as Gaby was pretty. There was nothing to be done about her long face and lank hair, and she had ceased to make any efforts. Everyone wore their hair very short in Paris, and even back home she noticed most women had cut off their shoulder-length bobs. Rita Hayworth was out and Jean Simmons was in. Carol's concession to fashion was to roll her mouse-brown locks into a bun that missed being chic by a mile. She did not mind. She was quite astute enough to know that her dilapidated look removed any kind of threat from her appearance. Her face and thin figure were overtly intelligent, and could have put people off. Her hairstyle and the way she wore her clothes cancelled all that.

She smiled helplessly as her gaze swept on around the tiny office. It wasn't much, but it was in a good address just off the Avenue Foch; the building had an imposing foyer and a fatherly concierge. And it was hers. Her office. She had hired Gaby, and she could fire her tomorrow if she wanted to. Her smile inverted at that thought; being the person she was, she could not fire Gaby tomorrow however much she might want to. Unless she caught her setting fire to the place or forging cheques for something. But that wasn't the point. She, Carol Woodford, was twenty-six years old, and in spite of looking like nothing on earth, being over-diffident and unambitious, she had come this far. She represented Universal Publications in France. She was their sole representative. And she hardly knew how it had happened.

Another self-deception: of course she knew how it had happened. Even now she became hot, then very cold, at the thought of the scene at Myrtle's wedding. She had had to get away from Northfield even if it did seem like desertion in the face of the enemy. Her mother had known. She had said, 'Take the job. Bessie and I are all right here – that rumour won't go any further unless we all move. If we stay put we shall outlive it. We can see you every holiday – you can come home weekends. Take the job.' And Ralph Morrish had been delighted when she obtained translation rights from such different authors as Sartre and de-Beauvoir – There had never been any question that the job was hers.

She had precious 'clout' now. And Bessie was almost ten. She'd be changing schools quite soon, no reason at all why she shouldn't change to one in France.

Carol smiled at her own secret plans. She was negotiating directly with her authors these days and many of them lived in the south of France. If she could persuade Universal to let her open another office in Marseilles, she was in a position to buy a villa inland. Maybe on the edge of Provence. Just where the Alps and the flowers began. There were convent schools there; she had visited several of them over the past few months. Most of them took children of other faiths and respected those faiths. Bessie had been with her one day and they had watched the sisters taking a group of children on a nature walk. 'They look like butterflies,' Bessie had commented delightedly. And she had been right. The wide coifs flapping among the flowers had indeed looked like cabbage butterflies on the wing.

Carol stood up and went to the window, unwilling to let her thoughts go further. She must open that drawer and begin to read Clive Hubert's manuscript. But not yet. It might be awful, and she couldn't bear that.

It was raining. So much for spring. However the rain partially obscured the view which was euphemistically described as *interne*; in fact the window looked out on a massive air shaft. She stared up. The cloud was like a cork on the top of the shaft. It reminded her of that day she and Liv and Myrtle and Monica had found the Haunted House. It hadn't been raining then, but winter had pressed all around them, making the heath private and very personal. How simple life had been. In spite of the war there had been an inner purpose which almost amounted to peace. She toyed with the thought that war might be a projection of personal battles, a kind of externalisation of emotions too much for one soul to bear. Like funerals. Like weddings. But then, she hadn't been involved in the war. She knew nothing of its miseries.

She turned impatiently from her own feeble ideas and went to the drawer. She hadn't matured since V.E. Day when she had vainly tried to reconcile her father's death with physical science. Surely she knew better now. Surely she knew that her stupid mental ramblings were a guard against other thoughts: speculations on the kind of marriage Jean-Claude and Gaby had. Thoughts of Jean-Claude himself.

She sat down and opened the drawer with unnecessary force. The string around the parcel defied her attempts to unknot it; she rummaged at the back of the drawer for scissors, and cut it. The brown paper was stiff and awkward and infuriating; she did not dare rip it in case it took some precious pages with it. Eventually

421

the pile of foolscap was before her. She remembered Clive saying doubtfully, 'If ever I do get anything on paper, will this size do? I've got so much of it from teaching days.' And she had responded instantly, 'Of course. Anything will do.' Though it was hard on poor Gaby when it came to typing it up. But Clive needed reassurance. He was a brilliant teacher and the British Council had sent him into Africa several times to advise on agriculture. But he had not written a book before.

She read his first words: 'It was almost dark when we arrived. The tiny mud hovels were silhouetted individually in this vast, flat land. I was conscious that we were in the sky; it was no longer above us, it was all around.' Her eyes opened wider and she sat back in her chair. This was going to be all right. Clive Hubert could write.

Some time later, when the reading lamp was making a pool of brightness in the gloom, the telephone rang. Carol reached for it without taking her eyes from the page before her. It would be her visiting femme du ménage, asking why she was not at home yet. But it was Jean-Claude Durant.

'You are still there! I thought you might be. You have started to read the book. It is good, yes?' 'It is.' Had Jean-Claude read Clive's manuscript? Or was it simply a polite surmise?

'Save the rest until tomorrow. Come to dinner.'

She frowned. Did he really expect her to intrude on his reunion with Gaby?

He anticipated her refusal, his voice came urgent. 'Please, Carol. I need to talk to you. It is important.'

'But Gaby—'

'Gaby and I . . . we do not enter into this. This is about your work.'

'Gaby and I work together,' she said stubbornly. 'Anything you have to say about our work, we can hear together.'

He seemed to take this as acceptance. 'I will be there in ten minutes to pick you up. Please lock the book away carefully. It is an important document.'

Her heart thumped. She knew suddenly that Clive Hubert was in some danger. And it was connected with the book which she had asked him to write.

She said, 'I think I should take it home and finish—'

The phone was humming emptily. She replaced it, frowning

422

slightly. She did not want to spend an evening with Gaby and Jean-Claude. Gaby would be scented from her bath, she would lounge around, pouting adorably, not a bit interested in work. Jean-Claude might simply want to talk about de Gaulle and French imperialism.

She opened the pile of papers in various places and read at random. It was going to maintain its atmosphere; it was a description of another world. Clive was pro-Moslem; that much was evident although he did his best to be the anonymous observer. Instead of setting the people impossible goals he had made himself one of them, trekking miles with the goats each day, treating disease on the spot, explaining pasteurisation as he heated their milk over an open fire. A sentence stood out on its own: 'To abandon old ways is wrong; we must adapt them, but keep their intrinsic harmony and rhythm.' It was typical of the man; she had met Clive Hubert only half a dozen times before he left for Algeria, but she knew that those words were the basis of his philosophy. He had gone in for agriculture because he needed to find an intrinsic harmony and rhythm of his own.

With a sigh she slid the wodge of paper into its packing and put it into the drawer again. She knew she could never marry; the 'physical side' of marriage was not for her. She had wanted a family, and Monica had given her that. But if she could ever consider the matrimonial state, then someone like Clive Hubert would be her choice. He was small, withdrawn to the point of secretiveness, but with a rich inner life.

She turned the key in the drawer, snapped out the light, and went into the corridor. The cage lift creaked as it climbed up the shaft, and creaked more loudly on the way down. She stepped out into the marble-tiled foyer. The concierge held the door for her and followed her through on to the wide steps above the Avenue. It was still raining.

'A taxi for madame?' He always gave her the courtesy title. 'Ah. Madame has no umbrella again.' He made a moue of despair.

'I like the rain, Henri.' She smiled at him. 'Besides, Monsieur Durant will arrive at any moment.'

He smiled back. French concierges were notoriously deadpan, but Henri could not resist Carol's English teeth. He waited with her beneath the awning until Jean-Claude's Renault squealed from the Avenue Foch and drew up much too suddenly beneath them. Carol ran down the steps and collected a large drip down the collar of her coat. She turned and waved to Henri. The last she saw of him was his Gallic shrug.

Jean-Claude turned in the road and made for the Place de la Concorde as if sheer speed could force him into the constant rotation of traffic there. It could. Cass gently closed her eyes so that she would not shame herself by screaming, and did not open them until much later. They were cruising down the Boulevard Saint-Germain between the acacia trees. It was almost dark and the rain had stopped.

Cass said, 'Where are we going? We're past the Rue Dauphine, surely?'

'The Reine Blanche. I always go to the Reine Blanche on my first night home.'

She caught a glimpse of his dark eyes as he turned his head momentarily. If only he were small and terribly diffident, like Clive Hubert. It was impossible to feel this sense of discomfort with Clive.

She said very calmly, 'Will Gaby meet us there?'

'I do not know. Perhaps.'

'She told me she was cooking coq-au-vin. At the flat.'

'Ah. That is her favourite. Coq-au-vin. All I need is onion soup. Very clear. Very full of onions. No goat's milk.'

She was forced to laugh but her discomfort did not go away.

'Jean-Claude. I thought you were inviting me to the flat. I really ought to have stayed at the office and finished reading. You said you needed to talk to me.'

'And that is exactly why we do not go to the flat and eat coq-au-vin, English Caroline.' He turned his quick smile on her for an instant. 'Please do not retreat into your shell. It was very important that you should be with me tonight.'

Her outward calm had gone. She hardly knew what to say. What would Monica reply to that sort of remark? She cleared her throat.

'I don't like it. It's not right. Gaby is a friend as well as a colleague.'

He actually laughed at that, tipping his head so that she could see his Adam's apple silhouetted against the side window.

'Gaby is nobody's friend, Cass! Only her own. And you

424

know that because you know people. Your blue English eyes see into them, inside them. That is why you are frightening. And endearing.'

'Please, Jean-Claude,' she said faintly.

'We are here.' he swerved on to the pavement, slapped the car into reverse and backed into a side street. The rain-soaked acacias smelled of the coming spring and everything shone wetly in the lamplight. Cass was suddenly conscious that her perceptions had gone into top gear, probably because of reading Clive's book. Sight and scent were emphasised by the touch of the cool damp air on her face and hands. She pulled on her gloves quickly as if to ward off danger, but she could not veil her face and she did not wear a hat. And her ears could not be blocked off either. The sound of water dripping from trees struck her as special, unique. She could imagine the languorous journey of each droplet along the length of each leaf until it gathered tremblingly on the tip. She must be going mad. How could she distinguish such sounds amidst the clatter of iron tables and pernod glasses? How did she sense that the river was close and darkly flowing beneath the Pont Neuf? How did she know that Jean-Claude's sudden silence as he piloted her inside was deliberate, so that she could absorb such sensory information?

He put her into a chair at a corner table where they could see outside to the lamplight without being cold: The way he settled her, taking her coat, pulling the table slightly away so that she could put down her bag and gloves, was very French. That was the trouble with him, of course: besides his ridiculous good looks, he was French. She tried to think of Clive Hubert and could not. In England she might have fallen gently in love with Clive and even married him if he'd asked her. But not in France.

She said. 'Seriously, Jean-Claude, this is not right. Gaby is expecting you.'

'No.' He shook his head firmly. 'Gaby is always surprised to see me. She would have you think otherwise, of course. You noticed her sang-froid when I turned up this afternoon. But when I touched her shoulders they were rigid. She never expects me to return.' He sat down and looked at her across the table. 'She thinks that I will be killed. One day, yes. Not today.'

He smiled, but she knew he was serious. He was an imperialist in a republic. Imperialists were outmoded. She thought sombrely

425

of her own country and the difficulties surrounding Indian independence. But much more important than thoughts of international affairs was the fact that Jean-Claude had found Gaby's shoulders rigid.

Carol swallowed and looked away from the hypnotically dark eyes opposite her.

A waiter came and took Jean-Claude's order. He did not ask her opinion. She knew he had orders six bowls of onion soup, and that this was not unusual. The waiter smiled and went away, and two glasses of pernod were brought. Cass did not like the drink, but she knew it had a high alcohol content and hoped it would deaden some of the peculiar sensations of the evening. She sipped it carefully.

Jean-Claude smiled again. 'You take it like medicine, Carol. Not permitting it to touch your tongue. Is it so distasteful to you?'

She had to smile back. 'I am not enamoured. But there is nothing I like better. However . . . this onion soup. I am not so sure about that.'

For the first time, he looked dismayed. 'I have ordered three bowls each!' he protested.

'I know. Perhaps you could manage five and I will—'

'No, no, no. You must choose something you would like. Carol, I apologise. I thought – I *felt* it - in my bones – that you were addicted to onion soup, as I am! Forgive me.'

She restrained his hand as it signalled the waiter.

'Leave it. Please. I would like to try your onion soup.'

At her touch he became very still. That stillness was more convincing than anything he had said or done. She removed her hand and felt up her sleeve for a handkerchief.

He said quietly, 'I have never seen anyone so English as you, Carol. So contained and secure in yourself, in your Englishness. Yet you are also the most vulnerable person I know. It is a paradox. A complete paradox.'

She flushed. She hated any limelight to fall on herself.

'And you are the most French. Though in fact you are cosmopolitan, multi-lingual. Another paradox.' She laughed, blew her nose, returned the hanky to her sleeve. He watched each action. 'Please, Jean-Claude,' she shook her head slightly. 'All this analysis! Tell me what it is we are to talk about.'

426

'You. Of course. You.' He gestured widely. 'Your Virginia Woolf face, your English skirt and jumper, the handkerchief in the sleeve, the scarf tucked into the neck, the blue eyes and the big mouth—'

'Jean-Claude!' She silenced him sternly. She was suddenly annoyed. And with herself. She should not have come; he was after all, the archetypal philanderer and by allowing herself to be aware of him, she was entering into his kind of game. She half rose, but he restrained her this time, and his touch had an immediate effect. She subsided.

The waiter arrived with the soup and placed the six bowls carefully around the table. Sticks of bread overhung their basket.

'Ah. Now these—' Jean-Claude pushed a bowl towards her, 'will be scalding. We drink carefully with lots of bread. The next one will be bearable. And the last will soothe the palate, tongue and throat, like balm.'

The waiter laughed. Either he knew English, or he had seen this performance many times before. Cass dunked her bread and felt her anger dissipate. An awful loneliness took its place. Not for her – ever – the joyous flirtation; certainly not the physical union of man and woman. Fleetingly she thought of Clive and knew that between them there could never be more than friendship. Because of this fear. She was frigid. There was no other word for how she felt. It was not the first time she had had to face that fact. She had known it in the Haunted House. She had known it when Malcolm Lennox had assaulted her drunkenly; she had known it a dozen times when reading books or watching films. Something was lacking in her: more than that, something was completely revolted by the mechanics of sex. She could know deep love: for her mother and for Bessie. Probably that kind of love was stronger than sex. She would certainly steal, perhaps even kill, for Bessie. But that kind of love was no bolster against the loneliness of eternity. She imagined, indeed she knew from her reading, that the joining of man and woman accomplished that. One became two; two became one; loneliness was impossible.

Jean-Claude said, 'I know, always I know, when you are . . . dissecting.' He leaned over his bowl with the French lack of inhibition when eating; he bit into his dripping bread. 'Please forget everything except onion soup. There is you and there is onion soup. Nothing else for the moment.'

427

Again she was forced to laugh. He continued to make non-sensical sounds through the mouthful of food, encouraging her to be silly. She forgot her fears, and the sense of desolation. Fleetingly she wondered if she were being inveigled into a flirtation. If so, it was painless.

'The next bowl, please Miss Woodford. No pause. No interval. The leisure, the savouring, the tête-à-tête comes with the third helping.' Even so he was slowing down, his eyes flicking over her face when he thought she would not notice. 'This is delicious.' She straightened. 'But I don't think I can manage the last bowl. Really.'

'Try.' His voice was no longer bantering. He sounded gentle and pleading. 'Please try, Carol. I would so much like you to be . . . replete.'

For some reason, she made an effort. Their spoons went back and forth. They ate no more bread.

She said, 'You have something to say. What is it?'

Still he parried. 'The soup first. Afterwards—'

'If you have something important to say, you had better be quick, Jean-Claude. I intend to return to the office when I have finished this. Now what is it?'

'You are offering me an ear – a shoulder? You write a column in the magazines for lonely hearts?'

She was in no mood for this stupid teasing. If it was nothing to do with Clive's book, it must be something to do with Gaby.

She pushed aside the bowl. 'I have no advice to offer on personal problems. You have chosen your confidante wrongly.'

'I don't think so.' He proffered a packet of Gauloises and when she shook her head, put them away again. But he narrowed his eyes as if he were smoking. 'Would you like coffee?'

'No, thank you. I would like to go back to the office.'

'Now? But why?'

She said with exaggerated patience, 'I wish to pick up Clive Hubert's manuscript, then take a taxi home.'

'That is ridiculous. It is late. Do you not intend to sleep tonight?'

'Jean-Claude—' she pushed back her chair. 'I am leaving. Thank you for the soup. Good night.'

He rose and got behind her chair, easing her out of it and into her coat with the same fluidity as before. It was beginning to rain again.

'Walk as far as the Seine,' he suggested, turning up his collar. 'It is special when it rains. The reflections dance crazily like the dervishes.'

She did not ask him whether he had actually seen dervishes in Algeria. All red herrings would be ignored, she decided.

'I haven't an umbrella and I don't wish to get wet to the skin,' she said instead, tightly. 'Will you drive me back or shall I get a taxi?'

'I will drive you, naturally. But please, Carol. Please walk to the river with me.'

'I'm sorry. I do not want to hear about your marital troubles,' she said straightly.

'It is not about Gaby. I promise you. I know about Gaby and Gaby knows about me. It is something else entirely.' he hesitated. 'It is something about your work. Nothing personal.'

She started to ask him whether they could talk in the car, but already he was walking down the boulevard, past the statue of Diderot. She joined him. It was a cold evening, but he had been right, the onion soup still glowed comfortingly inside her.

It was a long walk, much further than she remembered. They passed his apartment in Rue Dauphine, and she looked up, wondering which of the lights was his, or whether Gaby had given up and gone out herself. When they came to the Pont Neuf, he paused at last. They were both out of breath. Her awareness of him was softened now by sheer anxiety.

He leaned on the parapet and looked into the water, breathing deeply. After a moment, she did the same. The rain machine-gunned the river and the floodlighting gilding the Tour Saint-Jacques reminded her of war-time searchlights.

He lifted his head at last. 'Can you see the Palais de Justice?'

'No.' She dried her streaming face with the sleeve of her coat. 'Where is it?'

'Sainte Chapelle is rising out of it. There.' He touched her shoulder momentarily, and again the contact was electrifying.

She said hoarsely, 'You've brought me here to show me the heart of France? Remind me of its greatness? There is no need. I love France as you love her. I know Clive's book is pro independence. It will come anyway. There is no need for . . . protestations.'

'I know that.' His voice was low. 'People come first.

429

Always.' He took a breath. 'Are you in love with Clive Hubert?'

'No! Of course not! Why on earth do you ask me that?'

He turned her to face him. His hands on her shoulders were very hard.

'Because I need to know. Carol . . . English Carol . . . Clive Hubert is dead.'

The shock of it quite literally froze her. She was already turning to wrench herself free of him, and she stood there, corkscrewed, twisting her head to look at him.

He nodded. 'He handed the book to me. An hour later he was shot. And I smuggled the manuscript back inside my typewriter. My sympathies are known and it was quite safe.'

'But . . . why?' The words came out with her breath, a wail of perplexed anguish.

'He made no secret of his feelings, Carol. He had become the European representative of F.L.N.'

'I don't believe that. He was too . . . low key. He would never have taken an official stance with them.'

'You have read enough of his book to know that he believed in their aims.'

'He thought Algeria should belong to the Algerians – yes! He thought they should practise their own religion – he spoke of their harmonies, the harmonies of the soil . . . oh God!'

She put her hands to her face. The next instant she was in his arms, her head was cradled on his shoulder, he was whispering sympathy in her ear. She hardly knew why she was weeping. It was not entirely for Clive, but for the shocking waste of life, for struggling humanity, for everyone she had known who had suffered. She forgot about the intensity of physical feeling between herself and Jean-Claude. He was a fellow traveller, and for an instant in time they were united in a kind of universal grief. She clung to him; she felt his mouth against her wet neck and smelt the rain on his hair. When she tilted her head back to look at him, his face too was streaming, and she did not know whether it was rain or tears.

'Carol—' his voice choked. 'I did not want it. I did not want any of it. The end justifies the means, they say. But it is not so. I liked Clive Hubert, he was a good man. And he thought a great deal of you. I was so afraid that you too . . .'

'I did think a lot of him. Oh Jean-Claude—'

She stopped speaking and stared at him. One of the lamps on the bridge struck shadows across his already dark face. She thought he might be the devil come to tempt her. 'I must get back to the office and fetch the manuscript,' she said on a high note.

'No!' His hands were spread across her back, unconsciously kneading comfort into her spine. They became still and hard. 'No, Carol. You must not go back to Avenue Foch.'

'But I have to. Surely you can see that now?'

'I love you, Carol. That is all I know. All I care about. I want you to stay with me. Please.'

In spite of the awareness, which she had known he felt too, she was amazed at his declaration. Love. What had love to do with the kind of breathless attraction she had felt this evening? Love was friendship and loyalty and selflessness. What she had felt for Jean-Claude was based on their physical reactions to each other.

She stared up at him. The rain was still coursing down his face. She said, 'This is complete selfishness. Clive is dead. Gaby is waiting for you. She was going to have a bath. Specially.'

He barked a laugh and then brought his head down and kissed her. She had not been kissed since Malcolm Lennox had 'tried it on' as her mother put it, at Myrtle's wedding. She felt a quiver of fear, but he made no attempt to force an entry to her mouth. His lips touched hers and went, touched again, then went to her eyes. Her body felt heavy and voluptuous. Warmth flooded her. She linked her gloved hands behind his back and leaned on him. He kept on kissing her face and neck until she turned her mouth towards him and returned the kisses. Then he paused and looked at her.

'Is it all right, Carol? Is this all right?'

He sounded untypically tentative. She had her chance to withdraw then without hurt pride for either of them; with dignity and integrity. But she did not withdraw.

'Yes, Jean-Claude. It is all right,' she whispered.

After a long while they began to walk back down the Rue Dauphine, entwined like lovers. She could hardly believe what was happening. She had just heard of Clive Hubert's tragic death; she had long faced up to her own cold nature. Yet here she was walking in rain-soaked Paris, not knowing or caring where she was going, with a man she distrusted and disapproved of, who was married to a charming sex-kitten of a girl, a man who obviously had done this with many women before, who was . . . *practised* in the art of seduction.

They reached the Renault.

'We will drive for a while.' He settled her inside, carefully. 'Then we will go to the apartment.'

Her heart jumped and skittered. He came around the bonnet and got in beside her. He turned and took her in his arms and kissed her passionately. They looked at each other in the light from the street lamps. His face was luminous but still so dark. He kissed her again, lightly, and started the car.

She said, 'We cannot go to the apartment. Gaby will be there.'

'She will wait till midnight. Then she will go. Surely you know about Gaby?'

'We cannot go to the apartment.' She took a breath. 'We will go to mine.'

He glanced sideways and put a hand on hers.

'Thank you, my darling. But no.' He drew into the Boulevard Saint Germain. 'I love you, Carol Woodford. I love you and I am thankful for you.'

He drove to the river again and crossed to pass the Louvre and the Pont des Arts. And then, without warning, the sky was lit beyond the Place de la Concorde. Carol jerked in her seat and then was flung forward as Jean-Claude braked violently, stalling the Renault. It was like one of the worst land-mines of the war, as if the bowels of the planet itself were erupting. The blast burst the doors of the car and flung them out of it, still joined. They lay, shocked and sick, in the gutter, while flames silhouetted the Arc de Triomphe and the huge mass of the Louvre. Carol could hear herself begin to cry, though she wondered why; Jean-Claude was holding her very tightly but uttered no sound. She wailed, 'My God! My God! It's in the Avenue Foch. I have to get there!'

She tried to stand, and could not. Bells were ringing in her head. A police car screamed by, then an ambulance. Jean-Claude stood with obvious difficulty and pulled her up beside him.

'You are all right, Carol?' His voice was stern, cutting through her near-hysteria. 'You are all right? Answer me!'

'Yes. Yes. It is in the Avenue Foch. We must go—'

'No. It is not safe.'

'I must. Henri will be worried.'

'Henri?'

432

'The concierge. I should have gone before. You should have let me—'

'Don't be a fool, Carol. We shall not be allowed anywhere near such a fire. I will take you to the Rue Dauphine.'

She could not stop the tears. Where was his tenderness now?

He bundled her into the car and started it with some difficulty. The flames were leaping high and klaxons could be heard converging on the scene from all parts of the city. A gendarme appeared from the darkness and held up his hand. Jean-Claude muttered 'Merde!' and leapt from the car. Carol translated what was said laboriously inside her head.

'Ask him about Henri. Ask him whether the concierge—'

An ambulance flashed by and the gendarme said something. Jean-Claude interrupted him, but not quickly enough.

'Oh God.' She put her forehead against the windscreen and remembered how she had seen Henri last, shrugging acceptance of her mad Englishness. And the office, gone. The desk with the drawer containing Clive's manuscript. 'Oh God!'

The car moved again and when it eventually stopped they were outside the flat in Rue Dauphine.

She said dully, 'You knew. They were after the manuscript and you knew. I want to go home.'

'Your flat is less safe than the office,' he said brutally, and practically manhandled her upstairs.

She sat numbly where he had put her, drank the tea he handed to her later.

He said woodenly, 'I heard that Hubert was dead. I knew they would want to destroy his book. If you were with the book, you too would be destroyed. I had to separate you from that manuscript.'

'You could have stopped it. Henri . . . he could be alive now.'

'I couldn't be sure. I didn't know Henri would be there. I got you out. That was all I could do.'

She stood up. 'I need the bathroom.'

He indicated a door and she walked stiffly towards it. Afterwards he shoved her into a small boxroom furnished with books and a bed. She crept into the bed. There was a hot-water bottle there, freshly made. Weeping, she held it to her and fell asleep.

* * *

She arrived in Northfield before the news of the bombing had reached the rest of the world. Bessie was at school. Her mother opened the door to her and knew immediately that something was wrong.

'You're ill,' she said accusingly, taking the small holdall which had been packed for her by Jean-Claude.

'I've got one of my throats. Nothing much.'

'No, it's more than that. You're really ill. Run down.'

Mary backed into the living room where there was a fire and a low table laid for tea. Her eyes went over her daughter like twin probes. Carol tried to laugh.

'Honestly, Mother.' She went to the fire; she was terribly cold. 'Who is coming to tea?'

'Bessie, of course. It's cold enough for tea by the fire. And anyway she loves to be cosy.' Mary put the holdall on the floor and came closer. 'You're crying.'

'It's just so lovely. You and Bessie, cosy. Having tea by the fire.' The tears wouldn't stop, they dripped from her nose on to the hands which clung to the mantelpiece. 'I mean – Easter is always cold, isn't it?'

'Not quite Easter yet, darling.' Mary withdrew a hanky from her sleeve and put it into one of the clutching hands. 'Have a good cry, then sit down and we'll have our tea before Bessie comes in. I'll go and fetch it.'

She picked up the holdall again and went into the kitchen, wishing that she felt as briskly reassuring as she sounded. The kettle was simmering on the gas, and she put an extra spoonful of tea into the pot before making it. She hoped that just for once Bessie would be late home from school. She carried in the tray and set it on the table. Carol was sitting on the long box, staring into the fire. At least she was dry-eyed now.

Mary said, 'Have they given you the sack?'

'No.' Carol looked up with a fleeting smile. 'I wish it were that.' She spread her hands to the blaze. 'It's just that I've made a complete fool of myself. And one of my authors has got himself killed out in Algeria. And the office has been blown up by a crazy nationalist movement.' She smiled again at Mary's expression. 'Yes. Quite. I'm glad I can tell you before Bessie gets in. Better not say anything in front of her.'

'My God. Cass. My God. Were you anywhere near the place when this happened?'

'No. I saw it. Felt it. But there was no danger. But . . . an important book went. It was in my top drawer.'

'Oh darling. I'm sorry. But thank God – thank God – you escaped.'

'Yes.' Carol's voice was flat. 'Yes. I escaped.'

'You're suffering from shock. When did it happen?'

'Last night. Half-past twelve.'

'And you saw it?'

'I was out. I had dinner with Jean-Claude Durant. He brought this book out of Algeria.' She took a cup of tea from her mother and it wobbled dangerously. 'I'm all right. It's just that . . . I might have prevented it. Part of it. If only I'd taken the book and gone home straightaway.' She shook her head. 'They would still have killed Henri. You remember Henri, the concierge? He's gone.'

'Oh, dear God.'

'The thing is . . .' Carol looked up. 'I think I've been used, Mother. I think I have to take the responsibility for some of this.'

'Rubbish. I don't know what you're talking about, but I know that such an idea is rubbish.'

'I took Gaby on as my secretary and thought it was a great stroke of luck that her husband was a foreign correspondent who was very co-operative. I think now it was planned a long time ago. After the book about Cambodia, when Universal had got a reputation for international hot potatoes—'

'When you got that reputation,' Mary inserted.

'That was when Gaby appeared.'

'You think she was foisted on you? To report back?'

'I don't know what to think.'

There was a long pause. Some colour was returning to Carol's face.

Mary said, 'This whole business is very frightening, but I rather think you're jumping to conclusions, darling.'

'Possibly.'

There was another long silence. Then voices were heard outside the window. Someone said, 'Will you come to my house after Tina's party?' And Bessie replied, 'I'm not going to the party. It's Easter Saturday.' 'It's not church. It's church on Good

Friday and Easter Sunday. Not Saturday.' Bessie said smugly, 'Grannie and I go to Paris for Easter.'

Carol looked at her mother.

'Not this year. I shall have to go back and sort out what I can, but you must stay at home this year, Mother.'

'We'll see.'

Carol's eyes widened in panic. 'Mother. Promise me you won't bring Bessie to Paris. Promise. I mean it.'

The gate clicked and feet were heard running round to the kitchen door.

'I promise,' Mary said quickly, and put her hand over her daughter's before she went to let in her other daughter.

Six

Myrtle looked on the move from Bournemouth to Cheltenham as a new beginning. The tall Regency house overlooking Imperial Gardens boasted a real nursery, and the ground floor provided a luxurious waiting room for Malcolm's patients and two treatments rooms behind.

'Once I've had junior, I'll be able to take the occasional patient myself,' she said to Malcolm. 'I'm still a member of the Society.'

Malcolm glanced at her casually, making her immediately aware that her maternity smock was stained with milk from the baby's last bottle.

But all he said was, 'I remember you suggested that when we were still in Bournemouth.'

'Yes, but the babies came so quickly then. After this one we'll have a little pause, shall we darling? Then I can pull my weight in the practice.'

'It's up to you,' he said indifferently. 'I didn't want to leave Bournemouth particularly. But you seemed to think it was the answer to everything.'

'Darling, Bournemouth was full of osteopaths! We never stood a chance there. When I think how well you were thought of in Wales when I knew you first—'

'That was before we were married,' he said significantly.

'You mean when you could give your woman patients something a little more substantial in the manipulation department!' she snapped, diplomacy going to the winds. Then, when he merely smiled indulgently, she said quickly, 'Darling, don't let's quarrel. Let's make this a new start for us. I know you feel I've held you back, but don't you see – a wife and family add respectability to a practice. Especially if the wife is a qualified osteopath

437

too. Listen darling, I shall meet doctors and nurses at the ante-
natal clinic. I can make contacts. We might be outside the medical profession, but there must be some doctors who will blend
enough to make discreet recommendations.'

He said, '*I* never quarrel, Myrtle. You quarrel. And you repeat
yourself too. You said all this in Bournemouth.' He chucked her
under the chin. 'Be honest, Myrtle. You wanted to come here
because it's just as posh as Bournemouth, it included a very nice
house, and it's less than an hour on the train from Northfield and
your family.'

She smiled roguishly. 'You know me too well, darling. Just as I
know you!' She reached up to kiss him, but he stepped back.

'Myrtle, for God's sake – I don't want to smell of sour milk
for our first patient!'

'It's your fault I smell like sour milk, Malcolm Lennox!'

'Is it?' He held her gaze challengingly.

She was furious. 'D'you think I've got time to mess around like
you do! My God, I was pregnant before we came back from our
honeymoon, and I've either been pregnant or breast-feeding ever
since! Babies are a full-time job you know, Malcolm!'

'And you wanted them.' Suddenly his bored indulgence was
gone and he was angry. 'I know I fathered them, Myrtle. But it
was you who wanted them!' He assumed a high falsetto, nothing
like her voice. 'I want to be filled with babies, darling – I want
twelve children—' he caught her hands as she struck at him. 'You
know damn well it's true!'

'I say those kind of things to please you!' She was panting, on
the edge of tears.

He held her by the wrists at arms' length.

'And they do. Sometimes. But not all the time. There are times
when those little speeches make me feel as if I'm wearing fetters.
As if I'm chained to you.'

She lowered her eyes. She usually made those 'little speeches'
after she had discovered one of his liaisons. It was her way of
fettering him; he was quite right there.

His hands were very warm and she realised, from the change in
his grip, that he wanted her. She smiled slightly and whispered,
'I'm sorry, darling.'

But the smell of sour milk was not so easily forgotten. He
released her and said jovially, 'Oh, it's working at home, baby.

438

That's the trouble. If I were a nine-to-five man it would be different. We live in each other's pockets.'

He turned to go out and she slip up behind him and put her hand in his trouser pocket. He stopped and laughed throatily and would have grabbed her – she was sure of it – if there hadn't been a terrific crash on the front door knocker.

'Mrs Herron!' He pulled away and picked up his white coat from the chair. 'She's bloody early!' He went into the hall to intercept the new maid. 'Hang on Gilda – wait until I'm in the consulting room, for Christ's sake.'

Myrtle pushed the sitting-room door almost shut and peered through the crack. She wanted to see this Mrs Herron. And was Gilda going to be a threat too? Her skirt was fashionably long, but she had a tiny waist and a tiny, neat bust. Gilda indeed. Myrtle had to remind herself that Malcolm preferred big breasts.

Gilda opened the door as she had been instructed, backing away with it so that the patients had plenty of room for their walking sticks. Her white, pseudo-nurse's cap, sitting well back on her head, jerked with surprise. Obviously it was not Mrs Herron.

The next moment Myrtle was in the hall, arms spread wide.

'Borrie! Little brother! How marvellous – come here and be hugged by your big sis!' She folded the fourteen-year-old onto her smock and he did not recoil at any smells.

'Hiya, big cyst!' He grinned widely at his own joke. 'Mother said someone had to come down and welcome you to your new abode . . . so I volunteered!'

'Oh darling, I'm so glad to see you!'

And she was. Boris had been a nuisance when she was at home but she had been proud of him at the wedding, dancing with Bessie Woodford, and he was improving all the time. It wasn't really fair that he took after handsome Daddy, while she was a replica of her mother. But he represented her life in the Midlands. And she hugged him again.

The door knocker thumped.

'That'll be Mrs Herron. Come on upstairs and see your nephews, Borrie. They look a bit like you.'

It was fun having Boris. He could tell her all the news from home and he was at that satisfactory in-between stage of development, young enough to want to please, yet mature enough to know how to please. Occasionally he would become the typical smart-alec schoolboy, but most of the time she treated him as she would have treated a close woman friend – of she had one now.

'Honestly, Borrie, you don't know how I miss Cass and Liv and Mon. We were inseparable. Absolutely inseparable.'

'Don't I know it. You shouted at me if I just knocked on your door when you were all in you room.' He grinned and ran his hand through his crisp curls till they stood on end. 'I could have told you a thing or two if you'd let me in!'

'You were just a baby, for God's sake!'

'Well . . . you could have used me as an example of the male body!'

'Filthy little beast. You haven't changed.' She surveyed him affectionately. His eyes were bigger that hers and much greener. And his mouth was gorgeous.

'Take care of your teeth, little brud. You'll go a long way with those teeth!'

He bared them and growled much too loudly. Next door the baby woke and bawled lustily.

'Now look what you've done!'

She rushed into the nursery and picked up her youngest. He was nine months old and had had to come off the breast when she found she was pregnant again. As a result, he did nothing but burp up curds and whey, usually down her maternity smock.

Boris, watching her jog him, said, 'You ought to let him come down with Nicholas. They could play together.'

'Ridiculous child. Martin isn't a year old yet.'

'Well, Nicholas is only a year older than him – they'd amuse each other.'

'Malcolm couldn't stand both of them at meal times. It's bad enough with Nicky. At least I can give him all my attention while Gilda feeds Martin.'

'She just shoves a bottle in his mouth and reads the paper. I've seen her. No wonder he cries so much.'

'You have a go at it then, clever dick.'

'Okay.'

He took the baby from her. 'Go and have a bath and put on that silky kimono thing. Makes you look all oriental.'

She looked at him, startled. What with his previous remark and now this, she wondered if he might be rather precocious.

Then he held Martin beneath the armpits and gazed into the screwed-up face.

'Hiya, nephew. You gonna behave yourself for Uncle Borrie?'

It was incredible. The screaming stopped to be replaced by hiccoughing sobs.

Myrtle made for the bathroom.

That night Boris had Martin on his knee during supper. At first Malcolm was silent and tight-lipped, but when Boris kept up a stream of chatter which diverted the baby and delighted Nicholas in his high chair, he relaxed.

'See your big brother eating his meat and carrots?' Boris let the baby find his feet and look down on the plate of food. Nicholas immediately shovelled in a spoonful. Martin laughed. Boris said, 'There's a clever Nicky. Now shall we show him what we can do?' He took spoonful of mashed potato from his own plate and popped it into Martin's mouth.

'Borrie, I really think he's too young—' Myrtle began.

Malcolm said, 'Rubbish, Myrtle. Boris is doing a grand job.' He winked broadly at the boy and gave his wife a warning look. 'If it means you and I can eat our meal in peace . . .' He passed his plate for more of Myrtle's braised steak. 'You're looking rather charming this evening, my dear. That mandarin collar frames your face perfectly.'

Myrtle flushed and gave him more than his share. After all, meat was no longer rationed.

Malcolm approved of Boris not only because he was so good with the children, but because he kept Myrtle out of the treatment room. She had a bad habit of bringing in a cup of tea for his patient just when his sensitive fingers had discovered a knot of tight muscle in the base of the neck or across the shoulders. It was off-putting for all concerned. With Boris as a close companion, she tended to take the little ones out for walks.

Gilda felt the same way about the young visitor. Within two days of his arrival she was relieved of the boring chore of giving Baby Lennox his night-time bottle, and she no longer had to keep an eye on both children while Mrs Lennox popped in and out of the treatment room like a yo-yo. Gilda very much liked the idea of being a receptionist; she had not bargained for all the extras that went with it.

441

And Boris seemed to be enjoying himself. Just as Myrtle had, he was already wondering how soon he could get right away from the family home where his father treated his mother like a doormat, there were never any decent meals and the char dropped cigarette ash in his darkroom . . . Boris was a keen photographer.

He saw this visit as the first of many temporary escapes. Cheltenham was only an hour on the train from Northfield, and the new house behind the promenade was much better situated that his own. Besides, he had plans for the future.

He started laying a trail towards these while they walked up to Montpelier to view the first of the snowdrops.

'Bet these park places are a picture by Easter,' he commented as they passed the Queen's Hotel and had the first glimpse of the rotunda with King William guarding it. 'Half-terms are never long enough to see anything much. Can I come down in April, Sis? For a bit longer? That is, if I'm not a bloody nuisance.'

'Watch your language, young Borrie. I might put up with a lot, but pas devant les enfants, if you please. Dammitall you're only fourteen yourself!'

He looked at her and they both laughed. He said experimentally, 'I'm almost bluggy-well fifteen.'

'Bluggy?'

'A squashed up bloody and bugger.'

'Borrie!'

'That's nothing. You should hear what some of the seniors sat at school. In front of us juniors too. Ever heard of wanker?'

Myrtle stopped looking pleasurably shocked and remembered the Haunted House. 'Yes. Matter of fact, I have. But I was older than you.'

'Not much, I bet.'

'No, not much. Seems a lifetime ago.'

They crossed the road and entered the gardens. A chill February wind swept the empty tennis courts and the emptier trees. Boris tugged his cap closer to his ears and Myrtle pulled the hood of the pram higher to protect Nicholas who was perched on a pram seat.

Boris said, 'Monica Cook came home just before Christmas last year. I suppose she told you?'

Myrtle stopped fiddling with the hood and looked surprised.

442

'No. I've never heard from Mon. Not since she went to London for that hotel job. I wrote to her lots of times, but she didn't reply. I didn't think she'd come back to Northfield.'

'Several people saw her. She came for the day. Had sausage and chips in that awful caff where Mrs Cook works. Then went for a walk over the heath.'

'Good God, you had your spies out!'

'I thought you'd be interested.'

'I am. I am. A walk on the heath? I bet she met Cass at the Haunted House.'

'Carol Woodford? She's in Paris. Monica was with her brother.'

'Oh, was she? I thought she and Cass would be in touch. I thought Cass would have to tell her about the business at the wedding. Oh God, when I think of that! You were too young to understand, Borrie. I must have been mad! Fancy accusing Cass – of all people – anyway, as if it mattered! I've sent her a Christmas card every year.'

'She hasn't sent any to you?'

'No. Nor to Mon. Liv writes reams to me, of course. I mean, Reggie and Malcolm were friends, so obviously we're still quite close. But Liv hears nothing from Cass or Mon either. So there's no news from that quarter.' She pushed the pram ahead of him and kept her head turned away. 'Can't expect you to understand, little brud.'

'Well . . .' He hung back diplomatically. 'What it amounts to is that the four of you split into two and two. And you don't like it.'

Myrtle did no answer immediately. Then she said merely. 'Yes, That's it.'

She wheeled the pram to a holly bush which provided a wind-break, unstrapped Nicholas and set him down on the damp path. He walked stiff-legged to the edge of the grass and tried to pick a snowdrop through his mittens. She made a groaning noise and Boris produced a tennis ball and rolled it along the path. The next minute the two of them were running exaggeratedly after the ball aiming mighty kicks at it, laughing like hyenas. Myrtle sank on to the damp seat next to the pram and joggled the handle as she stared glumly at her family. They were all male. All so horribly male. Sometimes she thought she'd give anything to talk to

443

another woman. Of course there was her mother, besides dozens of sycophantic women who thought they might worm their way into Malcolm's affections via his unlikely wife. There was even Gilda. She wanted none of them. She wanted to be a girl again and squat on the floor of the Haunted House talking nonsense to the three girls who knew everything about her and accepted her faults with a scathing criticism that had nothing to do with unkindness of sadism. Yes, Malcolm was sadistic in his way.

'I say, Sis. You're not crying, are you?'

Boris was alarmed. He pushed the ball further up the path so that Nicholas would run after it.

Myrtle said crossly, 'Of course I'm not crying. It's this bloody wind making my eyes water.'

'Swearing!'

'Oh . . . . sod it!'

He had succeeded in making her laugh. She reached up to him.

'Sit down a minute. Nicky will be all right for fifty-two seconds. Then we'll go home and have tea and pikelets. Your favourite.'

He sat down and said brightly as if he'd just thought of it, 'Listen, Myrt. You could write and ask Mrs Woodford if Bessie can come and stay for a while. At Easter. She's crazy about babies apparently. Would that patch things up, d'you think?'

'Bessie? Bessie Woodford? But she was . . . I mean, it was about Bessie that we . . . what I mean is—'

'Sis, listen. If you said something horrid about Bessie, don't you see that to ask her to stay with you would show that you didn't mean it?'

'Yes. Yes, it would, wouldn't it? And she's a dear little soul – well, you know that. You danced with her that day.'

'I see her in park sometimes. And at church. Things like that.'

'How old would she be now . . . nine or ten?'

'Nine. She'll be ten next December.'

Myrtle looked at him sharply. He said sheepishly, 'We talk. I didn't like to tell you because it sounds awful. I pump her about Carol. It was Bessie who told me that someone had seen Monica Cook.'

'Well, for goodness' sake! Tell me about Carol!'

'Nothing really. Just that she is doing very well in Paris. She's supposed to be going to buy a house in the South of France

444

somewhere. Mrs Woodward and Bessie go out there a lot. If they go out there to live, you'll have lost your chance of patching things up.'

Myrtle stared wide-eyed. After a while she said, 'They'll be going to Paris at Easter then. She won't come here.'

'They're not going at Easter.'

'Why not?'

'Bessie doesn't know. Some trouble with Carol's work, I think.' He shrugged. 'Mrs Woodford is worried.'

'Might Carol have the sack?' Myrtle speculated. 'Or is there some trouble with a man? She might have to come home to nurse a broken heart. *She* could come to stay with me then.'

'Especially if you'd had Bessie here.'

Myrtle was brightening by the minute. Bessie might be only nine, but she was female.

'I think I'll write and . . .' she slumped suddenly. 'What am I talking about! They'll never let her come down here.'

'They would if she pestered. She's quite good at pestering.'

'Oh God, is she? But why should she want to some to see me? She doesn't know me – not as well as she knows Liv, for instance. Not that Liv would have a child within two miles of that house of hers.'

'Let me ask her. If I say I'm coming down here for Easter, she might want to come.'

Myrtle's look became very sharp indeed.

'Are you her hero or something, Borrie? What's going on? You're up to something. Like Daddy. Like Malcolm. My God, she's only mine!'

'Sis, calm down. What's the matter with you? I have a chat with Bessie Woodford in the park. For your sake. I'm suggesting she comes here. For your sake. And you jump down my neck.'

Her stare faltered, and went past him to Nicky.

'Yes. Okay. It must be because I'm pregnant. You wouldn't understand. Nobody would. Maybe Cass of course . . .' She shook her head, annoyed at the way her thoughts had gone again. 'Oh God. I don't know. It's too coincidental. But Cass, of all people!' Her eyes focused abruptly. 'Oh, Borrie. Why did you give him that ball? He's fallen over it and his coat will be filthy.'

Boris leapt up and ran to give assistance. Nicky stopped crying and allowed himself to be dusted off. He didn't look too bad,

445

Malcolm wouldn't be able to make any cracks about him coming from the wrong side of the tracks.

Myrtle let Boris plonk him back on the pram seat and strap him in. She smiled.

'I'll write to Mrs Woodford. And next time you see Bessie in the park you can tell her that you'll be here too.'

'Good old Sis. Cass won't be able to resist that.' And Boris looked very well pleased with himself.

Malcolm wasn't quite so certain. Myrtle said nothing to him until she had received a reply from Mrs Woodford. Then she broached it as 'rather a good idea to have someone to keep Boris company.'

Malcolm frowned. 'I thought the whole idea of having Boris was to use him to amuse the boys. He won't want to do that if he's got a pal.' Malcolm's practice had developed rapidly and it was all because of that first appointment with Mrs Herron. He now had a reputation to keep up in more ways than one, and he needed Boris to take up Myrtle's slack.

'Oh, it's not a pal in that sense, darling.' Myrtle put a hand beneath her enormous abdomen to support it. Unfortunately it also outlined it most unattractively. 'You remember little Bessie Woodford at our wedding? She's much younger than Boris and has the tiniest crush on him.' She giggled. 'She'll be marvellous with the boys. She'll want to play mummies and daddies.'

'Poor old Boris,' Malcolm grunted. 'I don't like the sound of it. Bit of a responsibility for us, isn't it? He's just at that age.'

'He's fourteen, Malcolm. And anyway I'm around all the time to keep an eye on things.'

'Oh well. That's different. Sorry baby.'

He sat on the sofa by her and cupped the abdomen caressingly. Then he kissed her. Then he kissed her again very deeply, massaging her stomach as he did so. When she closed her eyes, he glanced up at the clock. He just about had time. He pulled up her smock.

Bessie said politely, 'It's awfully kind of you to invite me to stay, Auntie Myrtle. It means Grannie can go to see Cass in France and not have to worry about me.'

'Hello, darling.' Myrtle kissed the girl with genuine affection. There was something about her that reminded Myrtle amazingly

446

of her own childhood. It must be a spiritual likeness to Cass; it certainly wasn't a physical one. With her black hair and eyes she was like a little gypsy. 'I've been longing to see you. What with having a family and a busy practice, it's been difficult. But we're nearer home now, and Boris is here to keep you company.'

'That will be nice.'

Bessie spoke with a kind of quiet satisfaction, as if Boris were an elderly uncle instead of a child.

Myrtle had determined not to fish for information, but she could not resist one question.

'Grandma tells me that you weren't keen on going to France this Easter, Bessie. I hope you haven't has a quarrel with dear Cass.' She made her voice teasing, hoping to goodness Bessie knew nothing of the scene at the wedding reception.

She didn't. She spoke with the kind of flat honesty that Myrtle also remembered from her own girlhood.

'I had to say that, else Grannie would have been upset. I knew they wouldn't let me go, you see. It's dangerous. If I'd pestered about it, then Grannie wouldn't have gone either. And Cass would have been lonely.'

'Dangerous?' Myrtle felt her heart beat hard in her throat. 'How do you mean?'

'Didn't you see it in the newspaper? Boris and I read it together and we knew it was the place where Cass works. It was blown up.' Bessie hung her matching coat and hat inside the wardrobe in the guest room. 'Boris said never mind, I could come to Cheltenham with him. He said he'd fix it. And he did.' She turned and smiled at Myrtle. 'It really is so awfully kind of you to invite me.'

Myrtle swallowed. Of course it didn't matter why the girl was here, but she'd certainly have a word with Borrie some time. Conniving little beast. Just like Daddy. Meanwhile this business of Cass' office was worrying, to say the least.

'There are so many dreadful things happening . . . must admit I didn't see . . .' she took a pile of navy-blue knickers and put them in a drawer. 'Can't Cass come home?'

'Well, yes. I suppose so. But she wouldn't. It would be like deserting her post.'

'Oh . . .'Myrtle just stopped herself from rapping out one of Malcolm's oaths. Really, Cass couldn't have grown up at all. She was as quixotic as ever. Myrtle knew she ought to let it rest there, but still she said, 'Why on earth would anyone want to blow up Cass' office, for goodness' sake? I thought she ran some little book agency. Translations or something.'

Bessie stopped admiring the real grown-up dressing table laid with powder bowl, hair tidy, ring stand and lace mats by the dozen, and looked round again with a different expression.

'Cass is a very important person, Aunt Myrtle. She works for the biggest publishers in – in – the whole world! And she runs the French office on her own – which shows they think she is very – very trusty. And good. And people like her. Even the French like her. Even the Germans. Everyone like Cass.'

Myrtle realised she had made a mistake. And Bessie was right, Cass was eminently 'trusty'.

She shifted ground.

'Yes, But books . . . why blow up books?'

That had evidently floored Bessie too. She tugged at one of her socks.

'Grandma says that the pen is mightier than the sword,' she suggested. 'Anyway, ackcherly it was the whole building that was blown up. Not just Cass's office. So it was a sort of accident.'

'Ah, I see.'

Myrtle felt impelled to give the small girl a sudden hug. They were both a bit embarrassed by it.

Myrtle laughed. 'I'm so glad you've come, Bessie. You make me feel I'm living my childhood over again. That must sound completely potty to you darling.'

'Oh no.' Bessie smiled forgivingly. 'Cass talks about the four of you. And Boris can remember you having secret meetings in your bedroom. I feel as if I know what it was like.'

Myrtle wasn't one hundred per cent certain she approved of such empathy. After all she was now the mother of almost three children and the wife of a very successful medical man. She wondered if Borrie had got his ear close enough to the keyhole to hear some of the things they had talked about in those days.

'Well, my love. You come to the nursery when you've finished putting all your things away. I'm going to get the boys ready for their walk. We can go and look at the shops if you like.'

Bessie watched her honorary aunt close the door. The stomach really was very big indeed, and Bessie wondered how on earth whatever was inside would manage to come out next month. Or even why it hadn't fallen out a long time ago. But Auntie Myrtle was nice. Grannie said she had been Cass' special companion when the two of them had gone on their country rambles. Bessie liked that thought. She had just read *Girl of the Limberlost* and the idea of exploring untamed country pleased her very much. She went to the window and squeezed behind the cheval mirror of the dressing table to lift the net curtain and look out.

She loved the smell of curtains and nets and the sort of flaky paint you always had on elderly windows. They smelled of all the suns that had shone on them and all the Jack Frosts that had painted them. She sniffed luxuriously as she surveyed the view. That was good too. There were railings around a sunken area, then the wide flagged pavement – that was a nice word, 'pavement' – then the road with its graceful trees, then Imperial Gardens. She repeated the words 'Imperial Gardens' aloud. They had a Russian sound. Not like the Russia the grown-ups meant when they moaned about the 'veto', but the Russia of sleighs and big fur coats and winter palaces. How lovely to have a winter palace and a summer palace. She decided that Cheltenham was very Russian.

At the moment, Imperial Gardens were full of daffodils in carved formal beds. Stabbing them at intervals were heavy tulips, and around the fountain were wallflowers. The grass was close cut. Bessie could not see one daisy or buttercup. She looked hard. If she concentrated on interesting words and views and looking for buttercups and daisies, she did not think of Grannie going over to France all on her own, and Cass being brave about the bombing.

Myrtle watched the children walking ahead of the pram down the length of Cheltenham's famous Promenade. Even Nicholas enjoyed window-shopping in the Prom. The pavement was so wide and the trees enabled a constant running game of his version of hide-and-seek, and the grown-ups never seemed to hurry. His new auntie called Bessie chased him satisfyingly; in other words, she never actually caught him unless he stumbled into someone's legs or someone's dog, or just went sprawling on an uneven paving stone. Then she would gather him up and give him to Borrie who was almost a man. And in her matching blue coat and hat she was very pretty.

Myrtle, reading her son's thoughts as if they were blazoned on

449

his own small cap, smiled smugly. She had done the right thing in inviting Cass' daughter to stay with her. Fleetingly she recalled that it had been Borrie's idea; even more fleetingly she acknowledged that if the bomb had not precluded Bessie spending Easter in France, Mrs Woodford would have turned down the invitation. Already she was well on the way to believing that she had arranged the whole thing; healed the terrible breach between herself and Cass. Her baby was due next month. If only – if only – if only it was a girl, she would call it Carol. That would do it. Anyway she wanted to call her daughter Carol, it was a beautiful name, reminding her of Christmas and candles and . . . Bessie's voice floated back to her.

'Boris. Let's pretend we're Nicky's mother and father, shall we?'

And to her amazement Boris, who should have cringed with embarrassment at such whimsy, said, 'Okey-dokey. You'd better take my arm. Or shall we swing Nicky in between us?'

Bessie put on voice. 'Oh, the latter, darling. Definitely the latter!'

They both doubled up with laughter and after a startled second, Myrtle leaned over the pram to hide her own giggles.

'Have we got a future match there, Martin?' she whispered. She kissed his adorable face. 'That would be one in the eye for Cass and her mother!' she murmured.

They got back when the wonderful spring afternoon had turned damp and chilly. Myrtle wanted a cup of tea and a welcoming fire so badly she was almost in tears. The last patient was just being driven away from the front door in a taxi, which meant Gilda wouldn't have to be a receptionist any more. With luck, the kettle would be on, and the fire lit in the sitting room. She dug Martin out of his wrappings and gave him to Boris. Nicky was clinging to 'Mummy's' hand.

'Be angels and take them up to the nursery,' she said. 'I'm absolutely dead on my feet.'

'We'll look after them, Sis.' Boris was far more sentient than she'd realised. Presumably that was why he could form a friendship with a small girl like Bessie. 'Go and put your feet up till dinner time.'

'You're a darling.' She blew a kiss at him. 'You too, Bessie,' she blew another one.

She tucked the pram into the large hall cupboard and made for the kitchen. It was empty. Of course. She filled the kettle and lit the gas. Gilda was doing less and less these days. Didn't the blasted girl remember she'd been taken on first as mother's help and second – very much second – as part-time receptionist? She had ideas above her station, that much was obvious.

Myrtle made tea and stirred it vigorously to hasten the brewing, then poured herself a cup and carried it to the sitting room. No fire. Not even laid. She felt the tears bubble up her nose. It was too bad. She'd had a lovely afternoon and everything was going so well. You would have thought that a fire wasn't too much to ask.

She put her cup on the mantelpiece with some force and it slopped tea into the saucer. Making little moaning sounds of self-pity, she got to her knees and began to place paper and sticks in the usual wigwam. She had to get up again to find a match, then down again to light the wigwam and feed in small coal. Then up again to reach her cup. Then down again to crouch like Cinderella over the first flickering flames. Thank God for Boris and Bessie. They at least helped and supported her. Where the *hell* was Gilda?

She began to feel better and to remember Malcolm clearing up in the treatment room. She would take him a cup of tea; that would please him. She glanced at herself in the mirror. She'd leave that smudge of coal dust on her nose, it looked rather sweet and might provoke him into having a word with Gilda. She went back into the kitchen and poured more tea. It was not steaming any more. She sipped experimentally. Malcolm did not like tea unless it was scalding. She poured it into the milk saucepan and boiled it over the gas. More washing-up for Gilda. Serve her right.

In the wide, thickly carpeted hall, the children's voices came pleasantly down the stairs. Malcolm would think she was with them, of course. He would be pleased and surprised to see that her idea for inviting Boris and Bessie together was working out so well.

She turned the handle and went into the all-white room. Then she stopped. The light inside the room was unusually dim; the heavy velvet curtains had been pulled over the thick white nets, though at half-past-five on a fine April day it would be light for some time. Even so she had no difficulty in discerning the main

451

event. On the treatment table Malcolm lay supine, fully clothed in white coat and serge trousers. However, his flies must have been opened because above him straddled Gilda and it was quite obvious that although she too was still dressed in black and white, even to her cap, she was without her knickers.

It took them all of two seconds to realise from the light that the door had been opened. Even then they were quite unable to disconnect for another two seconds. Perhaps it would have been longer, but the force of a cup and saucer hitting Gilda's shoulder, and the sudden shock of the scalding tea on bare thighs, hands, faces and other parts, accelerated their actions dramatically. Gilda screamed and fell to the floor. Malcolm sat up, clutching his revealed penis with one hand, his left cheek and eye with the other.

'Christ al*mighty*, woman! What the *hell* do you think you're doing?' he roared furiously.

Myrtle felt her self-control leave her. She rushed around the table and kicked Gilda as hard as she was able.

'Get out!' she panted. 'Get out of this house now! D'you hear me?' And she went on kicking as Gilda scrambled up, grabbed her knickers, which were hardly worth calling knickers, and made sobbingly for the door. Myrtle then slammed it hard and leaned against it, knees slightly bent, the back if her wrist to her forehead.

'I hate you,' she said fiercely. 'I hate you with all my soul! The patients – oh I suppose half of them expect it and pay for it! But Gilda! The maid!'

Malcolm swung his legs down and dealt with his flies. He was as upset as she was.

'Damned woman,' he kept repeating in varying registers. 'Damanblasted woman! Interfering. Things she knows nothing about.' He glanced up. 'Christ, you look like someone from the silent movies except that you don't know what the word silent means.'

'Good mind to throw you out after her.'

Don't seem to realise that when a girl like that keeps pestering, the easiest way to shut her up—'

'Lock stock and barrel. The new electro-massager. The lot.'

'She's been asking for it ever since she arrived. And you went off without a word this afternoon, taking everyone with you.'

'Once too often. That's what you've done, Malcolm Lennox. You've done it once too often.'

'Trying to scald me into celibacy! Christ, I've heard some stories about what women do to their men. But trying to scald the balls off me—'

They both stopped speaking as noises were heard outside. Myrtle looked a warning and turned the door handle. Boris' voice came loud and clear.

'Where do you think you're going, Gilda?'

'Leaving.' Gilda did not sound regretful. There was a small ring of triumph to her voice. Boris on the other hand sounded suddenly mature, and Myrtle realised his voice had completely broken.

'Not with my sister's fur coat, you're not!'

Blustering noises were suddenly cur off as Malcolm took the door handle from Myrtle and closed the latch by the simple expedient of leaning against her.

She looked up at him. He was laughing.

'Malcolm. We really should go and sort things out,' she whispered.

'Boris can do it. Good for him.' He rested his forehead on hers and looked at her. 'Did you want to castrate me? Really?'

'Yes. If it stops you making love to other women.'

'I don't make love to them. I—'

'Don't you dare use that word to me, Malcolm Lennox!'

'No. Not to you. Because I make love to you, Myrtle Lennox. That's what we do. Together. We make love. And we make babies.'

'There! You said it to me!' She glowed with triumph. 'It's not me who says it to you. Not always.'

'No.' He was breathing into her mouth. She was reminded of Cass telling her that you made friends with a horse by breathing into its nostrils. 'No. Not always.' He tilted his head so that he could kiss her. She moved slightly to free her mouth.

'It's all very well. But I don't like you doing – what you do – to every other woman in sight. Especially the maid!'

'Oh bunny rabbit. She did it to me. Honestly.'

'I know. I saw.' She tried to sound frigid. She tried to stiffen her body against his. But then she remembered throwing the tea at him and a little giggle shook the baby. He felt it.

'Myrtle. Myrtle. Myrtle. Myrtle . . .'

453

Each time he said her name he kissed her. Each kiss was different. Better. Or worse, depending on you point of view.

Boris called, 'Myrtle. Are you all right? What the hell is happening?'

Malcolm lifted his head.

'We've fired the maid, old man. And Myrtle and I are just clearing up in here. Can you cope for ten minutes?'

A slight pause, then Boris said, 'Yes. Is that okay with you, Sis?'

She was nearly swooning against the door, but she forced herself to sound natural as she called reassurances.

Then she was lying on the treatment table, wriggling her pants down beneath her smock.

'Are you sure you can manage?' She eyed him with sudden concern. He really was very red.

'Ask me in ten minutes.'

Thoughts crossed her mind hazily during that time. Firstly that though he was over-sexed she really wouldn't have him any other way. Secondly that it was almost worth catching him out each time, because it brought him so close to her for a few days; even sometimes a whole week. And thirdly . . .

She whispered to him afterwards, 'You know what Gilda . . . did . . . to you?'

'Baby-bunny-darling, I'm sorry. Forgive me. I adore you – you must know that—'

'Sweetheart, I'm not angry. But I thought . . . I wondered . . . shall *I* do it to you next time?'

'Oh . . . *baby* . . .' He was almost on his knees. She sat up and smiled at him as if he were a small boy. Perhaps that was the answer. To be Gilda as well as Myrtle. She took his face in her hands and was a long time kissing him, breathing into his mouth gently all the time. Yes, she must remember that. And something else too. Malcolm did not mind if she hurt him. It seemed to raise his passion to fresh heights.

She started to laugh quietly.

'What are you laughing at, naughty girl?' he asked.

'Just thinking. I could do with a nice hot cup of tea. Right now. Couldn't you?'

Clutching each other, almost helpless with laughter, they went into the kitchen where Bessie was tying on bibs while Boris laid the table. Myrtle was on top of the world.

454

'Darlings, you're absolutely marvellous. If you ever need references—'

Nicholas chanted, 'Gilda gone. Gilda gone.'

Bessie said indignantly, 'D'you know, she was going to take your fur coat, Auntie Myrt!'

'No, Was she really?'

'Yes. And she said you were a—'

Boris interrupted. 'She said some pretty insulting things, Sis. I bundled her out fast.'

'Well done, old man!' Malcolm took Martin on to his knee, an unprecedented action. 'Good job you were around.'

Boris said straightly, 'Yes, it was.'

Bessie put milk in four saucerless cups. 'She wasn't really insulting, Borrie, was she? She was on about Auntie Myrt being on heat or something.'

Boris looked apprehensively at his sister and brother-in-law. They could no longer contain themselves. They leaned over Martin, almost weeping with laughter.

After a while, with Bessie and Martin joining in, Boris said in the same stern voice, 'You shouldn't keep laughing like that, Sis. It's not good for the baby.'

Myrtle wailed anew. 'Not good for the baby! Did you hear that, lover man? Not good for the baby!'

Boris had had enough for one day.

'Better get the tea, Sis. Before your strength runs out completely!' he snapped.

Somehow, between them, they produced a scrap meal. It was like a party. Except that Boris was so glum. Even he cheered up when Bessie said contentedly. 'Gosh. I'd rather be here than anywhere else if I can't be with Grannie and Cass.'

That night, as if to justify Boris' gloom. Myrtle went into labour. It was her fourth pregnancy; she had had a miscarriage six months after her wedding. The first pain woke her with a jerk. It was bad, but she smiled into the darkness, glad it was early, glad it had been brought on by Malcolm's love-making, because it would be a future weapon in their constant duel. But when the pain did not stop her smile disappeared, and she held the edges of her mattress in sudden fear. She was stoical where pain was concerned and had been able to put up with the ripping convulsions of childbirth in the knowledge that each one had an ending. This went on and on. She had barely enough breath to call Malcolm, and wished – not for the first time – that he hadn't insisted on single beds for health reasons. He took so long to rouse, which wasn't surprising after his exertions that afternoon. She pulled the mattress upwards. It was a firm orthopaedic one, but by the time Malcolm had struggled out of his bed she had almost wrapped it around herself.

'It can't be yet!' He snicked on the light and narrowed his eyes at her. 'God. Myrt. Something must be wrong. You've never been like this before.'

She managed to croak the word 'doctor', then 'hospital', then she went into the private world of pain where there was just herself and this monster twisting her insides to bits. She knew she mustn't scream. For one thing it would take some of her concentration away from the enemy pain, for another it would wake Nicky and Martin. And Bessie. Oh God. She thought suddenly of Cass having Bessie, alone and sixteen years old, stuck somewhere god-awful, going through this. They should all have helped, all stuck together . . . they'd had something, something precious, and they'd let it go.

After that she could not put her thoughts together properly. Two things protruded like iceberg tips in the sea of frightfulness; one was that this time it must be a girl, because everything was so different; the other was that she and Liv and Cass and Mon must get together again. For Bessie's sake. One big family. For Bessie's sake.

Malcolm woke Boris when the ambulance arrived. He was by this time crazed with terror.

'She's going to die! It's never been like this before – I tell you she's going to die, Boris!'

Boris bundled out of bed and across the landing in time to look at his sister's face at one end of the stretcher. He turned with sudden venom on his brother-in-law.

'If she does, it's your fault! I know what went on in that room this afternoon! I've seen it at home! It's nothing more than rape – d'you hear me?'

Malcolm heard but barely comprehended. He shook his head as he trailed down the stairs with the pre-packed suitcase.

'You don't understand,' he muttered. 'I love her. I really love her.' He looked up from the hall and his face was running with tears. 'Take care of things, old man. I'll be back. As soon as poss.'

Boris stared after them. The front door closed and there were noises that diminished as the ambulance drove around the square and into Oriel Road. He tried to stay with his sister inside his head. He conjured up a picture of her distorted face and silent writhing body. Behind the picture he could see the scene of degradation that he imagined had taken place in the treatment room hours before. He had witnessed other scenes between his own parents and had no way of knowing that every seduction is different. His mother's was instigated by pleading: 'Please Ivan. I love you. I've said I forgive you. Please darling.' The ensuing copulation was abject on her part, impatient on his father's. Boris was certain that his father's acts of infidelity were his way of announcing his innate supremacy over his wife. In fact, a complicated system of rape.

Boris put his head on the newel post. He could not very well murder his own father. But Malcolm was a different case altogether.

He felt a touch on his shoulder and looked up with a spine-aching jolt. It was Bessie.

'What is it?' she whispered. 'You look terrible. Awful.'

She was just a kid. In her sprigged cotton nightie with her black curls wild, she looked younger than ever.

He whispered back, 'Myrtle's started having the new baby. She's gone to hospital with Malcolm. She looked very ill.'

'Oh poor Borrie. You're anxious. You're so sweet.'

He said, 'No. You're sweet, Bessie. You're sweet and innocent and good. You're the only truly good person I know.'

Her eyes were round and very black.

'Borrie. Are you crying?'

'No.' He swallowed. 'Promise me you'll stay the same. Promise me you won't ever do anything . . . horrible.'

'I'm always doing horrible things, Borrie. I forget to say my prayers, and I put salt in Cass' tea last time she was home.'

'You what?'

'It was a joke. But when she started being sick, I felt terrible.'

He spluttered. 'Oh, Bessie.'

'Listen.' She put on a busy voice that he recognised as Mrs

457

Woodford's. 'Just stop worrying about Myrtle, and go back to bed. I'll read you a story. And when you wake up everything will be all right. You're going to be an uncle again.'

She sat on the end of his bed and read from *Girl of the Limberlost*. He watched her avidly. She *was* good. She had been the only good thing about Myrtle's wedding, and since then he'd met her often outside her school and in the park, and each time she carried this air of purity with her.

He stopped thinking of Myrtle's tortured face, and drifted off to sleep. And Bessie crept back to her room and wished very much she was with Grannie and Cass.

At eight o'clock Myrtle was wheeled to the operating theatre and given a Caesarean section. After eight hours of agony she no longer remembered that she was in labour, and when she surfaced weakly for a few minutes she wondered why Malcolm kept talking and weeping.

It wasn't until another day and night had passed that she knew she had another son. And two days after that they told her the boy was a mongol.

Seven

Monica paid off the cab and stood outside the apartment block in Beekman Place, staring at it without her usual pleasure. The doorman came forward with an umbrella although the rain wasn't worth mentioning, and ushered her inside.

'Almost June,' he grumbled sympathetically. 'Wouldn't you think President Eisenhower would do something about it?'

Monica smiled obediently at the sally. Everyone in the block knew that Donaghue was an ardent Democrat and had actually wept real tears when Republican Eisenhower took over.

'It wouldn't have happened in Truman's time,' she said automatically as she went through to the elevator.

She had become adept at what dear old Gander had called the 'relevant rejoinder' in her days at the Albion. She eased the damp fur of her collar away from her neck and smiled briefly again and with cynicism.

The apartment was magnificent. In spite of her terrible ennui it hit her again as she went inside. Beekman Place housed the elite of New York and was opulently discreet – Bob called it down-beat. But in spite of his scoffing he shared her taste – her yearning – for 'quality'. They could have had a house on Long Island, a complex with fountains and a heated pool. But to reside in Beekman Place was to have made it in New York. The residents were nearly all connected with the Boston Five Hundred, and Bob had secured a lease solely because he had married an English lady who might well be the daughter of a duke.

She smiled again; at least she could be proud of that. At least she had brought something to the marriage. And perhaps this latest doctor was wrong. Perhaps this time next year she would have the baby she and Bob wanted so much. No-one could say definitely that she was unable to have children, it was impossible to predict such a thing.

But at the back of her mind she remembered Dr Martin talking to her all those years ago. Telling her seriously that the infection in her Fallopian tubes might well have damaged them.

She had been uncaring then.

'It doesn't matter. I'd never go through that again anyway.'

Her smile died and her whole body seemed to droop despairingly. She tried to recapture the stupid consoling thought of a moment ago: she might not be able to give Bob children, but she had given him a certain status. She trailed into her bedroom and kicked off her shoes. It was ironic: if she had gone ahead and married the first rich American she could find, she would have arrived here as a tart. By giving away her child and working for Dilly and Gander Gosling, she had come as a lady. That would tickle Gilly.

Nancy tapped on the door and came in. Monica surrendered her coat and lay back on the bed, exhausted. It was soothing to watch the tiny Korean girl hang up the coat, put away the shoes, ease the damp gloves on to stretchers.

'Tea please, Nancy. Plenty of hot water.'

If only she could go into the kitchen and make it herself. She desperately needed to be doing something. If Nancy was the sort of maid in whom she could confide, it would help. But Nancy, a refugee from Inchon, was a little short on colloquial English. Besides, brought up in a Japanese household, she served Monica solely because she happened to be married to Bob.

The tea arrived. Nancy made a great to-do of lighting the spirit lamp beneath the pot.

'No sugar, Nancy?' Monica queried. She did not take sugar, but somehow she had to make someone else feel a little of the total inadequacy that engulfed her.

'Pliss?'

'There is no sugar on the tea tray,' Monica enunciated.

'I t'ink Madam not take sugar.'

'Madam needs some sugar today, Nancy. And, for the future, kindly note that a tea tray needs sugar as a woman needs children.'

'Pliss?'

'Go and fetch sugar, Nancy.'

Nancy disappeared and Monica lay back and looked at the corniced ceiling. For a moment she felt ashamed at taking out her despair on someone like Nancy who had run from war. Then she said aloud. 'Who cares? I'm just as much a refugee as she is. And she can trot along to the South Korean Club and hobnob with fellow refugees. Where can I go?'

And then, with the honesty that gave her her integrity, she added, 'Self-pity, Mon. Be careful.'

Nancy returned with the sugar, and she said, 'Are you going out this evening, Nancy?'

'Maybe.' The girl gave her a wary look from those gorgeous almond eyes. 'If Mister Bob not want me.'

Monica squashed her irritation. Different culture, different language . . . She said, 'Look in my scarf drawer, Nancy. Choose one. Whichever you like.'

Of course the girl would have to choose the pure silk one that Bob had given for her un-birthday present four years ago. She could hardly retract her generosity now.

'Fine,' she said. 'The colour is good on you.'

Nancy draped it over her shoulders and smiled prettily.

'Very nice I t'ink.' She glanced over one shoulder into the mirror. Her smugness grated unbearably on Monica – she had to keep reminding herself that the girl was a refugee.

'That will be all,' she said sharply. 'Go as soon as you are ready.'

They had worked out the dinner menu this morning. Monica had thought it would be a celebration meal; tête-à-tête in the kitchen with coffee in proper big cups instead of the demi-tasses, and a steak for Bob that filled his plate.

Nancy disappeared again and Monica sat up slowly and swung her legs to the floor. She did not really want the tea. She wanted the comfort it could give, the sense of normalcy. She removed the lid of the teapot and inhaled the steam with closed eyes. She had felt twinges of homesickness before, but never like this. It had been enough to be Bob's wife, to be as rich as Croesus with a whole new world to explore. She reminded herself of her two sisters-in-law who had welcomed her into the family with overflowing American generosity. She had found herself saying, 'This is wonderful, Hildie. Leone. Wonderful. Has Bob told you I was adopted? I've never felt I had a family. Until now.'

461

It had been ridiculously sentimental; and untrue. She might have had unsatisfactory parents, but she had always had a brother. Oh God.

The steam made her eyes water, and she blinked angrily. How could she hanker after Gilly and that grotty little council house in Northfield when she had all this?

She said aloud again, and very calmly, 'I don't think I can bear it.' Then she poured her tea and drank it sedately.

Bob arrived home earlier than usual. She heard him talking to Nancy and Nancy's high-pitched giggle. Then he tapped and opened the door. No Englishman would tap on his own bedroom door: she was so damned lucky and she must remember that.

'Honey . . .' he came over and kissed her with great tenderness. 'How did it go? You're exhausted. Hell, I could kill that gynaecologist. Is it worth it, baby? Is it?'

She did not answer that.

'I'm a bit tired. I must admit. Has Nancy gone?'

'Yeah. Just wished her a good evening. What d'you suppose they get up to at that club of hers?'

'The usual. Music. Dancing. Flirting.'

He laughed and kissed her again. 'What do you know about it, miss? Is that the kind of thing you did when you were her age?'

'God, I'm not twenty-nine yet, Bob!'

'She's seventeen, hon. Can you remember that far back?'

She had to remind herself he was only teasing.

'Just about. Liv and I used to walk along Bristol Road eyeing up the boys. Nothing much changes.'

'What about the other two? Myrtle and Carol?'

'They tried to make things happen.'

'Huh?'

'Never mind. Let's go to the kitchen and I'll put the steaks on.'

'Hang on. I want to hear about your afternoon. And I've got something for you.'

Her heart sank. He'd bought her another present for this special occasion. And she had to tell him there was no occasion. Yet again.

To put off the moment, she reached up and took his velvet-soft ear lobe in gentle fingers.

'Come here, man,' she said, and drew him to her.

462

He came willingly and they made love in their usual profligate fashion. The detached part of her mind that always stood sentinel on such occasions thought how very useful sex was. The other half thought that she would tell him everything. about Gilda, about Elizabeth. Everything. She owed it to him, but more than anything she owed it to herself. Dammit, she'd had a baby, she couldn't be barren. She couldn't be.

They lay side by side, sated He continued to caress her and she closed her eyes.

'Was it all right, baby?' he whispered.

'It still is.'

'Oh honey. Was there ever another woman like you?'

'Lots. Don't stop. Kiss me.'

He did so and continued to do so.

'God. Monica. You know you drive me wild.'

'Yes.'

'I'm so bloody jealous! Just the thought of that doctor seeing you like this . . . being here . . . I can't stand it, honey!'

That meant she could never tell him about Gilly, of course. She held his head against her navel and opened her eyes to the same old ceiling, the same old cornices.

'You're crazy,' she whispered.

'Yeah. I just said so. Crazy about you.'

He moved and her body responded automatically. Yes. Sex was useful. Very useful indeed.

She had forgotten that she had stipulated oysters, and Nancy had gone to the market for them. Bob made jokes about their aphrodisiac properties and she pretended to be affronted. 'Who needs aphrodisiacs?' she said pertly.

'Not me, hon. And not you either.' He looked at her. 'I take it everything was okay?'

'I'm not pregnant, Bob,' she said bluntly, not meeting his eyes. 'Sorry.'

'Christ, hon. Early days.'

'You're taking it better than me.'

'I guessed it was negative when you went overboard in bed just now. I mean, when there's positive result, we'll have to be careful.'

'Rubbish.' She rather resented the implication that their recent

463

session had been all her doing. 'You don't know the meaning of the word anyway!'

He reached for her hand. 'Honey, when you tell me we are having a child, I'll be the most careful man in the world.'

She took avoiding action and stood up to see to the steaks. She should have said there would never be any need for him to be careful where she was concerned. But she didn't.

He waited in silence while she dished up the steaks and put salad on the table. Then he said, 'Okay, Monica. What's wrong?'

She kept her eyes on his plate while her heart jumped. He was too sentient. He knew.

'Nothing. Is there? It's practically raw. Just as you like it?'

'Idiot child. Your periods. Why did they stop? If there's something wrong for God's sake tell me, Monica. I'm your husband, remember?'

She laughed, surprised at her own relief.

'Oh that. Nerves. Apparently I was wishing pregnancy on myself. Did you know that bodies can do that sort of thing? It's okay, I'm not going funny or anything. It's quite common apparently.'

'Oh . . . shoot!' He leaned back in his chair, grinning again. He was so easily fooled. So easily.

She said, 'That's an Americanism I don't understand, darling. Shoot. What does it mean?'

'I'm not going to tell you. You'd be shocked. Oh baby, I thought – just for a moment—'

'Well, don't.'

'Okay. But in that case, why not? Something's wrong. Is it my fault? There are tests for men, surely? Look, I don't mind going for a test if it would make you happy. You're all screwed up about this baby business—'

'Not so.' She cut into her meat and thought that back home it would have been a month's ration a few years ago. 'Everything is okay. I don't need you to take any test, my darling. I know you'd pass with flying colours. It's just a question of time and patience.'

There. The lie was said. Everything okay. Hunky-dory.

He look as smug as Nancy had.

'Yeah. I reckon I would,' he said.

For a split second she hated him. Then she thought with the

464

objective half of her mind: what the hell, sex is useful. So it's just as well he's good at it.

Much later, he produced a letter from his jacket pocket.

'I forgot. Told you I had something for you, didn't I?'

It was a letter addressed to his office. She looked inside the envelope. It was from Dilly Gosling.

'Why addressed to your office?'

'She says you didn't leave an address, honey.'

'We had no address for ages. We went to Hildie's.'

'Yeah, sure. But we've been here over a year. I should have thought you would have found time to write to her. I kinda look on her as your family.'

Monica nodded. 'She was more my family than the Cooks, that's for certain. You've read it?'

'I told you I was jealous. I wondered who was writing to Mrs Gallagher at Mr Gallagher's office address.'

'Bob!' She was surprised. 'It has an English stamp.'

'Quite. You might have had a lover I didn't know about.'

She didn't like it. Just supposing . . . Gilly had written to her. She said tightly, 'Letters are private in my country, Bob.'

'Not from husbands, honey.'

She looked at him. His grey eyes were unfathomable.

'What about the other way round? May I open your mail?'

He laughed. 'Not on your pretty little ass, you may not!'

She was suddenly angry. 'Don't be so bloody patronising! Not on my pretty little ass, indeed! Typical. One law for men, another for women! Absolutely typical!'

He enveloped her in his arms and kissed her. 'God, I love you when you're angry,' he quipped. Then he tightened his grip against her struggles. 'Listen. Mon. There's some bad news in it. I guessed there would be and I wanted to prepare you. If you'd been pregnant . . . you know.' He kissed her again and she lifted her head an said, 'Is it Gilly? Is it my brother?'

'No. It's poor old Gander. He died last winter. Bronchitis. I'm sorry, Mon.'

She started to weep. Not for Gander Gosling. At least not only for Gander Gosling. But for Dilly and the Albion. And for Carol and Mrs Woodford. And for Elizabeth her baby. Hers and Gillys. Once started, she could not stop. Eventually Bob lifted

465

her in his arms and carried her bodily into the bedroom. There he cradled her in one arm and stroked her hair and face with his free hand.

She sobbed, 'I made lemon meringue pie. Hildie said it was your favourite, and Leone sent me the special recipe your mother always used, and I got the meringue to rise up like the Alps—'

'Oh baby.' He combed her hair with his fingers. 'Listen, how about if I bring it in here with a big pot of coffee and we plan a holiday for next month? Huh? I wondered about Yellowstone. We could hire a camper. What do you say?'

'Yes,' she said simply.

She knew how it would be. He came to the bedroom door half a dozen times to ask where was the pie. And where did she keep the dessert plates. And no, they weren't there.

'Nancy has moved them again. Try the dresser.'

'She's only seventeen,' he said inconsequentially.

'It's the oldest age there is.' She got off the bed and picked up Dilly's letter.

'What?' he yelled.

'Nothing. I'm going to the bathroom!'

It had been the only room in the house at Turves Green where she could get privacy. Nothing changed. She sat on the lavatory and spread the single page carefully.

Dilly wrote: 'My dear girl . . . do you remember how Gander called you his dear girl? For seven years you were our dear girl, Monica, and you are still mine. Yes, I am writing to tell you that Gander died on Monday, and nothing will ever be the same again. I keep telling myself that I lived forty years before I met him, but I cannot remember how I managed. Perhaps I shall feel better after the funeral. Well dear, the funeral was yesterday and I do not feel better. Just empty. The church was quite full because he was captain of the bowls and a sidesman as well. I wish now we had not sold the old Albion after you got married to your nice American. It would have done me good to work again. I am not seventy yet, it is nothing these days. Gander was seventy-five. Some people live until they are ninety. I wish you would write to me, Monica. You promised to send me your address and you didn't. But at least I know where your nice American works, so can get in touch with you there. It is a week later now, dear girl, and I have to tell you that Mrs Woodford came over from France last

Wednesday and stayed with me for three days. She read about Gander in *The Times* and came as soon as she could. She is a good woman. She wants me to go and have a holiday with them in France. I might do that, but I don't expect I shall really. Please write to me, Monica. This letter has taken me a fortnight. I must close now. God bless you, dear girl. From your old friend, Dilly Gosling.'

Monica folded the letter slowly and gazed before her. Poor Dilly. Why hadn't she met her Gander much sooner and had a few more years with him? How we all waste time.

Bob called, 'You're all right, honey? Why have you locked the door?'

She said very clearly, 'Because I can't go unless I do.'

'Okay. But I've got everything together in the bedroom. Don't be long.'

Monica sighed and pulled the flush. Sex was useful and invalidism was useful. But there were limits to both.

She stayed in bed for a week. It wasn't all put on, she felt really groggy and sometimes when she went to the bathroom it was like walking on the deck of a rolling ship. But she knew at the back of her mind that if she had a purpose in life, she would be instantly better. She and Bob planned to 'do' Yellowstone in the fall; Hildie came in from Connecticut with grapes and tickets for a concert. Nancy ate the grapes and although Monica got up and went to the concert, she fell asleep halfway through.

Hildie said, 'You come back with me to the farm, honey. Leonard will fill you up with good fresh eggs and butter.'

'You're sweet, Hildie,' Monica said sincerely. 'But I couldn't expect you husband to look after me.'

'Monica! Leonard is the hired help for godsakes! Surely you remember the name of my *husband*!'

'Oh lord. I'm sorry, Hildie. Of course I do.' But it had completely slipped her mind. She wondered if she were going mad.

'Wait till I tell George that! And he thought he made such a great impression on his English sister-in-law! Oh my dear! You always make me laugh! What a girl!'

Hildie did not often come to New York, so they had to do a lot of things in the two days she was with them. They shopped in Fifth Avenue, trailing around Macy's until Monica wanted to scream with boredom. She remembered how she and Liv had endlessly window-shopped during the war and wondered why. Perhaps it was only enjoyable when you couldn't afford to but anything. Now there was no need to shop. You saw a model you liked, you ordered it, it was delivered.

'The weather was suddenly glorious. 'Dwight might be getting the hang of things,' Donaghue said grudgingly. They went for lunch at Saks and Hildie talked. She loved talking and George was not a good listener. She was mad about the British Royal Family. She had actually met the Duke of Windsor back in '38 on board a yacht in the Mediterranean.

'I could understand why he fell for Wallis Simpson, my dear. She wasn't strictly beautiful but she had a sort of chic.'

Monica thought of Cass. She did not have chic, but she had the long nose and face of the Duchess.

'George always said I reminded him of Wallis,' Hildie confessed archly. 'Maybe that was why he fell for me!'

'Maybe.' Monica tried to make an effort. 'Did Bob tell you how we sat up all night along the Mall for the Coronation?'

'He sure did.' Hildie smiled. 'Leone and I knew you were right for each other after that. I mean – if you saw Lillibet and Phil-up getting crowned, well, what else could you do?'

Monica laughed at last, and let Hildie pat her hand.

Later, when the coffee arrived, Hildie was a little less reassuring.

'Listen, honey. I'm going to talk to you like a Dutch uncle now. You're good for Bob. You know that as well as I do. He hasn't looked at another woman since he set eyes on you. And that's something. I'm telling you, Monica, that is something.'

Monica murmured, 'We're very close.'

'I'm glad to hear it, honey. And make sure you clinch it. As soon as possible now, d'you hear me?' Her tone became teasingly hectoring. 'You give him a baby just as soon as you can, and he'll never look at another woman. That's what Bob wants . . . needs. A family of his own.'

Monica swallowed. 'Me too.'

Hildie looked partially reassured. 'Of course you do, honey. I said to George you were the maternal sort. But . . . well, you know . . . with your face and figure a lot of women would want to give child-bearing a miss. Like Tansy. I said to George, history

468

doesn't repeat itself and Monica isn't a bit like Tansy—'

'Bob's first wife?' Monica said faintly.

'Sure. Hasn't he mentioned her? Well, maybe it's all for the best. He was very bitter. She wouldn't have children, you see. She conceived – of course – and she had an abortion. Didn't bother to mention it to Bob. That was when he divorced her.'

'Oh, my God.'

'Maybe I shouldn't have told you.'

'No, I'm glad you did.' She was. But it made things worse.

Hildie said, 'You're looking peaky again, honey. D'you want to get back to Beekman Place?'

'If you're sure you're all through shopping.' Monica used the American phrase deliberately. She liked Hildie. She thought how marvellous it would have been to tell Hildie that she was pregnant and to live out here with these people for always.

When Hildie went back, Monica felt so tired she hardly knew how to dress in the mornings and undress at night. Invalidism had well and truly taken the place of sex now, and Bob even offered to sleep in the spare room until she was well again. She shook her head at him, but she was usually asleep when he came to bed anyway.

One evening at the end of June, he tried to talk to her about Indo-China.

'It's Korea all over again,' he said, 'De Gaulle had to give them independence, but the Communists won't be satisfied with a partition.'

She tried hard to be interested. 'I supposed if you believe in an ideology enough, it's natural to want to spread the message. Look at missionaries.'

'For chrissakes, Monica, what have missionaries got to do with Ho Chi Minh? Do missionaries kill people if they won't go along with Christianity?'

'Of course not. But I guess we thought God was on our side in the war. We killed for His sake.'

'Honey, you're unable to follow a logical train of thought. You'll be bringing in the Saracens and Crusaders next.'

'I'm sorry, Bob. It's a long way off. And there is no personal connection. It's difficult to . . . to identify.'

'Think of Nancy. Is that personal enough for you?'

'She's Korean.'

'You weren't listening. I said to you it's like Korea all over again. Nancy was a servant in a Japanese household in Korea. When the Japs left, the Commies came down from the north and she had to leave fast. Think of all the Nancies that will have to leave fast if Ho Chi Minh has his way.'

She did not want to think of Nancy. She suspected that the girl had been more than a servant in that Japanese family.

'Yes. Well. What can we do about it?'

Bob looked moody. 'At least think about it. The United Nations should take a hand, of course. But after Korea . . .'

Bob had had a desk job in the army and had been too old for Korea. She knew that part of him longed for action. Typically American, he had too much energy which sometimes festered into dissatisfaction.

She said. 'Let's go to bed, darling.'

He raised his eyebrows. 'Are you up to it, honey? I'd rather wait until you're strong again.'

'I'm up to it. I'm strong enough.'

'What about the dishes?'

'Nancy will do them when she gets in from her club.'

He hesitated. 'Tell you what. I'll scribble a note telling her to leave them till tomorrow.'

'She'll never be able to read it. Leave it, darling.'

'Go and get ready. I'll be with you in a minute.'

She crossed the hall to the bedroom, her good intentions already dissipating in dragging exhaustion. Her suspenders almost defeated her; tears pricked her eyes. Why hadn't Bob offered to undress her?

She heard Nancy's key in the lock and Bob's voice telling her about the dishes. Then nothing.

There was no point in putting on a nightdress; she slid between the sheets naked and lay on her side, waiting. Half an hour later, when Bob came to bed, he found her fast asleep with the light still on. Carefully he switched it off.

She woke with a start. She felt she had been asleep for two minutes, but when she looked at the clock it was three in the morning. Bob was not there. He must be in the spare room. Thankfully she closed her eyes again.

*   *   *

470

The next morning she could hear him singing in the bathroom. She pushed back the bedclothes and swung her legs to the floor, feeling weaker than usual. Also ridiculous without any clothes. Strange, if Bob had been with her last night her morning nakedness would have felt voluptuous. She drew on the satin dressing-gown that reminded her of Ginger Rogers, and went to the window. The view of the river never failed to give her pleasure, but this morning it was already shimmering with heat and she knew she would not be able to go out. Her heart sank. Another day to get through.

Bob breezed in smelling of cologne.

'Hi there, honey! How d'you sleep?'

'Like a log. Why didn't you come to bed?'

He sat on a chair and fiddled with a shoehorn.

'I did. You were dead to the world.' His feet clicked into his shoes and he stood up, marking time experimentally on the thick carpet. 'Honey. Why did you give that scarf to Nancy?'

'Scarf?' Her head throbbed as she thought back. It was almost two months since she'd tried to be nice to Nancy by giving her the scarf. 'Oh. Yes. Darling, I'm sorry. I told her to pick herself a scarf one day. She would have to take that one.' She went towards him. 'You don't mind too much, do you?'

His pumping legs took him past her to the window.

'You shouldn't open this, honey. It defeats the object of the air conditioning.' He closed the window. 'I don't mind about the scarf, baby. It was yours to give. Suits Nancy a lot.'

He pecked her briefly and was gone. And when Nancy brought her breakfast, she could tell from the girl's secret smile exactly what had happened.

She looked listlessly at the letter propped on the silver teapot, and sat up straight when she recognised Dilly's spidery scrawl. Eagerly she tore at the envelope.

'Dear girl,' it began, as before. 'Your letter was balm to me. Absolute balm. Yes, I can still sew a fine seam, Monica, and I took your advice and started straightaway. I've just finished a lovely wedding dress for the daughter of a friend. I wish you could see it, dear girl. You would be proud of me. The other thing you asked about was not so easy, as it was difficult to write to Mrs Woodford about the particular matter. I did drop a note enquiring for Elizabeth's health and well-being, but have heard

471

nothing to date. However, life is strange, dear girl. On Sunday last, the young lady mentioned above came for a fitting and enquired whether I would accompany her to Cheltenham to match up the headdress. I went with her and who should I see there but your friend, Myrtle Denning that was. My dear girl, what a change there! So ill-looking. It seems she has a little boy of two who is Not Quite the Thing. He is obviously wearing her out. But in the course of conversation she told me she would never be able to manage if it weren't for Bessie. Bessie Woodford no less. Bessie comes to stay with her quite often and has a way with the little boy. He will do anything for her it seems. So you see, Monica, Elizabeth must be a very special child. I hope that answers your question. And now, dear girl, for mine. When are you coming home for a visit? You and your husband can stay with me at any time. It would give me so much pleasure . . .'

Monica read on to the sentimental end, her eyes filling with tears. Then she found a handkerchief, dried her eyes, blew her nose and picked up the phone. She dialled Hildie's number.

'It's me. Monica. Listen Hildie. I'm leaving. For England. Can you tell Bob? Make it sound . . . okay?'

There were noises in the background. The farm was a busy place. Hildie said, 'What's that, honey? Tell Bob what? You sound better, honey. Why don't you come out to the far—'

Monica said firmly. 'I'm going home, Hildie. I might not come back. You see, I can't have children and I can't seem to tell him. And when I thought that one day . . . I mean I could put up with him . . . you know. But he slept with out Korean maid last night.'

'Oh my God. Oh Monica, honey. Are you sure?'

'Yes.'

'Fire her. Now. Put her on the line. I'll fire her.'

'There'd be someone else. You tried to warn me. Remember?'

'Honey. Don't take any notice of me. Bob loves you. He has told me often, you're the most exciting girl he's ever met.'

Monica said firmly, 'Hildie, sex is only exciting up to a point. It must have a meaning, an end result. Can you tell him – try to explain – make it easy for him—'

'Monica, wait. Listen. Don't you love him?' You must love him else you wouldn't be talking like this. You have to fight for him. You have to – you have to—'

Very carefully, Monica replaced the phone. Then lifted it and

472

laid it on the bedside table. She went to the bathroom and showered, then came back and dressed without too much difficulty. And then she began to pack. In a funny kind of way she was grateful to Bob for sleeping with Nancy. It made her feel less guilty.

She thought of Elizabeth, and a surge of excitement swept through her.

Eight

Liv had been close to Myrtle since that fateful wedding day back in '51. It was then she had met her own husband, and as he and Malcolm Lennox had been at school together, it was natural that the four of them should feel a strong bond. Besides, Liv and Myrtle felt they were the only survivors from the schoolgirl foursome of the war years. But they had never shared a roof before, and as Liv ushered Myrtle and her brood inside her four-bedroomed detached des. res. in Barnt Green, she knew a moment of pure terror. The hall and stairs were carpeted in grey and pink velvet, the woodwork pristine white. The lounge suite was pale leaf green with curtains and wallpapers to tone. The only room that would absorb fingermarks was the dining room which was pseudo-oak-panelled with parquet block floor and a refectory table to match. She led the way quickly to that room and held the door wide until they were all inside, then shut it firmly and stood against it.

'How absolutely lovely to see you all,' she said faintly, surveying them through the blue-tinted glasses that made her eyes look bigger than ever. 'We thought Malcolm would drive you up, Myrt. Reggie was looking forward to seeing him at dinner.'

Myrtle pulled out a dining chair which must have weighed a ton, and sat down, dragging Mally on to her lap. He turned in against her and put his fingers in her mouth.

She spoke with difficulty through the tiny fist.

'He had appointmentsh all day. He put ush on the train. Ghashly journey. Got a taxshi okay though.'

Mally started to laugh, so of course Nicky and Martin had to join in. They egged each other on until they were screaming hysterically. Myrtle made it worse by pretending to eat Mally's fingers. They weren't even clean fingers.

Liv said loudly. 'Would you like a cup of tea before dinner, Myrtle?'

'Absholuly adore one!'

Nicky mimicked screechingly,'Absholuly, shertainly!' And Martin clapped his hand over his mouth as if to hold his innards in place and immediately blew a huge bubble from one nostril.

Myrtle removed Mally's hand, and used a handkerchief on her middle child.

'Let me come and help you, Liv. My goodness, what a noise, I think they might be pleased to be here, Auntie Liv, don't you?'

'Yes. No. It's quite all right. Stay here and rest for a few minutes, Myrt. I'll bring the tea in, then we can take your stuff upstairs.'

She went into the hall again, sliding through the door as if frightened one of them might escape. Myrtle's luggage lay about where the taxi driver had dumped it. Refugees' luggage. Lots of soft leather bags bulging odd shapes, a basket overflowing with nappies and baby bottles, and a towel covering what was obviously a potty.

She felt completely helpless. She went into the kitchen and plugged in the kettle. The tea trolley was laid ready with biscuits for the children and scones for Myrtle and herself. As she put the pot on the brass stand, there was a flash of colour outside the window. She looked out. Nicky and Martin were running around the garden like puppies, jumping the flower beds, rolling down the grassed slope to the sunken garden, jumping for the apples on the laden tree. She went to the door and opened it, intending to call to them to come in at once, but she saw that Myrtle had somehow managed to open the French doors from the dining room and was helping Mally down the single step to join his brothers.

Liv withdrew and wheeled the trolley through the hall.

'Darling, how delightful!' Myrtle tapped Mally on the bottom to send him off, and came back to the table. 'And I'd forgotten how marvellous your garden is. If only the weather holds, we won't see much of the children. Look at them! They're like prisoners let loose! That train was so full, my dear. I just can't tell you how awful it was.' She sat down without grace and pulled up her dress. 'D'you mind if I take off my stockings, Liv?' She pulled at her suspenders and revealed unsavoury underwear.

Liv put a cup of tea on the table and went to fasten the French doors back.

'These haven't been opened for years. I wonder you managed it.' She stared anxiously. 'They won't trample the flowers, will they?'

'Relax, Liv. Make the most of their absence.' Myrtle smiled over her shoulder with real affection. 'Oh Liv . . . it's so good of you to have us like this. You don't know how I longed to get away. Having to keep them quiet when the patients come . . . well, you can imagine.'

'Yes. It must be difficult.' Liv smiled back, forgetting for a moment the furniture and flower beds. 'You're marvellous, Myrt. Everyone is full of admiration about the way you're coping. How do you feel these days?'

'Oh. About a hundred and eight. Mally's not easy, of course. And Malcolm is as demanding as ever.' But she laughed comfortably at this last.

'I wouldn't have that if I were you,' Liv said definitely. 'Malcolm should help you, pull his weight. When Reggie told me you were pregnant again, I couldn't believe it. Men are utterly selfish of course, but really—'

'Liv, it was me who wanted this baby!' Myrtle said frankly. Then she drooped. 'But I must admit I really do feel about a hundred and eight. And when Borrie said he was going on this camera course, I nearly died. He's such a *help*, Liv. You wouldn't believe it. He and Bessie Woodford between them take the boys off my hands entirely. The thought of the whole of August without them – ugh!'

'He's certainly healed the breach with Cass. I had a birthday card from her last month. Must remember to send her one next winter. Goodness, d'you remember my fourteenth when we had one of our après-midis in the Haunted House?'

'I can remember you playing that blasted violin of yours. And Mon and me pelting you with ink pellets, and Cass saying she thought you had talent. Just in case your feelings were hurt!'

'Cass was so – so kind.' Liv sipped her tea and tried not to notice the veins in Myrtle's bare feet and legs. 'I suppose that was why she got into trouble.'

'Yes. Oh God. I shouldn't have said anything to her, should I? I was just so mad to think she'd caught Malcolm off-balance on

476

our wedding day! Suddenly, just for a moment, she looked like some femme fatale. Oh I hated her!'

'No you didn't. You hated Malcolm. But you couldn't do much about that, so you hit out at Cass.' Liv gave her worldly-wise smile which had so irritated Myrtle once, but now seemed justified. 'What surprises me, looking back, is why Cass took it so to heart. Running off to France like that. Rather extreme.'

'Yes. But Cass . . .'

'Quite.'

There were sounds in the hall and Reggie came in, smiling broadly. 'Have the evacuees arrived, Mother?' he asked, pretending not to see Myrtle. Then, with a double take, 'It's them! All one and a half of them!' He scooped Myrtle up and hugged her soundly. 'Where are the other displaced persons?'

Liv thought he was going much too far, but Myrtle didn't mind.

'In the garden, trampling your flowers, Reggie dear,' she said sweetly.

But he didn't seem to mind that either. He went through the French doors and started chasing the boys all over the place. Little Mally screamed and dribbled and the next minute Martin screamed louder still as Mally went into the fishpond.

'Oh . . . *Christ*!' Liv practically sobbed.

Myrtle shook her head. 'Oh Liv. You'll never go to heaven. Swearing like that!'

'It's not funny, Myrt. The hall carpet . . .'

Myrtle looked at her pityingly. Sometimes she had the feeling that Liv didn't know what life was all about. She took the squalling Mally from Reggie and airlifted him over the precious floors and up to the bathroom. Reggie followed with the bags. Martin and Nicky sat up at the refectory table with Liv standing sentinel at the door.

'This is what family life is all about,' Reggie said enthusiastically from the bathroom door. 'May I come in and sponge my trousers, Myrtle?'

'It's your bathroom!' Myrtle finished stripping off Mally and stood him in the bath. She turned the taps on and stirred the water vigorously. 'Is Liv going to be able to put up with family life for a whole week, d'you think, Reggie?'

'Oh, she'll get to love it. That's why, suggested to Malcolm . . .'

477

he sponged away, leaning away from Myrtle so that she couldn't see his face. 'Thing is, old girl, life is a bit monotonous for Liv and me. It'll be like Christmas, having you and the kids. I just wish Malcolm could have come.'

Myrtle said nothing for a long time. Eventually she turned off the taps and sat Mally in the tepid water. He tried to put his muddy arms around her neck again, and she disengaged herself and reached for the soap. As she began to lather him, Mally went into what his father called his vegetarian state. She looked at him with the infinite sadness that came to her now and then since the birth and had replaced the anxiety and discontent of before. His body was stunted and squashed, rather like his flat mongolian head, his hair rigidly straight, but his tiny hands and feet were perfect. The doctors had said that the chance of it happening again was a million to one, and it would be good for them to have another baby. Malcolm had shaken his head decisively, but she had worked on him. She needed another baby to prove . . . something.

She let Mally lie back in his dream state, and straightened her spine. Reggie had his back to her still, and was rubbing at the damp patches with a beautiful, pristine huckaback towel.

She said quietly, 'You're an idiot, Reggie. I thought it was just Liv who didn't know anything about anything. But you're both as bad as one another.'

He said defensively, 'I don't know what you're on about, Myrt. Just because we haven't had to go through the hoop like you and Malcolm, doesn't mean we don't sympathise.'

'Oh my dear. Of course you sympathise. Which is very good and noble of you in the circs. Because you don't understand.' She sighed. 'Reggie, let me get this straight. Malcolm rang you to tell you about the new baby. You suggested that we have a holiday with you. Firstly because you care about us and want to help. Secondly because you found your life empty, you'd like children, and you thought that given a taste of family life, so would Liv. Am I right so far?'

Reggie wasn't used to this clear-thinking Myrtle. The girl he knew as his wife's friend and his friend's wife, was scatty, passionate and very laissez-faire.

He sat on the lavatory seat and looked at her. She was thinner than she'd been on her wedding day and her eyes were lined from

478

lack of sleep. She had disguised her incipient bump with a dirndl skirt which did nothing for her short figure, and the knitted top above it emphasised her enormous bust, but she had a definite earthy attraction and Reggie could feel it. He took a breath and looked away.

'Well . . . perhaps. Not quite so . . . but on the whole, yes, I suppose so.'

She sighed sharply. 'That's why you're an idiot, Reggie dear. Why do you think Malcolm jumped at your invitation and then didn't come? Because he'll have a clear field with his female patients, that's why. Don't get me wrong – he loves me and I know it. But . . . he still wants that clear field, and it's difficult when his pregnant wife and three children are swarming all over the place.' She laughed without a trace of bitterness and leaned over to pat his knee. 'It's all right, Reggie. Don't look like that. I could have refused to come, and I'm here, aren't I?'

She sat back on her heels and looked again at her supine child.

'The other thing is, Reggie, surely you know Liv by now? Having us here will put her off a family for life. Can't you see that?'

He was on firmer ground there.

'Rubbish. Oh I know there will be hiccups, especially at first.' He laughed determinedly and brushed at his trouser legs. 'I mean – it wasn't clever of me to chase the boys so that Mally fell in the pond, was it? I admit that. But give me credit for some sense, Myrt. Please. Liv and I . . . we go deep now. We've been married almost as long as you and Malcolm. Nearly six years. My God, hasn't time flown! Liv wanted a detached house near Northfield, membership of the golf club . . . all that. She's got it. Now she wants something else.'

Myrtle stood up and took the towel from him, then scooped Mally into it.

'All right, Reggie,' she said. 'All right. We'll see what we can do. I promise. Okay?'

'You're a good egg, Myrt.' Reggie stood up and put a hand on her shoulder.

A voice floated up the stairs.

'What on earth are you doing up there, Reggie? I need some help with these boys and their tea!'

'Coming, darling.' He smiled at Myrtle. 'See what I mean?'

He shut the bathroom door carefully on the woman and her child, and went downstairs.

By the end of the second day, Liv and Myrtle were both making secret plans to cut the holiday short. Myrtle was far more tired than she would have been at home where Tom and Doris, the married couple who had taken Gilda's place, would have kept an eye on Nicky and Martin and left her free to give all her time to Mally. The boys went to a select kindergarten each morning, where they were encouraged to 'explore their environment'. Suddenly that was not such a good idea; Liv's stipulation was that they should not explore.

On the phone to Malcolm, Myrtle said brightly, 'Fine, darling. Really fine. Liv and I are having such lovely natters.' And then, looking over her shoulder at the empty hall, she said in a low voice, 'It's dreadful, Malcolm. The boys don't know what to do with themselves and Nicky has broken two glasses . . . well, she gives them glasses of water at lunch time . . . yes, two of them . . . he simply bites pieces off them, darling. Of course it's dangerous. I nearly had a fit both times. I'm surprised I'm still carrying this baby . . . Mally? You now Mally. He loves everyone. Yes, even Liv!' She listened and gave a low laugh, then said hastily, 'Don't you dare say anything like that to Reggie! Seriously now, Malcolm! He's a nice man – a good man – and he's got a tough life here.' She listened again, lips thinning with exasperation. Then she said, 'You! You have an easy time of it, my lad, and don't you forget it! I wish you could try coping with Liv like Reggie has to! You might appreciate me a bit more then. What? Oh . . . yes, of course I love you too. But you're wicked. Yes, all right, I do . . . I do . . . very much.'

Liv appeared in the hall from the kitchen. She was wearing pale green linen slacks which looked wet.

'Myrtle! That son of yours has got into the fishpond again! I've left him to drip on the grass, but the other two will talk him into trying it again if you don't come quickly!'

Myrtle gabbled, 'Must do, darling. Mally, Bye.' She clapped down the phone and went quickly.

Liv did not follow her. She stood on her beautiful grey and pink carpet and stared down at the dark water-stain on her beautiful pale green trousers. A tear dropped from her eye. The phone rang.

480

'You're through, caller,' sang the exchange. And Malcolm Lennox's voice said, 'What has happened to Mally?'

'Oh Malcolm, it's you again.' Liv's voice lightened and her tears dried instantly. She had always been aware of Malcolm's attraction ever since that wedding day six years ago. 'Sorry to grab Myrtle away like that. My fishpond has a fatal attraction for your son, my dear! He simply has to get in it! He did it immediately on arrival last Monday. He did it yesterday morning. He did it yesterday afternoon. He did it this morning. And now, this afternoon—'

He said tersely, 'Is he all right? Can't you fence the bloody thing off?'

She tinkled an offended laugh. 'Hardly, my dear. This isn't a zoo, you know. At least, it's not supposed to be.'

He ignored that. 'Listen, Liv. Is Mally all right?'

She thought of the squat, ugly child who would climb on to her lap a dozen times a day if she didn't stand up quickly. How could he be described as 'all right'?

'Yes. Of course he's all right.' Malcolm's concern for his son made him endearing again. She decided to forgive his ridiculous question. 'He doesn't fall in, my dear. He goes in. He enjoys it.'

'Oh Liv. What an affected little devil you are.' Malcolm's laugh was an explosion of relief. 'D'you know what I'd like to do to you at times?'

'No. What?' Liv felt suddenly breathless.

'I'd like to put you across my knee and whack that pretty little backside of yours until you couldn't sit down for a week!'

She gasped, 'Malcolm! Stop messing about!'

'I haven't started yet! Listen, little Livvie Baker. If you want to avoid that tanning, here's what to do. Look after Mally, Cuddle him as often as he'll let you. He needs plenty of cuddles. It's his way of talking. Got that?'

'Tanning indeed. You wouldn't dare!'

'Wouldn't I? D'you want to come down and find out?'

'Reggie would kill you!'

'Reggie wouldn't know.'

'I'd tell him.'

'Oh no you wouldn't.'

He started to laugh. Then so did she. When she stopped it was to hear an empty buzzing in her ear. He had hung up. She looked at the receiver, her eyes bright and smiling. 'I bet you don't talk to your patients like that,' she said tartly. But she guessed he did, and she guessed they loved it.

Of course Reggie was highly tickled by Mally's fifth immersion. Liv wondered if the child was more intelligent than he seemed and was doing it just to amuse this new uncle. Powdered, pyjama'd and acceptably milky from his supper, he sat on Reggie's lap and rocked monotonously, making cooing noises.

Myrtle was upstairs putting the other two to bed. Liv poured sherry and thought about the casseroled chicken they were having for supper. This time of day was the best part of Myrtle's visit. The boys almost gone for the night, Reggie all soppy and sentimental about them, the supper perfectly organised as only she could organise things, and a blessed return to civilisation. Tonight something extra was added. She did not analyse what it was. She felt excited: very conscious of her small neat bust, her small firm buttocks, her perfect complexion, her long nylon-clad legs, her short curly hair-do. She felt beautiful and proud of her beauty. She wasn't thirty yet, there was a lot more life to live, she had got what she wanted which was an adoring husband and a modern home full of nice things; now she wanted something else. She did not know what it was but it seemed to be hovering on the horizon.

Reggie said, 'He really likes me, Liv. Have you noticed how he runs to me as soon as I arrive each afternoon? Funny, I was damned sorry for Malcolm and Myrtle when I heard they'd got a retarded kid. But they're both daft about him, and I can understand why. He's so full of love, isn't he?'

'Mmm.'

Liv sipped her sherry delicately and looked across at Mally. He was dribbling again. Yet he could swallow food all right so there was nothing wrong with his throat muscles.

She leaned over him. 'Swallow please, Mally,' she said firmly. 'Go on. Swallow.'

To her surprise he looked up at her and swallowed obediently. She took out her wispy hanky and wiped his mouth.

'Good boy.'

He seized the hanky and for a second there was a tug of war between them. Then she surrendered it.

'All right. You can keep Aunt Liv's hanky, if you'll remember to keep swallowing and wipe your mouth with it afterwards.'

He immediately shoved the scrap of cambric into his mouth and before they could do a thing began to choke.

'Oh my God! Oh – Myrtle – oh – Reggie—' Liv hit Mally fruitlessly on the back. He turned a nasty shade of purple-puce.

Reggie turned him face down across his knees, put his hands around the small body and pressed hard. With a gush of vomit the handkerchief landed on the carpet. He gurgled and turned his head to give them both his big, formless smile.

'You little . . . look at my carpet – just look! You're a very naughty boy!' Liv was beside herself with relief and horror. Mally's blue winceyette bottom was just beneath her hand. She smacked it. He began to cry. Myrtle entered the room at the double.

'What the hell—?' Myrtle took in the sick and the fact that Liv had just smacked her son, and she put the wrong two together. 'You . . . *bitch*, Liv! And you're no better. Reggie! Holding him down like that so that she could . . . there, there, baby. Come to Mummy. I could kill you, Liv. Bloody carpets. Who cares about them? Mally never cries. Never. And we're here for two bloody days and what happens?'

Liv made the mistake of trying to answer the rhetorical question.

'He was choking on the handkerchief, Myrt. We had to do something. Reggie saved his life – he was *choking* I tell you!'

'I saw what happened, thank you very much Liv. If Reggie . . . it sounds as if I should thank you Reggie. But what you did, Liv, was unforgivable. He's completely innocent. He—'

'Is he? He seemed to understand when I told him to swallow. And when I told him he could have my hanky if he kept swallowing, he put it straight into his mouth.'

'You mean you *told* him to swallow your hanky? Are you mad?'

'Don't be ridiculous, Myrt. Of course I didn't . . . oh, can't you shut him *up*?'

Reggie tried to take a hand.

'Listen Myrt, it wasn't like that – you're taking it the wrong way. The child *responded* to Liv. Honestly. It was amazing. He—'

'So she hit him, did she?' Myrtle said with abrasive bitterness. 'And he was supposed to respond to that too, was he?' She hoisted the heavy load further up her shoulder and turned. 'I'm going upstairs. I won't want supper. I'll feed Mally. That always soothes him.'

'You'll feed him?' Liv bleated. 'You mean—?'

Myrtle said deliberately, 'Yes. Breastfeed him. Does that disgust you too, Liv?'

'He's three years old!'

'African women breastfeed much later than that.'

'But you're English. And you're pregnant!'

Myrtle said a vary rude word indeed, and left the room. Liv began to cry. Reggie put his arms around her.

'It's just a storm in a teacup, darling. Natural, in the circumstances. Myrtle is under strain—'

'What about me?' Liv wailed, trying to keep her spouting eyes away from the shoulder of his suit. 'I'm under far more strain that she is! All she has to do is sit around all day and eat the meals I get for her! I have to put up with those children – clean up after them every five minutes. You should see the bath after they've used it – go on up and look at it now – go on!'

'Yes, but you shouldn't have smacked Mally. It would have been bad enough if it had been Nicky or Martin. But Mally.'

'He did it deliberately! I know he did! He deserved that smack. Anyway, whose side are you on?'

'Nobody's. You can't have sides in a case like this. Look darling, go up and make your peace. Please.'

'I have to dish up supper.'

'She won't come down if you don't go up and ask her.'

'You go up. Tell her what happened. She'll listen to you. And while you're about it—' she disengaged herself and made for the door ahead of him – 'have a look at the bath.' She glanced back and remembered the sick. 'Oh my God. If I don't get some water on that, it'll be stained for ever!' She rushed away and Reggie said to thin air, 'I've never heard you call on God so often before, darling.' Perhaps it was as well she didn't hear, he reflected as he went upstairs; that sort of bantering never made her laugh.

The door to the bedroom which Myrtle was sharing with the boys was ajar, and Nicky's and Martin's voices could be heard within, arguing more or less amicably. Reggie put his head inside and saw them on one of the single beds, conducting a fight between two toy soldiers. In a pale gold Lloyd Loom chair by the window, Myrtle sat with open blouse, Mally – looking bigger than ever – at her breast.

Reggie would have withdrawn very quickly indeed, except that Myrtle looked up, saw him and smiled a was welcome.

'Come on in, Reggie. I'm sorry about all that. Have you come to tell me what an unreasonable cow I am?'

In the circumstances the appellation was almost too apt. Reggie felt his face become explosively hot; he stood fidgeting in the doorway.

'Not at all. She – Liv – just wanted me to say that she's sorry and won't you please come down for supper?'

Myrtle's smile became less wan. 'I bet she didn't apologise! But of course I'm coming down. As soon as I've got this little lot settled.' She stood her head gently at all their foolishness. 'I'm sorry, Reggie. It's not much fun for you, is it? But you know, my dear, this is what family life is like. Are you still as keen as ever?'

He had to stay and reassure her; he couldn't very well leave after she'd come full way to meet Liv.

'Of course I am. Let me put the boys to bed. May I?'

'Help yourself.' She sounded very tired. He knew Liv was right, she shouldn't be breastfeeding a two-year-old child, especially when she was pregnant again.

He went over to the single bed and took another soldier from the box. The boys welcomed him as an 'umpire' and allowed him to pronounce a draw fairly speedily. He put the lid on the box and stowed it out of reach on top of the wardrobe. Then he tucked the boys into their beds and told then an edited version of Jack and the Beanstalk. He tried to feel paternal, or at least avuncular. All he could feel was desperately lascivious. He was sideways on to Myrtle and when Mally's head dropped back in sleep, he could see quite clearly the huge bell of her breast with its shining wet nipple. When she stood up carefully to carry the boy to his bed, he had to clench his hands in Nicky's bed cover; she was now wearing a brassiere and made no attempt to button her blouse. Both breasts were fully and shockingly visible. His palms ached to hold them.

'What if the giant wasn't really dead at all, Uncle Reggie?' asked Nicky. 'What if he jumped up and began to chase Jack?

What if—' Martin wailed and put his head under the bedclothes.

'Oh, he was definitely dead,' Reggie said, swallowing frantically. 'He never moved again, you see.'

Nicky looked at the writhing shape of his small brother and said scornfully. 'Anyone can shut their eyes and pretend to be dead.'

'But his eyes weren't closed. That was how Jack knew he was properly dead. When your eyes are closed, you're asleep. But when they're open and you can't move, then you're dead.'

'Oh.' Nicky had no more shots in his locker and Martin was convinced that the giant was dead. Reggie tucked them up and drew the curtains, then turned to face Myrtle. She had buttoned her blouse and was combing her wiry hair.

'Bless you, Reggie,' she whispered. 'I'll be with you in a minute.'

The only trouble was that now he knew what was under the blouse, she might just as well leave it off.

He whispered back, 'Okay,' moved swiftly into the bathroom and locked the door. There he stared at his reflection in the cabinet mirror and breathed very deeply. Then he looked at the ringed bath and got down on his knees to begin cleaning it.

Later that evening when two girls were chattering away as if nothing had happened, he told them he would take the next day off.

'I'll drive you over the Lickeys. We'll take a picnic. What do you say? The boys would love it and I think it would do both of you good to get out of the house for a bit.'

'Oh Reggie, you are sweet,' Myrtle said unguardedly.

'Quixotic is the word, Myrt,' Liv said, smiling indulgently at her husband. 'D'you know, when there was all that Hungarian business last year, he wanted to take in a family of refugees!'

Myrtle knew she was being firmly put in her place, but a sudden empathy with Reggie carried her past discretion.

'Oh I wanted to do something too,' she said to him. 'But of course, Malcolm . . . the practice . . . it wouldn't have done it much good.'

'I should think not,' Liv helped herself to more potatoes though she was cutting down on carbohydrates. 'And where on earth would you have put them, darling?'

Myrtle shrugged diplomatically, recognising the endearment as a sign of Liv's extreme annoyance.

Reggie altered the subject smoothly. 'Last year was grim all round. Suez – what a fiasco. Eden should never have withdrawn. My God, France and Britain built the bloody canal and have maintained it all these years—'

'Language, Reggie,' Liv interrupted lightly.

'And this Khrushchev chappie. All smiles and Father Christmas on the outside, but it's his deStalinisation business that started the Hungarian troubles. Not to mention Poland.'

They were getting back to refugees again. Myrtle said hurriedly, 'When Malcolm and I went out to dinner last week, one of the men was saying that Russia would be putting some kind of capsule into space before this year is out.'

'Rubbish.' Liv took another spoonful of gravy to go with her potatoes. The taught of Myrtle and Malcolm going to dinner parties together was not welcome. She had imagined she could bring a little glamour into Malcolm's life. Surely Myrtle spent all her time being pregnant and washing up? She knew for a fact they did not have an automatic dishwasher. 'Surely you remember you physics lessons, Myrt? Miss Edgeworth told us that if anything ever did get out of the earth's atmosphere, it would explode instantly.'

'Mm. She was wrong about the atom though, wasn't she?' Myrtle smiled at Reggie. 'She said that if one atom was split in two, the energy released would split the next and the next and the next and the next and the next . . .'

They were both giggling helplessly and foolishly. Liv spooned the remainder of her gravy into her mouth in the way Mrs Cook's customers fed themselves at the cafe; as if they were starving.

'Right. Has everyone had enough? I think you've had too much, Reggie darling. You're overflowing. There's potato on your chin and is that some chicken on your tie? Really, Reggie?'

She'd made an apple pie for pudding. Myrtle spent the rest of supper time extolling the shortness of the pastry and the delicate flavouring of cloves with the apples. Mollified, Liv fetched her recipe book and offered to copy out the particular recipe. They took their coffee into the pristine lounge, and Reggie opened the doors of the television and they watched a programme called 'Little-known talents'.

'That name is familiar.' Myrtle leaned forward, frowning. 'Clive Hubert. Good lord. He was one of Cass' authors.'

Liv, interrupted in mid-flow, also frowned.

'Cass and her very important career! She's just a middle-man. Or woman. Isn't she?' Like a shopkeeper.'

Myrtle did not reply; she was listening to the broadcaster with untypical concentration. When he went on to something else, she sat back and looked at Liv with wide eyes.

'I say. Did you get all that? They thought this Clive Hubert's book was blown up in Paris a couple of year ago. Now it turns out there was another copy or something.'

'Fascinating,' Liv said.

'No, but don't you remember the Paris explosion? It was in Cass' office. The book must have been in Cass' office. My God, no wonder she didn't want Bessie over there that Easter. They could have been after Cass herself. I mean if she knew what was in the book.'

There was a little silence. Liv said slowly, 'Clive Hubert. I've never heard of him. Is he famous?'

'He's dead, Liv. That's why they're just been saying. He was killed, then his book was destroyed.'

Liv made a downward moue. 'Melodrama. Who would have thought it of our Cass? No wonder she moved to the South. I imagined it was for the weather, but obviously there were other reasons.' She sipped her coffee. 'Was there anything in it? With this Clive wotsit I mean.'

'That doesn't matter now. What does matter is that they've found another copy of the bloody book!'

Reggie took a tentative hand in the conversation. 'Surely that's good for your friend? The book can be published – it's saving something from catastrophe, I should have thought.'

'But if someone thought it worthwhile to kill because of it . . . .' Myrtle put her cup on the table without its saucer and Liv leaned forward with her handkerchief at the ready '. . . Mrs Woodford and Carol will send Bessie home. Mrs Woodford won't leave Cass. I'm certain of that. But they won't risk Bessie's safety. She can come to me.' Her face lit up at the thought. 'Boris has gone off on this camera course, but she will be all right with me.'

Liv stopped polishing and said dryly, 'And she's so good with the boys, isn't she?'

Myrtle nodded unoffended, 'And she adores Mally. And they all adore her.' She smiled at Liv. 'She is quite special, Liv. Rather like Cass when she was a kid. She seems to understand things. Instinctively. I mean, she's much too young to work things out. But she knows about people.'

'I have met her. I knew her quite well until you wedding, Myrt. She didn't seem a bit like Cass to me. Much too dark and pretty.'

'I didn't mean she looked like Cass. But she'd got all her mannerisms. Gosh, I hope Cass will be all right. I loved that girl – really loved her.'

Liv tucked her handkerchief away and looked back into the past. 'We had something special then, didn't we? Me and Mon were so different from you and Cass, but there was a very strong link.'

Myrtle stood up.

'I'm going to write to her tonight. Suggesting it.' She smiled. 'I'll go upstairs now. Liv . . . I'm sorry about Mally and the fishpond. I really will try to impress on him—'

Reggie said heartily, 'Don't bother, Myrtle. We're out all day tomorrow – give them all a chance to run wild.'

Myrtle started to tell him again how sweet he was, then stopped herself and left them to it.

Liv said, 'Reggie dear. If Cass isn't that keen on sending her daughter to Myrtle's – where it's quite obvious she is some kind of skivvy – we could have her here if you like.'

Reggie realised his plan was working. He stood up and pulled his wife to her feet.

'Oh darling. I love you.'

He began to kiss her; her eyes, her nose, then down her face to her neck.

She said, 'Just let me stack this stuff in the dishwasher, and we'll have an early night, Reggie.'

'Bugger the dishwasher,' he said.

'Language,' she replied. But she met his mouth with her own when he came around her chin, and allowed him to come inside, thankful that she had already cleaned her teeth. He would have done it then and there on the carpet, but she couldn't go that far. Laughing breathlessly, she let him pretend to chase her up the stairs and into the bedroom, and even to unzip the placket of her slacks, but after that she had to draw a line. The thought of going to bed without creaming her face and hands was impossible for Liv. She was lucky that her hair was naturally curly and needed no pinning. When she came out of the bathroom slippery with cream and a new satin nightgown, he was already on the bed, stark naked, holding out his arms to her.

'Why on earth did you bother with a nightie?' He laughed at her as he practically tore it off. 'You're mad, Olive Bradbury. Mad. D'you hear me?'

There was no time to answer, because the kissing began again, but she hadn't liked him using her full name. She had been eight years old when she truncated it, and apart from at her wedding, it had been rarely heard since. She pursed her lips against his.

It was then that the screaming began.

At first she thought one of the children had wandered into the room and seen their two bodies entwined on the bed. There was a split second when she imagined what it must be like, the horror of it, the damage done to the innocent child for the future. Then she realised that the screams came from the room down the passage and must indeed be piercing to penetrate two walls so clearly.

Reggie would have run to investigate as he was, but she threw his dressing-gown at him even as she dug her arms into her own. They burst into Myrtle's room neck and neck.

Myrtle already had Martin in her arms and was rocking him soothingly. His screams threatened to burst their eardrums, so she merely shook her head uncomprehendingly above his. Incredibly, Mally and Nicky did not move in their beds. Reggie crouched opposite Myrtle and touched the child's face, and as if by magic, the screams stopped. The boy turned tear-swollen eyes towards him and hiccuped, 'He closed his eyes, Uncle Reggie. He weren't dead at all. He closed his eyes.'

Myrtle whispered, 'Oh God. The giant in Jack and the Beanstalk. You little idiot. I'll give you dead tomorrow morning!'

Reggie felt in his pocket and found a handkerchief; he dried Martin's face.

'Listen, old man. It's just a story. But the giant was dead all right. They closed his eyes before the funeral. But he was dead. No doubt about it.'

Liv watched it all in astonishment. Not only was Reggie crouching there with his dressing-gown doubtless flapping open,

490

but it was obvious, in spite of the cradled child, that Myrtle slept in the buff. She could hardly believe it. Reggie must see . . . what she could see. It was indecent. Myrtle was as brown as a berry, too. Did she also sunbathe in the buff?

She said bracingly, 'All right now, then? Can we get back to bed?'

'Sorry.' Myrtle surrendered Martin to Reggie who carried him back to bed. At last she seemed to realise her own nakedness and with what seemed like brazen slowness, she reached for a sort of shawl and draped it inadequately around herself. 'Very occasionally he gets nightmares. I should have warned you.'

Reggie finished tucking Martin in and whispered, 'No more dreams, old man. Sleep tight. All right?' And Martin giggled sleepily at the rhyme and closed his eyes immediately.

Reggie stood up.

'I should be apologising. I'm sorry, Myrtle. I'll be more careful about stories in future.'

They both laughed. Everyone said goodnight. Liv led the way back down the landing.

'Poor Malcolm. That's all I can say.' She spoke tightly, not removing her dressing-gown, sitting on the edge of the bed with ramrod back. 'She's gone to pot, hasn't she? Her bust . . . and those stretch marks. Poor Malcolm.' She saw in the mirror that Reggie had taken off his dressing-gown and was very aroused. 'And poor you, too. Quite a shock.'

He reached over the bed and slid his hands over the silk.

'Mmmm, nice.' He grinned. 'Not really. She was feeding Mally earlier, if you remember.'

She did remember now. And she had sent him up to see that! And no doubt all this rampant passion was a direct result of what he had seen.

She said, 'Darling. I'm sorry. But not now. I simply couldn't. It was too disgusting. Put me right off.'

She stood up, picked up her nightgown and made for the bathroom. And Reggie, astonished, rolled on to his back. Then thought of Myrtle.

The next day Liv told them she had had a telephone call from a friend in Worcester who was ill. She did not want them to postpone the picnic, in fact she had packed a hamper that would have

491

fed an army, but she felt she must visit his friend. Someone she had known in her Civil Service days. And she did not need the car because she would take the train. She kissed the boys and Mally, then Myrtle.

'Have a wonderful day,' she instructed. 'And look after my husband for me!'

Myrtle held her warmly for a moment and would have asked more, but Liv broke away. Reggie said nothing at all. He seemed relieved when a taxi arrived and whisked her to the station.

'Right. Let's get packed up. Ready boys?'

Myrtle said, 'Look, Reggie. If you'd rather not . . . honestly we shall be quite all right here. Nicky adores the television and I'll take them down to Northfield this afternoon to see Mummy and Daddy—'

'You've planned to do that tomorrow, Myrtle. Today we're going on an expedition to them thar hills! Aren't we boys? We're going to make a camp fire and cook sausages—'

'Liv has done a huge picnic!' Myrtle protested through vociferous approval from her brood.

'Bugger the picnic!' Reggie declared, and Nicky echoed, 'Yeah. Bugger the picnic.' And Martin said, 'Let's bugger the picnic.' Mally snorted his laugh, and Myrtle threw everything to the winds. 'Okay. I'll bugger it out to the car. Then you can bugger it to the camp site. How's that?' She picked up the hamper and marched outside. Reggie shouldered Mally, laughing like a drain. They looked like a gaggle of gypsies as they loaded up with fishing rods and frying pans. It was what family life was all about. On a sudden crazy impulse, Reggie leaned over Martin's head and planted a kiss on Myrtle's mouth.

'We're going to have a lovely day,' he said.

She looked at him, amazed. Then returned the kiss.

'We are,' she agreed.

They did. Reggie put his heart and soul into everything. The fire was one hundred per cent successful: crackling flames that they could war-whoop around at first, then a long-lasting glow over which sausages spat and sizzled satisfyingly. Then, while Mally slept and Myrtle read the newspaper, there was French cricket and tree-climbing and finally fishing in the reservoir.

Myrtle knew now that he wanted her. It made her feel proud

492

and special, guilty and conscience-stricken. They must have had a row, the two of them, and it might even have been over her. She couldn't think way. Compared with Liv she was downright ugly; besides, she was mother of three and pregnant again. Men didn't lust after the likes of her. But he was lusting. She knew it and felt a response in her own fertile body.

Of course she would let nothing come of it. Liv would be home when they got back and she would make sure the two of them had the rest of the evening together. She did not want anything to come of it. She loved Malcolm. And even more importantly. she loved Liv. Her loyalty was flawed where Malcolm was concerned because of his own constant infidelities. But it was strong for Liv.

Meanwhile each time Reggie's shoulder brushed hers, she deliberately enjoyed the thrill. It could harm no-one.

They got back to the house at seven o'clock to hear the phone ringing. Myrtle hopped out of the car and answered it. It was Liv. She wasn't going to be able to get back home that night. Could Myrtle possibly manage supper on her own? There were chops in the fridge and veg in the crisper. Reggie needed fresh greens each day, so Myrtle must not open a tin under any circumstances.And she was to let Reggie load the dishwasher.

Myrtle said, 'Never mind all that. Of course I can manage – how do you think I cope at home with five months to feed? But listen. Liv. *Listen*. What has happened with you and Reggie? You *are* coming back, are you? I mean, this is ridiculous. Reggie adores you – you must know that—'

'I've told you, Myrt. My friend *needs* me! Surely you don't mind looking after things for another day? Good lord, I've done everything all this week, I shouldn't have thought it was too much to ask you to hold the fort for one day!'

Myrtle said wearily, 'Of course it's not. What's your number in case of emergencies?'

But the phone was dead in her hand.

Reggie got the supper while she put the boys to bed. When she went downstairs she wondered how they would get through the evening. Maybe she could ask him to baby-sit while she borrowed the car and went into Northfield. It was a frightful cheek. But then he would probably understand her motives. She knew, even as she planned it, that she would not do that. She was tense as a spring. She wanted to be with him.

In the same state of mind as a drowning man reaching for a lifebelt, she grabbed the phone at the bottom of the stairs and dialled the operator.

'Cheltenham, please. Five, four, seven, four.' She cleared her throat and repeated the number. Malcolm would save her. He would talk to her over the line, stake his claim as he always did. Reggie would become just Reggie again. Liv's husband.

'You're through, caller,' said the disembodied voice of the operator. And them someone said, 'Hello?'

Myrtle was transfixed. She gripped the receiver frantically and stared at the virgin-white newel post as if it had spouted wings.

'Is that Cheltenham five, four, seven, four?' she asked tremblingly.

The line went dead.

'What is it?' Reggie was in the kitchen doorway, apron on towel over one arm à la waiter, even a makeshift chef's hat atop his fair hair. 'My God. What has happened, Myrt? Tell me. Quickly.'

She began to weep, and he leapt forward and gathered her into his arms. She held on to him desperately. His hat fell to the floor. He kicked it away and pressed their bodies together.

'It's Liv—' she sobbed into his neck. 'Oh Reggie. Liv is with Malcolm. Liv is with Malcolm. What shall I do?'

His mouth came over her open one. He kissed her fiercely as if he could drive out physically the horrific pictures that formed and re-formed in her head. It was answer enough. She continued to cry for a while, but already she was conscious of him and against her; already she responded to his kiss; already her hands slid into the nape of his neck and behind his ears. She knew so well the mechanics of sex. After a very short interval in the hall, they found themselves in the lounge where the brand new television was switched on low. Before Cliff Michelmore's eyes, they undressed each other with indecent haste and took to the carpet. The chops congealed in the kitchen as their love-making continued and the evening darkened. Myrtle's passion now had something vengeful about it. When Reggie would have finished, she put his hands on her breasts and leaned over him as she had seen Gilda lean over Malcolm. Reggie groaned, 'Oh darling . . . I

494

worship you . . . I worship you . . .' And it was balm on an open wound.

When it was completely dark and a man in a dog collar appeared on the screen and talked about eternity, she rose at last and they went into the kitchen to eat. They sat naked in front of the cooker, tearing at the cold meat like animals. Occasionally they would laugh, almost hysterically.

After the meat, Reggie shovelled the fresh vegetables into the waste disposal and looked at her.

'Upstairs or downstairs?' he asked.

She baulked at using Liv's bed.

'Downstairs.'

She led the way into the lounge again. The screen was dark and emitted a high-pitched whine. She switched off the set and they continued where they had left off.

Liv arrived at the house in Imperial Square at eleven o'clock that morning. She told herself she was going to talk to Malcolm about Myrtle's health. There was a residential nursery school for mentally subnormal infants in a remote corner of the Cotswolds between Broadway and Evesham. Her women's club had entertained a speaker from there not long ago. It would be the ideal place for Mally. With the other two boys in kindergarten, Myrtle could rest during the day. It was so obvious.

The door was opened by Tom, a prematurely elderly man, who usually did the outdoor work. His wife, Doris had taken the opportunity of Myrtle's absence to visit her sister for a few days, and Tom was doubling as receptionist. He knew nothing of appointment systems, and assuming Liv was another patient, showed her into the waiting room. Mercifully it was empty. Perhaps Malcolm was not as busy as Myrtle made out. Even so she waited nearly an hour before he appeared. When he did, he was minus white coat and his thick hair was almost standing on end. The woman he ushered out was in her fifties, maybe even older. In spite of the heat she wore a fur cape over a black crepe de chine dress. She had a walking stick over one arm, but she must be almost cured now as she walked without trace of a handicap. Malcolm was bending over her deferentially and did not immediately spot Liv.

'Let's make your next appointment right away, shall we?' he

was saying. He laughed in his throat. 'How long do you think you can wait?'

But she had seen Liv. She said haughtily, 'I did not realise anyone else was waiting. Mr Lennox. I'll telephone you.' And she swept into the hall and out of the front door without waiting for Tom's assistance.

Malcolm looked round.

'What the hell are you doing here?' he asked unwelcomingly.

Liv felt like a schoolgirl. She stammered, 'I wanted to talk to you about Myrtle. I'm worried about her.'

'Why? Is she ill?' he asked urgently.

'No, of course not. She's tired, that's all. She's doing too much.' She paused, then burst out suddenly, 'Do you know she still breast-feeds Mally?'

He laughed at that. 'Of course I know, you idiot. There's nothing there. She does it to comfort him. She does it for me sometimes.'

He intended to embarrass her and he succeeded. She turned bright red and gasped as if he had struck her. He laughed and ran his fingers through his hair, returning it to its usual Brylcreemed splendour as if by magic. Then he laughed again and reached for a clean white coat behind the door.

'My midday appointment will be here soon. Was that all you wanted to say?' he asked, leaving the coat unbuttoned and digging his hands in its pockets.

'I . . . yes. I suppose it was. Perhaps I'd better go.'

'Oh no you don't. You came here for your punishment and you're going to get it. Meanwhile I can make use of you. Come with me.'

He walked out of the room and after a split second of token and silent rebellion when she told herself she was going to leave that minute, she followed him meekly to the kitchen.

It was a total wreck. The sink was piled high with dirty dishes, more were on the big scrubbed table in the middle of the floor, a heap of unwashed laundry was pushing open a door at the far end, and an unpleasant smell told of unemptied bins. A bluebottle droned around the light flex.

'Right!' he said briskly. 'I want this lot cleared and a meal cooked. Something light. Scrambled eggs, you know the sort of thing. Myrt tells me you're an angel in the kitchen. Can you prove it?'

He smiled at her and she felt again the unexpected charm of the man. He was all the things she loathed, yet . . . yet . . .

'I can prove it,' she said, holding his stare somehow.

He came very close to her. 'Good girl.'

Her breathing went to pieces as she waited for his kiss. It did not come. When she opened her eyes he had gone.

She had worn a new dress, green cotton to go with her oddly flecked eyes. The skirt was too tight for comfort, her heels too high. And the weather was very hot. She had not worked so hard for a long time. Myrtle's housekeeping concentrated on essentials, and little luxuries like clean sinks and store cupboards were left out of her timetable. Liv could not cook a meal until she had clean crockery, and she could not wash up until the sink was scoured and disinfected. She thought longingly of her dishwasher and the new electric cooker. She eyed the ancient gas stove beneath its huge hood, filled the sink again and began to take it to pieces. By the time Malcolm returned to the kitchen there was a cloth over the table, flowers in the centre, a rack full of toast and a covered dish full of the fluffiest scrambled eggs she had ever made. But she was red and shiny-faced and she had a nasty feeling her deodorant was not working.

He surveyed everything with a smile.

'Congratulations.' He sat down. 'Sauce? And where is Albert?'

'Albert?' she asked faintly.

'The bluebottle. I haven't eaten without the company of Albert for many moons.'

'Oh Malcolm!' She laughed and collapsed on to a chair.

'That's better. You looked like a coiled spring.'

'I'm fine. But how on earth Myrtle lives in these conditions I do not know.'

'I'll show you in a minute.' He spread butter on toast and scooped the ethereal egg on to it. She was having trouble with her breathing again. He cut off a wedge of toast and crammed it into his mouth, then pushed the plate across to her.

'Go on, get on with that,' he ordered through his food. 'I can't stand it without sauce.' He got up and fetched the bottle from the dresser. 'God. You've scrubbed the shelves too, haven't you? No wonder you look so hot and bothered.'

She said, 'I can't eat anything. Honestly.'

'Get on with it, woman.' He swallowed and grinned companionably. 'I really am a good osteopath, Liv. Myrt lives and thrives with me for a lot of reasons, and that is one of them. When she gets wound up I make her eat, then I give her a massage. So . . . eat.'

She took a forkful of egg, then another. He ate greedily and massively. She had made eight pieces of toast, never dreaming it would all go. It did.

He sat back.

'It's not going well at home? Mally upsetting you?'

'Oh, it's not that.' She took the plates to the sink and ran water on them. 'Though as you've mentioned Mally, I was going to tell you about a little nursery school I've heard of. Near Broadway. Very beautiful.'

'And very remote. Is that so no-one will hear them yelling, d'you think?'

'Oh Malcolm, Mally doesn't yell.'

'No, he's a good kid.' He stood abruptly and picked up a grubby tea towel, 'I don't think Myrt and I could face life without him now.'

She said, 'I haven't washed up properly, only rinsed.'

He ignored her and rubbed at the plates busily.

'Funny. When he was born I was horrified. Horrified for Myrt and horrified for myself. But I'd heard mongol children were very lovable. It's true.'

'He's always on Reggie's lap. Reggie loves him.'

'And you?'

She said, 'Malcolm, have you got a washing machine? The little scullery place is full of laundry.'

'I'll show you. Come and have that massage first.' He flung the towel at the drying rack and it missed. 'We'll have to do it in two parts. I've got another appointment at two.'

She did not know whether she was coming or going. She could not have a massage if she was smelling. But if she had a massage she would have the strength – surely – to go for train and get back home before Myrtle and Reggie returned from their picnic. But was he really intending to give her a massage? Or was he going to rape her? And would he have to rape her?

That was the most difficult question of all.

Still, she went with Malcolm into the treatment room.

He did not rape her. She took off her unsuitable shoes and her nylons, her dress and petticoat, and lay face down on the high table. There was a hole for her face and her arms hung over the edge. It was amazingly comfortable. He sponged her with tepid water, lifting the top of her pants to go around her waist, holding up each arm. Amazingly there was so embarrassment, he was so professional, so clinical. When he put his hands on her spine she knew without doubt that he was good. She felt so relaxed it was as if she were melting and would end up a small pool on the floor. His thumbs went into her lumbar region and undid knots she hadn't known were there. She closed her eyes and surrendered to him. She hoped quite desperately that he would kiss her. He did not.

'That's all for now, Little Liv,' he said. 'Get dressed and go out of the other door, will you? I'll finish you off before dinner, never fear.'

The doorbell rang while she was putting on her stockings and she heard Malcolm go into the waiting room and greet his next patient. It was an exquisite relief to heat it was a man. She crept into the hall holding her shoes in one hand. No-one was about. She went in to the kitchen and picked up the fallen towel. In the scullery, beneath the mountain of dirty washing, she found a machine and began to sort the clothes. When the first load was pounding away she searched the fridge for food. There was nothing worth mentioning. In the cupboard were tins of salmon. She began on a salmon mousse.

At five o'clock Malcolm came in and drank a cup of tea. He was sweating profusely, which was something she hated normally. Not it struck her as exciting physical, proof of his strength, his maleness. He opened the fridge and eyed the mousse and salad.

'God, I'm hungry. We'll eat at six an d go straight to bed.' He looked at her. 'You are staying?' The shock of his words was almost too much for her. She did all the movie star things: gasped, clutched her throat, felt for a chair and sank into it.

'They . . . they've gone for a picnic. They're expecting me to be there when they get back.'

'When will they get back?'

'I don't know. In time to put the boys to bed, I suppose. Half-past six.'

'You can phone then. Let's finish your massage.' He was gone again.

She was slightly more assured this time. If he thought she was staying the night he wouldn't do anything now. And afterwards she could catch the seven twenty-eight back home and feel that she'd struck some sort of blow for herself. Yes. She didn't need a host of children to prove that she was a complete woman. She had herself.

So she went into the treatment room and took off her dress and stockings again and lay on the couch. But she had forgotten the magic of his hands. In ten minutes she was enslaved again. All thought of the seven twenty-eight left her mind. In was the most sensual experience of her life and she longed to conclude it with a kiss, but, as before, he walked away from her to the wash basin and she went behind the curtain and dressed hurriedly.

He was in a jocular mood now.

'Food, Liv. D'you know, I haven't lived so well since I married Myrtle! Salmon mousse. And fruit salad. And then . . . your punishment.' He glinted at her. 'I'm looking forward to that. It's what you came for, isn't it?'

'Oh. Really Malcolm! I don't know what you're talking about! What about the old man who answered the door? Is he going to eat with us?'

'Tom? He's gone now. The house is ours. No-one to hear your cries.

'Stop it, Malcolm. I have to go home. I must go home.'

He shrugged. 'Another time then. If there is another time.'

It had the inevitability of a dream. She washed up and took coffee into the sitting room. He indicated the telephone and she rang the Barnt Green number and got Myrtle and told her about Marion Lonsdale being ill. When she replaced the receiver he started to laugh, then he got up and moved menacingly towards her. She shrieked and ran and he chased her through the kitchen and hall and upstairs where he cornered her in the nursery and got her across his knee. He gave her a token beating which occasionally hurt even through her clothes, then he stood them both up and kissed her. She had waited all day for that kiss. She was exhausted with work and anticipation and almost collapsed in his arms. He wasn't mad for her as Reggie had been last night; he lingered over her mouth as if it were a glass of wine to be

500

savoured. His hands outlined her body like a sculptor's, discovering her shape and glorying in it. Every move was calculated, and she didn't mind. After a long time, he lifted her bodily and carried her downstairs. It crossed her mind that she must be a very light weight after Myrtle; that was the first time she had thought of Myrtle all day. She banished the thought quickly. He put her down in the hall.

'Go into my room, Liv. I'll get a bottle of wine. We'll do the thing properly.

She was lost when he went. His voice said the wrong things: shocking, brutal things. His hands were sweet and sensitive. She needed his hands. The heat of the day was going and she shivered convulsively.

The phone rang.

She waited, thinking he would answer from the sitting room, but he didn't. Perhaps the house had a proper cellar and that was where he was. The phone rang again. She lifted the receiver and was connected with a long-distance caller.

'Hello?' she said faintly.

There was a pause, then Myrtle's voice asked, 'Is that Cheltenham five, four, seven, four?'

Liv replaced the receiver very carefully and Malcolm came through the kitchen door.

'Where are you, woman? Don't hang about there.'

Liv went slowly into the treatment room again and accepted a glass of wine. She drank it quickly and passed it back to be refilled.

'Dutch courage?' He grinned and gave her the bottle. She stood there, drooping, hearing again the incredulity in Myrtle's voice.

She whimpered, 'I can't, Malcolm. I'm sorry. I can't.'

He didn't believe her. He remove the bottle and began to kiss her again and undo the buttons of her dress. She kept repeating no, no, but he completely ignored her and at last she found the energy to push him away and run for the door. Her shoes had gone and her dress flapped around her waist. She ran down the hall weeping, wanting to get away, yet at the same time desperate for him to run after her and make her go back.

She opened the front door knowing she couldn't possibly go down the steps to respectable Imperial Square. But there was no

501

need. Standing on the top step, hand raised to the bell, was a woman. She was not tall, very dark, her long hair pleated neatly around her head to form a coronet. Her make-up was the most perfect Liv had seen and her clothes the most expensive.

Behind Liv, Malcolm started to laugh. She looked round at him, startled. He couldn't possibly know who it was.

Then she turned back to the picture of elegant simplicity before her.

'Mon. What the hell are you doing here?'

And Monica smiled. 'You've changed, Liv. You never used to swear.' She looked down the hall. 'And you must be Malcolm. I expect Myrtle is seeing to the children, is she?' She leaned forward and touched her sweet-smelling cheek to Liv's. 'D'you think I could come in? I'll help you with your dress, my dear. It seems to be undone.'

Nine

Cass opened her eyes on a perfect August morning and listened for the single tolling of the bell at the tiny église further up the mountain. The sun was already over the cypresses which provided a windbreak for the Bergerie in the winter, but the air coming from the High Alps was still cold and clean and she relished the goosefeather quilt on the four-poster.

She thought luxuriously, 'Sunday. Church with Mother and Bessie. Lunch. Siesta. Walk. Oh . . . oh . . . bliss.'

The door opened a quarter of an inch, and Bessie's voice hissed, 'Can I come in?'

Carol groaned theatrically, and Bessie took this for assent and came giggling into the bedroom. She wore no slippers and her pyjama trousers ended just below the knee. She would be thirteen this winter and she was tall for her age.

'If you get a splinter in your foot, don't blame me,' Carol said, not very seriously. The bare boards of the Bergerie were polished into a diamond-hard surface. The furniture was old and heavy and they enjoyed moving it about; it never scratched the floors.

'Never mind that.' Bessie galloped over to the bed and got beneath the quilt. 'Can you smell the flowers?'

'Yes.' Carol sniffed. 'Yes. Those little roses. And honey suckle, and that bed of godetia—'

'I saved the seed from last year. And the nicotina seeds. All the flowers from Northfield too – forget-me-nots and marigolds and stocks. Gardening is much more interesting here, even Gran's salad garden really *grows*.'

'Where is Gran?'

'Gone to early Mass.'

As if in agreement, the bell began to toll. It sounded tinny but very commanding.

Carol rolled out of bed.

'Come on. Let's go and cook her a real breakfast.' She dragged a skirt under her nightie and turned her back to fasten her brassiere. Bessie, who stayed with uninhibited Myrtle fairly often, made a wry face at the narrow back and went off to her room to dress.

They met in the big kitchen which had been a barn in the days when the Bergerie really was used by shepherds. Mary Woodford had already opened the damper on the range and filled the kettle; Carol lifted down the big iron frying pan and fetched bacon from the cold slab in the larder. Bessie darted about like a fly, laying the table, rushing out to pick flowers and arrange them as a centrepiece.

It was often like this on a Sunday when the maid, Sylvie, did not come. The Woodfords had a talent for making an occasion out of everyday happenings. For just over two years they had lived in the converted Bergerie. Carol had an office in Marseilles, but she worked a great deal from home, and most of her writers preferred to see her there.

In the village further down the mountain the English women were known affectionately as 'les trois' and were dealt with almost protectively. Their foibles were indulged – newspapers and post delivered before nine in the morning, fish and liver twice weekly . . . for the cat if you please! But they were proud of young Bessie who could sing like a bird and draw every flower which grew on the mountain; and if they could not afford a visit to the doctor, Mrs Woodford offered excellent medical advice. As for Carol, she could pen a better letter the the notary himself, and if there were any local disputes she could often sort them out with her quiet diplomacy.

When Mary came back from church they ate bacon and eggs and drank a great deal of tea, and discussed the week that had gone and the one to come. Bessie's school had closed for the summer and she wanted Carol to take her holiday too so that they could go on one of their treks up the mountain.

'It's going to get hotter and hotter, Cass,' she pointed out. 'We could take the tent and live like gypsies wherever we chose. You always say that August is the silly season for your job anyway. Nothing happens.'

'I thought you'd want to go and stay with Aunt Myrt. You did

504

last year and the one before.' Carol helped herself liberally to marmalade. 'I thought we might all go home for a couple of weeks. It's about time I took an interest in my godson.' She looked over at her mother. 'Perhaps Dilly would come back with us, if we really pressed her?'

'I don't think so.' Mary poured more tea. Provence suited her so well, she felt younger and more alive than she had for years. She sipped blissfully. 'Why don't you and Bessie go and stay with Myrtle? She asks you every time she writes. I think she'd like to feel the old breach was well and truly healed.'

Carol glanced at Bessie expecting her to ask 'What breach? but she was wrinkling her nose in disapprobation.

'Don't let's split up. Let's all stay here. It's no fun at Aunt Myrt's unless Boris is there, and he's gone on a camera course with his school.'

Carol shrugged helplessly. 'Fine with me. I thought you'd like to go back home before winter comes.' She smiled warmly. 'I'm delighted you want to stay at the Bergerie. When I remember how worried we were about moving out here . . .'

'It was the best thing we ever did,' Mary Woodford said definitely, remembering Carol's distress three years ago. 'This place has given us so much.'

'Let's go camping,' Bessie urged again. 'Follow the river up to its source. We could swim in it. We could—'

Just then Sylvie's husband, Pierre, arrived with milk and post and rolled newspapers. Carol looked idly through half a dozen envelopes, froze for a moment on one then passed casually on. Bessie was chattering to Pierre about the flower festival which preceded harvest, and featured a battle of flowers. Mary was clearing the crockery into the big stone sink; her French was not up to Bessie's and she smiled at Pierre, but made no comment. Carol said quietly, 'I must go to the bathroom, Mother. Will you come to church again with Bessie and me?'

'Certainly.' Mary glanced at her daughter. 'Is something the matter?'

'No. Nothing. I'll be with you in a moment. Leave that.'

She did not wait for a reply. The corkscrew stairs had never seemed so inconvenient. She closed her bedroom door carefully and went to the window. The letter was heavy in the pocket of her gathered skirt, though it was only a thin airmail sheet. Even so she left it there while she stared out at the distant peak of their special mountain, the view which had become so dear to them all over the past three years. She had fought quite consciously to make this life all in all, to blot out the memory of that night in Paris when she had so nearly lost her very soul to Jean-Claude Durant. And she had succeeded. He had never attempted to get in touch with her which had been a help in one way, but a terrible blow to her damaged pride in another. Now, suddenly to see his name on the back of this air letter, to see the address 'Algérie', had, quite literally, taken her wits. She needed to orientate herself again. She was Carol Woodford of the Bergerie, near Aix-en-Durance. She could no longer be manipulated or used by . . . anyone.

She took a deep breath of the clear air. Below her, Pierre and Bessie emerged from the house, and Bessie – still chattering-took Pierre to see les haricots blancs, also transported from North-field. Carol reminded herself that she had Bessie too. She had wanted children, and Monica had given her Bessie. She looked beyond the garden to the terraced fields which belonged to her farmer neighbour, Monsieur Lassevour. His sheep had gone further up the mountain for the summer, and he was growing crops of flowers for the parfumeries at Grasse. The French rarely grew anything for mere ornamentation. He had thrown up his hands when she told him that their flower garden was not destined for the scent factories.

She smiled at the thought and drew the letter calmly from her pocket, walked to the chest of drawers for scissors, and cut carefully around the glued edge. She glanced at the signature and read 'Ever yours, Jean-Claude' and sat down on the edge of the unmade bed very suddenly.

Just for a moment she closed her eyes, then began to read determinedly.

'My dear Carol . . .'

Not even his writing looked French. Instead of the typical slanting, spidery spikes which she was used to from all her French contacts, his script was upright and bold.

'Please do not throw this letter away until you have read it – I beg you. It is of great importance, not only to your-self, but to your family. As you see I am in Algeria again

506

and have managed to spend some time on the plateau; in fact last week I travelled with Berbers who knew of Clive Hubert. I cannot explain my anxiety to walk the ground he walked. It is not for his sake of course, but for yours. I will not enter into a one-sided dialogue about that night, Carol. Please believe that I had no idea your regard for Hubert was so deep. You must have realised my feelings for you, and I know your solution was the right one. I have always respected your wish to cut yourself off from Paris and me, until now.

'Carol, the Berbers took me to a Sufi mystic. Did you know that Hubert had been converted to Islam and especially Sufism? I talked with the mystic for some time. Eventually he handed me a tin box which he said had belonged to the pasha. Inside was the original of Hubert's book, hand-written, almost illegible after all this time, but certainly substantially the same as I handed to you in Paris. I wanted to bring it to you. I wanted to impress you, Carol! You see, I am still love-sick and ridiculous! But also I thought it would dispel any suspicions that you might harbour against me. Though surely you must have known I could not have had anything to do with the explosion? I would never have given you the manuscript had I realised its potential danger. It was only later, when I talked with friends, that I learned of the plot, and even then it was so rumour-laden I could not be certain.

'I soon realised that to send you Hubert's book was to put you under threat again, so I resisted that temptation. Instead, I posted it immediately to your publishers in London, and asked them to hold it until the trouble over here is settled . . . which I think will not be long now. There is talk of asking de Gaulle to come out of retirement and put an end to the war. However, Carol, as you will see from the newspapers, some-one has told the press that the book has turned up. Frankly, my dear, I think the risk is very small, but it is there. Please will you leave your cottage for a while? Could you go to England for a holiday? At any rate, do not stay there, where I under-stand you are very vulnerable.

'When I leave here I fly to London to see what is to happen next. I shall stay at a small hotel near Paddington station called the Albion. If you wish to contact me, that is where I shall be. Gaby and I were never together after the night of the explosion. Ever yours, Jean-Claude Durant.'

Carol folded the single sheet of paper and smoothed the crease to knife sharpness. Her heart was hammering and she was breathing quickly. She controlled herself with an effort of will and opened the letter again. She tried to read between the lines: Algeria was war-torn, the Front de Libération Nationale, composed mainly of Arabs, were inflicting savageries which had shocked decent French people into acts of retaliation as bad if not worse in many cases. After Clive's death in 1955 there had been a clamp-down on foreign journalists travelling in the country, but this was probably relaxed now. She knew that Jean-Claude had been in Egypt reporting on the new President Nasser and his nationalisation of the Suez Canal. During *that* ill-fated war she had followed the casualty lists with a trepidation she never consciously admitted to herself. He must have badgered his paper to let him re-enter Algeria as soon as he returned from Egypt.

And Gaby . . . Gaby whom she had suspected of being in collusion with him . . . Gaby and he 'were not together'. Exactly what did he mean by that? She closed her eyes again. She wished he had not discovered Clive's original manuscript. She wanted to forget the whole terrible episode.

She went downstairs and the three women left for church. Theirs was a strangely sedate way of life in the Bergerie, not unlike that of three ladies in the English countryside fifty or sixty years ago. There was more freedom of course; but Bessie's schooling at the convent, their attendance at the village festivals, the enormous interest in the garden and growing things, all gave a structure to their lives that was slow and rhythmical and very pleasant to them. It was not surprising that Carol and her mother appreciated it, but it was unusual for a twelve-year-old girl to feel the same way. Perhaps Bessie's regular visits to Myrtle's chaotic household provided the necessary comparison. Even so she was glad when the service was over and they could walk through the village square in the sunshine and talk to the people they knew. Solange and Brigitte Metier from her class were trailing behind their parents, and Bessie caught them up and asked what they were doing for the vacances.

Brigitte made a face. 'Grandmère is coming. It will be sewing and prayers.'

'All the time?' Bessie asked, wide-eyed.

'Oh no,' Solange grinned wickedly. 'Sometimes it is prayers and then sewing.'

The three of them giggled, then Solange asked, 'You go to England as usual, I suppose? You are so lucky, Bessie.'

It was Bessie's turn to make a face. 'I am not sure. I would rather stay here and go camping. I don't know that Cass has decided.' She added quickly, 'Listen. If we go, could you come with us? Would your parents agree?'

The French girls raised their brows expressively, registering doubt and hope at the same time. Bessie ran back to Carol who was staring aimlessly at the slightly different view of the mountain peak, and put her request. Carol seemed to have some difficulty in understanding.

'Solange and Brigitte . . . where, Bessie? Ah yes. Of course. We could go tomorrow, couldn't we? This afternoon is rather soon, but I think we had better leave tomorrow.'

Bessie stared at her big 'sister' who she knew must really be an aunt, and who made the plans for the little family.

'I thought . . .' she changed her mind, and nodded vigorously. 'Yes. We had better leave tomorrow. Can you talk to Madame Metier?'

So it was arranged.

They took a tent as usual but there was an ancient shepherd's hut six miles up the side of the Victoire mountain, which provided a more permanent shelter for the nights and a fireplace for cooking. They could see as far as the Camargue one way and Nice the other. But the real attraction was the profusion of wild flowers. It was as if the tiny hut had been dropped from the sky into a carpet of aquilegia, gentians, giant saxifrage, moon daisies and a myriad tiny flowers which Bessie and Mary would spend hours identifying and pressing.

On the day they arrived they felt it was sacrilege to track through them with their haversacks, and they did so in single file and on tiptoe. When Carol lifted the wooden latch of the hut and everyone crowded beneath its overhanging eaves, Solange, looking back, immediately exclaimed, 'But they grow again after us!' And Bessie said, awed, 'It's like the Red Sea.'

Mary laughed. 'Not quite. And I don't think Sister Michael would be exactly delighted with the comparison. Come and help me open the shutters.' She went inside the found Carol standing by the fireplace. 'Is everything all right, darling? I can't see a thing. Don't tell me it's full of dead birds!'

Carol seemed to pull herself together. She laughed.

'No, Mother. I don't think anyone has used it since we were here before. Bessie stacked fresh logs in a criss-cross pattern, and here they are, untouched.'

'Good.' Mary knocked up the retaining beams of the shutters and began to lift them down. The one-roomed hut was flooded with sunlight. 'What is it, Carol? Aren't you well?'

'Sorry. I'm dreaming.' Carol smiled quickly and went to the table where five haversacks were piled anyhow. 'What are the girls up to?'

Mary said accurately, 'They are running and screaming.'

Carol managed a laugh, then she walked around the table peering into the rough bunks which had been mangers when the shepherds lived with their flocks. She said, 'I'm glad we came. 'It – it's so normal!'

Mary laughed too. 'Two Englishwomen with three small girls alone on a mountain plateau with the minimum of provisions – normal? You must be mad!'

'Normal for us!' Carol began to unwind sleeping bags. 'If that clothes line is still at the back, I'll hang these out to air. Then we can send the girls for fresh hay. They need a task!' She paused by the door. 'We must be fairly normal, Mother. Otherwise the Metiers would not have entrusted us with their daughters.'

Mary cocked an ironic ear. 'Don't you think they might well have been thankful to be rid of them? With Grandmère arriving too?

Carol laughed again and went out to deploy her forces. Pierre had arrived with a laden mule and the rest of the luggage. Mary spent some time reassuring him that they would be quite all right, the farmhouse was only a mile away and walkers used this route frequently. Then he went away and the wonderful peace of the high place descended on them. Mary knew that Carol had had

510

some bad news, and this was a kind of escape for her. She watched her daughter sweeping out the bunks and the hut as if her life depended on it. And she closed her eyes momentarily and said inside her head, 'Please John, let her be happy. Always.'

It was a halcyon time for all of them. After the heavy heat of summer by the river, the mountain air gave them a new energy. They spent all day out of doors making forays up their special peak to discover new vistas, a waterfall, a bubbling spring, different flowers. They would eat their supper beneath the eaves of the hut, watching wonderful sunsets night after night; then they would spread fresh newspaper over the straw in the bunks and climb into their bags with much crackling and laughter. For the first two nights if one of them turned over the others would wake at the sound, but after that, the air did its work and they slept through Mary rising at six with the dawn, to light the fire and make tea.

The three girls declared they were 'going native', but after an hour of walking barefoot, they took to their sandals again, and the joy of bathing in the stream kept them all very clean. It was Monday when they arrived. On Thursday Pierre came again with fresh food and letters. One of the letters was from the London office telling Carol what she already knew and suggesting that as she had seen the final draft of the Hubert book, she might like to help sort out the jumbled script which was now safely with them. She handed the letter to her mother as soon as they were alone, and Mary read it and pulled her mouth down.

'I knew it was too good to last. When?'

'No hurry. They know I'm on holiday. I could be in Timbuctu for all they know.' She smiled at her mother. 'We'll have another week. It's doing us all good. And then . . . darling, I want you and Bessie to come with me. I know you're not keen on going again so soon after your visit to Dilly Gosling, but . . .' her voice petered out and she coughed. 'If I'm going to see Myrtle again, I'd like you there.'

'Not me. Bessie is your ambassador in Cheltenham.' Mary laughed, then stopped. 'Cass, what is it? Really?'

'Jean-Claude is in London. Incredibly enough he is staying at the old Albion. Can you believe it? Life is so strange. No word from Monica for years, but the links cannot be cut.'

'Of course they cannot. Bessie will always be the link.'

Carol was silent for some time. Then she said, 'You will come with me?'

Mary smiled. 'Yes. Yes, of course.'

That night they heard cowbells. It was an unusual sound during the hours of darkness, and Carol opened the door and peered in its direction. She was suddenly terrified. If they had been 'vulnerable' at the Bergerie, they were doubly so here. The safety of the hut depended entirely on its secrecy, and they had not asked the Metiers to keep silent about their daughters. And Pierre was coming up very fourth day . . .

Lights flickered at the far edge of the plateau. Carol's heart was hammering suffocatingly. She reached behind the door for one of the stout pieces of wood which barred the shutters. Should she wake the girls and send them scurrying into the night to the farm?

Then Bessie's head bounced under her arm.

'Cass! Oh joy everlasting! Angélique is having her calf! Solly! Gitte! Wake up, mes petites! Quick. Coats – socks – where *are* they?' Mary was lighting the lamp, her eyes flashing around in wild surmise. Bessie babbled, 'Gran, didn't we tell you? One of the cows is having her accouchement! Isn't it wonderful? Old Beppo – the cowman – he said we could go. D'you want to come? Cass, what about you?'

They were gone without waiting for an answer. Now that her eyes were used to the darkness, she could recognise Beppo's burly silhouette holding the cow by the horns while Mrs Beppo and the little Beppos crowded around the operational end.

She relaxed tremblingly against the door jamb and closed her eyes.

Mary said, 'All right, darling?'

Carol did not want to mention the word danger to any of them. She did not let it enter her mind. But it was there. She remembered that night when the building off the Avenue Foch and gone up like a torch, killing Henri so needlessly. Somehow that had been partly her doing. She must not let it happen again.

'Fine, Mother. But I imagine we shall have more peace in England!' She tried to make it sound funny, but Mary did not laugh. 'As Professor Joad would say,' she commented, 'it depends on what you mean by peace.'

They called the calf Bluebell, and Bessie pronounced it like the French girls: Bleu-beel. Beppo fenced it off with its mother who was neurotically possessive except where the three girls were concerned. She would actually nudge Bluebell to the fence so that they could stroke her and tell her how beautiful she was. Mary took a lot of photographs of them, and Bessie made sketches of the animals with elongated Disney eyes and smiling mouths.

'Your flower drawings are far more accurate,' Mary commented.

'Oh I know, Grannie. But these are *fun*!' Bessie explained.

On their last full day, the girls roamed further than usual. They were playing at mountaineers and scrambled up a long chute of scree to another very small and unexpected plateau. It was a hard climb and they were breathless and gasping when they reached the top.

Then Gitte saw the hut.

'It's another shepherd's hut!' she exclaimed. 'But why here? There is no grazing – not even for goats.'

The girls approached the tumbledown hovel curiously. Inside, the single room was much smaller than 'their' hut and there were no mangers nor a fireplace.

Solange said knowledgeably. 'It's a climber's hut. Yes? Perhaps halfway up the Victoire?'

Bessie said, 'I claim it in the name of S.B.B.'

'S.B.B.?' the other two asked in unison.

'Solange. Brigitte. And Bessie!'

They all laughed, but then Solange said seriously, 'Yes. Let it be ours. And let us meet here every summer until we are ancien!'

Bessie said, 'Oh joy everlasting! A secret tryst!'

'Where we share our secrets?' asked Brigitte.

'If you like.' Bessie frowned. 'I have no secrets.'

Brigitte giggled. 'We have. Shall we say, Sollie?'

Solange shrugged, embarrassed. 'It is just our parents. We saw them. You understand. Bouncing on the bed.' She shrugged again. 'Anyway, you have the biggest secret of all, chérie. You are adopted.'

Bessie, still puzzled regarding the Metier secret, raised her brows. 'That is a secret, polichinelle! I am—' she struck an attitude - 'a chosen child!'

Brigitte giggled. 'Yes, but the secret is . . . who bounced up and down on a bed before you were born?' She sighed with impatience at Bessie's incomprehension and her sister's red face. 'Who were your parents – your real parents?' she enlarged.

'Does it matter?'

'Naturellement it is of great import. And . . . Maman says she thinks that Carol is your true mother. She thinks that Carol had a wonderful affaire de coêur when she was very young, and when you were born, Mrs Woodford adopted you!' She spread her hands. 'Is it not very romantic?' Bessie was stunned.

When at last she got her breath, she said slowly, 'Cass . . . my mother? She is too young, I think.' She did some calculations in her head. 'She would have been sixteen when I was born.'

Solange shrugged expressively. 'It is possible.'

There was another silence, then Bessie said, 'But why would she not tell me? It would be wonderful!'

'Ah . . .' Gitte rolled her eyes. 'It would also be a disgrace!'

She and her sister started to laugh at the ridiculousness of adults, and after a while Bessie joined in. But she was laughing with sudden excitement. She had never thought about her parentage before; Grannie and Cass had shared their family anecdotes and made them hers as a gift. But if Cass was her real mother, then they were also hers as a right. She felt a great upsurge of joy. She stood on the lip of the plateau where it disintegrated into the long slide of scree, and she shouted at the top of her voice, 'You belong to me! My plateau! My secret hut! My mountain!' Her voice bounced back off the sides of the chute, and before the echoes died she turned to her two friends and said exultantly, 'And I have a boyfriend! There! Another secret which you must tell no-one. I have a boyfriend who thinks I am the absolute bee's knees!'

She spoke in English and very quickly. They could not translate it and before they could ask what she had said, she squatted on her heels and took off down the scree. The back of her cotton skirt was in tatters when she got to the bottom, but she was still laughing.

Carol walked down by herself to tell Pierre to bring the mules unloaded next week, so that their things could be carried back down the mountain. She arrived at the Bergerie without anyone knowing she was there. From the flower terraces of M. Lassevour the surveyed the house and garden carefully. It was exactly as they had left it ten days ago. No broken windows, no ravaged plants. Pierre had obviously been watering the night before, but other than that she could have sworn no-one had crossed the grass to the door.

She slipped her key into the lock as quietly as she could, swung the door wide and stood listening while she counted sixty. Then she went from room to room doing all the things she'd read about in crime books, even to sniffing the air and looking under the beds. Nothing.

Smiling with relief, she left the house again and went down to the village. She met Pierre en route and gave him her message. When she told him they would soon be off to England on business, he threw up his hands.

'The little one will miss the flower festival!' he mourned.

Cass had forgotten that. She hoped they would not have trouble with Bessie.

'Has anyone called at the Bergerie while we have been away, Pierre?' she asked casually as she turned.

'No-one madame.' Like poor Henri, he invariably gave her the courtesy title of madame.

She smiled. 'Of course, I should not enquire. How could you know. You are there infrequently for the watering of the plants.'

He spread his hands. 'I would know, madame. There is only one way to the Bergerie and someone would always tell me if anyone took it.'

'Naturally.' She nodded, well satisfied. 'Thank you, Pierre. Thank you very much.' He looked surprised, and she went on quickly, 'So, we will see you on Thursday. Early, yes? I will begin to pack our things now, but we shall need to clean up and sort the laundry. So . . . early.'

'Certainement, madame.' He took off his cap and held it across his midriff respectfully while she turned and went back up the track to the Bergerie again. He was a comfort and a support, and at that moment she loved all the villagers who kept an eye on the Bergerie, even if they probably did it from sheer curiosity.

She pulled out cases and opened them wide on her bed. The first was easily filled with underwear and night clothes. The second with blouses, skirts and summer dresses. The third was for her files. She went to the desk in the corner, and stopped. The second drawer was not closed.

She stared at it, mesmerised by it, trying to remember whether in her lightning check an hour earlier she might have given it a careless push which hadn't quite closed it. That must be the explanation. No-one could have come to the villa in that hour; she would have passed them on the track; Pierre would have seen them. Nevertheless however carelessly she pushed at drawers, she always waited for them to click into place. She would have shut that drawer properly.

She swallowed and forced herself to walk forward normally in case she was under some kind of surveillance. Her heart hammered frantically, just as it had done two nights ago. She was terrified. She glanced over her shoulder at the dressing-table mirror which invariably tipped forward. It reflected the base of the bed. No-one was beneath it. With a sob of sheer relief she reached the desk and looked carefully around the drawer for a telltale wire. There was nothing. She left it and went downstairs again for a broom. On the cooking range was Mary's enormous iron frying pan. She picked that up too.

Once more she searched the house, catching glimpses of herself in the mirrors, frying pan held high: a ludicrous sight that could not raise even a smile. At last she was back in her own room, allowing her breathing to be very audible now. Crouching low, her pillow held in front of her face, she inserted the broom head into the open drawer and pulled. She jumped and screamed a little as the drawer clattered on to the polished boards, scattering its contents everywhere. Nothing else happened. After a long time she removed the pillow and gazed at the empty drawer. She knew she should laugh. First the calving, and now this. But she, who was usually good at laughing at herself, could not do so now. She only just stopped herself from weeping.

With forced calm, she replaced the pillow on her bed and knelt down to clear up the mess on the floor. It must have been her own doing; it must have. But she knew it wasn't.

Everything went according to plan. It had been a wonderful holiday and though the French girls wished it could have lasted longer, they accepted without question that Carol's work was taking her to London and that Bessie and Mrs Woodford must go

516

with her. Carol knew that her mother would be a willing companion once her first reluctance had been overcome, but she had expected objections from Bessie. After all, Boris Denning was away. But Bessie was strangely elated about everything. She said, 'Families stick together, don't they? Through thick and thin!' And although it was the sort of clarion call Bessie often made, this time it was different. Carol couldn't put her finger on the difference, but it was there.

She was like a cat on hot bricks. Moving slowly down the mountain in the wake of the loaded mules, she constantly glanced around her, and when they reached the neighbouring farm she ran ahead and was there to welcome them at the door when they arrived.

'Everything is fine,' she panted. 'And a letter from Liv by the look of it—' She brandished an envelope.

'Of course everything is fine,' Mary said rather tartly. 'You were here only a few days ago.'

Bessie called, 'I'll go on down with Sollie and Gitte, Cass. See you for déjeuner.'

'We have a great deal to do if we're to be off tomorrow, Bessie,' Mary objected. But Carol seemed relieved.

'It'll give us a chance to get cracking,' she explained to her mother.

By the oddest coincidence, the letter from Liv was to ask them all to come and stay for as long as they liked. Carol couldn't get over it.

'Myrtle is staying with Liv too. She's expecting again – how marvellous. Oh, it will be much easier if we're all there. How very sweet of Liv!'

They flew out the next day, landing at Stansted without mishap. It was tea time when their taxi drew up outside the Albion. The August day had turned brassy and breathless; thunder was on the way and the smell of sulphur from Paddington station made Carol feel sick.

The new owners had filled the foyer with flowers and each doorway was striped with multi-coloured plastic strips. It was a jumble of such contradictions: Irish linen curtains and bedspreads, paper towels in the cloakrooms. But the welcoming atmosphere was still prevalent. Mary said to Bessie, 'Your Aunt

517

Monica was the manageress here. She had this room built on to the back of the house. Isn't it nice?'

Bessie, who had never met Aunt Monica, though she knew her from the many apocryphal stories told by Carol and Mary, glanced around without much interest.

'It's all right. But I don't like the place very much. Right in the middle of all these streets—'

'The park isn't far,' Carol said quickly. 'And anyway, you and Grannie will be going to Northfield tomorrow. You'll see all your old friends.'

Bessie shrugged, withholding co-operation, her esprit de corps a thing of the past. 'They'll have gone away for their summer hols. And Boris isn't back yet. And Aunt Liv doesn't live in Northfield.'

Mary glanced at Carol and said, 'You could have stayed with Solange and Brigitte, Bessie. You chose to come with us.'

'S'ppose so.' Bessie shrugged again, clinging to her Frenchness. She added, 'Anyway, I came so that the three of us could stay together. I didn't know you were going to stay in London, Cass.'

'A few days. A week at the most.' Carol was ill at ease. She had not seen this new room before. Big French doors opened into the small sooty garden, and a handful of people sat outside, swatting at the gnats. She checked them over with a quick glance and saw no-one she knew, but she was anxious to get out of this public place to their rooms. They need not have come here. Some sense of fairness had made her force a meeting with Jean-Claude; she knew now that decision had been a mistake.

For at least the third time she explained the arrangements to Bessie. 'I have to check a special manuscript that has turned up out of the blue, darling. That's all. It won't take long.' She looked helplessly at their luggage. 'I thought Mrs Arlen had gone for someone to help with the bags.'

Mary said soothingly, 'She has, darling. You and Bessie are so impatient. Look, I'll see to the luggage and settling us in our rooms. You two go outside and sit quietly.'

Carol said eagerly, 'No. You go, Mother. Please. I'm fidgety.' She blinked. 'It's this place. We shouldn't have come here, perhaps.'

'Why on earth not? It seems entirely appropriate to me. And

518

you need to be here to liaise with your Monsieur Durant.' Mary watched her daughter closely. That had been Carol's excuse for staying at the Albion; Mary thought it was probably her way of facing her own particular weakness.

Bessie said impatiently, 'Oh come on, Grannie. I'm fed up with standing about like a potted palm in a patisserie.'

Carol and Mary laughed as Bessie had intended, and Carol left them and went into the hall in search of Mrs Arlen.

There was no sign of Jean-Claude, either that evening or at breakfast the next day. Carol felt her nerves were as taut as violin strings; every time a door opened she jumped. Finally, just before she took her mother and Bessie to Paddington, she enquired at the desk for him.

'Ah, Mr Durant. He has gone to Paris for the rest of this week, Miss Woodford. To see his wife apparently.' Mrs Arlen smiled. 'You know the gentleman?'

Carol swallowed. The sense of anti-climax was appalling.

'We are colleagues,' she said. 'Publishing. Books.'

The smile became roguish. 'I wondered if he was a film star. So handsome.'

Carol forced an answering smile. 'Yes.' She wished it were not so. His classic Latin good looks somehow denigrated everything she had felt that night two years ago. Had it been just a schoolgirl crush for a handsome man? She turned away, sickened by her own thoughts. 'I won't be in for lunch, Mrs Arlen. I'll go straight to my office from Paddington and work through until this evening.' It was the obvious thing to do; she would need to take her mind off from Bessie and her mother, and she ought to start work as soon as possible.

It was agony saying goodbye. They were often apart, and in any case she would be joining them at Liv's in two or three days; nevertheless this parting was particularly painful. Carol took a taxi to Blackfriars, trying not to think of Jean-Claude and his return to Gaby. He had lied to her in his letter, but that should not surprise her. Nothing should surprise her about human nature. And she was lucky; she had Bessie. She had wanted a child, not a husband. She surely had the best of both worlds.

Ralph Morrish greeted her in the tiny foyer of the offices. People coming here for the first time had difficulty in realising that this old Dickensian building housed the most important

519

publishers in Europe, but Carol was always delighted that the two brothers who still held the reins refused to consider major modernisations. She shook Ralph's hand warmly; he had created the French post and made sure it went to her six years ago, and it was he who had made it easy for her to move to Marseilles after the fire.

'Carol. We did not expect you so soon. Monsieur Durant has taken a couple of days off to see his family. He particularly wants to collaborate with you on this book.' He drew her closer and kissed her cheek. 'It is good to see you, my dear. Are you alone? Is Bessie with you? Your mother?' Ralph had met them both and was a firm favourite.

'Yes and no. We arrived yesterday, but they have gone to see friends at home. I hope to join them as soon as I have finished here.' Carol smiled. 'They send their love of course. How are you, Ralph?'

'Very well. And it is obvious you are, too. You are so brown, Carol.'

She could accept compliments from him without suspicion.

'We've been camping – living outside for nearly a fortnight. It suited us all.' She asked after his family and colleagues. Someone brought coffee and they went up the first flight of stairs to his office and settled themselves in chairs by a window looking out on the river.

Ralph leaned forward. 'This book, Carol. Quite a find. Wonderful from the point of view of the firm. I understand, however, it could be dangerous for you. Monsieur Durant is most anxious to dissociate you from it. But we need you to look through it, verify it, if you like. You read the finished copy, didn't you?'

'Not all of it. About half. I don't see it as dangerous now, Ralph. You have it and will publish it whatever part I play. I should think Monsieur Durant is in an invidious position, however. His newspaper will not like him giving the manuscript to you. And he represents the imperialists' views. Clive Hubert's book is pro Algerian independence. Very much so.'

'You are not worried for yourself, then?'

'No. I am a very small cog in a very large wheel.'

'I can't agree there. But I am inclined to agree that you are in no personal danger. Otherwise we would not have asked you to come over. As you say, it is different for Monsieur Durant. But he chose to come – he was adamant actually.'

'Really?' Carol thought of her panic on the plateau; the half-hour of sheer terror in the Bergerie. Had Jean-Claude deliberately planted that fear in an effort to drive her into his company again? Or was that her schoolgirl wishful thinking?

She took a deep breath. 'Anyway I'll work on it in the office, Ralph, if I may. Then obviously I shall be perfectly safe.' She put her cup down. 'In fact, I'll start now. Have you got the manuscript here?'

He stood up and went to a safe in the wall.

'Durant has frightened us into locking it away!' He laughed wryly as he took out a bulky package and put it on his desk.

She did not respond. The sight of it reminded her of the first time she had seen it; how free she had been then. She stood up. Of course she had been free since then. The Bergerie had offered solace and a new life. Coming here like this had been her choice. There had been no coercion at all.

'I'll read it in two or three days, Ralph.'

He shook his head, still smiling. 'I don't think so, my dear. Wait until you open it.' He drew out a chair. 'Come on. Sit here where you can still see the bend in the river. Do you need the fan? No? Then I'll send up more coffee and collect you at one o'clock sharp for lunch.'

He was as good as his word, and by that time Carol knew that to do Clive's work justice, she would have to give at least a week to her reading. She sipped her coffee and closed her eyes against the almost illegible script and the wide sweep of the Thames, as she tried to remember again the small, self-effacing man with the enormous sense of justice. It was necessary to hold him in her mind and to forget the other man who was so different.

She worked through the weekend and by the following Thursday the end was in sight. Jean-Claude's continued absence made it easier by the minute to forget him. Clive's enormous word canvas of a country still living in the eighteenth century was breathtaking. At times she could smell the gunpowder from the cannon of deys, at others the French war-time government seemed little different. She worked chapter by chapter; reading, typing, some of the more illegible passages and making notes. Sometimes there were insertions, then deletions. But she was gradually pulling the book into some kind of order so that the typist could begin to make a finished copy.

The weather was still sulphurically hot. Ralph wanted her to go to his home in Maidenhead where it was comparatively cool by the river, but something took her back to the Albion each night. She was living in a curious limbo peopled by the Arabs from Clive's book, and the sultry weather made it more real. After dinner in the front of the house, she would sit in the new extension with her coffee and respond to desultory remarks from the other guests. Nobody remembered Mon, certainly no-one had heard of the Goslings.

She telephoned Liv's number twice a day and spoke to Bessie and her mother. They seemed odd; distant, even evasive. She put it down to her own peculiar state of mind. On Thursday evening she told them that one more day would see an end to her work. She could join them at the weekend.

'Oh, joy everlasting,' Bessie responded in a flat voice. 'Can we go to the baths or something? It's stifling here.'

'Well, of course. Anything you like.'

'You might change your mind. Your haven't had an all-girls-together meeting since you were sixteen, Auntie Liv says. You might want to do that.'

'Don't be silly, Bessie. Auntie Myrt will be much too busy with the children for us to go off together. We shall have our chats when you're in bed.' There was a silence and Carol frowned at the receiver. 'Let me talk to Grannie, darling.'

But her mother did not sound quite right either.

'Of course everything is all right, Cass. Why on earth wouldn't it be?'

'I simply wondered whether there was an atmosphere or something. So many of you in Liv's house at one time. She's rather house-proud, isn't she? Is it awkward for you to talk. Just say yes or no.'

'No.'

'Is Myrtle behaving badly?'

'No.'

'What about Liv?'

'Same answer.'

'Well, all right then. Listen, I'll see you on Saturday definitely. And if it's too much of a good thing, we'll go to an hotel. How's that?'

'Fine. Just fine. Take care of yourself. And be prepared.'

'For what?'

There were muffled voices on the line, then her mother said quickly, 'Anything. Goodbye, darling.' And the line went dead.

She went back to the office that evening and worked until she had finished. It was quite dark; the desk lamp made a pool of light around the typewriter and scattered papers. Outside the glitter of the river was just discernible beneath a murky moon; the heat made the air feel thick and tangible. Carol tipped her chair and stretched enormously. Her eyes felt gritty yet damp. Clive had died for this book and she had done her best to ensure that his death had not been in vain. She should feel relief; she had done the entire backbreaking job without Jean-Claude's doubtful help. She could leave earlier than she had planned and thereby avoid seeing him. And she could surprise Bessie and her mother.

But there was no relief. She wondered now why she had returned this evening to finish off. She had effectively scuppered her reasons for staying and seeing Jean-Claude, if that was what she had really wanted all the time.

She closed her eyes and put her hands over them. Tears oozed between her fingers. She did not know what she wanted any more. Poor Clive. At last he had known. Beneath that diffident surface he had been a great man.

Wearily she found a handkerchief and dried her face, then tidied the papers into a pile and locked everything away in the safe. She scribbled a note for Ralph and propped it on the typewriter. She would call into the office before she went back to France, but she left Liv's telephone number in case there were any queries. Then she rang for a taxi.

It was two o'clock when she let herself into the Albion. Mrs Arlen had given her a key and told her to make herself a hot drink if she felt like it, but her one thought was to go to bed and find oblivion in sleep. The plastic door strips stirred momentarily as she closed the door behind her, then subsided into the stillness of the breathless night. She crept upstairs and went to the bathroom, then unlocked her door.

At first it did not register that the light was on. She leaned down to unbuckle her sandals, and then froze in an awkward stoop. Even without the light she should have known she was not alone in the room, and her immediate thought was that the intruders who had visited the Bergerie had found her here in

523

London. And then she saw a pair of feet in very feminine high-heeled sandals; she let her eyes travel up a pair of very beautiful nylon-clad legs, until she could see a whole person sitting in her bedside chair. A woman, hair as black as a raven's wing, a book face down on her lap, a strange, twisted sort of smile on her beautiful face; it was Monica.

Carol gave a gasping sob and straightened, arms already extended in welcome.

'Mon! Dear God . . . it's you! Oh my dear girl – where have you come from? Oh Mon—'

She cast herself on the unresponsive figure, her previous state of mind forgotten in a mixture of relief and joy. After a hiatus of perhaps two seconds, Monica too gave a sob and scrambled her arms around Carol's neck. The book fell to the floor; somehow Monica stood up and the girls did a kind of dance, clutching each other convulsively, speaking single-word sentences, laughing meaninglessly.

'How—?'

'Surprise—'

'Where?'

'Liv's. Over a week now.'

'See you.'

'Mother.'

'Nearly gave the game away.'

'Oh . . . Mon!' Carol drew off slightly to look into the familiar face. It was eleven years. The brown skin was smoother, almost enamelled; the plucked eyebrows were thicker but just as definitive; the pouting mouth was firmer, the eyes as guarded as before. 'You . . . you're beautiful! Like a film star! Oh Mon!'

'And you haven't changed either.'

'Worse luck.'

'Stupid woman. You're lovely and you don't know it. Hasn't anyone told you that?'

'Stop it, Mon. Sit down. Tell me. Everything.'

'How can I? You're punch-drunk. Get to bed. I've got a room down the hall. I'll see you tomorrow. Midday.'

'No. Mon, stay. I can't sleep, I'm too wound up. This is absolutely right, you coming – being here – now. At this moment. I'm in a state. I need you. Don't go.'

'Okay.' Mon opened her hands in a gesture typically American. She turned to the bed table. 'There's coffee here in a Thermos. I've been drinking it to keep me awake. D'you want some?'

'Yes. Please. You shouldn't have waited up. But I'm glad you did.'

'I nearly didn't. Then I got damned worried. I was going to give you another hour then ring the police.'

'You could have rung the office.'

'Yes. But I still wanted to surprise you.'

'You did. Oh God, you did.' She took the proffered cup and laughed hysterically. 'I thought you were the terrorists again. Oh God.'

'I heard. From your mother and from Myrtle. You shouldn't be caught up in this F.L.N. business, Cass. For Christ's sake. There's Bessie to consider.'

'I know. I'm out of it now. The whole thing is finished and done with.' Carol sipped, eyes closed. Then she sat on the bed and after another pause, Monica sat by her. Carol opened her eyes and smiled. 'You being here . . . you've changed things. You've sort of taken hold of fate . . .' she giggled. 'You're a kind of deus ex machina.'

'You mean I've thrown a spanner in the works?' Monica said, not smiling.

'I don't know. Just banished the nightmares, I think. Done away with the uncertainty.'

'You're bushed.'

Carol nodded. 'I'm bushed.' She drank the coffee and put the cup from her. 'Mon. I'm so pleased to see you. Of course.' She looked into the black eyes, so like Bessie's. 'How long are you here?'

'I don't know. It sort of depends on you.'

'What about your husband? Bob.'

'I don't know about him either. He's got someone else.'

'Mon. I'm so sorry. So sorry.' She looked at her friend. There was no expression on the carefully made-up face. She said, 'Come back with us. To the Bergerie. You'll love it.'

'I've got my own place, Cass. And – with Elizabeth – it could be a home.' There was a pause, then she added very calmly, 'And I want Elizabeth. I want to make a home for my daughter, Cass. I'm in a position to do that, you see. And you always said if ever I

525

wanted her back, I could have her.' She stood up, picked up her handbag and went to the door. 'I wanted to tell you immediately even though you're so tired. I've met Elizabeth. We've been together a great deal over the past few days. We get on well.' She opened the door. 'Sorry. I always believed in dropping my bombshells quickly, if you remember. Get to bed now and we'll talk about it in the morning. Good night.'

Incredibly, she was gone. Carol made no attempt to stop her. She felt frozen to the bed, literally frozen solid in spite of the heat. She might have told herself the whole interview had not happened, except that the bedside table held two empty coffee cups.

After a long while she took off her dress and slid into her old-fashioned nightdress. Then she lay on top of the bed and closed her eyes.

526

Ten

Carol fell into a fitful sleep just before the early dawn. She was conscious of the hotel coming to life with the sound of bathrooms and breakfast, but she did not have the will to struggle out of her murky half-world and face reality. Even when she forced herself to roll over and look at the clock, she played a kind of gruesome mental game. Just out of sight where she knew her hairbrush lay on the dressing table, were some unpleasant facts. She couldn't quite see them though she knew they were there. She registered the time, nine-thirty, and closed her eyes quickly in case her gaze should stray to the hairbrush. Then she forced herself to think of the Bergerie and the little shepherd's hut halfway up the Victoire, where they had been only a few days ago.

After five minutes tears oozed from her closed eyes and ran saltily into her mouth, and she sat up, angry with herself.

'Maudlin,' she said aloud and very calmly. And then, 'Whether you had stayed there or come here, it would have been the same. Mother and I always knew that we had Bessie on loan. We've had her for nearly twelve years. Wouldn't you think we could be grateful for that?' She closed her eyes again and took a long trembling breath. Then she whispered, 'Monica is my best friend. My best friend.'

She swung her legs out of bed and sat for a moment, holding her head. Fleetingly she remembered the fuss about Clive's book; her palpitations about whether she might meet Jean-Claude again. That all seemed petty now. Her ridiculous fear on the mountain and in her bedroom at the Bergerie had been practically self-delusion. She had wanted to run into Jean-Claude's arms, so she had fabricated reasons for so doing. And all the time, fate had this in store. A blow more terrible than any explosion.

Her head throbbed and she felt very sick. She had eaten dinner

527

last night before going back to the office – she recalled all that with difficulty – but perhaps she needed food. As if in reply to the thought there was a knock on the door and Mrs Arlen appeared with a tray.

'Are you all right, Miss Woodford?'

Curious eyes glanced at the ravaged bed and carelessly discarded clothes. Already the hotel owner knew that this guest was normally very neat.

'Your friend Mrs Gallagher said you weren't very well last night after all that work. She asked me to bring you your breakfast at ten o'clock if you hadn't come down. And give you this letter from her.'

Carol switched her eyes from Mrs Arlen's face to the tray. Her head throbbed alarmingly.

'Come on now. Sit back on the bed.' Mrs Arlen put the tray down and tried to lift Carol's legs. Carol flapped her away feebly.

'I'm better up. A touch of migraine. That's all.' She forced a sickly smile. 'I didn't realise Mrs Gallagher was leaving. She *is* leaving?'

'Oh she's gone, my dear. She wanted to leave before the traffic got bad. It will all be explained in her letter. Here, let me pour you a nice cup of tea and you'll fell better. Do you need an aspirin?'

'No. Fine. Honestly.' Carol took the tea and gulped too quickly. The roof of her mouth burned agonisingly.

'I'll leave you then.' Mrs Arlen made for the door, excusing herself at some length. Thankfully Carol closed her eyes again and let the steam from the cup soothe the front of her face. She wondered if she really was ill. She put the cup down and fumbled in her handbag for aspirin. She would have some after all and lie still until she felt better. She couldn't face Monica's letter yet.

An hour later, with her head still thumping as thoughts milled inside her brain, she opened it. Words hopped about on the single page; she picked out 'sorry' and 'barren' and then blinked hard and brought the whole thing into focus. Monica's writing had always been atrocious. Carol had to concentrate.

'Cass. I cannot face you so am leaving early. I'm not exactly running again, but almost. I'm sorry, my dear. I did not realise how hard it would hit you. But Cass, she is my daughter, and the doctors in New York say I cannot have any more. Can you imagine what it is like to be barren when you already have a child? My

528

marriage is over. Elizabeth is all I have. Can you understand? I shall say nothing, but please help me. Join us as soon as you can and suggest Elizabeth and I have a holiday together. Or something. Anything, Cass. Please. Forgive me. Mon. P.S. You still have your mother.'

Carol closed her eyes again and lay very still. Unbidden mental pictures of Monica flashed by like flipped pages in a photograph album. Monica clouting Liv with her satchel; Monica telling them brutally that she had 'lost her virginity'; Monica announcing she was pregnant. There was something ruthless about the girl; when she felt she had to do something she did it as quickly as she could. Like ripping off a bandage. Like grasping a nettle.

With heart-stopping suddenness, the telephone rang. Carol snatched at it, convinced it was Bessie full of questions, full of . . . anger? It was Ralph.

'I can see you have finished, Carol. But are we not to see you again?'

'I should not be here now, Ralph. I want to join my family as soon as I can.'

'You worked all night and overslept,' he guessed.

'Yes. More or less.'

'Listen, Carol. You've been wonderful. I will send the proofs to the Bergerie. And if there is anything – not only with work. I like to think we're friends.'

'Thank you, Ralph. I do too.' She could so easily have wept again; she must be sickening for something.

'This whole thing has been a strain, Carol. Are you going to be all right? Marion keeps asking me to get you to come down to Maidenhead for a break. Bessie and your mother too, of course.'

'No. Really. Thanks, Ralph, but . . .' For a moment she almost told him then and there. 'Actually there are a few domestic problems. I need to go to Birmingham. But thanks again.'

'Bear it in mind. Any time.'

She replaced the receiver carefully and nibbled at some cold toast. Then she got up and began to tidy her room. There was a train at two something. She would catch that. She needed to be in Birmingham. Monica might say something to Bessie. And why had Bessie sounded odd on the phone? Her mother too. She must get up there as soon as she could.

She put her case near the door for Mr Arlen to collect, shouldered her bag and pushed her hat down to meet the knot of hair at
her nape. Then with a final checking glance around the room, she
opened the door. Jean-Claude stood there, hand raised to knock.

For a long moment they stared at each other. She saw that he
had changed physically. His black, crisp hair was blotched with
grey, and his dark eyes were no longer knowing and confident,
they were wise and rather tired. His shoulders were slightly bent.
It was only three years since they had shared that night together,
but he was different.

Seeming to become aware of his lifted hand, he made a small
apologetic sound and put it in his jacket pocket. He still did not
look French. His jacket was leather-patched, his flannels would
be out of the place on the Champs Elysées. He wore an open-
necked shirt. After Ralph's formal office suits, he looked as if
he'd just returned from a conventional seaside holiday.

She said, 'It's you.'

The small apologetic sound came again. 'Yes. I wanted . . .
I'm sorry . . . you were leaving. I should have let you . . . go.'

'The book is read and I have to go to Birmingham.'

'Ah yes. Your mother. And your small sister. I understand.'
He seemed to droop, as if surrendering to something, or someone, much stronger. But neither of them moved from the
doorway.

She said, 'Gaby? Was Gaby all right?'

'Yes. She will not divorce. We do not go to church, we had a
civil marriage at the mairie. But she claims she does not believe in
divorce.'

'I did not know. I mean that you wished for . . . wanted . . .'

'It is you I love. You know that.'

'No!' It was a protest rather than a negation. She blurted, 'You
don't know about me! There's Bessie—'

'Of course I know. She is your child. I always knew that.
Perhaps it was one of the reasons . . . not so, I always loved you.'

Carol cried out again, 'No!' And then she put her hands to her
face. 'Bessie belongs to my friend. My schoolfriend. And now
she wants her back. And I cannot stop her – we always agreed –
she was a trust – Mother and I had her on trust – she was a kind
of honour for us. And Monica cannot have any more children
and she wants Bessie back!'

Tears spouted between her fingers. One hand was gloved and she tried frantically to wipe at the tears with the soft kid.

He said, 'A-a-ah,' as only a Frenchman could say it, and she noted fleetingly that his origins were still there somewhere. Then she was in his arms and his cheek was against hers and he murmured in her ear, 'Reposes. Ma pauvre . . .' and the tears ran between them, into his neck and hers. She could no longer control herself; the silent weeping escalated into tearing sobs. He lifted her feet clear of the floor and moved inside the room, closed the door with a kick, sat her on the bed.

'Now. Now. chérie.' He found a handkerchief and mopped. 'Don't speak. It is nothing. An eruption of the heart, of the soul. It is good. It is good.' His hand beneath the handkerchief cradled her face. 'That night after the fire . . . this should have happened then. So much control is not good.'

Her hat was hanging from a hairpin. She tore it off.

'I look a mess,' she wailed. 'I wanted so much to see you yet I was determined it should not happen. And now – now – this!'

'Carol. Darling girl. Darling woman. You are beautiful to me always. So un-un-obvious. You know?'

Her sob hiccoughed into a laugh. 'Of course. So unobvious no-one can see it!'

'Always you must laugh at yourself. Listen, my Carol. You are a special human being. Such a special human being cannot be kept in an obvious body. Obvious hair. Obvious face. It has to be . . . encased . . . in something very special. A kind of asceticism. A kind of strength.'

She had to stop him. She looked up, eyes and nose liquid. 'Oh . . . Jean-Claude.' And she kissed him.

It was a circumspect English kiss, but it stunned him into silence. Words, conventional gestures, solace, concern, all went out of the window. He let the handkerchief fall and stared at her again, one hand on her shoulder, the other lying against her neck.

After a long time when she too neither moved nor seemed to breathe, he whispered, 'So be it.' And then he cupped her face and bent his head to hers.

At first his kisses alarmed her and she had to hold herself still against an urge to run. Then she sensed a reverence about them which was infinitely reassuring. He touched her mouth with his over and over again, as if sipping were, and very tentatively she began to relax. Her eyes closed; she let his hands take the weight of her head. She moved her own hands to his neck and held him to her longer. The ungloved hand felt his ears, the rough short hair at the base of his skull. She remembered them from before. She remembered that it was not like Malcolm Lennox at the wedding party. It was not an invasion, a demand. It was not like that. Together they tasted the wine.

At some moment, he unpinned her hair so that it fell around her shoulders, still in sun-bleached stripes from her mountain holiday. It gave her confidence; she knew it was ample and deeply waved. Incredibly, beneath his touch, she did indeed begin to feel beautiful.

'Carol.' He traced the contours of her face with his thumbs. 'I would like – so much – to consummate this love. But I cannot offer . . . respectability.'

She began to laugh. His Frenchness had come to the fore just in time to sabotage any hint of a sordid seduction scene.

She sat back, seeing his uncertainty, remembering the suave Parisian of two years ago who had been so sure of himself.

'A-a-ah,' she deliberately mimicked his accent. 'A-a-ah, Jean-Claude. You can offer me the whole world. What would I want with respectability?'

He smiled wryly. 'Shall I ever really know you, Carol? Will you always surprise me completely?' He slid out of his jacket then touched the back of her hand. 'Are you certain, my darling? I cannot lose you now.'

She stood up and with calm deliberation unbuttoned her blouse and took it off. She unzipped her skirt and let it fall to the floor. As his hand touched her shoulders she was conscious of his warmth melting her cold and knew that this could not have happened if Monica hadn't turned up when she did and claimed Bessie. Somehow this blinding happiness now lightened that awful event. She saw, in its clarity, that Bessie could never be taken from them; she could live elsewhere perhaps, be happy elsewhere, but she belonged to the Woodfords. Everything seemed inevitable and leading to this moment. The horrors were woven into the good things to make a whole: the Mussolini man, ludicrous and sickening, juxtaposed with the tragedy of her father's death and led relentlessly into the adoption of Bessie. The terror of the explosion at the Avenue Foch had seemed pointless. Now she saw that it had enabled Jean-Claude to go back to Algeria and find Clive's manuscript, so that she knew without doubt that he loved her.

Her thoughts described a full circle in that protracted moment of awareness between them, and then, gently, they came together like travellers at the end of a long journey.

He wanted to come with her to Birmingham, but she could not agree to that.

'I have committed myself to you, my dearest. But it would be unfair to expect Mother . . . Bessie . . . the others – no, I cannot present them with a fait accompli just yet. Forgive me. I am not ashamed of our union. You know that.'

He nodded. 'I am being selfish, Carol. I do not want to be away from you ever again. Also, I am frightened. That you will change.' He was propped on one elbow, looking at her. She lay, totally relaxed, her arms above her head. He touched the pale, blue-veined underside of her elbow, then the swell of her breast, then the concave curve at the top of her hip. 'I cannot believe it, my darling. You have been inside my head for so long. And now, you are here.' He laughed. 'I thought always you would run. But you are . . . here!' He put his face into her neck and held her close, and she cradled his head and smiled blindly at the ceiling. There was a word game she and Mother played with Bessie on journeys: word collections, Bessie called it. She started now with happiness . . . not enough. Happiness. Joy. Ecstasy. She said aloud, 'Deliriosity.'

He lifted his face, dark eyes wide. 'Deliree what?'

'That's what I'm suffering from. Deliriosity.'

'Oh, my Carol. You are so English. So mad.'

'And you . . . you are so very dear to me.'

They were lost again in laughter and tears and their special kind of communion. But at last it was settled that she would go to Birmingham that evening and he would stay in London, see Ralph, check her work on the manuscript and wait until she could join him. Then they would make more decisions.

'Will you be all right, chérie? This Monica, will she really take your Bessie?'

She said soberly, 'I don't know. Monica is – used to be – a very determined person.'

533

'She will have to take into account Bessie's wishes. I do not think the child will want to leave you and your mother.' He spread his hands, 'And yet . . . how will she take me, Carol? Might my sudden arrival in your life drive her away?'

'I don't know that either.'

'Carol, I will not interfere with your life in Provence. I will visit you sometimes . . . whenever you tell me I may do so.'

She smiled. 'A clandestine affaire? I am hopeless at intrigue, Jean-Claude.'

'I know that. But if – I want you to know that you may tell me always when to go. I will understand.'

She almost wept again. She kissed his eyes and nose and then his mouth. And then she laughed. 'When did I take off my glove?'

He laughed too. Like all lovers they firmly believed that tomorrow would take care of itself.

Liv thought she might die: either of sheer exhaustion or terrible, soul-shaking loneliness. Two weeks ago she had returned home with Monica. Inexplicably – because after all she had not been going to succumb to Malcolm's undeniable charms – she was disgraced. She had explained everything to Monica, and Monica had accepted her explanations and smiled into Malcolm's eyes and he had smiled back.

Monica had said to Liv as if humouring her, 'We'll go back to Northfield together, shall we darling? Perhaps I can help to keep Mallie out of your fishpond. I shouldn't worry too much about Myrtle. I think she is probably coping very well in her own way.'

Malcolm had actually laughed aloud at this, all through Liv saying defensively, 'It's all very well, taking it so lightly. She's expecting again at any minute. It's just too much for her. I thought Malcolm might listen to my suggestion about a residential school for Mallie. But he's as bad as Myrtle—'

'Mallie's best at home,' Malcolm had said defensively, closing the subject for good and all. 'But it was good of you to come down to see me, Liv.' He turned that glinting smile on her. 'I appreciated it. No regrets?'

She flushed dark red again. She had grabbed at a coat in the hall and told Monica she was going upstairs for a bath, but she was aware that Monica did not believe her. She wanted to say,

'Yes, I'm full of regrets. I've made an idiot of myself. Acted like a bitch on heat one minute and a frigid schoolgirl the next. I wish I'd never come.'

But she didn't say that.

'Not at all, Malcolm.' She turned to Monica, though she did not meet her amused gaze. 'The four of us have been friends for years. We're like one big happy family.'

Monica nodded. 'So I gathered. Sorry to barge in. I've been staying with Dilly Gosling and she told me that Cass and Elizabeth might be here. So I turned up on the off-chance.'

'Not this year. Myrtle was rabbiting on about some book or other which might bring Carol to London – to see her publishers, you know.' Liv began to feel in control again. 'Anyway, I shall have to get back home. Reggie is expecting me. Have you booked into a Cheltenham hotel, Mon?'

'No.'

'Why don't you come with me then? We've got heaps of room and we three girls have got a lot of talking to do!' She attempted a laugh. It sounded slightly hysterical.

Monica said, 'Actually, I've hired a car. It's outside. Perhaps we could drive up together? Could we make it tomorrow though – I'm bushed. I'd love it, Liv. If you're sure . . .' She had lost some of her veneer; she wanted to come. Liv straightened her back. It was all so ridiculous. Of course everything was going to be all right.

But back home it was obviously not all right. She had done nothing, but Reggie acted as if she had. And Myrtle too, was curiously distant. They both kissed Monica with surprise, but not amazement. They were in a world of their own. Not that night, because she was so tired, but the next night, she put her arms around Reggie and asked if she should take off her nightie.

'No thanks, darling,' he said as if she'd offered him a biscuit. 'I'm rather tired. Heavy day at the office.'

'And I bet Myrtle had you running after the kids every minute on Tuesday, didn't she?' She wanted him to criticise Myrtle. To reassure her that he would prefer to be without children.

He said coldly, 'We both ran after them, Liv. That's how it is with children. I enjoyed it and it didn't tire me at all.'

The trouble was, it did tire Liv. It was lovely for the three girls

535

to be together again, and at Mon's suggestion Liv wrote to Cass and asked her to join them. Mon had lots to tell them and she had gifts for them too. Lingerie such as they'd never seen before, and make-up by the sackful. She talked about Fifth Avenue and Macy's, and the wonderful apartment she had in Beekman Place. She hardly mentioned her husband. Liv felt that she and Mon still had a great deal in common; funny, it had always been the two of them pairing off in the old days. She would have liked a tête-à-tête, with Mon, but the opportunity could not arise just yet. There was so much to organise, so much to do. Meals were endless, so were bath times, play times, reading-aloud times.

Then came the phone call from Carol. It was incredible that Myrtle had been proved right; it was all something to do with this wretched book she kept on about. Anyway whatever it was, Carol and Bessie and Mrs Woodford were coming home, and Carol chose to stay with Liv.

Liv thought this might give her an edge over Myrtle. Myrtle was the one who had Bessie and wrote to Carol. Yet Carol had accepted Liv's invitation.

Myrtle said, 'It'll be nice for Mrs Woodford to be able to pop into Northfield and see all her old friends.'

'Yes.' Liv could afford to be generous about it. She smiled. 'Perhaps we could get along to the Haunted House one afternoon. That would make the reunion absolute, wouldn't it?'

Mon said quickly, 'Don't tell Carol I'm here. Let it be a surprise.'

'Okay.' Myrtle hugged Mallie to her shoulder and spoke over his head. 'She'll be so pleased to see you, Mon. You two were always close, weren't you?'

And Liv felt lonely again.

Mrs Woodford looked different. Not really younger, but more relaxed, more free-and-easy. She had been a mother, a matronly figure, respected by everyone who knew her in Northfield. Now she was not matronly. Her grey hair could look ash blonde in sunlight, and it was very short and brushed upward like Ingrid Bergman's, and the lines in her face shot upwards too when she smiled, which was often. But as far as Liv was concerned, the real shock was Bessie.

Liv had not seen Bessie for some time, probably since Myrtle's wedding. She had always thought of her as 'belonging' to the Woodfords. She was convinced that Bessie was the result of some ghastly experience Carol had suffered as a teenager. Now she had to reverse her ideas; turn them inside-out. Because with Monica and Bessie side by side under one roof; it was quite obvious who belonged to whom.

Monica watched the child with a kind of avid curiosity; she listened to every word she said even when she was telling one of the boys, 'ferme ta bouche!' She laughed inordinately at her jokes, then stopped herself as if she were afraid she might miss another gem. And as the days went by and she gradually used less make-up and let her black hair fall straight to her shoulders, she looked so like Bessie it was incredible.

Myrtle couldn't – or wouldn't – see it.

'It's a coincidence. Matter of fact I don't think Bessie belongs to anyone local. It was just like Cass told us at the time – her mother needed something to fill the gap, especially when Cass was at Bristol, so she decided to adopt a baby.'

'You're just saying that because you want to forget what an idiot you made of yourself at your wedding!' Liv snapped unguardedly.

Myrtle did not get angry. She looked at Liv consideringly and then said – as if she were actually sorry for Liv – 'Yes, maybe you're right.'

Somehow they prevailed on Mrs Woodford and Bessie to keep Carol ignorant of Mon's presence, though neither of them seemed to see any point in it, and Mrs Woodford obviously did not like it. Whether she spoke to Mon privately, Liv never knew, but on the Thursday after their arrival, Mon suddenly announced she had some people to see in London, and swung out of the house, into her hired car, and was off before anyone could say a word. Liv, perspiring as genteelly as possible in the kitchen, felt again the sense of isolation, almost desertion. None of the children really liked her, not even Bessie; Myrtle and Malcolm were completely absorbed in a world of fecundity which Malcolm might well have extended to her if she'd had the nerve to enter it. Now Monica had simply up and gone, and if Bessie was her child, then she was not the special friend Liv had thought she was.

There was a yell from the garden; Bessie went sprinting by the kitchen window; five minutes later she appeared at the door holding a dripping Mallie.

'I suppose your Aunt Myrt is sunning herself somewhere!' Liv said acidly as she took the wet clothes and dumped them in the washing machine.

Bessie looked up from the grinning child and grinned herself.

'She's reading that book by Iris Murdoch,' she said. 'You know, the one where all the husbands and wives change over.'

Liv looked at the dark, gypsy face that was so full of life.

'You shouldn't know about books like that!' she said.

Bessie laughed. 'I don't. But I've heard Cass talking about it with one of her authors. It's funny – they were both laughing.'

'Yes. Well. In books maybe it is.' Liv pursed her lips. The child had stayed in Myrtle's house three or four times. She must have seen Malcolm getting . . . up to things. 'It's not in the least funny in real life,' she finished austerely.

Bessie did not reply. She took Mallie up to the bathroom and brought him down to lunch looking angelic. Liv wondered what went on in a thirteen-year-old mind. She herself and deliberately gone to see Malcolm in the hope of being seduced . . . hadn't she? So wasn't that funny? Or was it just fun? And what was the difference?

Liv wasn't used to such introspection. Her perspiration turned sweaty and she wanted to cry.

Mrs Woodford said, 'Bessie and I are going to the village today, girls. Shall we take the boys? Then you two could have a nap.'

Mrs Woodford was an angel. Both Liv and Myrtle told her so unreservedly. And the boys – even Mallie – raised a cheer.

Liv slept the sleep of the exhausted. Around six o'clock she heard Reggie's car draw up . . . or perhaps Monica's . . . semi-conscious, she waited for a cup of tea to arrive. She would have a cool bath and suggest that she and Reggie went out for dinner. Myrtle could then take over the kitchen and cook up one of her revolting high teas: beans on toast with curdled scrambled egg, or something similar. She stretched luxuriously on the bed. A little breeze stirred the curtains. She wondered how they would manage when Cass arrived. It was rather a coup that they should all decide to meet at her house, but it was also a great strain. She smiled; she would put it to Reggie that they move out and let everyone else get on as best they could. No, she wouldn't. Reggie wouldn't realise

538

it was a joke, and he'd start talking about the joys of a big family again.

The tea did not arrive. It was too bad. Her tongue was cleaving to the roof of her mouth. She rolled her head on the pillow and looked at the bedside table. Last night's glass of water sat there, but it had air bubbles in it and looked as tired as she felt. Sighing gustily, she sat up. She'd have to get her own tea. As per usual.

She wandered on to the landing. There was a sound from Myrtle's room: as if she were having a bad dream. Liv thought it served her jolly well right, then she softened. Poor old Myrt, misshapen with yet another child, burdened with little Mallie, plagued by Nicky and Martin – she probably didn't get much cosseting from Malcolm. Liv knocked on her door.

'Wakey wakey!' she called like Billy Cotton. 'How about a cup of tea, Myrt?'

There was no reply save for a ghastly snuffling sound. Suddenly alarmed, Liv opened the door just in time to see Reggie scrambling off the bed. In his birthday suit. She closed the door quickly and went on downstairs. Reggie joined her three minutes later, clothed if not in his right mind, and started babbling something. She glanced at him wide-eyed.

'Are you all right, darling? I didn't realise you were home yet. I'm just making some tea for Myrtle and me. Would you like some?' He didn't say anything, just stared at her with his mouth open. She giggled insanely. 'Did you hear that? I'm a poet and don't know it. I'm just making some tea for Myrtle and me.'

She marshalled a tray and cups, poured boiling water into an empty pot, and carried the lot upstairs. And still he did not move or speak.

She didn't go in to Myrtle. In the shattered security of her own room she poured herself a cup of hot water and milk and sipped it; little finger cocked automatically. It hadn't happened. It had been a dream.

But that was when she thought she might die from soul-shaking loneliness.

Monica found herself applying her make-up again when she came back from her overnight visit to London. Her blood seemed to stop flowing in the middle of her neck and her sun-tanned skin looked like rather ancient dough. Every morning she smiled fiercely at herself in the mirror and applied rouge to the cushions of her cheeks, then powdered and blotted in the required fashion until the necessary sheen was achieved. She was at once thankful and aghast when Carol did not turn up that afternoon. Thankful because to face her after their interview and her subsequent note was a frightening prospect. Aghast, because Carol might have done anything. Or she might be ill. Monica recalled her face that Thursday night and felt physically sick at what she had done. And what she must still do. She must stiffen her spine, and do it. After all, Carol had always known Elizabeth wasn't her child. She'd always known that.

Monica tried to avoid Mrs Woodford. In the unnaturally large household, it was not difficult. Sometimes she caught Mrs Woodford regarding her and knew that the older woman would like to talk privately. Probably she only wanted to ask about Mrs Gosling, or to say 'D'you remember how we played Monopoly when we were at Rhyl?' Or to ask Monica about Bob . . . or . . . anything. But Monica could not risk a direct question. Carol would explain it all to her mother. She would know best how to do it. After all, it might be quite a relief to Mrs Woodford. She wasn't getting any younger and she probably worried herself sick about Elizabeth's schooling and . . . things.

Monica told herself now that she had not run away from Bob at all. She had always known that Bob's ideas of fidelity were his own; and he had many good qualities to offset his . . . wandering eye. No, she had run from herself. She had run because she had failed to produce children and failed to tell him she could not produce them. And if . . . when . . . Cass and Mrs Woodford honoured the promise they had made thirteen years ago, then at least one of those failures could be redeemed. She would go back to Bob with a child.

But she had to win Bessie first.

She thought about the problem until her head ached. The solution was simple, of course. If she took Bessie back to the States, the child would be a long way from old associations. She would have a new world to explore and new people to meet. She would charm Bob and when he had got thoroughly used to her, Monica would tell him and she would be his daughter too. Bessie would love America and she would love Bob, and Hildie, and everyone. In fact they could go to Hildie's first. She would talk it all over with Hildie.

But she had to win Bessie first.

She found reasons for taking the girl to America. Carol's involvement with the F.L.N. was irresponsible to say the least. And the entirely female household was not good. Then surely France could not offer the same educational and social opportunities as America. Also she did not like the way they had renamed Elizabeth. Bessie was an unfashionable diminutive, reminiscent of comfortable old housekeepers or faithful dogs. So far she had avoided calling the child anything but 'honey', but she intended asking her whether she wouldn't prefer Liz or Ellie. Once they were back in the States she'd be able to increase the closeness of their relationship so that it would dawn on the girl gradually and naturally that she was Monica's daughter.

It would all work so well if only Bessie would agree to come with her. She would make it work. In a year's time they could be a proper family again.

Just before lunch on Friday, a taxi crunched over Liv's immaculate gravel and Bessie shrieked, 'It's Cass!' and dashed down the hall to rip open the door before it could be knocked on.

Even Cass herself seemed surprised at her welcome. Bessie hugged her so passionately her hat was knocked askew and a glove pulled off.

'Oh Cass – Cass – oh I've missed you so much!'

'Darling – you've been here just a week without me! When you're at the convent I'm often—'

'Oh it seemed like forever! Besides, it's different now! I mean, we're family and when we're in a strange country we should stick together!'

'A strange country! Bessie, what are you saying?' Cass was laughing and hugging and paying off the taxi and gathering up her cases, all at the same time. Monica could have sworn she was happy; really happy. She felt a sense of anti-climax. After the way she'd worried and fretted, consumed with guilt, here was Cass taking the whole thing on the chin.

Mary Woodford encircled them both.

'Well, anyway. So everything is all right. Really all right.'

It was sort of question. Monica noticed that Cass didn't answer it. Or maybe she did because as soon as she was able, she kissed Monica. Monica saw Mrs Woodford's eyes widen and felt she was being identified by Carol as the traitor in their midst. A Judas kiss.

541

'Well. So what's happening?' she asked, sounding like Bob arriving at the apartment and finding her once again in bed. It was a meaningless question and should have been answered accordingly. Carol could have said, 'Ghastly journey' or 'It's still as hot as London.' Or Myrtle could have started on about little Mallie. Or Liv could have ordered Reggie to collect the luggage.

Instead, everyone looked at her oddly, and after a pause Carol said hesitantly, 'Well. Let me see. Tentative plans only, of course. But I did wonder . . . if you'd like to take Bessie for a holiday in the States, Mon.' She flashed a smile at the girl. 'Auntie Mon and I met up in London, did she tell you or is it surprise? We talked and talked. And I told her you were at rather a loose end for the rest of the vacances, and she suggested—'

'I'd rather not,' Bessie said flatly.

'Darling, why ever not?'

Monica said swiftly, 'I'd simply love it, Eliz . . . Bessie. You'd be doing me a great favour actually.'

And Liv said, 'Good idea. Get to know each other.'

Bessie said, 'But we could go back up the Victoire.' She looked at Mrs Woodford who appeared to swallow and then said enthusiastically, 'It's the chance of a lifetime, Bessie. New York! Who will be able to say they've been to New York in the summer holidays?'

Bessie stared at her, then Carol, as if they had stabbed her. Monica said quietly, 'Not if you don't want to. Of course.'

There was a strange silence. Then came a screech from the garden and Nicky's triumphant yell of 'Mallie's in the pool again!'

Bessie said, 'I'd love to, Aunt Monica. But I have to be back for the end of September.'

Monica took a long slow breath. 'Yes. That will be okay, honey. I'll see to Mallie. You have a chat with Cass.' And she made her escape into the garden.

She booked a call to Hildie and asked whether she could bring Elizabeth to the farm for a week or so. Hildie was delighted. 'Bob is mad to see you, honey! If you'll see him, everything will be okay. Believe me!' Monica began to feel hopeful; so far so good. Bob had continued to pay her allowance into her account, and had written to her twice, care of Dilly Gosling, saying that he

542

'understood'. It might be possible to pretend everything was all right. Elizabeth would then have a father as well as almost limitless wealth. Monica told herself firmly that the child would be getting a very good bargain indeed.

Carol spoke to her mother and Bessie that night in the privacy of their communal bedroom.

She said quietly and directly, 'I've met someone, my darlings. A Frenchman. I knew him . . . before, and wondered then if we loved each other. Now I am certain.' She looked at them in turn. 'I love you more than ever, because of him. Can you understand that.'

Mary Woodford's eyes filled with tears. She reached for Bessie with one hand and Carol with the other.

'I can understand. You are loving for two people now, Carol, not one. I love you and Bessie in the same way, for myself and for Daddy.'

'Oh Mother . . .'

Bessie said, 'Is that why you want me to go to America with Auntie Monica?'

The two women turned to her, shocked.

Bessie said defensively, 'You want to send me away. So that you can be by yourself with this – man!'

Carol began to protest, but Mary stopped her.

'In a way she's right, Cass. You're not sending anyone away. Naturally not. But you need to be by yourself for a while. It is important for you.' She pressed Carol's hand meaningfully and smiled at Bessie. 'You're going on this really special holiday with Aunt Mon. And I think I'll stay on in Northfield for two or three weeks and look up all the old friends.'

Carol did not know how to respond to this. She said lamely, 'There's no need. Jean-Claude and I cannot marry, Mother. We shall simply be friends.'

Bessie said pressingly, 'He won't live with us? He won't be proper family?'

'He won't live with us. No.'

Mary said, 'Ah. Jean-Claude.'

'Yes. Jean-Claude Durant. He is the foreign correspondent for *La Planète*. It was he who rescued Clive Hubert's book from Algeria.'

Bessie looked a little less defensive. 'An adventurer?' she queried.

'I hope not.' Carol walked to the window and looked out. Liv was standing by the fishpond, gazing into its depths. 'He has to go to places that are often dangerous.'

'Does he take photographs?' Bessie asked unexpectedly.

Carol said, 'He usually has a photographer with him. Why do you ask that, darling?'

'I might know a good photographer. Who could help him out,' Bessie said. She joined Carol at the window. 'I'm sorry I was horrid about Aunt Mon. I'll be a sort of foreign correspondent in America, won't I?'

'You certainly will.'

Carol smiled again, determined not to think about the possible consequences of Bessie's visit to New York. Tomorrow she would be with Jean-Claude again. If her mother stayed in Northfield, she could be with Jean-Claude at the Bergerie. She understood fully the selfishness of lovers.

Bessie said, 'What on earth is Auntie Liv doing?'

They stared through the window in disbelief. Liv was wading into the fishpond. Even as they looked she slipped on the slime at the bottom and fell forward on all fours.

Mary said, 'Oh my God—' and was gone through the bedroom door. But it didn't seem all that serious, and Carol and Bessie continued to watch as Mary appeared at the kitchen door and dashed down the garden.

And then Bessie was in Carol's arms and they were transfixed with horror. Liv had staggered to her feet holding something. She began to pull. Mary joined her and they pulled together. And with a sudden jerk, the lily roots gave up their dead, and Mallie's small muddy body was beached on the crazy paving that edged the pool.

544

Eleven

The funeral seemed to last all week. There was an inquest; there was Malcolm clinging to Myrtle, bent, a pathetic ex-Lothario; there were thrice-daily phone calls for Carol from London; there was Liv repeating, 'If only I'd seen him before – I'd been standing there of ages – if only—'; there was Myrtle stunned and white-faced with guilt; there were Carol and Mrs Woodford reading endless stories to Nicky and Martin in an effort to divert their bewildered grief; there were Monica and Bessie cooking and washing and 'seeing to things'; there was Reggie inexplicably saying, 'I'm sorry, Myrtle, so terribly sorry.'

Neighbours called and were kind to their faces and condemning behind their backs. Bessie, standing in a queue for liver, heard someone say 'too busy with Mrs Bradbury's husband I daresay'. She wondered if she should spring to Aunt Myrt's defence, but wasn't entirely sure the remark was derogatory.

Aunt Mon, waiting outside with Mallie's pushchair full of vegetables, frowned slightly when Bessie told her what had been said. Then she sighed deeply.

'I suppose everyone will think poor Myrtle should have known he wasn't in his bed. But she couldn't keep an eye on him all the time, and he did love that bloody pond.' She looked at Bessie, her huge black eyes suddenly swimming. 'The four of us were there, darling. In a way we share all you children. So in a way we were all responsible for Mallie.'

Bessie liked that. Sometimes the small family unit of Grannie, Cass and herself seemed somehow beleaguered. Monica extended it threefold with her words.

Bessie put the liver on top of the kidney beans, and said briskly, 'That's good then. No-one is to blame. Come on, let's get back and tell Aunt Myrt what you said.'

545

Monica blinked hard, then smiled. 'My God. You're like your mother, Elizabeth.'

That pleased Bessie still more. She grinned and relaxed fully towards this American aunt.

'I wish you'd call me by my proper name,' she remarked.

'Oh . . . shoot.' Monica laughed. 'Okay. Bessie.'

Monica's words, reported faithfully by Bessie, had little effect on the sombre company at the Barnt Green house. Liv had completely lost interest in her grey carpets and pale furniture and already the place looked far less than pristine. The people in it looked the worse for wear too. Liv's naturally curly hair was limp and flat, and Monica's sophisticated veneer had rubbed away. Only Carol retained the shine she had acquired so recently; it was subdued, but it was still there.

She knelt before Myrtle, repeating what Bessie had said.

'You see, Myrt? It must have been a pure accident, mustn't it? The four of us here . . .'

Myrtle said suddenly, 'Cass. I don't want this new baby. I don't want it. If I can't have Mallie, I don't want any other children at all. Nicky – Martin—' her voice began to rise hysterically. Carol leaned forward and encircled the heaving shoulders with her long arms. Malcolm, hunched up by his wife, put his big manipulative hands to his face, and started to cry.

Carol said over her shoulder, 'Mother. Bessie. Take the boys into the garden for a while, will you?' She stroked Myrtle's frizzy hair and made soothing sounds. 'Listen. Both of you, listen. This is going to get better. Just hang on to that fact and take the present as best you can. It's going to get better. Honestly.'

She continued to stroke Myrtle. Reggie crossed the room and clapped a manly hand on Malcolm's shoulder. Liv and Monica exchanged glances.

Monica said, 'Shall we go for a walk? I think you should get out of this house for five minutes, Myrtle. Come on. Let's go down to the heath.'

Malcolm blubbered, 'I can't come. Can't face it again. After that court business and the funeral . . . can't face anyone again.'

Reggie tightened his grip. 'We'll let the girls go by themselves, old man. Shall we? Perhaps at opening time we could go down to the Swan for a swift one. Break the ice as it were.' He looked

546

meaningfully at Liv. 'Don't hurry back, girls. Find somewhere for tea. Take it easy.'

For the first time in two weeks, Liv met his eyes and gave a slight answering smile. Somehow they got Myrtle on her feet and draped a cardigan over her awful misshapen floral frock. Monica waited with her in the hall while the other two went to the bathroom; she squared Myrtle's shoulders and moved her to the mirror. Myrtle looked at her reflection as if she'd never seen it before. Monica picked up the clothes brush and brushed out the wire-wool hair and smiled encouragingly.

'It's like Cass says, darling. You'll heal. Gradually.'

Myrtle whispered, 'No. I'll adapt. A man who loses a leg has to adapt. But it doesn't heal. And it doesn't grow back.'

'Okay. Then you'll adapt.'

'I still don't want this baby. 'It'll come between me and Mallie. I don't want it.'

Monica said lightly, 'Then give it to me. I want it.'

Myrtle's dead, haunted eyes focused for an instant on Monica's film-star face.

She whispered, 'Like your mother gave you away? Like you gave Bessie to Cass?'

Monica stiffened into alertness, and gradually Myrtle subsided into her private hell again.

'It's all right,' she said dully. 'Liv saw it first. I've told her she's talking rubbish. I won't say anything. No-one will say anything.'

Monica continued to stare into the mirror for a long moment, then she put her forehead on Myrtle's shoulder.

'Oh my God,' she whispered.

'I don't think He wants to help us,' Myrtle commented with unusual bitterness, and made for the door.

They walked for over an hour in almost complete silence. It was not as hot as the previous week, but Myrtle soon removed the cardigan from her shoulders and trailed it along the footpath like a disconsolate child. They left the road as soon as they could and clambered over a stile to skirt the golf course and eventually drop down to the heath. On one of the small country roads they had to cross there was a black and white cottage advertising teas. Remembering Reggie's words, Liv led the way through the gate

547

to one of the small iron tables in the front garden. They sat themselves down, suddenly tired.

'God. We've got all that way to get back home,' Myrtle said mournfully. 'Look at my feet.'

They looked as she stuck a leg ungracefully above table level. Her bare foot bulged over the straps of her sandals.

'Well, it's not for want of rest,' Liv said with a sudden return to her old self. 'You had them up all morning on the sofa. I don't understand it.'

Monica said, 'It's fluid. What does the doctor say?'

'Haven't been to the doctor yet.'

'You damned fool.'

Carol intervened. 'Tell you what. We'll ring for a taxi back. It's been marvellous getting out, but probably we've done enough. Let's have boiled eggs and loads of bread and butter and go home when the gnats come out.'

'Sounds lovely,' Myrtle managed a smile. 'You're right. It is good to get out. My feet don't bother me actually.' She leaned forward. 'Girls . . . thank you.'

Everyone looked embarrassed. Monica saved the day by using one of her American phrases again. 'Oh shoot,' she said.

She gave the order to the matronly figure who emerged from the front door, and then went on talking, suddenly enthusiastic.

'Honeys. I think I've been this way before. If we strike across country we shall get to our part of the heath. If Myrt is up to it, we could look for our house again, then get a taxi from Northfield. What do you think?'

Liv said cautiously, 'How far is it? I mean, Myrtle's feet do look bad.'

'A mile? Maybe two? I'll ask the woman when she brings the tea. I went to the Haunted House three or four years ago and when I left I didn't want to return the same way as I'd come. So I struck away from the brook. You remember the way the Mussolini man appeared from? And I came out on this road.'

'You were here before? You didn't contact any of us.' Liv regarded Mon wide-eyed. 'You simply disappeared off the face of the earth. Why didn't you get in touch?'

Monica flushed. 'I had to see the Cooks. Before I married Bob. Just to tell them. That was all. I was here for about six hours.'

Carol intervened. 'It would be rather special to find the house again, wouldn't it? I mean, it's thirteen years since we were there together.'

'Since we were anywhere together,' Liv said.

The woman came out with a tray of tea and bread and butter and Monica asked if they could get across the fields to the West Heath road. The woman was almost certain they could.

'Hubby's got an ordnance survey map in the cottage. I'll bring it with your eggs. Three minutes each?'

They looked at her uncomprehendingly then Carol said, 'Oh, the eggs. Yes. Fine.' And they all laughed almost normally.

The map arrived with the eggs. All the footpaths were marked and they pinpointed where they were with some excitement. Suddenly the afternoon had an objective, and with the objective, perhaps a meaning which might be revealed later. It became of paramount importance to find the Haunted House again.

'How long d'you think it'll take?' Myrtle asked.

'Not sure. Depends on the state of the footpaths I guess.' Monica rummaged in her pocket and found a pencil. 'Anyone got any paper? I'll copy this bit of the map. See, we have to go through this little wood . . . I don't think it's far actually.'

Liv had tissue in her pocket, always kept there against the possibility of a public lavatory minus toilet roll. Somehow Monica managed to transfer the relevant details. The woman came out again with a bottle of lemonade.

'Best take this. It's warm weather for hiking.'

'We can drink a toast when we get there!' Carol hugged Myrtle's arm. 'D'you remember that night we slept there?'

Liv said, 'D'you remember the time I pinned up Mon's hair and she whipped it all out?'

Mon said, 'What about when we found it first of all? We were soaked to the skin and I was certain I was covered in leeches.'

Myrtle said, 'We were happy then. The four of us. No-one else. Just the four of us.'

They started off again and located the footpath immediately. It was a good omen. They trudged single file along the edge of a field of acid-yellow rape, over another stile, and down a steep sheep-bitten slope of a stream.

'There was a bridge marked on the map,' Monica said, squinting at her tissue copy. 'Right here.'

'Well, it's not here now.' Myrtle sat down and negotiated the stream's bank on her bottom. She put her feet, sandals and all, into the crystal-clear water. 'Oh, this is good. Better than wading up the mini-Orinoco that time in midwinter.'

They splashed across and ploughed soggily up the other bank. It was all so reminiscent of that time when they had been twelve. The intervening years might never have happened. Myrtle said, 'This is better than looking for boys along the Bristol Road, isn't it Cass?'

Carol thought of poor Malcolm back home with Reggie, then of Jean-Claude waiting for her in London; she said nothing.

Unexpectedly, Liv, who had notched up her conquests like the Battle of Britain fighter pilots, said, 'Oh, yes. Much better.' And Monica agreed fervently, 'I'd rather be here with you three than anywhere else.'

They crossed another two fields, climbed another two stiles. The sun was perceptibly lower in the sky.

Mon said triumphantly, 'The map is right. There's the wood. And the other side of that will be our heath.'

With renewed energy they plunged into the wood. It wasn't much bigger than a coppice: a sudden different environment. Shadowed and breathing a life of its own, it silenced the girls again. They slowed and walked two abreast, smiling and pointing out wood anemones and strange lethally red berries in fleshly green sheaths. Monica, walking behind Carol, noticed again the still-awkward length of her body, the striped brown and beige hair knotted into a bun slightly higher on her head than usual in small deference to fashion. Liv watched Myrtle's large hips swaying from side to side beneath her multi-coloured frock, and tried not to remember that awful afternoon before Mallie had died. Myrtle looked up and caught Carol's wide grey gaze and smiled a question. She needed Carol now more than ever; it was no longer a game. She needed her more than she needed her parents or Malcolm. It was so ridiculous, that awful row. Bessie had turned out to be Monica's anyway.

She whispered, 'I'm sorry, Cass. Forgive me.'

Carol smiled back. Her own shining happiness had had to be tucked away in the face of the tragedy of little Mallie, but it was there.

'Nothing to forgive,' she murmured, and pulled Myrtle's hand through her arm.

550

They emerged quite suddenly on the other side of the trees. There was a fence, and they leaned on it surveying the landscape with complete bewilderment. Gone were the undulating fields with hedges and stiles; a strip of muddy green grass protected the coppice, then the land was gouged into baked mud-heaps; mounds of bricks and topsoil rose from the desert, metal skeletons of buildings lined the horizon, tunnels of sewage pipes lay waiting burial.

'My God. It's all being developed,' Liv said blankly.

'Daddy was talking about it, wasn't he?' Myrtle remembered. 'Slum clearance from the middle of Brum. Or something.'

Monica wailed, 'It's gone. Our house. It's been razed to the ground!'

They stared again, unable to find any familiar landmark until Carol pointed to the long cleft below them.

'There's the brook. They've left one of the willows. It might be the one by the house.'

'Let's go and see.' Myrtle was already clambering over the fence. 'I just can't bear it. Perhaps there will be something left. Just something.'

It was hard going, crossing the building site. The hot weather had fired the mud into ragged, rigid shapes, razor sharp at times. Carol and Monica got either side of Myrtle and half carried her down towards the brook. There was no-one around; no workmen climbed the scaffolding or operated the apparently abandoned machinery.

'Must be late.' Liv was panting. 'About seven o'clock. When does it get dark?'

'Soon. And we don't want to be caught here.' Monica edged around a pothole and reached back for Myrtle. 'They must have brought a road in, though. We're going in the right direction.'

The banks of the brook were blessedly untouched. They walked to the willow and tried to work out where the Haunted House would have been. It was Liv who found the raked remains of wood and broken glass that appeared to be all that was left of the tumbledown building.

'There was a dresser in the kitchen with wood like that . . . and here are some tiles from the roof.'

Myrtle gave a sudden screech.

'Look what I've found! Girls, look!'

She held aloft a flattened paint can. They crowded around her, unimpressed. She turned it over to show, faintly, an old war-time utility mark.

'It's the can we pinched from school, Cass! You know. We buried it in the garden and the digger thing has turned it up! Don't you remember, we painted the post office wall—'

'Of course – of course!' Carol was ecstatic. 'The paint pot! The incriminating evidence! Oh God – this was it then – where we hid. Where we saw . . . things. Where we talked and did our work and you played the violin, Liv, and—'

Monica produced the lemonade bottle.

'Come on. I'll pass it round. Phoenix from the ashes and all that!'

'Phoenix from the ashes,' they intoned in turn, tipping the bottle back so that it foamed and glinted in the dying sun.

'Who has the can?' Myrtle looked at Carol. 'You have it. Tell Bessie about it. Give it to her.'

Carol took the can and leaned down from her great height to kiss the top of Myrtle's head.

'Thanks, Myrt,' she said.

Bessie was completely captivated by the story of the paint pot. She said, 'Funny, Cass, but I don't mind going off with Aunt Mon half so much now.'

Carol quickly squashed a feeling of foreboding.

'Why? Because of an old paint pot?'

'No. Though yes. Somehow. Oh I don't know, she seems like our family.'

'Yes.'

Bessie said, 'Besides, it will be lovely to get away from here. This place . . . it's awful, Cass.'

'Because of poor little Mallie.'

'I didn't like it before that happened. Everyone was so unhappy.' Bessie ran her fingers through her thick black hair. 'I guess Auntie Myrt won't want me to go to Cheltenham any more. She only had me because of Mallie.'

'Oh Bessie. She didn't. She had you for all sorts of reasons, and it was a bonus to her that you and Mallie got on. Really. Really and truly.' Carol smiled rallyingly, determined not to notice Bessie's unconscious Americanism which she must have picked up from Mon.

552

Bessie's reaction was unexpected. She cast herself bodily on Carol and hugged her suffocatingly.

She whispered in her ear, 'Listen. I'm going to try to like this newspaper man. I really am, Cass. I know everything now, you see. Everything.'

Carol held the child's waist to steady her. She said carefully, 'I see. Who told you, darling?'

'No-one. Well, in a way Solange told me. It made all the diff. All the diff in the world.'

'What are you talking about?'

'You and me. It's why I'm jealous of your boyfriend.'

'He's not my boyfriend.'

'Don't go all prudy-rudy, Cass. If you can't get married to him then he'll have to be your boyfriend, won't he?' She sighed sharply.' And I shall have to learn to like him. And I will. I just . . . will.'

She drew away. 'What I mean is, don't worry about me in Connecticut. Aunt Mon being family-ish makes all the diff. I think I'll pack the paint pot. If that's okay with you.'

'It's okay with me.'

Carol watched Bessie 'make a hole' in her suitcase and push down the paint pot. The child was such a pragmatist. Like her mother. Strangely, Bessie's obscure words reassured her. There was no sense of imminent loss any more. Maybe she would come back with an American accent, calling Monica 'Mom'. It would make no 'diff'. Carol smiled.

'May I tell Jean-Claude what you said?' she asked.

Bessie hesitated, then nodded. 'Okay.' She added grimly. 'I just hope he'll try as hard to like me!'

Carol joined Jean-Claude two day later. They stayed at the Albion overnight, making love with an insatiable passion that secretly shocked Carol. She had not known such feeling existed in the world, let alone in herself. Jean-Claude had only to touch her for her body to flame into a life of its own. Suddenly and miraculously she could understand Malcolm Lennox and Myrtle. Monica and her adopted brother Giles, even perhaps her own parents. Sexual love was not an isolated emotion between one man and one woman: it encompassed the universe because it was universal.

553

Carol wanted Jean-Claude to see the Bergerie; she thought of this time together as a honeymoon, and knew that it might have to last them for a very long time.

'If we can live together for just a few days in the Bergerie, it will make it our home. So that afterwards, when we only see each other at intervals, your presence will be there.'

Tears filled her eyes at the mere thought of his absence. He kissed her and held her to him.

'Chérie, it will not be for long. Bessie will grow up and leave home and your mother would always understand. She *would* understand?'

'Yes. Of course.' Carol smiled tremulously. 'It will work out, I know it will. It is just a stupid feeling I have. I never expected – never knew about – this kind of happiness, my darling. It seems too precious, too ephemeral, to last. Forgive me.'

'There is no more danger, Carol. The book will be published. No-one can stop it now.'

'There may well be recriminations, Jean. And you are so vulnerable. Travelling the world, always where there is fighting.'

'Carol. I was not a member of the reactionaries. Nor the F.L.N. I was over there to report on what was happening and my newspaper had a nationalistic bias. Perhaps I also was biased that way at the time – remember the only thing I had to hang on to during the years of the war was my love for France. But neither one side nor the other can see me as a threat.'

'If anyone finds out that you collected that original manuscript from the Sufi—'

'How could anyone find out?'

'If you could discover the manuscript, Jean, then so could others.'

'I had a very important reason for discovering it.' He smiled into her eyes. 'Listen. Carol. The political climate is changing all the time. De Gaulle has been recalled to deal with the problem. I still have strong connections with him. I am safe. I promise you, chérie. I am safe.'

They flew to Nice and took a train to Marseilles where she had left her Renault. They drove slowly north to Aix-en-Durance, bought groceries and paraffin and took the track which led to the base of the Victoire. The flower harvest, which started in April and went on until October, was evident in the baskets of flowers awaiting collection at every gate. The few south-facing vineyards were being picked; already there was a sense of summer's end. 'The happiest summer of my whole life,' Carol murmured, then turned to face Jean-Claude with a stricken face. 'How can I say that when Mallie died right under our very noses? And Monica is going to claim Bessie?'

Jean-Claude turned his mouth down. 'That is why it is so precious. It has flowered from fear and tragedy. Don't question it, Carol. Accept it. Be glad.'

She could do nothing else, the whole thing was out of her hands. As she unlocked the door she glanced on the kitchen floor for a telegram or letter, and when there were neither, the outside world retreated for her; future and past were shadowy and irrelevant and her tiny span of life here with Jean-Claude was the only reality.

It was a time of deliriosity indeed. For the sake of her mother and Bessie she did not want to advertise Jean-Claude's presence in the Bergerie, through she was sure that the sharp eyes of Pierre would miss very little. However, for the time being she declined Sylvie's offers of help and delighted in lighting the fire in the range and doing her own cooking. Jean-Claude proved unexpectedly adept domestically. He scrubbed the huge table bleach-white and rolled out pastry that melted in the mouth. He dealt with the overgrown crop of haricots from Northfield, cutting them up and salting them down in the big stone jars beloved by Mary. And in the darkening evenings he would light the candles and wind up the ancient gramophone and they would dance around the uneven flagstones while the onions were cooking for his favourite soup. Choice of music was limited for dancing: Mary favoured Offenbach which was too sprightly, Bessie like Tommy Steele. Half a dozen scratched records from schooldays sufficed. There were some Cole Porters and 'Dancing in the Dark.' When Carol rested her chin on Jean-Claude's shoulder and swayed slowly to that haunting melody, she knew it would always evoke this time.

'Like the paint pot,' she murmured.

'Is that one of your significant non sequiturs, chérie?' he asked.

'A symbol. The paint pot is a symbol. You see it and immediately a whole era comes to mind. Now, when I hear "Dancing in the Dark'', I shall be here. The candles flickering, the shadows, the scent of burning apple logs and . . . and you.' She closed her eyes on the present which would so terribly soon become a memory.

'Carol, I know what you are still thinking. Ephemeral. Yes? It cannot be so. I would feel it too. And I do not feel it. I see us growing old. Perhaps quite soon Gaby will change her mind and divorce me. And we will be an old married pair. How do you say it in England – Darby and Joan?'

'Yes.' She opened her eyes and tipped back her head. 'We will not talk about the future. I forgot to tell you. Bessie is quite determined to like you. And she is hoping that you will try to like her.'

He laughed. 'It sounds as if she intends to come back here fairly soon then? Even though she knows that Monica Gallagher is her mother?'

Carol sighed. 'I don't know, Jean. I really don't know. I haven't talked about any of it with Mother, but *she* seemed quite content with the situation. But then she is a very special woman.' She shook her head slowly. 'When I look back I see that she takes the awful things that happen and makes something good from them. Daddy's death and Monica's pregnancy. The bombing in Paris . . . the way she made this place into a home . . . it's amazing.'

She moved away from him and carried the pot of soup to the table and they re-enacted the first meal they had shared in the Reine Blanche. She told him about Liv and her chapel background, her sharp little mother and rather nice father. She spoke of her own father and his long illness; the grandparents she could only just remember. And about Mon and the Cook family.

'That is sad,' he murmured. 'How did she bring herself to give away little Bessie?'

'She wouldn't look at her. It was as if she had internal bleeding: there was a raw look on her face. You see, I don't think she ever stopped loving Giles. She told us last week that she went back to Northfield just before she married Bob. It must have been to see Giles. It sounds as if she took him to the Haunted House.'

'This house was important to you girls?'

'Just another symbol. The paint pot will do.'

They both laughed.

Jean-Claude told her of his family and his rigid upbringing.

'My brother and I were destined for the Church. It never occurred to me to rebel. I was actually in the seminary when France fell.' He grinned boyishly. 'I was sixteen. It sounds like the *Boys' Own Paper*, Carol. Yes? I left the seminary that very day and made my way to the coast. I joined the Free French Army as soon as de Gaulle arrived in London. It probably broke my father's heart. I do not know. Both my parents were shot for harbouring Jews. My brother is on the Vatican staff. They would be proud of him.'

'They would be proud of you too, my dear.' Carol touched the back of his hand. 'I do not believe there were any broken hearts on your behalf. You did what you believed to be right. To do anything else *would* have been wrong. They knew that, I am sure.'

'Perhaps. I am not so sure of my own motives. For me it was a great adventure. Just as my work since the war has been a series of adventures. Until I met you nothing seemed very important. Gaby began working with you and I came into the office – do you remember? I was covering the Indo-China business and had met that other reporter who wished to write a book. I told him about you. Do you remember?'

'I remember.' She smiled. She had fought against admitting any attraction. His good looks and easy charm had worked against him.

'Gaby had spoken about you, of course. For the first time since I knew her, she was interested in something beyond her hair and make-up and clothes. So I knew you were special. I thought at first – the English blue-stocking. An academic. But you did not go into any mould, Cass. You would look up when I came into the office, and I felt I was looking into another human soul. I questioned Gaby. I learned that you were indeed a blue-stocking. And you were kind and very loving to your family. But I did not know I loved you until I heard that night that you might be in danger. And then I knew.' His smile widened. 'They talk about falling in love. It truly was like that. I had a physical sensation of falling all that evening. Until the explosion. And then we both landed. Hard, I think.'

She looked at him for a long time without speaking. He was holding both her hands in his and she realised she was gripping his fingers as if he were physically pulling her through the experiences of the past few years.

He said at last, tentatively, 'And you, Carol? Did you feel . . . anything . . . for me in that time?'

She relaxed and laughed, throwing back her head and showing the classic line of her throat.

'Jean-Claude! You are fishing! You know very well how I felt – you knew before I knew myself. How could I dare to admit any feelings for you! The plain, gawky Englishwoman – you said yourself, a typical blue-stocking! And you – you were the Rudolf Valentino of Paris!'

He silenced her with a kiss, and they were serious again.

She said at last, breathlessly, 'Remember, my love, I compared myself always with Gaby. She was pretty and vivacious and all the things I was not. And when I thought you had organised the job for her so that she could tell you what kind of manuscripts were coming in—'

'You did not think that? Not seriously?'

'Of course I thought it! I thought everything! Everything underhand and cunning and—'

He stopped her again with a kiss.

And then he said in a low voice, 'I am sorry, my love. My only love. If I had explained about Gaby right at the start, perhaps you could have looked on me separately. Seen me in my own right. But it is not done . . . to talk of one's wife so. Even now—'

'It's all right, Jean. She said something herself – that very evening. But, after all, you were still together. She was still cooking your meals and – and—'

He said steadily, 'The room you slept in on the night of the explosion, Cass. That was my room. We did not sleep together. Whatever she told you, she did not cook for me. It was a marriage of convenience, chérie, and that was all. Until you, there was no reason to move out of the apartment. It cut down on expenses – she would not divorce me. Perhaps she was still frightened that some of the patriots had long memories and would seek revenge. I do not know.'

They came together again, there were no barriers, no more shadows between them. But just before they slept that night, Carol wondered what the future might hold. What would happen if her mother did not like him. Or if Bessie could not overcome the jealousy she had spoken of.

It was the next day that Pierre brought a telegram from Ralph saying simply 'Please phone.' She stayed only long enough to find Jean-Claude in the small room next to Bessie's which he had been using as a study, and tell him what had happened. She was certain it was something to do with Bessie or her mother. She reversed the Renault into a bank of pansies outside the kitchen door and roared down the track, passing Pierre on his bicycle long before he reached the road.

The telephone was in the post office which also sold everything else, and was always full of customers. At least none of them spoke English. While she waited to be connected with London, she half heard the topic of conversation. It was about the English lady and her amour. So much for all their discretion.

Ralph's voice was blessedly reassuring, if indistinct.

'It's not for you at all, Carol. The *Planète* office assumed that Durant was still working here. He told me he was holidaying in Provence and might drop in on you. If he does, tell him he's needed back in Paris. Pronto.'

Her heart contracted painfully. She wanted to cry a protest. They had had only five days together. But all she said was, 'Thank you, Ralph. Is everything else all right? What about the book?'

'Publicity are formulating a strategy. 'What about you?'

'Bessie has gone to America with my friend. Mother is staying in Birmingham doing the rounds. I'm taking it easy here.'

'Feel like contacting Demetier again?'

Maurice Demetier was a playwright who summered in Antibes. He was one of Carol's less popular coups.

'Yes. Perhaps. All right.' Carol wondered whether Ralph knew that Jean was here. Was he giving her a job to fill her hours when *Planète* wanted Jean to fly off somewhere?

'No hurry. Take the rest of the summer off if you feel like it. You've already done your stint over here with Clive's book.'

She said her goodbyes, then asked to be put through to the *Planète* office. She told the girl on the other end that she could forward any messages to Monsieur Durant. A silence fell in the tiny shop.

A male voice came on the line, speaking English.

'Madame Woodford?' She did not correct him. 'Durant is to cover the Civil Rights march in Washington next week. We have air tickets – everything – here'.

Carol took a deep breath. This was it: the end of their time together. The future was here, now.

'I will tell him. Thank you.'

She replaced the receiver carefully, and prepared to leave the shop with head held high. To her surprise everyone smiled at her as if in congratulation. She went into the sunshine and slid into the hot leather seat of the car. The French were . . . different. She could be proud to be the chère amie of Jean-Claude Durant. Her mood lifted.

Monica wondered why she did not feel happier. She had achieved her aim; Bessie was with her, and what was more they were already very good friends. And this end had not been achieved by Mallie's death – Bessie had agreed to come to America before that awful event. And it had not been achieved at Carol's expense either. Carol had been pathetically honest before they left Barnt Green: she had fallen in love. Monica had been pleased – personally pleased – about that. It explained Carol's enormous strength all through the inquest and funeral.

But it still did not seem to make everything 'all right'. Monica told herself it was because the hurdle of Bob had to be jumped. Once he knew Bessie, he would accept her. The child was delightful, unspoilt, beautiful, and with a sense of humour that would win Bob's heart immediately.

The trip over had been perfect: Bessie appeared to put her old life behind her almost physically; she was the ideal travelling companion, excited one minute, peacably happy the next. They landed at Gander for refuelling and after that she slept until La Guardia and the customs. It was only six weeks since Monica had left the country, but now she saw it through Bessie's eyes, and the sheer efficiency of the place impressed her anew. Besides, she had left New York a failure. And she was returning a success. She should be on top of the world.

George met them, driving the enormous Oldsmobile that was so ideal for the boys and the dogs. Bessie was entranced.

'They're *gorgeous*,' she said, referring to the dogs. 'And their names are so right!'

Douglas and Fairbanks gazed at her from their drooping eyes and drooled thanks. They were bloodhounds, supposed to protect Hildie and the boys when George was away from the farm, but apart from barking loudly at strangers, they were harmless. Bessie sat in the back and reached through the dog guard to stroke them. They wined ecstatically.

George was apologetic.

'Hildie would have been here except she might be . . . not too good in the mornings. Guess you two just want your beds and a cup of coffee, anyway.'

'Sounds heaven, George. Is this all right, really? We could have stayed at an hotel, but I wanted Bessie to see the farm. And I wanted to talk to you two before I contacted Bob.'

George took his eyes off the road long enough to swivel them questioningly at Bessie.

'Bessie understands.' Monica had said nothing at all to the child about Bob, and amazingly no-one had asked her about him. She recalled saying something to Carol about her marriage being over; probably Carol's tact had kept everyone else silent on the subject.

Monica turned to face her daughter.

'You'll like Bob, darling. And he'll like you, I'm certain. We had a bit of a bust-up before I left, so I want to phone him first.' She smiled easily. 'As it happens it worked out for the best.' She turned to George again. 'It's been a strange six weeks. Did Hildie tell you? Not all tragic. But I was very, very glad to be there when it happened.'

'Sure. We understood that.' George grinned in the mirror. 'We're just glad you've come home. And brought this young lady with you. Say, you didn't warn us she was a budding Jane Russell!'

Bessie giggled. Jane Russell was considered very daring at the convent. She couldn't wait to fell Solange that she looked like Jane Russell. She leaned back so that the dogs could breathe in her ear. She was still very tired. She thought about Carol and Grannie. Her mother, and her grandmother. It was good, so good, to belong to them properly. She mustn't be jealous of this French newspaperman. Carol wouldn't let it make any difference. And, in an odd way, it was good to get away from everything just now; poor little Mallie. And poor Aunt Myrt. If only Boris had been there. If only . . . She slept.

America was 'fantastique'. Bessie loved everything about it. The Connecticut farm was like no farm she'd seen before; it wasn't all mud and manure. Aunt Hildie and Uncle George weren't real farmers at all; their 'help' had originally owned the house – which was called a salt-box though it was hard to see why – and had sold it with the proviso that they stay on and work it. Uncle George did something with real estate and had an office in New York. Aunt Hildie and Aggie ran the house and looked after Aunt Hildie's two children between them. Aggie's husband saw to the farm and showed George's visitors around when they came. Aggie and Jim lived in a flat over the garage which had its own bathroom. Everyone else lived in the salt-box which had six bedrooms and three bathrooms and a basement which was called a rumpus room. They weren't quite rich enough yet to have their own swimming pool, but they shared one with their neighbours who lived in the next 'lot'.

Bessie loved Aunt Hildie. Aunt Monica told Bessie that Aunt Hildie was a bit scatty, a bit pretty, a bit clever, and very wise. She pretended to find her nine-year-old twins, Leo and Ossie, distasteful, but when they went to summer camp, she phoned them every day and spent a long time cleaning up their room for the fall. Bessie missed them too, though she had only known them a week before they went off. They weren't like her convent friends who liked talking and giggling. And they weren't a bit like Boris who understood everything even when you couldn't explain it. They woke each day with a 'program'. Usually the program started with a swim in the pool, then it might take in an inspection of the farm animals with Jim. Then there would be a run before lunch. They literally took to their heels and ran until they could run no more. 'Just like the dogs,' Uncle George commented in disgust, rumpling their heads fondly as he said it. When Leo brought home an injured pigeon and it died, they ran as if their very lives depended on it. Bessie gave up and went to her room where she hung out of the window and watched their distant stick-shapes tearing around a field of stubble. 'They'll sweat it all out,' said Aunt Hildie, turning her mouth down wryly. Aunt Monica said, 'That's all very well, but where do they get their energy?' 'From good American steaks,' Aunt Hildie replied. 'And it looks as if the two of you could do with a course of them, too.'

Aunt Hildie did not want them to go to New York.

'Bessie is used to the countryside,' she told Aunt Mon repeatedly. 'Sidewalks and stores aren't for her this weather. Let's wait till it breaks, huh?'

Aunt Mon waited until Bessie was watching the Beverly

Hillybillies on the giant television set, then said quietly, 'Why don't you want us to see Bob? Is he will with Nancy?'

'No. I told you he wasn't, honey. My God, he went crazy when you left. Sacked her on the spot. He's written you, surely?'

'Yes. And I didn't exactly *leave*. I had to see Bessie. She was in some danger . . . too long to explain.'

Hildie spoke quietly but with emphasis. 'You left. When you phoned me that morning, you were leaving. At least be honest with yourself.'

Aunt Mon was quiet for some time, then Bessie saw her dim reflection shrug in the television screen and she said, 'Oh shoot!' Then they both laughed. Then Aunt Mon went back to the beginning and said, 'Why don't you want us to see Bob?'

'I want *you* to see Bob. I think a certain person might be rather a shock for him.'

There was another pause, then Aunt Hildie sighed sharply and said in an exasperated voice, 'Surely you can see that, honey?'

'Yes. But if he loves me . . . listen Hildie, if it comes to a choice I have to choose . . . her.'

'Honey. For Pete's sake. She's already got a family. You could end up with nothing. And Bob might – if the worst came to the worst – get away with zero alimony. In the circumstances.'

Aunt Mon got up and walked to the window. She called, 'Bessie! Jim is taking the tractor up to the high field to plough in the stubble. D'you want to go with him?'

Bessie did not take her eyes off Ellie May.

'In a minute,' she droned, concentration obviously otherwise engaged.

Aunt Mon came back to where Aunt Hildie sat in a chair doing her nails.

'I have to do it this way. Or not at all. And I want to get it over and done with. Will you come, Hildie? Please?'

Hildie laughed. 'I wouldn't miss it for anything,' she said. As if it were a bullfight. Or Wimbledon.

They went in with Uncle George. Bessie wore her cotton frock with daisies all over it. It had pockets in the side seams of the skirt and she liked pushing her hands into them and making it stick out at the sides. The last time she had worn this frock had been when they came over to England at the beginning of August. Maybe it would be lucky. Maybe they would decide to go back to France today. Maybe it was a travelling frock.

But she was still loving America.

Fifth Avenue was amazing. She had expected the buildings to reach into the sky and make all the streets into tunnels, but she hadn't expected trees. Nor the street vendors, nor the politeness of the girls in the shops, nor the expensive women with little dogs, nor the screaming traffic. They bought presents for each other; Aunt Hildie bought earrings for Auntie Mon, and Aunt Mon bought an expanding gold bracelet for Bessie.

'Shall we have them sent to Beekman Place?' Aunt Hildie asked half-teasingly. Aunt Mon shook her head.

'Stop making a big thing out of this,' she chided. 'Bob was perfectly all right on the phone. He's looking forward to meeting Bessie. We don't have to lay claim to the place by having stuff delivered there! Besides, I'd like to wear my earrings if that is okay by you.'

'Sure. How about you, Bessie?'

So Bessie wore the bracelet and they took Aunt Hildie to buy things for the new baby which she seemed to be concealing more successfully than Aunt Myrt concealed hers. Then they went out to lunch.

Aunt Hildie said, 'You don't know what a treat this is for me. No kids, no husband . . . do you realise, Aggie and me – we're the only women on the farm? Apart from the cows of course.'

They all giggled and people looked round at them and Bessie put one hand over the back of her chair so that everyone could see the bracelet.

'Having a good time, honey?' It was strange how Auntie Mon seemed to be talking American now.

Bessie grinned. 'I sure am!'

They laughed again.

Central Park was like a very big Cannon Hill in Birmingham. On the paths there were people running for no reason, like Leo and Ossie, but then there were huge areas of grass and trees and bushes and emptiness.

They took a horse and carriage and meandered slowly down a wide driveway lined with drooping aspen trees. The driver was a coloured man with a beautiful white smile; he told them they had better leave the park by four p.m. at the latest.

'There's a rally today, ladies. It's running at the same time as the big Washington march. It's going to be mighty crowded in an hour or two.'

Bessie said, 'Why are they marching? Is it like the changing of the Guard?'

'No.' Aunt Mon glanced at the driver's broad back. 'It's a freedom march.'

'I thought America was free already?'

The driver looked round. He was still smiling.

'Not everyone isn't free, little lady. Down in the south, people like me can't go to the same places as people like you. And white children can't go to school with coloured children.'

Bessie was mildly surprised. 'We have coloured girls at the convent. They come from Morocco mostly.'

Aunt Hildie said quickly, 'It's different in France, honey.'

People were already arriving when they left the park. They were carrying flags and big notices on poles which said starkly, 'human rights'. For some reason they made Bessie remember again the dark and terrible two weeks at Barnt Green after Mallie's death. She forgot her pretty dress and new bracelet and took Aunt Mon's hand.

'All right, baby?' asked Aunt Mon.

'I was just wondering what Carol was doing now,' Bessie said in a small voice.

'She and Grannie are getting the French house cleaned up for the winter, I expect,' Aunt Mon suggested.

Bessie wondered whether Aunt Mon knew about Jean-Claude Durant.

'Have you ever heard a newspaper called *La Planète*, Auntie Monica?' she asked.

'Vaguely. One of the Paris newspapers, isn't it?'

Aunt Hildie said, 'They have offices in New York.'

She hailed a taxi and they all got in and Aunt Mon gave the Beekman Place address. They both seemed suddenly nervous and preoccupied and no-one asked Bessie any more about *La Planète*. She sat back in the slippery leather seat and put her hands in her pockets.

The apartments were more like a big London house than anything she'd seen in New York. There was an awning over the pavement at the front door and a concierge like in Paris who seemed delighted to see Aunt Mon.

'Say, Mrs Gallagher! I've missed you. What about the marches? Comes of having a Republican in office, that's what I say. My old lady's sister says they're bringing in the troops in Arkansas. The army! Can you believe it?'

'Is Mr Gallagher at home yet, Donaghue?'

'Sure is, Mrs Gallagher. And he went up that elevator with the biggest bunch of roses you ever did see. And a grin from ear to ear!'

'Thank you, Donaghue,' said Auntie Monica, and Auntie Hildie said very clearly, 'Familiarity.'

They took the lift for miles. Bessie didn't look at the indicator because it made her feel worse. She, who had climbed the Victoire, could not stand lifts. When the doors opened, a man was waiting on the sumptuous landing. It must be Uncle Bob. He carried flowers and he was grinning. Maybe Donaghue had telephoned him.

'Hello. Hello. Hello. Hello. Say, is this wonderful, or just wonderful? Hello Sis. Hello Honey. I thought I might never . . . hello. Gee you look wonderful. How was the trip? How is George? And the boys?'

He couldn't seem to stop talking. He didn't give Auntie Monica a chance to say anything about Bessie. They all moved – shuffled – to a big carved door with an enormous brass door knob and letter box. Uncle Bob, still half hidden by the flowers, let them go in first, then he followed, shut the door and stood with his back against it in case anyone tried to escape.

Auntie Mon said, 'It looks great, Bob. You've had help, obviously.'

Bob said, 'Listen honey. She's about eighty-four and she goes home at nights. Honest to God. Her name is Mrs Bergdorf, and I got her from an agency. Hildie will bear me out.'

Aunt Monica said, 'Pas devant l'enfant, please Bob.' Then caught Bessie's eye and grinned. 'I was forgetting you speak the language like a native, honey. Come here and meet your Uncle Bob. Bob, you've heard me talk of my friend, Carol Woodford. This is her small sister, Bessie Woodford. She came back with me for a holiday. I have to take her home at the end of September.' She closed one eye, reminding Bessie of her own words. Bessie felt a surge of thankfulness. Even if she was enjoying America, even if Carol did have a man friend, even if Uncle Bob was as nice

566

as Aunt Hildie said, she still wanted to know she was going home in two weeks' time.

'How do you do,' she said politely, extending the hand with the bracelet.

He dumped the flowers at last, and took the hand.

'Say, that's some bracelet. And some wrist it's on.'

She explained about the bracelet and he said, 'Mon's got an eye for jewellery.' He kept her hand and led them all through to an enormous sitting room with windows looking out over a river. The sense of space was amazing. Bessie wanted to be thoroughly childish and run about and even jump on the huge squashy sofas that were everywhere.

Hildie said, 'Can we have some tea, please Bob? We've done the town all day and we're exhausted.'

He twirled Bessie around and sat her down.

'Tea. I'll get it.' He had hardly looked at Auntie Mon since they came into the room. Now he glanced at her. 'Give me a hand, hon?'

'Only too pleased.'

They left.

'Well,' Aunt Hildie said. 'Well, well, *well*.'

Bessie said, 'They've made up the quarrel, haven't they?'

'Temporarily, at any rate.' Aunt Hildie looked at the open door speculatively. 'She chickened out. Temporarily at any rate.'

'Chickened out?'

'Yes. She ducked out of telling him something important.'

Aunt Hildie transferred the speculative gaze to Bessie.

'Hope it's not temporary.' She seemed to shake her shoulders. 'My motto is, least said soonest mended, Bessie Woodford. What d'you think?'

Bessie thought to Carol having to keep her secret all these years. She nodded.

Aunt Mon and Uncle Bob were gone ages. Aunt Hildie asked if she wanted to see the apartment, then took her into the bathroom and a bedroom and another bedroom. She slid back some doors.

'Your Aunt Mon's clothes,' she said, as if introducing another person. The cupboard went along the whole length of a wall and was full of clothes. Aunt Hildie grinned. 'Go on, try some on. Monica won't mind. I have to go to the bathroom.'

Bessie didn't think she wanted to try on any clothes, but after a very few minutes she found herself pushing at the hangers to get a better look at the dresses, skirts, suits, blouses – everything. There was a long satin dance dress in pale cream. It had a boned top. Bessie had never seen anything like it before. She unbuttoned her daisy dress and pulled it over her head. The dance dress slid into its place. She looked at herself in the mirror. The boned top did not touch her body at all. She opened a drawer and found handkerchiefs, and stuffed them into the gaps. That was better. She giggled. She went to the dressing table where lipsticks and rouge were laid out on a glass tray and began to apply make-up with a liberal hand. A blue scarf hung over a chair and she pulled that through her bracelet. She looked gorgeous. Like Jane Russell. Sultry. She half-closed her eyes and pouted at herself. If only Solange could see her now. Or Boris. But Aunt Mon would appreciate her too. She fluffed out her hair with spread fingers, and made for the kitchen.

At first it was just embarrassing. Aunt Mon was engulfed by Uncle Bob's enormous shoulders and arms, it was as if he had wrapped himself around her. She had seen Aunt Myrt and Uncle Malcolm having a cuddle, but Aunt Myrt was bigger than Aunt Mon and she didn't practically disappear into Uncle Malcolm. Even so, it was Aunt Mon who caught sight of Bessie first. Sideways and almost upside down, her wide-open eyes dilated then narrowed with amusement as if sharing a joke with Bessie. She put a hand to Uncle Bob's neck and moved her face sideways.

'Darling. Bessie is here.'

It was when Bob surfaced and registered her appearance, that embarrassment became bewilderment and then alarm.

He obviously didn't remember who she was. He lifted his head and stared at her as if she were a ghost. Auntie Mon looked up at him and gave a nervous laugh. 'It's Bessie, honey. In my dress.' But he went on staring and staring and Bessie started to stammer in apology, and Aunt Mon moved to her and said, 'It's all right, darling. I don't mind a bit. You look gorgeous.' And Uncle Bob blurted, 'Christ, she's yours. Don't deny it. She's your kid! Christ—' And Aunt Mon said, 'Go and get changed, Bessie. We'll have some tea in just a moment.' And as Bessie fled, it was as if Uncle Bob exploded with a final '*Christ*!' And then the door slammed on them as Aunt Mon said, 'Shut *up*, Bob!' And she was in the thick, silent hall again by herself.

She did not let herself recall any of those two minutes. Like an automaton she went back into the bedroom, stripped off the gown and let it lie on the floor with its tumble of handkerchief-paddings. She put on her daisy dress and smoothed her hair with the palms of hands that were trembling slightly. She found her handkerchief in one of the skirt pockets and scrubbed at her face. Then she walked across the hall once more, through the heavy door, on to the landing. She pressed the button by the side of the lift and a moment later it arrived and the doors opened silently. She squeezed her hands inside her pockets and closed her eyes. It was worse going down, but she didn't care.

The nice concierge asked her how she was doing and she said, 'Fine.' And he said, 'Say, where are you off to, little lady?' And she said, 'Going for a walk.' And she was gone.

It was so easy. The pavement was wide and small trees grew in tubs along its edge. She thought she would go as far as the first tub, and when she got there she decided to go to the second. The concierge shouted something behind her, so she ran to the third and fourth, then there was a corner and she went around it and did not hear him any more.

She had to get to Carol. Or to Grannie. Yes, Grannie would know and tell her the truth about everything.

Twelve

After the first overwhelming impulse to get away had been satisfied, Bessie did not know what to do. Her day of shopping and sight-seeing in New York had not prepared her for using its transport facilities. She knew nothing about the mysterious subway, and the yellow taxis that cruised along the kerbs of the hotels cost money; she had no money. She kept walking because someone might speak to her if she stopped, and she had not made up her mind what to say to the inevitable question, 'Have you lost your way, little girl?'

The streets around Beekman Place looked the same; she needed to see some shops, though she had no idea why. She kept walking. When she saw it, she would know what it was she wanted.

It was a policeman. He was talking to a lady with a white poodle dog. He had his truncheon swinging from his wrist, and he pushed his hat to the back of his head and said something about the weather. As Bessie drew near, she heard the woman say, 'I always go north, for the summer, but this year I decided to stay put. I sure have regretted it. What a summer!' She turned and saw Bessie coming towards them. She smiled. Bessie in her daisy frock was unmistakably a nice little girl.

'Hi there, honey. You're new around here, aren't you?'

Bessie leaned down and stroked the poodle.

'I'm visiting.'

Her accent caused ecstasy.

'Say! You're English!' The poodle lady turned to the policeman. 'Officer, did you hear that? She's all the way from England. Visiting New York!'

The policeman grinned amiably. No trouble here.

'Welcome to the city, little lady. But you shouldn't really wander around on your own.'

Bessie straightened and looked at the policeman, and knew what she had to do. It wasn't a welcome decision, but the alternative of going back to Beekman Place was worse.

'Actually, I'm looking for my uncle. We were going back to his office, and he was talking to someone, and I went round the corner, and – and I seem to have lost him.' Somehow it was better to have lost her mythical uncle than be lost herself.

They were concerned.

'Hey. That's not good in a big city like New York.' The poodle lady picked up her dog as if she expected him to dash off and get himself lost. 'Maybe you'd better come back to my apartment, honey, while this officer puts out a call for your uncle.'

Bessie said, 'There's no need for that. If you can direct me to his office, I'll be fine. I can meet him there. Or they will phone him. Or something.'

'Do you know the name of his company?' The policeman looked less relaxed.

'Oh yes. He works for *La Planète*. The French newspaper, you know.'

'I ain't heard of that one.'

'They share an office with an American paper. I can't remember the name . . .' She began to feel really frightened. She had to get back to Cass, and *La Planète* was the only link she had.

'Listen, honey. I'll take you along the block and phone in for a car. They'll drive you to your uncle's office. They know every inch of the city. Relax, honey. We'll take care of you.'

'I'm not a bit worried,' Bessie lied. 'My grandmother told me when I was a little girl that if I was in any difficulty I only had to ask a policeman for help.'

The policeman looked gratified, and the poodle lady said, 'Isn't that cute? Isn't there some little old English song about asking a policeman? And you've really done that. Just that!' She trilled a laugh. 'What's your name, baby? I just have to tell my ladies' group that I've met a little English girl.'

Bessie swallowed. 'Elizabeth . . . Durant,' she said. 'I am English, but my uncle is French.'

It didn't make much sense, but they accepted the name instantly. Bessie said goodbye to the poodle lady and walked alongside the policeman to a phone booth, where he made his call. In less than a minute a car drew up at the kerb and Bessie sat inside it while the driver spoke on a radio to someone called Frank who was given the task of finding out where the offices of *La Planète* were. Then they were driving through the evening traffic on the wrong side of the road, sirens screaming, the driver shouting remarks back to her about taking more care next time. Nobody seemed to realise she was running away from danger, not into it.

La Planète had an office in the enormous Herald building in Thirty-Second Street. The revolving doors did not stop. The policeman took Bessie's hand and ran to catch them up and held on to her tightly as they were ejected the other side. It was blessedly cool in the big foyer.

Bessie said, 'I'm all right now. Thank you very much.'

'I'm not letting you go till I can hand you over to a responsible citizen,' the policeman said, only half humorously.

He went to the desk and found the floor occupied by *La Planète*, then led her into the elevator. 'My chief would have my badge if I reported half the story!' he grinned. 'Took us ten minutes to get you here – it'll take half an hour to write it up!'

'I'm sorry,' she said in a small voice. She wondered how much longer it would take when the people in the Planète office disclaimed all knowledge of her.

There was just one person in the small room at the end of the corridor. He had round owl eyes behind glasses, and when he stood up behind the large desk where he was tapping at a typewriter, he was still very short indeed.

'How can I help you, officer?' He held out his hand, and Bessie knew that in spite of his American accent he was French.

The policeman said, 'Picked up this little lady on the East side by the river. She says she is meeting her uncle here. Name of Durant.'

Bessie took a step forward. 'Jean-Claude Durant. I am Elizabeth Durant.' Deliberately she closed one eye. Then she waited without hope.

The little man was momentarily silent, then he beamed.

'Jean-Claude. One of our best foreign correspondents. He is covering the Washington march.' He came around the desk. 'I am the New York representative, officer.' He removed some papers and revealed a name board. 'Louis Gotthard. I cannot sufficiently thank you for bringing in Elizabeth.'

572

'Washington?' The office frowned. 'He is in Washington?'

'Was in Washington,' Monsieur Gotthard said smoothly. 'You became lost, chérie?' He looked at her questioningly and in spite of her astonishment at this turn of events, she took up his cue.

She spoke in French. 'He was showing me the city and stopped to talk to someone and I went on for a few metres, then I could not see him.'

The policeman said sharply, 'What did she say?'

'She was explaining how she came to be lost. Of course, Jean-Claude has such a short time in New York, he would want to show her the sights.' He turned back to Bessie. 'Will you wait here for him? He will surely arrive very soon and be very worried.'

'I will wait. Please.' She went to the window and closed her eyes on the view. In her head she began to pray very hard.

'Okay. I'll have to report this to the Juvenile Department. They will want to check it out.' The officer produced a notebook and Monsieur Gotthard had to sign it as if she were a parcel being delivered. And then at last the door closed.

She said in a very small voice, 'Thank you, monsieur. Perhaps . . . could I stay here tonight?'

'You really know Jean-Claude?'

'Yes. Sort of. He knows my . . . mother.'

'Ah. I see.'

There were sounds. Bessie turned her bowed head and looked beneath her arm. Monsieur Gotthard was filling a kettle and plugging it in. He turned quickly and forced her to meet his glinting spectacles.

He said, 'I went along with you because I thought there might be a story for the paper. I am wrong?'

She swallowed. Was he still going to give her up?

'Yes. I mean, I can't explain anything. But I have to get home to France somehow. And I remembered that Jean-Claude's paper . . . is he really in America?'

'Yes. Washington. He is covering the Washington march.'

'I know about that. There was another one in Central Park.'

'You're a bright child.' He stared at her for a long moment, then made up his mind. 'Come, we will drink tea and you can tell me what you would like to tell me.'

573

She looked out at the view. They were so far up she could not see the street below. 'Thank you God,' she said in her head. Then she went to the chair Monsieur Gotthard indicated and sat down. Her legs were trembling.

Bob said for the umpteenth time, 'You choose. The kid or me. My God, when I think that all the time you had this on your mind . . . no wonder you were ill. No wonder you were bloody ill!'

Monica quelled a flutter of panic. She said, 'Bob, I have to go to her. She didn't know a thing till you spoke. She'll be upset—'

But he wouldn't move from the door and he was very large.

'You stay here until you've made up your mind. I mean it, Monica. You've twisted me round your finger till I can't see straight, but I know this isn't right. If you want me for my own sake, then you'll have no trouble making up your mind. But if you've come looking for a father for your bastard kid, then I'll know it, won't I? What's the big idea? For Christ's sake, what goes on in that mind of yours?'

'Bob. You keep asking me questions then you don't let me answer. Just listen.' She couldn't stop thinking of Bessie, stripping off her finery, bewildered and perhaps frightened. With difficulty she brought her mind back to Bob. 'Listen. It was when I was a child. Sixteen. It was my brother – my adopted brother. I was farmed out when I was born then . . . then . . . oh God . . . I had to do it to my baby!' She sobbed suddenly and she hadn't meant to do that. She mustn't get upset, for Bessie's sake. She gulped. 'The doctor said – back in the summer – he said I couldn't have children. But I've got a child. I've got a daughter. Can't you understand – I had to find her and get to know her—'

'And then palm her off on me. Was that it? Someone else's kid? The child of your *brother* for Christ's sake! Incest!'

'He was my adopted brother – I just told you that—'

'Moral incest then! That makes it all right, does it? Did you love me in the first place, Monica? Or were you planning even then to foist your daughter on to me? When I think of you – the way you practically seduced me – night after night—'

It could have been hilarious. But it wasn't.

She said. 'Bob. Stop it. We'll talk about this another day. When we're both calmer. I have to go to that child.'

But he wouldn't move. He started again. 'You'll stay here until you've made up your mind. The kid or me. That's the offer, Monica. The kid or me.'

Behind him came a knocking. It was Hildie. He turned and pulled open the door.

'We've got some trading to do, Sis. Get lost for half an hour. Take the kid with you.'

Hildie said, 'Never mind that. Where *is* Bessie? I've looked in the bedroom and the sitting room and—'

Monica made an animal sound. 'Oh no –!'

Bob said, 'Go find her, Hildie. Bring her back here and keep her in the living room—'

'She's run off.' Monica's nails tore on the door. She thrust herself past Bob and Hildie and ran into the bedroom. 'Bessie – darling – where are you? It's okay – it's me, Auntie Mon. Bessie – where are you?'

It was obvious that Bessie had gone. Hildie was wide-eyed and as frantic as Monica herself.

'How long ago? Where—? Ring Donaghue – Bob, *do* something!'

He rang downstairs and heard that Bessie had 'just stepped out five minutes ago'. He looked at Monica.

She said, 'She's in this city. Alone. Oh God.'

Hildie said, 'What happened? Why has she gone?'

Monica did not look at her. Her eyes never left Bob's.

'You said we were doing some trading.' Her voice rose until it was a scream. 'I will trade you for my daughter!' She lifted her head and shrieked at the ceiling. 'Do you hear me, God? Give me back my daughter and I'll never go near this man again in my life!'

Bob caught her as she fell.

Immediately she saw him, Bessie knew why Cass loved Jean-Claude. And quite soon after that, she knew too that he was her father. It was suddenly so obvious. Cass would not have loved twice, it was not in her nature. She had fallen in love with this man, then he had gone away and Cass had had a baby. Then she had found him again. It was simple. He had dark hair like Bessie herself had, he had black eyes like she had. And he was somehow oddly familiar. Her body and bones knew him already.

He arrived late that evening in response to a telephone call from Monsieur Gotthard and they met him at the airport. He had cameras with him because the message had been so obscure he thought the New York rally had exploded into unprecedented violence, and he was to cover that angle for the newspaper.

Confronted by Bessie, he was still uncomprehending. When Louis introduced 'Miss Elizabeth Durant' he began to wonder. Then she blurted, 'I'm sorry. I'm Cass' daughter, Bessie. Bessie Woodford. I didn't know how to contact you. I have to get back to Cass. I must. I didn't know how . . .' An enormous tear of sheer exhaustion blurred her vision, and she blinked hard.

He unloaded his bags and sat down so that he was on a level with her. He did not ask a lot of questions. Obviously the child was terribly confused about her true parentage. It did not matter to Jean-Claude. He knew that Cass loved Bessie and Bessie loved Cass. That was all that mattered.

He held out his hand.

'Bessie. I have wanted to see you very much. I am very honoured that you too wanted to see me.'

She took his hand, intending to shake it politely. It was warm and dry and infinitely reassuring. The tear ran down her face and was followed by others. He drew her on to his knee and she hid her face in his shirt and behaved like a baby. And it was then she knew he must be her father.

He took her to a drugstore and bought her a soda and some food and she told him what had happened. She kept talking about Mallie's death and Boris, and how unhappy Aunt Liv was, and he held her and rocked her and finally said, 'The sooner we get you back to the Bergerie, the better. Do you agree with that?'

'Oh yes, monsieur.'

'And you had better call me by name. Jean will do. Could you manage that?'

'Oh yes. Oh Jean, Grannie and Cass will be disappointed that I ran away. Can you explain to them? Monica's husband did not recognise me when I was dressed up, and I felt so ashamed and . . . sort of . . . frightened.' She looked up, tears already drying. 'I don't know why. Not now. It was just – after Mallie – and Boris not being at home—'

'And Cass telling you about me, perhaps?'

She flushed darkly.

He said quietly, 'It is nothing to be ashamed of, chérie. Cass

576

belongs to you and you thought I would take her away. Yes?' He did not wait for an answer. 'It is not so, Bessie. Can you try to think of all love and concern and friendship being pooled – a lake of it – a sea of it—' He stopped and smiled at her. She was only thirteen, he would probably drown her in his sea of concepts. But she smiled back at him.

'Like Mallie. Always wading into the fishpond at Aunt Liv's. Perhaps that was why he did it.'

He thought about it, then nodded. 'Perhaps it is so,' he agreed.

He telephoned the Connecticut farm and spoke to Aggie. He told her that Bessie had become lost and had asked a policeman to take her to the office of *La Planète*. He would bring her back to the farm himself. Bessie watched him, wide-eyed, aghast that he was betraying her.

'You understand this is best, chérie?' He replaced the telephone. 'This Aggie – she will now telephone Monica and by the time we all meet at the Connecticut farm, everyone will be calm. I will introduce myself as a colleague of Cass' and suggest that you come home with me at the end of the week. So we all avoid unpleasantness – perhaps a rift between Monica and Carol – you understand?'

'Yes. Of course. You are . . . good. But—' she breathed deeply. 'You see, Jean, Aunt Mon won't agree to it. She will want me to stay with her and Uncle Bob.'

'I do not think so, Bessie. Trust me. If she asks you to stay, simply tell her that you think it would be best to go home now. Then I will talk to her. Trust me.'

Bessie trusted him. She would have told him that she knew he was her father, but innate good manners insisted that she must wait for him to mention it. She nodded and sat back on the high stool. She felt suddenly very tired and relaxed. Jean was telephoning about hiring a car. He was so competent. He would look after them all. He would train Boris to use a camera. He might even make it all right for Auntie Liv and Auntie Myrt.

Monica did not know what to think or do. She had never fainted in her life before and by doing so now, she had lost them all valuable time. She sat with her head still between her knees; her tears dried; she stared at the carpet. Unexpectedly she thought of Myrtle and the new baby. No wonder Myrtle did not want it any

more; Monica would give up anything – anything in the worid –
to see Bessie walk through the door.

Hildie was crouched by her side.

'Listen, honey. I'll go and look. Right now. You and Bob get
on to the Juvenile Department. When I get back – if I haven't
found her – Bob can wait here for calls and we'll get a cab and
scour the area. Okay?' She stood up. 'She can't have got far – I'll
find her. Okay Bob?'

Monica heard him mumble something; he sounded like a sulky
schoolboy. Hildie said sharply, 'I don't know what you said to
scare away that kid, but you'd better pull yourself together now.
She's thirteen years old dammit, and New York is a big place.'

She left, and Monica stood up and made for the phone much
too quickly; the pale walls of the apartment swam around her.

'Sit down. I'll do it.' But he went to the kitchen first and
returned with a whisky. She could have wept at the delay. 'Drink
this.' He thrust the glass at her, and at last went to the phone. It
was a long business. First of all they put him through to something called Missing Persons, and after he'd told the story and
made it sound almost unimportant, he was put through to the
Juvenile Department.

'Description? Well . . . she's kind of tall for her age, and she
has dark hair and eyes. Dress?' He looked over his shoulder.
'What dress was she wearing, Mon?'

Monica put the glass down on the floor and made for the
phone. He surrendered it without argument.

'She was wearing a blue dress. Covered in white daisies. And
white sandals. Yes, socks. And a gold bracelet. No, no other
jewellery.' She began to shiver. 'She hasn't got a coat or anything, and when the sun goes down . . . yes, I know it's been less
than an hour. No, there was no argument. Not exactly. Yes, she
might have been upset. No, she wouldn't be hiding in the apartment – we've looked. Searched? No, not really, but yes, we will
search. And the elevators. Yes. Yes, of course.' She put the
receiver down and looked at Bob. 'They think she's playing us
up. Hiding. To worry us. Sort of . . . punish us.'

'Well, that's what she's doing, isn't it? She didn't like me
yelling at her – she didn't like me, period.'

Monica said wearily, 'Bob. She heard what you said. And she
doesn't want to be my child. She wants to belong to Cass and

578

Mary Woodford. Like I wanted to belong to Gilly. Belonging. That's what it's about, Bob.'

'Weren't you going to tell her? Were you going to trick the pair of us? For the rest of our lives?' He was still rigid with anger.

'Bob. Please. You wanted me back. I couldn't have come back without Bessie. If you'd accepted her, then I would have stayed and told her one day. She might have just come by the knowledge gradually. Herself.' She gave a dry sob. 'Oh, I don't know. It sounds crazy now. I didn't work it out. It just happened. I was miserable – you'd rejected me – I wanted to see Bessie and Cass – and the others. And when I saw them, I just wanted to – to – borrow Bessie. First of all for my – my self-esteem. And then because I loved her. And I told myself that she was in danger with Cass and that I was doing her a favour taking her right away from Europe. And then Myrtle's child was drowned in the garden pool and it was so awful, I wanted to get back here myself. I thought we might make ourselves into a family. A proper family. If Myrtle can put up with Malcolm playing around with every woman in sight and still make something good out of it, I thought I could too.' Monica stopped speaking, listened, and said, 'Is that the elevator? Hildie might have her—'

'No, it's not the elevator. It's the fridge.' Bob came and stood by her. 'Listen, Mon. Nancy threw herself at me. She was nothing to me and I was nothing to her. It was just that . . . nothing. I've never played around, as you put it.'

'Hildie told me how much you wanted children. I can't have them.'

'You're enough for me. I thought I was enough for you.'

She bowed her head. She knew he wanted to take her into his arms and comfort her. And she knew if she let him she could eventually make him agree to keep Bessie. But she had cheated enough.

She said in a low voice, 'I can't think about that now, Bob. I can't think about us.'

'All right, honey. All right. Listen, finish that whisky and Hildie will be back with the kid.'

'With Bessie.'

'Yeah. Okay. With Bessie.'

She downed the whisky and as if on cue the elevator whined. They met it, the doors slid back, Hildie was alone.

* * *

579

The cab driver was almost too keen on his mission: he became Philip Marlowe and did unnecessary U turns every time he glimpsed a child on the sidewalk. They went back to Central Park but there was no hope of seeing any one individual in the ordered crowds marching solemnly with banners and placards. 'She wouldn't have come back here,' Hildie declared. The cab driver agreed. 'The Empire State. That's where she'd go. That's where they all go.' Monica was silent. Bessie had thought the march might be something like the Changing of the Guard; might she have joined it? Either for its ritual ceremony, or in a bid for her own freedom of choice? Monica dropped her head for a moment, fighting off nausea again, then raised it quickly in case she missed a glimpse of that slim schoolgirl figure in her blue and white dress.

After an hour they drove back to Beekman Place to see whether there was any news from the Police Department. Bob had heard nothing. He met them at the elevator doors; he was smoking fiercely. The hour had given him a lot of time to think, but his thinking had got him nowhere. He wanted to yell a disgusted 'Women!' and leave for the nearest bar. He couldn't do that.

Hildie rang the Juvenile people. She was incisive, almost hectoring.

'There's only so much we can do.' She looked at Monica then quickly away – it was like staring at a recent wound. 'Where would a twelve-year-old go in a strange city? We've tried all the drugstores round about. We've been back to Central Park . . . yeah, we were there earlier . . . no, hopeless, the place is packed with marchers. We can't cover every angle and you've got the manpower. Sure I realise she's not your only problem, but we're asking for action now. It could actually save time in the end.' She held the receiver, breathing hard while she listened. 'Go back home? Home is France or England for this kid.' She nodded. 'Okay. She just might have tried to get back to Connecticut. We'll cover that angle.' She replaced the receiver without saying goodbye, and immediately picked it up to dial another number. 'George,' she explained over the mouthpiece.

Bob said, 'Monica, honey, come into the kitchen and have some food. Another drink.'

She was going to shake her head, then thought that anything

580

was better than sitting on the chair in the hall. She went through to the kitchen and automatically filled the kettle at the faucet. She thought of Nancy. Then by an incomprehensible link, of her adoptive mother, Nelly Cook.

'We'll have some tea,' she said as if it were a line in a play. She looked round at Bob and realised that he was at a complete loss. She said, 'I'm sorry, Bob. I really am. You were so good, oh better than good – you were wonderful. Lots of men had tried to get through my barrier in the old Albion days. You just didn't see there was a barrier there.' She laughed shakily. 'You battered it down.'

He made an enormous effort. 'Like Sleeping Beauty I guess. Huh?'

'I suppose so. Maybe.' She poured hot water into the teapot to warm it and swilled it gently around as Liv did in her immaculate kitchen. 'I didn't want to cheat you in any way, Bob. I loved you. I went back home and saw my brother. If there'd been anything there . . . anything left . . . I would have called off our wedding.' She measured tea carefully. 'But he didn't love me. He didn't understand about love. It was just fun . . . all those nights . . . just fun. He thought he knew about Bessie, but he wasn't going to try to find out in case it made things difficult for him. I couldn't love a man like that. So I came back to London and married you.'

He swallowed. He did not like her references to Gilly. But still he said, 'And it was wonderful, hon. Wasn't it?'

There was no tea cosy, the silver teapot was vacuum sealed, but she fetched a clean tea towel from the drawer and wrapped it around the teapot as best she could. Then she put three bone china cups on a tray without their saucers, and went for milk from the refrigerator.

'Yes, it was.' She remembered the desperation with which she had made love with Bob. As if by sheer exertion she could shut out memories of Gilly and Bessie.

'Then it could be wonderful again.' He shook his head as she started to speak. 'I know. You can't talk about the future with this hanging over your head. But . . . there is a future, honey. I want you to know that it could be wonderful again. It's up to you.'

She did not ask him whether his ultimatum still held. She poured tea almost steadily, and let him carry the tray to the kitchen table. Hildie joined them.

'I've rung George. I've rung home. I've rung George again.' She

581

sat down heavily. Monica remembered she was pregnant. She put a hand on her shoulder, and Hildie covered it with hers. It was as if Hildie was standing in for Cass. Or Myrt. Or Liv.

An hour later the Juvenile Department came through. A woman spoke to Hildie at some length, and for once Hildie listened intently.

She put a hand over the mouthpiece.

'Listen. A girl in a blue dress was picked up earlier by a cop car. She was taken to the offices of the *Herald* – she wanted to talk to some reporter in a French newspaper office, called *La Planète*, which hangs out in the same building. The guy who vouched for her was called Louis Gotthard, and she gave a name – Elizabeth Durant. D'you think it's Bessie? Didn't she ask about *La Planète* earlier?'

Monica was completely thrown. The name Durant meant nothing to her. She vaguely remembered hearing the name of the newspaper. She looked wildly at Bob.

He said, 'Get the address. We'll go straight there.'

Hildie returned to the telephone. She spoke, then listened again, then lifted her head.

'They say they will follow it up and be through again in a few minutes.' She avoided Monica's eye. 'There's no answer from this newspaper office. The reception desk says the Gotthard man left with a child half an hour ago. He says Gotthard is completely trustworthy.'

'What can they do, then?' Monica asked wildly.

'Go into the office. Look for notes . . . something.'

So again they waited. It was dark. The lights of the city seemed to twinkle heartlessly. They drank more tea and Bob switched on the television to get the news. No bodies had been found that day.

George rang through. There was no sign of Bessie at the farm. Someone from the Juvenile Department was with him and they had searched the buildings.

Half an hour later another call came through. An officer was waiting outside Gotthard's apartment in Brooklyn. He had not arrived home yet. As soon as he could be interviewed they would come back with more news.

At half-past ten, Monsieur Gotthard returned home and the crucial information filtered back to Beekman Place. The child, Elizabeth Durant, had indeed been wearing a gold bracelet and a blue and white dress. She had wanted to contact her uncle Jean-Claude Durant. Monsieur Gotthard had telephoned him in Washington. He had then taken the child to the airport to meet the plane. When he had seen them installed in a nearby drugstore; he had left. Gotthard was a reputable newspaperman, so was Durant. There was no reason to worry; but it might be as well if Mr and Mrs Gallagher reported to headquarters now. It would be necessary to find out why the child had run away from them, and exactly to whom she belonged.

Ten minutes after replacing the receiver, when they were still affronted and baffled, the phone rang again. This time it was George speaking from the farm. Bessie and her uncle were on their way.

They were all exhausted. Bob shook Jean-Claude's hand, but his jaw was clamped hard and the muscle under his ear twitched rhythmically throughout the garbled explanations.

Jean-Claude provided most of these.

'It seems that Bessie was reminded of my assignment in America. The march in Central Park and – er – so on. She took a walk – got lost and decided to find her way to the newspaper office.'

Monica said faintly, 'I'm sorry. Who are you? Bessie has not mentioned an uncle at all . . .'

'I am a very old friend of Carol's. We have worked together – I was with her last month when she edited a book in London. Perhaps she mentioned it.'

'I know about the book. Yes.'

'But she did not speak of me?' He smiled with all the charm he could muster. Cass had said Monica was beautiful, but this gaunt creature with sallow face and staring eyes looked menacing to him. He wondered how soon he would be able to extricate Bessie from this situation. It wasn't good for the child. The sister-in-law was normal enough, but the Gallaghers seemed on the brink of a furious marital breakup. If Bessie had triggered it, there was nothing to be done except spirit her away.

He said, 'Probably there was much to talk about. I heard that the four of you met for the first time in twelve years. Also I heard of the tragedy of the small boy. It was most kind of you to bring Bessie away for this holiday.'

He stared into Monica's eyes and she stared back. She told herself this was another reason why Bessie should stay in America. First the danger from the publication of this mysterious book; and now the presence of Cass' lover.

There was a long pause. Everyone seemed to be looking at Monica. She felt a physical pressure from these looks. She blinked hard and turned her own gaze on Bessie. The child was strained and white, her dress crumpled, her hair like rats' tails. She seemed to be holding her breath and Monica knew what she wanted to do. What she wanted to do more than anything else in the world.

Monica blinked again and turned to the Frenchman.

'I'll have to talk to Bessie's mother on the telephone. You understand that? And if she is agreeable, I see no reason why Bessie shouldn't return with you.'

She felt Bob's arm across her shoulders, she saw Bess' smile. She could have been referring to Mrs Woodford when she said 'Bessie's mother', but everyone knew who she meant.

Hildie, the only person beside herself who was not smiling, said, 'Are you sure that's for the best, honey?'

'I think so.' Monica let Bob take some of her weight. 'If it's what Bessie wants.'

'There's so much to do before school, Aunt Mon,' Bessie began diplomatically.

Hildie cut across the careful words.

'Let's have milk and cookies then. And go to bed.'

Of course Bob thought she'd 'chosen' him. He knew the kind of sacrifice she'd made, and he wept that night, holding her like a child and whispering in her ear, 'Thank you, honey. I love you – you know that. I'll never look at another woman.'

Monica, lying on her back, wide-eyed in the milky darkness, wished she'd done it for Bob. She wished she could turn into his shoulder and whisper, 'I love you too, darling.' But she couldn't. Giving Bessie back to Cass this time was worse than it had been thirteen years ago. Then she hadn't looked at the baby's face; it had been an anonymous creature. Now it was Bessie. Had she done it for Bessie's sake? Or for Carol's? She did not know.

Long after Bob was asleep, she went on staring. Around four o'clock she heard Jim go across the yard to the cowsheds to start the milking machine. The whole ethos of the farm emphasised her own barrenness; she felt herself shrivelling and drying. Surely there was supposed to be some sort of satisfaction gained from making a sacrifice? She searched her soul for an atom of satisfaction, and could find none.

Carol met them both at Marseilles. Monica's phone call had been enigmatic to say the least, and until she saw them walking across the tarmac together she did not let herself believe that they were both all right, that they were both being returned to her.

It was obvious they knew each other intuitively. On the long double flight back to France they had not talked of their pasts at all; it seemed from Bessie's usual insouciant chatter that she had questioned Jean-Claude in detail about the techniques of his job.

'Boris wants to be a photographer, you see,' she explained to them both.

She had chosen to sit in the back of the Renault, and Jean-Claude then chose to sit by her. There was no embarrassment or awkwardness between them; Carol could hardly believe it. If it had been anyone else, she might even have felt excluded. But Bessie hung over the passenger seat, explaining, turning to Jean-Claude for corroboration now and then, making the events of the last two days sound almost normal.

Carol drove out of the city and followed the north bank of the Rhône into the country. She glanced in the mirror and saw Jean-Claude sitting relaxed and smiling, directly behind her. That was incredible in itself. She had said goodbye to him only a week ago, trying to blot out the insidious feeling that she would never see him again. Her mother had returned home, and in the relief of having her back at the Bergerie, Carol had wept and said, 'I know he will be killed, Mother. I feel it. I'm not meant to have a normal life with him. I'm sorry . . . I can't help it . . .'

And here he was. And with Bessie. The impossible had happened. When she was a child herself, she might have prayed for this. 'Please God let Bessie and Jean be friends. Let them meet in America and come home together safely.' As an adult, it would have seemed a ridiculous request. Yet it had happened.

Jean-Claude said, 'Why are you smiling, Cass? Do you think Bessie is exaggerating? I can assure you that Providence had a hand in what happened. It is as she says – the march in Central

Park reminded her of me – the friendly policeman talking to the woman with the dog—'

'Oh, I agree!' Carol shifted her head so that her reflected smile could include both of them. 'Actually I was just thinking that God must have read my mind. I didn't like to bother Him with such a big thing. But He knew what I wanted and . . . here you are!'

They all laughed. It was, after all, nothing short of miraculous.

At the Bergerie, Mary Woodford waited for them. If she had any qualms about the direction their lives were taking, she hid them well. When Jean-Claude shook her hand solemnly, Bessie sprang between them and hugged her with her usual thoroughness. And as she did so, she whispered in her ear, 'Give him a kiss, Grannie. He wants so much for you to love him.'

For a startled moment, Mary stared at the child. Like Cass, she could hardly believe that this instant relationship was real. Bessie, for all her good intentions, had been guarded about the advent of Carol's 'friend'. She had been ripe for a good old-fashioned bout of jealousy. What had happened in America?

But Mary could not refuse the urgent request.

She looked at the clever dark eyes of the man who had swept Cass completely off her feet, and gave a rueful laugh.

'Oh . . . come here!' She held his face in her hands and felt the strong jawbone, tense beneath her fingers. 'I've never had a son,' she said with a little break in her voice. 'I think we should do more than shake hands though.'

He was overwhelmed. Mary knew all about the strong sexual attraction that could batter down all barriers, and she had been terrified that Carol had been 'smitten' by such an attraction. But in his delighted smile and the sudden release of the tension in him, she saw the likeableness of the man.

Carol lugged in the last case and said disgustedly, 'Thank you for all your help.'

And again, everyone laughed.

586

Thirteen

At the end of January, Myrtle went into a nursing home near Pittsville pump rooms, and gave birth to another boy on February 1st.

It was an easy birth; the baby was perfect, a carbon copy of Nicholas and Martin, who had both been ridiculously like Malcolm. Myrtle looked at him lying in the webbed canvas cot, and felt nothing at all.

But Malcolm was thrilled.

'What shall we call him, darling?'

He was always thrilled by babies, it was one of his endearing qualities. He seemed to have forgotten Mallie. He hung over the monkey-like scrap dotingly, offering his finger and searching the crumpled features for likenesses to himself.

'I don't know. Not Malcolm.'

'Of course not, baby. We can't replace Mallie. But this . . . this is a chance to start again. Myrt. Can't we start again now?' He looked up at her from where he knelt by the cot. His eyes pleaded. He wanted the excitement again: the running battle of marriage which had been so sadly absent since last August. Myrtle never brought tea into the treatment room any more; she couldn't care less if he made love to every patient he had, male or female.

She said, 'I suppose we've got to.' She tried to smile at him. 'It's just that I'm so tired, Malcolm. That's all.'

'We'll take a holiday this summer, honey. Look up our old friends in Bournemouth. Good hotel. Sit on the beach.'

'We haven't got any friends in Bournemouth any more, Malcolm. I never had time to write . . . keep in touch. Anyway there was no-one we wanted to keep in touch with.'

'Well, we'll have a holiday somewhere, darling. You deserve a rest.'

'A rest? With Nicky and Martin and this new baby?'

'Just the two of us, then. We could get a nanny. How about going to France to see Cass?'

She said half-heartedly, 'Perhaps I'd be better going somewhere alone. I'm not good company at the moment.'

He looked at her steadily in a way that in the old days would have made her melt. 'You'd trust me with a nanny? Those white overalls? Those caps? You know what I'm like.'

She couldn't make more of an effort. 'In any case, Malcolm, Cass is fully occupied at the moment. She doesn't want us barging in on her little love-nest.'

There was a deadening effect in her complete lack of interest; he wished he could generate one of their old-style rows. But the doctor had bandied words like 'post-natal depression', and he knew he had to be very, very gentle with her.

He said pacifically, 'All right. We'll see, this summer.' He returned to the baby. 'God, he's lovely, Myrt. You're a bloody clever girl. In fact we're a bloody clever pair, aren't we?'

Her eyes clouded. She was thinking of Mallie.

He went on quickly, 'Come on. Let's think of a name. What about Ivan after your father? Or Chester after mine?'

'Whichever you like.'

'Well, Chester is my name too of course. And he's the spitting image of me.' He smiled. 'Christ, Myrt. This is what immortality is all about. All these boys. God, it makes me feel randy. I love you, Myrt.'

She said definitely, 'I'm not having any more. That's final, Malcolm. I mean it.'

'All right, bunny rabbit. All right.' He smiled. She'd change her mind. It had always been Myrtle who wanted the babies. Always.

The nurses thought Chester was simply hilarious for such a tiny baby, and they simply shortened their own 'Baby Lennox' to 'Lennie'. And Lennie he became.

Myrtle called him nothing. She knew there was something wrong with her, but she did not know what to do about it. She told herself that when she got home everything would start to be all right again. But she dreaded going home. The tall house in Imperial Gardens was so empty without Mallie. When they'd

588

returned from Barnt Green last August it had looked messy and old after Liv's suburban luxury; the kitchen was so dark, her bedroom – where she spent a lot of time – was so cold. She couldn't go back to Liv's because of Reggie; Monica was trying to get her marriage back on its feet in far-away New York; Carol had, of course, made a newly structured and blissful family with the addition of the boyfriend. Myrtle was completely and utterly alone.

On bonfire night she stood in the long narrow garden with the boys and watched while Malcolm and Tom let off the fireworks, and in an effort to feel something, she took a burnt-out sparkler from Nicky and held it in her bare hand where the end still glowed redly. She dropped it very quickly, but she did not scream and it was much later that Malcolm discovered the blistered hand and dressed it.

She had hoped that after the shock of Mallie's death, she would miscarry. The thought had been in her mind during the long walk with the girls to find the Haunted House. But her short sturdy body had a strength of its own beyond her will. She continued to expand; her legs continued to swell; she even had obsessive eating fads. She craved Worcester sauce on everything, but when Doris brought some from the Maypole Dairy, she no longer wanted it.

She never complained, but Malcolm still said, 'It'll be all right once the baby is born, bunny rabbit. Don't worry, it'll be all right.' Whether he was comforting her or himself was a moot point. One night when again she turned from him, he asked sadly, 'Don't you love me any more, Myrtle?'

She replied automatically, 'Of course I love you. I'm just so tired, that's all.'

But how could she know whether she loved him when she had no feelings left?

She would have liked to have seen the girls; she knew that much. When they'd been together on that walk, just the four of them, she had almost forgotten Mallie. She had felt normal; she had been a human being with her feet on Mother Earth.

Carol wrote to her:

'Have you heard from Monica? Bessie's visit to New York was cut short and she came back to France with Jean-Claude. I

589

think you will like Jean, Myrt. In fact I pray you will like him, because if he can get a divorce we shall be married. Has that shocked you?'

It did shock Myrtle. It removed Cass in some way: she was no longer the property of the girls. If Cass was going to marry a man, it meant she was wholeheartedly in love with him. And it was obvious that Liv, Mon, and Myrtle herself, were no longer wholeheartedly in love with their husbands.

She sat on the edge of her bed and tore the letter up into postage-stamp pieces. They stayed on the floor until Doris vacuumed a week later.

The day she went home with Baby Lennox, it was snowing. She sat in the big front room and watched Doris taking the boys across the pristine expanse of the Gardens to a birthday party at the Queens Hotel. It was going to be a posh affair and Doris had bought them minuscule suits and white shirts with attached bow ties. They had come into the front room where she sat by Lennie's cot, and showed themselves off smirkingly. Nicky had grown up suddenly; he no longer bedevilled Martin, they were quite good friends.

'You look beautiful,' she said as if by rote.

Nicky made a terrible face. 'Boys don't look beautiful, Mummy. We look handsome.'

'All right. Handsome.' Before last summer she would have grinned at that.

'Say goodbye to Mummy and Lennie,' Doris prompted. 'Goodbye Mummy. Goodbye Lennie,' parroted Martin.

Nicky dragged him over to the cot and insisted they went through the usual performance.

'Bye bye then, baby,' Nicky cooed in perfect imitation of his father. 'Be a good boy while we're gone.'

Martin said more naturally, 'I'll teach you to play football next week, Lennie.'

They planted dry boy-kisses on Myrtle's cheeks and went into the hall to be booted and capped. Myrtle whispered, 'They're lovely kids. I love them. I must love them.'

They pretended to skate on the slushy snow, then turned and

waved at the window, though they did not know whether she was there or not.

Malcolm's head came round the door.

'Did you see the boys? I waved a towel from the treatment room and they must have seen me and waved back. We've been doing that while you were away. I'm going to teach them semaphore.'

He was gone. She almost smiled. The boys hadn't been waving at her, or clowning for her. They could live without her just as she could live without them. Which was good.

Malcolm reappeard with tea and told her he had a long appointment so wouldn't see her for a while.

'Will you be all right, bunny rabbit?'

'Of course.'

He crouched before her chair. 'Why don't you try to feed Lennie yourself, Myrtle? You had so much milk for the others, there must be something there. And it would help you to begin to feel like a . . . mother.'

'I'd rather not.'

He sighed. 'All right.' He went on giving her one of his looks. Her eyes slid away from his. He said, 'Not long ago it would have been you bringing *me* tea. Right into the treatment room. Keeping your predatory eye on me, bunny rabbit!'

She said nothing. He whispered, 'Aren't you worried about what I might be getting up to in the next hour?'

There was a pause. Then she said, 'No.'

The monosyllable was objective, passionless. She did not mean that she trusted him for the next hour. Simply that she did not care. He almost recoiled. He wanted to shout at her, call her names, tell her that it was Mrs Herron he was seeing. But it would make no difference.

He stood up, and, like the boys, gave her a chaste kiss on her cheek. Then he left.

After a while the baby started to whimper. She unwrapped the bottle from its clean nappy and shoved the teat in his mouth. He sucked until the teat turned inside-out, then started to cry again. She pulled out the teat, put the bottle back, moved closer to the fire. Ten minutes later, the crying began again. She let it go on for a while then looked into the cot. The bottle was empty, the baby had wind. If it went on crying, Malcolm would come to investigate. But she did not want to pick it up to wind it. Instead, she picked up the discarded nappy and folded it into a thick six-inch pad. Carefully she put it over the baby's face and went to the window. The cries went on, but they were muffled.

A car drew up outside the front door right behind Mrs Herron's. She looked at it incuriously. It was vaguely familiar. It drove away again, chugged slowly up the road as if looking for an address, then turned at the top to go down the back lane where the mews had been turned into garages.

The baby's cries grew louder. It had turned its head away from the nappy. She went back and looked down on it. It was not a bit like Mallie. She wondered who was looking after Mallie now. She didn't want to replace Mallie. She took the nappy pad and put it on the baby's face, and pressed gently.

The door opened. Someone came in, tentatively at first then with a rush. Myrtle was pulled backwards, the nappy fell to the floor. The baby cried in earnest. Myrtle flailed her arms against the sort of thick camel coat beloved by all auctioneers, and then said in amazement, 'Reggie!' And Reggie, almost weeping, said, 'Oh my darling. My darling girl. What has happened to you?' and held her to him in a hug that could not be resisted; a hug that was as cold as the snow outside and as warm as that summer's day when they had first made love.

He did not know she was dead inside. He kissed her repeatedly, her eyes, her ears, her mouth. He smoothed her rough, frizzy hair, and buried his face in her neck.

She said, 'Reggie. Reggie . . .' but it was not a protest, more a murmur of continuing surprise.

He said, 'I saw you standing by the window. I thought you knew it was me. I went round the back so that Malcolm wouldn't see me. Oh my darling. I couldn't keep away. I love you so much. I've missed you so much. I think of you all the time. I think of Mallie. I blame myself, darling. It was my fault. If we hadn't been together that afternoon, you would have been with Mallie. I've tried to keep away, but . . .' he broke down and sobbed tearingly.

She heard herself telling him it wasn't his fault. She felt her arms pushing him into a chair and cradling his heaving shoulders. She actually kissed the top of his head and smelled the familiar smell of his hair. She was transported back to that time, that wonderful time, when she had managed to free herself from Malcolm and love someone else. When Mallie had been alive.

She whispered, 'Perhaps we were both to blame, my dearest. Perhaps we're both guilty.' And she began to cry.

It was Reggie who eventually dealt with the baby. The cries were filtering through the house and he knew someone must come soon. He lowered the crumpled Myrtle to the hearthrug and let her rest her head on the chair; now she had started to weep she could not stop. He picked up the child and hung it over his shoulder. Immediately it gave an almighty burp and a trickle of milk went down his overcoat. He cradled it in his big hands. The sudden silence was bliss. Myrtle breathed sobbingly and closed her eyes.

'He's lovely, Myrt. What's his name?'

She did not answer immediately, then she remembered.

'Chester.'

'Ah. Malcolm's family name.'

'Yes.' She opened her eyes and looked at him. 'He's Malcolm's. Nicky and Martin are Malcolm's too. Mallie was mine.'

'Malcolm loved Mallie. He's terribly grieved . . . that day at home . . . I didn't know what to do with him.'

'He's got the others. And his women.'

'Oh Myrtle.'

'I don't mind. I'm glad in a way.' She went on looking at him. She hadn't really looked at anyone for a long time. She said, 'I haven't been with him since . . . then.'

He swallowed visibly. Then he stood up and put Lennie back in his cot. He said, 'I haven't been with Liv either.'

She said with some of her old realistic cheerfulness, 'We shall get over it, Reggie. We shall have to.'

'We don't have to.' He sat down again and looked at her sitting on the floor, her arms on the chair. She was looking so ill, white as a ghost, her body beneath the awful jumper and skirt was flabby and loose. 'Myrtle. Why were you trying to suffocate Chester just now?'

'I don't know. Perhaps I'm going mad.'

'You're not going mad. You're the sanest person I know. Don't you love him?'

'No. I didn't want him after Mallie died.' She puffed a laugh. 'I tried to get Mon to take him. I tried to have a miss.'

'Why?' he asked again.

'Don't know. Because after Mallie, everything is different. And this baby is forcing me to go back to how I was. And I'm different. But now I've got to stay and look after it. I've got to sleep with Malcolm. I've got to take Nicky and Martin to school, and give dinner parties, and . . .' She stopped and looked at the cot. The baby was asleep. 'I suppose I thought that without him I could go away. Stay with Cass. Or Mon. I don't know, Reggie. I don't know.'

He said in a low voice, 'Will you come away with me, Myrtle?'

That really did shock her. Her head came up and her grey eyes were wide.

'With you? What about Liv? What about having a family? I don't want any more children, Reggie.'

'Liv and I – we're nothing any more. I'd have to tell her, of course. But I'd go. Whatever she said.'

She went on staring, not moving.

'You fell for me first because of the kids. Because I was pregnant. You know you did.'

'Okay. I admit it. But now . . . I can't think of anything else. Anyone else.' He put out a hand. 'Come with me, darling. I'll get a job somewhere else. We won't have much but we'll be together.'

'Oh Reggie.' She drooped. 'I can't. I haven't got the energy to feed the baby, let alone pack up and leave my husband. And I couldn't do it to Liv.'

'You did it to Liv before when you realised she was here with Malcolm. Nothing has changed.'

'I can't. Reggie. I *can't*!' She started to cry again with a new kind of despair.

He knelt and took her in his arms again. She thought he would 'do a Malcolm' and try to seduce her with repeated kisses and his hands on her body. But he did none of those things. He cradled her as he had cradled the baby, making soothing noises into her hair and rocking her gently. When she was still again, he put her in the chair, found a rug and tucked it under her knees. He looked at the untouched tea tray on the table.

'I'm going to make some fresh tea, my love. Then I'll

announce my arrival, in the treatment room. Everything is all right. Perfectly all right. What I have said is what I mean – what I want. But I'll not say it again. You can put it away from you. We will be friends. I am your friend, Myrtle. Remember that.'

He did not wait for a reply. When the door closed behind him, she looked at it and knew that he was a good man. He was the sort of man she needed – and before her, her mother had needed. She put her hands to her face and wept again. But this time her tears were not for Mallie.

Perhaps nothing would have come of it if Liv hadn't forced the issue. The winter had seemed unbearably long to her and her old routine did not fill her days. The golf course had been under snow most of the time and anyway she wasn't that keen on the game, it was really the social life and the status she went for. She spent a lot of time with her parents, but the constant round of bazaars, whist drives, and jumble sales, which were bound up with chapel life, no longer appealed. Her parents still had rigid standards of behaviour which at times had little to do with Christianity and more with keeping up with the Jones'. Mrs Baker noted religiously how often the minister's wife washed her curtain nets, and Mr Baker kept his front lawn shaven and knife-edged like a bowling green for the sake of his public image. Laundry and lawn-cutting gave neither of them any personal pleasure.

Her mother was appalled at what Myrtle's children had done to the carpets at the Barnt Green house.

'You should have them steam-cleaned properly, Liv,' she said, down on her hands and knees shifting the pile with a manicured finger. She looked up suddenly, a smile dawning. 'Or you are planning to get new carpets out of Reggie?'

Liv, who would indeed have planned just that at one time, stared down at the revealed stain without interest.

'Of course not, Mother. That was a top quality carpet. It'll last out my marriage.'

Mrs Baker was seriously shocked. She sat up on the armchair, wide-eyed.

'My dear girl, no carpet is intended to last out a lifetime!'

Liv nearly said, 'Who's talking about a lifetime?' But she stopped herself in time; she had no wish to deal with a fit of hysterics from her mother.

'I don't want new carpets, Mother,' she said definitely, closing the subject.

So the house wasn't using up her slack as it always had in the past. As for Reggie, he might as well have moved out of his body. The body came home, was fed and watered, clothed and cleaned, but the man himself was somewhere else. He replied to her questions, he poured drinks for guests, he worked in the garden at weekends, he even accompanied her to chapel on Sunday evenings, but beyond smiling vaguely, he did not respond to her on a personal level at all. She tried to break through to him by what she considered cheap, erotic methods. In other words she bought one of the new shortie see-through nighties and dabbed Chanel No 5 behind her ears before she went to bed.

Perhaps she did get a response, though it was not the one she wanted: two days later Reggie complained of a sore throat and suggested he should move into the spare room. It was the room where Myrtle and the boys had slept. Liv could not obliterate that particular memory any more. She had not contacted Myrtle since last summer, and when the news of Lennie's birth had come through she had sent her flowers and a card but no message. Somehow she had managed to hold on to the memory of Myrtle on the walk: the old Myrtle, pregnant and scruffy and down-to-earth with no pretensions at all. But when she took Reggie's clean shirts into that room, she saw again the fertile naked Myrtle. And then her own husband scrambling off the bed.

One Wednesday afternoon in May when an icy wind blew across the Lickeys and boredom hung tangibly in the shining house, the phone rang. Liv dived for it, delighted that someone was disturbing her 'afternoon rest'. If it was her mother she'd suggest coming down to Northfield and going to the cinema. They were showing an old film of John Wayne's called *Red River*. Liv felt like fantasising.

It was Ron Jameson, one of the clerks at the office.

'Just ringing to see if Mr Bradley could cover a farm sale tomorrow, Mrs Bradley. Copse Elms out at Bitton.'

Obviously Reggie must be out at a sale. Liv have asked him what he was doing that day, and he had mumbled a reply which she hadn't heard.

'I should think so. You'll see him before I do though. I'm going to the cinema so I won't be around when he gets home.'

'Oh sorry. But he won't be coming into the office tonight as it's his golfing day. Perhaps you could leave him a message.'

Liv was rocked back on her heels. Reggie's golfing day? Did he have a regular golfing day? Her pride would not let her enquire further.

'Of course,' she said.

She did not go to the cinema. She waited for him to come home, planning what she would say, discarding plans then remaking them. Sometimes she hated him with a fierce hatred because he was hurting her pride so much. At other times she felt something much deeper, a keen sense of loss, of aloneness, of standing on the edge of eternity. It did not really matter where he went on Wednesdays. What mattered was that he had a life which did not include her. She was going to scream at him, shake him if necessary, make him see her again.

But when he came in at seven o'clock, he did not look like a man who had had a good day out. His face was grey with tiredness and she saw suddenly how much he had aged in the past year. She was concerned enough to feed him first and wait for the explosive row that would make or break their marriage.

But apparently not even her cooking was good enough now. She had poached a Severn salmon and scraped a pound of tiny new potatoes. He ate perhaps half a dozen mouthfuls and pushed his plate to one side.

'Delicious,' he murmured. 'Shall we go in the other room and see if there's anything on the box?'

'I've done rhubarb fool,' she commented without emphasis.

He said in the same tone, 'Jolly good.' And made for the door.

She followed him into the lounge, went to the socket in the wall, and removed the television plug. Then she faced him.

'I want to know where you've been, Reggie. Shall we sit down or stand?'

Her action and words got through. He looked startled for a moment, then almost relieved. He took a deep breath.

'Let's sit down, Liv. Let's sit down.'

They both sat. He leaned forward, elbows on knees; she sat determinedly back as if she was relaxed, fidgeting slightly with a cushion, then forcing herself to be still.

He said slowly, 'Liv, I can't go on like this.' He glanced up at her then looked again at the floor. 'And I imagine neither can you. Shall we call it a day?'

Now that it had come – and from him, not her – she was appalled. She could have gone on; she was quite good at blotting out unpleasant thoughts. She'd had practice.

She left her first question and asked another. 'What was wrong with supper, I'd like to know? That was fresh salmon. I got it from Prewett's.'

'I had chips, Liv. With Nicky and Martin.'

'Chips? D'you call that a meal?' Her mouth was dry; she tried to swallow and nearly choked.

'There were a lot of them. We had salt and vinegar and bread and butter, and a great deal of tomato sauce.'

When she said nothing he looked up again. She was so pretty with her curly hair and big eyes.

He said in a low voice, 'That's where I go every Wednesday, Liv. To see Myrtle. She's ill and I know you won't go to see her, so I go.'

It was something to hang on to. 'You go in my place, d'you mean? Well, I didn't know she was ill, did I? You've never said. I'll go next week if you like. I thought she'd had enough of us. After Mallie.'

He nodded. 'Perhaps she has. But I can't keep away. You must know I love her, Liv. She is the only thing that matters in my life now. I'm sorry. I can't do anything about it. I tried. I didn't go to see her until after the baby. Then Malcolm told me how ill she was, and I was terrified she might die, and I'd never see her again. So I started—'

She said sharply, 'Shut *up*! Can't you see you're making it worse? She's married to Malcolm and they have three sons!' You're married to me. For better or worse – remember? We've got to put up with it and you're making the worse worse!' The odd syntax gave her words a biblical sound. She tried to get out of the chair so that she could switch on the television and pour a drink, but her strength had gone. She sobbed suddenly, 'We'll have a baby if that's what you want! All this ridiculous nonsense just because you want a family—'

He interrupted sternly. 'It might have been that at one time. It's not any longer. Myrtle does not want any more children, but if she'd come away with me I would look after her for the rest of my life and ask nothing more!'

She cried out with the pain of such complete rejection. Then, at last, bitter anger came to her rescue.

'You swine!' she yelled. 'You filthy swine! Under our own roof! Don't think I don't know what went on! Here – in my lovely house . . . oh my God . . . when I think—' She sprang up and paced the floor like an animal.

He said, 'I'm glad. Glad you can talk about it at last, Liv. Because now I can tell you why it happened. Oh, I'm not trying to shift any blame – Myrtle and I were fully responsible for our own actions. But she wouldn't have let it go further . . . she knew how I felt that day and she would have stopped it for your sake. But then she rang Malcolm and heard your voice. And that was that.'

She wailed aloud again with a new pain.

'I didn't do anything – you must believe me! Nothing happened that day! Ask Monica – she arrived – she will tell you . . .' She collapsed into the chair again and bowed her head to the arm. 'I knew something was wrong when I came home. I knew you were angry with me—'

'I was not angry, Liv.'

'I admit that I intended to – to – flirt with him a little. That was all. He's got a reputation and I was curious and fed up with Myrtle and the kids . . . but when he got serious. I couldn't bear it. I ran off and Monica came . . . ask her. Ask Monica if you don't believe me!'

He watched her for a long moment, then said tiredly, 'Liv, of course I believe you. All I can say is . . . I'm sorry.'

'Sorry I wasn't seduced by your best friend, d'you mean?'

'No. Sorry Myrtle got the wrong end of the stick.' He sighed. 'Oh Liv. If we're being really truthful, then that was a lie. I'm not sorry. I want to belong to Myrtle. How that was brought about does not matter.'

She lifted a tearstained face.

'But Myrtle belongs to Malcolm!'

'No. She did. Even when we made love she belonged to Malcolm. But she doesn't now. She is in a no-man's-land now, belonging to no-one, not even herself. When she comes out of that land, I want to be there.'

'But nothing can come of it, Reggie! Don't you see? Myrtle has three children – you can't take them away from Malcolm, and she won't leave them!'

'Maybe not. I'm not so certain. Myrtle has never been her own woman. She could be that with me.'

'Reggie, you can't do this! Deliberately lure away your best friend's wife! It's not in you to do such a terrible thing.'

'You don't know me. I did not know myself until I began to love Myrtle. I would do anything for her. If she doesn't want me, then I will never see her again. But if she does . . .' he looked at her directly. 'Liv. When I went to see her first – after the baby was born last February – I quite seriously considered killing Malcolm. If there had been a way—'

'Be quiet!' She put a hand over her eyes. 'I don't want to hear this!'

He obeyed her and for a long two minutes there was silence in the room, broken by Liv's breathing.

Then slowly she put a hand on each of the chair arms and levered herself back until her head was supported. She kept her eyes closed.

'So. What do we do?'

'I don't know. I know what I do. I don't know what we do.'

'All right then. What are you going to do?'

'I'm going to keep on visiting Myrtle. Until she's better. Then I'm going to try to persuade her to come away with me.'

'Have you had any thoughts about me?' Her voice was suddenly bitingly sarcastic, and in spite of his professed indifference he flushed.

'Of course. We've been married for seven years. I shall sell my share of the business. You'll have half. And the house of course.'

'Of course. Of course. Of course.' She was trembling on the edge of hysteria again and made a visible effort to control herself. 'Perhaps I should go and live with Malcolm. Do a complete changeover.'

'Is that what you want?'

She thought of the culmination of that ridiculous day in Cheltenham last summer, and shuddered. 'No.'

'You'll have enough money to stay on here. Nothing need change for you. You'll marry again.'

'Stay on here? Mummy and Daddy would die of shame! I'd have to leave the golf club! I couldn't face anyone in the village!'

'Perhaps you could have a holiday with Carol.'

'Play gooseberry, you mean? Thank you again.'

'Liv, we're finished. Before Myrtle we didn't have much. Be honest. But if Myrtle sends me away and you want what is left—'

'Oh my *God*!' She leapt from the chair and threw herself at him. Her nails scored red blood down his face. 'You condescending, patronising . . .!' she screamed. 'D'you think I'll stay here another minute now?' He held her off, at last thrown from the single track that he had made for himself all these months. She shouted and spat in his face. Words emerged somehow. '. . . hate you . . . hate Myrtle . . . we were friends . . . we had something – loyalty – you've taken that . . . she's a bitch . . . permanent heat . . .' He removed his right hand from her flailing arm and hit her across the face. They both collapsed on to the maltreated carpet.

'Liv, I'm sorry. I'm sorry.'

But he had cured the hysteria, and she said almost sadly, 'This is the end then. This really is the end.'

Monica was delighted to see her. Hildie had had her new baby and did not go far from the Connecticut farm these days. Monica and Bob had joined a select club which offered everything from riding to poker, with people who had either money or breeding. Bob loved it. He loved some of the women he played tennis with, and he loved to see Monica attracting the men she swam with. Monica hated it.

Somehow she was in a worse position than she'd been before she left for England. Bob was treating her like a prized possession, or – which was worse – as if she might have a nervous breakdown at any minute. She had given Bessie back to Cass and she was missing her friends and what she privately thought of as a 'real life'. Mallie's tragic death had cut through so much superficial rubbish: they had all shared Myrtle's grief, and from this distance and in retrospect her two months back home seemed like the real ale beneath the froth. It might have been bitter, but it had some kind of meaning, some kind of purpose.

She did not write letters, but she heard from Carol occasionally and sent Myrtle a card when the new baby was born. Liv's request was like a shaft of light. She cabled back 'Come. Stay long time.' She got Mrs Warren, the latest in helps, hopeless and helpless, to prettify the guest room with flowers and a new lace bedcover and bows on the pillows. It was sentimental and sickening but,

601

remembering the house at Barnt Green, it would please Liv.

It became immediately obvious that Liv was not going to notice flowers or bows. She was like a coiled spring, tense yet on the point of collapse. The exclusiveness of Beekman Place was lost on her. They did the usual sightseeing trips and as she gazed up at the tops of the canyon buildings, she murmured, 'It's a foreign country. I hadn't realised that. It's a foreign country, and I'm a foreigner.'

Monica said, 'The Americans don't want you to feel that, Liv. Bob's family and friends made me one of them immediately. I don't think I've ever felt a foreigner.' She purposely did not recall last year when she had been ill; nor the month after Bessie's departure.'

But Liv shook her head. 'I don't mean America. I just mean . . . it brought it home to me.'

'Brought what home, Liv?' Monica felt a sharp concern for her friend. The big baby eyes were not just tired any more, they were frightened.

'Oh. Nothing.' Liv laughed suddenly. 'Actually, I've got quite a lot of money. Shall we go and buy something?'

'Darling. Why not? There's a pink cocktail dress in a little place down here. It's ballerina length – and pink was always your colour. If you like it, I'll give a party especially for you to show it off.'

It was hard to know whether Liv liked the dress or not, but she bought it and Monica hired caterers and gave a select little dinner party and got tickets for a concert featuring the Russian violinist who had recently defected. Hildie and George came; one of Bob's colleagues who was divorced; a couple from the club called Rosa and Jerry Palmer. Bob asked them. Bob admitted he was 'making a play for' Rosa. It sounded so innocent: making a play. And in a way it was just a game to Bob. But Monica knew what he meant; she knew they would end up in bed together.

But that evening at any rate, the Palmers were still a happily married couple. They hardly left Liv's side. And they couldn't stop touching her; first they kissed her in turn, then they escorted her to the window so that she could show them the view. They both put their arms across her shoulders and kept their heads close to hers. The pink dress made her feel like a stick of candy floss, and she wondered whether they might take a bite out of her at any minute.

Jeremy Palmer said, 'And what do you think of our little city, Liv?'

She said truthfully, 'It's what I've dreamed of all my life.' And she should have added, 'And I'm still dreaming it because it can't be real.'

She was very popular with everyone. Her girlish prettiness captivated the women as well as the men. Hildie thought she was innocent and charming. Danny Connell, the divorced man, sat next to her in the theatre box and took her hand. It didn't worry her too much, she was wearing gloves.

'You're making me feel alive again,' he said when the orchestra were tuning up. 'Ever since Margaret left me, I've been half dead. No-one has wanted to listen. You've listened.'

She felt a twinge of surprise. Had she listened? She certainly had not heard. But this attention was good for her damaged pride. She smiled into the darkness and allowed her hand to be kept while the young Russian bowed deeply and took his place close to the conductor. Monica whispered, 'He looks so bewildered, poor man.' Liv nodded.

Reggie took a room in the Bath Road, drove to Cheltenham after work, and visited Myrtle every evening. Malcolm's ego took this as a personal compliment.

'It's good of you, old man. Oh I know with Liv in America you're at a loose end, but to come down and keep an eye on us . . . it's what friendship is all about.'

Reggie's concern for Myrtle did not allow guilt feelings. He said, 'I think she's getting better. Don't you?'

'She's not ill, old man. Just a bit twitchy after all that's happened. She should have fed Lennie. It's taking a long time for her to feel maternal again.'

'I don't think she wants Lennie.'

'Not want her own baby? You don't know anything about mothers, Reggie!' Malcolm tried to laugh. 'What would you suggest? We drown the poor little devil?'

Reggie said, 'She could do with getting away from the children. Haven't you noticed how she avoids them if she can?'

Malcolm, who had just picked up Nicky and Martin from school, helped them to change into cricketing gear, then driven them out to Dean Close for a match, downed his early drink violently.

'Of course I've bloody well noticed!'

He coughed explosively and grabbed his decent handkerchief from his breast pocket. Reggie beat his back.

'Sorry, old man.' Malcolm looked up, eyes streaming. 'It's just that there's nothing to be done. I've tried. Don't think I haven't tried. I wanted her to come up to you and Liv. She wouldn't have that at any price.' He wiped his eyes. 'Have they had a row or something?'

'Not that I know of. But come on, old man. Barnt Green is where Mallie died.'

Malcolm flinched visibly.

'Yes. But I suggested she and Liv went away together. Bournemouth. Or somewhere. Anyway, now Liv's in Yankee-land. And Carol is too occupied with lover-boy apparently. I don't know. Her mother would go with her. Or Boris. But no.'

Reggie said, 'If I could persuade her to go away, would you agree to it?'

'Haven't I just been saying—'

'With me.'

'With *you*?' Malcolm stopped pouring himself another drink and turned. 'With you? What the hell's going on, Reggie, for Christ's sake?'

'You've heard the Royals are giving one of their places on the north-east coast to the National Trust? Hardfanger Castle? We requested permission to catalogue the books – the firm, I mean. They've got original stuff from Lindisfarne stored there. It's a big job. Four firms are involved.'

'Well. Congratulations, old man. What the hell has that got to do with Myrtle?'

'It's a wonderful castle, for God's sake. No-one has seen its treasures. She could come with me whenever she felt like it. Other days she could explore the country – my car will be there.'

'Well . . .' Malcolm finished pouring the drink. 'Sorry, old man, but all I can say is, big deal. The north-east coast even in the summer doesn't sound exactly the kind of thing I had in mind for my wife!'

'It's within an hour's drive of Alnwick. Berwick-on-Tweed. Holy Island. Hadrian's Wall. We're taking over most of a hotel at Alnmouth.'

'Okay, okay.' Malcolm took his drink more slowly this time.

'I've got to get back into the treatment room. Two evening patients.' He sighed. 'Look Reggie, I don't want to hurt your feelings. It's a great thought. But she needs another woman. You know how they are. Symptoms. Knitting. Babies.'

'May I put it to her while you're working?'

'Well, if you . . . Sure. Okay. I suppose. But don't push her, old man. I'm not having her pushed.'

'I won't push her.'

But he had to talk to her for a long time. She laughed at him at first. Sometimes he could make her laugh.

'Don't be silly, Reggie. I can't walk out on Nicky and Martin. Malcolm wouldn't let me go away.'

'He says he will. And Nicky and Martin don't need you. They've got Doris.' Neither of them mentioned Lennie.

'Darling Reggie. You're so kind. But it's no good. Can't you see that? I'm not the Myrtle you fell for. I'm completely changed. I couldn't sleep with you.'

He wanted desperately to pick her up and hold her again, but since that visit in February he had not touched her.

He said, 'I told you ages ago we would be friends – just friends. I meant that, Myrtle.' He stood up and began to pick up the newspapers littering the chairs and floor. 'You need a holiday away from the family. You need not see me in the day at all. The beach at Alnmouth is wonderful, the sand is white and the waves churn in like trains.' He began to tell her about Hardfanger and the Farne Islands and the glories of Hadrian's Wall. When he paused and looked at her she was smiling.

'You're very like Liv,' she said. 'A place for everything, and everything in its place.'

He felt a terrible pang of disappointment; she hadn't heard a word he'd said.

But then she said, 'I'd like to come with you very much, Reggie. Thank you for asking me.'

He was so happy he almost cried. All right, it was just a holiday for her, but it was also the thin edge of the wedge. He would make her well again. Then he would woo her. He almost ran across the room to kiss her. But he managed to hold back.

'Thank *you*, Myrtle. I'm sure you won't regret it.'

* * *

He would have been very surprised if he could have seen the letter she posted to Monica, care of Dilly Gosling, the next day. It was brief.

'My dear Mon, d'you remember I said you could have my new baby. Do you want him? He weighs sixteen pounds, which is really too heavy, but he is bottle-fed and that puts on weight. He is very healthy and Doris looks after him most of the time. I am going away with Reggie. It is just for a holiday until I get better, but I don't think I shall come back. I don't love Malcolm any more, and Nicky and Martin are like him. I don't know how you can work it, Mon dear, but you've not done too badly up till now. Love, Myrtle.'

Fourteen

Boris was eighteen that summer. His National Service papers arrived the day before he left for his trek up the Victoire with Bessie. He had to report at Corsham in Wiltshire on 10th September.

His mother chose to take it as another tragedy.

'First Myrtle, now you,' she wailed. 'Just as you got that place at the art school! Everything is ruined!'

'Myrtle is having a holiday, Mother. That is all. And my art school place is being saved for me.' He looked again at the railway pass. 'I'm glad they've given me such long notice. I would have hated missing out on France again this year.'

'You've always had a thing about Bessie Woodford. I hope it's natural, Boris. I've not got over last year when you wanted to become a monk. You are all *right*, I suppose?'

He said steadily, 'It depends what you mean by all right. I hope I'm not like Father. Or Malcolm Lennox.' The fact that he had not been with his sister or Bessie during the tragedy of Mallie's death had weighed heavily. He had been convinced during that winter that Myrtle was either dying or going mad, and Bessie's obvious happiness with the new situation in France had seemed like a rejection. His natural inclination to celibacy had persuaded him that the monastic life was for him.

Then at Christmas Bessie outlined one of her famous 'plans.' She told him that they might be able to get jobs together one day, he with his camera, and she with her drawing, and he had dropped the monastery idea like a stone. Bessie had said, 'My favourite things at school are botany and art.' Boris had dismissed the first. 'Bots is boring. But art . . . and travelling the world together looking for unusual plants would be marvellous. But who would pay us?' 'I'm working on that,' she'd assured him.

607

He smiled at his mother, to take the sting out of his words. 'Anyway, Bessie Woodford isn't on her own over there, you know. I thought you wanted me to bring you back news of the others?'

Mrs Denning nodded. 'Especially how Mary is coping with that very *vairy* tricky situation.'

Boris had no intention of reporting back in detail, but he too nodded. Already he knew enough of the three Woodford women to guess that they would cope very well with the new situation.

Jean-Claude was an accepted part of the menage now. He travelled from Paris most weekends, and when he was on an overseas assignment he invariably flew home directly to Marseilles and was met by Cass or her mother.

Cass could never take his safety for granted. During the Paris riots – which he covered for *La Planète* – she was certain he would be killed. Although his old imperialist ideas had mellowed a long time ago, he was still publicly known for them, and could easily have been a target for the new liberalism sweeping France. When de Gaulle was returned to power and began to remodel the constitution, Jean-Claude wrote a leader in support of the new policy and was granted an interview with the President. As one of the war-time Free French, he managed to break through the stiff-necked reserve of the statesman.

Cass was partially reassured by this contact; as a supporter of de Gaulle he could no longer be seen as a threat. But, deep in her subconscious, there still lurked a belief that she must pay fate somehow for the unexpected gift of happiness which was so well and truly ensconced in the little shepherd's house in Provence. The fact that Bessie and her mother both loved Jean too crowned everything and made it perfect. Bessie, particularly, liked to get him to herself. 'Jean, I've drawn the inside of an anemone. Would it do for a flower book, d'you think?' Carol realised the child was asking a professional for an opinion, but there was more to it than that. She saved special things for Jean: the first of the Northfield beans, the crop of tiny onions 'for his soup', a poem she wrote about freedom. The immediate rapport she had felt for him in New York had ripened into love. Carol felt – physically – overflowing with this happiness. She told herself it was worth whatever price she might have to pay.

* * *

608

They used the same donkeys as before, and as Pierre did not come with them, the animals would remain this year and enjoy good mountain grazing.

'Let's hope we can stay yonks this time,' Bessie said as she cut down one of the bean sticks for a staff. 'We had to come back early last year because of that book you found, Jean!'

'I beg your pardon, Bessie,' Jean said gravely. 'But if it had not been for the book, I would not have seen Carol again. Which would have meant I would not have seen you. Or Mary.' He grinned at Boris. 'Or Boris.'

Bessie nodded. 'Or Aunt Mon. Or Aunt Hildie. Uncle George. Leo and Ossie . . . oh no, they were at camp.'

Boris said, 'Funny to think of all those people over there . . . funny that you know them, I mean.'

Bessie said acutely, 'Funny that, I know them and you don't? But you know hundreds of people I've never seen, Borrie. And when you go into the Navy, you'll know thousands. I hate you going into the Navy. You'll be so . . . controlled. Not free any more.'

He had said nothing about his call-up papers. 'I hate me going too.' He grinned at Bessie. 'But at the moment I'm on my way up the Victoire. Which is wonderful!'

They reached the shepherd's hut and set about sweeping and fetching fresh hay for the palliasses. It was good to have the strength of the two men this year. Mary opened the shutters and went round with the Flit gun and left them to clean out the hearth and start a fire. She had worked out a menu for the whole of their two-week stay; if she could buy flour from the farm she intended making their own bread.

'Mother is in her element,' Carol said to Jean as he fed kindling into the stove. 'She feels she is turning the clock back when she gets away from her own kitchen. She says it reminds her of the war in the best possible way!'

Jean-Claude nodded. 'Survival. In one way a challenge. In another . . . simplicity.'

They smiled into each other's eyes. He did not touch her. He had made a point of not touching her at first in case it was an affront to Mary and Bessie. Now there was no need. Their union was absolute.

Bessie lost no time in taking Boris to the tiny climbers' hut

609

which she and the Metier girls had discovered the previous year. It proved to be further than she remembered, and the knapsack of food which she had insisted on shouldering knocked awkwardly as she scrambled up the scree.

'Must have been in better shape last year,' she panted, accepting Boris' hand at the top. 'Now I'm nearly in my teens I'm ageing!'

'Poor old thing,' Boris commented. 'Already decrepit. And what on earth have you got in that sack? It's all lumps and corners.'

She flopped on to the grass plateau; it was as she remembered, like a box at the theatre.

'Well, food for a start. Grannie showed me how to make Cornish pasties yesterday, so I did four.' She ignored his threatrical groan. 'And my drawing stuff. And a paint pot.'

As if reminded, he unhitched his camera and removed it carefully from its case. It was one of the new ones with a telescopic lens. He squinted through it, already seeing the enormous panorama in terms of photographs and frames.

Bessie coughed loudly. 'I said "and a paint pot".'

'You're going to paint as well as draw?' he queried without lowering the camera.

'No. It's an empty paint pot.'

She waited for his surprised eye to appear, and grinned smugly.

'Thought that would intrigue you. We're going to bury it. Right here. Or next to the hut. Anyway somewhere on this plateau.'

He tried to retrieve his sang-froid.

'Before or after the Cornish pasties?'

'I could kill you!' But she was giggling. 'Hasn't Aunt Myrt told you about the paint pot? It's like a family heirloom really. And it's sort of connected to my mother and your sister, so I asked Cass if I could bury it again on the mountain. And I wanted you to be in on it.' She frowned. 'It's not really like an heirloom. More like a symbol of eternal friendship.'

'You sound like a schoolgirl comic. And what's this about your mother?'

She said flatly, 'Carol is my mother. Didn't you know? Even Solange and Brigitte guessed, so I thought you probably knew from Jean-Claude, or your parents, or someone.'

Boris stared at her for a long time without speaking.

She said, 'Don't look like that. I know what you're thinking. I'm illegitimate. All that stuff. I'd rather be illegitimate a million times over and have Cass as my mother. Surely you can see that, Borrie? She and me – I – we're – we're blood sisters! All that love . . . it had to mean that we were from the same body. Yes?'

Her acquired Frenchness took him aback. He stammered, 'Bess. Are you certain about this? Has Cass actually said—'

'Of course not!' She was impatient. 'I don't want her to have to – to con*fess* – nothing like that. I've told her I know, and that is enough!'

Again he was silent. He had heard his parents talking, and he could remember Monica at Bessie's age. They could be identical twins.

'And of course,' she went on, 'I've said nothing about Jean. Immediately I saw him, I knew he was my father. I've asked questions since then, and it fits in. He came over to join the Free French in 1940. He was only sixteen. I expect he met Cass at a dance. They used to go to a lot of dances in those days.' Her eyes took on a far-away look. 'They fell in love. Then Paris was liberated and he was trapped into marriage by Gaby.' She flashed him a look. 'That's his wife. Remember he was still only twenty.' She crooked her knees and hugged them. 'It's obvious. Cass would love just one man. Only one. So when she told Grannie and me about Jean, it didn't take me long to realise that he must be the one. And then when we met at the airport in New York, I just knew.' She waved a hand airily.

Boris swallowed. 'I see.' He had heard only vaguely about the business with Monica in New York; Myrtle no longer talked to him as she had done, and Bessie herself had been reticent.

They sat spine to spine. The sun was hot but the air was very clear and cold: a heady combination. Bessie knew that if she leaned further, the top of her scalp would fit into the nape of Boris' neck. Especially if he, too, lifted his face to the sun.

She said in a low voice, 'Boris. When can we get married?'

His spine tightened against hers. But at least he did not move away or laugh at her.

After what seemed to her like a year, he said, 'I have to report to Corsham. On September 10th.'

She said, 'Oh.'

'Bessie.' His voice was rough. 'You are thirteen years old!'

'Fourteen in three months. And I shall get older.'

'You'll meet boys. Men.'

'Of course. You'll meet girls.'

'I'm different.'

'Because you wanted to be a monk for five minutes? I knew why you wanted to be a monk, Borrie. You were disgusted. That night Myrtle had Mallie. That was the end, wasn't it?'

'Oh God. How did you know? You were nine!'

'Don't keep telling me how old I was. I started to love you at Myrtle's wedding. So where you're concerned, I've always been grown-up.'

'Yes. But . . . it's not the same. Being married needs something extra to . . . love.'

'It'll be all right, Borrie. Because we're so close to start with. We've always played at mummies and daddies. We've had . . . practice.'

He managed a laugh then, and his back seemed to relax a little against hers. He said, 'I love you, Bess. I want to protect you and look after you.'

'That's all right then. You're like Jean-Claude, you don't know about these things. Women do. Cass knew. I know. That's why I want it settled before you go away.' She took a deep breath. 'I want us to be engaged, Borrie.'

'Oh Bess. One minute you sound like a woman of thirty. And the next you're such a *kid*!'

'I know it sounds like that. I can't help it. I've got to have it out in the open, cut and dried. That was one of the reasons for the paint pot. And for this.'

She did not move her back from his, but her hand reached behind her and found his. He took the gold bracelet from her.

'Aunt Mon bought it for me in New York last year. It's the only valuable thing I've got. It's real gold, you see. I want you to keep it. You could wear it on a string around your neck. No-one would see it underneath your shirt. Anyway, keep it. Somehow. It means you belong to me and you can't get married to anyone else. Is that clear?'

'Oh Bess. I can't do this—'

'Is that *clear*?' Her voice was fierce.

He looked at the bracelet in his palm which had been bought by

612

her real mother; and she did not even know it. One day she might need him properly; there were so many dangers, so many shipwrecks . . . He closed his fingers over the gold.

'Yes. That's clear.'

She smiled sightlessly at the pearly view. Gradually her head tipped back. His came to meet it. They sat in the sunshine supporting each other easily and naturally. When they eventually stood up to eat their lunch, the grass was flattened evenly and there were no visible joins.

Liv was not surprised by Myrtle's letter. Monica showed it to her almost accusingly.

'What has been going on?' she demanded. 'I thought you and Malcolm were up to something. But Myrt and Reggie? It doesn't make sense.'

Liv stared at the flimsy airmail paper without a great deal of interest. She said unemotionally, 'I was very stupid, Mon. I've always been stupid about boys, haven't I? D'you remember I used to notch up how many had asked me out? Like the fighter pilots used to clock up victories?'

'We're talking about men, Liv. Not boys.'

'That's it, you see. I still thought of them as boys. To be won. To be notched up.' She let the single sheet of paper fall to the carpet. 'I went down to Cheltenham that day, to notch Malcolm up.' She shrugged. 'I suppose I didn't think that when you're grown-up, you . . . you . . .' She flushed slightly.

Monica finished for her. 'Malcolm went a bit far for you, Liv, didn't he? You wanted a kiss. You wanted him on his knees, begging for you. You wanted to be able to turn him down.' She picked up the letter and folded it with a deep sigh. 'Oh God.'

Liv said, 'I wish Myrtle had known that. But Myrtle has grown up. And when she rang the Cheltenham number and I replied, she thought . . .' a tear formed in her right eye. It was Liv's misfortune that it looked theatrical. She swallowed. 'Anyway. She and Reggie . . . Reggie is so good at – at being kind. And he must have been angry with me. And it started from there.'

'That's why you came out here,' Monica said flatly.

'I had to get away. You don't know what it was like, Mon. He is obsessed with her. He can't live without her. I mean . . . Myrt! of all people!'

Monica was silent, staring through the window at the enormously expensive view. She remembered Nancy. It had been her pride that had hurt then; that was all. Was it the same for Liv?

She said at last, 'Has it ever occurred to you, Liv, that you and I haven't got much love in us? We were the ones who played around when we were at school. Perhaps we've gone on playing around ever since. Carol and Myrtle were different. Even then I knew that Cass was special. And Myrtle was so – so – *giving*.'

Liv snorted a laugh which turned into a sob.

Monica said, 'You're not interested in men. Not really. Are you? Material things come first for you. Admit it.'

'All right. But I do love Reggie. Or I did love him. Oh, I don't know. He was so insulting, Mon.' She began to cry in earnest. 'At one stage he said that if nothing came of him and Myrt, I could have what was left! I tried to scratch his eyes out.'

'Really?' Monica asked with interest.

'Yes. I hated him so much at that moment. Myrtle is my friend. And she's not even pretty. Both of them – both of them – were betraying me! I couldn't bear it!'

Monica patted Liv's shoulder almost absent-mindedly. The objective side of her reviewed the whole scenario with complete detachment. Somehow she could not see it as a tragedy, unless poor Reggie and Myrtle were eventually consumed with guilt. They had fallen in love and gone away together. That was the only fact that mattered. Once that was accepted, the problem to be dealt with was Myrtle's family, and Liv.

She waited until Liv was dabbing at her eyes, then she stood up and began pacing.

'The thing is . . . are you coming with me?' she asked briskly.

Liv blew her nose miserably. 'Where are you going?'

'To England of course. Cheltenham. To look after the boys.' She made a face. 'And Malcolm I suppose. He's going to be more trouble than the other three put together.'

'Me? Come with you to Cheltenham? Myrtle's home? Don't be silly, Mon. How could I do that?'

'With great ease. Come on, Liv. What else can you do? You can't stay here. If we go together, it will shut Bob up. It will shut up most of the Cheltenham gossip. And, as you want to get back at Myrt and Reggie, I should think it would heap coals of fire on both their heads!' She began to smile. 'From where I'm standing, it looks the ideal move to make.'

Liv stared, mouth slightly open. 'You're so cold-blooded, Mon! It's not a game of chess, you know!'

'Might be better if you tried to see it in that light!' Monica paused and looked down at the big eyes. 'Listen, Liv. You're not that badly hurt. You might not have Reggie. You might not have poor old Myrtle. But you've got me.' She sat on the arm of a chair and stared right at Liv. 'I'm pretty strong you know, Liv. I was only sixteen when I had Bessie, and I worked for eight years getting the Albion on its feet. The only person I've ever really wanted is Bessie, and I gave her back to Carol last summer. You can lean on me till you learn to stand on your own two feet.'

Liv was shocked at the sudden confession. Her eyes seemed to focus anew. After a long pause she said merely, 'Thank you, Mon.'

Monica stood up again, energy tingling through her.

'I want to go to Cheltenham. I want to look after Myrtle's kids. It's a terrific challenge.'

Liv focused on another thought.

'What about Bob?'

'Yes. It might be the end for Bob and me. I don't know. He's pretty tied up with Rosa at the moment. So he won't object too much if I go home with you.'

'What about if he does object.'

Monica flashed a smile over her shoulder. 'He's given me an ultimatum before. He thinks he won then. He thinks I gave up Bessie for his sake. I didn't, of course. Well, he'll know this time that he's lost.'

'You can't do it, Mon. You can't give up . . .' she spread her hands '. . . all this.'

Monica looked around the room calmly. 'I shall miss it. And America. Hildie and the boys and the new baby.' She smiled. 'But for a while, I shall be much too busy to think about that.'

Liv began to cry in earnest. She dropped her face into her hands. Monica said, 'I'll make some tea. Have a good cry in peace, then you can make up your mind what you're going to do.'

She left the room and Liv wept on for a while obediently, then dabbed at her eyes. Her voice catching childishly, she said to the empty room, 'You're not just cold-blooded, Mon. You're hard.'

Because after all, there was really no decision to be made. Monica was right, she couldn't stay here with Bob and she didn't want to go back to Birmingham and the total shame of being a deserted wife. Maybe later she could go to Carol, but not yet. She'd have to stick to Monica. She'd have to.

By the time she'd drunk a cup of tea, she had accepted the preposterous idea of living in Myrtle's house and looking after Myrtle's husband and children. It had its ironies. It might even embarrass Reggie and Myrtle.

Slowly over the damp summer, Myrtle learned to love Reggie. There had been no doubt about their physical attraction in Barnt Green; it had been difficult to keep their hands off each other once they were committed. Even that frightful afternoon when Liv had discovered them together had not ended the affair. They had thought it was the end, but that night Reggie had crept into Myrtle's room again, and after the first shocked refusal – 'I can't, Reggie darling, not now that Liv knows' – she had welcomed him into her arms until dawn. But if she hadn't been with him that early evening, she might have known that Mallie was in the garden on his own. Reggie assured her it was not so; how could she have known that the boys had climbed the fence on to the golf course and left Mallie to his own devices? If anyone was to blame, it was himself. He always played with the boys for an hour when he got home from work. But his time with Myrtle had been running out, he had known that. And Liv was sitting on the terrace relaxing before dinner.

Myrtle was adamant about the holiday.

'I really cannot sleep with you, Reggie. I'm terribly fond of you. I'd rather be with you than anyone else in the whole world. But I can never sleep with you again. You do realise that?'

'Darling girl. You know how I feel. Whatever you want . . . whatever.'

If she wanted to be with him more than anyone else, it must mean that beneath that awful frozen exterior she loved him. He was certain of it. For him, last summer had not been merely a crazy sexual fling. He had always seen Myrtle as a 'good sort', uncritical and easy-going. He had liked her from the moment he had met her at the wedding. Later, he had seen her as a good influence on Liv. Her careless happiness with her three boys must surely show Liv that families need not be the fraught, destructive units she thought they were. And then, later still, he had felt a strong sexual attraction. The attributes which Liv thought disgusting drove him mad with desire. The breasts made pendulous by three avid babies, the distended abdomen, the thighs diagonally marked with stretch marks, gave her a reality Liv had somehow lost. And then she had turned to him for comfort. As they had made love that first time he had thought of a phrase in the marriage service: 'mutual comfort'. They had given each other mutual comfort.

Maybe it could have ended there if Mallie hadn't drowned. He might have transferred his heightened feelings to Liv and battered down her primness somehow. Myrtle would certainly have returned to Malcolm and taken a kind of pride with her; pride that another man had found her beautiful and irresistible.

But Mallie had drowned. And everything had been turned upside down.

They drove north that early June, along the interminable A1 past Scotch Corner and Newcastle and signs announcing Newbiggin-on-Sea and Seahouses. Reggie turned back there, and they had a high tea at a little cafe overlooking the workaday harbour with the boats leaving for the Farne Islands.

'We'll go there one day,' he told her, smiling into her inward-looking eyes. 'We'll see the puffins and the seals and pretend we're marooned.'

She said, 'I'd like that, Reggie. To be marooned. Away from everything.'

'I know, darling. But you are away from everything now. With me. You'll realise that quite soon.'

'Reggie. You're so sweet.'

'Only you think so, Myrtle. But then, your opinion is the only one that matters to me.'

She knew that Malcolm didn't love her like that, had never loved her like that. She tried to respond by reaching across the table for Reggie's hand. He took her wrist and eased off her glove and held her fingers in his warm ones. It made her wish for an instant that she hadn't made the gesture in the first place. Then she thought that it didn't really matter because nothing really mattered any more.

But when they drove into Alnmouth that night, she liked it.

The few houses and hotels, huddled behind dunes from the north sea and its winds, had a friendly look about them. They promised sanctuary. Reggie signed the register and pushed it over to her; he had booked separate rooms. Their hotel was called the Lobster Pot. He explained that everyone in the Hardfanger working party had booked their own rooms. They would work as a team, but they were by no means tied to each other. She need not meet anyone if she did not wish it. He would introduce her as a family friend so that she need feel no embarrassment either. She could mix, or she could be private.

'I'd prefer to be . . . private,' she said as they sat over a drink in her room.

'All right, Myrtle. That's all right.'

She liked her room, too. She could hear, very faintly, noises from the bar below, but nothing intrusive; just a reminder that her isolation was chosen rather than forced. The room itself was small with two deep window embrasures where she could sit and look at the sea. The walls were an aged cream colour, dissected randomly by beams. After she'd unpacked she ran her fingers over some of the beams. They were split and pitted and she could smell the tar in them. They gave her comfort.

She told Reggie she didn't want anything else to eat.

'That boiled egg filled me up. Where did we have that?'

'Seahouses. D'you remember me saying we'd go to the Farne Islands?'

'Oh yes.' She smiled at him. 'I think I'll have an early night, Reggie. If that's all right.'

He smiled back. 'It's all right.' He took her face in his hands and kissed her forehead. She stayed very still. He said, 'Would you like to walk to the seashore before you settle down? Have some fresh air?'

'Yes. That would be nice.'

'And would avoid me kissing you again?' His smile deepened. 'Myrtle, please believe me. I am not going to force anything. Anything at all.'

They walked down the sandy road and came upon the shore unexpectedly. The white beach rolled away into the distance and the waves came greyly along it, pounding it indiscriminately. The air was damp and cold on their faces. Myrtle shivered.

'Come on. Let's run!'

Reggie took her hand and pulled her over the sand. Her legs moved leadenly. She was immediately out of breath.

'Reggie, stop! I can't—'

'Do you good, Myrt! Come on – down to the sea with you—'

'Reggie, we shall get wet!'

'That's the idea! Jump that rock! Come *on*!'

He did not realise that her sobs were in earnest. She never cried. Her white strappy sandals sank into the sand as it grew damper. Suddenly a wave came up the beach and soaked them both to the knees.

Myrtle started to scream.

He picked her up and held her closely against his shoulder.

'It's all right, Myrtle. It's only the sea. I was trying to make you feel like a child again. Running into the sea on the first evening of the holiday!'

She held him so tightly he thought he might suffocate.

'Oh Reggie. That's how it was, wasn't it? For him. For Mallie. And it crept up and up and then he fell down.'

Reggie carried her to a rock and leaned her against it. She could not stop weeping.

'I'm sorry. So sorry, darling. I should have thought . . .' he kissed her hair. 'It's good to cry. You haven't done enough of it.'

She calmed down at last and they went slowly back to the Lobster Pot. As she said goodnight to him at her bedroom door, she smiled directly at him for the first time.

He whispered, 'Goodnight, Myrtle. Get out of those wet shoes quickly and snuggle down like a good girl.'

She went into the room and noticed that the floor was uneven. How Mallie would have loved it.

'The first day of the holiday,' she murmured.

He did not go to work immediately. He took her to Bamborough Castle and Alnwick. In the tiny, expensive shops of Alnwick she bought herself a new dress and shoes. He chose them for her: a lime green linen dress, sleeveless, with a mandarin collar and gored skirt. Ridiculous shoes with heels that gave her height. She had always worn gathered skirts and flat shoes. The tailored dress made the most of her slim waist and big bust, the gored skirt kept her hips smooth, the plain green court shoes did wonders for her legs if not her balance. She wore her new things and held tightly to

619

his arm as they toured the castle. He thought or another phrase from the marriage service. 'With my body I thee worship.' His body worshipped Myrtle's. It was much more than a sexual feeling.

The next day he went to look over Hardfanger and meet his fellow workers. Myrtle had decided to stay in her room, but after lunch she changed her mind and went for a stroll. It was a grey, windy day and unless she strode out for a long walk there was not much to do in the tiny village. She wasn't up to striding out, so she went into a cafe and ordered tea and cakes. The elderly owner brought them on a silver salver.

Myrtle was suddenly inspired.

'Is there a hairdresser in the village?' she asked.

'Aye, pet. Two of 'em. Jeannie does home perms if that's what you were after.'

'I don't know what I want. Something different.'

'Then Meggie's the one for you. She's just above the gown shop, a few steps down the road. Aye, Meggie's the one with the imagination.'

The words were spoken without much approval, and Myrtle wondered what Meggie would do for her. It did not worry her unduly; she knew that a visit to the hairdresser would please Reggie. Reggie was so kind. She wanted to please him.

As it happened, Meggie was inspired when it came to Myrtle's dry and frizzy mop. She cut out all the old perms that had built up over the years and got down to Myrtle's fine, schoolgirl hair that lay flat to her head like a cap. She shampooed the inch-long locks and styled them layer on layer in the popular urchin cut. Suddenly Myrtle was emerging as a small girl, no longer flabby and overweight. Since the birth of Lennie, she had lost interest in eating and was in any case much slimmer than she'd been for years. Now, with her close-cut hair and tailored dress, she looked quite different. She surveyed herself in the mirror with a feeling that was almost pleasure.

'Madam is pleased?' asked Meggie in her careful voice.

'Reggie will like it,' Myrtle replied.

Reggie was delighted. It was a positive sign of her recovery. That evening he spotted one of his colleagues in the hotel dining room. He risked introducing Myrtle, and she took it well, shaking the man's hand and smiling politely. He then suggested that the next day she should go with him to Hardfanger to see the library which he and Alan Forrester were cataloguing. She agreed to that in the same way she had agreed to come away with him, like a small obedient child taking medicine she didn't much relish. But once in the tall library with its beautiful mobile staircases on the ground floor and gallery, she changed. It was such a subtle change that Reggie did not recognise it for a while. He explained the system they were using and showed her the entry books and the catalogue cards. Her absorption could have been the same politeness she had shown before; it was not until they broke for coffee that he realised she was turning pages and checking the entries in his handwriting with the relevant file cards.

He said, 'We'll go and find a pub for lunch, Myrtle, shall we?'

'Didn't you say that the housekeeper prepared a snack lunch in the kitchen?'

'Yes. But I rather assumed you wouldn't want to mingle with the others.'

'I'm not keen. But you can mingle and I can have a look around. Would that be all right, Reggie? This castle belonged to the King of Northumbria when the Danes were here – did you know?'

'Yes. That's why it's such an important gift.' He tucked her hand in his arm and led her through the vaulted hall to the staircase. 'See. It's like an upturned boat. All the architecture around here of that time seemed to be based on the sea.'

'There's some stuff about Bede entered in your writing.'

'I'll look it out for you this afternoon. Would you like that?'

'I won't understand it, Reggie. I was hopeless at school.'

'There are notes to go with it.' He led her down a narrow passage incongruously ribbed by metal gas pipes. His voice was suddenly husky. 'Darling. Don't ever call yourself hopeless. Not to me. You see . . . you are my hope.'

Unexpectedly, tears came into her eyes again. She said nothing and had blinked them away when they emerged into the enormous cellar-kitchens, but she felt suddenly as if she might be starting to melt. Quite literally and physically.

She went to Hardfanger with him most days. There were other women in the party: wives of the curators, secretaries and administrators. They would have liked her to join them occasionally for shopping and exploring, but they were not offended when she declined. Myrtle discovered that she had a talent for not giving offence. She thought back and realised how often she had smoothed the ruffled feathers of Malcolm's patients – and the husbands of patients. She smiled at the motley collection of people she met in the castle kitchen most days, and asked them whether they had enjoyed their trips to Lindisfarne or Scotland, or even the Lakes; and they seemed to respect her isolation and told her she really must go before the summer was over. Meanwhile she was actively helping Reggie: transforming his scribbled notes into legible entries, sorting cards for him, enthusing when he showed her a first edition or a handwritten manuscript.

'I'm beginning to understand how Carol feels about books,' she said one day when they drove through Hexham towards Hadrian's Wall. 'Perhaps it's one of the ways we can get inside people's heads. Share thoughts.' She smiled at Reggie. 'Those books bridge time. They almost make you feel you're beginning to understand eternity.'

Reggie nodded. 'You remember what Carol said to us about that book she was editing? The one smuggled out from Algeria?' He returned her smile tentatively. 'She said something about it being the author's immortality.'

Myrtle was silent for a long time. She asked at last, 'What are you trying to say, Reggie? Mallie couldn't write his name. He couldn't hold a pen.' Her voice was as steady as a rock.

He said, 'But you can write. You could write about Mallie.'

'No. No, I couldn't do that. I couldn't bear to do that.'

He did not push it and there was another silence. They came to Haltwhistle and found a car park. The weather had improved in the last three weeks, but it was still blowy, and Myrtle's new haircut blew around her head like a cherub's halo. They clambered up a rise and surveyed the view of the Wall and a distant fort.

Myrtle said, 'Let's walk along it. Let's pretend we're from one of the Legions.' It was the first positive suggestion she'd made; he let her take the lead, though his instinct was to go ahead and help her over the rough places. She climbed a rickety ladder and turned to smile at him. 'Wouldn't Nicky love this?'

He paused, his hand on the top rung of the ladder. They looked into each other's eyes, and for the first time he faced the possibility that her 'cure' might also mean she would return to her children.

She took his hand.

'I could write to you, Reggie. I could write to you about Mallie. About everything.'

Almost immediately, she turned and walked along the grass track on top of the wall, leaving him to scramble up and follow her. He wanted to shout, 'You won't have to write to me. I shall be with you. You can talk to me.' But he said nothing, and they walked on until they came to the round buttress of the fort. She turned then, and gave him the Roman salute. But when she saw his face, her fist dropped to her side and she came to him, put her arms around his waist, and pressed her head against his shirt front.

She said very seriously, 'I love you, Reggie.'

They were the words he had wanted to hear. He did not know why he kissed her short silky hair as if they were saying goodbye.

She spent some more time alone. She went into Newcastle, driving the car cautiously, parking on the outskirts and taking a bus into the shopping centre. She bought some more clothes and made a phone call home. Monica answered and was her usual brisk self. She said, 'Why don't you have a word with Malcolm, Myrt? He phoned your hotel about six times last night and you weren't there.'

'I was there, actually. I go to bed at eight o'clock. I'm still very tired.' She looked through the glass of the phone box. She could see the gilded cupola of the university building and the long length of Newgate Street. She should have felt disorientated and lonely, but she didn't. 'How are the boys?'

Monica said, 'First time you've asked that. Liv has taken them out for a walk.'

'Why aren't they at school?'

'Holidays, idiot. Can you speak up? You sound a million miles away.'

'Three hundred, almost.' She'd forgotten about the holidays. 'Are they all right?'

'What, with Liv? She's not giving to suffocate them or anything if that's what you mean.'

Myrtle flinched. But of course Monica did not know that she had put a nappy over Lennie's face.

'I just meant . . . are they all right?'

'Fine. I'll say this for Malcolm, he's a good father.'

'Yes. He is. I know.'

Monica said, 'And you're a good mother. Don't worry, I make sure they know that.'

'Oh Mon.'

'I'm loving it. I'm properly tired at night. When you come home I could stay on if you like. Help you.'

'What about Liv?'

'She wouldn't stay on.'

'Is she . . . very unhappy?'

'Of course.'

'It's awful, Mon. Isn't it?'

'Depends what you want from life. Most of us aren't wonderfully happy. Liv will be okay.'

'Mon. I can't thank you enough. I'd have ended up going mad.'

'Yes. But you're all right now. Aren't you?'

'I think so. I haven't wanted to know about the boys before.'

'Quite. Well, my offer stands. I'll help you when you come back.'

'I . . .' Myrtle looked at the golden dome and tried to picture Malcolm and the boys and the sitting room overlooking Imperial Gardens. She said, 'I don't know about that, Mon. I'm different. I don't belong to the boys any more. I certainly don't belong to Malcolm.'

'You belong to Reggie?'

'No. I belong to myself.'

Monica's voice became suddenly stronger. 'That's good. Then you can choose. You can make your own choice.' There was a pause. Then she said, 'Goodbye, Myrtle. Ring again.' And she was gone.

Myrtle replaced the receiver carefully, and waited for a pang of some sort. Guilt, or maternal anguish, or plain homesickness. Nothing happened. Further down Newgate Street was a bookshop, she wondered if they had anything interesting about Bede. She looked in the small mirror above the telephone and checked that her nose wasn't shiny, then she pushed the door with her shoulder, and stepped into the sunshine.

624

Malcolm rang before she was in bed that night; he sounded jovial and assured her everything was fine and Monica had everything under control.

'Don't want to cut your holiday short or anything, bunny rabbit, but can you give us some idea . . .'

'No, Malcolm.' She was surprised at the steadiness of her voice. So was he, and his joviality became hectoring.

'Look here, old girl, it's not right going off with your best friend's husband! She's stuck here looking like a yard of pump water. It's embarrassing to say the least. And Monica's a good egg, but she's bossy.'

Suddenly Myrtle wanted to laugh. She said, 'So long as she's taking care of you and the boys—'

'Dammit Myrtle! You're my wife! It's your duty to come home! I don't care if the place is like a pigsty if you're here! I order you to come back – tomorrow! The next day! By the end of the week at the very latest!'

She said gently, 'Malcolm, I'm tired. Good night.' And she passed the phone to Reggie and went upstairs.

After that, Reggie took all the calls that came for her. If it was Monica he would pass the telephone over, but most evenings he would hunch a shoulder and listen hard for a long time, then make a few remarks before saying goodbye.

June went out in a blaze of sunshine and July came in with a thunderstorm and then sultry weather that made Hardfanger's thick walls very welcome. Malcolm's phone calls became less frequent. Myrtle rang Monica during the day when she knew he would be in the treatment room, and Monica said that he had been in touch with Reggie's firm of auctioneers and knew that his work was coming to an end.

Myrtle said, 'Next time Malcolm rings, Reggie, let me speak to him.'

'Really? I don't want him to upset you, darling. You're looking wonderful. You're almost better.'

'I am better. Thanks to you. I'll talk to him next time he phones.'

Reggie looked at her. 'Tell me first, Myrtle. Are you going back to him?'

'No.'

'But you are going back to Nicky and Martin and little Lennie?'

'No. Monica will stay on. Perhaps eventually she will be

divorced from her husband, and she might marry Malcolm. But she will be a good mother for the boys.'

He couldn't believe it. 'Myrtle. Does this mean you're staying with me?'

'Do you want me?'

'Myrtle—'

'Yes. All right.'

He had to be content with that for the moment. It was not the sort of wholehearted commitment he had hoped for. But she did not wait for Malcolm to ring her; that evening she got through to trunks and asked for the Cheltenham number. He made a move away to give her a spurious privacy but she put a hand on his sleeve and kept him near her.

She said directly, 'Malcolm. It's Myrtle. My dear, I'm sorry, but I'm not coming home. I thought I'd better tell you the minute I'd made up my mind.'

Reggie could hear sounds but no words. Malcolm could have been spluttering with rage; he could have been weeping.

Myrtle said very calmly, 'Why? Because I love Reggie, that's why. You must have guessed that.'

She continued to listen with strange politeness for a very long time, but she did not speak again. Eventually she put the telephone down.

'He is confused,' she said, not looking at Reggie. She turned and went upstairs and he followed. At the door of her small and very private room, she paused as if considering something. Then she said, 'We'll be together now, Reggie. Shall we?'

He could have wept. He said, 'Only if you want that, Myrtle.'

She nodded briefly, went through the door and held it open for him.

It wasn't as it had been before, there was no crazy abandonment. Afterwards, Myrtle pillowed his head on her shoulder and ran her fingers from his forehead to his chin.

She said again as she had said that day on Hadrian's Wall, 'I could write to you, Reggie. You wouldn't mind about my spelling and grammar, would you? I was terrible at school.'

He said throatily, 'I wouldn't mind, darling.' He held on to her tightly and pushed his cheek into her shoulder as if he could weld himself to her. After a while he whispered, 'But Myrtle, you won't need to write. You can tell me everything you want me to know.'

626

She stilled her fingers and cupped his face to her.

'I know' she said.

But she was seized with the idea of writing. She began to write to Carol, short letters at first, about Hardfanger and Alnwick and the white sand at Alnmouth. One day she added a postscript: 'Mallie would love it here, it's so empty and there is so much water. Do you remember Miss Edgeworth saying that all life came from the sea? Perhaps Mallie was going back to the beginning of everything when he kept going into Liv's fishpond.'

Just before they left Alnmouth, she had a reply. 'Myrtle, I am in love with a married man and so are you. How strange life is. I think you, too, feel a sense of temporary happiness only and that is why you write to me: to record this happiness and make it eternal whatever happens. In the same way you are remembering Mallie, cherishing him still. Myrtle, Bessie did this sketch of Mallie during your stay in Barnt Green. It comes with great love, and a belief that it will not hurt you. I make no comment about Liv. It is obvious that Reggie loves you very much and had to do his best to protect you. You are lucky, Myrtle. I am too.'

Sandwiched between pasteboard was Bessie's sketch. She had drawn a back view of Mallie, but it was unmistakably him. In the raised hands, the bowed head, the hunched shoulders, it was possible to see delight as he dipped one sandalled foot into the scribbled water.

Fifteen

In a strange way the summer of '58 was the happiest period of Monica's life. She was coping with an impossible situation which involved no personal heartache; she was making normality from abnormality; she was daily dressing invisible and unhealing wounds. She felt like a nurse for Liv and Malcolm, and a mother to Nicky, Martin and Lennie. She organised Malcolm's professional life so that gossip and speculation were kept to a minimum. Most of his regular clients had known that Myrtle was ill after the loss of Mallie, and the birth of the new baby, so to mention discreetly that she had gone away to convalesce was logical enough. That she and Liv were Myrtle's best friends and had stepped in to help was no less than laudable.

If anything, Malcolm's popularity increased. Favoured lady patients who thought that Myrtle had gone into a private lunatic asylum hoped that they might step into her shoes eventually, and made more regular appointments. Local doctors, who had held out against his paramedical status, were sympathetic and charmed by Monica. They began recommending him to their own incurables. Malcolm might not be able to effect a cure any more than the doctor could, but he had a definite facility, and his soothing hand and high bills convinced people they were improving.

Luckily, Nicky and Martin had liked Monica's straight and open approach when they'd met her at Aunt Liv's. Now, after the uncaring chaos of their mother's recent rule, they welcomed her wholeheartedly. As Nicky said one day, 'If we can't have Mummy, we might as well have you, Aunt Mon.' And Monica took that as the enormous compliment it was.

But Lennie was the real joy for her. He had been born at almost the same time of the year as Bessie, and she felt she was living the time she had missed then. Every day she saw a difference in him;

when she arrived he lay flat in his cot or pram, doing amazing press-ups when he was on his tummy, lifting his head with agonised grimaces when he was on his back, but flopping sideways if she propped him up. Within two weeks of her arrival, he was sitting up in the pram when they went across the park to meet the boys. After a month he could sit on the floor scuffing his legs ecstatically and clutching at the air with pudgy hands. By the time Myrtle rang Malcolm to say she was never coming back, he was crawling everywhere, lifting his arms to Monica when she came into his line of vision, finding his mouth and filling it with whatever came to hand.

Monica looked at Malcolm's haggard face and said, 'Don't worry, Malcolm. Myrtle won't be able to stay away from the children for ever. She'll come back. And until she does, I'll stay.'

Until she saw him flinch she did not realise she had been cruel. She added quickly, 'It's a temporary thing. After losing Mallie. And having the new baby. She is still your wife, Malcolm.'

He allowed himself to be rallied; he was easily convinced because he could not really believe anyone would prefer Reggie Bradbury to himself.

Liv was different.

'I can't stand it much more, Mon. It was different when they were officially on holiday. But now . . . And they don't *care* that I'm here – they don't care who is here. They're obsessed with each other – totally and absolutely obssessed!'

'Listen, Liv. It'll burn itself out. Can't you see that? These intense affairs always do. Myrtle will come home, and so will Reggie.'

'Don't *you* see that I wouldn't want him again? Not after . . . Myrtle.'

Monica was tempted to ask what alternatives there were; but she did not. She did not look into the future herself. She had had the perfect excuse for returning to England. Bob had understood that her friend was ill and needed her; besides, he had Rosa Palmer in mind. But there was a limit to Bob's understanding, and his letters were becoming short, terse, and infrequent. Monica's happiness had not entirely suppressed the calculating side of her nature, and she thought there might come a time when she would want to return to Bob. She might not love Bob passionately, but she was very fond of him; and she felt part of his family.

So their odd, triangular life limped into August. The boys were starting a different school that autumn, and Monica and Liv took them to Cavendish House to be fitted out in the wine-red uniform. Monica carried Lennie on her left hip and held Martin's hand. Liv walked by Nicky's side and waited ostentatiously for him to open doors for her. It was very hot and Lennie was unusually fractious. The boys stood in front of mirrors in their new blazers and said they itched all over.

'Just let's get you fitted out,' Monica told them briskly. 'And we'll have tea at the Gloucestershire Dairy and go on to the lido. How does that appeal?'

'Haven't got our swimming stuff,' Nicky objected instantly.

'If it's too far for you to get it, then we won't bother,' Monica said in a friendly voice. 'Aunt Liv and I will take Lennie, and you two can help Tom in the garden.'

'We'll come,' Martin said quickly.

But on the roof garden of the cafe, eating ices from metal sundae cups with flat spoons, it was Liv who became recalcitrant.

'I'll have Lennie. You take the boys. I can't face all the noise. It'll be packed out.'

Monica looked at her sharply; she was pale and her lovely Shirley Temple curls were sticky with sweat.

'We can manage Lennie. All the stuff will go in the pram anyway. You go and lie down, Liv.'

So in the end they left Liv in her room; Monica put a swimsuit under her dress, collected all the necessary paraphernalia and stuck a scribbled note for Malcolm under the tea-tray in the kitchen.

Really, it was easier without Liv. The boys walked either side of the pram and chattered without restraint. Monica chipped in now and then, but mostly she smiled at Lennie and made noises at him when he gurgled at her. It was less than a mile to the open-air swimming pool, and at that time in the afternoon the queues had disappeared and people were beginning to leave to go home for tea. Monica bought the tickets and waited for the gate to be opened for her to take the pram through. The boys insisted on using the turnstile, and somehow Martin got stuck halfway through. She rescued him and they walked through to the grounds around the pool and found themselves a base. Lennie began to whimper again. The boys put on their trunks and went off to the children's pool while she undressed Lennie. The she slipped out of her dress and piled everything on to the pram. The boys crowded delightedly at the edge of the pool when she slid in with Lennie in her arms.

'He likes it, Aunt Mon!' Nicky peered into the baby's surprised face. 'He's stopped crying!'

'It'll just cool him down.' Monica dangled him experimentally. 'I think he might have a touch of the sun.'

'Will you wait for us at the bottom of the chute, Aunt Mon?' asked Martin.

'You don't need to be *caught*, do you?' scoffed Nicky.

'He wants to make sure Lennie and I get splashed,' Monica covered for him. The boys went off, honour satisfied, and Monica waited at the bottom of the chute and dipped Lennie now and then. Yes. Yes, she was happy. She did not want Myrtle to come back. Ever.

Liv could not sleep, she could not even lie still.

Monica had explained that her unhappiness was due merely to wounded pride, but it did not seem to make much difference what caused it. It was perpetual and debilitating. Sometimes she felt ill with it.

She got up and went to open the window wider. The clock on the parish church struck five. Malcolm would be finishing off his last patient and going into the kitchen for his tea. It was a pity she could not face him unless it was in a crowd, because she and he had something in common now. He looked as she felt, haggard and frightened, and utterly bewildered. It was two weeks since Myrtle had telephoned him from Alnmouth and announced she wasn't coming home. He had gone downhill badly since then. He had cancelled three appointments at very short notice and shut himself up in his room.

Her window overlooked the walled back garden. Old Tom did his best with the raised borders, and there was an ancient apple tree in one corner with a swing suspended from it, but otherwise it was simply a square of grass bounded by the high wall of the old mews. Down the centre of the grass was a worn line where the boys kicked their footballs against the wall, and under the swing another worn patch. Next door they had a pergola and roses everywhere and a hammock. Liv had had roses and a hammock. Her eyes filled with tears.

The kitchen door opened and Malcolm came into the garden holding a cup. Liv drew back, but watched him with morbid curiosity. It was like watching herself, or at least, her own actions. He wandered around the garden aimlessly, pausing now and then to stare at a clump of flowers as if admiring them. When he got to the swing, he put the edge of his bottom on the seat and sipped at the cup. Liv moved to the windowsill again and put out her head. He had taken off his white coat and where his braces crossed his back, his shirt was darkened with sweat. She'd never noticed Malcolm perspire before; nor herself. Yet her hair was stuck to her head today and though she wore dress shields she knew that her Moygashel suit was ruined.

He took another token sip from his cup then stood up again and walked down the other side of the garden. His head was bent, the sun glinted on the immaculate waves, and the reddish-coloured hairs on the backs of his hands were burnished. They were large, competent hands. She remembered them searching the bones of her back last year, and closed her eyes on renewed pain. If she hadn't left home that day . . . if . . . if. Malcolm stopped suddenly by a blazing bed of godetia, stared at their colours as if offended by them, and suddenly tipped the cup of hot tea over them. They crumpled where it fell, instantly spoiled.

Liv must have made a sound because his head came up and he saw her. They looked at each other, both frowning as if at intruders.

Malcolm said, 'Have you had any tea? Monica's left it ready in the kitchen.'

'No. I was resting.'

'Come on down. Let's have a cup together, shall we?' He looked at the scalded flowers. 'I've just spilled mine.'

She did not want to be with him, but something made her nod. Guilt or pity, she did not know which it was. She picked up a comb as she passed the dressing table, and ran it from the nape of her neck to the crown of her head. For a moment the hair stayed glossily loose, then fell back again. She would have changed her linen jacket for a blouse, but nothing seemed worthwhile.

At least the kitchen was cool and cavernous. Monica and Liv between them had organised it beyond recognition, and with the door open on to the garden it was pleasant and homely. Malcolm was at the gas stove, making fresh tea. Strangely he was more domesticated than Reggie. Perhaps it was because his work kept him in the home. Or perhaps she had never given Reggie a chance.

She fetched two cups and saucers from the dresser and set them out; poured milk into each. He brought the teapot to the table and sat down heavily.

He said, 'Why didn't you go to the lido with Monica and the boys?'

'I felt too tired. Couldn't face the people.' She looked up at him. 'You know.'

He snorted a mirthless laugh. 'Oh yes, I know. We both know. We can't help each other, but at least we both know.'

She was surprised at his empathy. She had always thought it was just animal attraction that kept Myrtle tied to this man, but sometimes lately she wondered.

She swallowed. 'It was my fault. I know that. I'm sorry, Malcolm.'

'I wondered about blame too. Wondered if I should have sent you packing that day. But . . . dammit, Liv. Myrtle. I could have trusted her with anyone. And *Reggie* – he was my best friend!' He stood up violently and his chair fell to the ground with a clatter. 'I'll never forget last May when he told me he was going to take her on holiday. He made it sound so bloody reasonable. But . . . he was *ruthless*!'

She put her elbows on the table and looked at the backs of her hands. 'I know. That's how he was with me. Ruthless.'

'Myrtle didn't stand a chance, Liv.' Malcolm paced to the sink and back again. 'She was ill. He was determined. I should have kicked him out then and there. Never let him in the house again. I thought she'd laugh at him. But she didn't have the will to do it. He – he practically abducted her!'

'Yes.' It still stuck in her throat. Myrtle. Of all people.

'She told me there was nothing in it. All those weeks in that blasted hotel up there. Nothing, she said. She helped him with his stupid work, and he looked after her. She let me think she'd be back. Just a holiday. She'd come back and be her old self again. And then . . . oh *God*!'

She said dully, 'I know.'

He kicked at the fallen chair and winced with the pain of it.

'Liv.' He leaned on the table and stared at her. 'She's gutted me. I can't live without her, d'you know *that*?'

She said nothing. In one way the thought of living with Reggie again was repulsive.

He said tensely, 'I haven't touched a woman since Myrtle went off with Reggie. I've lost . . . that. It's as if she's castrated me!' Tears suddenly flooded his eyes. 'No-one can help me, Liv. Only Myrt. Only Myrt. Only Myrt . . .' He was sobbing, almost hysterical. She had to do something.

Quite suddenly she knew what to do. She would give herself to Malcolm. She would allow him to take her this time. Fully. And with that one action she would prove herself an attractive woman again, and she would help Malcolm to realise that he could indeed live without Myrtle. She would make the sacrifice now. She put a hand over his as she stood up.

'It's all right, Malcolm. All right. Don't cry. We're both in the same boat. But they'll come back. And we'll show them that we don't care. We're all right. That way they'll come back very quickly! Oh yes, they're not going to give everything up for some silly attraction . . . you'll see.' She moved round the table as she spoke, not removing her hand from his, massaging his knuckles gently. When she stood in front of him she lifted the hand and turned him towards her.

'We can help each other, Malcolm. Myrtle hasn't . . .' she could not bring herself to say the word 'castrated' and searched for a frantic three seconds for an alternative word. 'Myrtle hasn't damaged you. Of course she hasn't. You're a very attractive man. Very attractive.'

She released him to reach in her pocket for a handkerchief. She dabbed at his eyes and less efficiently at his nose. He put his hands on her shoulders to steady himself. She remembered his touch all too clearly and an unexpected tremor centred itself in her pelvic area.

He sobbed breathlessly, 'You and Mon. So good. But you've taken me over. I'm no-one any more. Nothing. Nothing.'

She let him lean on her, reached up and touched her lips chastely to his. She knew again what he meant. But together they could restore each other.

He was startled and held his breath on another sob to stare at her.

'Liv?'

'Yes. I know,' she whispered as if they were magic words.

634

'Liv. You can't. Don't you remember? Before?'

'It's different now. We need each other.'

He went on staring for a long moment, still leaning heavily on her shoulders. She dabbed again, more effectually, and touched his lips with her fingers. Automatically, his mouth opened and he held them gently with his teeth. Then he lifted the padded shoulders of her jacket and wrenched hard. The buttons flew off and the jacket slid down her arms. He took her wrists and held them down. The jacket fell over the chair.

Liv was startled. It was so practised, so sudden, so violent. Thoughts of them comforting each other were gone. This was to be a fierce, animal coupling. She told herself wildly she didn't care. This time she would do all that was expected of her. The jacket had been spoiled by her sweat anyway. Before he could tear the straps of her petticoat and brassiere, she slipped them quickly from her shoulders.

He cupped her small firm breasts and bent quickly to them. Her pelvic tremor spread to her legs and she would have collapsed if he hadn't held her so firmly. He knelt before her and stripped her expertly. His hands were on her buttocks, his thumbs in her groin. She couldn't bear it. Yet she could not stop him, did not want to stop him. She took his leonine head in her hands and turned his face upwards, afraid of what he might do next. And that was her mistake. His eyes were closed, screwed up like a child's. He was breathing fast through his mouth, panting fiercely as if he were racing time. He might have gone through with it if she had let the race continue. But she had interrupted it. He opened his eyes and saw her. His face twisted in agony. She fell to her knees too, trapped by her own clothes. The fallen chair scraped her bare back.

She babbled, 'It's all right, Malcolm. I don't mind, honestly. Whatever you want to do. Whatever—'

But he was crying again, this time like a dog, head thrown back, howling at the moon.

She deciphered words and put them together in some sort of order. 'No good. Only Myrtle. Can't do it. Myrtle.'

He pushed her quite hard so that she fell back against the upturned legs of the chair, then he was up, scrabbling his braces back over his shoulders, still howling incomprehensibly. For some reason he banged his fist on the table and the teapot skidded across

635

the scrubbed surface. He must have been burned, because his voice rose still further; then he stood up and bowed his head. 'She burned me. With tea. Once.'

And he stumbled across the kitchen and was gone. She heard the door of the treatment room close. She was left with dripping tea, her clothes in tatters around her feet, her body indecently exposed. And completely unsatisfied.

When Monica returned, Liv had tidied everything and gone to bed. She lay on top of the covers, bathed and in her best nightie. She wondered whether she was going mad. She recalled once before when she had obliterated something from her mind – though she could not remember what that something was – and she tried to do it again. What had happened in the kitchen must be torn out of her life somehow. Otherwise she could not bear it. She must not – she must never – remember that she had tried to seduce Myrtle's husband. She must never remember that he had rejected her. She must never picture the upturned chair, the slavering man, the dripping tea, the naked depraved woman. Never. She put her fist in her mouth and bit down hard, and as the pain registered like balm, so Monica knocked on her door.

'Liv, are you all right?'

'Yes, Fine.' Her voice sounded completely normal; it was amazing.

'Are you coming down for supper?'

'No.' She could not think of an excuse, so repeated, 'No.'

Monica sighed audibly and called through the door again, 'I'm a bit worried about Lennie. He seems very hot. And Malcolm won't come out of the treatment room to look at him. He just shouted at me to go away.'

Liv said, 'Come on in.' She swung her legs to the floor. She should never have left her own house. At least she could have had some privacy there. Mon came in looking not her usual calm self.

'What's going on, Liv? Surely you're not going to bed yet?'

'You told me to lie down!' Liv felt her head throbbing alarmingly. She tried to pull herself together. 'Tell Malcolm about Lennie. That will bring him to his senses.'

'What do you mean? Have you talked to him? Is there something the matter?'

'I really don't know, Monica. I'm not a doctor.' She felt with her bare feet for her slippers. 'I'll come and help you to put the boys to bed.'

'No. No, it's okay. You're right, I'll have to tell Malcolm about Lennie. If he's ill *he* should have a doctor.'

'I'll see to Nicky and Martin. You see to Lennie.'

Nicky and Martin were hard work and did not obey Liv as they obeyed Monica, but if she was up with them in their room she would not have to face Malcolm.

They were tired anyway, and thoroughly clean after their swim. She stood over them while they cleaned their teeth, folded their clothes while they got into the pyjamas, opened their window as wide as it would go to catch some of the cooling air.

'D'you want a story?' she asked grudgingly.

'No thank you, Aunt Liv,' Martin said. And Nicky asked, 'Can we look at our books by ourselves for ten minutes?'

'Yes. All right.'

Martin said, 'Aunt Liv, when is Mummy coming home?'

'Soon.' Liv let her mind think of Myrtle and Reggie. They were behaving cruelly . . . evilly . . . but if only they would come home everyone would forgive them. Even she herself. 'Soon, I hope,' she said.

She trailed out on to the the landing. She was wearing her old dressing-gown because putting the boys to bed was not always a pristine activity, but the sight of the over-ironed satin depressed her unutterably. She went into her room and slung it over the bed. She had worn this nightie when she'd gone home from Cheltenham last year . . . to please Reggie. It had been packed in tissue since.

She heard Monica coming along the landing and climbed quickly into bed. Nothing would make her face Malcolm across the supper table. Monica was breathing rather heavily. She burst into Liv's room without knocking. Her face looked muddy.

'What—'

'Quickly . . . Liv . . .' Monica could hardly speak. She hung on to the door handle. 'I've phoned the ambulance. Come down quickly!'

'Oh my God. Is it Lennie? Not again . . . please not again . . .' Liv shoved on her slippers once more and grabbed the dressing-gown.

637

'No. It's not Lennie. It's Malcolm.' Monica bent low and sucked in a deep breath, then straightened. 'Oh Liv. He's taken a bottle of the painkillers he gives his patients and locked himself in the treatment room. He told me it's too late to do anything! I didn't want to start screaming . . . the boys mustn't know anything is wrong . . . kept knocking on the door. Tom and Doris aren't anywhere—'

'It's their day off. It'll be all right.'

Quite suddenly Liv felt almost her old self; slightly impatient with Malcolm for making such a fuss, rather surprised at Mon for going to pieces. She clutched her old dressing-gown around her again and ran down the stairs and across the wide hall to the treatment room. She tapped lightly.

'Malcolm! It's Liv. I want to talk to you about this afternoon. Let me in, please.'

She put her ear to the door. The silence was thick.

Monica panted behind her, 'He hasn't spoken for ages. That was why I phoned the ambulance. Liv, if anything happens to him – to any of them – it will be my responsibility. D'you realise that? I practically forced my way in here – I didn't ask him whether he wanted me to come – and I dragged you with me. My God, I never realised before . . . I never thought . . .' her beautiful dark eyes looked haggard. She took Liv's arm and her nails dug through the crinkled satin. 'Liv – I've been happy! Can you believe it? While you've hated every minute, and Malcolm has been slowly sinking into this state, I've actually been happy!'

Liv said, 'Yes, I know. The thing is, how are the ambulance men going to knock this door down? It's mahogany or something.'

'It's too late. He said it was too late.'

'He didn't mean it. Not Malcolm.' Liv frowned. 'The waiting room. It looks over the garden. Maybe this hot weather one of the windows will be open.'

'He'll have closed all the windows.'

But he hadn't. Liv wasn't surprised. She wasn't angry with him either. If she'd known more about drugs, she might well have done the same thing. She grabbed a trowel from the trug outside the door, kilted her dressing-gown and nightie and pulled a bench beneath the window and scrambled on to the sill. The sash was open at the top. She stood up and closed it with difficulty – the windows were six feet high and very heavy. Her nails broke and her slippers came off at the heel. She kicked them behind her and pushed at the lower window with all her might. It came up half an inch. Grimacing with triumph she squatted on the sill and levered the sash with the trowel. She scrambled inside; there was no sign of Malcolm. If he'd locked the inner door they were no better off. She pushed her head out of the window.

'I'll let you in from the hall, Mon. You'd better unlock the front door. See if the ambulance is coming.'

The hall door was bolted. She opened it wide, then went to the inner door. It was unlocked. She went inside.

Malcolm was lying on the treatment table. The Venetian blinds were closed against the evening sun and it was unbearably hot in the room. Instruments lay everywhere. On the soap dish at the wash basin was an empty bottle. She looked at the sleeping face.

'You covered every angle, Malcolm,' she said.

He did not move. His breathing was stertorous and saliva ran from a corner of his mouth. Monica came in with a rush. She took in the scene at a glance and groaned aloud.

Liv said, 'It's all right. He's still alive and he's left the bottle for the medical people to see, so probably there's an antidote.'

'What can we do? There's no sign of the ambulance!'

'Get him to wake up if poss.' Liv took one of the flaccid arms and hauled hard. 'Give me a hand. He's too heavy for one of us.'

Somehow they propped him up. His head lolled alarmingly. Liv did the things she'd seen in films: talked at him, moved his body, and – not at all reluctantly – slapped his face. It was terribly hard work; she and Mon were breathing as heavily as Malcolm, and it was some time before they realised that the sounds coming from him contained complaining notes.

'He's coming round,' Monica panted. 'My God – Liv – you've done it!'

'We have to keep it up.' Liv delivered a stinging blow across his cheek and shook his arm. 'Come on Malcolm! Wake up!'

'I think I heard a bell.' Monica stopped breathing to listen. It was the bell of an ambulance. The next moment two uniformed men appeared, bringing sanity with them. There was a stretcher and another man. Someone said, 'Will you come with us, madam?' He spoke to Monica as she was dressed, and she looked helplessly at Liv.

'I'll see to things here,' Liv assured her. 'He won't want to see me when he comes round.'

And then they were all gone, and the house was blessedly silent. Liv did the rounds of the boys. They were asleep. Little Lennie looked like an angel. Liv hung over his cot for a moment, feeling a very slight maternal pang. Suddenly she knew quite definitely that Myrtle would have to come back to the children.

Liv went to her room and began to dress again. When Monica got back they would need to talk. But she had already made up her mind. She'd had enough of inactivity, of running away from her problems. She would go up to Alnmouth tomorrow and see Myrtle.

Monica was not sure it was the right thing to do, but then, Monica was not sure of anything any more. She had no time to wonder about Liv's decision however, there was so much to do. She sat for two hours with the appointment book on her lap, telephoning Malcolm's clients while Doris took the boys for a long walk and Tom painted the window which had been scarred with the trowel. She visited Malcolm and tried to talk to the blank face without success. He was kept in the General Hospital for the next day only, and then, because he was not fit to be seen by his sons, she arranged for him to be transferred to a private nursing home in the Park. Seizing the opportunity, she spring-cleaned the treatment room, sterilised the instruments, boiled the sheets from the table, booked professional cleaners to steam-clean the carpet and curtains. She tried to telephone the hotel at Alnmouth and got through eventually, but was told that Mr Bradbury and Mrs Lennox had left there a week ago. She asked about Liv. 'Yes, Mrs Bradbury stayed overnight here the night before last. I believe she was then travelling south to catch the ferry.'

Monica could hardly believe her ears. 'Ferry?'

'Mr Bradbury left a forwarding address in Paris.'

The voice was withdrawn and disapproving. Melodramatics were not encouraged in small northern hotels, and Liv's arrival must have made it obvious that Reggie and Myrtle were absconding.

'Could you give it to me, please?'

'I'm sorry—'

Monica said with a return to her old authoritarian voice, 'I am looking after Mrs Lennox' children. Her baby son is not well and her husband is in hospital. I think she should know.'

'Um. Yes. Just a moment, please.' Muffled sounds of consultation came across the wires. Then the voice said huffily, 'Hotel Crillon. Place de la Concorde.'

'Thank you.' Monica replaced the telephone and stared down the hall. The Crillon. It was like the Savoy or the Ritz. What the hell did Myrtle think she was playing at?

A key turned in the lock and the door opened to admit Doris with Nicky and Martin. They clamoured towards her.

'Can we go swimming again, Aunt Mon?'

'I want to go down the chute head first!'

They felt that their father's mysterious illness and Liv's departure warranted a relaxation of all rules amounting to anarchy.

Monica said, 'Perhaps. Let's get lunch first. Salad in the fridge, Doris. I just want to book a call to France.'

'Salad?' howled Nicky. 'Rabbits' food! Ugh. And double ugh!'

Doris rolled her eyes at Monica. 'Shall I do them a few chips, Mrs Gallagher?'

Monica felt so helpless. She shrugged. 'All right. Tom is still painting and keeping an eye on Lennie in the pram. Could you check on them first?'

She booked a call to the Crillon, and one to Carol who had recently had a phone installed at the Bergerie. Then she went down to the kitchen. Lennie had graduated to Mallie's high chair and sat up there squawling for his lunch, rubbing the soles of his feet together convulsively and banging with a spoon. Tom was washing his hands at the sink, ignoring everything. Nicky and Martin were pouring salt on to the table and throwing it over their shoulders with much laughter. Poor Doris was trying to fry chips at the stove.

Monica stood in the door and shouted at the top of her voice, 'Shut *up!*' which certainly worked with the children, but probably damaged Doris' heart. Tom did not flinch. The only sounds to break the startled silence were the running tap and sizzling chip fat.

'That's better.' Monica removed the salt cellar and Lennie's spoon. 'Go and wash your hands up in the bathroom while your chips are cooking.'

'We've already washed, Aunt Mon.'

'Then do it again, and this time use the nail brush on your finger-nails. Also comb your hair.' She moved to the dresser and began to open a tin of baby food. 'Any future trips to the lido depend entirely on your behaviour.'

The boys disappeared meekly.

Tom turned off the tap and dried his hands laboriously. 'Well done, Mrs Gallagher. Lick 'em into shape early, I say.'

But Doris, obviously still suffering from shock, was less approving. 'Mrs Lennox never has any trouble with the lads,' she said, banging the wire chip basket on the side of the pan with unnecessary force.

Monica tightened her lips as she approached Lennie.

'Then the sooner she comes home, the better,' she said. It was the first time she had wished Myrtle back. Lennie looked at her as if she were Pontius Pilate, and turned away from the proffered spoon.

The lines to France were hopeless. The Crillon did not have anyone by the name of Blackberry, whether they came from Chester Lennox or Timbuctu. Baffled, Monica asked for someone who spoke better English than her French, and when a cultured voice said, 'The English secretary here,' she spelled Bradbury and then Chester Lennox. 'We do not have a Mr Bradbury. Nor Mrs Lennox. But Mrs Bradbury has booked a room. She is out at the moment. May I ask her to telephone you when she returns?'

'Yes please.' Monica gave the Cheltenham number without much hope.

Her call to the Bergerie was more successful. Mrs Woodford answered the phone and sounded clear and immediately under-standing.

'Carol has gone to the village for some groceries, Mon dear. We have just come back from camping in the mountains. Yes. Delight-ful. Bessie? She enjoyed it very much. Boris Denning was with us. They are very close. I wonder if perhaps, later . . . Cass calls me the ancient romantic!' Her laugh sounded blessedly normal. She resumed more seriously, 'Mon, we realise how difficult it must be for you and Liv over there. Carol would like to help. She writes to Myrtle, you know. She thinks Myrtle will soon be well enough to return home.'

Monica told her the latest developments, and Mrs Woodford's horror was consoling.

'You're there on your own? Oh Mon, I am sorry. How rotten. Listen, Jean-Claude is in Paris at the moment. Perhaps he could contact Myrtle? Yes, but I do not think Liv is the best person to act as conciliator, do you? All right, my dear, I'll tell Carol exactly what has happened, and she will contact you as soon as she can.'

That meant they could not go the lido that afternoon. Monica did not feel she could ask Doris to take the children out yet again. Instead, as if to prove something, she gave her the afternoon off, and lugged Nicky's inflatable pool into the garden. Tom tipped the bench across the window so that no-one could climb up and touch the wet paint, and disappeared without suggesting that he could fill the pool via the garden hose. She organised a chain with buckets from the sink and tried to ignore the puddles all across the kitchen floor. The boys pretended to slip in the water and spilled even more. They ran in and out and turned the lawn into mud. Lennie sat in his pram and bawled. The phone rang and Monica left the sink and ran for it.

'Carol? Is that a call from France, operator?' she babbled.

'This is Mrs French from next door. I'm sorry to be a nuisance, Mrs Gallagher. I do realise that you are doing your best. But I have a tea party for the Ladies' Circle this afternoon, and I wondered if you could possibly make a little less noise?'

Monica almost sobbed her apologies and ran back to the kitchen to find Martin sitting in the sink splashing Nicky whenever he approached.

Somehow she had organised them into making paper boats, when Carol's call eventually came through. At least that offered some hope.

'I'm going to Paris myself, Mon. I've got hold of Jean-Claude, but obviously he does not know Liv – he doesn't know any of them – and if they're signed under false names, we can only identify them on sight. I think Liv has made a mistake to chase after them, but I suppose she couldn't sit and take it any more.'

'No.' Monica felt guilty again. 'I didn't realise it was telling on her so much, Cass. She was so different when Malcolm took those tablets – she seemed to know what to do – she absolutely took over.'

'Yes, but it means you're there on your own. Too much for you, Mon.' She paused but Monica did not contradict her. She went on, 'Boris could come and help out, but he has to go to Corsham next month. And Mother needs to be here to look after Bessie—'

'I'm all right, Cass. Honestly.'

'No, you're not. I can tell. I'll come over from Paris. Hopefully I'll bring the others with me. But I'll come anyway.'

'Oh Cass. Could you?'

'Of course. It will be compassionate leave. Don't worry.'

Monica could only say, 'Oh Cass.'

She replaced the phone and listened to the sounds from outside. Mrs French's tinkling teacups were almost submerged beneath yells from the boys. The paper boats were engaged in a naval battle. Monica sorted them out and stood on the bench to look over the wall.

'I'm terribly sorry, ladies. We won't disturb you any more.' She gave them all her sweetest smile, but melted very few hearts. When she looked around and saw Martin had righted the bench and Nicky was climbing on it and hanging on to the wet window like grim death, she could have wept all over again.

'Right. That's it. Inside. Baths and bed.'

'It's not tea time yet, Aunt Mon,' waited Martin.

She scooped Lennie out of his pram and he yelled again.

'I don't care if it's breakfast time. In you go.'

She herded them before her, ignoring their protests. Just let Myrtle come back and she'd tell her what she thought of her. She was so tired her head ached, and she felt thoroughly alone.

The door bell rang just as they turned to climb the stairs. With Nicky holding his paint-stained hands high, Martin as naked as the day he was born, Lennie raising Cain under his arm, she opened the door.

Bob stood there.

She said, 'Bob! What in heaven's name . . .'

He blurted. 'I had to see you. Rosa Palmer is pregnant. I want a divorce.'

It was as if he had hit her across the face. She flinched and grabbed Lennie with her other hand as if afraid she might drop him. Suddenly Martin started to cry.

'Don't go away, Aunt Mon! Please don't go away! We won't be naughty any more.'

Nicky put his paint-hands around her skirt and held her hard. 'We love you, Aunt Mon!' he shouted.

She began to cry.

Sixteen

The room at the Crillon overlooked the Place de la Concorde and was vast. Myrtle could not get over it.

'Reggie, how will you afford it?' She went from canopied bed to Empire escritoire, feeling materials, sliding across the rosewood with her fingertips. She opened a door into an enormous and elegant bathroom. 'Gold taps! Oh Reggie, I do believe they are gold taps! And this thing – what's this thing?'

'A bidet, honeybun.'

He was delighted his extravagance was so successful. She was moving quickly, like a girl. She wore a slim linen suit with a bolero-type jacket that flattered her full bust. He loved her so intensely that he could have wept when he looked at her and saw her happy and carefree again.

She noticed him watching her and came to him.

'Darling. I do love you.' She rubbed her cheek against his with a familiarity that surpassed a kiss. 'I never knew it could be like this, Reggie. You give me so much.'

'You give me more than I could ever give you, darling.'

'No. It is an equal giving.' She cupped his face and looked at him intently. 'For a long time it wasn't. You gave and I received. Now, I think it is equal. It is as if I was born for you, and you for me.' She kissed him. 'I am not talking about this room, Reggie. You know what I mean.'

'Of course.' He put his hands to her waist and drew her body towards his. 'I was nothing until I loved you, Myrtle. All that stuff about being an empty vessel – dammit, it's true!'

She smiled into his eyes. 'For me too. More so, perhaps.' She laughed, a sound which was still unfamiliar and which entranced Reggie. 'Oh darling, Reggie. Shall we? On the bed? Now?'

They did.

645

Last year at Barnt Green, Reggie had had to remind himself that Myrtle's expertise in bed had been learned from Malcolm. But since her calm declaration of love a month ago in Alnmouth, he had gradually known that their love-making owed nothing to anything or anyone. The Myrtle he had coaxed from the ashes of despair, brought a kind of innocence to their bed. At first it was passive; she would lie on her back looking just past his head, and when he roused her she would cling to him desperately, panting his name as if she were drowning. Then she had started to watch him as he undressed; she had touched his appendix scar: 'I didn't know you had that,' she said, as if it were important to her. Later she said, 'I need to know you, Reggie, every inch of you. Without you I am nothing at all, so I must know you.' Her investigations, even of his fingernails, had been at once the most erotic and spiritual experience of his life. She made him conscious of the sanctity of his own body. When she responded to him it was a sacrament.

But in Paris, the canopied bed took away any seriousness from their coupling. They romped on it like children and he tickled her until she giggled helplessly.

Reggie had made up a name for them to use in Paris. They had driven to Dover, inventing and discarding the most ridiculous identities. Myrtle had wanted the Honourable and Mrs Dalrymple. Reggie had suggested Alf and Gladys Mudd. In the end he had phoned a booking from the Railway Hotel in Dover where they left the car. Mr and Mrs Turner Stubbs. 'My two favourite artists,' he explained to her on the boat going over.

It seemed to impress. They were given what Reggie called pre-war treatment. His tweeds and brogues made him the archetypal English gentleman, and her round feminity was indefinably French. They had the best of both worlds: the reluctant respect accorded to the indomitable British, and the courtesy given to a womanly woman. Reggie hired a car and they 'did' the countryside around Paris. So it was that when Liv enquired for them at Reception, they were at Versailles and did not return until she had gone to bed. They slept late the next day, breakfasted in their room, and walked in the Tuileries while Liv enquired at neighbouring hotels. The Crillon was so vast they could have been in the foyer together and not known it. For three days they lived in the same building and came and went at different times. On the fourth day, Carol arrived from Provence, and enquired for Liv. She was out again, roaming art galleries, sure that Reggie would want to see all the pictures he could. Liv was feeling a sense of purpose she hadn't experienced for a long time.

Carol waited for her in the long blue and white gallery of the hotel. She drank coffee and corrected proofs and thought of how she would surprise Jean-Claude that evening at the Reine Blanche. He had told her that he ate every evening there, in memory of that first meal together; they had promised each other that they would go back one day and drink onion soup again, but they had not done so. Until now. She turned back a page of her manuscript and nibbled at her bottom lip, feeling suddenly guilty that her mission to Paris was not entirely disinterested.

She glanced up, hoping that Liv would appear and enmesh her in the tangled web that had spun itself so inexorably since Mallie's death last year. She was becoming selfish in her happiness, and somehow she was still haunted by the feeling that she was in debt to fate. It had come so easily: Bessie as a daughter, Jean-Claude as a mate; the love between Bessie and Jean-Claude and between Jean-Claude and her mother. She still wondered, every time he left the Bergerie, whether she would see him again. She could never forget the terrible anonymous hatred behind that fire bomb.

A waiter hovered, and she ordered more coffee. It was no good, she could not concentrate on the manuscript. The train journey had been tiring; she had picked up the Côte d'Azur at Marseilles with a boatload of sailors going to Paris on leave. One of them had been sick in her carriage and the smell had lingered until they ran into the Gare du Nord.

She slid the sheaf of paper into its folder and made room before her for the tray of coffee. She forced herself to think of Monica alone in Myrtle's house, coping with Myrtle's three children and suicidal husband. It was all so awful. Yet she could not condemn Myrtle as the others must be doing. Myrtle's letters came regularly now, at least one a week. They had been disjointed at first and full of unconscious pathos; now they were full of Reggie. Anyone else might have found them unbearably immature. Carol did not.

She poured coffee and reached across the damask-covered sofa for a copy of *Paris-Match*. There were some graphic illustrations of the student riots around the Sorbonne. She stared at them intently. Jean-Claude had another appointment with General de Gaulle to discuss these very issues. She wondered when they would ever be resolved. Britain appeared to be giving up her colonies more readily than France. Perhaps that humiliating surrender in 1940 had hardened France's innate nationalism into a canker. Jean-Claude prophesied a lot more trouble before the Algerian problem was settled.

She shivered and turned a page to the fashion spread. Yves St Laurent had taken over the house of Dior and was shocking the world with his mannish designs. Carol smiled at a picture of a girl dressed in black leather. Then stopped smiling and peered closer. The model was Gaby Durant. Jean-Claude's wife.

She leaned back and stared unseeingly down the gallery. Gaby. The same Gaby who had sat beneath the window in the office on Avenue Foch and typed so busily; who had prinked at her Brigitte Bardot hairstyle in the tiny mirror. Before Carol had known of Jean-Claude, Gaby had been a colleague, and the sight of her in newspaper should be a shock. No more than that. Nothing more than that. Just an insignificant coincidence.

But she felt cold in spite of the weather, and she took a gulp of coffee as she might have taken medicine. She glanced at her watch. Almost midday. At least six hours before she could go to the Reine Blanche.

And then she saw them. It was incredible. All three of them. Liv was several yards in front, obviously looking for Carol after getting her message in the foyer. Reggie and Myrtle had no idea that their secret hideout had been discovered, and were wandering along the gallery on their way out, or to lunch, their hands linked loosely; they had eyes only for each other. Reggie looked exactly as Carol remembered him last year, tweeds and white shirt, dark blue tie; Myrtle was quite different, slimmer, smaller altogether, her head erect and neatly framed in a Byronesque haircut not unlike Gaby's, a straight linen strawberry-coloured dress with a mandarin collar making her look taller than she really was.

Carol half rose and Liv saw her and hurried forward. Myrtle's attention was caught by the sudden flurry of movement: she switched her gaze from Reggie and saw Carol and Liv embracing. Frantically Carol signalled to her to go away. For a split second

Myrtle hesitated, then she turned to Reggie and said something urgently; the next minute they had disappeared through the doors to the foyer.

Liv said, 'Cass – my dear – what on earth are you doing here? Did you know?' She withdrew and smiled up at the familiar plain face. 'Oh of course. Mon phoned you. I suppose she's worried to death?'

'Well yes. She is rather. Oh Liv . . .' Carol shrugged with Gallic helplessness. 'Sit down. Have this coffee – I've only just poured it. No, I'm awash with the stuff. Oh, I'm glad to find you. I wasn't sure if you'd come back before tonight.' She watched Liv settle herself with her usual fussy movements. 'My dear, you look fine. I thought – I was afraid – Mon did not know how you'd be.'

Liv finished smoothing her skirt.

'I'm better now actually. I shouldn't have run to Mon like I did. It was just so awful, Cass. And I've never had to be on my own . . . oh you wouldn't understand of course, you're so independent—'

'Not any more.'

'No, but . . . anyway, I did go to Mon. I sort of plonked all my worries on to her. I don't know what I expected her to do. She produced some answers of course, but they weren't the right ones for me. It's been a dreadful summer, Cass. Like some waking dream in New York which turned to a nightmare in Cheltenham.' She sipped her coffee and dabbed at her lipstick with the monogrammed napkin. 'Mon thought me being there and helping to look after Myrt's children would bring Myrt back quickly. Guilt. That sort of thing. All it did was to make her throw in her lot with Reggie officially.' She sighed, opened her bag, fished out a compact and snapped it open to look at her reflection. 'You heard about Malcolm?'

'Yes. He's going to be all right, Mon says.'

'Oh, of course. He had no intention of committing suicide. Not really.' She snapped the compact shut. 'God, Cass, it's such a *mess*!'

'And why are *you* here? That's what I cannot understand.' Carol let her eyes flick towards the double doors. There was no sign of a strawberry linen dress. She sat back on the sofa again.

Liv shrugged. 'I had to do something. Off my own bat. I know

Reggie is besotted. Even now I can't bear to remember some of the things he said to me, Cass. But Myrtle . . . surely she intends to go back to the children and to Malcolm? I want to tell her about Malcolm myself.' She leaned forward. 'I know how he is feeling, Cass. He told me.'

Carol was at a loss for words. She could not see that anything Liv might say to Myrtle would help anyone.

Liv drank her coffee and put the cup down with a click.

'Strangely enough, now that I'm . . . on the trail . . . I feel better.' She lifted her brows at Carol. 'I know it sounds utterly heartless, Cass, but there was nothing I could do until Malcolm took that overdose. The inactivity was simply terrible. I knew that Mon was half despising me too. Oh she's been kindness itself, don't get me wrong. But sometimes she would look at me in a way that I knew was . . . well . . . critical. After all, look at the terrible knocks she's had to take. No family, nothing.'

Carol felt like protesting; there had been herself, her mother, Dilly and Gander Gosling.

Instead she said, 'What *about* Mon? How long will her husband put up with this situation?'

Liv shrugged. 'She doesn't love him. She and I, we're quite similar in that way still.' She laughed mirthlessly. 'Unloved, and unloving.'

'Rubbish,' Carol said without conviction. She leaned across and put a hand on Liv's arm. '*We're* still friends. All of us.'

Liv laughed again. 'Speak for yourself! Oh you can speak for Mon, I suppose. But Myrtle has opted out of friendship, I'd say. Wouldn't you?'

'No.' Carol's voice was strong. 'No. I certainly wouldn't say that. Our friendship is still there. Remember last summer? Finding the paint pot?'

'Oh come off it, Cass.'

'I mean it. It wouldn't matter what happened. We four would have something left. Something.'

'Well, if you mean Myrtle would have my husband, and Mon would have Myrtle's kids, and you would have Mon's kid, and I nearly had Myrtle's husband . . .' Suddenly and unexpectedly, Liv's eyes overflowed with tears. 'Oh damn! I thought I was over all this soppy stuff. I thought I'd pulled myself together by now.'

'You have. That's why you're crying. Because it's hit you that you've still got Myrtle. And me. And Mon.' But Carol was white-faced at the brutality of that summing-up. She said desperately, 'Liv, I know it sounds crazy, but in a strange way, what you said just now . . . doesn't it show that we still share those things? Oh God. I don't mean that we should share our husbands. I don't mean that. I don't know what I mean. But there is something, Liv. Something.'

'*You're* upset now.' Liv passed a handkerchief. 'God. Here. In the swankiest hotel in Paris.'

'That doesn't matter. What matters is that we don't hurt each other more than we can help. Listen.' Carol blew loudly and smiled. 'Not to that!' She tried to laugh as she tucked the ridiculous square of cambric into her sleeve. Then she stopped laughing and looked very serious. 'Liv. I don't think you should see Myrtle. Not this time.'

Liv stared at her. 'Surely she has a right to know about Malcolm?'

'Yes. But he can tell her himself when she's back in England. She's been very ill, Liv. Close to a complete breakdown. She's been writing to me and I've been able to chart her recovery. If you confront her with this news, other things will be said – they're bound to be, Liv, you won't be able to control your words once you start. Forgive me, my dear, but you are the worst person to tell Myrtle. You're doing it for the wrong reasons. You want her to go back to Malcolm so that you can return to Reggie.'

Liv protested angrily. 'No such thing! I thought I'd explained to you – I thought you realised – I cannot go back to Reggie, ever!'

Carol looked down at her hands. Like Monica she could see no other future for Liv. She said quietly, 'I wasn't criticising the idea, Liv. Not at all. I was just saying that this is not a good way to bring it about.'

'Haven't I just *said* –!' Liv half rose as if to flee, but Carol put out a hand and she subsided again. 'Cass. I don't want to talk like this. Please. I felt better – coming out here – I had a – a mission—' she sobbed a laugh – 'sorry. But you know what I mean. Something definite to do. I don't want to lose that feeling. Don't try to talk me out of it. Please.'

Carol swallowed. 'All right. Pax. For now.' She took Liv's hand and held it tightly. 'Will you give up your "mission" – just for a few hours? Let's go and have lunch somewhere. Let's talk about . . . anything. I think whatever your motives it was terrific of you to look after Myrt's children. Tell me about them. And New York.'

'Mon was in charge of the boys. Well, I suppose I put them to bed sometimes. Nicky is quite a little gentleman – he opens doors . . . that kind of thing.' Liv looked helpless and lost again.

Cass said, 'That's what I meant about sharing things. We share the children. You and I have none, Liv. But it doesn't matter because we share Mon's and Myrtle's. Does that make sense to you?'

'I suppose so.' Liv managed a wry smile. 'But I'll give you this, Cass. I don't think I could have got through the last few months without Mon. And now you. After what Myrt has done to me, I needed to feel your support.'

Carol thought about Myrtle: the Myrtle she had known in baggy dirndl skirts and blouses and the Myrtle who was in the Crillon with Reggie Bradbury, using a false name and wearing a straight dress with poise.

She said, 'Don't hate Myrt. It . . . happened.'

'You've always been an idealist, Cass.'

'Not really. Most friendships are based on sheer pragmatism. I like to think ours isn't.' Carol stood up, then bent to pick up her bag and added softly, 'I know I'm going to sound like the manuscript I'm reading, but I actually believe this – the more love you give, the more you get.'

Liv did not reply. But when Carol proffered a crooked elbow, she pushed her hand through it affectionately, and they walked through the swing doors and the foyer and into the Place to find a cafe for lunch.

Reggie and Myrtle, sitting in the foyer behind a screen of palms, registered the linked arms with foreboding.

Myrtle said, 'What does it mean? Liv here. And Carol too. What are they doing? They must be looking for us – they must be! But then, why did Carol wave us away?' She pushed a hand through her careful urchin cut and it stood on end. 'Reggie. I'm frightened. I'm really frightened.'

'I know, Myrtle.' He stared after the two women, frowning. He knew that of all four friends, Carol Woodford was the most reliable, the most staunch, the most faithful. All those years ago at Malcolm's wedding he had wanted to know her, and when finally they had met last summer, his first impressions had been confirmed. 'Those letters she has written to you, darling . . . Carol is on your side. I'm sure of it.'

'She understands. Yes.' Myrtle's initial panic had abated. 'But she won't be on anyone's side, Reggie. Carol isn't like that.' She looked at him. 'It might be something to do with the children. Carol wants to stop Liv blurting it out.'

'Rubbish. If there was anything wrong with your family, Carol would be the first to come and tell you so. You know that.'

Myrtle swallowed. 'Yes. Yes, you're right of course. Then Liv is going to try and get me to go home, Reggie. Or to make you . . . Reggie, what are we going to do? We've never talked about the future properly. I know I said I was leaving Malcolm . . . but I didn't say that I was leaving the boys.'

It was Reggie's turn to be frightened.

'You wouldn't – Myrt, you couldn't – we're everything for each other. You've said that—'

'And I've meant it. I still mean it. Now and in the future.'

'You wouldn't feel you had to make any sacrifices? You know that if you sacrifice your happiness, you sacrifice mine too.'

'Yes. Yes, I know.'

She met his eyes but looked away before they could make their usual connection. He had no children. He loved hers, but they weren't his. If Liv and Carol had come to tell her that something was wrong with one of the boys, she might have very little choice.

Bob lay propped on pillows in Malcolm's bed, wearing Malcolm's pyjama top and watching Monica give Lennie his early-morning bottle.

'He should be sleeping properly now, hon, surely?' he asked, running his hands through his hair. 'And I thought babies had their own rooms these days?'

'Not when I'm looking after them.' Monica tore her gaze away from Lennie's blissfully closed eyes and frantically bellowing cheeks, and glanced at Bob. He grinned at her, but she did not grin back. She knew how he felt; the feeling of a secret shared, the secret of their love-making. It convinced her – even more than his admitted infidelity with Rosa Palmer – that is was over between them. Bob saw absolutely nothing wrong in sleeping with his wife after he had asked her for a divorce so that he could marry a woman he had made pregnant. Monica hated herself for surrendering so abysmally to his blandishments.

She said abruptly, 'The trouble with me is I'm too good in bed.'

He laughed. 'You are, hon. But that's no trouble. Take it from me.'

The teat of Lennie's bottle turned suddenly inside-out and he opened his gums to yell. She lifted him expertly on to her shoulder while she released the vacuum in the bottle. She resettled him.

She went on as if Bob had not spoken. 'I can't relate love and sex. Love is something I feel for Lennie and Martin and Nicky. And Carol and Liv and Myrtle. Sex is something else.'

He was affronted.

'Are you saying you never loved me, Mon baby?'

'I'm not sure.'

'What about last night?'

'That's what I mean. I certainly don't love you now. I might have done earlier. I simply do not know.'

'You're saying this because of Rosa. Okay, so I have to marry her. I want to marry her dammitall – she's carrying my child. But I still love you. There. If I can admit it, so can you!'

'Bob . . . for goodness' sake. I'm trying to be honest. I don't want you going into this new marriage with an albatross around your neck! You're free! And you're lucky – you're going to have a family!'

He returned stubbornly to his point. 'And what about last night?'

She looked him straight in the eye. 'Bob. I'd had an awful day. An awful week. I felt totally alone. Any man would have done.'

For an instant she thought he might hit her. His eyes narrowed coldly and his right hand clenched on the bedspread. Then he shook his head as if to clear it. She could almost follow his train of thought: Monica was making it easy for him . . . good old Monica . . . typical English sportswoman.

She finished winding Lennie and put him back in his cot, smiling down at him reassuringly as she smoothed the covers around his shoulders. He should sleep again until nearly nine; long enough for her to get breakfast for the boys and send them off with Doris for a walk. She felt a renewed energy as she thought about the coming day; her smile became wry, perhaps that was what last night had been about. He misinterpreted the smile.

'Christ, Mon. What will you do? You're bored enough when we're up to our eyes in the sports club and the theatre and everything. What are you going to do here? Your friend, Myrtle, whatever her name is – she can't stay away for ever. You've got yourself in the middle of a godawful mess. How are you going to get out of it?'

She shrugged. 'I stay in it until it solves itself. I'm not in the solution business, Bob.' She transferred the smile to him. 'You should know that.'

He smiled back, reassured, relieved . . . enormously relieved.

'You're a nice woman. You're a stunner. If only . . . But anyway Mon, I'll always love you. If ever you need me, just yell. Okay?'

'Okay. That's the nicest thing you've ever said to me actually, Bob. And I'll yell. In fact I'm yelling now.'

He reached for her. 'Again? Christ, you're insatiable. But then, so am I—'

She slapped him away. 'Not that! Idiot. I want you to shave and dress now, while the bathroom is free. Then I want you to have breakfast with Nicky and Martin and take them out for an hour. It'll be good practice for you.'

He pretended to be henpecked and grumbled all through getting dressed. She watched him. It was the last time. There was something very intimate about lying in bed watching a man tuck his shirt into his trousers and fit a tie beneath his collar. When he was ready she put on her dressing-gown and kissed him chastely on the cheek.

'You're a nice man. Completely amoral, but nice.'

'Immoral? I'm no such thing . . .'

She didn't explain the difference. They trailed downstairs, bickering like any old married couple. When she saw how good he was with Nicky and Martin she could have loved him properly, but she wouldn't let herself. It was too late. But the one thing about being too late was that you had to make new beginnings. Carol would be phoning today.

Carol did not tell Liv that Myrtle and Reggie were staying at the Crillon.

They ate lunch together and talked about the past, and gradually

Liv was able to reveal her pain and unhappiness as if it were a running sore to be healed by the clean air of Carol's understanding.

They walked down the Champs Elysées to the Tuileries and sat in the gardens in the sunshine. They had so little in common, yet there was no difficulty in talking. Carol spoke of her feeling for Jean-Claude and Liv admitted for the first time that Reggie's defection had made her realise how deeply she loved him.

'When he comes home you'll be able to show him that. So that he isn't consumed with guilt.'

'Oh Cass. He won't come back. That was why I came here . . . yes, you were right of course. I can't get him back like that. But it's still the only way. He'll never come back to me of his own accord.'

'I think he will. You see, he'll want to be with someone . . . make someone happy. If you were at home, waiting for him . . .'

Liv laughed uncomfortably. 'I wanted to be independent. Tough. Like Mon.'

'You're not like Mon. You're Liv. There's a lot to Liv Baker – show Reggie the side he hasn't met yet.' Carol shifted the fine gravel with her toe. 'You've found out that Reggie is a very passionate person. Can you fill that need in him, Liv?'

Liv stared. 'You've changed. You couldn't have said that when we were girls!'

'No.' Carol blushed faintly and smiled at her friend. 'Jean-Claude has made the difference, of course. But I think Bessie would have done, anyway. She is very . . . frank.'

They both laughed.

Liv said, 'You're so lucky, Cass.'

But Carol said quickly as if touching wood, 'Happiness is only on loan, remember, Liv. Like Bessie. Only on loan.'

'Rubbish. You'll never lose Bessie. Oh, I suppose one day she'll learn that Mon is her real mother, but she won't forget you and your mother. Never.' She tipped her head back and closed her eyes on the sunshine. 'Any more than I can forget Reggie and Myrtle.'

Carol stood up briskly. 'Come on. Enough of that. Let's find somewhere and have a cup of tea. I'm meeting Jean-Claude this evening to tell him what is happening. Then tomorrow you and I will go back to Cheltenham and help Monica.' She pulled Liv to her feet. 'Listen. If Reggie and Myrtle had been – say – victims of an earthquake – you would nurse their injuries. That's what they were. Victims of an earthquake.'

Liv tried to laugh.

Arm in arm they walked back towards the Place, unmistakably English, though so different. If they noticed the small knots of students hurrying in the direction of the Bastille, they did not find it remarkable. President de Gaulle was even now discussing the future of Algeria, where he had kept alive the idea of a Free French Government all through the war years. If anyone could sort out the muddle it was he. Student groups were always volatile, whether they were French, English, American or whatever.

In their room at the Crillon, Reggie wondered whether there might be a demonstration in the offing. The traffic, whirling around Concorde at high speeds as usual, was diverted, even halted momentarily, by strings of young people like threads of molecules, running between the cars. Reggie fetched his binoculars and in an effort to divert Myrtle from her constant worrying about the sudden appearance of Liv and Carol, watched them carefully, reporting back to her where she lay on the bed.

'They've got some kind of banner, darling. Black. I can't see what is says.'

Myrtle turned on one side and pillowed her cheek on the palm of her hand.

'Could that be why Cass is here? Maybe she is with that reporter – Jean Durant – and she asked Liv to come for a holiday and they—'

Reggie seized on this explanation gladly.

'Of course that's it, Myrtle. Why didn't I think of that? It's obvious, isn't it? Nothing at all to do with the boys. Liv was with Cass in Provence. Durant was given this assignment in Paris. They thought it was a good opportunity to show Liv the city—'

'But why come to the Crillon? I mean, it's not Cass' sort of place. And she didn't seem surprised to see us, Reggie.'

'But she couldn't have known we were here, darling. If she'd known – I mean, if she was looking for us – she'd hardly wave us away like that, would she?'

'No. She wouldn't want Liv to see us. But supposing Liv had

657

come to find us. To tell us something about the boys. Or Mon.
And Cass saw her by accident. And—'

'Honey. Cass knows we are here. She doesn't know what name
we're using, but she knows we're here and she'll find a way to
contact us. All we have to do is sit tight. Which is okay by us,
yes?' He smiled over the binoculars, then put them to his eyes and
swept the enormous circus again. 'Those youngsters seem to have
met up and gone into the Métro. I'll ring down for some newspapers.'

'We could switch on that wireless.'

'Can't understand the lingo unless it's written down, can you?'
He steadied the binoculars and concentrated.

'Let's go down for dinner, Reggie. We shall pick up more from
the waiter than from the newspaper.'

He watched carefully. It was Liv. By herself. She was beneath
them now. He went to the window and saw her disappear under
the awning.

'Let's have dinner sent up, Myrtle.' He came over to the bed
and kissed her ear tenderly. 'I don't want to share you with all
those people.' He moved his lips from ear to cheek and murmured, 'If I never saw you again, my love, I'd always remember the
feel of your skin under my mouth.'

She turned and tried to focus on him.

'You're just as frightened as I am,' she whispered. She put her
arms around his neck. 'Ah, Reggie. Don't be. We're here and it's
now.'

And she held him to her.

Carol's taxi crossed the Pont Neuf at six-thirty and was stopped
in the Rue Madeleine by a column of people in the road, waving a
banner proclaiming 'Liberté pour Algérie.' She wound down
the window and heard them chanting the words like a mantra.

'What is it?' She spoke in English after being with Liv for so
long, and the taxi-driver replied in English too.

'They are young and impatient. Not willing to wait. There is
much ill-feeling.' He leaned on his horn and received some black
looks. 'They are congregating around the Sorbonne. Also the
Bastille. Do not be out late, mademoiselle.'

'Thank you. I do not expect to be.'

But the hold-up continued and by seven-thirty she was

beginning to wonder whether she might miss Jean-Claude.

'I'll walk.' She leaned forward to pay the driver. 'I am sorry, you are well and truly caught in this crowd.'

He let her alight with many warnings which she hardly heard for the sheer press of people around the vehicle. However, as soon as she went into the crowd, there was a furious honking behind her and she saw the taxi do an about-turn and honk its way back towards the river. Unexpectedly she suddenly felt isolated and very foreign among the motley collection of students.

A young girl with hair and eyes as black as Bessie's spoke to her.

'You are English? You would join us?'

Carol hated crowds and could hardly think straight. She tried to work her way diagonally to the other side of this impenetrable mass.

'I'm trying to find a friend,' she panted.

'Ah. One of us?'

'Yes. I suppose so.'

'Bien. Then come – come – venez ici—'

The girl took her arm and wormed her way between two young giants labelled 'Maquis'. She shouted something at them and they shouldered another opening, and the next minute Carol was among the stragglers on the other side of the column.

'Thank you. Thank you so much,' she gasped at the dark-haired girl. But she had already gone and the young giants roared 'Vive la liberté!' and marched on.

She moved on down the Avenue, and leaned against one of the acacia trees to watch the last of the demonstrators. She hoped Liv had got back to the Crillon all right and that she would not see Reggie and Myrtle. Perhaps she should have told her that they were in fact staying in the same hotel, presumably under a false name. But she hadn't, and it was too late now.

She took some deep breaths and relaxed her stiffened spine. She was wearing a blue dress with a deeper blue cardigan, both rather the worse for wear now. She straightened the cardigan self-consciously. Jean-Claude would say it was typically English, but it seemed to her that on a summer's evening there was really nothing else to wear. Certainly Liv had worn a linen suit and Myrtle appeared to be wearing something vaguely Chinese, but such fashions were no good to Carol.

659

She began to walk towards the Reine Blanche. If Jean-Claude wasn't there, she didn't know where to find him. She hoped very much – in fact with all her soul – that he would be there. She was experiencing a strange sense of déjà vu. As if there might be another explosion, another fire.

But he was there.

She paused in the little side street where he had left the Renault that time, and saw the familiar outline of him in the same seat that he'd occupied that night. She could see the shape of a bowl before him, and there were other bowls too. She wondered how many he had managed tonight. She walked along the wide pavement towards the entrance, picking her way between the outside tables, transferring her bag from one shoulder to the other, thinking he would glance up and see her and come running to meet her. She looked up again. He was with someone. Of course he would be. There would be other reporters, and some of them would be women.

But this woman was vaguely familiar. Carol stopped beneath an umbrella and blinked her eyes clear. The woman was leaning over her bowl, laughing, spooning soup into her mouth. Carol had seen her picture just that day.

It was Gaby.

There was an instant's hiatus of thought and action. And then small things clicked into place. Gaby was happy. She was actually laughing at this man who was her husband – laughing with him. Yes, he was laughing too. And Gaby had never laughed all the time she had worked with Carol in the Paris office; she had been secretive and mysterious and entirely without laughter. And all those soup bowls. Six soup bowls. They were on the last two. They had shared six bowls of onion soup. Gaby was a model now, featured in *Paris Match*, used to more exotic fare than onion soup.

Carol turned and walked quickly across the road and behind the screen of acacia trees. She closed her eyes and told herself she was being a fool and it was all right. But she couldn't face them now. She couldn't look as if she'd followed him here.

She began to walk briskly, intending to go back to the Crillon to find Liv, eat dinner with her and be normal again.

At the Pont Neuf she met up with the column of marchers. She turned away, almost sobbing with frustration, wondering how she could get across the river. Coming towards her was another column of people. Gendarmerie. They appeared to be carrying dustbin lids in front of them. She glanced from them to the marchers. They had seen the police and were turning to meet them with a concerted howl that sounded animal-like. Carol searched their anonymous faces for the familiar one of the dark-haired girl, but could see only open mouths and aggressive flags.

She was suddenly possessed by an unnatural terror. She knew it stemmed from the previous incident four years ago and was activated by everything that was happening to her here and now: Myrtle and Reggie, Liv and Monica, Jean-Claude and Gaby. She tried to use mental logic to calm herself, but the only logic she knew was Jean-Claude. She should have stayed at the cafe and seen him. She had to get back there quickly.

For some reason the police were beating the dustbin lids with their truncheons. The noise from the marchers had escalated to a near-scream, and they were moving towards her.

She began to run towards the police.

At the Reine Blanche, Jean-Claude offered Gaby a gauloise and sat back in his chair. He wondered what he ever seen in her. She was so pretty, so smug and self-satisfied, so egotistic.

He said, 'Are you sure you'll be all right, Gaby?'

She smiled again, showing perfect, pointed teeth.

'Certainly. Marcel is a film star you know, chéri. He understands that I, too, am in show business. He will get me a part quite soon.' Her smile widened. 'Oh yes, I shall be very all right.'

He lit her cigarette and nodded slowly.

'You know I have wanted a divorce for some time now. I am . . . grateful.'

'You would not have it if it did not suit me, Jean-Claude!' At least she was honest. She exhaled smoke through parted lips. 'Though I refused before, chéri, for you own sake. I did not think your infatuation with the English Carol would last. She is not suitable for you, chéri. She is not . . .' she searched for a word, her eyes narrowed in concentration. 'She is not *amusant*.'

Jean-Claude considered for an instant trying to explain to Gaby what fun it was to be with Carol, then gave up the idea. She would never understand.

He said, 'Well. Perhaps you know her only in one way.' He must be diplomatic. She was capricious and could change her mind on a whim. 'After all, Gaby, in the office it was a little different.'

She shrugged. 'It is of no importance.' She smiled again. 'It has been *amusant* for me—' she waved her cigarette to indicate the small cafe. 'Meeting like this – so *mystérieux* . . . you must have wondered who wanted to see you. And when you got here, why there were six bowls of onion soup all ready to be eaten!' She laughed deliciously and leaned forward. 'Or did you recognise my voice on the telephone and wish to see me again, Jean? Was that it? A double secret?'

He smiled obediently. He had known his anonymous caller was Gaby, and he had come here tonight in the ever-present hope that she wanted to marry someone else. At last it had happened, and now he could ask Carol if she would marry him.

He said, 'You were always up to such tricks, Gaby. I should have remembered.'

'It was why you fell in love with me first, yes? You called me your taste of happiness!'

'Yes. Yes, I did.' The recollection made him suddenly sad, as if he had been disloyal to Carol.

She was serious. 'And you saved me from much unpleasantness, Jean. I am still grateful for that. I had enjoyed the war. There were people who resented me enjoying myself. Then you came along – the brave Free Frenchman – and you married me! Who could criticise me then?' She shrugged again. 'Pouf! There are still people who resent me enjoying myself. I do not care a fig for them.'

He waited until she finished the cigarette, then said, 'Gaby, I told my photographer to meet me here at eight o'clock to cover the student demonstration. When he arrives I must go. The lawyers will send me the papers no doubt?'

'It is all organised.' She stood up. 'Get me a taxi, Jean. I am having a proper dinner with Marcel later.' She smiled roguishly. 'My days of onion soup are over!'

It seemed a fitting epitaph. He waited with her beneath the pavement umbrellas until the taxi arrived. Down towards the river there was a constant noise from the demonstrators. They must be crossing the Seine to meet up with others from the university. He wondered where his photographer had got to, and wished he had brought his own camera.

'Listen.' Gaby looked up at him in surprise. 'Is it drums? They must have a band.'

He frowned, then said, 'It is police batons. Beating their shields. They're trying to disperse the students before they can become threatening.'

'Young fools,' Gaby said unemotionally. 'Causing inconvenience to good citizens.' She looked the other way. 'Ah. Here is my taxi.' She got in and slammed the door. 'Au 'voir, Jean. We shall meet again. Of that I am certain.'

He did not watch her drive away. He began to run towards the noise. He was used to violence and he could smell it in the air, hear it in the muttered roar of the students and the beating of the police shields. If there was a story he had to be there to report it. But it was more than a journalistic urge that sent him accelerating along the Saint-German; he did not know what it was. His heart was hammering in his chest and his head was filled with a nightmare terror that he had never experienced before.

He saw the backs of the police, a solid phalanx across the boulevard. Beyond them there was a mass of people and the usual array of banners; not waving in the slight breeze as they would have done if held still, but jerking spasmodically as their bearers became aggressive. He saw the whites of faces and gesturing hands and knew that they were all young people. Probably unwise, even foolish, but idealistic and with the terrible power of idealism.

He came to the police guard as the first stone crashed among them.

'Let me through,' he panted. '*La Planète* – I can talk to them – they will listen to me. Let me through!'

'Retirez monsieur!'

An angry face was turned on him, and someone – obviously an inspector – came and took his arm.

Then another hail of stones caused a momentary gap in the line of police, and he saw someone running towards him. He could not believe, for an interminable second, that it was Carol. She was back in the safety of the Bergerie with her mother and Bessie. The girl running so desperately in his direction wore a blue frock very like Carol's, and a blue cardigan identical to the one

Carol had bought in London last year. But it could not be Carol.

And then something hit her. He could not see what it was, but she went down in a sprawled heap, her arm stretched out, her shoulder back at an angle to her body. And he saw that it was Carol.

In the sudden shocked silence, his cry filled the air. He was through the gap and running towards her. The police inspector shouted a warning, but if the stones had been machine-gun bullets it would have made no difference. He was on his knees, skidding to a stop by her head.

'Cass – my Cass—' he heard his own voice, high, like a child's. Blood was oozing from the back of her head and darkening her sun-striped hair. The hair hung in loops from its pins and he pulled them out frantically, frightened that the pins themselves might have impaled themselves in her scalp. She was unconscious, but she was breathing.

'Get an ambulance!' He lifted his head. He knew he was weeping but did not care. 'Vite! An ambulance!'

Someone knelt by him.

'She was with us earlier, m'sieu. She was looking for you.'

He glanced sideways and saw through his tears the wavering face of a young girl not much older than Bessie.

He said, 'She'll be all right, won't she? It's just a surface wound – she'll be all right?'

But the girl had disappeared, wrenched away by official hands. The police, doubtless trained in first aid, were all around. There were blankets and a white box with a red cross printed on it. And then the blessed sound of the ambulance.

He said, 'I must go with her. Let me through . . .'

But there was no need for further struggle. The crowd had magically dispersed and the way was clear. The stretcher slid on to its shelf and he followed it in and knelt again, his arms protectively over the blanketed figure.

They told him she would be all right. The ambulance man who travelled inside tried to help by saying that she had done the police a great service because the demonstration was over without anyone being hurt. Then he realised what he had said and tucked the red blanket around Carol's neck carefully, Jean-Claude found himself abandoning the enormous question of why Carol was there at that precise time, and asking himself whether the red blanket was to disguise bloodstains. He tried to recall how he had dealt with emergencies on his many travels, especially in Suez where he had taken over an ambulance and driven twenty miles through enemy territory. He remembered feeling very calm, almost detached. Not like this. Not weak and shaky and completely helpless.

He said suddenly, 'She's wet – oh God – she's wet! She's bleeding somewhere else!'

The ambulance man pushed him out of the way and flipped back the blanket.

'Urine.'

It sounded simple enough, but still the man crouched above her clamping an oxygen mask over the white face.

'Hold this if you please,' he said to Jean-Claude brusquely.

Somehow they changed places in the cramped confines of the van. Jean-Claude knew suddenly that this was an emergency. He felt the weakness in his limbs drain away, and he became very cold. He leaned close to Carol's ear and said quietly, 'My strength is going into you, beloved. Feel it. Know it.'

The ambulance man was pounding on her chest. The ambulance took a wide turn somewhere and they all swung inwards. For a moment Jean-Claude imagined that Carol was leaning on him responsively, and his right arm went beneath her head to hold her to him. And then, with terrible certainty, he knew she was dead.

He pushed aside the mask and held her face to his in a spasm of grief that seemed to explode his soul. At his left shoulder the ambulance man had given up his attempts at artificial respiration. He said quietly, 'I am sorry, m'sieur. Very sorry.' Jean-Claude made no reply. He was conscious that something was happening. He held Carol to him quite gently and knew that they were in a void together. They were still together. Then he was alone, yet not alone. He was filled with her. She had told him once that he had become Jean-Claude-Carol and he had thought he had known what she meant. He had not known. He did now.

Very gently he laid her head back and took away his arm. He remembered that void and wished himself back there; yet knew she was no longer there. She was here.

Even so his voice said, 'She cannot be gone. It is not true.' The ambulance man responded instantly to the new emergency and pushed him firmly back on the other stretcher. And then everyone else took over. It was in their behaviour that Jean-Claude knew of his own outward state. Inside he was calm and whole. Nobody else knew this. He sat very still and let Carol's being fill him again and again. He was lifted and taken into a hospital and heard someone say the word catatonic, and thought how amusing it was.

Liv waited in the foyer at the Crillon until ten o'clock, when she knew she and Carol had missed the train. The old fear and isolation began to overtake her. She wondered whether she had dreamed the whole episode of meeting Carol yesterday. It was possible. She had read an article in one of Malcolm's osteopathy magazines about something called psychosomatic pain and hallucination. She tried to remember exactly what it had been about, but could not. She could barely remember why she was in Paris at all. When she looked up and saw Myrtle and Reggie coming towards her, she thought they really were part of the dream she must be having. Then she saw that Myrtle was weeping and Reggie was holding out his arm to her as if to include her in their grief. She held back, telling herself she hated them both. Myrtle did not look like Myrtle at all, she was small and smart and strangely French. But Reggie was the same, and Reggie had been cruel.

Reggie said briefly, 'We telephoned Mrs Woodford. The girl – I expect you've heard about it – it was Carol.'

Myrtle took her by the upper arm; her weeping was uncontrolled and embarrassing.

'It's our faults, Liv. All our faults. And Carol . . . oh God, Liv, Carol is innocent!'

Liv said, 'What has happened to Carol?' At least it wasn't a dream. None of it was a dream.

Reggie said, 'She's been killed. During the riots last night. Mrs Woodford said you were here and Carol had come to see you. We thought you must have heard.'

Liv drew back slightly and looked at them both. The news was at once unacceptable and inevitable. There had had to be a sacrifice. It had not been Mallie; Mallie's death had caused the events that followed, not atoned for them. It had not been Malcolm; his suicide attempt had been almost ludicrous. No. It was Carol.

Nevertheless, she said, as Jean-Claude had done, 'It isn't true – it can't be true!'

Reggie tried to gather her in again, but she held back. 'We've asked for a taxi. We're going to the hospital. Come with us, Liv—'

'No! I have to meet Carol!'

He repeated gently, 'Come with us. We should be together now.'

The realisation that she would not be meeting Carol and going home with her hit Liv like a blow in the solar plexus. As she bent with the pain of it, Reggie's arm encircled her at last and drew her to him. She felt Myrtle's hand on her shoulder. They stood together. Carol's death had brought them together.

Seventeen

Bessie survived. She did not want to survive. For a long time she thought quite seriously about trying something like Uncle Malcolm had tried that awful summer – and making it work. But there were things that stopped her. There were people who stopped her. Grannie, Boris and Jean obviously topped her list of people, but her aunts came close behind. Especially Aunt Myrt. She did not know why, but her feeling for Aunt Myrt changed with Carol's death and became painful and protective. Aunt Liv and Aunt Mon had to be protected too, but she knew instinctively that if she did an Uncle Malcolm on them they would cope with it eventually. Not Aunt Myrt. Aunt Myrt needed them all now: her husband and her children, Uncle Reggie and Aunt Liv, Grannie, Aunt Mon, Bessie herself, even Jean-Claude. Then when she thought she must go mad with her unhappiness, she discovered a way to deal with it. She invented a yellow curtain – manufactured it quite carefully in her mind – and drew it with a circular motion right around the events of that September evening. She did not think Carol would return, she did not fool herself or live in some childish make-believe world, but she simply did not look at the actuality of Carol's death, and thus it was possible to live almost normally.

She tried to share her imagined curtain with Jean-Claude and Grannie. They all stayed at the Bergerie, but not because they wanted to, just because they did not know what else to do.

Jean-Claude said, 'I like that colour, chérie. I think always of Carol being bathed in sunshine.'

But that had not been Bessie's intention at all. Her memories of Carol were strong, often monochrome. She had no wish to blur them in any way. She flung her arms around him and hugged him hard as if she could drive the terrible unhappiness out of his soul.

668

He suffered her embrace and returned it only half-heartedly. She knew that he still loved her, but that he had also distanced himself from her. She did not know why. Sometimes she considered blurting out that she knew he was her father, but something always stopped her. Something to do with Aunt Mon. Something which she had also shrouded in her memory.

When she told Grannie about the yellow curtain, she had a much better response.

'It's like bandaging a sore leg, darling. Isn't it? You know it's still there, but it helps to make it better.'

Grannie obviously used the same method. Together they limped along as best they could.

Everyone survived.

Myrtle knew she had to, not even dear Mon could look after Nicky, Martin and Lennie as she could. She agreed with Reggie that it would be a temporary arrangement, until the boys were grown-up. But she knew neither of them could make the gigantic leap together again.

She wrote to him every week. In the autumn of 1962 Lennie started kindergarten. Myrtle left him there with a strange feeling of release. He could no longer be seen as a substitute for Mallie; Mallie had never gone to school. Lennie had a life of his own now. She watched him run confidently into the playground with the other children and wondered whether she might even make friends with him.

That afternoon she wrote to Reggie. 'Lennie started school this morning. I waited by the gates and watched him. He is so like Malcolm. It never occurs to him that people might not like him. He rolled across the playground like a small red barrel in his new red blazer, grabbed someone's hand and had organised a game of Poor Mary before the other kids had said goodbye to their mothers. I never worry about him like I worry about Nicky and Martin. Sometimes, Reggie, I think Mallie took most of my love and concern with him when he died. You started to resurrect it during our time together and if it hadn't been for you I could never have come back to Malcolm and cared for the children again. I think you knew that at the time, Reggie. Didn't you? In a way you always knew you were making me better in order for me to go back home. And if it hadn't been for my illness,

Reggie, we would never have gone away together in the first place, would we? This is such a difficult letter, my darling. I shall always love you, but can we be really honest, Reggie? Will either of us be able to hurt Liv and Malcolm all over again? I don't think so. Perhaps in a year or two we might be able to spend more time together without hurting either of them. Just a day. Just to talk – nothing else – just to look at each other. Darling, when Lennie went off to school, without a backward glance, my thoughts came to you. My dearest love. I am so hopeless at writing letters. Carol understood them, and I can only pray that you will too. Now that all three boys are at school, there are some hours in every day which are my own, and in those hours my thoughts will always be with you. Not with Mallie. Not with Cass. But with you. I bless you for this because it means I want to live. Dear Reggie, I hope so much that you want to live too. Ever your, Myrtle.'

Liv knew that the letters which arrived so regularly were from Myrtle. She would pick them up from the hall floor and put them carefully on the table for Reggie to find when he got home from work. She was surprised that she felt so little resentment or jealousy at their regularity. Perhaps she no longer looked on Reggie as hers; certainly they did not sleep together and though they would spend evenings at home companionably enough, they never went out together either.

The love which had flared when she lost him was quite different now, changed by Cass' death into a concern for him and his well-being. In an odd way she would worry if Myrtle's letters stopped.

This time when she placed the envelope meticulously next to the clothes brush, she felt that it was heavier than usual. Letter-writing was anathema to Myrtle – Liv remembered only too well from schooldays what Myrtle's spelling was like – and her notes to Reggie were usually as flimsy as airmails. This one was not exactly bulky, but it had some substance.

That evening she waited until the dinner things were stacked in the dishwater and they were sitting at right angles to the television ready for a serial called 'A for Andromeda', then she said, 'Everything all right down in Cheltenham?'

Reggie glanced at her warily. 'Fine.' He cleared his throat, then shifted in his seat. Then he added, 'Lennie started kindergarten yesterday apparently.'

'Oh.'

She had known that, of course. Monica had rung from Exeter to say she was sending him a school satchel and it hardly seemed like three years since they had wheeled him along the Prom, did it? Liv had agreed, but she hadn't sent Lennie anything. The science-fiction serial was announced and the credits rolled up.

She said, 'So Myrtle is free again.'

Reggie became still.

'You read her letter?'

'No. I've never read one of Myrtle's letters to you, Reggie. Surely you know that?' She was hurt more than angry.

He breathed normally and stared at the screen. 'Sorry.'

She said, 'Look. Reggie. If you have to go to see her . . . then go. I mean it. I came back to you to try to make something else – not what we had – neither of us wanted that back again.' She sighed sharply. 'And I certainly did not expect you to fall in love with me.' She leaned forward. 'Reggie, I know you loved Myrtle. I know you still love her.'

He was almost shocked by her honesty; she had indeed changed.

'You came back to make something else? What do you mean by that, Liv? What were you trying to make?'

'I don't know. I still don't know. Carol's death had to mean something. It brought Myrt back to her children – you can't deny that.'

'No. I don't deny it. But I think she might have done that anyway. Quite soon.'

'Well . . . I don't know. Maybe. But we wouldn't have joined up again – I'm sure of that. I was too bitter, too . . . oh I don't know. It doesn't matter now, I suppose. I just want you to know that if you have to see Myrtle, you do not need to – to pretend you're playing golf.'

He remembered the lie he had lived that frightful winter when he had thought Myrtle would die.

'Liv . . . I'm sorry.'

She was surprised. Since Carol's death three years before, he had never apologised to her.

She said slowly, 'I'm sorry too. It was an earthquake. We were all injured in one way or another.'

671

'I meant . . . the lies. But, I suppose you're right about the earthquake.'

'Carol said that.'

'Ah.'

They watched the screen but saw no more than moving shapes.

After the news, Reggie stood up and switched off. He said quietly, 'I want to see Myrtle. But she doesn't need me like she did before. I'm not going to Cheltenham.'

Liv closed her eyes momentarily. When Reggie was at the door, she said huskily, 'If you have to go – at any time – will you tell me?'

He paused and looked back at her. For the first time he noticed that the baby curls were pale with grey threads. He said, 'Yes.'

Monica survived better than any of them. In 1962 she was State Registered and working in the Children's Hospital in Exeter.

Before Carol's death Monica had been determined to become a nurse, but when she had the frantic telephone call from Liv that glorious September morning her decision had become resolution. Hard work had got her through tragedy before, and she knew it would again. For perhaps ten minutes she examined the idea that now Bessie would need her. Then she discarded it. She had less right to Bessie than ever now. And if she tried to offer herself, Bessie might well end up hating her.

Monica was the ideal nurse. She was not sentimental, but her compassion was limitless – or at any rate she had not yet reached its limit. She could supply what the patient needed, from a bed-time cuddle for homesick toddlers, to tough tactics with the convalescents.

One night she nursed a five-year-old from this world into the next, and went off duty two hours late.

The night sister followed her down the ward.

'Thank you, nurse. Are you all right?'

'Yes.' Monica was surprised at the question.

'Would you like a sleeping tablet?'

'No. Thank you, sister.' Monica smiled, reassuring her senior. 'I never lie awake.' She nearly added 'when I sleep alone' but luckily did not. But it was true. She went to her tiny cubby-hole in the nurse's home, and fell into bed. If she thought of the child who was now being moved into the mortuary, it was with deep thankfulness that he had escaped all pain and distress for ever. Once, she had found herself murmuring, 'Another one for you, Carol.' But only once. In Monica's opinion, so much of religion was akin to whimsy.

Mary Woodford knew that one day her grief would catch up with her and she would be quite literally pole-axed. She postponed that day by some pretty desperate methods. Bessie's 'curtain' was one; work was another; the reasons for the postponement, were, in themselves, yet another.

Those reasons were, simply, that Bessie and Jean-Claude needed her. Bessie's need was obvious: the child could not manage alone, and though Monica would provide a home for her at the drop of a hat, any kind of transferral – physical or mental – was out of the question. Mary prayed constantly for life and strength until Bessie finished school.

Jean-Claude's need was perhaps less obvious. His life went on much as it had when Carol was alive. He spent blocks of time abroad or in Paris, and then would come home to the Bergerie and take up a domestic life with apparent relish.

But Mary knew that although he wanted to be with her and Bessie, the relish was entirely forced. He had nowhere else to go, nothing else to do. Gaby and he were divorced. He was free . . . and lonely. He had no official capacity at the Bergerie. He was not a grieving widower, nor a loyal son-in-law. He was, as he had always been, just a friend.

Mary could think of no solution. Bessie's eventual career – or marriage – would make things worse. She wondered what the future could hold for him, and knew that he too, being an intelligent man, would wonder also. She shivered. There would come a time when she could do no more for Jean-Claude. Carol had always thought he would be the one to be killed. It had happened the other way round. And Carol would have managed far better than he could.

Boris Denning spent two very boring years learning how to be a signalman and was determined never to lose his freedom again. In the autumn of 1961 he managed to visit Bessie in France, and they talked as naturally and as easily as they always had done.

'I'd shoot my foot – like they used to in the Great War,' he said to Bessie. 'Or be a Bevin Boy. Anything.'

He'd met her out of school as a surprise. She was nearly sixteen then, leggy and very beautiful. He was more like his father than ever. They made a striking pair, and Bessie's friends hung back, whispering and giggling. She put her nose in the air and ignored them.

'It would be different if there was a war, or another emergency like Suez,' she said wisely. 'At least it wouldn't be a waste of time, then.'

'I was worried about you,' he explained. 'Oh God, Bessie. When all that happened just as I'd gone in—'

'You wouldn't have got compassionate leave however long you'd been in,' she said matter-of-factly. 'We're not related, you see. Jean-Claude told me that.'

'I would've,' he maintained stubbornly.

They swung into the track and walked between the massed chrysanthemums; the smell was pungent and very autumnal.

He said, 'How are you? D'you realise I haven't seen you for a whole year, and that was only a four-day leave?'

'Of course I realise it, idiot.' She glanced sideways, unsmiling. 'Have you still got my bracelet? Did you keep it with you all the time?'

'Yes. And yes.' He produced it from a pocket and made to return it to her. She pushed it away.

'It's our engagement thing!' She sounded annoyed. 'If I take it back it means we're not going to get married!'

He laughed uncomfortably. He was twenty and she was still only fifteen. But he replaced the bracelet in his pocket and was thankful. He had wondered whether Carol's death might have changed their relationship. However unsuitable it might be, he couldn't have borne that.

He talked to Jean-Claude about his career. They had always got on well even when Bessie wasn't around: they had a lot of interests in common.

Jean-Claude approved his plans to go back to art college and specialise in camera work.

'So much design work will be redundant in a very few years, my friend.' Jean-Claude shook his head regretfully. 'But the accuracy and immediacy of the photograph . . . especially the television film. How would you feel about that?'

Boris grinned. 'Bessie and I used to talk about travelling the world filming.'

Jean-Claude did not return the smile. 'Bessie has her education to finish, Boris. You must understand that.'

'Of course . . .' Boris found himself almost stammering or calling Jean 'sir' or something equally silly.

'I might be able to get you something. A trainee cameraman with a film crew. Yes, it would certainly mean travelling.'

Boris stammered in earnest; he was overwhelmed. 'Could you? Really? It would be marvellous.'

'It would mean being away. For long periods.'

'I . . . understand.' Boris looked at the older man frankly. 'You want me out of the way. While Bessie grows up.'

Jean-Claude lifted his shoulders. 'I am not as definite as that, Boris. But the crew I have in mind produce films of exotic locations. Pearl-diving. Primitive tribal living. It would mean being away for a year. Perhaps more.'

'No holidays at the Bergerie for a while.'

'Probably not.'

'You know that I will come back? You know that I love Bessie?'

'That is understood.' Jean-Claude inclined his head as if bowing to the inevitable.

'She will be . . . thrilled.'

'Then try to angle your course towards filming. And I will see what I can do.'

'That's . . . wonderful. I can't thank you enough.'

In 1962, he went to say goodbye to his sister.

Lennie had been at kindergarten for two weeks and already Myrtle was taking a few patients in the old waiting room and talking of making it into a second treatment room. It was as if her letter to Reggie had released her in some way and though Boris knew nothing of that, he could see the re-emergence of his down-to-earth commonsensical sister. This time with something added: an independence; a freedom from all kinds of fetters.

It was good to see her enthusiasm when he told her about his job. He had secured a trainee position with one of the new commercial television companies and was being sent to Australia to do some underwater filming around the Barrier Reef. There had been several interviews with film companies, overtly arranged by Jean-Claude. Boris was not absolutely certain how much influence Jean had exerted in this case; as the project entailed at least fifteen months' filming at the other end of the world, he assumed – wryly – that Jean had pulled quite a few strings.

He said diplomatically, 'I think it was something to do with Jean-Claude. There were about forty applications from all the art colleges in the country – they interviewed fifteen and I didn't have the qualifications of some of them!'

'Rubbish!' Myrtle told him stoutly. 'You've always been able to do anything with a camera. Besides, how would a Frenchman know anyone in British television?'

'He's an international journalist, Myrt! He told me he would pull a few strings.'

Myrtle smiled. 'Bessie's been nagging him then. I sometimes think the only reason she took to Jean was because she saw him as being a help to you!'

He said quietly, 'She thinks he is her father, Sis. That's the real reason she is so devoted.'

'My God! You're joking, Borrie!'

'No. She told me before Carol was killed. It has been her one consolation.'

Myrtle was appalled. She stared at her brother who was so like his father. Yet so completely different.

'You'll have to tell her the truth, Borrie. You're the only one who can. You do *know* the truth, do you?'

'That she is Monica's child. Yes. I think she knows it too. Something happened in New York, when she went there . . . she never talks about it, but I think in her heart of hearts she must know.'

'Yes, but do you know who her father really is? Obviously you don't. No-one does except we girls, I suppose. It's Giles Cook. Monica's adoptive brother.'

It was Boris' turn to be appalled.

'That . . . layabout? Bessie's father? Oh no – Myrt, are you certain?'

'Monica told us herself that summer. It's true.'

Boris was silent, assimilating this unwelcome news. Finally he said, 'Well, I couldn't have told her about Jean-Claude before. I certainly can't now. The only way to convince her that he's not her father is to tell her the name of her real father. And I'm not telling her that it's Giles Cook!'

Myrtle saw the point of that.

She said, 'Well. I suppose it doesn't matter. Not really.' She glanced at the clock. 'It's time to meet Lennie, Boris. Are you coming?'

Bessie would be seventeen that Christmas and she wanted to leave the convent and join the staff of *La Planète*.

She had expected resistance from Jean-Claude, but not the complete barrier put up by her grandmother.

'It's the most ridiculous idea I've heard of!' Mary looked at Jean-Claude. 'Tell her, Jean. She has always wanted to use her drawing skills – there is no place for that in journalism!'

'Grannie – I wanted to draw flowers when I was a little girl! Now I want a career! Cass worked with books and Jean-Claude works on newspapers. Surely it is obvious—'

Jean-Claude interrupted calmly. 'Listen, chérie. The day of the cub reporter is gone. Now you need to go to journalists' college and learn all there is to learn about newspapers. And in order to get there, you will have to stay at school for at least another two years.'

Mary said, 'But in any case, Jean—'

'That is necessary whatever Bessie eventually decides to do, Mary.' Jean looked at the older woman meaningfully. 'If she should then decide to turn to botanical research—'

'I only wanted to do that because I thought Boris and I could work together,' Bessie declared hotly. 'Now I know that is impossible, surely it is natural I should wish to work with Jean?'

Mary said carefully, 'Perhaps it is natural in our circumstances, darling. We are very close. Perhaps too close. You know that you are adopted, so that legally you and I belong to each other. But—'

Bessie began to feel desperate. 'Then if it's natural, that's all right. Isn't it?'

'What I meant was, *we* understand how you feel. We think it is natural. Outsiders will not agree.' Mary folded her hands. 'I'm sorry, Bessie darling. But I think it would be much better if you

677

went into something else. And botanical research sounds just your thing.'

'Grannie – stop it!' Suddenly Bessie could bear it no more. She stood up. 'I know Cass was my real mother! I understand that! And I know Jean is my real father! I am not a child any more – I can understand how it happened! I want to follow in their footsteps, Grannie. I want to work with my father. Why can't we bring it into the open – I know when I was a child you wanted to shield me . . . but—'

Jean-Claude too stood up. His face was chalk-white and his voice, when he spoke, was hoarse.

'Bessie! Stop! You do not know what you say.' He took a deep breath. 'Let us be clear about one thing, child. I am not your father.' He made for the door. 'I am not Carol's husband. I am nothing. Nothing to either of you.' He opened the door and turned to look at Mary. 'I think you should tell her. And then I think you should finish her education in England among her friends.'

Mary said, 'Jean – please! Do not go! I think of you as Carol's husband and my son – you must know that—'

But the door closed quietly after him.

Bessie made to follow him and then stopped and looked around at Mary. She was shaking, near tears.

'What did he mean? Grannie, what is happening?'

And so . . . wearily . . . Mary began to tell Monica's story.

In spite of Mary's reassurances, Jean-Claude moved out the next day. Only a week later he applied for, and got, a post as correspondent in Algiers. The country had at last gained its independence, and Jean-Claude, as de Gaulle's unofficial envoy, had been responsible for many of the negotiations. He had seen his work there as a tribute to Carol, but he knew that this new post – to report on the country's progress – was nothing to do with her. This was self-inflicted banishment.

Mary and Bessie went home. It was as if all the things that had happened came home to roost at last and they could no longer face the Bergerie. They spent two weeks packing up all the things they wanted to keep and arranging for them to be put into store. Bessie cast a thought to the mountain plateau where the symbolic paint can lay buried, but it was meaningless now. She felt empty and utterly helpless; all her schoolgirl energy and enthusiasm had gone. She was reading Shelley's poetry and the life of Byron, and she wondered whether she might be going into a decline.

Mary had plans for buying back the old house in Northfield and sending Bessie to the grammar school at Kings Norton, but the house was not for sale and the autumn term was well advanced: Bessie would need to do a lot of reading at home to qualify for the university entrance course. They stayed with the Dennings and though Bessie had Boris' old room, she could not settle to any books. She missed the view of the mountain terribly, but had no desire at all to go back there. She was in a curious no-man's-land where nothing much mattered and though she wasn't ill she certainly wasn't well, either. She took to walking in the park where she and Boris had met so often and so coincidentally when she had been a small girl.

Mary rang Monica and told her that Bessie knew everything.

'She's taking it badly,' Mary reported. 'Will you come up and talk to her?'

On the other end of the phone, Monica studied her red nurse's hands carefully. Life was so damned ironic; at one time she would have leapt at such a chance, but now . . . what could she offer a girl of seventeen? Did she really want to give up her nursing and make a home for her?

She said, 'Has she asked to see me?'

'No. It's the lack of curiosity that has me bothered, Mon. It's not natural.'

Monica said astutely, 'She's known inside her head for some time. She's angry with herself.'

'Perhaps that's it. It's more than that though. She's losing Carol all over again.' Mary began to weep. 'Sorry, Mon. It's . . . awful. We'd got something together between us in France . . . we didn't dream – Jean and I – that she was seeing him as a father. A father figure perhaps. But not a real father. She's lost them both, Mon. Something has to fill the – the vacuum.'

'Yes, but if I force myself on her . . . listen – will you ask her outright if she would like to talk to me? She can ask me anything she likes. I'll come then.'

Mary swallowed her tears. 'Yes. All right, Mon. Thank you.' She knew what Bessie would say. And she was right. Monica was the last person Bessie wanted to see.

* * *

It was the worst winter for years. The snow began before Christmas and by the middle of January was piled everywhere in drifted, abstract shapes that bore little relationship to the objects they covered.

Bessie had still not started school, still not started a serious course of work. She hated everything now: hated the snow, hated living at Dr Denning's big house on the Bristol Road, hated the old familiar Brummy accents all around her, more especially hated herself. She knew she was making Grannie ill and Mrs Denning even more anxious than usual. Mrs Baker had called yesterday and Bessie had heard her say that it was a case of sparing the rod and spoiling the child. When Bessie went into the lounge she pretended she had been talking about her eldest daughter's little boy, but Bessie knew that was not true. She wondered whether she really did need a good beating; impossible to imagine Jean administering punishment, but supposing he appeared and suddenly smacked her across her face as if she were hysterical. Would it snap her out of this dreadfulness? If so, she would willingly put up with it. But nor from anyone else. Not even Boris. Especially not Boris.

She went for her usual afternoon walk in the park. No-one had used the swings that day and the seats were three feet thick with snow, the chains solid white ropes. She swept one of the seats with her forearm and shook the chains vigorously until they emerged from their sheath, then sat down and began to swing idly. Her breath vaporised before her; already her fingers and toes were numb and her nose hurt. She'd have to go home again and make another pretence at doing some work.

Then a voice said, 'What's a pretty girl like you doing out of school on a day like this?' And she looked up to see a man just beyond the rank of swings, blowing on his gloved hands, red with cold, short and rather fat and not attractive, but grinning at her cheekily as if they were old friends. She had never seen him before.

She said, 'Killing time. Feeling fed up.' At least with this stranger she could be honest.

'That won't do.' His grin became wider. He moved closer, beating his arms around his barrel chest now. 'You're playing truant, en't you? Nice girl like you too. What's the world coming to?'

680

She knew she should brush him off now; pleasantries had been exchanged and that was that. But in spite of his unprepossessing appearance she felt strangely at ease with him. She said, 'Oh, it's not really like that. I haven't started school yet.'

He laughed. 'Not started school? Where's your trike then? Where's your dolly's pram?'

And she laughed too. 'Oh, I wish I had them still!'

'Do you?' He leaned against the supporting posts and looked at her, still twinkling. 'D'you know, that's something I never wish for. Going back. Oh I've had some good times – don't get me wrong – I've had some great times! But there's better ones yet, I reckon.'

It was her own philosophy; or it had been until last September. She nodded sadly.

He said, 'Come on now, girl. Give us a smile. That's better! I can't abide long faces – life's made for fun, I reckon.'

She smiled again, nodded again.

He said, 'Listen. Let's go to the pictures. What d'you say? I've just come off early shift – give me ten minutes to get changed and I'll treat you to fish and chips and Cliff Richard down at Longbridge.'

'Cliff Richard?'

'His latest. "The Young Ones". Come on, what d'you say? I'm nearly old enough to be your dad, so there'll be no hanky panky. And I reckon it's about time I was seen around with a really pretty girl again!'

She had to laugh; he was so frank and open.

She said, 'I don't even know who you are. My grandmother would have a fit if she thought I was going to the pictures with a stranger!'

He sketched a ridiculous bow.

'Giles Cook at your service, madam. But you can call me Gilly.'

She stared at him speechlessly for what seemed a long time. He kept laughing and flailing his arms and repeating, 'Come on now, say yes. No strings attached.'

It was so strange. She had considered looking him up, but not seriously and not for long. She didn't want a new father; she had a new mother and that was too much. She wanted Jean-Claude to be her father.

But here he was. Aunt Mon's adopted brother. Her natural father.

She said, 'All right then. If you're sure it will be okay. I love Cliff Richard and it's too cold to stay out for long.'

'Never a truer word spoked!' He crooked his arm and she took it. She didn't know why she was doing this, why she wasn't telling him that she was his daughter. It was as if she were trying to punish someone. Monica. She was trying to punish Monica for having her in the first place.

Amazingly, she enjoyed herself. Afterwards when she had left him at the edge of the snow field which was really the school playground, she tried to analyse why that had been. Grannie had described Giles Cook as an 'ordinary man' which had sounded damning to Bessie's young ears. But it was his very ordinariness that made him such easy company.

She told him her name was Lizzie Durrant; as far as he knew they were complete strangers. So there was none of the tangled string which made life with Grannie and everyone so tricky. She didn't have to think about what she said: quite stupid remarks, like 'the snow makes lots of things private', went down with him like Einstein's theory. He came back with, 'In the summer I miss my hot-water bottle', and she knew just what he meant. Especially now when going to bed was a kind of escape from everything.

Walking back up the long hill to Turves Green, they had talked about the film. He must be about the same age as Jean-Claude, yet he had enjoyed seeing Cliff and Hank and Una in their improbable story, and they had discussed it from the same standpoint. Perhaps it wasn't complimentary to him to think he was so immature, but it certainly made him easy company.

They had reached the colony of bungalows past Kalamazoo, when the rooks, disturbed from their roosting by the laughter, squawked a protest. Giles immediately parodied the title song of the film: 'The young ones, always want the breadcrumbs . . .' It had been ridiculous, not a bit funny, but they had laughed uproariously.

'Let's do this again,' he'd said impulsively. And she smiled secretly and said, 'Let's.'

Grannie was waiting anxiously for her.

'Darling, where on earth have you been? I went round to the park – it's been three hours – so dark tonight—'

'I met someone and we went to the pictures.' Bessie felt better still. Somehow, all powerful. She had been a puppet for too long. 'Don't be cross, Grannie. It was Cliff Richard and it was great.'

Mary looked at the sparkling eyes and rosy cheeks and decided against asking questions. It was wonderful to see Bessie looking her old self again. She would find out more about the new friend in due course.

But Bessie was strangely evasive. She disclosed that the friend was male and that he lived in Northfield, but more than that she kept to herself. Mary respected that. Outside the convent, Bessie's friendship had been limited almost exclusively to Boris. And because she had always been happy, everyone had thought this was perfectly all right; but perhaps it had not been. Girls of seventeen usually had a host of boyfriends. Perhaps Bessie was merely reverting to normality.

Mary said tentatively, 'Listen, darling. I hope I don't sound over-protective at this late date, but you will be careful, won't you?'

For some reason Bessie flushed bright red. 'Sometimes, Grannie, adults can be . . . disgusting!' she said unexpectedly.

Mary persevered. 'I am thinking of your safety, Bessie. Not the proprieties – though they are set basically for safety reasons.'

'Grannie. Take it from me. I am as safe as houses with this particular friend.'

Mary spread her hands. 'All right. But if you go to the pictures again, I would like to know about it beforehand. And I would very much like to meet this young man.'

'I'm dying for you to meet him, actually. And Aunt Mon, too.'

'Really? Darling, Aunt Mon would love to come and see you – and any of your friends. You know that. She is in a very invidious position where you are concerned—'

'*She* is in an invidious position! That's rich!'

Mary frowned slightly. That was not the sort of thing Bessie said. She hoped the new friend was not going to be a bad influence.

They went to the pictures again. Then they met in a greasy little cafe run by his mother. It came as a shock to Bessie to realise that Mrs Cook was her real grandmother. She began to feel a tiny sympathy towards Aunt Mon which she suppressed quickly, reminding herself that somehow everything was Aunt Mon's fault and all this way by way of sweet revenge.

Revenge or not, Giles Cook's company was consoling. She found that with 'project Giles' in mind, she could actually begin to study properly. She took to spending mornings in the little library at the top of Turves Green hill. It got her away from the irritation of the Dennings and the constant reminder of unhappiness which showed in Grannie's anxious expression. When Giles was on nights at the factory, he would sleep all morning and often see her in the afternoons. He would sit opposite her in the small reading room and make faces at her until she succumbed to stupid, schoolgirl giggles and was glared at by the librarian. Then they would go outside and throw snowballs at each other all the way down the hill. One day he said out of the blue, 'This is crazy. I haven't had a friend like you since . . . oh, a long time ago.' And she responded automatically, 'Nor me.' And then realised she meant it. She wasn't thinking of Boris either. She was thinking of Jean. Maybe she had fooled herself for a long time now where Jean was concerned; maybe that's what he had been, a good friend.

But she didn't want to soften at this stage, and she said quickly, 'Would you like to come and have tea with us one day, Gillie? My aunt is coming for a weekend soon. I'd like you to meet her.'

He flushed with pleasure. 'Say when, girl, and I'll be there,' he accepted promptly.

She never achieved the vindictive pleasure she had been working for.

She planned it all carefully: Monica arrived just before lunchtime from Exeter, she had left at the crack of dawn and had to change trains at Bristol and was exhausted. Mary had planned a quiet afternoon in front of the fire. Just the three of them – Mrs Denning had been prevailed upon to go visiting . At three o'clock, when she could see Monica's eyelids begin to droop, Bessie sprang her surprise.

'I've invited my new friend to tea,' she announced brightly. 'I want him to meet you, Aunt Mon, and as Mrs Denning has gone out, it seemed the ideal opportunity.'

'Why on earth didn't you warn me?' Mary was not so much

flummoxed as disappointed. She excelled herself at afternoon teas. 'I would have made some potato scones or something nice.'

'Oh, he's not coming for the food and drink. Just to meet you.' Bessie smiled as the knocker sounded. 'I'll go. Just relax. You'll feel as if you've known him all your lives. I promise you.'

It was Monica she wanted to hurt. Not Grannie. Not Giles. But it was Monica who threw back her head and burst out laughing when she registered who the 'new friend' was, and it was Grannie and Giles who looked at her as if she'd stuck a knife into the pair of them.

Monica saved the day by being so frank it made Bessie feel small.

'Well. You certainly exploded a bombshell here, Bessie,' she said as if it were a Christmas cracker. 'Let me have your coat, Gillie. Is it snowing again?' She went behind him and pressed his arms as she slid the coat sleeves down over his jacket. 'Did you know about it?'

It was obvious from his face he hadn't known a thing.

'You said your name was Lizzie,' he said accusingly to Bessie.

She was defiant, her plan in ruins. 'It's Elizabeth. And you—' she threw Monica a challenging look. 'You never liked Bessie. You wanted to call me Lizzie once.'

'So I did.' Monica put Giles' coat over the back of a chair and came forward, still smiling. 'I've grown up a lot since then.' She indicated a chair. 'Sit down, Gillie. Don't look like that. After all, what's in a name? I'm glad you and Bessie have made friends.'

But Giles had had enough of being conned. He looked from Monica's determinedly smiling face to Mary's ashen one.

'We haven't. I don't make friends with people who lie to me.' He picked up his coat. 'I don't know what's going on here, our Mon, you always were a devious one. Looks like she's the same too.' He jerked his head at Bessie with something like contempt. 'I'll be on my way. And I don't want to hear anything more about this. Is that understood?'

Even Monica was silent at that. Mary began to apologise. Actually to apologise.

Bessie cut across her stammering words. 'And we don't want to hear any more of *you*, either! I haven't lied - I don't *know* what my proper name is, do I? I told you Durrant because that's the name of the man I thought was my father until six months ago! I just wish he was . . . oh God, I just wish he was!'

And she left the lounge precipitately and went to her room which was bitterly cold in spite of the central heating. And would never be home. She heard Giles leave shortly afterwards and got off her bed to watch him trudge through the snow to the front gate. She hadn't wanted to hurt Giles Cook, her new friend. But oh, she had wanted to hurt Giles Cook, her natural father.

It was an hour later when Monica knocked on her door and said briskly, 'I think you'd better come down. I don't seem to be able to console your grandmother.'

Bessie called, 'She's not my grandmother. My grandmother runs a horrid little snack bar along the Bristol Road!'

And Monica said, 'It's not that bad, actually. Have you tried her sausage and chips?' And then, even more aggravatingly, she did not wait for an answer, but went back downstairs.

Bessie went down too because in another hour Mrs Denning would be back and life would be even more intolerable. And she wanted tea and toast and the warm fire.

Mary and Monica were talking about the weather. Monica was telling a story about them airlifting a pregnant mother from Exmoor to the maternity unit at Exeter. And Mary said yes it was really incredible, though of course there had been fairs held on the frozen Thames in Elizabethan times, so . . .

Bessie interrupted rudely, 'Well? What are you going to do about me? A reform school? Pity I haven't got an aunt in the country somewhere, isn't it?'

Mary looked down at her lap. And Monica said thoughtfully, 'Actually, you have got an aunt in the country. That's a good idea, Bessie.'

'I'm not going to Aunt Myrt's. Now without Boris. Besides I want to go to your old school. Cass' old school.' Bessie was suddenly white-faced and determined. 'I know I've made a bloomer, but you can't take that away from me!'

'I was referring to Aunt Liv, actually. Plenty of countryside around there. Good train service to Kings Norton. Lots of peace and quiet for studying. And . . . I rather think Aunt Liv needs you.'

'Needs me? You mean Grannie.'

'Grannie too. But I meant you.'

'Why?' Bessie's self-esteem was so low she could not imagine anyone needing her.

Monica paused, then said bluntly, 'Because if she hadn't gone over to find Myrtle and Reggie in Paris, Cass would probably be alive now.'

Bessie was wide-eyed. 'That's a terrible thing to say! You might as well blame Aunt Myrt for going off to Paris in the first place! And Cass never blamed *her* for anything! She said that if Myrtle hadn't gone with Reggie, she would have died!'

Monica said calmly, 'I'm just telling you how Liv feels. Not how I feel.' She looked at Bessie. 'I've been to see Aunt Myrt, Bessie. And I've talked to Grannie about it all. You're more than welcome there. And I don't think you want to stay here much longer, do you?'

Bessie swallowed. At the moment she did not want to stay here another minute.

'No,' she said.

Monica drew out her cigarette case. 'Then that's settled.' She smiled at Mary reassuringly and turned again to Bessie. 'Look. I know you're very miserable at the moment. Everything has gone wrong – or so you feel. You're raw and it's awful. There's a cure. And it's work. Quite simply, work. Get yourself settled at Liv's – Reggie will love it and he'll be Giles and Jean rolled into one. You'll fill a gap for Liv, believe me. And then start school, work hard at it. This time next year, you'll wonder what this was all about.'

Bessie said soberly, 'No, I won't.' She looked at Mary, still big-eyed and white-faced. 'I don't want to forget. This is . . . important.'

And suddenly she began to cry and cast herself on the woman she had always called Grannie. Not for the first time, they comforted each other.

Mary and Bessie settled in to the Barnt Green house very easily. They gave Liv a purpose in life; she enjoyed cooking – she enjoyed housekeeping – but the days of being houseproud were over, she needed a reason for making a home now. Reggie was his usual gentle self, but she knew that if she put fish and chips in front of him every day he would not notice. Half of him was still with Myrtle.

Reggie too was delighted to have them in the house. His taste for family life was still there, and they filled a yawning gap for him. He timed his homecomings for when Bessie got off the train each afternoon, and he ran her home and heard how her day had gone.

An unexpected bonus was the way they could talk about the past; the past before Mallie's and Carol's deaths. Reggie spoke of his childhood with Malcolm: football and paper chases and camps in Scotland.

'We ought to take a holiday in Scotland, Liv,' he suggested. 'It's completely unspoilt, you'd love it.'

She looked at him in surprise, but all she said was, 'Yes. Yes, I'm sure I should.' It was the first time she realised that he was missing Malcolm as well as Myrtle; perhaps more than Myrtle.

For her part she spoke of the Haunted House and Monica's complicated hair-do's and their days at school.

'You're in time for the tennis, Bessie. The courts are so lovely. There's a little grove of lime trees just beyond them where we used to sit and talk, and Cass would read us the Shakespeare sonnets, and Myrt would tell jokes, and Mon and I . . .' her voice died and Bessie said, 'Go on. Please, Aunt Liv.'

'Oh, nothing really. Mon and I used to talk about boys. That's all.' She sighed. 'Mon must have been so unhappy. Finding out she was adopted and had no family that she knew about. She'd never been one of the Cooks.'

There was a silence. Then Mary picked up her knitting.

'Mon loved Giles. Let's get that straight. She loved him as a brother, then she loved him as a man. And while she made no demands on him, she was wonderfully happy.'

Reggie said, 'I've never thought about it before. It must have been an impossible situation. If only Giles had had the gumption to leave Northfield and take her with him. Make a home somewhere else.'

'She knew he couldn't – wouldn't – do that.' Mary dropped a stitch and spent a long time picking it up. Her gaze flicked to Bessie and back to her knitting. 'D'you know, on V.E. day she was on her way to London to find an American who would marry her and be a father for you, Bessie. Luckily she called in at the Haunted House to say goodbye to Cass, who persuaded her that we could help.'

Reggie said strongly, 'Thank God. Talk about a happy ending
. . .' he cleared his throat. 'She gave you what she hadn't had herself. An enormous family!' He tried to lighten his voice. '*We've*
shared you, for a start, Bessie Woodford!'

Everyone laughed obediently. Liv said, 'Cass was saying something like that. The afternoon before she . . . before it . . .
happened.'

Bessie, who had been staring at Mary's knitting, looked at Liv,
then got up and went to sit on the arm of her chair.

'If she'd died any other way—' she too cleared her throat – 'she
wouldn't have had that time with you, Aunt Liv. I'm so glad she had
that. It sort of connects us all together again, doesn't it?'

Liv bowed her head. Almost as if receiving absolution.

Much later, when she was sitting up in bed reading, there was a tap at
the door.

She smiled, certain it was Bessie.

'Come in,' she said, 'I'm not asleep.'

The door opened tentatively and Reggie was there. She put down
her book and sat away from the pillows.

He said, 'Liv. Until today – tonight – I didn't realise how you
felt. About Carol.'

She was bewildered. 'Carol? You must have known how close we
were. The four of us.'

'Yes. Of course. But the way Bessie spoke to you . . . surely you
do not feel responsible for what happened?'

Liv swallowed. 'I . . . of course. You know I was responsible,
Reggie. You all knew. If I hadn't come over to Paris to look for you,
Carol would have been safe at the Bergerie when those students
marched that night.' Her throat muscles worked convulsively.

Reggie closed the door and came further into the room.

'Come off it, Liv. Ask yourself why you were there. You can trace
responsibility any way you like.'

She gripped the sheet and closed her eyes. 'Doesn't it all come
back to that day before Mallie? When I went to see Malcolm and
threw you and Myrt together?'

He said strongly, 'No. You and I . . . we weren't a proper couple,
Liv. If that hadn't happened, something else would have triggered
off the train of events.'

He sat on the edge of the bed.

'Listen. Liv. It's almost four years since . . . all that. I'm not suggesting the wounds are healed, my dear, but even if we're limping along – surely we're limping in unison?'

She heard the smile in his voice and opened her eyes. She thought how strange it was to fall in love with one's own husband; and to accept that she would always come second for him.

She whispered, 'Don't feel . . . sorry for me, Reggie.'

'Why not? I hope you're sorry for me, Liv.'

She sobbed suddenly. She was sorry for him; it was true.

He held her and stroked her hair.

He said, 'May I come back here, Liv? Are you as lonely as I am?'

She did not stop weeping for a long time. She had not imagined that making love could be an act of intense compassion.

Much later still she whispered to him, 'Oh Reggie. Bessie was right. I am so glad I had that time with Carol before she died. So glad. So . . . thankful.'

Eighteen

That summer, Mary and Bessie went back to the Bergerie for a holiday. In response to a carefully worded letter from Mary, Jean-Claude suggested that he joined them for a week at the end of August.

Bessie thought she was all right. She had survived a year back home with the frightful knowledge of her true parentage gradually settling into some kind of sense. The move to Barnt Green had been a good one: in Reggie she had found at last a father figure worthy of the name, and she knew that Liv was comforted by the presence of Mary and herself. She respected Monica for the way she had dealt with her confrontation with Giles Cook, and when Liv and Reggie spoke of her, she began to feel a certain pride that this woman was her mother. And of course Myrtle was always there when she was needed; a Myrtle who was different, stronger and more independent, but still full and overflowing with love. And a link with Boris, who was, after all, Bessie's assured destiny. Yes, she had grown up, she was certain of that. She and Grannie, they were all right now.

She was a loner at school, but she was not lonely. The sixth form was small and friendships had already been made when she arrived in the spring term. But she was respected for her difference; her wide knowledge of French literature and history set her apart from the others. In some ways she was younger than her peers; in others much older. She knew nothing of sex, and many of her contemporaries had gone 'almost the whole way' with their boyfriends. On the other hand she was used to the company of males and able to hold a conversation with them without embarrassment or giggling.

She thought she probably felt as Monica felt: not so much independent as sufficient within herself. Yes, she was fairly

691

certain she had negotiated her particular valley of shadow.

And then Mary announced that Jean was coming home for a week.

'It will be like old times,' she said brightly, knowing that old times had gone for ever. 'We'll make lots of onion soup and you can bake that favourite cake of his.'

'Marble cake,' Bessie said, swallowing.

'That's it. Marble cake. D'you remember how you used to play that silly game to see if you could eat one colour at a time?'

'That was ages ago, Grannie. When I thought he was my . . . that was ages ago.'

Mary looked out of the window at the Victoire soaring over the little house. 'Darling,' she said slowly. 'The three of us . . . we're a family. We're not united by blood ties, but we're still a family.'

Bessie nodded and swallowed again. 'We're united by Cass, Grannie. Aren't we?'

'Yes darling.' Mary's eyes were full of tears. It was the perfect answer. They would always be a family because of Cass.

But though Bessie had provided the answer, though it seemed obvious to her, it did not bring the pleasure it should. She had adored Cass; now, unexpectedly and shockingly, she felt that Cass might come between them in some way. It was ridiculous and she pushed the thought away quickly.

But there was no ease any more with Jean. He arrived a day before they expected him, driving up the track in a new Citroen that looked like a police car. Bessie knew he was inside it; she saw it turn off the village road and bump between the clumps of chrysanthemums, and she sensed that it contained Jean. She did not move from the hammock where she and Mary were sitting shelling the second crop of peas.

Mary said, 'What can the gendarmerie want with us, I wonder? It cannot be news from England. They would phone us direct now.'

'It's the Renault,' Bessie confessed quickly, as if she could change the occupant of the car somehow. 'Pierre's cousin who is a policeman saw me driving it through the village yesterday, and he knows I am not yet eighteen.'

'Bessie! How could you? Well, you'll have to eat humble pie and hope for the best.' Mary put down her colander and stood up as the car swirled to a halt outside the door. 'My God.' She looked wildly at Bessie. 'My God, it's Jean!'

It was only then that Bessie realised how much Mary had missed the man who had been almost a son-in-law to her. The older woman flew to the car and pulled Jean-Claude from it, laughing and crying at the same time. Belatedly, after she had hugged him soundly and scolded him for not telephoning ahead, and telling him he had lost weight, she realised that Bessie had risen from the hammock but not moved one step forward.

'Bessie – it's Jean – look how brown he is!'

He was very brown, and had somehow acquired an Arabic look. His black eyes were perpetually narrowed against the sun and his hands seemed longer and thinner than ever.

They stared, and he protested quickly. 'Please. I am not used to so much attention.' He glanced at Bessie then swiftly back to Mary. 'It is good to be back. Thank you for asking me.'

Mary was confused. 'I didn't mention it to Bessie. I wasn't sure you'd come and I wanted it to be a surprise.'

'Ah. I wondered at the state of . . . shock.'

He smiled and his long intelligent face was transformed. Bessie held herself against crying out.

He said, 'Mary tells me it has been hard, chérie. But you have come to terms with . . . everything.'

She managed to nod. She had thought she had. Now she knew she had not.

He held out his hand. 'Come. Do not hold it against me. I am here for one week. Let it be a good one.'

At last she came forward and took his hand. It was warm and dry and blessedly familiar. She felt tears behind her eyes and did not know why.

Her happiness that week was poignant and painful and almost too much to bear. He was determined to behave as if nothing had happened, and up to a point, he succeeded. But the spontaneity had gone from their relationship. She was a woman now and she knew he was not her father; she could no longer throw her arms around his neck and sit by him on the old leather sofa and jabber to him insouciantly. Yet he was so precious to her, so dear, that she wondered how she would exist when he went back to Algiers. He talked to her about his work as he had always done, but when the conversation became more personal he spoke indulgently as if she were still a child.

'What would you like to do, chérie? Shall we drive to one of the parfumeries? Or go down to Antibes for a day? Whatever you wish.'

'I'd like to trek up the Victoire,' she said.

Mary pulled a face. 'I can't spend a whole day walking, like you two. Count me out.'

Jean hesitated then gave his wry upside-down smile.

'Very well, Bessie. A trek it shall be. How far?'

'As far as we can. We'll start at six and be back before dark.'

His smile became a laugh. 'I asked for it, I suppose. I am an old man now, Bessie. How can you ask this of me?'

'You are not old. You will never be old in that sense. You are . . .' she searched for a word to describe him. 'You are universal.'

'Mon Dieu! I thought you were going to call me ageless! I must be thankful for small mercies I suppose.' He lifted his shoulders. 'Only at sixteen could the word "universal" be made to apply to age!'

'I am nearly eighteen, Jean,' she reminded him, but without undue emphasis.

He had genuinely forgotten. 'You were sixteen when we parted so unhappily, chérie. To me you have not changed at all.'

She too gave a Gallic Shrug. 'I also am universal,' she told him. 'Age has very little relevance sometimes. It is simply a . . . convention.'

His smile died as he looked into her serious dark eyes.

They went, lightly loaded with small haversacks and sticks.

It was a splendid morning; September was a few days away and the sun held a different warmth: gentle and golden. Jean had switched on the wireless before they left and pulled a face because the main item of news concerned the Beatles and their latest hit record.

Bessie said, 'It's so much better than war and disasters, Jean. You have dealt too much in them. You should listen to the Beatles.'

'Yes, ma vieille,' he said pseudo-solemnly.

They walked until eleven, and then stopped for their sandwiches. They had passed the tiny shepherd's hut some time before, and were well on the way to the slide of scree and the mini plateau.

Jean fetched water from the stream that was fed by last winter's snows. He gave the beaker to Bessie and watched her drink.

'Do I gather this is a sort of pilgrimage for you, chérie?' he asked. He drank himself, and waited for a reply. She nodded.

'Ah. I have to guess, is that it?' He was using his indulgent voice again. 'Now. Let me see. Boris.' She nodded again. 'The summer we all camped up here.'

She said, 'The Metier girls first of all. We found this special place. Then I brought Boris. I'll show you why, when we get there.'

'Ah. A secret. A mystery.' He drained the water and put the beaker away. 'Come then. En avant.'

She went ahead. She did not know why, but sometimes the feeling she had for him was liberally mixed with anger.

They reached the plateau at midday and rested, heads against the haversacks, while the sun spent its noon heat and settled into a lazy afternoon. Bessie sat up at last, opened her sack and removed a trowel. Jean watched her, surprised and amused, as she began to dig. She could not remember the exact place and had to make several attempts before the trowel clinked on metal. At last, after a tussle with the springy turf, she resurrected the paint can.

He said quietly, 'I know about it, Bessie.'

'I thought you might,' she panted. 'Well, this is it. I want you to have it.'

He stared at the battered tin and his eyes were no longer smiling.

'No. It is for you girls. Not me.'

'I am not one of them.'

'Then give it to Myrtle. It was she and Cass who took it in the first place. Give it to her.'

She sat with it between her legs, staring at it. For some reason she had wanted to get rid of it. She did not know why. But she was glad Jean-Claude did not want it.

She said, 'All right. Perhaps I will.' She knelt again and packed it carefully away. Then she sat down once more.

695

He said, 'This . . . ritual. With Boris. It was special? Perhaps though you were so young, he asked you to marry him?'

She smiled into the sun.

'No. We've always sort of known we would get married one day. I engaged myself to him a long time ago. With Aunt Mon's bracelet.' She looked into the past. 'My mother's gift to me. I didn't know that at the time, of course. Or perhaps I did.'

The silence stretched between them until Bessie was breathless with it.

Then he said, 'You are angry with me. Because I arranged work for Boris that would take him away for a long time.'

She was surprised out of her tension.

'No. I did not realise . . . no. Not angry.'

She had missed Boris of course. Often. But there had not been the anguish she associated with missing Jean-Claude.

He seemed to feel the need to explain.

'I knew how it was between you two. And I wanted very much for you to finish your education, chérie. To look around. To see other things. I told Boris this.'

'What did he say?'

'I think he understood. But he said that one day he would come back and marry you.'

'He said that?'

'Are you surprised? I thought it was settled between you?'

'Yes. But I was the one who had to settle it.' She was pleased Boris had said that. She felt enormously flattered.

Jean said very dryly, 'Ah. Yes. I can imagine that.'

She looked at him, and for the first time they laughed together wholeheartedly and without inhibitions.

As they wandered down the mountain and into the warm dusk of the flower farms, she knew that part of her pleasure had been because Jean had taken a hand in her fate. He had sent Boris away. He had kept her . . . safe.

The agony of parting was upon her before she was ready for it. She extracted a promise that he would come again at Christmas, but he made provisos about his work schedule, and she did not trust him.

Then she had an idea.

'Grannie will stay on here – won't you, darling? It's only three

696

months till Christmas . . . just over. Why don't you stay? Jean would come home much oftener then, wouldn't you Jean? Like you used to.'

Mary's refusal was automatic.

'Bessie, I wouldn't dream of leaving you in your A levels year!'

But Bessie was adamant. This was her link with Jean-Claude. The few letters they exchanged meant nothing. But if he came regularly to the Bergerie, she would get news . . . he would be joined to her by Mary.

Unexpectedly he too thought it a good idea.

'The English winter does not suit you, Mary. And you love this house and the kitchen and the garden.'

'I'm all right with Aunt Liv and Uncle Reggie, Grannie. I'll be able to work much harder if I don't have to worry about you!'

Mary laughed reluctantly. The idea appealed to her very much; Liv shared her house as best she could, but it was still her house.

Bessie warned, 'I'm going to keep on at you, Grannie, until you agree!'

Mary groaned. And so did Jean-Claude. And then they laughed. It was almost like old times. Almost.

She got her way. And back in Barnt Green she continued to take Monica's advice and worked furiously. Time flew. Christmas was wonderful; to be reunited with Mary and Jean-Claude was enough. But Jean had arranged a party for practically the whole village. She met again with Solange and Brigitte, was introduced to Grandmère and danced with all the young men there. Jean did not dance. He watched smilingly and helped Mary to give out the presents.

As they walked back up the track that night, he said quietly, 'It is all right now, yes?'

Mary replied immediately, 'Oh yes, Jean. It is all right.'

Bessie said, 'What is all right?'

'We are a small family again. We go our separate ways. We come together and pool our *contente* – is it not so?'

She did not answer. The start were brilliant; she stared up at them until she stumbled and would have fallen if Jean had not grabbed her elbow.

He said quietly, 'She is not up there, Bessie. She is with us here. You know that.'

'Of course. Yes.'

He was right. In everything he had said, he was right. She was surprised it did not give her more pleasure.

As soon as Bessie's examinations were over, Monica went to stay at Barnt Green. Mary Woodford was already there – had come back with Bessie after the Easter holidays and stayed ever since. Liv's four double bedrooms were filled again and she obviously enjoyed it. Monica smiled remembering the old Liv.

Reggie escorted all of them to the school on the last day of term to see Bessie receive her leaving gift: a copy of the controversial New English Bible. Afterwards they waited in a queue to be introduced to the headmistress. Thankfully Monica saw that old Miss Jenson had been replaced by a fairly young woman who even smiled now and then.

'My grandmother,' Bessie murmured. 'Uncle . . . aunt. And my mother.'

Monica took the proffered hand, but could no longer see the face. Somehow, with an enormous effort of will, she controlled her tears. Bessie took her arm and led her towards a display of work.

'It's lucky in a way,' she said in Monica's ear. 'I've never called anyone Mother. So now, I can learn all about it.'

Monica knew that Bessie had thought about it carefully, it wasn't a spur of the moment thing. She remembered the barren years when she had so much wanted to possess this girl and call her daughter. By letting her go, pushing her away almost, it had happened.

She held on to the young arm very tightly. Without it she thought she would probably fall down.

That night they were to have gone out for a celebratory meal, but it was raining and the house was warm and cosy.

'Let's stay in,' Bessie begged. 'We could play Monopoly. When I went to see Aunt Myrtle at Easter, the boys had a craze for it and it was such fun.'

Liv rose to the occasion. 'Why not? And I've got some steaks for tomorrow. I could do steak and chips. And we could have a bottle of wine. Shall we?'

Suddenly it was a party. The rain ran steadily down the French windows and the sunken rose garden which had been the fish pool filled with water. Inside Liv produced a wonderful meal and they played Monopoly.

'The last time I played this so-and-so game was at Rhyl. D'you remember, Mary?'

'Yes, I remember.' Mary smiled into the eyes of the girl who had at last taken her rightful place. 'You won immediately of course.'

Monica gave her old wicked grin. 'I think I cheated actually. I often did.'

'I can vouch for that,' Liv agreed, shaking the dice so vigorously it flew on to the floor. 'Ooops. Sorry everyone.' She shook again, moved, then said, 'You know, you two should adopt each other. You get on so well, you've got Bessie between you – you're made for each other.'

Reggie said quickly, 'Happy endings are for books, Liv.'

Liv flushed. 'Oh I didn't mean . . . I'm sorry.'

Mary said calmly, 'You didn't mean that Monica could replace Cass. Of course you didn't. Monica had always been an extra blessing. I think that's a marvellous suggestion, Liv.' She smiled again across the table. 'Anyway, Mon, you haven't got much choice. You are Bessie's mother and I am Bessie's grandmother. So it follows—'

Bessie chanted from her literature syllabus, 'as the night the day . . .'

Monica said, 'My God! Have I got a mother and a daughter now?' She tried to laugh. 'It's too much.'

Bessie was grinning like a Cheshire cat. 'What she means is it's two more birthday presents to buy!'

That night Monica talked to Cass as she so often did when she was alone.

'Darling, I was going to thank you for Bessie. Now I have to thank you for Mary too. I don't know what to say. I'm not too good at being deep, am I, Cass? Never was. But . . . well, you know that my one fear was having no-one of my own. Later. When I can't work any more.' She laughed. 'Yes. I'm being morbid, darling. Sorry.' She grinned into the darkness and took a deep breath. 'Thing is, Cass, I'm a great one for believing that there's a way of saying thank you for these sort of things. Cass, I want to do something. What can I do? I mean, in one way I'd like to go and see poor old Giles, and tell him that everything is all right now. But . . . well, I can't do that, Cass. It still wouldn't work between us – never will – but he can still melt my heart with that crumpled smile of his. So what can I *do*?' She waited for few moments, then sighed. 'Okay. I'll sleep on it. But . . . it's been the best day of my life, Cass, it really has.'

The next morning she sought Liv out in the kitchen. It was still raining and the others were discussing a trip into Birmingham to buy presents. Boris was coming home that summer and Bessie was paying her usual visit to Myrtle and Malcolm to see him. She wanted to buy a cricket bat for Lennie and fishing tackle for the other two boys. She had been going to get a special lens for Boris' camera, but was now deciding to buy an umbrella. 'He'll need it. And he won't have one. And it will make him laugh,' she was saying to Reggie and Mary in the living room.

Monica said, 'Liv, it's been a wonderful time. Thank you.'

Liv looked round, surprised. 'Mon. You've made it wonderful. You always do. You're so full of energy. You take us all and – and – make us into something!' She laughed. 'I don't know. I always feel better for seeing you. And it was lovely for Bessie.'

Monica leaned against the new freezer. 'I suppose you're thinking up something to replace the steaks for today? And we shall have a marvellous lunch produced in minutes. And the dishwasher will do its job—'

Liv said quickly, 'I know. Same old Liv. I can't help it, Mon. I enjoy it.'

'My God, I wasn't criticising! And you're not the same old Liv. You didn't used to enjoy it, my girl. Admit it.' They both laughed and Monica said seriously, 'Liv. I don't want to step on any toes, but couldn't you forgive Myrtle now? It's been six years. A long time. And I think Cass would like it if we got together again, don't you?'

Liv looked round. She still had her baby face, but paradoxically it was no longer young.

She said simply, 'Yes. Yes, of course she would. And I would too. And obviously so would you. But . . . there are obstacles, Mon.'

'Reggie.'

'I don't think he could bear it.'

'It would be a shock, but I think it's the answer, darling. She was a dream, that's all. She's not the same now, Liv. She's no dream. She is very, very real.'

Liv said nothing for a long time. She forgot her meal preparations and put her back against the sink to stare into the past which appeared to be just left of Monica's knee.

'I just don't know. He wouldn't agree to it. But even if he did, there's Malcolm. He has had nothing to do with Reggie since then. Nothing at all.' She looked up and smiled slightly. 'Actually, Reggie misses him very much.'

Monica smiled back. 'Incredible.'

They both laughed, then Monica straightened.

'Well, that *is* something I can do. I'll go down to Cheltenham with Bessie and Mary and stick my oar in there.'

'Steady on, Mon. You might get hurt.'

'That doesn't matter.' Monica gave her indefatigable grin again. 'If I've inherited Cass' mother and Cass' daughter, then I've got to do what she would have done. And the sooner the better!'

She walked into the hall. 'Is everyone ready? I suggest we go now and treat Liv to a slap-up lunch at Rackham's. Everyone in favour say—'

Bessie yelled, 'Aye!'

Boris had changed. Bessie had expected him to be different after two years in the outback of Australia, but not in this way. He was more . . . enclosed . . . than before. Where she could have expected a confidence and a free-and-easiness from his outdoor life, she was met with a strange self-containment that did not exactly exclude her, but was nevertheless impenetrable. For one thing he accepted the umbrella as if it were the Holy Grail instead of a bit of a joke.

'I'll treasure it always,' he said.

'I thought you'd probably wear one of those special hats to keep off the rain.'

'Hat?'

'You know, the kind the Australians wear. Like a cowboy hat with corks all around.'

'Oh. Yes. They're to keep the flies off, actually.'

'I know *that*! Idiot.' She laughed and aimed a kiss at his cheek and the boys, who were dancing around with fishing rods and cricket bat, gave knowing catcalls and wanted to know if they were going to play mummies and daddies again like they used to.

Boris turned bright red and Bessie missed his cheek and rounded on the boys and chased them out of the room. Myrtle was just seeing off her last patient. She herded them down to the kitchen where Monica had started a meal.

'Give Boris and Bessie a bit of peace,' she ordered, laughing. She stuck her head around the door before closing it. 'For goodness sake talk him out of this latest thing, Bessie. If anyone can do it, you can!' And she left.

'What's this? A new job?' Bessie was so pleased to see him she could hardly stand still. She took one of his hands and swung around him as if they were still children. 'Come on, tell Bessie!'

'Later. It's something to talk around. But not now, not here.'

She respected that and knew it must be serious. But still she pestered him, enjoying reverting to their old camaraderie.

'Give me a clue. Is it work?'

'Oh Bessie.'

'Come on, come on. Is it a different life?'

He looked at her dancing around her like a gadfly.

'Yes. If . . . it would be a different life. But . . . I just don't know, Bessie. Leave it for now. Please.'

She stopped and stared at him, not laughing any more.

'Will it be the end of us, Borrie?'

She saw his Adam's apple move as he swallowed. Then he said steadily, 'You know that I will never stop loving you, Bessie.'

She said just as solemnly, 'Nor I you. So that's all right then. Let's go and have tea with everyone. And laugh again.'

He smiled and pulled her hand through his arm in the old companionable way. As they went into the hall, Malcolm emerged from his treatment room.

'Ah. The heavenly twins,' he greeted them. He kissed Bessie chastely and shook Boris' hand. 'I feel safe with you two.' He shook his head. 'My God, you've seen us through some tough times, haven't you?'

He put his arms around their shoulders and led them down to the kitchen. And it was the same as ever, darkly cavernous and inconvenient, and totally homely.

* * *

702

After two days, Mary decided she would go and see Dilly Gosling and then return to France, and Mon took over the kitchen. Like Bessie, she enjoyed its old associations, and the challenge of making it nearly efficient again.

Nicky was almost twelve and he and Martin had inherited their father's domestic streak; they were pressed into service. Lennie, a fully-fledged horror now, had been recruited into as many organisations as would have him, so was not much in evidence. Monica packed him off in Doris' care most mornings, and left his room till last.

Myrtle bemoaned the fact that it was no holiday for Monica.

'I'm in my element, Myrt!' Monica folded and turned her puff pastry. 'Next month I get my own little place. This is great practice.'

'Oh Mon. You're marvellous.' Myrtle unconsciously echoed Malcolm's words. 'You've seen us through it all, haven't you?'

'I've certainly been around.' Monica floured the rolling pin and paused. 'I'd like to be around more in the future, too.'

'My God. You know you're always welcome here, darling. Any time at all. I mean that—'

'I'd like us all to be around in the future.' Monica rolled out an oblong piece of pastry and folded it again into three. 'You. Me. Liv. The others of course. But we're the middle. We're important. We should be together again.'

Myrtle pulled out a chair and sat down quickly.

'I'd like it more than anything. But how can I expect . . .? After what happened . . . Liv could never . . . And Malcolm hates Reggie. Hates him.'

'I don't believe that. And Liv wants to heal the breach. And Reggie misses Malcolm.'

'Liv would actually be willing to see me? Be friends again?'

'She is worried about Reggie. Naturally. What do you think?'

'It's gone – like Mallie – like Cass. Gone.'

'I agree. So it's just Malcolm.'

Myrtle stared as Monica put the pastry over a bowl full of apples and began to crimp the edges.

'Are you going to have a go at him, Mon?'

'Why not? I've got nothing to lose and a lot to gain.'

'Yes. Well. If you really think . . . It would be marvellous if we could . . . I miss Liv. They used to come down quite often. And occasionally she'd invite us up there. Without the boys of course.'

'She's different now. She'd have the boys. Even Lennie.'

They both laughed.

Monica said, 'Look, Myrt. No time like the present. Tell Malcolm his coffee is ready.'

'Oh my God.'

But Myrtle stood up and went to fetch her husband. Then she tidied away her own instruments and wished she'd remembered to tell Monica about Boris. He and Bessie had gone for a walk to the Devil's Chimney, an outcrop of rock on Leckhampton Hill. She wondered what would be the outcome of that. And of Monica's interview with Malcolm.

They sat on the side of the hill, the whole of Cheltenham and Tewkesbury spread below them. For once they were without Nicky and Martin. It was an overcast day with a chilly wind blowing; the boys had decided to go to the Gaumont where *Summer Holiday* was showing.

Bessie took a deep breath of the wind.

'It's a splendid view, but it's not in the least like the Victoire, is it?'

'No. The air tastes differently and there's no sun.'

'It's very English. And the Victoire is very Provencal. The taste is because of the flowers.'

'Will you go up the Victoire next week? When you and Mary go back to the Begerie?'

'What do you mean – me and Mary? You're coming too, aren't you?' Bessie was dismayed. She turned on her wrist and looked at him. He lay on his side, his jacket turned up at the collar, his eyes on the grass by his supporting elbow.

'I'm not sure. I have the chance to go to Prinknash Abbey. A sort of retreat.'

She waited for more and when it did not come, frowned her puzzlement. 'Prinknash is Roman Catholic, Boris. You won't be able to go there.'

He glanced up. 'Bessie. It is one of the things I want to talk about. I was accepted into the Roman Catholic Church last January.'

'You never said anything. In your letters. Nothing.' She was hurt at the omission, but not surprised. Borrie had been attracted to that religion for many years now. She leaned down. 'Why didn't you tell me? It's not a secret or anything, is it? You're not ashamed of being a convert, surely?'

He sat up quickly. 'Of course not. I am proud, my dear.' He picked some grass and examined it carefully. 'I could not tell you what was happening, Bessie, because I did not know. I still do not know. I wanted . . . whatever was happening to my soul, to happen. Not to be influenced by . . . anything.'

'Oh Borrie. I wouldn't have tried to influence you. I went to a convent. My friends in France are all Catholic.'

He nodded but was silent. He began to discard the blades of grass, piece by piece.

She said, 'It's more than that, Borrie. Isn't it? You wanted to be a monk before. Is that what it is?'

She saw by the contraction of his ear that he smiled briefly, but all he said was, 'You know me very well, Bessie.'

She took another breath. The wind filled her chest and seemed to give her courage.

She said, 'You thought I would hold you to our – our engagement, Borrie. Was *that* it?'

He laughed then. 'No. Of course not. That is not your style, Bessie Woodford.' He turned and looked at her and she saw so much love in his eyes she gasped. 'I can see that already, now, you are preparing to . . . what is it called? Give me my freedom?'

She could not return his smile. For so long she had counted on Boris for her future. For so long.

She said, 'We were children, Borrie. It was nothing. You have always been free, you know that.'

He continued to look at her until she dropped her own gaze. She thought in a sudden panic, I do not love him like that . . . I could not give my life for him . . .

He said quietly, 'I want to marry you, Bessie. God needs me. He has called – if you like. Quite literally called. It happens. But I cannot give you up. I love you more than I love God. Will you marry me?'

It was such an enormous thing to happen; she felt her heart beating – thumping – in her chest, the wind lifting her hair, an incipient blister on her heel beginning to sting; and inside herself and Boris, in their souls, there was this awesome statement. To be loved more than God.

She was not conscious of making a decision. She was not conscious of sifting thoughts and feelings and coming to a conclusion. Boris was there, infinitely dear to her, always special, always different. And here was she; understanding him because she had acquired so much sensitivity from Cass; yet irrevocably Monica's daughter, her feet always on the ground.

She said matter-of-factly, 'Darling Borrie. I do love you. I've always loved you and always will. But I cannot marry you. Oh Boris, I'm in love with Jean. Help me. Help me if you can. I did not know till now. Oh Boris . . . Borrie . . .'

And she crumpled where she was on the short grass. And after a very small hesitation, he gathered her up and held her tenderly. Like a shepherd holding a lamb.

Nineteen

It was a week later. Mary and Bessie had gone to France without Boris. He was still with Myrtle and Malcolm and gradually moving out of the curious limbo-state in which he had been for some time. Bessie's 'confession' had released him in may ways; he knew worldly love was not for him. Probably he had know it since that ghastly day Myrtle had given birth to Mallie. Now, quite suddenly, the horror he had felt for some time at the outward manifestation of that wordly love was dissolving. It was something to do with Bessie, but he didn't know what. In turning him down, Bessie had quite literally set him free. It was curious. Like Alice, he felt it was becoming curiouser by the minute. But fascinating and interesting and almost overwhelming. There was nothing ethereal or otherworldly about the love he felt for God. It was tremendously exciting. He waited impatiently for a reply to his letter to the Brotherhood.

Monica had gone back to Exeter feeling such intense irritation with Malcolm she would dearly have liked to smack him.

'I haven't given up,' she warned Myrtle. 'And neither must you. Immediately you see a chink ın his armour, attack! I am absolutely determined we shall get together again. It is my mission in life.'

Myrtle felt almost sorry for Malcolm. She said, 'He can be very stubborn. And after all, when you think what happened—'

'He brought it on himself!' Monica wouldn't give an inch. 'How about withholding conjugal rights?'

Myrtle correctly concluded Monica was fishing. She laughed. 'Blackmail, Monica.'

Monica reverted to her American days. 'Oh, shoot,' she said. It was strange that her irritation with Malcolm did not extend very far at all. She was so happy these days she thought she might write to Bob and ask how his son was doing now. Or maybe . . . just maybe . . . get in touch with Gilly. No, not that. But it was a pity. As she had said over and over again to Malcolm, they were all getting too old to harbour grudges.

Liv stood, like Sister Anne, waiting at the window for Reggie's return from the farm sale in Malvern. Immediately the roof of the Humber Snipe appeared, gliding along the top of the privet which bounded the front garden, she whipped into the kitchen and began on the hollandaise sauce. The salmon lay on its dish. The meringue was drying in the oven, the cream whipped and in the fridge. She would leave the wine to him; she did not know whether this was a celebration or not.

She saw immediately that he was tired and her heart sank. He had been subdued since Mary and Bessie left; different. She wondered whether he was finding the house intolerable without them. Whether he was thinking of Bessie . . . with Myrtle.

He stood in the kitchen doorway, loosening his tie.

'D'you mind, Liv? It's so damned hot. Do I stink? It turned out to be mostly sheep to be auctioned. Can't get the smell out of my nostrils!'

'You don't smell at all, Reggie. But why don't you have a bath before supper? Go on. I'll bring you a cup of tea if you like.'

'Will you?' He sounded surprised, though it was a long time since Liv had ruled that no food or drink went in the bathroom. 'I must admit that sounds good.'

Even so, he sat on the kitchen stool and watched her stirring the sauce as if he did not have the energy to climb the stairs. Her heart went six inches lower. He was going to tell her something. It could only be that he could not live any more without Myrtle.

He said, 'D'you mind me collapsing here for a few minutes, Liv? There's something soothing about watching you cook.'

'Of course not. Here.' She left the pan and wooden spoon to reach inside the fridge for a carafe of lemon juice. She poured him a glass. 'Have some of this. Fresh lemons. Mary showed me how to do it. They used to drink it in France.'

He accepted the glass gratefully, but she wished she hadn't mentioned Mary, She went back to the sauce. It was unnerving the way he was watching her. He sipped, looked, sipped, looked. He was trying to find the courage and the moment to tell her something.

She said brightly, 'It's your favourite. Salmon with hollandaise sauce.'

'Lovely.'

'I thought we might sit in the garden afterwards. The television is a bit . . .'

'That would be nice.'

He stood up and reached around her to put the glass on the work surface. At close quarters she could smell the sheep. She wanted to throw her arms around him and hold him to her physically. Force him to forget everything that had happened.

He sat down again. 'Liv. How you've changed. Do you realise how much you've changed?'

'Yes.' Her voice was stifled.

'Oh I know. We've all changed. Some of us more strikingly than others. But I don't think anyone realises about you. They think you're the same. And you're not.'

She said in the same muffled voice, 'I know.'

But he wanted to tell her anyway. He said, 'You're an artist, Liv. Did you know *that*?'

She did not know that and she glanced up in surprise.

'I thought you meant my hair going grey. And all my lines.'

He actually laughed. 'If you're looking for compliments . . . you have all of twelve grey hairs, and they seem to be making you look blonder than ever. And there are no lines, Liv. You are far more beautiful than when I knew you first. Then you were pretty. Now you are . . . beautiful. Yes, beautiful.'

'Oh Reggie. Reggie.' Her eyes suddenly filled with tears and he forgot what he had been going to say.

'What is it, Liv? What's the matter?'

'Nothing. Nothing at all. But . . . I know you're building up to something. Go on. Finish now, Reggie. Please.'

'Finish?' I was just thinking about you, love. How different you are. You would have swept me out of the kitchen at one time. Got me into a bath before I could fill the house with the stink of sheep! He laughed; but without condemnation. 'Now, all that – that – what do you call it – house pride? You've refined it, Liv. You're a home-maker now. You've made a home – a sanctuary – for Mary and Bessie. And for me before that. When we got back from Paris. I didn't realise it then, of course. I could only think of Myrtle. But when I saw you looking after Bessie, then I knew what you'd done for me, Liv.' He smiled right at her, 'Yes, you're an artist.'

She swallowed and moved the saucepan from the ring.

She said in a small voice, 'When Bessie goes, for good I mean, will you stay? I mean, will be the same, Reggie?'

He did not answer for a long time. He knew suddenly that this was an important moment, and he needed to choose his words.

At last he said quietly, 'I'll stay for as long as you'll have me, Liv. You must know that I love you. Surely – now – you know that?'

She said, 'Myrtle?'

'Liv. Myrtle is part of me. I cannot wrench her out. But I couldn't *live* with her. I couldn't live without you, now. I can't explain it, my darling. Can you . . . take me on trust?'

She tried to laugh. 'I trust you to be honest. I know you would be.'

He knew she was thinking of his . . . brutal honesty . . . about his love for Myrtle.

'Oh God. I'm sorry, Liv. I'm sorry.'

'No. Don't be. We wouldn't be here now if anything had been different. We mustn't waste time on regrets.'

He made no attempt to touch her, and she wanted him to put his arms around her very much indeed.

He said, 'It's six years now. Six years ago. Would your Carol be disappointed, d'you think?'

She kept her head turned from him, tears dripped into the sauce. It would be inedible.

'Not altogether. Bessie will marry Boris. Myrtle is working. Monica is happy – very happy.'

'What about you, Liv?'

She whispered, 'Reggie, I don't want you to feel . . . tied. Or anything like that. But, I'm pregnant.'

He didn't shout or jump, or react in any way for a long time. Then he stood up slowly behind her and put his arms right around her and held her against him. She could feel his breath moving the curls on top of her head.

He said, 'Darling. Listen. I know you don't want this, but believe me, you will be happy. You will be the best mother in the world. You've got talents, Liv, and those talents need other outlets, not just me. Please be happy, Liv. Please. This is the

710

most wonderful thing that has happened to either of us.'

She howled then, lifting her head and letting cries burst from her. He turned her within his arms and held her tightly against him so that she could hardly breathe.

She babbled through his soothing words, through her own tears, 'You idiot. You absolute idiot. I'm so happy I could burst. But I thought – I thought – you'd be thinking of Myrtle and I couldn't bear it! I want this baby more than anything in the world, Reggie. But not unless you want it too. It's yours. At last – at last – I am giving you something! Can't you understand that?'

He smoothed her curls, then held her away from him so that she could see that he, too, was weeping.

Somehow, saltily, they kissed. And then they kissed again. And then they held each other as if they might be drowning in their own tears.

The year before, Bessie had arrived at the Bergerie assuring herself that she was 'all right' and had discovered over the holiday that she was not all right. She had not known why, but it had been a fact. She had gone home to follow Monica's instructions and work through it.

Back in the refined and perfumed air, she knew at least that she was most definitely not all right. And she knew why.

She wondered how long she had been in love with Jean-Claude. She remembered the instant connection she had felt with him when she met him in New York and wondered if it could have been then. She wondered if it had been her love for him that had made Cass into some kind of barrier. She wondered how it was that Boris' love differed from hers. She wondered why she was happy one minute and bewildered and frightened the next. She wondered what she should do. She wondered whom she could tell.

The last question was the only one she could answer. She could tell Monica. She had told Boris and he had come up with no answers. She could not possibly tell Grannie . . . because . . . because of Cass. Solange or Brigitte would treat it as a giggling secret and that would be unbearable. Liv and Myrtle were pretty hopeless when it came to being in love. And on the surface so was Monica. But only on the surface. Bessie knew by now that

711

Monica would always – hopelessly – love Giles Cook. Monica would understand. And would come up with some practical answers too.

Meanwhile Bessie was on the see-saw of emotions; delirious one minute when Jean-Claude talked to her properly, or laughed with her and not at her, or was simply there; derelict the next when he saw her looking at him with her shining dark eyes and became immediately avuncular.

She found herself resorting to ploys she'd read in magazines. They went to Nice for the day and swam in the tideless, rather murky Mediterranean. She wore one of the new bikini two-piece costumes, named for the atoll in the Marshall Islands where the Americans were testing nuclear bombs. When they sunbathed afterwards, she passed the sun oil to Jean-Claude without a word and rolled on to her front.

Obediently he smeared some on her back, stopping short half-way down her spine.

'Legs too, please Jean,' she said, her voice muffled by her arms. And while he tackled her calves, she reached behind her and undid the ties of the bra.

When, half an hour later, she rolled on to her back, he did not look at her for a long minute and then was suddenly furious.

'Cover yourself, Bessie! Do you wish to be arrested?'

She felt like a defiant schoolgirl.

'I don't see why I can't do it. Lots of others—'

'What would Mary say? If she had not gone to the shops you would never have dreamed—'

'You're so old-fashioned, Jean!'

'Certainly I am. Especially where you are concerned.'

She put on a towelling robe and hugged her knees.

'There is no shame in the human body.'

'The shame is when it is used provocatively.'

Her face flamed. She thought he had guessed the reason for what she had done. But when he said no more, she had to conclude otherwise.

After that he made sure they were rarely alone together. When Mary left the room to cook or simply to walk in the garden, he would get up and follow her, offering her his help even though she patently did not need it.

Mary herself noticed something was wrong.

'Have you and Jean had a row?' she asked bluntly one morning when they were picking the last of the tomatoes. 'He hates shopping, but he offered to go down this morning as if he couldn't wait to get away from us.'

'Well in that case, perhaps he's had a row with you?' Bessie said pertly.

Mary tightened her mouth. 'No. He has not had a row with me. How about you, I ask again?'

'Oh Grannie. He's just a bit cross with me about something.'

'What?'

Bessie had the decency to blush. 'I took off the top of my costume when we were on the beach in Nice. I wanted to get one of those all-over tans. You know, like Bardot.'

Mary did not display immediate disapproval as Bessie had expected. She rubbed the bloom off a tomato with the palm of her hand and placed it carefully in the trug.

'Darling. This is difficult to say. I think – I am certain in fact – that Jean-Claude sees Cass in you.'

Bessie did not like that at all. 'I'm not a bit like Cass,' she protested.

'No. Perhaps I don't mean it quite in the way you think.' Mary bit her bottom lip then tried again. 'He reveres you, darling. He's put you on a pedestal. You are the part of Cass that must be kept . . .' she ran out of words.

'Pure?' Bessie was incredulous. 'Mon *Dieu*! Should I get inside the china cabinet or something?'

'Don't be silly, Bessie. It's just that anything like that would make him – er – react strongly.'

'Yes. Certainly.' Bessie's face was suddenly set and determined. 'Well, I must get off the pedestal, mustn't I? He must see me as I really am.' She glanced at Mary. 'And that is not even Bessie Woodford, Grannie. It is Bessie Cook.'

She put a tomato in the trug as if physically making a point, then she turned and walked down the garden, over the wall and through the roses that were even now being cut for the perfume factories. One or two of the pickers called to her, but she ignored them. Mary watched as she reached the boundary of the cultivated land and started on the real mountain. She had been wearing a hat, but she took it off and swung it by her side. Her hair – black like Monica's and curly like Giles' – fanned out behind her

713

almost down to her neat waist. She wore an old cotton frock and espadrilles, but there was nothing childish about that figure.

Mary sighed, then to her own surprise she began to laugh.

Bessie walked until she could walk no longer. Her heel, which always blistered unless she wore proper walking shoes, was burning protestingly. It was late afternoon and there were goose pimples on her arms in spite of all the exercise. She found the stream they always used for drinking water, and sat above it, hypnotised by the rushing glitter as it passed over stones and made miniature weirs and waterfalls. To wake herself up she got down the bank on her bottom, and dabbled her feet, but then she felt really cold and her shoes wouldn't go back on and the scramble back up the bank was difficult and when she got there it was almost dusk.

'Damn, damn and double damn! she said loudly. She wanted to throw back her head and scream her resentment and frustration to the skies, but sound carried a long way on the mountain and there were a few farms not far below her.

She crammed her feet back into the espadrilles somehow, rammed her sunhat on until it covered her ears, and started back down. And, like her mother, she talked aloud to Cass.

'I don't want to take him away from you – I don't want that! I don't know what I want! I don't want him to think I'm you, either. I'm not you, Cass. We were like blood sisters – spirit sisters, but we weren't alike. I want him to see me as me. But if that means he has to forget you, then he can't. Not ever. Can he?' She stopped and lifted her head and said as loudly as she dared, '*Can* he, Cass? *Can* he? Oh why don't you answer me – just put a thought in my head or something! Don't you see what is happening, Cass? You are haunting us! Just like Mallie haunted Myrtle! I want to stop it, yet I don't want to send you away, Cass.' She began to weep. 'I love you, Cass. I love you and always will love you. But I love Jean-Claude too. What am I going to do, Cass?'

She huddled down, clutching her cold legs to her, letting her tears drip on her knees. But there was no answer and after a very short while, feeling slightly ridiculous, she stood up and began to plod grimly on. If Cass couldn't help she would have to take matters into her own hands.

It was quite dark when Jean-Claude met her almost on the Lassevour boundary. She was limping badly and her face was streaked with tears, but he could not see that and his anger was cold and cutting.

'You think you are grown-up, yet you have no consideration whatever for your grandmother, have you! She will tell me nothing but I suppose there was an argument and off you go like the spoiled brat you are!'

She would say nothing to excuse herself, but she fumed with the injustice of it, and tried to walk tall and make her silence dignified rather than piqued.

He jumped over the wall and waited for her to do likewise. She sat on the top, swung her legs over and promptly collapsed in a heap, catching her bare arm on some rose thorns. She could not hold back a cry.

'Let me see.'

She tried to struggle up but he practically shoved her back down, found a torch in his pocket and shone in on her.

'Mon Dieu! You are in a state, are you not?' For a moment his voice softened, then he saw the blood oozing from the back of her espadrille. 'You wore those for walking on the mountain? You deserve everything you got! Little fool!'

She could stay silent no longer.

'How dare you call me names? What right have you got to – to disapprove of me! None at all – you have made that quite clear over and over again! I realise you are here on behalf of Grannie – well, now you have found me so you can go back and tell her everything is all right!'

She tried to stand up and immediately collapsed again. He wasted no more time on words, but bent and picked her up as if she were a sack of potatoes. There was nothing romantic about it; nothing she could look back on later and enjoy in retrospect. Her head hung level with his waist, her hands clutched the top of his trousers in panic. He hoisted her back slightly to balance her weight, and ripped off both her shoes. The cold air on her bleeding heel was bliss. She closed her eyes momentarily, surrendering to the inevitable, and the next minute they were trudging between the roses and she was jolting up and down and from side to side, trying to brace herself, failing, losing every scrap of dignity, hating him more with each step.

Mary took her gently from Jean's bowed figure and laid her back on the sofa. A bowl of water appeared and she put her feet

715

in it. Somewhere there was another bowl and Mary bathed her face and hands. When she opened her eyes, Mary's were smiling at her without reproach.

'Well, darling. You walked it out of your system well and truly, I should think. Bed now. I'll bring you some cocoa and a sandwich. Supper in bed. You always enjoyed that.'

She wanted to decline it if only to prove she was no longer a child, but she was famished and the thought of bed and food at the same time was delightful. She avoided Jean-Claude's eye. He sat at the kitchen table, a book open in front of him. He did not say goodnight when she limped past him so neither did she. The stairs were difficult to negotiate and she would dearly have liked to go up on hands and knees. The sight of her bed, turned down neatly, the pillows arranged like an armchair, was too much and she started to cry again. She hardly ever cried now, and it was, of course, all his fault. When Mary came in with a tray she had mopped herself up, but it was no good.

'Bessie . . . Bessie. Don't force it, darling. Something will happen and he will realise you're a woman.'

'What – what do you mean?' Bessie was startled out of her self-absorption. 'What's he been saying? Has he been moaning about me behind my back?' She pushed back the clothes, already recovered enough to go down and do battle.

Mary laughed as she put down the tray. 'He has said nothing at all – though his face is grim enough for anything.' She shook her head gently. 'He was very anxious, Bessie. He said it was for my sake, but it was for his own. I knew you would all right – the Victoire is your mountain and you would have called for help if necessary.' She went to the door. 'He loves you very much, darling,' she said quietly. And was gone.

Bessie stared at the closed door. Even if Mary had not disappeared so quickly she could not have asked her for further information. But surely she must mean that Jean *loved* her?

She ate her supper appreciatively and thought how she would get up early tomorrow and light the fire in the range and make breakfast and be . . . wonderful. Then she wondered if Jean-Claude would notice; or if he would just see her as a penitent child trying to get back into everybody's good books. She bit her lip and flung back the clothes to examine her heel. He hadn't even looked at it properly.

716

She needed to clean her teeth and go to the lavatory. She got up quietly and crept across the landing. Below in the kitchen, Mary and Jean was talking. Mary's voice was soothing and reassuring – as usual. Bessie hardly heard it, she knew what it would be saying. But then Jean spoke. 'She is just a child, Mary. In many ways we have over-protected her. She is more than just innocent – she is naive.'

It was the way he said it. Not exactly with contempt, but certainly not affectionately. There was a weariness in his voice. As if he were sick and tired of the whole problem.

Bessie went into the bathroom, did what was necessary, and went back to her room. She sat bolt upright in her high French bed, listening. First Mary went to bed. Then Jean. Then the old house creaked into a kind of silence. Outside, a little breeze got up. It would be cold on the mountain. Bessie shivered.

At midnight precisely she got out of bed, ignored her slippers and dressing-gown, and padded silently over the bare boards to the door. Unfortunately they, and the door, creaked at the slightest pressure, but by the time she had got herself on to the landing nothing was stirring. Jean slept in Cass' old room. She lifted the latch millimetre by millimetre, then pushed on the door. It swung inwards quite silently. Sitting up in bed, a book on the cover in a pool of light from the bedside lamp, Jean-Claude looked at her. He said nothing. Anything would have been better than nothing. For a few moments of indecision, she was paralysed.

Then she said in a high voice, 'My heel hurts.'

He did not move but he said levelly, 'Go back to bed, Bessie. Now.'

She said, 'But Jean, my heel hurts. And I can't sleep.' She advanced into the room and pushed the door shut behind her. He flung back his bedcovers and swung his legs to the floor. He was wearing ivory-coloured pyjamas that she had seen often on the ironing board, but they looked different on him. She could hardly breathe and a sensation developed in her pelvic area and spread down her legs.

He snapped, 'Go back to your room immediately, Bessie!'

She whispered, 'No. I'm not a child, whatever you think. I'm grown-up. I'm a woman. I want to sleep with you.'

He stopped feeling for his slippers and looked at her in total disbelief.

717

'You what?' His voice was dangerous, but she refused to back down now.

'I don't care what you think. When I took off my bra I wanted to do it for you. Look – I'll do it again!' She dragged her nightie over head frantically. The buttons got caught in her hair and pulled it unmercifully, but she ripped them away and flung the whole thing on the floor. Then she had to hang on to one of the brass knobs at the foot of the bed because she thought she might collapse with the nightie.

He stared at her, his black eyes burning. He did not move, but she was suddenly terribly conscious of her body. It was as if he touched her, ran his hands over her. Like Eve, she was ashamed of her nakedness.

He said very quietly, 'Put your nightgown back on, Bessie. Go to your room. We will never speak of this again. But I would like you to try to imagine how Cass would view it.' He got back into his bed and picked up his book.

She was totally dismissed. Her love, her desire, rejected. And because of Cass. She could not fight a ghost.

She shook like a leaf as she struggled into her nightie. And when she got outside the door she had to go to the bathroom again. She leaned over the basin and brought up her sandwich and cocoa. Her own actions had made her sick.

She arrived at Exeter before her letter. But Monica knew she was coming because she had received a frantic phone call from Mary the day before. It seemed Bessie had left the Bergerie very early in the morning, taking with her two thousand francs and a bag containing two cardigans, a mac, a pair of shoes and a toothbrush. She had written a garbled note for Mary, saying merely that no-one was to worry, she was quite old enough to travel by herself and she was going to see her mother.

Monica had reassured Mary and promised she would telephone as soon as she had some news of Bessie, but as she had no idea by which route the girl would come, she had to sit tight and wait. Mary had phoned twice when Monica was in, and the porter reported that her phone had rung several times while she had been on duty. As a sister, Monica now had a flat in the grounds of the hospital. It was in a block of almshouses built in the last century, and she felt a positive sense of homecoming as she opened up and went into the tiny lobby after being on duty all night. It was a quiet grey morning, windless, full of the scent of stocks from the little cottage garden around the block. She took a long breath before closing the door and leaning against it with her eyes shut. She was tired in her very bones, but knew there was no hope of sleep.

She went into the kitchen and plugged in the kettle.

'It's all very well,' she said aloud. 'I haven't got the experience. Yes, I know it's marvellous – running home to mother – just marvellous. But I don't know what to do about it, Cass.'

The kettle bubbled and she made tea, laid a tray and carried it into the little sitting room. It was chilly in there, and she switched on one bar of the electric fire and pulled her cardigan closer over her uniform. Then she sat down and poured her first cup of tea. It tasted wonderful. She closed her eyes against the steam and inhaled with the same pleasure with which she'd breathed in the flower scent ten minutes ago.

'The trouble is, Cass, I'm so damned content! We've got a little outbreak of meningitis – towards Barnstaple – quite a country district. Two children came in during last night. Took lumbar punctures . . . results just been confirmed. Told the parents . . . got them tea and toast. Told them it will be all right – kids already responding to penicillin – thank God for penicillin, Cass.' She sipped, still with eyes closed. Then went on. 'You know, Cass, if ever I get time, I'd like to do a paper about the necessity of nursing the whole family in these cases. Kids respond so much quicker if ma and pa are there. D'you know, in Africa, the patients invariably bring half a dozen close relatives with them when they're admitted.'

She sipped again and opened her eyes quickly before she nodded off.

She said, 'Cass, why has she run away? That's what I need to know. She'll tell me something of course, but it might not be the truth. And I need to know the truth, Cass. Otherwise what can I do?'

She drained her cup and poured another one.

'I know what you'd do. Listen. Not advise, not interfere. Just listen. But I'm not like you, Cass. I want to do something. And it's often the wrong thing. I mean, I shouldn't have married Bob. And maybe I shouldn't have taken over Myrtle's family. Or lugged poor old Liv along with me. Maybe if I hadn't done that, you wouldn't be dead now, Cass.'

The second cup of tea did not taste as good as the first one. She needed to go to the bathroom and clean her teeth and maybe take a shower.

'Oh, shoot,' she said wearily.

And the door knocker thumped.

Bessie did not look too bad. Her hair was combed and her face and hands were clean. She wore French espadrilles, one pencilled with the name 'Paul', the other 'Ringo'. There were traces of blood around the top of one of them.

She stood in the doorway clutching a small zipped bag and looking chilly.

'Did you get my letter?' she asked by way of greeting.

'No.' Monica stood aside and guided her into the sitting room and the one-bar fire. 'I knew you were coming of course. But no letter yet.'

'Do you mind? I had to get away. And Boris is still with Myrt, and I couldn't possibly tell Liv after what happened to her and Uncle Reggie.'

'I don't mind. I'm on night duty so after tonight I shall have four days off. If that helps.'

'Yes, it does. I want to go up to Liv's and get my results. But . . . I don't know what to do, Mon. I just don't know what to do.' She sank down on the floor by the fire and shivered. 'I've done something awful. Really awful.'

'Mary didn't say. So it couldn't have been that bad.'

'She doesn't know.'

'Oh, I think she'd know.'

'No. It's got nothing to do with her really.' Bessie put her head on her knees. 'Except . . . except now I think of it, it would probably kill her! Oh God, oh God!'

Monica took the cosy off the teapot and felt the outside. It was still very hot. She poured Bessie some tea in her own cup and handed it down saucerless.

'Drink this. I'll get some food. I suppose you're starving?'

'No. I mean, I'm not hungry. I'm probably starving though. Mon, don't go. I have to tell you straightaway.' The head came up and the eyes were black in the white face. 'Listen. When Boris

720

told me he was going to be a priest, I didn't mind. Not at all. It was right – I could see that. Boris had always been different. Trying to get away from the things people do. He should have gone into that monastery when he wanted to . . . ages ago.'

'Boris, a priest? I didn't know.' Monica wondered whether she'd got hold of the wrong stick together. 'Are you sure you didn't mind? I mean, you've always . . . you and Boris . . . only kids, I know, but it's amazing how these things grow up . . .'

'I was sort of relieved. And of course, once that was out of the way, I realised the truth.' She slurped some tea and wiped her hand over her chin. 'I must have known all the time, of course. It was so obvious. When I was in France before . . . I should have known then.' She drank more tea. 'The trouble is . . . Cass. Oh Mon, I never thought I'd want Cass to go away – right away—' she began to cry and Monica leaned down and took the cup away from her, then crouched opposite her. She wondered whether she should take the girl into her arms, then decided against it.

After a while, she said briskly, 'You haven't told me yet. Just why do you want Cass to go away? Or shall I guess?' She took a breath; Bessie did not speak. Monica said bluntly, 'You're in love with Jean-Claude. And you think Cass would mind? You're an idiot, Bessie Woodford. You're an absolute idiot. Cass would be overjoyed. The people she loved best in the world coming together? Use your head, girl!'

Bessie looked up, startled. 'How did you know? Oh my God, is it that obvious?'

'No. But the only reason you might see Cass as an obstacle as if you thought you were on her territory.' Monica leaned towards her daughter and took her face in her hands. 'Darling. You do Cass such an injustice.'

She continued to hold the head that was so like her own, while Bessie's tears began again. Then at last she put her arms around the shaking shoulders and held them close.

'Don't cry, Bessie,' she whispered. 'It's natural. And beautiful. Nothing to cry about.'

'He – he – he thought I was disgusting! I *was* disgusting! I had to make him see me – really see me! And I went into his room and took off my nightie and asked him if I could sleep with him. And he said – he said – what would Cass . . . Oh Mon . . . I was so ashamed! I wanted to die! I was sick. Then I tried to sleep. Then I went downstairs and wrote a letter to you and to Grannie, and then I left. I got a lift to Marseilles and there was this horrid old ship coming across the Plymouth and I—'

'My God! Bessie – you fool – you could have been abducted—'

'White slavery?' There was a tiny hint of a smile in the girl's voice. 'Mon, I'm not that much of an idiot! When I said horrid, I meant it stank. It was full of salted fish. It was quite respectable otherwise. There was a vicar on board.'

Monica tried to take into account that she had worked all night; even so, the conversation was more than just bizzare.

'A vicar?' she asked faintly.

'He'd done the whole of ancient Greece on fifteen pounds. Of course he was pretty thin by then.'

'Bessie. Can you sit up in the chair now, darling. I need some food. Toast or something.'

'I'll make it. Really. I love your little house. I'm so glad you've got . . . something . . .' she began to cry again.

'Oh for goodness' sake!' Monica struggled to her feet. 'Listen, my girl, I've got everything. And if you end up without Jean-Claude, you can still have everything. It's there for the finding, for the . . . listen, Bessie. Stop crying a moment. You might have to do without him. But you might not. He knows now how you feel. Give him time. If you're still free in two or three years—'

'Two or three *years*? Besides, he hates me. I disgust him. I—'

'Bessie. Shut up.' Monica went to the door. 'I don't want you to help me. I want to do it by myself. We'll eat, then we'll sleep. And then, perhaps, we can talk properly.'

She went into the kitchen and began to make toast and scramble eggs. She wondered how it was possible to want to laugh and cry at the same time. It could be hysteria of course. But she didn't think it was.

She said quietly, 'You know all about it, Cass don't you?'

As she took the tray of food into the sitting room, the post dropped through the door. She recognised Bessie's round handwriting. It reminded her that she must telephone the Bergerie immediately.

The girl looked up as she went into the room. Her face was streaked, but she was no longer crying.

'I know what you're going to say, Mon. I did it

722

before – worked, I mean – and you're quite right, it's the only thing to do.' She took the tray and put it on the floor in front of the fire. 'But I'll never forget him. Just as you've never forgotten your Gilly.'

Monica stared. Then gently sank to her knees and began to serve the eggs on toast.

Twenty

Two days later, refreshed and subdued at the same time, Bessie went to St David's station in Exeter and caught a through train to Birmingham. She telephoned Monica to announce her safe arrival and to say that her results were very good and she could go to Bristol University to read Zoology. It was where Cass had gone.

Two hours later she rang again.

'Aunt Liv says I can tell you, Mon! They're having a baby! Isn't it marvellous? Yes, of course you can speak to her. Hang on.'

Monica duly spoke to Liv.

There was a lot of laughter amidst the congratulations, then Monica said quietly, 'So it's all right now, Liv? It was worth it?'

'I can't answer that, my dear. But it looks as if something good is happening for most of us, doesn't it? And . . . and I couldn't have done anything without you, Mon. And Cass of course. And Myrt . . . yes, Myrt especially.'

They talked almost incoherently for ten minutes, then Bessie came back on the line.

'Listen, Mon. Will you tell Grannie? Somehow, this makes the – er – situation – seem better. It's so great it kind of dwarfs all that – drama – at the Bergerie. D'you know what I mean?'

'Yes. I think so. It might make all the difference to Malcolm, too.'

'Malcolm?'

'I meant to tell you. I tried to arrange a big reconciliation. Nothing doing. Malcolm is too insecure, too frightened he will lose Myrt again. But now . . . Bessie love. If I can get Mary over here for a spell, how would you feel about meeting up at Cheltenham? All of us?'

'Well, fine. If it's okay with everyone else.'

'You're certain that Boris—'

'I told you. I'm glad about Boris.'

'But before that, you said you couldn't go to Myrt's – tell Myrt – because of Boris.'

Bessie actually managed a little chuckle. 'Can you imagine me confessing to Boris what I'd done. And him about to enter the brotherhood?'

'Sorry, love. That's fine then. I'll see what I can do. Perhaps you can work on them your end?'

Monica replaced the receiver. It would give Bessie something to think about at any rate. If nothing came of it, it was worth it for that.

She made her phone call to France with an enormous sense of déjà vu. Events seemed to be piling up as they'd done before. Somehow she ought to have more wisdom than she'd had then, and knew she had not.

She had postponed her nights off in case she might need them for the future. Bessie had slept for twenty hours after they'd breakfasted, and Monica had gone on duty at eight as usual and napped for three hours the next morning. Today, she was beginning to wonder if her eyes were focusing properly; she had already dropped two cups of tea and burnt her toast.

Jean answered the call. Monica had met him twice: once in Connecticut at Hildie's farm, and once at Cass' funeral. She felt she knew him intimately because of Cass and now because of Bessie, but she could so easily be wrong.

She said, 'Is Mary there? This is Monica Gallagher.'

'She is here.' He covered the receiver but she heard him call Mary. Then he came back to her. 'Monica, we were so glad . . . Bessie must feel very close to you. It is good she had somewhere – someone – to go to.'

'It is, isn't it?' Suddenly Monica forgot all her qualms about rushing in where angels feared to tread. 'As she was forced to run somewhere – anywhere – it is very good she could come here.' She heard her own voice, fierce with anger and sarcasm. It wasn't the way to do it. But she could not stop now. 'It was clever of you to find the one way you could really cut her down, Jean. But then, I suppose you are trained to do just that.'

There was a pause. She wondered if he had walked away and left the receiver dangling somewhere. But then his voice came on the line again. 'Monica. Mary is here. I would like to talk. Afterwards. Shall I telephone you?'

She said crisply. 'That is entirely up to you.'

Mary's voice came next. She did not sound anxious.

'Mon. I've telephoned Barnt Green, so I know Bessie has arrived safely. My dear, she sounds so much steadier. Thank you.'

'Nothing to do with me. She has common sense and as you know, I'm short on that.' Monica tried to laugh. She said, 'Mary, did she mention anything else to you? About Liv and Reggie?'

'No.'

'Liv's pregnant.'

Mary's joyous comments echoed resonantly. The kitchen at the French cottage must be big, or maybe stone-flagged.

Monica said, 'The thing is, Mary. It might make it possible for us to get together again. And I'd like that. I feel it would be . . . right. I wondered if you could come over too? Go straight to Myrtle's – I'll fix it all up. Just for a few days. What do you think?'

'Well . . . yes. Why not? I was coming over anyway to be with Bessie obviously. And Myrtle can always do with help. That kitchen . . . and Lennie . . . Mon – leave it to me. I'll ring Myrtle. Good idea.'

They made their farewells. Monica put down her receiver and sat by the phone, waiting for it to ring. She drank more tea and made more toast. If he didn't come through in the next half an hour she would have to go to bed and that was that.

After thirty-five minutes, it rang.

'I had to wait for Mary to go into the garden. It was necessary to speak privately, Monica. Obviously Bessie has told you what happened and you are very angry with me.'

'Obviously,' Monica echoed icily.

'It was cruel. Yes, I see that it was the cruellest thing I could have said. But it had to done quickly. Finally. In the end she will thank me.'

'In the end? What end is that, Jean? Your end? Or hers?'

'Monica, please. I am twenty years older than she.'

'So you think you might die sooner than she dies, then she

will be glad she's not a widow? Is that what you mean?'

'Monica, you know what I mean. The child still loves me as a father.'

'So she tried to seduce you.'

'She is confused. The point is one that is still escaping you.' His voice no longer pleaded for understanding; it was stern. 'I do not love Bessie Woodford as my child, Monica. I love her as a woman. If I had not sent her away very quickly the other night, I might have indeed have taken her into my bed. And that would have been unforgivable.'

Monica was silent. She closed her eyes.

Jean's voice came across the wires again.

'Are you still there, Monica? You are disgusted perhaps? You too are thinking of Cass?'

'No. I was thinking of Giles. My adopted brother. Bessie's father.' She took a breath. 'Jean. Bessie is my daughter and I know her instinctively. She does not love you as a father, she loves you as a woman loves a man. She loves you even more because you were Cass' man. If you truly love her, you cannot leave her in ignorance. I meant it, Jean. You can go to Timbuctu afterwards. But first you have got to tell her that you love her.'

'That is exactly what I am trying not to do.'

Monica said levelly, 'And I am trying not to interfere in this. Sometimes when I interfere, things do not work out properly. But I say this to you, Jean. If you do not tell Bessie, then I will. Goodbye.'

She replaced the receiver once more, and began to clear away her breakfast things. Later she would ring Myrtle and Liv. Later on still she would arrange to have next week off and she would buy a new dress to wear in Cheltenham. But now . . . she had to sleep.

The first reunion was stilted affair to begin with.

Liv, Reggie and Bessie arrived at Imperial Square a week later to find Mary already there. It was tea time and the boys were dressed in their best; Malcolm was with a patient, Myrtle had just finished her appointments for the day and was frantically trying on dresses in her bedroom. It did not matter what she looked like, yet she wanted to look . . . all right. Not beautiful as she had looked for Reggie; she would never look like that again. But she

727

wanted to look . . . all right. She actually tried to get into the lime green she had bought in Alnwick, but it would not pull over her bust any more. Probably just as well.

By the time she had decided on her usual gathered skirt and v-necked top. Malcolm had joined her.

'I don't know whether this is good idea.' He looked as nervous as a schoolboy. 'You should hear them in there, laughing and talking as if they're quite at home!'

'That's what we want, darling. We want to be natural. Normal. Don't worry. The boys are there. And Mary. It will pass off easily. And by the time they've been here a couple of days we shall feel easier.'

'It's ridiculous filling up the house with visitors at our busiest time!'

'It's not a busy time by any means. I had to cancel just two appointments and Doris and Tom will put up the double bed in there this evening – it will be no trouble at all.'

'Not to you. You let everything like that sail over your head. But I'm still working, trying to see patients—'

She came close to him and kissed him. 'Darling. I'm just as nervous as you are. But do it for my sake. Please. You and Reggie were good friends and I came between you—'

'It was him! The bastard! Even now when I think of it, I could bloody well kill him!'

She kissed him again, sensed him beginning to feel heavy against her and realised there wasn't time for that.

'Come on, sweetheart. It'll soon be tonight.'

'Oh bunny rabbit, I do love you. I'm doing it for you, then. Is that quite clear?'

'Perfectly clear.'

They went downstairs holding hands.

Unfortunately, Mary rounded up the boys and disappeared with indecent haste as soon as they came into the room. Lennie, who had a summer cold and could not go swimming, whined a protest which Nicky amputated with a surreptitious clip. The two couples were left facing each other across a loaded tea-trolley. Liv and Reggie had scrambled to their feet as soon as the door handle turned, Malcolm and Myrtle appeared to have forgotten where the chairs were placed in the room. They all stood and stared.

Myrtle hardly glanced at Reggie, her eyes were all for Liv. On Liv depended everything as far as Myrtle was concerned. And Liv was scared; Myrtle could see that Liv was still scared that she might whip Reggie away. Oh God.

Myrtle said, 'Liv. I'm so sorry if I hurt you. And I'm so pleased – so very, very pleased, about the baby.'

It was as if a spring was released in the region of Liv's shoulders. She gave a gasping sigh and ran at Myrtle. They embraced thoroughly, laughing and weeping and rocking from side to side so that they appeared to be doing a strange sort of dance.

Malcolm cleared his throat.

'Well, Reggie.'

Reggie said, 'It's good of you to invite us here, old man.'

'I know it bloody well is. But actually it wasn't me. It was Myrtle.'

'Well . . . you must have agreed to it.'

'Suppose I must.'

'The baby. Amazing what babies can do isn't it?'

Malcolm looked at him. 'Yes. Amazing.'

'Sorry, old man. Look, can't we – somehow – be friends again?'

'Don't know. Not very likely.'

The girls had finished their foxtrot and separated, laughing sheepishly.

Myrtle said, 'Let's have some tea. Sit down, Liv. Relax every moment you can, it's terribly important.' She risked a quick look at Reggie. 'Do you still take sugar, Reggie?'

Malcolm said, 'They've had tea already. I heard them at it when I came out of the treatment room.'

'Then we'll have some, darling.'

Myrtle sat down by the trolley and began to pour. Liv sat too. Malcolm and Reggie remained standing.

Then the door opened and Bessie's head came around it.

'Okay? Sorry to disappear like that. Boris and I went for a walk. We're going down to the kitchen to help Grannie.'

Malcolm turned quickly. 'No. Don't do that, Bess, old thing. Come and have tea with Myrtle and me. Is Borrie there? Get two more cups, Borrie and join us.' He almost carried Bessie into the room. She had been a friend to everyone all through. With her sitting next to Myrtle, the two men could also sit down.

729

Myrtle smiled at Liv. It wasn't going to be easy. But they'd made a start.

That night as she got ready for bed, Myrtle let herself think about Reggie and the time they had spent together. She was not introspective, and soon after Lennie started school she had know that she could no longer continue to cherish her time with Reggie as the perfect relationship. Its perfection relied entirely on its brevity and its complete lack of responsibility. Reggie had probably saved her sanity; he had made her well; and when Myrtle was well she did not dwell on the past, she lived in the present. Myrtle saw those three months now as lived by other people – actors in a drama – nothing to do with the Myrtle who was undressing here and the Reggie who was undressing downstairs.

She only hoped that Reggie felt the same way.

She sat on the edge of the bed to roll down her stockings; gone were the days when she slopped around bare-legged in the summer. Her legs were more veined than ever. She held one of them out and wondered whether she might have the veins stripped soon. They did not ache or trouble her in any way. She remembered Reggie tracing them from thigh to ankle. Dear Reggie. If he could see them now he would realise that she was not the same girl.

Malcolm came into the room with a rush. She smiled at him over her shoulder. He was looking better these days; celibacy had not suited him.

'Myrt – honey-bun – there are noises coming from your treatment room!'

She looked at him in surprise.

'Well, of course, Malcolm. Reggie and Liv are sleeping there. Have you forgotten. It's so that Monica can have the—'

'I know they're *sleeping* there, Myrt! But these noises . . . it's disgusting, darling.'

He was genuinely shocked. She began to laugh.

'It's not a laughing matter, Myrt! Under our roof!'

She could not control herself. She rolled about on the bed like the old Myrtle, convulsed with schoolgirl giggles.

'You! Of all people, Malcolm Lennox! My God! That treatment room was more like a boudoir—'

'They're in *your* room, Myrtle! Not mine! And it's many years

730

since . . . Myrtle, will you kindly stop laughing! In the circumstances you have to admit it's in pretty poor taste.'

She got off the bed and went to him.

'Darling. They're having a baby. So they must have done it before.' She kissed him. 'Did you tell me so that you could gauge my reaction? Well, it's this . . . I'm glad that Reggie and Liv are making love under our roof, Malcolm.' She kissed him again. 'Would you help me with my brassiere, please, darling? And are you too tired to give me a massage?'

'No.' His voice was hoarse. He slid her shoulder straps to waist level and kissed her breast very gently. There was a reverence in his love-making that had not been there before.

He whispered, 'Oh bunny rabbit. I do love you.'

She looked at his handsome head, touched the crisp hair and the outside edge of his ears.

'I love you too, Malcolm.'

Monica arrived the next day in time for lunch.

'Why didn't you telephone? Myrtle fussed around her like a mother hen. 'We'd have met you at the station or something.'

'I didn't come by train. I had a lift. Practically to the door.'

'Isn't this wonderful – all of us together after so long. And Liv having a baby. And everything.' Myrtle seemed in a state of euphoria.

Liv said, 'You look tired, Mon. Bessie told us about the meningitis.'

'It's not the worst kind. I think it's all right.'

Bessie said mock-soberly, 'It's motherhood. It's tough for Mon. You'll come to it gradually, Aunt Liv. Mon tends to jump in at the deep end.'

She was referring to herself but suddenly realised there had been another time when Monica had taken on motherhood. But they all laughed, which was a good sign.

They went upstairs and helped Monica to unpack. Lennie jumped on the bed and Nicky and Martin held him down.

'Where are Malcolm and Reggie?' Monica asked, wondering whether a week would be too long in Cheltenham. Her head was already aching; she had worked everything out with great care and forgotten the children.

'Boris and Reggie have gone to see a photographic exhibition at the town hall, and Malcolm has appointments today.' Myrtle put a navy-blue dress on a hanger. 'You do sound rather done up, Mon. Is everything all right?'

'I hope so. I wondered if we could have a day out. Weather permitting.' Monica smiled brightly at Liv and passed her some underwear. 'You see, I got a friend with me. The chap who gave me a lift, actually. And I said I'd show him Stratford – you know how foreigners are, they always want to see where Shakespeare was born.'

'One of your American in-laws?' Liv laid the underwear in a drawer and closed it. 'It would be great fun, girls, wouldn't it? We lived so near but we only went with boring school parties to see productions of the plays we were reading.'

Myrtle groaned. 'D'you remember Donald Wolfit in *King Lear*? Cass thought it was too marvellous for words and you got off with one of the actors, Liv—'

'We could go on the river!' yelled Lennie. 'Super-duper! I'll row. I know how to row!'

'We could have a picnic,' said Martin a little less exuberantly. 'Cold sausages and ham sandwiches and strawberries from Evesham—'

'It's September, idiot!' said Nicky. 'But there'll be plums. Pershore plums. And Victorias. And—'

'Who is your friend from America, Mon?' asked Bessie.

There was a little pause, then Monica turned and faced her daughter.

'It's Jean-Claude. He's staying at the Queen's.'

'Jean? Cass' Jean?' Myrtle was astonished. Neither Mary nor Bessie spoke of him often. 'I didn't realise you knew him, Mon! Whyever didn't you bring him here? We could have managed.'

'He wouldn't do that. But he wanted to see us all.' She turned again to her case. 'He has to go back to Algeria for at least a year.'

Bessie said, 'When? When is he going to Algeria?'

'Next week.'

'So you asked him to come over,' Bessie concluded flatly.

Monica smiled. 'No. As a matter of fact, I didn't ask him to come over. We spoke on the phone. Then he turned up on my doorstep. Rather like you did.'

'Why?'

'He had a rather marvellous idea he wanted to put to me. He assumed you'd get your place at Bristol all right. And he thought I might try for a job at the Children's Hospital there and join you and Mary.' She turned her smile on Mary. 'I don't know what you think about it, but it sounded good to me.'

Mary beamed. 'And to me. And meanwhile he'd like to see Stratford.' She hauled Lennie off the bed. 'Come on boys. Let's go and see what's in the larder. We shall need at least four loaves and an enormous picnic hamper.'

'We could take a tent in case it rains,' Lennie suggested.

'Can we swim?' Martin asked. 'Aunt Mon used to take us swimming—'

'Shut up, Martin.' Nicky ordered tersely. They went off and the room was quiet again.

Bessie said, 'I can't face him.'

'Rubbish.'

Myrtle said, 'Why not? Has there been a row?'

Bessie said, 'Yes.'

Monica said, 'No.'

Liv said, 'Don't let there be any more rows. Please.'

Monica said, 'He wants to talk to Boris. He hasn't seen him since he came home from Australia. Then he simply wants to say goodbye to you and Mary, Bessie. That's all. He doesn't want to disappear without a word like last time. We'll all be with you, don't worry. Just be there. If nothing else, it will paper over the cracks. And that's important just now, isn't it?'

Liv said, 'It is. It is, Bessie.'

Myrtle said, 'So there was a row.'

Bessie sighed. 'No. Not really. Monica is right, there was no row. And . . . I suppose . . . if everyone else is there, I will be too.'

Monica hugged her. 'You'll be glad. Afterwards, you'll be glad,' she assured her.

Nicky lost no time in detaching Lennie and persuading a willing Martin to come with him to the Queen's. At twelve years old, he was suddenly curious about adults and there was a mystery somewhere which he had been unable to solve. It could well be that Monsieur Durant was the missing link.

They presented themselves at the reception desk with aplomb

733

and were taken into the lounge where Jean-Claude was drinking tea and looking disappointingly English. Nicky introduced himself and his brother and graciously accepted a place at the low table.

'We thought we'd better come and tell you about the picnic tomorrow,' Martin explained. 'Lennie wants to row but of course he can't – he's only five. But after you've seen the town and everything, the river might be a good idea. Before the whole thing gets boring.'

Jean-Claude inclined his head. 'It sounds enchanting. A picnic by the Avon river. Yes.'

Nicky said kindly, 'Actually it's called the river Avon, not the Avon river, monsewer. And it won't be exciting like Algeria of course. I saw a film that took place in Algiers. There was this man with a knife who captured English ladies and sold them to—'

'It certainly has an exciting history,' Jean-Claude agreed. 'The Kasbah is intact still. It was the headquarters of the old pirates.'

'Golly,' said Martin. 'Are you allowed in there, monsewer?'

'Yes.'

The boys were momentarily dumb. Jean-Claude took the opportunity to order more tea and some buns. His popularity kept rising.

After more conversation about the Algeria of the deys and pirates, Martin said hopefully, 'I think you might be some relation of ours, monsewer. If you were married to Aunt Carol, then you're sort of Bessie's stepfather. And—'

'Bessie was adopted,' Nicky interrupted scornfully. 'And anyway, she's not our real cousin.'

Jean-Claude added gravely, 'I was not married to Carol unfortunately. We were to be married.'

'Ah.' Nicky looked apprehensive. He'd thought men never cried, but he'd seen his father in tears not long ago and that had been connected with Carol in some way.

He said quickly and without giving his words due consideration, 'Of course, if you were to marry Aunt Mon, then you would be Bessie's real stepfather, and—'

Martin said triumphantly, 'But she's still not our real cousin, so monsewer wouldn't be related to us.'

Jean-Claude passed the buns again. 'Actually, I am not going

734

to marry Monica. But I could still invite you to see Algeria when you are a little older.'

'Golly. That would be great,' said Martin without bothering to swallo. 'Thank you tons, monsewer.'

Jean-Claude brushed crumbs from his shirt front and Nicky said, 'Sorry about that, monsewer. Martin is a pig at times.'

But all Jean-Claude said was, 'I think you had better call me Jean. You can pronounce it as John if you prefer.'

'Oh jolly good. French is stupid really, isn't it?'

The next day was Saturday and Malcolm had no appointments. It was slightly overcast but nothing was going to stop them now. Jean-Claude had hired a car in Exeter; he managed to pack in Boris and the three boys. Reggie's Humber Snipe took Malcolm, Mary and Bessie, leaving Myrtle to drive Malcolm's car with Liv and Monica. They stopped at Broadway for coffee at the Lygon Arms. Bessie did not look at Jean, and he did not look at her. But, as Monica had said, they were together, and that must count for something.

They went slowly through Willersey so that Jean could see the ducks.

Boris said, 'The first time Bessie and I came to stay with Myrtle, my father drove us this way. We stopped and fed the ducks. It doesn't seem very long ago.'

'It is not very long ago. Nine years. No more.'

Martin said, 'That's a lifetime, monsewer . . . John. Lennie wasn't even born then. Crikey, imagine life without Lennie . . .' There was as skirmish on the back seat during which Boris said quietly, 'Time is so relative. Nine years for you is not long. For Bessie it is the difference between childhood and maturity.'

Jean-Claude murmured, 'You know.'

It wasn't a question but Boris replied. 'I know she loves you. And . . . actually . . . I know quite a bit about love. So I really do *know* that she loves you.'

Jean sighed. 'To think I got you that job in Australia to keep you apart. And all the time . . .'

'You kept yourself fairly apart too. You must have known subconsciously that you loved her. You do love her, Jean, don't you?'

Martin said, 'Who? Who do you love, monsewer . . . John? If

you've changed your mind about Aunt Mon, we'd better tell you that she is very strict.'

'But very nice,' Nicky added.

Boris turned in his seat.

'Shut up, boys,' he said pleasantly.

They parked the cars and walked to Shakespeare's birthplace. The boys were restless. They went on to the church and the boys were more restless still.

'We'll save Anne Hathaway's until after our picnic,' Myrtle decreed.

They took out three skiffs. Skimming past the Memorial Theatre and beneath overhanging willows, they felt suitably Arcadian. Bessie and Monica sat in the stern of the first skiff, trailing their hands and smiling at each other. Boris sculled the boys; Malcolm and Reggie took on the other two boats.

They stopped for lunch at a jetty upstream.

'Someone else can row back,' Boris panted.

'Me – me!' Nicky offered.

'I'll do it,' Lennie said. 'We've gone canoeing with the club and it's easy-peezy.'

Martin said, 'Well, you're only five, so hard cheese.'

They went off across the grass, wrangling amicably, while Boris and Bessie began to lay out the picnic. Jean-Claude put some bottles to cool at the edge of the river. It was halcyon. And still very easy to avoid any kind of confrontation.

After lunch it clouded over. 'Thunder,' Myrtle forecast. 'Lennie will have a fit.'

'Lennie?' queried Jean incredulously.

Malcolm said, 'He's like his father, all front and no back.' Then he realised what he had said and started to laugh. So did Reggie. They went so far as to punch each other on the shoulder. Myrtle looked at Liv and smiled. 'Filthy devil,' she commented.

They began to pack up hurriedly.

The boys were playing French cricket. It amused them greatly that though he was French, Jean-Claude had never heard of the game. Lennie had been in for a long time simply because the bat completely protected his small knees. Nicky and Martin were fed up with him, and glad the game had to end.

736

'You're cross because I'm so brave,' Lennie mentioned matter-of-factly. 'I've got the heart of a lion!'

'And the brains of a donkey,' returned Nicky tartly. 'Mother is packing up because it's going to thunder, Lennie the Lionheart!'

Lennie's reaction was craven, much to the joy of his two brothers.

There was an immediate scrabble to load the skiffs and embark. Jean-Claude waited his turn politely, and somehow Bessie got behind him. He passed the last basket.

'I would very much like to walk along the bank. Malcolm, it will make the boat lighter and you will be able to get Lennie back more quickly. We will meet you in the hotel by the car park.' He turned and took Bessie's arm. 'Come. We can be back as soon as them if we step it out.'

She thought it an obvious ploy, but everyone seemed to accept it naturally; Monica pushed off the last skiff and Malcolm sculled into midstream. The boys were catcalling from ahead; Lennie hid in his mother's arms.

'So. Do not be distant, Bessie. You must know that I came to Cheltenham with Monica especially to see you.'

'I thought . . . just to see each other . . . papering over the cracks Monica called it.' Bessie could feel her heart jumping around quite wildly. She managed to disengage her arm fairly casually and went ahead of him. 'Personally, I think it's a case of least said soonest mended.'

'I do not agree. I am going away next week—'

'Monica told me. Not even the occasional weekend back at the Bergerie?'

'No. And in any case the Bergerie is only home for me when you and Mary are there.'

'Oh. But it was yours and Cass'.' She picked a huge frond of cow parsley and sniffed it luxuriously. It smelled rankly of river.

He said, 'Cass is dead, Bessie.'

She took a breath and swallowed it.

He said, 'I wish to congratulate you. And I hope the three years at Bristol will be very happy. I like to think of you and Monica and Mary making a home together and sharing your experiences.'

She said lightly, 'You sound like the complete stuffed shirt, Jean. What you mean is, you hope that we will make another life,

737

that I will meet suitable young men, and not embarrass you again.'

He said, 'I do not hope that. No. Because I am very selfish. But if it happens then . . . I will dance at your wedding. Is that the saying?'

She flung away the cow parsley. 'Oh, shut up,' she said rudely.

Incredibly, he laughed. She wanted to turn round and hit him. Instead she increased her pace until she was almost running.

She heard him panting and laughing behind her.

'Bessie, if you are trying to prove that I am much older than you, you have succeeded. I cannot keep this up for long!'

She stopped abruptly and he almost ran into her. She said, 'I think I hate you, Jean.'

'Ah chérie. Do not say that.'

'I do say it. Because you are playing with me. You are treating me like a child again. You know I love you. You know that I want to marry you. You know that I feel terrible because of Cass, but that I still want you. You think because I am nineteen, I am a child. I loved Boris, now I love you, next week I shall love someone else. But it is not like that, Jean. I have always loved you. Ever since I saw you first at the airport in New York, I have loved you. I thought you were my father and I loved you as a father. But I know now, it wasn't for that reason at all. I fell in love with you when I was twelve years old, Jean-Claude! And I didn't even know it!' She turned and looked at him. 'I cannot force you to love me. But surely I deserve something more than a pat on the head and good wishes for the next boyfriend?'

He bowed his head as if he expected – wanted – her to strike him.

He said, 'Bessie. I cannot look at you. You are too beautiful and it hurts too much. When you came to my room . . . I had to send you away. Otherwise I would have made love to you as you wanted me to. And chérie, it would have been wrong. Not because of Cass. But because for so long I *was* a father to you. You must understand that, Bessie. It would have been the betrayal of a trust.'

She heardly heard his last words. She whispered, 'What do you mean? What are you saying, Jean?'

He did not look up.

'I am saying I love you. I am saying I want you. And I am

738

saying that I am going away and giving you time . . . giving us time. Because that is the right way to do things.'

She breathed, 'You love me. Say it. Look at me and say it.'

He lifted his head. His black eyes met her black eyes. He said, 'I love you, Bessie. I am twenty years older than you. But I cannot help myself. I love you.'

She sensed his helplessness, amounting almost to a fear of this second total commitment. She put her arms right around him and held him tightly.

'Then that is all right, my darling. All right. There will be no other boys, Jean. I will wait. I will work and you will be proud of me. And then, if you still love me, we will be together.' It was strange that the crazy joy she should be feeling was suddenly muted to this protectiveness. She tightened her grip. 'Trust me, chéri. Trust me. This is right. There will be no more pain.'

She felt his tears before her own. And then his arms came around her and held her to him, and her joy began.

Twenty-one

Jean-Claude and Bessie were married in 1967. The ceremony took place in the same church as Myrtle's wedding fifteen years before, at the top of the hill in Northfield overlooking the enormous housing estate where once had stood the Haunted House.

Boris gave her away. He had not yet entered a seminary, choosing to spend a few years with the Franciscan order in a small friary near Bristol, and in his brown robes and sandals he brought an air of simplicity to the packed church. He had of course returned the bracelet, and Bessie was wearing it over the white cuff of her wedding dress. He put his hand over it lightly as they walked up the aisle together. He had arrived at his happiness as tortuously as the others, and the bracelet was a poignant reminder of how near he had come to another life together. He smiled sideways at the exquisite gypsy face beneath the froth of lace. She had not changed that much from the girl he had danced with at his sister's wedding; and she was as much his sister as Myrtle – more in many ways.

Nicky and Martin had refused to be attendants, but had agreed to the less embarrassing tasks of ushering. Lennie followed Bessie up the aisle, resplendent in velvet and jabot. Behind him, Liv, as matron of honour, carried Helen instead of a bouquet. Bessie had insisted on it. 'We can't leave her out, Liv. She's got to carry the torch for all of us.' And Helen, at two and a half, seemed to accept this responsibility. She had her mother's curls and her father's warmth; she eyed the guests carefully and smiled happily at a selected few.

Myrtle, frankly dumpy again, stood next to Malcolm and smiled all the time. She had been sorry that Boris and Bessie had never made a match of it; like her mother, Myrtle felt they had all 'lost' Boris. But his presence today went a long way to banishing

740

this conception, and it gave more meaning to Bessie's marriage to Jean-Claude. Somehow they were all part of this match, even Cass. Cass would be so pleased; it made the wastefulness of her death have some kind of meaning. When the Rector intoned, 'If they be any just cause or impediment why these . . .' she felt Malcolm's hand fumbling for hers in the folds of her full skirt, and she took it and squeezed it gently. Malcolm was so emotional, so dependent on her; sometimes it was like having a fourth son; almost like having Mallie back again. She leaned forward slightly to smile at her mother who was standing next to her doctor husband, looking as anxious as ever. No, Myrtle hadn't wanted to follow that particular family pattern, and she hadn't. And neither had Borrie. Some time she would talk to Mother and try to reassure her about Borrie going into a monastery. It was so right for him. He was special. She hadn't seen it before, but that's what he was, special.

Reggie had opted to sit on the groom's side as Jean had no family. He too smiled, looking at his wife and daughter, then Bessie, then Jean-Claude. Reggie was almost certain it would be all right. The man did not even look French, and though he was so much older than Bessie, there was no generation gap. Bessie had come midway between the two generations. Reggie did not want to be fanciful, but he could almost imagine the very English Carol drawing them together, bridging any gaps there might be. He blinked and smiled across the aisle at Mary Woodford. What must she be thinking? Eight short years ago at Carol's funeral, her life had been shattered. And yet she had carried on somehow and put the pieces together. It was so good that she had had three years of Bessie and Monica; the trio had made up an odd little household in their flat off Whiteladies Road in Bristol, but how would she manage now? He had to remind himself that eight years ago his life too had been in ruins. That affair with Myrtle . . . how had it happened? He looked further down the church and saw Myrtle and Malcolm holding hands like a pair of lovers. Myrtle was forty and looked older; she also looked competent and in control of everything, Malcolm included. He recalled the lost and terrified girl on Alnmouth beach; the tremulous mistress in the room at the Crillon. They had gone. This was the real Myrtle.

Malcolm looked across heads and saw Reggie staring. For a

second he was startled, almost frightened. Then Reggie smiled and lifted a hand, and Malcolm relaxed against the stalwart shoulder so near his breast pocket. Well, he would never take Myrtle for granted again, he hardly needed Reggie to remind him of that. And he hoped that Reggie would never take Liv for granted either. Malcolm looked back at Liv, standing small and slim by Lennie. Helen had moved in her mother's arms so that she could see her father. Malcolm was a loving father, and seeing the link between Reggie and that baby girl melted his defences. Neither Reggie nor he deserved their happiness: let them both remember that. As if to underline that thought, the rector's voice boomed out, 'Those whom God hath joined together, let no man put asunder.'

Mary listened to the words too, and felt a deep thankfulness that Cass and Jean had never actually married. She remembered Cass' conviction that her union with Jean-Claude could not last. Well . . . it had not, but in a way Bessie was continuing it. Mary dared not let that train of thought go further. She heard the awe-inspiring words and knew that if they'd been said before, they would have stayed in Jean's head for ever and come between him and his love for Bessie. They were words that should be said only once in a lifetime.

She moved to the vestry slowly, forcing Monica to go ahead and sign the register first. She looked around her smilingly and caught Giles Cook's eyes. So he had come to see his daughter married. On an impulse she went back down the aisle and took his arm, urging him up.

'Would you walk with me?' she whispered. 'Then Mon can go with Boris.'

He flushed bright red with pleasure. And, better still, when Bessie saw him in the vestry she beamed at him and said, 'Oh, I'm glad you're here. Are you all right?' And he nodded, quite unable to speak.

Monica felt strange; apart from all of it. For three years now, she, Bessie and Mary had shared a flat in Bristol and lived in almost perfect harmony. She and Mary were to continue living together. Everything was working out well. Yet she stood in a corner of the vestry, watching the smiling faces, feeling like an observer and not knowing why.

When Mary walked in with Gilly, she felt the usual soft squeezing of her heart muscles, a tenderness oozing through her insidiously, and wondered for a moment whether Giles might, after all this time, be her true destiny. But the very next instant she knew it was too late; had been too late even before Bob.

Liv came up and gave Helen to her.

'Bessie wants me to sign too. Hang on to Nellie, will you, Mon?'

Monica took the child, her godchild, and was rewarded by a smile and a quick, snuggling hug. And quite suddenly she knew what she wanted to do. She couldn't wait to tell Mary all about it. Mary loved children too. If she felt up to it, she'd be as keen as Monica herself.

Giles came up to her.

'Nice little kid,' he said awkwardly, standing stiffly to attention. 'Whose is that, then?'

'Liv's. You remember. Liv Baker that was.' Monica waited until Helen turned and said hello. Giles chucked her under the chin too familiarly and she buried her head in Monica's neck.

Monica said, 'I've wanted to look you up, Gilly.'

'Aye, aye,' Gilly said. 'What have I done now?'

Monica said, 'I hoped you weren't too shattered by that business four years ago. Is it too late to apologise?'

Unexpectedly, he grinned. 'She did that already,' he said. 'Couple months after if all happened. Didn't she tell you?'

'No.'

'She's quite a gal. Invited me to the wedding too. Probl'y didn't think I'd come, but I couldn't've missed it.'

'No,' Monica said again. She never cried, but she could have cried at that. Bessie was special, so very special.

Giles said frankly, 'Reckon she's giving us plenty of chances to get together again, our Mon. But I don't think we could, do you?'

Monica swallowed and pressed her cheek against Helen's curls. 'No,' she said.

'I mean. If you've got leanings that way—'

'No.'

'That's all right then. 'Cos I'm a bit set in my ways now. Couldn't really fancy anyone else after you, our Mon, but couldn't be bothered either. Know what I mean?'

'Absolutely.'

He said, 'Right. Then it's just as well I'm walking along of Mrs Woodford. We don't want to give no-one ideas.'

'No.'

They gathered around the car which was to take Bessie and Jean to the airport.

Mary said to Monica, 'Are you sure we'd be allowed to foster children? I thought there had to be a father figure somewhere around?'

'Short-term fostering . . . difficult children . . . that kind of thing we can do. What do you think?'

Mary said thoughtfully, 'We'd have to buy a house somewhere of course. Or maybe a bungalow would be better.'

Monica smiled and squeezed the older woman's arm. 'It would be fun to do something together, wouldn't it? Make a family again . . .'

Mary said, 'Mon, you're not suggesting this simply for my sake are you? What about your nursing career? You're doing so well.'

'I'm suggesting it for my sake. Selfish to the end, you see. But I can't do it without you, Mary. And we can offer so much – a foster mother and a foster grannie!'

They both laughed.

Bessie had changed into trousers and shirt. She and Jean would be in the Bergerie within three hours. Their goodbyes were laced with instructions: most of the people there were coming out for their holidays before the end of the month.

'Don't do a thing, darling,' Mary told her. 'I'll give the place a good clean and do masses of cooking—'

Monica said, 'You'll want to get away from all of us! Are you sure—'

Jean said smilingly, 'We're sure. And perhaps in any case we shall not be there. Bessie is taking me up the side of the mountain – tomorrow morning very early. I believe we shall be accompanied by a mule.'

Everyone laughed. Then Bessie looked at Boris. 'I've got something here. Something Borrie and I buried a long time ago and Jean and I dug up. We all think it's too important to be kept in one place. It's going to do the rounds. Like a talisman.'

'What is it?' Myrtle asked curiously.

Bessie transferred her gaze. 'It's your paint pot, Aunt Myrt.

It – it's a sort of proof. Of Cass. Of Mallie. Of everything.'

Myrtle looked and said nothing. Suddenly Liv went to her and put her arms around her. And Mon followed suit. The three women were quite silent, standing there in the sunshine. Then Myrtle held out an arm for Bessie.

She kissed each one in turn. And then went to Mary. It did not surprise her to find that Jean was there before her, holding Mary gently to him. If was he who said, 'Cass is still here. In each one of us. We shall never lose her.'

They got into the car and drove away.

For some reason, Mary heard herself say, 'It's not finished. It will go on and on.'

Monica asked, 'Do you mind?'

Mary said, 'No. There are so many kinds of happiness. I have one kind in abundance.'

Monica said, 'So have I.'

Liv said, 'So have we.' And, instead of looking at Reggie and Helen, she added, 'Haven't we, Myrt?'

Myrtle took out a large man's handkerchief, wiped her eyes and blew her nose. 'Yes.' She grinned, and was her old self, the Myrtle who had scrambled up the bank of the brook with Cass' help. They looked at each other anew. None of them had changed at all. They could have been still thirteen, with all of life before them.

'Of course,' she said emphatically.

Bessie placed a tureen of onion soup on the kitchen table next to the basket of rolls. It was a heavy tureen and her hands trembled slightly as she sat down. She put them quickly on to her lap.

Jean-Claude said in a low voice, 'I am frightened too, Bessie. Do not let us hide our fear from each other.'

She swallowed visibly, then tried to smile.

'You are frightened that I will come between you and Cass. I understand that, my darling. I will never do that, Jean. I will never . . . usurp . . . Cass. This – thing – this love between you and me – it is something different. Something separate.'

He said nothing, but he smiled at her and lifted his shoulders as if helpless to explain the deep flow of their feeling for each other.

She said briskly, 'Let's have your wretched soup while it's hot enough to scald out tongues! And – and – just – take it as it comes.'

He held his plate, his smile widening. She said, 'What? What have I said?'

'Nothing. It is the way you speak. So like Monica. How could anyone have imagined you were Cass' child!'

She flinched and gave a little cry and he leaned forward and grabbed her wrist.

'Darling! Bessie – I did not mean to hurt you. She was closer to you than a mother could have been!'

The tears flooded her dark eyes. 'I know. I know. I know. But . . . if I'd actually belonged to her – been her daughter – you could have loved me – sort of – through her . . . don't you see?'

The grip on her wrist tightened painfully.

'No. I don't see! It would not have been like that, Bessie. Not a bit. It would have been wrong – practically incestuous!' He pushed back his chair and came around the table, not releasing her wrist. 'Listen, chérie. What you have just said . . . it makes sense in an upside-down way!' He lifted her and held her tightly and she pressed her face into his shoulders and let the tears flow. 'Ah . . . listen, Bessie.' His mouth was close to her ear. 'You think you need to be one with Carol for me to love you. But it is the other way round, my darling. I have to tell you something . . . and I cannot find words.' He laughed briefly. 'Jean-Claude Durant, bereft of words! Mon Dieu, c'est incroyable!'

He was trying to make her laugh, but she could not. It was as if all her grief and love had come together at once and fountained from her in tears. He cradled her, smoothing her hair back from her hot forehead. Then he carried her to the old settle by the range and pillowed her head on his shoulder. And gradually she became quiet.

He said softly, 'Darling Bessie. I want to talk about Carol's death. Can you bear it?'

For a long time she did not speak or move. Then he felt her head jerk up and back. He kissed the parting in her hair.

'I have never spoken of it to anyone, dearest. They thought – at the time – that I was suffering from shock. And perhaps I was. Who can tell? It seemed to me then, and still does, that those moments of Cass' dying, were the most real of my life. Until now.'

Her hands which had been clutching his shirt front, slid slowly around his chest and held him.

He went on very quietly. 'Bessie. I wanted to go with Cass. I wanted to die with her. But she would not let me. She sent me back. For a reason of course. We know why, don't we?'

Another pause, then Bessie's head nodded again.

And again he kissed her and went on.

'I came back to this life, not . . . empty. Not without Cass.' He sighed. 'This is the difficult part to explain, Bess. Yet is so simple. Cass and I were one. We are still . . . one. The person you love, my darling, is not just Jean-Claude Durant. It is Jean-Claude-Carol Durant. That is why I tell you that your words were upside-down. Can you understand that?'

Her hands held him tightly. She nodded.

He whispered, 'Do you see that Cass can never come between us, yet never be dismissed into the past? Can you see why our love is amazingly strong?'

She cleared her throat. 'Yes,' she said hoarsely.

They were still. Neither of them spoke. They held each other tightly as if afraid one would fall down without the support of the other.

Jean-Claude said, 'I have put it badly. You are more frightened than before.'

At last she sat up. Her eyes were still shining with tears, but he could see into their depths and was instantly reassured.

'I am not frightened, Jean,' she whispered. 'I am just . . . amazed. I was thinking back. Thinking of everything that has happened. And it seems to lead . . . here.'

It was his turn to weep. She held his head in her hands and kissed his eyes. And then the bridge of his nose. Finally his mouth. And then they came together. Without haste, or embarrassment; with perfect naturalness, they undressed and made love on the kitchen floor while above them, the tureen of onion soup grew cold. And congealed.

And it was as if all the roads from the Haunted House so many years ago, had indeed led to this place, and this time. A real time. A time when all the laughter and all the weeping were given a wonderful significance. An even more wonderful immortality.

THE END